SPIES OF THE MIDNIGHT SUN:

A TRUE STORY OF WWII HEROES

VOLUME THREE OF THE WORLD WAR TWO SERIES

SAMUEL MARQUIS

MOUNT SOPRIS PUBLISHING

"In his novels *Blind Thrust* and *Cluster of Lies*, Samuel Marquis vividly combines the excitement of the best modern techno-thrillers, an education in geology, and a clarifying reminder that the choices each of us make have a profound impact on our precious planet."
—Ambassador Marc Grossman, Former U.S. Under Secretary of State and Co-Author of *Believers: Love and Death in Tehran*

"When I read a book about World War II these days, I look for something new...*Lions of the Desert* by Samuel Marquis delivered this in spectacular fashion. He has written another great book about the war that we should never forget."
—Ray Simmons for Readers' Favorite (5-Star Review)

"A simply riveting read from beginning to end, *Spies of the Midnight Sun* is impressively informed and informative, and a work of solidly researched history."
—Midwest Book Review

"In the richness of the texture of his material, Marquis far exceeds the stance of a mere raconteur and entertainer of the masses—he, in fact, becomes a public historian."
—Lois C. Henderson, Bookpleasures.com (Crime & Mystery) - 5-Star Review

"A combination of *The Great Escape*, *Public Enemies*, a genuine old-time Western, and a John Le Carré novel."
—BlueInk Review (for *Bodyguard of Deception*, Book 1 of WWII Series)

"*Cluster of Lies* has a twisty plot that grabs hold from the beginning and never let's go. A true page turner! I'm already looking forward to the next Joe Higheagle adventure."
—Robert Bailey, Author of *Legacy of Lies* and *The Final Reckoning*

"If you haven't tried a Samuel Marquis novel yet, *The Fourth Pularchek* is a good one to get introduced. The action is non-stop and gripping with no shortage of surprises. If you're already a fan of the award-winning novelist, this one won't disappoint."
—Dr. Wesley Britton, Bookpleasures.com (Crime & Mystery) - 5-Star Review

"Marquis is the new Follett, Silva, and Clancy rolled into one."
—Prof. J.R. Welch, Editor of *Dispatches from Fort Apache*

"Reminiscent of *The Day of the Jackal*...with a high level of authentic detail. Skyler is a convincing sniper, and also a nicely conflicted one."
—Donald Maass, Author of *The Emotional Craft of Fiction* (for *The Coalition*)

"Readers looking for an unapologetic historical action book should tear through this volume."
—Kirkus Reviews (for *Bodyguard of Deception*)

"Samuel Marquis picks up his World War II trilogy with *Altar of Resistance*, a well-researched and explosive ride through war-torn Rome with Nazis, booming battles, and intense cat-and-mouse chases....Grounded in historical fact but spiced up with thrilling imagination with the fate of the world in balance."
—Foreword Reviews

BY SAMUEL MARQUIS

WORLD WAR TWO SERIES

SOLDIERS OF FREEDOM
LIONS OF THE DESERT
SPIES OF THE MIDNIGHT SUN
ALTAR OF RESISTANCE
BODYGUARD OF DECEPTION

NICK LASSITER-SKYLER INTERNATIONAL ESPIONAGE SERIES

THE FOURTH PULARCHEK
THE COALITION
THE DEVIL'S BRIGADE

JOE HIGHEAGLE ENVIRONMENTAL SLEUTH SERIES

CLUSTER OF LIES
BLIND THRUST

BLACKBEARD: THE BIRTH OF AMERICA

SPIES OF THE MIDNIGHT SUN:

A TRUE STORY OF WWII HEROES

VOLUME THREE OF THE WORLD WAR TWO SERIES

SAMUEL MARQUIS

MOUNT SOPRIS PUBLISHING

SPIES OF THE MIDNIGHT SUN
VOLUME THREE OF THE WORLD WAR TWO SERIES
Copyright © 2018 by Samuel Marquis

MOUNT SOPRIS PUBLISHING
Trade paper: ISBN 978-1-943593-23-1
Kindle: ISBN 978-1-943593-24-8

Second Mount Sopris Publishing premium printing: April 2020
Cover Design: Christian Fuenfhausen (http://cefdesign.com)
Formatting: Rik Hall (www.WildSeasFormatting.com)
Printed in the United States of America

To Order Samuel Marquis Books and Contact Samuel:
Visit Samuel Marquis's website, join his mailing list, learn about his forthcoming novels and book events, and order his books at www.samuelmarquisbooks.com. Please send all fan mail (including criticism) to samuelmarquisbooks@gmail.com. Thank you for your support!

ATTENTION: ORGANIZATIONS AND CORPORATIONS
Mount Sopris Publishing books may be purchased for educational, business, or sales promotional use. For information, please email the Special Markets Department at samuelmarquisbooks@gmail.com.

Dedication

To Dagmar Lahlum (March 1923 - December 1999) and Annemarie Breien (August 1915 - April 2003), two of Norway's most courageous anti-German Resistance operatives who were falsely and unfairly labeled as *tyskertøs ("German whores")*. Their significant contributions to the Allied war effort should have long ago been officially recognized by their countries (Dagmar should be honored by both Norway and Great Britain), as history has indisputably shown that they risked their lives and fought the good fight on the side of the Allies in the name of democracy and freedom.

SPIES OF THE MIDNIGHT SUN:
A TRUE STORY OF WWII HEROES

Anything that can be aligned with resistance against the Germans must necessarily be done. No one may voluntarily provide his labor, his expertise, or his business to the Germans...Not the slightest attempt at Nazification, not a single thought or sound, must penetrate into the soul of our people. We are fighting not only for the destruction of Nazism but for the reconstruction of our democratic country. This idea is to serve all of our actions.

> —Norwegian Underground Resistance Editorial in Nazi-Banned Newspaper

If there is anyone who doubts the democratic will to win, again I say, let him look to Norway. He will find in Norway, at once unconquered and unconquerable, the answer to his question.

> —U.S. President Franklin Delano Roosevelt

To keep one flame through life
To live in wintry age the same
As first youth we loved
To feel that we adore with such refined excess
Although the heat could break,
We could not live with less
This is love, perfect love
Such has kindled the hearts of the saints above

> —Eddie Chapman, Agent Zigzag, Dagmar Lahlum's lover and fellow spy in Occupied Norway

CAST OF HISTORICAL FIGURES

NORWEGIANS: RESISTANCE OPERATIVES, MILITARY/ POLITICAL LEADERS, AND CITIZENS

Dagmar Mohne Hansen Lahlum: Working woman and clandestine Norwegian Resistance operative (Milorg); Eddie Chapman's lover and unofficial spy for MI5.

Annemarie Breien: Resistance operative informing on German Police activities on behalf of Milorg; contact and short-term secret girlfriend of German Gestapo officer Siegfried Fehmer to gain intelligence and secure the release of Resistance members.

Roald Breien: Head of Milorg Upper Buskerud Cell of the Norwegian Resistance; father of Annemarie Breien.

Jens Christian Hauge: Chief of Milorg; lawyer and secret senior operative of the U.S. Office of Strategic Services (OSS).

King Haakon VII: His Majesty the King of Norway; leader of the government-in-exile in London and source of inspiration for the Norwegian people.

***Løytnant* Max Manus**: British Special Operations Executive-trained Resistance fighter specializing in sabotage; member of the Oslo Gang.

Vidkun Abraham Lauritz Jonssøn Quisling: Head of Norwegian pro-Nazi puppet government (Quisling regime dominated by ministers from *Nasjonal Samling* Party) in 1940 and 1941; Minister-President of puppet regime beginning in February 1942.

Kjell Bügel Langballe: Oslo lawyer; husband and later ex-husband of Annemarie Breien.

***Løytnant* Peder Olav Gleditsch (fictional)**: First lieutenant in Norwegian Resistance Group Milorg; fictional control officer of Dagmar Lahlum since real-life agent not known; code name Ishmael.

Mary Larsen: Friend of Dagmar Lahlum.

BRITISH: INTELLIGENCE OPERATIVES, MILITARY OFFICERS, AND CITIZENS

Edward Arnold "Eddie" Chapman: Professional safecracker and thief; double agent code-named "Zigzag" by British Security Service (MI5) and "Fritz/Fritzchen" by German Foreign Intelligence Service (Abwehr).

Lieutenant Colonel Thomas Argyll "Tar" Robertson: Scottish MI5 intelligence officer; chief of MI5's B1A counterintelligence section; creator of the Double Cross Spy System.

Lieutenant Colonel Robin "Tin Eye" Stephens: Commandant of London's Camp 020; worked closely with Tar Robertson; first-rate interrogator as well as a raging xeno- and homo-phobe.

Major Sir John C. Masterman: Distinguished Oxford don and chairman of the Double Cross Committee that ran and controlled German double agents living in England.

Captain Ronnie Reed: Chapman's impressive first B1A counterintelligence section case officer.

Major Michael Ryde: Chapman's despicable second B1A counterintelligence section case officer.

Captain Ewen Edward Samuel Montagu: Senior naval intelligence officer on the Double Cross Committee.

Anthony Faramus: Chapman's cellmate and partner-in-crime in Jersey and Romainville prison.

GERMANS: ABWEHR, SS, AND WEHRMACHT OFFICERS

Rittmeister **Stephan Albert Heinrich von Gröning**: Head of Abwehr Nantes spy school in Occupied France; senior Abwehr control officer for Eddie Chapman; anti-Nazi German aristocrat; alias Doktor Stephan Graumann.

SS-*Obersturmführer-Hauptsturmführer* Siegfried Wolfgang Fehmer: Clever and brutal German police investigator (*Kriminalrat*) and head of infamous *Sicherheitspolizei* (Sipo) *Abteilung IV* (Gestapo) at Victoria Terrasse, Oslo.

SS-*Oberführer* Heinrich Fehlis: Chief of the German Security Service (SS, including *Sicherheitspolizei* [Sipo] and *Sicherheitsdienst* [SD]) at Victoria Terrasse.

SS-*Oberleutnant* Walter Praetorius: Chapman's junior control officer and chaperone; rabid Nazi and Anglophile obsessed with English folk dancing; alias Walter Thomas.

Kapitän **Johnny Holst**: Hard-drinking and amiable Abwehr officer and Chapman chaperone.

Oberst **Alexander Waag**: Chief of the Paris Abwehrstelle.

Josef Antonius Heinrich Terboven: Rabid Nazi and *Reichskommissar* for Norway during the German Occupation; a humorless martinet with control over Regular Army and SS.

Generaloberst **Nikolaus von Falkenhorst**: Planner and commanding general of German invasion of Denmark and Norway in 1940; Wehrmacht commander during German Occupation of Norway through December 1944.

SS-*Hauptsharführer* Axel Etling: Leader of the Gestapo motor transport; enemy acquaintance of double agents Chapman and Dagmar Lahlum.

SS-*Obersturmführers* Hoeler and Bernhard: Brutal Gestapo interrogation officers in *Abteilung IV* at Victoria Terrasse.

SPIES OF THE MIDNIGHT SUN: A TRUE STORY OF WWII HEROES

VOLUME THREE OF THE WORLD WAR TWO SERIES

TO THE READER

The primary hero of this story was originally going to be the legendary British double agent Eddie Chapman, known as Agent Zigzag by his British handlers and Agent Fritz by his German control officers. Having read Ben Macintyre's enthralling *Agent Zigzag: A True Story of Nazi Espionage, Love, and Betrayal*, I immediately identified with the iconoclastic British safecracker and WWII spy. Why the inglorious bastard was just like me growing up. As the ninth great-grandson of Captain William Kidd, I always fancied myself a pirate, and as a boy I was a troublemaker, girl-chaser, and hyperactive athlete who, like the restless Eddie, had at least a modicum of roguish charm and lived for the thrill of illicit adventure. But then, when I read Nicholas Booth's *Zigzag: The Incredible Wartime Exploits of Double Agent Eddie Chapman*, I realized that the most intriguing character in the Eddie Chapman story wasn't Eddie at all—but rather his Norwegian girlfriend Dagmar Lahlum, an aspiring fashion model and Resistance operative, who hated the Nazis with a passion, smoked Craven A cigarettes from a long ebony holder, and wore high heels and fashionably risqué dresses like Marlene Dietrich to deceive the Germans and bring down the Reich.

Once I had read both Macintyre's and Booth's books, it was clear that Dagmar needed to be on equal footing with Eddie, not his subagent. She was no mere Ingrid Bergman in *Casablanca*—she was a real-life Norwegian spy in a male-dominated world that didn't even know she existed. Here was a smart-as-a-whip and gorgeous woman of twenty years of age—that's right, twenty—who risked her life for the Allies just as much as her lover Eddie, but that history has neglected. How would you like to be a daring spy risking your life coming into close contact with German intelligence officers and rabid Nazis to bring Hitler to his knees, and yet your fellow countrymen don't give a damn about you and even unfairly persecute you as a collaborator for getting too cozy with German agents? Now that's a character with internal conflict and a story worth telling.

And then I found out that Dagmar wasn't the only brave Norwegian woman overlooked by history and wrongly abused by her countrymen. Annemarie Breien, whose father and siblings were also in the Norwegian Resistance, was just as courageous and equally unknown despite her undeniable heroism. To me, it seemed incredible. How could such WWII heroes be overlooked and even mistreated by their own countrymen for six decades after the war? It seemed grossly unfair. Surely, they must have had some serious character flaws or inhabited the gray area between active resistance and Nazi collaboration. Only they didn't. Their contributions to the

Allied war effort are many and incontrovertible—and yet history has never properly recognized them for their achievements.

Until now. This book is *their* story—the true story of Dagmar Lahlum and Annemarie Breien—a story that should have been told long ago. It is also the story of the colorful Eddie Chapman and three important WWII intelligence officers: the inestimable Scottish gentleman spymaster Tar Robertson of MI5 and the Germans Siegfried Fehmer (Gestapo) and Stephan von Gröning (Abwehr), all three of whom figured prominently in the real-life events depicted in this novel. I hope you enjoy this tale of WWII espionage, romance, and derring-do.

CHAPTER 1

GRAND HOTEL
KARL JOHANS GATE 31
OSLO, NORWAY

APRIL 9, 1940

THE CONQUERORS HAD CONQUERED YET AGAIN. For the past twelve hours, Dagmar Lahlum had anxiously anticipated their arrival, and a part of her still couldn't believe the Norwegian surrender flag had already been raised. But like the odor of a skunk defeat clung to the air of the capital. The Army had been caught flat-footed and given up the city with barely a whimper of resistance—and now Oslo belonged to General Nikolaus von Falkenhorst and his seemingly invincible Wehrmacht.

Throughout the night, she had heard the shrieking air-raid sirens, and all morning her ears had been assaulted by the roar of Messerschmitt and Focke-Wulf fighter engines and the clatter of anti-aircraft machine guns. But the fighting had long since ended. Now the moment that everyone had been dreading was upon them. In less than twenty-four hours, the Germans had taken the city, and now they were about to parade down the main thoroughfare in a triumphal march. The very idea sickened her. Only a half-hour ago, at precisely 2:30 p.m., the word had spread like wildfire through the luxurious Grand Hotel that any minute now von Falkenhorst and his victorious army would goose-step their way down Karl Johans gate. And no one was doing a damned thing to stop them.

No one.

Standing at the hotel's front desk, Dagmar Lahlum still couldn't believe it had come to this. The seventeen-year-old receptionist from Eidsvoll—who had moved to the capital only three weeks earlier—hadn't even set eyes upon the invaders yet, and already she hated them with a passion. Though young and innocent in the ways of the world, she had no illusions about Hitler and his Third Reich, or his foreign barbarians in the green-gray uniforms who had passed virtually uncontested through the city's gates and were about to parade brazenly down Oslo's principal boulevard. What made it even worse in her eyes was that the Germans were apparently counting on the fact that they would be greeted as fellow Nordic liberators, like some sort of long-lost cousin here to re-forge an alliance with their vaunted Viking brethren. But unlike many of her countrymen, Dagmar would not greet the Nazis as liberators. Not her. In fact, she didn't even want to give them the satisfaction of seeing her watching them march past the hotel. But she *would* watch them. If for no other reason than to see with her own eyes what her beloved country was up against.

"They'll be here soon," she said to her friend Mary Larsen, who had come by the hotel to visit her and see the Germans. "We can go upstairs now to watch, though I wish I could instead line them all up and shoot them."

"They would just hang you and you would never get a chance to become a famous fashion model."

"With war upon us, I will probably never get my chance anyway."

"Oh, yes you will. You are a true beauty."

"But not as beautiful as Rita Hayworth. Come on, let's go."

She grabbed the key for Room 301, which was unoccupied. A few minutes earlier, when her supervisor had granted her and the rest of the Grand Hotel staff two hours off to watch the German conquerors march through Oslo, Dagmar had telephoned her friend Mary and invited her to watch the spectacle from the hotel, which looked out upon Karl Johans gate. Now they snatched their jackets from the coatrack, took the stairs to the third floor, and made their way briskly down the hallway to 301. Once inside, they opened the French doors and stepped out onto the narrow balcony overlooking Karl Johans gate and the park across the boulevard. Below, thousands upon thousands of nervous Osloans wearing spring overcoats and hats stood waiting for the approaching German Army along both sidewalks. Many had pedaled here on bicycles; some stood gripping the handlebars, others had leaned the conveyances upon the pavement or against streetlights.

Beyond the park, Dagmar saw cars and open-topped trucks packed with young men of military age screaming down Rosenkrantz gate, Eidsvoll plass, and Akersgata. The traffic funneled into Stortingsgata and Nedra Vollgate like streams feeding a mighty river. The young men were hurrying to get out of town before the enemy took full control of the city. Now that Oslo had fallen, they must have been fearful the Germans would begin rounding up the youth for work camps or military conscription, or arresting some for their subversive, anti-Nazi political views or probable ties to the underground. Watching her fellow Norwegians fleeing in panic, she wondered if the Germans were about to turn Oslo into a living hell, as the BBC had said they had done to Warsaw, or merely an uncomfortable place to live, as they had reportedly done in Prague and other less brutalized European cities. Looking to the south and east, she could see that the streetcars had stopped running and people were escaping on foot or on bicycles.

She wondered if she and her friend Mary should be making their escape, too, while there was still time. But where would they go?

Today was the first time she had witnessed firsthand a city threatened under a German occupation, and it frightened her. After Parliament had voted unanimously to resist the Nazis in the early morning hours, King Haakon and the royal family had been forced to flee the city. The remaining government had swiftly ordered a general mobilization, but the capital had fallen quicker than anyone expected. The only officials on the street below appeared to be policemen clearing a path for the German invaders. The remaining population seemed to be divided between those attempting to escape the city, the curious onlookers lining the boulevard below, and those that had shuttered their windows and bolted their doors, hoping to be left alone by the new belligerents that had invaded their country.

Dagmar considered the latter prospect unlikely. As an occupying power, the Germans would never just leave Norway alone. Hitler would prod and poke her, stymie her, lie to her, and attempt to rule her like the angry tyrant he was—and Norway would have no choice but to resist such bullying. And one day, in hopefully the not-too-distant future, her country would defeat the tyrant and his thus far unstoppable armies. But Norway was going to need British help, Dagmar knew. That's what everyone was saying.

"Have you heard the latest ultimatum?" asked Mary as they scanned northwest towards the Royal Palace for the enemy column. "I heard it on the radio. The Germans have said that they are going to occupy every single Norwegian port."

"Where is the king now?"

"He and the government have reportedly been evacuated to Hamar. There is nothing more they can do here."

At that moment, they heard the low hum of distant airplane engines to the west. They looked worriedly at one another. The noise grew louder. Dagmar searched the sky. The dull pewter backdrop was broken in places by white, wedge-shaped clouds with gray rims. Overhead, she saw a squadron of geese flying north in tight formation, a symmetrical V against the sky. But there were still no planes visible.

And then, like phantoms emerging from the darkness of night, they materialized from the clouds in the distance, coming in fast, engines wide open.

They swooped in low over the Royal Palace, a triumvirate of German Messerschmitt Bf 109-F's. Dagmar and Mary didn't know what they were called or that they were fighters not bombers; all they knew was that the aircraft looked as menacing as a swarm of hornets streaking across the sky with their battle camouflage and their black iron crosses emblazoned across the fuselages below the wings. They came in low and violent, roaring like hungry lions, nearly shaving off the rooftop of the three-story Neo-Classical building with the facade of stuccoed brick. The citizenry stood fearful and breathless on the streets, in the windows, and all along the balconies as the fighters swept down the full length of Karl Johans gate and then, after grazing another set of rooftops, flew off to the south.

"Good heavens, look at them," exclaimed Mary, as their heads turned in unison to follow the German planes. "Was that all just for show?"

"They want us to know who is boss. It was meant to be intimidating."

"Well, I think they made their point."

They watched as the three Messerschmitts raced towards Oslo Fjord, then rose again towards the heavens, their tail exhaust plumes streaking, spiraling, and crisscrossing across the pewter sky. Then Dagmar and her friend returned their gaze to the street.

Directly below them, a burly German officer and half dozen soldiers shoved their way through the crowd and began shouting out orders in Norwegian to a group of Oslo policemen. The entire group then pushed their way up the boulevard giving commands to clear the streets of all foot and bicycle traffic. Within two minutes they had accomplished the feat.

It was then the German marching column came into view.

"Here they come," said Dagmar expectantly. The column wheeled to the right at the foot of the hill before the Royal Palace and started marching down Karl Johans gate.

She looked at her watch: 3:03 p.m.

The column was led by six Norwegian mounted police escorts. Directly behind the mounted Norwegians, forming the head of the German column, was the victorious General Nikolaus von Falkenhorst in all his military finery, along with two other officers. In the general's wake marched the granite-faced Wehrmacht regulars, three abreast, wearing heavy *feldgrau* overcoats, black boots, and steel coal-scuttle helmets. On their shoulders, most carried simple rifles, but a minority of the officers and non-coms had *Maschinenpistole* 40 light machine guns, or Schmeissers as the British and American Allies called them, on their shoulders. As the troops passed the University Square with the *Domus Bibliotheca* and other buildings on their left, Dagmar and Mary got an even better look at them. Most of the Germans looked straight ahead, but some shot triumphant smiles at the balconies and winked at the smattering of women in the crowd. Several times von Falkenhorst acknowledged Nazi salutes from persons in the crowd whom Dagmar knew were the followers of Vidkun Quisling and his pro-Nazi *Nasjonal Samling* Party.

She shook her head in disgust. "Look at those quislings down there," she grumbled. "Why it's as if they are welcoming the Germans to take over our country."

"Quislings?"

"Traitors. Three weeks ago, when I left Eidsvoll, my father told me that's what the treacherous followers of Vidkun Quisling are called. He said to watch out for the 'quislings'—they would turn on their own countrymen and do the bidding of the Nazis."

"With the Germans occupying Oslo, their numbers will only grow."

"Unfortunately." Dagmar frowned as she saw another exchange of Nazi salutes on the street below. "This is a sad day for Norway," she added.

"It's not over yet. The Army will continue to fight to the north, don't you think?"

"Yes, I'm sure of it. But look at the enemy down there. I don't see how we can beat them."

"They do look like they know how to fight," agreed Mary. "In fact, they scare me."

Nodding in agreement, Dagmar studied the first wave of officers and soldiers more closely as they passed the hotel with a military brass band on their heels. They presented a formidable and orderly-looking picture, marching in lockstep with perfect precision. They were obviously well-trained, highly disciplined, and battle-hardened, with grit and iron on their faces. But what made the marching German column even more terrifying was the handful of SS officers walking alongside the troops in the wake of the mounted Norwegian police. The SS policemen wore jet-black uniforms with red swastika armbands, jackboots, and skull-and-crossbones insignias that leered hideously from their lapels.

"German police?" asked Mary with a note of fear in her voice.

"The Gestapo," said Dagmar, eyeing them closely. "I've heard bad things about them. We're going to want to avoid them like the plague."

"I'm going to keep away from all the Germans. They frighten me."

"Yes, they frighten me too," agreed Dagmar, though at the same time she was intrigued. "But most of all, I don't like them."

They continued to watch the military procession in silence. She thought of her friend from the university, whom she had talked to an hour earlier when he had come by the hotel. He had told her that he had stumbled upon an advanced German patrol

4

down by the harbor and had asked the Germans what they were doing here in Oslo. They had replied, "We were sent here to help you against the English," which both he and Dagmar found puzzling. On his way to see her at the hotel, the young man had later come across a group of Norwegian firemen who told him that the Norwegian Army had not surrendered at all but had thrown up an "iron ring" around Oslo and was preparing to deal a stunning counterblow to drive out the German invaders. But then another group of Norwegian fishermen told him that the Germans had already taken every Norwegian port and the country was lost.

After hearing so many conflicting stories, Dagmar wasn't sure what to believe. But as she gazed down at the German Army marching down Karl Johans gate, and then beyond at the thousands of people struggling to escape the city in cars, trucks, bicycles, and on foot, she knew that the Norwegian capital was lost. She looked back at the triumphant von Falkenhorst and his vanguard marching boldly down Oslo's main thoroughfare, while tens of thousands of her fellow citizens just stood there dazedly watching. It seemed unthinkable that the Germans had, in a single day, taken complete possession of Oslo and were now marching through the streets as if on national holiday parade. But there the bastards were.

She wanted to believe that her country's capital had been overtaken because of German wickedness and Quisling's treachery. She wanted to believe that Hitler's enemy army had used trickery: Norway's courageous defenders had only been defeated because it had been an unfair fight and the Germans had been secretly supported by a small army of traitors, "quislings" who marched to the drumbeat of their treacherous *Nasjonal Samling* Party leader. But she knew that wasn't true. The Germans simply fielded the better and bolder army. Her country had been unprepared for war, as had Norway's British allies, while the Germans were not only well-trained and well-equipped, but daring, audacious, and acutely aware that their Nordic opponent would not be able to mount an effective resistance.

In short, they were a *real* army.

That was the lesson the seventeen-year-old had learned here today. And as she gazed down upon the receding German column, Dagmar Mohne Hansen Lahlum knew that her life would never be the same.

The Nazis had invaded Norway.

And they would not be leaving any time soon.

CHAPTER 2

EDDIE CHAPMAN—SAFECRACKER AND PROFESSIONAL THIEF—stared out the steel-barred window of his dank prison cell, wondering if he and his fellow Englishman and partner in crime Anthony Faramus were going to rot away in this hellhole for the entire war. They had been locked up here at Fort de Romainville for four months now and the Germans still had not accepted their offer to serve as Hitler's spies against their native country, Great Britain.

Built in the 1830s on the crest of a hill, Fort de Romainville had a long and dark history. The bloated limestone monstrosity ringed with a 12-foot barbed-wire fence was originally constructed to serve as a defensive bastion to ward off foreign invaders and French insurrectionists, considered of equal threat in the wake of Napoleon. Since 1941, it had been converted into a German prison and transit camp. The convicts called it "death's waiting room" for here civilian Resistance fighters, political prisoners, prominent Jews, communists, intellectuals, and suspected spies were held hostage, interrogated, tortured, and held as reprisal fodder for French partisan attacks committed against German soldiers outside the prison walls. Those captives fortunate enough to survive without dying of disease or being sent to the wall were deported to Auschwitz, Ravensbrück, Buchenwald, or Dachau where they would be subjected to even greater horrors.

Feeling a little melancholy, Eddie Chapman peered beyond the main courtyard of the prison at Sacre Coeur in the distance. The great white church was ablaze in the mid-morning sunlight. To the left, the Eiffel Tower poked above the misty clouds and caught the sun's rays. It was a beautiful sight. But somehow, the majestic scene only reinforced that he was behind bars and the Germans still had not accepted his offer to spy for them. As a political prisoner and suspected saboteur by the Gestapo, Chapman knew offering to spy for the Nazis was likely his only chance to get out of the living hell on earth known as Fort de Romainville.

As he stared out the prison window, he heard the crackle of a pair of rifles. He was no longer surprised by such incidents and knew instantly what had happened. Two more unlucky souls had been executed by firing-squad in reprisal for some act of resistance in Paris. The number of prisoners the Nazis plucked from their cells and shot depended on the severity of the infraction: the more serious the incident, the higher the death toll. Sometimes, hostages were informed before they were executed which specific act of defiance was about to cost them their lives, but usually they were simply yanked from their cells and told nothing at all. With the execution of only two prisoners, Chapman surmised that the infraction must have been merely an injury inflicted upon a German officer or the killing of a single enlisted man.

He looked up at the sentries. Armed with machine guns, they stood in the guard towers at either end of the barracks. They showed no visible reaction to the shootings. Then he looked at Faramus, lying on his rotting, straw-filled bed mattress. They both shook their heads.

At that moment, he heard a footfall outside the cell in the corridor followed by the jingle of a set of keys and the sound of the jail door opening. Two middle-aged guards, whom Chapman had christened Tweedledum and Tweedledee upon his arrival four months earlier, stepped into the cell and instructed him to follow them. Chapman looked again at his young friend Anthony Faramus before looking back at the two German corporals.

"You're not here to take me before a firing squad, are you mates?" he said in German.

"No, not today Englishman," replied Tweedledee. "Come with us to the *kapitan's* office. There are men waiting to see you."

Chapman and Faramus exchanged knowing glances. "Visitors you say?" inquired the safecracker.

"Yes, two this time. Let's go."

He and Faramus looked at one another again. "Good luck," his friend seemed to say, "and don't forget about me."

"Don't worry, I won't," Chapman responded back reassuringly with his eyes.

Tweedledum and Tweedledee led him from the prison cell to the office of Captain Brüchenbach, the Romainville prison commandant. Scowling-faced, short, and stocky, Brüchenbach was a brutish thug who had banished him to solitary confinement on several occasions, where Chapman would have frozen to death if not for piling up loose gravel around himself in his cell to conserve body heat during the frigid winter. The commandant, already red-eyed from the influence of alcohol though it was not yet noon, grunted out in slurred German to follow him and led him to a meeting room next to his office where two men were sitting. Chapman instantly recognized one of them—the young German intelligence officer who went by the name Walter Thomas had interrogated him last December shortly after his arrival to the prison—but he didn't recognize the older man who was clearly Thomas's superior officer. The senior German intelligence man was a new visitor to Romainville. When Brüchenbach closed and locked the door behind them, Chapman was alone with his two inquisitors.

"Allow me to introduce you to Herr Doktor Stephan Graumann," said Thomas, gesturing to the older man at the head of the table.

"Please have a seat," said Graumann in an old-fashioned, upper-class English accent. Then, with a courtly gesture, he waved his hand towards the lone unoccupied chair at the table.

"Thank you." Taking his seat, Chapman appraised the two Germans. From his first interrogation, he was familiar with the younger man, *Oberleutnant* Thomas. He was a tall, spare, and scholarly-looking Anglophile with pale blue eyes that missed nothing, hollow cheeks streaked with broken red veins, and a Southampton College tie at his throat. In contrast, the senior officer Graumann that he was meeting for the first time was a pleasantly rotund, middle-aged man with an amiable and vaguely amused expression on a moon-shaped face. Perhaps six feet tall, he wore thick-

7

rimmed spectacles and carried himself with an intellectual and aristocratic bearing. He was dressed in the uniform of a cavalry rittmeister, the equivalent of a senior captain, and at his throat dangled an Iron Cross, Second Class—*Eisernes Kreuz* II. Both men had thick open files on the table in front of them.

"How are they treating you here at Fort de Romainville?" asked Graumann to open the meeting. Though he and Thomas both spoke English like true upper-class Brits, from their excessive precision, formality, and pronunciation Chapman could tell that they were both German and English was their second language.

"Badly, but that's to be expected in a rathole like this," responded Chapman good-naturedly. "The cells are unheated and lit by a single bulb, and all we have to sleep on are rotting straw mattresses."

"I see. I hear you have spent some time in the *cachot*, which I take it is even worse."

"You'd be right about that. Prisoners in solitary get only one meal of bread and soup every three days, and the cells have no lights and are freezing cold. At times in early March, it was so cold that frost formed inside the walls of my cell. I was forced to scrape the gravel from the floor and cover myself just to survive. And unfortunately, the commandant seems to have it out for me. I was just back in the *cachot* on his orders a few days before you chaps showed up."

The two German officers chuckled. "Captain Brüchenbach is but a trained brute," said Graumann, his eyes sympathetic as he offered him a British Dunhill cigarette from a full pack.

Chapman nodded appreciatively and took a cigarette, which Graumann lit for him with a silver Zippo lighter. "You should have seen the commandant in February," he said, blowing out a cloud of blue smoke. "He flew into a rage when he heard about my nocturnal activities."

"And what would those be?"

"I was picking the lock to my cell at night and making love to my beautiful Paulette. She is a redheaded French prisoner that I am a bit smitten with here in the camp. Well, somehow one of the guards found out about it and told Brüchenbach. He came to my cell in a fit of rage and started waving his revolver around."

Graumann gave a bemused smile. "As I said, the man is a Neanderthal. He has no understanding of a gentleman's needs."

"Indeed not. What's funny is even though I was a month in solitary, I continued to pick my lock to visit my sweet Paulette. But a few weeks ago, I was discovered again. This time Brüchenbach barged into my cell, drunk out of his mind, drew his revolver, and threatened to shoot me."

"What did you do?" asked Thomas, intrigued just like Graumann.

"The incident was so bloody absurd…I invited the bastard to go ahead with it. The commandant leveled his pistol at me and hurled a string of obscenities before coming to his senses and stuffing the gun back in its holster. Unfortunately, I remained confined to the *cachot* on bread and water for a whole month. But I still picked the lock and snuck away at night to cavort with my dear Paulette."

The two interrogators looked at one another again and chuckled. "Well, we're glad that your punishment wasn't too severe. And for God's sake, please don't regard Herr Brüchenbach as a typical German," said Graumann with the cordial grace of a lifelong aristocrat. "And now that we have the preliminaries out of the way, Monsieur Chapman, I would like to know more about your career as a professional criminal and safecracker in London. I know you have recounted your rather colorful history to Lieutenant Thomas here, but I would like to hear about your past exploits from the horse's mouth so to speak. If you would please indulge me."

"Of course. Where do you want me to start?"

"How about when you first became a prince of the underworld back in Soho? From there, you can fill me in on your more recent crimes, experience with explosives, imprisonment in Jersey, and proficiency in German. Lieutenant Thomas and I, of course, know every detail of your criminal record, but I want you to tell me your story in your own words."

"Very well. It all started when me dear mum passed away."

"Excuse me?"

"My life of crime began nine years ago when my mother died of tuberculosis. I was with the Coldstream Guards at the time, and her death sent me off the rails."

"Sent you off the rails how?"

"Turned me against society."

"I see."

"I grew up in poverty in Northern England and I didn't want to be a piss poor bloke with nary a penny to my name my whole life. Seeing me poor mum dying away in the TB ward of Wearmouth Hospital, I said to myself if this is what society does to my mother then fuck society. I went AWOL from the Guards shortly thereafter and was arrested, imprisoned, and discharged from the service. That's when I began to mix with all kinds of dodgy types in the criminal underworld: racehorse crooks, cat burglars, forgers, fixers, prostitutes, and the like."

Graumann leaned back in his chair, curling the index finger of one hand into the side pocket of his rittmeister's uniform while stroking his thinning brown hair with the other. "And when did you acquire your experience with safecracking and explosives?" the German officer asked.

"That was later, after I had been some time forging checks and snatching suitcases with a dash of housebreaking, light burglary blackmail, and other petty crimes thrown in. By then I had developed a taste for disreputable women, cognac, and the gaming tables."

"And then you got caught."

"Yes. I was thrown in the slammer at Wormwood Scrubs and Wandsworth Prison."

"So, when did you go big-time?"

Chapman puffed on his Dunhill thoughtfully. "Must have been 1934 after my stint in Wandsworth. Inside, I had befriended the best cracksman in London."

"James Wells Hunt."

"Aye, together we formed the 'Jelly Gang.'"

"You used gelignite to burst open safes."

"Yes, with Hunt's help I became something of a gelignite artiste. It's safer than nitroglycerine because it's less combustible. We were able to leave behind the safe and safebreaker after the explosion. We used to steal detonators by the hundreds and packets of gelignite from unprotected mines. For two straight years, the Jelly Gang knocked off fur shops, pawnbrokers, cinemas, dairies, and other shops all over London. Sometimes, we'd just smash a hole through the wall of the shop next door, haul out the safe, and drive it back in the Bentley to Hunt's garage in Notting Hill and blow the safe there."

"You appear to be well-versed in explosives and demolition."

"That I am."

"And I am told that you took a liking to the nightlife and mingled with the rich and famous during these times. Is it true you are friends with Marlene Dietrich?" Graumann pulled off his thick-rimmed spectacles, smiled at him, and delivered a knowing glance to his partner Thomas.

"Yes, Marlene and I are chums, or I should say we were chums before I went to Jersey. By this time, around 1937 or 1938, I was a notorious underworld criminal of means. I wore Saville Row suits, drove a fast sportscar, had my own table at the Nest in Kingsley Street, and held court with the sketchy politicians, businessmen, film directors, actors, models, journalists, and other assorted rogues who enjoyed slumming it with the upper criminal class."

"It would appear you have the ability to mingle with all sorts of people."

"Yes, in addition to Dietrich, I was on friendly terms with the filmmaker Terence Young as well as the playwright Noël Coward and the composer Ivor Novello. I also became something of a bookworm to elevate my standing in artistic circles. In short, I was an underworld grandee hobnobbing with the semi-respectable rebels of the London scene. I had plenty of booze, money, and disreputable women. I have to say, in all honesty, it was the best time of me life."

Graumann smiled to himself, as if enjoying a private joke. "And now you are here in Hôtel de Romainville. Quite a reversal of fortune for a fair prince of the underworld, wouldn't you say?"

"Yes, well, no one said life was going to be easy. But I make the best of it, I do."

"From what you have described of your liaisons with Paulette, I can see that you have certainly done that. You are quite resourceful."

"Yes, that's true. But I'm mostly just randy."

The Germans laughed again, and this time he couldn't help but chuckle himself. He found himself warming to Graumann in particular. He considered himself a good judge of character and he had a positive feeling about the rittmeister with the thick-framed glasses and thinning brown hair. The portly gentleman had a lofty and scholarly yet benevolent air about him. He seemed to be a German officer of understanding and tolerance, which seemed at odds with Nazism and the idea of a Thousand Year Reich.

"Now tell me what happened to you in Edinburgh and Jersey?" asked Graumann.

Chapman proceeded to describe the details of the Jelly Gang's arrest in the Scottish capital and their subsequent bail, flight to the British island of Jersey off the French coast, arrest, and imprisonment while the island was still a dominion of Great Britain. He followed this by describing his release from jail and re-arrest by the Gestapo once Jersey had earned the embarrassing distinction of becoming the only part of Great Britain seized by Hitler. Two hours into the interrogation, he could tell that his German overseers intended to follow through and have him join their secret intelligence service sooner rather than later. All he could do was to continue to tell the truth and keep his fingers crossed.

"And now, Monsieur Chapman," pronounced Graumann with a grandiloquent air, "it is time to ask the more delicate questions."

"Fire away, chaps. As you can see, I have nothing to hide."

"What can you do for the German Secret Service?"

"I believe I can be quite useful in spying and sabotage."

"And your fluency in French and German?"

"As rock solid as bully beef, as Lieutenant Thomas here can attest." He nodded towards the file on the table in front of Graumann. "The lieutenant, and the female interrogator that questioned me last month after his visit, asked me many questions in both languages. Both times I believe I passed the test, though my accent could use improvement."

Thomas looked at the senior officer and spoke in rapid-fire German as if Chapman wasn't there. "He is competent in both languages, but he still needs work for our purposes."

Graumann nodded and returned his gaze to Chapman. "Language proficiency is important, but I'm more interested in what motivates you to want to spy for us," he said, taking over the questioning again in English. "Is it money or hatred of your country?"

"Money. But given that I would still have to serve out my sentence if I was ever caught on British soil, I have to say that I am just as motivated by my hatred of the police and a strong desire not to return to prison."

"And suppose after spying for Germany you didn't want to return to us?"

"You're going to have to trust me on that score, old boy. But I think I've made it quite clear to you that, as a former member of the Jelly Gang, I wouldn't be too tempted to stay."

"Yes, I can see your point. So, Eddie—you don't mind if I call you Eddie, do you?"

"No, Eddie works just fine."

"We have to ask you one last time. Are you prepared to be trained by the German Secret Service and serve as a spy for Germany?"

"Yes, I am. In fact, I would be quite thrilled to do so and would like to start right away."

"Once again, are you motivated more by a hatred of Britain or the promise of financial gain?"

"As I said before, both are factors. I have no love for my country, it is true, but mostly I'd like to earn some money and I don't want to end up back in jail but in a different land. That would be rather pointless, exchanging one prison cell for another, don't you think?"

"You value your freedom then?"

"I'd say that sums it up rather well. I suppose I'm just an adventurous and free-spirited sort."

Graumann smiled at him, like a father to a son, his watery blue eyes seeming to reach out to him. In that instant, Eddie Chapman—discharged soldier, professional crook, inveterate liar, and serial womanizer—saw a kindred spirit. Here was a partnership in the making with a man he felt certain was destined to become a close friend, adviser, and fellow conspirator, this well-humored and highly placed member of the German Secret Service. Or was he bloody dreaming?

"Very well," said Graumann. "Here is our offer. If you agree to be trained in sabotage, wireless telegraphy, and intelligence work, and you are willing and able to undertake a mission to England, I can promise you a substantial financial reward upon your return."

He tried hard to contain his excitement, but he couldn't help a little smile. *Finally, the Germans have accepted my offer!* "I am at your service, Herr Graumann."

"Good, then we shall arrange for your release. If you can keep out of trouble, we will have you out of here in a fortnight."

"As I said, I am at your command, gentlemen. But what about my friend Faramus?"

Graumann's heavy brows knitted solemnly. "Unfortunately, we can't accept his offer. He is of no use to the German Secret Service."

"I see," said Eddie, feeling deflated and dreading breaking the news to his friend.

The burly German seemed to pick his next words carefully. "In times of war, we must be careful. That is why one of you must remain here at Romainville."

Eddie tried to conceal his disappointment. It was clear the Germans wanted to hold Faramus as a hostage. By keeping his friend in custody, they knew that he would be less likely to double cross them and would be more inclined to follow through with his assignments and be on his best behavior.

Graumann stood up from his chair, signaling that the three-hour meeting was over. As they shook hands, Chapman noticed the bulging and expensive-looking gold ring with five black dots on the captain's little finger. He also noted the suppleness of his pudgy hands. As soft as a baby's, they had never performed a lick of manual labor. The voice, the hands, the signet ring: there was no doubt in Chapman's mind that *Herr Doktor* Stephan Graumann was born of German nobility and had enjoyed a coddled, upper-class upbringing. *What an unusual soldier and spy,* he thought of the man who was about to become his control officer and whose real name he would not learn until well after the end of the war: Stephan Albert Heinrich von Gröning.

"I look forward to seeing you in a fortnight then, Doctor Graumann and Lieutenant Thomas," he said in German, and he was escorted back to his barracks cell by a guard.

He was both relieved and ecstatic that he would soon be set free. But he was also troubled by the veiled threat to his friend Faramus and that he would have to keep the details of his agreement with the Germans from him. But he wasn't about to jeopardize his chances of getting out of here by telling Faramus the Germans didn't want him and he would have to stay behind as human collateral.

"Well, what did they say?" asked Faramus as soon as the guard had closed the cell and walked down the corridor.

"You have to swear to secrecy."

"All right, I swear."

"I will be leaving soon under the care of the Germans. I am sorry, but I can't tell you any more than that I will be spying for them."

Faramus let out a heavy sigh, went to the prison window, and stared out at Sacre Coeur in the distance. The afternoon sunlight slanted off its great white dome.

"I am sorry, Tony."

"I knew it would come to this. I was always worth nothing to them. What use does the Reich have for a twenty-year-old hairdresser whose only crime in this world has been stealing nine measly pounds on bloody Jersey Island? And now you get to go free and I am stuck here."

"Yes, well at least you can now have Paulette all to yourself."

"That's not funny."

"A feeble attempt to make you feel better. I'm sorry."

Faramus continued staring out the window. "Suppose you slip up. Then I'll be the one to get it in the neck. And what if once you have set foot back in England, you don't want to come back? I don't fancy being shot. I'm too young to die."

"Look here, Tony," he said, his tone more defensive than he intended, "you've got to let me play this my way. I am gambling with my own life, too, don't forget."

"I know, but it's still hard."

Feeling badly for him, he walked over to the prison window and patted him reassuringly on the shoulder. "I can't control the Germans. They have to do things their own way."

"Our fates are intertwined now. If I am pulled from my cell someday, I will know why. You would have betrayed me."

"I will never betray you, my friend. You know that."

Faramus continued to stare off despondently at the great church, set against a backdrop of billowy gray clouds. "I hope you succeed in this game of yours. My agreeing to play by your rules could very well cost me my life. Talk about bad luck."

"You can't feel sorry for yourself when there is no other way. The Germans have made it clear where they stand and there isn't a bloody thing we can do about it. Don't tell me you're asking me not to take them up on their offer and stay here?"

"No, I'm just angry is all." He sighed again. "And yet, a part of me can't help but wonder if this bold bluff might actually succeed." He smiled with a glimmer of hope.

"I'll make it work, Tony. I promise."

"Desperately and fearfully, I hope so. For your sake as well as mine."

CHAPTER 3

GESTAPO HEADQUARTERS
VICTORIA TERRASSE, OSLO, OCCUPIED NORWAY

MAY 14, 1942

STARING UP AT INFAMOUS VICTORIA TERRASSE, Annemarie Breien felt her throat go dry. Stealing inside the Gestapo headquarters and accomplishing her mission was not going to be easy—but coming back out alive might prove even more daunting. Some Norwegians who set foot inside the building were never seen alive again, and today she could only pray that she wouldn't be among them.

The massive, chalk-colored edifice was like a great white whale: awe-inspiring but with a hint of violence. With its ornate façade, slate rooftop, multiple towers bearing fluttering Nazi flags, and life-sized portrait of the Führer in the lobby, the building had been taken over by the German Security Service—the *Sicherheitspolizei*, or Sipo, and *Sicherheitsdienst*, or SD—in April 1940. It had quickly been converted into the enemy's primary military intelligence and police headquarters, holding area, and interrogation center.

In the last two and a half years of the German Occupation, the name Victoria Terrasse had come to strike fear into the hearts of the indigenous population as a place of unmitigated police brutality and torture. The citizens of Oslo—but particularly anti-fascists, Home Guard partisans, Jews, communists, former Norwegian Army soldiers and intelligence agents, and those harboring fugitives wanted by the Nazis—were very much aware that terrible things were happening behind the closed doors and sound-proofed torture rooms of Victoria Terrasse. In fact, the place had such a fearsome reputation that several prisoners had jumped out of third- or fourth-floor windows, choosing to end their own lives rather than submit to the heinous tortures of their interrogators.

Annemarie Breien felt a shiver up her spine as she pondered the stories she had heard about the Gestapo headquarters. Though she suspected some were exaggerated, many were undoubtedly true, and these were the stories that terrified her most as she tried to figure out a way inside the gloomy place where civilization and the rule of law did not apply. With her palms now sweaty, she turned her eyes from the soaring white building to the machine-gun nest flanking the front entrance. There were two well-fed armed guards standing behind the sandbags. Indeed, they were almost plump. She frowned as she heard her own stomach growl. While the caloric intake of most Norwegians was subsistence level at best in the war's third year, the German occupiers received the best selections of available food and produce and rarely went hungry.

She studied them carefully, sizing them up. They didn't just look well-fed, they looked formidable in their SS uniforms, black boots, and steel coal-scuttle helmets, with Schmeisser light machine guns slung about their brawny shoulders.

You can't be afraid of them, Annemarie—you must get past them. You must get past them without getting killed.

The question was how?

She gazed up to the fourth floor, trying to locate the office of the German officer she had come to Victoria Terrasse to speak with today. Talking in private with this well-known and greatly feared man was her all-consuming mission. As if on cue, she saw a tall, blond-haired officer in a well-tailored gray suit a Norwegian businessman might wear appear in the sixth window from the right. The figure stood gazing out at the cityscape from behind the glass, as if deep in thought.

She couldn't believe her eyes: it was him!

She felt her heart begin to beat wildly. It suddenly dawned on her that she might never get a chance like this again and had to act fast. The officer was *SS-Obersturmführer* Siegfried Fehmer, the lead police investigator in the infamous *Sicherheitspolizei Abteilung IV*, better known as the Gestapo. His job was to break the Resistance in Oslo and he was damned good at it. She had seen him up close on two prior occasions but had never met him in person. But today was her day.

She was here to plead for mercy from Fehmer on behalf of her father, who had been arrested the night of January 8 and was being held at Grini concentration camp. Though the Germans didn't know it, Roald Breien was the head of *Militær Organisasjon's* Upper Buskerud Cell of the Norwegian Resistance, and Annemarie was here to appeal to Fehmer to use his powerful influence in a gesture of goodwill and set her father free. She had written countless letters to the German Occupation authorities, tried to set up appointments with them, and spoken with countless influential Osloans to secure his release—all to no avail. Now she was desperate. She had decided to take matters into her own hands by making a personal appeal to Fehmer, but to do that she had to somehow find a way to sneak inside Victoria Terrasse and talk alone with him. He was there right now—she just had to find a way to slip inside undetected.

But again, how?

She continued to study him in the window, running through her options in her mind. But to her dismay, after a moment Fehmer disappeared from the window and didn't reappear. Had he sat back down in his chair and returned to work, or was he leaving the building? If he left, her opportunity would be lost. She felt a sudden wave of desperation.

You have to go now, Annemarie!

She started for the front entrance, her legs seeming to move as if through a will of their own. Fifty yards, forty, thirty, twenty…now the SS guards at the front entrance turned their heads towards her and studied her intently, like wolves scrutinizing a deer. She continued walking briskly towards them, pretending that she was a secretary returning from an errand. As she drew closer, they seemed to regard her as little threat and their faces relaxed. But they still looked as though they had no intention of letting her pass without presenting identification.

"Halt," one of them said when she had closed to five paces. He stepped out from behind the sandbag to question her on the purpose of her visit and review her papers.

This was it, the moment she had dreaded: without an appointment or some sort of written authorization to call upon Fehmer, she would be turned away like a whimpering dog. But she couldn't allow that to happen. Her father was not only a man she loved that had raised and nurtured her, but as one of the regional leaders of Milorg he was a key figure in the Resistance. She could not allow him to sit rotting away in Grini with a death sentence hanging over his head. No, she had to act. In a last desperate attempt to secure her father's release, she had decided to lobby Fehmer personally—and she intended to follow through with it.

"Stop, I said," growled the SS guard, his sharp Teutonic staccato like a knife.

She felt her heart thundering in her chest as she realized what she had to do if she wanted to save her father. She knew it was an act of desperation, but she had no other choice.

"Don't shoot! I am here to see Siegfried Fehmer!" she cried, and she dashed past the two guards and flung herself through the door, nearly colliding with a young lieutenant with an SS insignia on his lapel and dueling scar on his cheek, who looked at her in startlement.

"I have a meeting with Siegfried Fehmer!" she cried again, hoping that by invoking the well-known Gestapo officer's name she would not be shot.

Now she could hear the guards muffled voices as they cried after her again to stop. "*Halt mal! Halt! Halt!*"

But she didn't stop. Instead, she picked up speed as she swept past the stunned lieutenant, entered the cavernous lobby, and bolted for the main staircase. The receptionist at the front desk at the foot of the stairs called for her to stop but she blasted past him without slowing down. As she started up the stairs, she heard the front door crash open behind her and the two armed guards dashed into Victoria Terrasse. Glancing over her shoulder, she caught only a glimpse of them and the SS lieutenant as they ran after her, screaming for her to stop.

"Halt oder wir werden schießen!"

She ran up the stairs as fast as her legs would carry her. Her low pumps clattered against the polished marble staircase, resonating loudly in the hollow stairwell and raising a note of terrified urgency. When she was midway to the third floor, she looked over the railing to see how close the Germans were.

From one floor below, the SS lieutenant with the snake-like dueling scar and two sentries glowered up at her. "Stop where you are! Do not move!" commanded the lieutenant in a strong Prussian accent.

Ignoring him, Annemarie dashed on and her pursuers resumed the chase.

Feeling her survival instincts kicking in, she moved at breakneck speed, taking three steps at a time and swinging herself around the hand rails to go faster. But she could hear them gaining on her, and making matters worse, others had joined in the chase. To her dismay, she realized that they would catch her before she reached Fehmer's office.

Hurry, you can't let them cut you off!

Reaching the third floor, she decided that she would have to perform a clever ruse to elude her pursuers. She dashed down the hallway, spotted a room marked "Cleaning," and jumped inside. Panting heavily, covered in perspiration, terrified out of her wits, she quickly ducked behind a bevy of brooms and mops. Then she waited.

She heard the sound of shuffling feet and urgent voices. Then the sounds receded down the hallway and up the stairwell before fading out altogether. Had they gone to Fehmer's office on the fourth floor to warn him, or were they still searching for her on the third floor?

She counted off ten more seconds before going to the door to check. She felt certain the last noise had come from the stairwell leading to the fourth floor and pricked her ear in that direction.

But she heard only muffled, distant voices.

Were they fanning out now to search for her?

She leaned towards the door and listened. Now the voices were loud and close-by again and she heard many clomping footsteps. She had a whole army after her now.

Oh dear, what am I going to do?

She opened the door a crack and looked down the hallway. The SS lieutenant with the scar had taken charge and was shouting out instructions to men and women to search the building. If she stayed here, they would find her eventually.

She decided to make a run for it.

It was then fate intervened on her behalf. The lieutenant led a handful of troops in the opposite direction from the cleaning closet where she was hiding, and a second group led by the two guards went downstairs to see if she had backtracked. This was her chance. Grabbing one of the brooms to look like a cleaning lady, she stepped out into the hallway and started for the fire exit stairs in the opposite direction of the lieutenant and his team.

Halfway to the fire stairs, she heard footsteps behind her. Without breaking stride, she chanced a look over her shoulder.

A female clerk had stepped out of one of the offices. Breathing a sigh of relief that the clerk seemed unaware of the commotion, she walked quickly down the hallway but not so fast that she would draw attention.

The female clerk went into a ladies' room.

Annemarie continued walking, struggling to remain composed. But she hadn't gone five paces when she heard footsteps again, this time coming from far down the hallway. She was gripped with a sudden urge to dash down the fire stairs and run away altogether to save her life. But she could not do that when her father's life was at stake. She kept walking without turning around to see who might be watching her movements or following her, moving quickly but still resisting the urge to run. Again, she told herself not to be afraid, but instinct told her she was about to be caught.

She began to walk faster.

Then, to her horror, she heard the SS officer shout at her, "Halt!"

Heart hammering in her chest, she continued briskly towards the fire exit door, broom in hand.

"Halt or I will shoot!"

Stifling the urge to scream, she ran as fast as her legs would carry her the last fifteen feet and drove her shoulder into the heavy steel door. To her surprise no shots rang out. Just before dashing up the stairs, she glanced back to see how many were coming after her.

The lieutenant had with him five stout German soldiers. But why weren't they shooting at her? Was it because she was a woman?

Slamming the door, she looked for something with which to jam it. Finding nothing, she ran up the stairs to the fourth floor. As she stepped into the hallway, she realized that coming this way was to her advantage, as Fehmer's office was closer to the fire stairs than the main staircase.

Once again reminding herself not to panic, she started to walk briskly towards Fehmer's office. But as she rounded the corner past a row of cubicles, she saw the SS lieutenant with the scar and three of the armed soldiers coming at her from the main staircase.

Oh dear, oh dear!

Survival instinct took over as she turned left and darted towards Fehmer's office, just three offices down. Her feet flew like a magic carpet across the floor.

"Halt! Halt!"

But she didn't halt. There was no reason to unless she wanted her father, Roald Breien, to die. Her only chance to save him and herself was to get to Fehmer and beg for his mercy.

She ran to his office and flung open the door.

CHAPTER 4

GESTAPO HEADQUARTERS
VICTORIA TERRASSE

MAY 14, 1942

TWO MINUTES BEFORE ANNEMARIE BREIEN burst into his office and changed his life forever, Siegfried Wolfgang Fehmer was staring out his window thinking about how much he hated communists. Though he loathed Russian Bolsheviks the worst of all, Norwegian Reds still rankled him, and not solely because of their politics. The fact was the Norwegian communists—represented by Asbjørn Sunde and his Osvald Group—comprised the toughest and most militant Resistance group in Occupied Norway. They were skilled saboteurs who liked to blow things up, just like his other nemesis, Max Manus of the Oslo Gang, who to his dismay, had become something of a cult hero when the seriously injured freedom fighter had rappelled down a rope from a second-floor hospital room and escaped from Fehmer a year ago. The worst part about the communists was that they ran a tight, Soviet-style security network, which had thus far made them one of his most elusive adversaries within the Resistance movement. Three months earlier, in February 1942, the Osvald Group had set explosives at the *Østbanehallen*, blowing up a large portion of the train station to protest the inauguration of Vidkun Quisling, the leader of the pro-German *Nasjonal Samling* Party, as Minister-President of Norway.

He thought back to his time growing up in Russia when he had first learned to hate the communists. Born in Munich of Baltic-German parents, he had spent most of his early years in the Ukraine and Moscow and had Russian citizenship until 1918, when his family moved back to Germany and settled in Berlin. It was in his last year in Russia, when he had witnessed the Revolution of 1917, that he had developed his longstanding hatred of Bolsheviks. It was the most explosive political event of his life—at least until Hitler had come into power in Nazi Germany—marking the end of the Romanov dynasty and centuries of Russian Imperial rule as the leftist revolutionary Vladimir Lenin seized power and began a campaign of murder and property seizures that destroyed the lives of hundreds of thousands of hard-working people. He remembered the fear and uncertainty of life as the Russian Empire collapsed with the abdication of Emperor Nicholas II and the vacuum was filled by Lenin and his gang of murderers. Moscow became an unsafe place to live, and his father decided to pack up and move the family back to Berlin.

Turning away from the window, he returned to his chair and the pile of paperwork at his desk. His office had a masculine flair that reflected his genuine affection for Norway and its culture as well as his unflinching devotion to Hitler's Reich. On his desk stood a hand-carved wooden lamp with a Viking emblem; several tin soldiers of Norwegian Knights in glittering armor; a silver plaque with the inscription of an Iron Cross; a gold-plated rotary telephone with finger-holes in hunter green; and today's copy of the conservative Oslo newspaper *Aftenposten*, which had been sympathetic to Fascist Italy and Nazi Germany since the beginning of the war. The bookcase lining the wall to his left was packed with Gestapo handbooks on interrogation techniques, police procedurals, legal documents, and counterintelligence briefs. In contrast, the bookcase on the opposite wall provided him with an escape from his Sipo work. Stuffed into its top two rows were leatherbound copies of *Mein Kampf* and Hans Grimm's *People Without Space*, as well as other works by state-approved, pro-Nazi writers such as Werner Bumelburg, Gottfried Benn, Agnes Miegel, Rudolf Binding, and Börries von Münchhausen; and packed into the bottom two rows were the complete works of the pro-Nazi Norwegian writer Knut Hamsun, who had been awarded the Nobel Prize in Literature in 1920. Hanging from the walls were reproductions of two famous paintings from the late 1800s of peasants in bucolic landscapes: *Shepherds at Tåtøy* and *On the Plain*, created by the reputable Norwegian artist and illustrator Erik Theodor Werenskiold.

In the corner of the office lay Fehmer's coal-black German shepherd, Wolfie. After a moment, the fearlessly loyal canine made eye contact with him, rose from his fleece dog mattress, and walked over to him to be petted. Smiling down at him, Fehmer began stroking his neck and whispering soothingly.

Suddenly, his door flung open, taking him by surprise.

"Captain Fehmer, I need to talk to you! It is most urgent!" a young woman cried breathlessly in German.

Before he could react, Wolfie jerked free from him, rounded his desk, and charged the woman, barking aggressively and baring his sharp teeth.

"No, Wolfie, down!" At his command, the German shepherd stopped in his tracks but continued barking loudly at the woman, protecting his master. Fehmer jumped out of his chair, grabbed the dog by the collar, and restrained him as a handful of armed soldiers burst into the room right behind the woman.

"Are you all right, Herr Fehmer?" one of them cried, and he reached out to grab the woman.

She jerked her arm away. "Let me go! I am here to see Captain Fehmer!"

Holding back Wolfie, Fehmer looked at the woman more closely. She had blonde hair, blue eyes, luminescent skin as smooth as silk, and a fine Norwegian figure that he would have been more than happy to intimately explore. Her cheeks were flush with color and she was short of breath; she must have run up the stairs to his office, eluding guards and receptionists along the way. Desperation mingled with resolve showed on her face, and he couldn't help but think to himself: *What a beautiful and remarkably brave young woman.*

"Please, Captain Fehmer, I must speak with you! The matter is of the utmost urgency!"

Though her German was quite good, he could tell that she was Norwegian, so he spoke to her in her native tongue. "And just who am I speaking to?"

"My name is Annemarie Breien. I am sorry for the intrusion, but I had no one else to turn to."

Again, Wolfie barked at her and bared his teeth. He took the dog firmly by the collar and guided him towards his fleece mattress. "Stay!" he commanded, and the German shepherd lowered his head submissively and obeyed.

When he turned back around, an SS lieutenant whose scarred-face Fehmer recognized but name he didn't know stepped forward. "This woman should be arrested, sir! She ran past the guards at the entrance and refused to stop when requested to do so several times!"

Fehmer looked at her. "Is this true?"

She was still catching her breath. "Yes, but I only did it because I had to see you!"

"You had to see me?"

"I have called here at Victoria Terrasse more than a dozen times and sent several letters regarding my father, who has been wrongfully imprisoned at Grini, but no one has answered me back. That's the only reason I ran past the guards to see you. I am desperate and am here to plead for your mercy!"

So that's what this is about, he thought: *the young woman wants me to free her father.* "What is your father's name?"

"Roald Breien."

"What crime has he been charged with?"

"Working for the underground as an enemy of the state. But as I said, it is not true."

The lieutenant scoffed. "You don't actually believe this woman?"

He looked at her, letting his eyes linger sympathetically, before casting a harsh scowl at the impudent young officer. "It is not your place to question me, Lieutenant. Now please leave us." He made eye contact with the others. "That means everyone. I need to speak alone with Frøken Breien here."

"But this woman is a criminal! She should be arrested!"

"I will be the judge of that, Lieutenant. Now please leave my office at once, or you will force me to report your insolent conduct to Colonel Fehlis. Have I made myself clear?"

The scar on the young officer's face visibly reddened at the mention of the *SS-Oberführer.* Heinrich Fehlis was Fehmer's boss and chief of the German Security Service in Occupied Norway, which included Sipo, the branch tasked with investigating alleged crimes and acts of sabotage committed by the Norwegian Resistance against the Reich, and the *Sicherheitsdienst,* or SD, the official security service of the SS and Nazi Party.

"My apologies, sir. I will leave you now then," said the lieutenant meekly, and he and the others left.

When the door closed, Fehmer smiled cordially at the woman and waved her to the upholstered leather chair in front of his eighteenth-century desk. "Please take a seat, Annemarie. You don't mind if I call you Annemarie, do you?"

She looked at him warily as she took her seat. "No, I don't mind," she said.

"Good, and you may call me Siegfried."

"Very well, Siegfried." Her voice was still tentative.

He sat down and leaned back in his high-backed black leather chair, which bore an emblem of the *Parteiadler* of the Third Reich—an eagle violently clutching a swastika in its claws. Then he smiled to put her at ease. He could tell that she was afraid of him, which made him feel a touch ashamed. He loved Norway, spoke its language fluently, and enjoyed its people, considering Germans and Norwegians members of the same Nordic-Aryan tribe with a common heritage and folklore. Sometimes, it tore him up inside to have to crack down on a kindred people whose culture and history he so greatly admired. He even dressed like a Norwegian. Though he sometimes donned his stiff gray-green SS uniform, black peaked cap, and black boots, he typically dressed like an affluent Oslo businessman. Today, for instance, he was wearing a double-breasted gray suit with a white silk pocket square, blue tie, and handsome brown leather dress shoes. Fehmer—who was known to be quite a ladies' man in Occupied Norway—had fine taste in clothing and always liked to be smartly dressed.

"Now tell me how I can help you?" he asked her in a soft voice.

Her response was forthright. "I would like you to get my father out of prison. He is not a member of the Home Front and has been wrongly rounded up and put behind bars. As I said, he is being held at Grini."

"Is trial pending?"

"Yes. He will be sentenced to death if the allegation against him is proved. But he has done nothing wrong, as I have told you."

"Then why was he arrested?"

"Many innocent people have been arrested, Captain Fehmer, and my father is one of them."

"Just so you know I am not actually a captain."

"You're not? But you're the head of Sipo *Abteilung IV*—the Gestapo."

"No, I'm actually not. At the end of the day, I am but an overworked first lieutenant with the responsibilities of a captain and several demanding bosses above me. Which means that if I'm going to have any chance of helping you, I'm going to need to know more about you." A meticulous record-keeper like most Germans, he took up his pen and held it poised above a small black leather notebook imprinted with a blood-red swastika. "What is your date of birth and where are you from?"

"I was born on August 19, 1915 in Vestre Aker."

"An Osloan, I see," he said, as he began taking notes. "And what did you do before the war?"

"I grew up in Slemdal before my family moved to a farm on Ringerike. I trained in gymnastics at the National Gymnastics School, and in 1937 I traveled to Munich to study rhythmic gymnastics."

"So, you have been to the Fatherland? Did you enjoy your studies there?"

"Very much so."

He looked at her wedding ring. "I can see you are married."

"Yes."

"What is your husband's name?"

"Kjell Langballe."

He continued writing in his notebook without looking up. "You did not take your husband's name?"

"I did, but I go by Annemarie Breien Langballe and sometimes forget to say my full name."

"How long have you been married?"

"Two years. Kjell and I were married in 1940."

"What does your husband do for a living?"

"He is a lawyer."

He had found that most lawyers were subversives with ties to the Home Front, but he did not say this to her. He made a note to investigate her husband to determine if he was on any of the political lists or had any known ties to the Resistance. "What about your parents?"

"As I told you, my father is Roald Breien. My mother's name is Nancy, and she is terribly worried about my father." She leaned forward impatiently in her chair. "Please, can you help me, Lieutenant Fehmer? He is just an ordinary working man who has not lifted a finger against Germany. He does not belong in prison."

He offered no reply, instead forging on with another question. "When was your father arrested?"

"On January 8."

He was surprised that her father been held for three months, but the wheels of the criminal justice system in Occupied Norway often ground along slowly. "Do you have brothers and sisters?"

"Yes. My two brothers are Roald Jr. and Oscar, and my sister's name is Nancy. Like me they are in their twenties."

"Are you the oldest?"

"Yes."

"Are they with the *Hjemmefronten*?"

She gave a look of shock. "No, of course they are not with the Home Front. And like I said, neither is my father."

"I don't suppose, though, you would tell me if they were. And what about yourself, are you in the Resistance?"

"No. If I was, Lieutenant Fehmer, do you think I would venture here into the lion's den? This is Gestapo headquarters."

"Perhaps it is a reverse psychological ploy and you are trying to fool me. In any case, I have to pose these difficult questions because I will be unable to help you if you or your family members are in the Resistance. And please call me Siegfried. We don't need to be so formal here."

"Very well, Siegfried."

"And if I asked you if your husband was in the Resistance, what would you say?"

"I would say no because he is a practicing lawyer, as I have been informed you used to be. Now I think you have asked enough questions. Can you help me or not, Siegfried?"

He couldn't help but admire her for her courage in coming here and for her directness. He closed his notebook with Teutonic flourish. "I have to be honest with you, Annemarie. The only thing I can promise you is I will look into this matter personally. If your story checks out, then I may be able to arrange for your father's release."

Her face lit up with hope. "Really?"

"Yes, but even if it can be done, it will take time. It is important for you to understand that."

"I do," she said.

He smiled at her, hoping to win over her trust. There was an appreciative gleam in her eyes, and he knew he was smitten. She possessed an unusual combination of sweetness, bravery, intelligence, and determination—and he most definitely wanted to see her again. He wondered if such a thing as love at first sight, or at least love upon a first encounter, was truly possible. He also wondered if it was fate or just plain random luck that had brought her flying through his door. Regardless, Annemarie Breien was an extraordinary woman, and he resolved that he would win her over so he could see her again. He suspected that she wasn't as innocent as she pretended, and most likely had ties to the Resistance even if she wasn't an active member of Milorg or one of the other partisan groups. Which meant that she might prove useful to him from a practical standpoint by serving as a possible link to the Norwegian underground. For Fehmer, the Resistance wasn't always an entity to be hounded and crushed; there were also diplomatic angles and negotiations to pursue with its leadership to limit bloodshed, ensure stability, and exchange information. But he didn't want her to know that.

"You are a remarkably brave woman, Annemarie. You do realize that, don't you?"

She nodded humbly but said nothing.

"Not many people would have the courage to do what you just did. To have rushed past the guards like that…well it's quite amazing. At the same time, you do realize you could have been shot?"

"I just wanted to save my father. He doesn't deserve to die."

"I understand. But it was still quite a risk you took."

"If I hadn't tried, I would have felt ashamed. I love my father and don't want him to be executed for something he didn't do."

"He is a very fortunate father to have a daughter like you."

"And to have a reasonable man like you working on his behalf. You are going to help me, aren't you, Siegfried?"

He liked the way she said his name. "If I want to see you again, do I have a choice?"

Her gaze was direct. "No, I'm afraid you don't. And in the end, you'll have to come through for me. I will not allow my father to be executed."

My God, she is both brave and demanding—but with such sweetness and innocence. How is such a thing possible? "If your father is innocent as you say, I have every intention of helping you, I can assure you," he said with a seductive smile, unable to suppress his urge to flirt with her.

But she seemed unseduced by his charms. She reached across the desk and took his hands in hers, like a kindly niece to an uncle, and looked into his eyes. "I believe there is quite a bit of goodness in you, Siegfried. Please tell me I was not mistaken in coming to you today."

Siegfried Wolfgang Fehmer—one of the top five most powerful Nazis in Occupied Norway—sat there completely captivated and speechless, as if a spell had been cast over him. A full ten seconds passed before he found his voice. "You are not mistaken. But even once I have checked up on your story, it is going to take some clever maneuvering, as well as time, to secure your father's release from Grini. I cannot emphasize that enough."

She touched his hand above the thumb and he felt a shudder of excitement; her hand was warm and as soft as the underside of a baby's chin. Then she stood up from her chair, signaling that the meeting was over.

He wished that she wouldn't leave.

"Thank you, Siegfried, for hearing me out," she said. "I know you will do the right thing."

"I will most certainly try," he said. "Of that, I can assure you."

"May I call upon you in a week then to see where the situation stands?"

He felt his heart palpitate. "Yes, that will be fine. In fact, I will be delighted to see you again."

"Good. So, we have an accord?"

"Yes, if your story checks out, we have an accord," he said, but deep down he already knew that she had won him over and he would do everything possible to get her father released from prison.

CHAPTER 5

ABWEHR NANTES SPY SCHOOL
VILLA DE LA BRETONNIÈRE, OCCUPIED FRANCE

AUGUST 29, 1942

SPYMASTER STEPHAN ALBERT HEINRICH VON GRÖNING—known to Eddie Chapman as Dr. Stephan Graumann—stared out his second-floor study window at his prodigy. The young Englishman was sitting in the garden smoking, talking, and petting the Alsatians with three fellow spies that Chapman knew only as Albert, Leo, and Schmidt. To their right, in the direction of the ornamental pond, Walter Thomas was practicing English dancing steps in his ever-present Southampton University boating tie. Von Gröning took a puff of his *Eckstein cigaretten*, blew out a bluish cloud of smoke from his nostrils, and looked at it appreciatively. Unbeknownst to Chapman, "Albert," "Leo," "Schmidt," and "Walter Thomas" were in reality: a former traveling salesman named Albert Schael, a toothless prizefighter and criminal named Leo Kreusch, a saboteur named Franz Stetzner who had traveled to London before the war to work as a waiter sponsored by a British hotel association, and a dedicated Nazi and Anglophile with English ancestry and obsessed with Morris dancing named Walter Praetorius.

To the German spymaster's delight, Chapman had already taken to spy games like a fish to water, and he was bonding with his German hosts. After four and a half months of rigorous training here at La Bretonnière and in Paris under the tutelage of multifarious experts of varied nationalities, he was now an expert in his own right in explosives, radio communications, parachute jumping, clandestine operations, photography, map reading, firearms, and committing acts of sabotage without getting caught. In fact, von Gröning, who ran his Nantes Dienststelle spy shop in Occupied France as his own personal fiefdom, was so impressed with his new golden boy that he had bestowed upon Agent Fritz the code name Fritzchen, the diminutive form of Fritz, as a term of trust and endearment. He had big plans for the safecracker.

It had been a glorious summer: the liquor had flowed copiously, the food and weather had been superb, and the men had formed a strong comradery singing songs and bibulously swapping stories at night. Von Gröning and his team of operatives lived like princes and suffered few of the discomforts of war while performing their espionage training. Most days, the French country *maison de maître* on the outskirts of the industrial port of Nantes hardly seemed like an Abwehr spy training center at all. The villa was graced with fine oil paintings, solid oak floors, marble fireplaces, crystal chandeliers, and double doors that opened onto a spacious grassy lawn and sumptuous gardens. The grounds were flanked by a thick stand of elm, oak, and beech trees and a high, vine-draped wall to keep nosy neighbors and the French Resistance from eavesdropping. To the west, the land sloped gently towards the beautiful Erdre River. The woods, orchards, and verdant fields along the river banks served as a quiet refuge for grazing red deer, felines, rabbits, squirrels, and a host of waterfowl.

The only thing that everyone agreed was disappointingly lacking was women. Chapman and the others frequently joked that they lived "like bloody monks." Unfortunately, the only antidote was the sporting ladies from the red-light district of Nantes, whose favors Chapman and his comrades were allowed to partake in on occasion, albeit discretely, so as to not raise the suspicion of the locals or the Gestapo. Chapman had had two girlfriends—one named Freda Stevenson and the other Betty Farmer—back in England, but that had been before the war and he now spent most of his time with good-time girls and prostitutes. Von Gröning knew that Agent Fritz had too much of a wandering eye to be faithful to only one woman, and the lad had admitted as much to his German handler. The man was a restless spirit, which von Gröning knew was not a bad attribute for a spy.

Today, the Abwehr officer had decided, was the day that his protégé would be told about his first assignment. Though Chapman was developing into a first-rate spy, he was growing increasingly bored, restless, and frustrated with the relentless training and enforced chastity at the Dienststelle itself. It was obvious to von Gröning that what he needed was a chance to perform some real spycraft. After surviving a harrowing parachute training drop in high winds that had left him requiring major dental work and after passing a battery of tests with flying colors, including a successful mock explosives raid on a French locomotive works, Chapman had in recent weeks become moody and withdrawn. To make matters worse, he had been insisting on writing his left-behind friend Tony Faramus in Fort de Romainville. Of course, for security reasons von Gröning refused. He told him that he would send the young man a food parcel, but Chapman was insistent that more be done to help his old friend. Not usually one to raise his voice in anger, von Gröning brusquely responded that such a thing was impossible. Realizing his folly, he then softened his voice and mollified Chapman reassuringly: "Don't you worry. We're going to send Faramus a parcel and he'll be well looked after." It was a lie, of course, but he hoped it would appease his protégé.

But the former safecracker was not convinced and asked him on the spot if he could be sent back to the French prison. That's when von Gröning realized that if he didn't dangle a carrot in front of Chapman soon, by offering him the opportunity to finally put his training to good use, he ran the risk of losing him altogether.

He called down from the second-story window. "Fritzchen, I'd like to have a word with you please."

Chapman tossed a ball to one of the Alsatian puppies. "I'll be right up," he said.

When Chapman entered the villa and was out of earshot, von Gröning leaned over the balcony and gestured at Walter Praetorius and Franz Stetzner, so-called "Thomas" and "Schmidt." "Give us five minutes, Walter, and then you and Franz come on up." He didn't give any further explanation than that, and the two men nodded.

A minute later, Chapman appeared.

"Have a seat, Fritzchen," he said pleasantly from behind his desk. When Chapman was seated, he took the typewritten sheet of paper in front of him and passed it across to him. "I have prepared a contract, written in English, for your professional services to spy against your country. I would like you to read it over and sign it—and then I can go over the details of your mission."

A flash of excitement crossed Eddie Chapman's face. "It's about time," he said, taking the sheet of paper from him. "Where do I sign?"

Von Gröning tried to conceal his own elation. He had been right: this was precisely the remedy Fritzchen needed to get out of his melancholy funk. "You should read it over first while I summarize the key points."

"Yes, of course."

"As you can see, the contract is between you, Fritz Graumann, and the Third Reich and calls for you to be paid one hundred fifty thousand reichsmarks—or, if you prefer, the same amount in pounds sterling, at a rate of ten pounds to the mark—for the proposed sabotage operation and associated espionage activities in England."

"Yes, I see it here in the second paragraph."

"While in France, we will pay you twelve thousand francs per month, and once you leave for England you will receive three hundred reichsmarks per month. In addition, you will be given the sum of one thousand pounds for spending money upon your departure and all incidental expenses will be reimbursed upon your return to Occupied France or Germany."

"And if I'm captured?"

"As you can see in the agreement, you will continue to be paid."

"How much?"

"If for any reason you are imprisoned while in Britain, you will automatically receive six hundred reichsmarks per month."

"For how long?"

"Until the end of the war."

"And as I said, upon your return to us, you will receive the full payment of one hundred fifty thousand reichsmarks, assuming you have successfully completed your mission to the satisfaction of the Abwehr. As you can see, there are several conditions."

"Yes, I'm reading the first paragraph."

"First, if you somehow do manage to be caught, you are to keep quiet. By signing this contract, you are agreeing not to divulge any of the names of people who have trained you, that you have worked with, or that you have had contact with in Jersey, France, or Germany. In short, you can tell them nothing about any of the places you have been or anything you have learned since the Gestapo arrested you in Jersey."

"And the penalty for violating any of these conditions?"

"Execution, I'm afraid. You can see it in the fourth sentence of paragraph one."

"Yes, I see."

"Furthermore, this clause extends to not only those you have trained and worked with or come into contact with, but any of the chemical formulae or techniques you have learned under our direction."

Chapman reread the paragraph again before looking up. "I understand, Doktor."

At that moment, Walter Praetorius and Maurice Schmidt walked into the study.

"Ah, yes, gentlemen, good timing. I believe Agent Fritz here is ready to sign the agreement we have prepared for him. I need you to act as witnesses."

"Of course," said the man Chapman knew as Walter Thomas.

"Wait just one minute. I am still looking it over," said Chapman.

"Yes, of course," said von Gröning as Praetorius and Schmidt took seats at the conference table in the room.

"What's this about taxes?" asked the young Englishman.

Von Gröning smiled graciously. "Oh yes, paragraph three. You are legally responsible for paying all taxes on your earnings as an intelligence asset in France since this is where the agreement has been drafted."

"Wait a second. I'm about to parachute into enemy territory and perform a major act of sabotage—and Hitler is worried about me paying bloody taxes?"

"Blame it on the bean counters in Berlin. They do things that I will never understand."

"Paying taxes is the last thing I'd be worried about. Hell, I'll be lucky not to get caught."

"You have raised an interesting point. If you were caught by the British authorities and they learned of your criminal past, how long of a sentence would you receive? Your best estimate?"

"I'd say my sentence would be in the neighborhood of fifteen to twenty years. It would be me fifth or sixth time in the slammer."

Von Gröning looked at Praetorius and, with an exaggeratedly somber expression, said, "I don't suppose there is much danger of him surrendering to the police then. Wouldn't you agree?"

Praetorius nodded. "No, I wouldn't think so."

"Yes, well, I think that settles the matter," said von Gröning. "Are you ready to sign then, Fritzchen, so I can get on with the details of your mission?"

With the mention of the cross-channel operation again, Chapman's expression changed from sober reflection to alertness. "Yes, I will sign the agreement now," he said, reaching for the ink pen on the desk in front of him.

Von Gröning smiled discretely at Praetorius and Schmidt then reached for the additional copies on his desk. "Here, you have to sign all six copies. And make sure to use your alias, Fritz Graumann," he added. He pushed the small pile towards Chapman. He had already signed each copy with his alias: *S. Graumann (Doktor).*

The young Brit proceeded to sign all six copies. When he was finished, Thomas and Schmidt left to lock the signed copies in the safe.

Von Gröning took a moment to gather his thoughts before launching into the mission details. He hadn't meant to make Chapman angry by suggesting disloyalty on his part, only to remind him that if he made the mistake of surrendering himself to the authorities in England, he would be looking at serious jail time. The truth was von Gröning and Chapman had grown quite fond of one another in the past five months. The avuncular German spymaster had become a mentor and father figure to his protégé, and he admired Chapman for his boundless energy, wit, enthusiasm, and his fearlessness. At night, when spy school was done for the day, they would drink brandy together and discuss art, music, and literature, and Chapman would regale him with colorful stories of his criminal past. They quickly found that they both had a passion for the novels of H. G. Wells and the poetry of Tennyson and talked for hours on end on these subjects.

Although they had grown close, von Gröning kept their relationship in perspective. Chapman was his secret weapon to be harnessed against the enemy across the channel: Great Britain. In raising the prospect of incarceration if Chapman turned himself in to the British police, he was letting his prodigy know that he had selected him to be his personal spy not because he was special, but because he was a valuable resource. Chapman gave von Gröning the opportunity to not only survive but thrive within the Abwehr without the possibility of being sent to the front or coming under the scrutiny of the SS.

"All right, Fritzchen, let's go over the details of your mission to Britain. Your primary target will be the de Havilland Aircraft Company factory outside London that manufactures the new Mosquito fighter-bombers that have been wreaking havoc upon the Reich."

"You're talking about the factory in Hatfield, Hertfordshire?"

"Yes, your mission is to blow it up."

"The whole factory?"

"No, we understand that would be difficult, if not impossible. We would regard the mission as a success if you could blow up the boiler house or destroy the electric plant, or preferably both."

"I see. That's quite an operation."

"You will be parachuted north of London with a wireless and enough money to last for six months. You would then find a place to hide out and gather a quantity of explosives, with help from your previous criminal associates if need be, provided they are not wanted by the police."

"So that's it: the target is the de Havilland factory?"

"We have secondary objectives for you as well. First, we want you to report on troop movements, particularly the Americans. We want to know where they're stationed along with the corps signs displayed on American transport vehicles. Second, we want you to identify secondary aircraft factories and conduct sabotage operations there, if practicable. Third, we would like you to send reports on the positions of flak artillery around London. While these secondary operations are important, blowing up the de Havilland factory is to be your primary objective."

"Why do you want to destroy the factory so badly? Is a single airplane really tipping the scales of the war?"

"Unfortunately, yes. What we refer to in jest as the *Anopheles de Havillandus* has been a thorn in our side since shortly after the war began. The reason is that the Mosquito fighter-bomber is made almost entirely of wood, requires only a two-man crew, and doesn't man defensive guns. That's why the bloody thing can carry four thousand pounds of bombs and has an effective range of seven hundred miles. They call it the Wooden Wonder. It can clock in at over four hundred miles per hour, fast enough to outrun most of our fighters. Plus, it's incredibly cheap to build and highly accurate in targeted bombing runs. *Reichsmarschall* Göring has declared holy war on the airplane. He wants it taken off the assembly line."

"I didn't realize it was such a powerful weapon."

"The Mosquito is so easy to build that even cabinetmakers and carpenters can put together the damned things. Not only that but it can be used in almost any type of operation. Besides targeted bombing missions, it is well-suited for aerial photo reconnaissance, night fighting, V-boat destruction, minelaying, and even transport. If you can cripple the de Havilland plant, Fritzchen, you will be a living legend and I promise you will be well-rewarded for your efforts."

"I'd better succeed then. Here's hopefully to an Iron Cross and not a coffin."

"Come now, Fritzchen, there will be no coffin for you. You have the luck of an Irishman about you and I am confident you'll see an Iron Cross in your future."

"You truly think so?"

"Yes, I do. If you can do this for us, you will have nothing more to worry about. Your whole future will be set when you come back. And upon your triumphant return, we will drink champagne and I will say to everyone, 'I always knew my Fritzchen would win the Iron Cross. It was his destiny.'"

And with that von Gröning fingered his own Iron Cross at his throat—and smiled the smile of a true German spymaster.

CHAPTER 6

KARL JOHANS GATE AND VICTORIA TERRASSE
OSLO, OCCUPIED NORWAY

SEPTEMBER 25, 1942

THE TWO LUFTWAFFE FOCKE-WULF FW 190S swept in from the southwest, screaming across the tops of the buildings. The pair of fighters had flown in from Stavanger for the parade flyover, and the crowd of Norwegian Nazi loyalists along the length of Karl Johans gate roared its approval, with people waving their arms and tossing their hats in the air in celebration. Despite the excitement, Dagmar Lahlum frowned at the sight of the fighters. She didn't so much mind the German pilots showboating for the crowd's entertainment; what she objected to was what the two planes represented. They reminded her—as if she needed to be reminded yet again—that Hitler's Nazi Germany controlled her country and was tightening its grip on the Norwegian people with every passing day.

Over the past two and a half years, since Falkenhorst's victorious German Army had marched triumphantly into Oslo, she had grown to despise the Nazis. They weren't just to blame for shortages of food, clothing, and other basic necessities; their draconian rules and regulations had put a muzzle on *all* forms of freedom and posed a daily burden. Even worse, the ubiquitous presence of an occupation force made her feel insecure and paranoid, like she was always being watched. But as she looked around her at the crowd that had gathered to celebrate the 8th Congress of Minister-President Vidkun Quisling's *Nasjonal Samling* Party, she knew that she hated Norwegian collaborators more than even the Nazis.

Reportedly, more than thirty thousand traitorous "quislings" had joined the NS—Norway's answer to the Nazi Party—since the beginning of the Occupation. She couldn't believe that so many of her people were going along with Quisling and German *Reichskommissar* Josef Terboven's program for Nazifying the country. For her part, she was vociferously anti-Nazi and anti-*Nasjonal Samling*, at least in the private company of friends since publicly denouncing either could get one thrown into prison. Despite her disdain for the German occupiers and their Norwegian collaborators, she had come to watch the Quisling parade out of morbid curiosity. Her apartment was only a fifteen-minute walk away in Frydenlundsgate, and she had decided to spend her day off from work to witness firsthand how low her fellow countrymen had sunk. She had planned on going to the *Marka*—the beautiful hiking and cross-country skiing forest surrounding Oslo—to enjoy an invigorating stroll through nature for the day, but at the last minute she had changed her mind.

The fighters roared past, engines gunning, and raced off to the west in the direction of the airport in Fornebu as the people in the procession and spectators on the sidewalks continued to wave their hats and cheer. Dagmar shook her head in disgust as she watched the German planes and their trailing white plumes of tail exhaust recede in the distance. *The Nazis don't belong here in Norway,* she thought bitterly; *in fact, we should never have allowed them to set foot on our soil in the first place.*

It was then she saw a man wearing a fedora, wire-rimmed spectacles, and a trench coat discretely studying her.

She felt the breath catch in her throat. Was he Gestapo? She pretended not to notice him staring at her and looked to the southwest towards Victoria Terrasse. A bright red Nazi flag with a swastika fluttered in the breeze above the Gestapo headquarters. Feeling a sudden chill down her spine, she started down Karl Johans gate in the opposite direction of the Royal Palace, heading towards the *Universitetsplassen.*

The man followed her.

She felt her heart begin to beat faster.

She parted her way quickly through the crowd, continuing southeast. When she was even with the *Domus Bibliotheca*, she turned sharply to the left and made her way through a gap in the parade. Reaching the far curb, she paused for a moment and glanced casually across her left shoulder to see if the man was following her.

To her horror, he still was.

She turned on a heel and started moving again through the crowd, which had grown thicker in University Square. She saw people craning their necks to get a better view and realized someone important must be passing through the square. Then she caught a glimpse of Vidkun Quisling himself. He and what appeared to be a contingent of NS Party leaders were heading in the direction of the *Domus Media* building escorted by an armed escort of uniformed Norwegian policemen. Near the front of the iconic Neoclassical façade designed by Christian Heinrich Grosch, Quisling stopped and waved to the crowd. Wearing a dapper, navy-blue suit with a white handkerchief, he appeared to be on his way to make a speech for the 8th Congress occasion. Hundreds of NS supporters in the crowd cheered as he waved to them and took a moment to shake a few hands.

Dagmar frowned. Here in the flesh was the bastard who had betrayed her county and was remaking Norway into a Fascist state. The sycophant who had, through his Nazi backers, removed all those not loyal to the so-called "New Order" from positions of authority. Political leaders, judges, clergy, teachers, administrators, business leaders, policemen, journalists—he had replaced thousands of them with Nazi-sympathizing NS Party members. For a moment, she imagined herself shooting him dead where he stood in front of his quisling followers. But the image had only just begun to form in her head when *Reichskommissar* Terboven's lap dog was off again, heading towards the old hall of the university with his phalanx of policemen.

Realizing she had been momentarily distracted, she looked around for the man that had been following her. She no longer saw him, but there were now so many people packing into the *Universitetsplassen*, it was hard to tell. She decided to take advantage of the opportunity and start walking again so she could hopefully lose him for good.

She looked at her watch. It was ten minutes to four.

She walked down Karl Johans gate and crossed the street again through the parade crowd at Universitetsgata. A marching band member barked out archly to her as she squeezed her way through the band, but she ignored him and ducked into the crowd on the far sidewalk. From there, she strode quickly into Eidsvoll Square, filled with public gardens and neat rows of evenly spaced poplar trees just beginning to lose their leaves. When she had passed the central square and made it to the trees beyond, she chanced another look over her shoulder.

The man in the trench coat was staring at her from the edge of the trees off Karl Johans gate, his hands stuffed into his pockets.

My God, he's like a ghost! How does he do it?

She dashed through the park to Stortingsgata, keeping the embowering row of trees between her and her mysterious pursuer. The man started moving east-to-west through the park, following her movements.

She felt a razor's edge paranoia, as if she was a fugitive on the run. Why, she asked herself, did she have to come to see the Quisling parade? If she had just stayed at her apartment in Frydenlundsgate, she would never have gotten herself into this situation. She could have been at home quietly enjoying a Sigrid Undset novel instead of being on the run.

She picked up her pace.

The man matched her stride for stride. For the first time, it struck her that he looked familiar. She had the feeling she had seen him before today, but she couldn't remember where. *My God, has he been following me for some time?* she wondered.

She looked around the street, wondering if she should ask for help from some stranger. But to her surprise, the pedestrians seemed to be looking at her suspiciously. Suddenly, she felt like an imposter in her own city.

Crossing the street, she took a soft left onto Roald Amundsen gate, named for the famous Norwegian polar explorer.

She glanced again over her shoulder, searching the trees along the edge of the square. The man walked swiftly between a pair of poplars and started to cross the street. She couldn't help but feel as if she was in some sort of spy novel.

She was gripped with a sudden urge to run, to flat out tear down the street and dash into the police station. But she couldn't trust the police; they were pawns of the Nazis and would probably arrest her for some minor offense or take her name down and put her on a list of suspicious Norwegians to keep an eye out for. She told herself to remain calm and not be afraid: it was best not to panic despite her overwhelming urge to flee.

She began to walk faster.

To her infinite horror, she could now hear footsteps behind her. She turned again and saw that the man was moving quickly now and gaining on her.

Damnit!

She picked up her pace as she made it to Dronning Mauds gate. The Oslo docks were on her left now, just a hundred feet to the south, and the scent of the sea was potent. As she started to take the corner, she heard the distant drone of airplanes.

A whole squadron of airplanes.

She paused to look southward in the direction of the sound, but she couldn't see the planes yet. But there was no doubt they were coming: the sounds were growing louder. It must be the German fighters returning for another aerial demonstration above the parade. But why then was the sound coming from the south?

Before resuming walking, she flicked a glance back up Roald Amundsen gate for her pursuer, but he had stopped on the sidewalk to look up at the sky.

This was her chance.

She started walking northwest at a brisk pace, hoping to put some distance between herself and her pursuer. The roar of the aircraft grew louder. As she neared the intersection of Dronning Mauds gate and Munkedamsveien, she looked up again at the sky.

Now she could see the planes.

There were four of them, screaming in from the south like a swarm of angry hornets, skimming the waves of Oslo Harbor as they skirted the eastern side of the Oslo Fjord. From their low approach and aggressive-looking formation, they couldn't possibly be German planes making another pass over the parade, though she couldn't yet make out any markings. And then to the west, she saw a pair of Focke-Wulf's fighters with black swastikas and yellow trim on their tails like the ones she had seen earlier. They appeared to be flying in to intercept the four aircraft and she knew then that the airplanes grazing the top of Akershus Castle did not belong to the Nazis. Were they going to bomb the parade?

Instinctively, she turned and dashed northwest towards Munkedamsveien. She wondered why no air-raid alarm was sounding near Akershus Fortress or along the shore. And then she heard the sound of machine-gun firing as the anti-aircraft shore batteries opened up on the new interlopers. Looking back over her shoulder, she saw that the man in the trench coat had come to a stop fifty yards behind her and was staring up at the approaching aircraft and the Luftwaffe planes streaking in to intercept them. She studied the man for a moment before turning around again and heading up the street. She wanted to get as far away from him and the incoming planes as possible.

To her surprise, she quickly came upon Victoria Terrasse. With machine guns rattling her ears and airplane engines roaring, she looked up at the monstrous Gestapo headquarters then back at the four incoming planes. Unbeknownst to her, they were de Havilland Mosquito B Mark IV Series 2 DK338's from the No. 105 Squadron of the British Royal Air Force under the command of squadron leader George Parry. The twin-engined light bombers were extremely fast and bore British markings. They were flying so low over the parade that she could swear they would clip the marching band.

And then she realized what the British planes were doing here: they were going to bomb the Gestapo headquarters.

She had to get the hell out of here.

She started running down Munkedamsveien, seeing people up and down the street in the direction of Karl Johans gate scrambling for cover. But she hadn't gotten ten steps before the bombers veered hard left from the Royal Palace and swooped in. The bulging bomb bay doors opened up like a chasm and disgorged their bombs from no more than one hundred feet above Victoria Terrasse.

What happened next unfolded as if in slow motion. She stood there breathlessly, unable to move her feet, as four whistling bombs dropped and smashed into the Gestapo headquarters. At the same time, the two German Focke-Wulf's intercepted the British planes and opened fire. For a brief instant, it was like some great pageant as the bombs plummeted downward through the air and the machine guns crackled and the six, engaged aircraft raced across the backdrop of blue sky, the men inside the flying machines heavily engaged in combat and fighting desperately. The red tracer fire flew past like comets streaking across the heavens. It was so visceral and violent that up close it seemed surreal to her.

She covered her ears and braced herself for the explosions. But to her surprise, there weren't any. Instead, the heavy bombs augered their way through the roof of the massive building and exited through the rear wall without detonating. And then, after what seemed like a long delay but was really only a matter of seconds, the bombs went off. Three explosions, one right after the other, rocked the Gestapo headquarters and surrounding neighborhood like an earth tremor. She realized that the bombs must have been delayed-action devices for the pilots' protection since the planes were flying so low.

She felt a wave of searing airborne heat from the blast. A cloud of black smoke erupted from the corner of Victoria Terrasse and the building beyond. She waited expectantly for a fourth explosion, but there wasn't one. As smoke, debris, and a great quantity of dark red dust enveloped the Gestapo headquarters, she realized that the fourth bomb had failed to detonate.

The British bombers climbed to a higher altitude and flew off to the south with the two German Focke-Wulfs hot on their tail. She saw more tracer fire as the aircraft battled it out in a running dogfight. With their payloads dropped, the British bombers were racing back to the safety of England, while the Germans were intent on stopping them. They worked their way southwest along the edge of the Oslo Fjord, following the jagged coastline, until she saw one of the German fighters clip some trees and break off from the chase and one of the British bombers lose part of its fuselage and crash somewhere near Lake Engervannet and the town of Baerum.

As the smoke began to drift to the north, she looked back at Victoria Terrasse. The building was partially damaged rather than destroyed. Several nearby civilian residences had borne the brunt of the bombing. Although the Gestapo headquarters building had not taken a direct hit, it was thankfully still damaged from the bombs plowing through the walls and the subsequent explosions. The flames dancing around the exit holes sent up a cloud of billowy black smoke. By now a crowd had gathered all along the perimeter of the Gestapo headquarters, all eyes fixed on the separate blazes in awed silence.

Dagmar felt someone grab her by the arm.

Spinning around, she came face to face with the man in the trench coat that had been following her. She felt her heart leap from her chest and her eyes widen with fear. Now the face looked even more familiar. But where had she seen him before?

"I am not what you think," he said to her, nodding towards Victoria Terrasse with the backdrop of black smoke hovering overhead. "In fact, I wish the whole damned building had been flattened to the ground."

CHAPTER 7

THROUGH THE HAZE OF SMOKE, the man escorted her to Café Seterstua. The German clientele from Victoria Terrasse and other nearby government offices that normally frequented the establishment had vacated the premises en masse when the bombs were dropped, and now the café was empty except for the owner and his two teenage daughters. While the two men stepped to the back to confer in private, one of the girls showed Dagmar to a table by the window and poured two cups of steaming *kokekaffe*, while the other calmly placed a closed sign on the door. Neither of them said a word. The rich, dark-black coffee had become a rarity in Oslo given the severe war rationing imposed by the German Occupation, but you could still get it occasionally.

Outside, the streets were pandemonium with ambulances, fire engines, and police vehicles racing onto the scene. Nazi and NS police scrambled towards the building, and sirens sounded all over the city. Dagmar found it peculiar that the man who had been following her, the café owner, and his daughters seemed unfazed by the bedlam happening out on the street. Had they known about the attack in advance? And why did the man seem familiar to her? Where had she seen him before?

Here at Café Seterstua, Dagmar Lahlum found herself in new and different territory, and somehow it felt like a dream to her. Of course, she didn't know that the establishment was a front for the Resistance. Located a mere stone's throw from the headquarters of the *Schutzstaffel* and Luftwaffe, serving as a partisan listening post right under the very noses of the German High Command, the café was privy to some of the most coveted secrets of the Reich in Occupied Norway, courtesy of the hundreds of loose-tongued German officers that drank and dined here daily, thinking their conversations in rapid-fire German could not be overheard and understood by the café's Norwegian owners or their native clientele. To members of the Oslo underground, the café was known as the Wolf's Lair, an unflattering reference to Hitler's military command post in East Prussia. But for the valuable intelligence information that could be gleaned from the gossipy Germans, it was more appropriately regarded as the "Gold Mine" by those in the underground.

After a minute, the man returned, took a seat at the table, and quietly stared out the window at the commotion while nonchalantly sipping his coffee. Dagmar studied him discretely. He was not quite thirty with strong shoulders, glacier-blue eyes tucked behind wire-rimmed spectacles, and a face that looked as if it had been chiseled from granite. Up close, he was more handsome and affable-looking than he had appeared from a distance. She could tell now, up close, that he was Norwegian.

She still couldn't remember where they had crossed paths before today, but she was sure she had seen him before.

"You're with the Resistance," she said in a quiet voice, so the owner and his daughters who had taken positions behind the counter could not hear them.

"What makes you say that?"

"The look in your eyes."

"And what if I said you have the same look?"

"I would say that you were a good judge of character." She nodded towards the window and the street beyond where ambulances and fire engines continued to arrive on the scene and police began cordoning off the streets. "Are you behind that out there?"

"No. That's a British operation. Unfortunately, they didn't even tell us they were coming."

"They just bombed our capital and didn't even bother to forewarn us?"

"I doubt even the king and the rest of our government-in-exile in London were informed in advance of the raid. One of Churchill's aides is probably just getting around to telling Haakon now."

"Why is it that you don't seem surprised about the bombing? I mean, here we are sitting in a café as if nothing is happening." She looked at the owner and his daughters. "And what about them?"

"What about them?"

"They don't seem surprised either."

"You don't need to worry about them. What you do need to know is that when the Germans are distracted, it is a good time to talk. And to watch. Right now, you should be concerned with recording in your mind everything that is going on out there." He pointed outside. "We, of course, don't know the numbers yet, but there are bound to be many civilian casualties. Unfortunately, not one of the bombs was a direct hit."

"I know. I saw all four of them go through the building. They didn't explode until they exited out the other side."

"You are observant. The apartments to the north took the brunt of the attack. But thankfully, Gestapo headquarters is still damaged. And now the Germans will have to live and work in fear of another bombing attack every day throughout the war when they go to work."

"The planes that dropped the bombs...I have never seen anything like them before."

"They're the new fighter-bombers the British have been working on for some months. They're called Mosquitoes."

"Mosquitoes? That seems an apt name."

"I'm sure it will be announced on the BBC and in all the underground papers tomorrow."

"Even though the bombs only partially struck their target?"

"The British never pass up an opportunity to toot their own horn. And the bombs did, at least, damage the building and scare the crap out of the Nazis. Those quislings at the rally had to run for their lives. That was priceless. But unfortunately, from what I saw there was only superficial damage at Victoria Terrasse itself, and the

Gestapo will be open again tomorrow for the gruesome business of interrogation and torture."

"You can count on it. Now what is it you want from me?"

"That is the question, isn't it? What is it that I want from Dagmar Mohne Hansen Lahlum?"

She felt herself straighten up in her seat. "How do you know my name?"

"Believe me I know a lot more than that. I know, for instance, that you were born in Serumsand, but you grew up in Eidsvoll. And I know that you are the daughter of a shoemaker and that you had a hard childhood."

"I don't like being talked about as if I am a character in a book."

"Actually, a *hard childhood* doesn't even begin to describe it," he continued, as if she wasn't even there. "There was hardly any money for you and your mother, or your much-older sister and two step-brothers. It was so bad that your poor father struggled just to put food on the table to feed the family during the crisis years in the 1920s and 1930s. That's why, to save money, you learned to mend and sew your own clothes. It's also why you are a skilled seamstress to this day, in addition to your work as a hotel receptionist. You hate poverty. You hate it so much that by the time you were a teenager, you wanted to put the little rural town where in 1814 our constitution was signed—and the hardship and ruin it represented—behind you."

Feeling outrage at this intrusion into her life, Dagmar stood up from her chair. "I don't think I want to hear any more of this."

But the man calmly motioned her to sit back down. After taking a deep breath, she did, a defiant expression on her smooth, oval face. When she was settled, he continued.

"Dissatisfied with your family's situation, you were hot-headed and opinionated as a teenager. The neighbors and local gossips claimed you were far too attractive and snooty for their respectable town and they were just as glad to see you go as you were to leave them behind. Meanwhile, you had an aunt in Oslo that used to send you the latest fashion magazines and you were intent on making a name for yourself in the fashion and modeling world. So, three weeks before the German invasion, you moved to our fair city and took a job as a receptionist at the Grand Hotel. Have I forgotten anything so far?"

"How do you know all this?"

"It's my business to know such things. Shall I go on?"

"I don't know, can you?"

"Indeed, I can. While working as a receptionist, you've continued your work as a seamstress trying to reproduce the latest fashions with your needle and thread. You have a tiny flat in Frydenlundsgate. At night, you read books about art and poetry and paint elaborate clothing designs, but you've also been taking modeling classes. You've already learned how to sashay and swivel your hips like Betty Grable. Having fantasized of escape all those years in Eidsvoll, you came to Oslo thinking you were going to take the world by storm. That's why you left your fellow small-town girls behind and came here. You wanted to do something, to make a difference in the world. You were going to design the finest fashions, dance, become fluent in English, and see the world. You wanted adventure and you wanted to improve yourself and become famous. But it hasn't quite turned out that way, has it Dagmar?"

She stood up again, glaring. "How dare you! I have dreams, you know!"

"Yes, and the Germans have stolen them from you and all the rest of us. So get in fucking line!"

"Why are you doing this? Are trying to make me angry to convince me to spy for you?"

He tipped his head at the Germans on the street. "Every day, we have to sit by and watch those bastards plunder more and more of our resources and turn us into quislings, fighting against one another for the Reich's leftover scraps. Would you like to do something about that? Would you, Dagmar? And I'm talking about doing more than wearing a paper clip, painting H7 on a wall for our king, or wearing a stupid red bobble hat."

Again, he nodded towards the window. She looked out at the heavily armed German soldiers cordoning off the street and yelling at the crowd on the corner to stand back. They were the very picture of oppression and belligerence—a nation of murderous invaders driven by the insane ideology of their Führer. She thought of her Viking forbearers, but even at their worst they were nothing like these barbarians in gray-green and black.

"Who are you with? The SOE? The Oslo Gang?"

He shook his head.

"Milorg?"

He didn't reply.

"All right then, you must be a communist with the Osvald Group."

He took a sip of his *kokekaffe*. "Do I look like a communist?"

"I don't know. I only know two communists and I am not sure whether they are typical or not. What about the XU? Is that the group you are with?"

"You don't even know what XU stands for."

"X stands for unknown, U for undercover agent. So XU is *unknown undercover agent*. The name comes from Lauritz Sand, one of its founding members."

"What do you know of Lauritz Sand?"

"I know he is a hero of the Resistance. Just like Max Manus and his Oslo Gang."

"You are just spouting off names."

"It is true, I have only heard stories. But I have listened to them closely nonetheless. And you know that—otherwise you wouldn't be here."

"What do you know of Milorg?"

"Oh, so it is Milorg."

"I asked you what it stands for. Do you even know?"

"It is the abbreviation for *Militær Organisasjon*. But many people on the streets just call it the Home Front."

"I must say you know an awful lot for a simple girl from Eidsvoll."

"It must be the company I keep. Obviously, you have spoken with several of my friends, and probably my aunt and uncle and perhaps other people from Eidsvoll, to know so much about me. Are you trying to recruit me?"

"I have not decided. You have a hot temper."

"If I were a man, you would never say that. You would say I was determined and did not suffer fools."

He smiled. "Against my better judgment, I find myself liking you, Dagmar Lahlum."

"That's too bad because right now I don't like you. What is your name?"

"You know I can't tell you that. But since I like you, you may call me Ishmael."

"Are you toying with me or are you a fan of the American novel *Moby Dick*?"

"I cannot tell you that either but I can tell you it pleases me you recognize the Melville reference. And now I shall come to the point. I was directed by someone you do not know to recruit you to join our movement. There, I've said it."

"How do you know I am not a quisling?"

"You have been thoroughly investigated and found to be more than acceptable for the task I have assigned for you."

"I need to know more about the organization I will be working for."

"No, you don't. Not yet."

"I want to help. But can I have time to think this over? Can I at least talk to my parents, or my aunt and uncle who live here in Oslo?"

"Absolutely not. No one must know that we have spoken, and you will never be able to talk to anyone about the work you do for us. Even after the war is over."

"Even after the war is over? But why?"

"Because we take secrecy extremely seriously."

"Then why were you following me and making such a scene doing it?"

"Because I wanted to see how you would react. I also wanted to see if you could pick me up again after you thought you had lost me, or if you were perhaps good enough to shake my tail. That's when the British attacked."

"What would my duties be with this group you won't tell me the name of?"

"That I cannot reveal either. If you decide to join us, you will learn more when I meet you again."

"When will that be?"

"Tomorrow. That's when you're going to give me your decision on whether you accept our offer."

"I have only until tomorrow to decide?"

"Yes. If you decide to join, you will walk out of the Grand Hotel tomorrow at precisely twelve noon when you are on your lunch break. From there you will walk west along Karl Johans gate. Somewhere along your route, a car will pull up beside you with the front and rear door windows rolled down, and you will get into the car without saying anything. Stay close to the curb and make sure you are carrying a copy of *Fritt Folk* in you left hand with the front-page headline facing out towards the street and visible."

Fritt Folk—or *Free People*—was the official Norwegian newspaper of the NS. With all democratic, non-state-controlled newspapers having been banned or forced to move underground, *Fritt Folk's* only remaining competition was the popular *Aftenposten*, controlled by the Nazis, and the occupier's own German-language newspaper, *Deutsche Zeitung in Norwegen*.

"How do you know I am working tomorrow?" she asked him.

"Because you had today off. If you fail to appear, we will know that you have chosen not to join us. If you so decide, you must disregard this entire conversation."

He then withdrew a printed sheet of paper from his coat and handed it to her. "Here, I want you to read this over. And tonight, when you are alone in your apartment in Frydenlundsgate, I want you to read it over again and then think carefully about it. If you decide not to join our organization, you will destroy it. The Gestapo already has a copy of the directive, but we don't want them to be finding any more."

He handed her the sheet of paper and she read over first the bold-faced heading and then the entire document. It read:

HOME FRONT SECURITY DIRECTIVE

The work is absolutely secret. None with whom you do not have organization contact shall know you belong. Gossiping is the unpardonable sin. Do not choose an associate unless you have complete confidence in his silence. Caution must characterize the work. No one has a right to take unnecessary risks. Results of such carelessness affect not only him but others and the organization. It is not courageous to take unnecessary risks but is a betrayal of the cause. Remember that carelessness is the Gestapo's best ally. Operate under an assumed name. Use your assumed name with others. Everyone should know the fewest real names.

Never talk loudly about secret things and do not talk on busses, sidewalks, trains, boats, restaurants, or any place where you might be overheard. Use the telephone as little as possible. Never call from your own telephone but from some store. Always assume that someone is listening. Do not talk obliquely. Write nothing secret in a letter. Do not write to anyone with whom you have not previously corresponded. Do not use envelopes with names.

Under no circumstances should you hide writings around your home, office, in or under such as rugs, books, or coin banks. Suggest burying in a fruit jar. When you have to carry important papers do not hide them in your shoes or under your hat but have them where you can quickly reach them and dispose of them if you are being followed. If you have not met your contact man for some time call him up to assure yourself that he is at home—and not with the police! Remember that you can be shadowed. Do not go to a meeting place directly without looking about, but do not do that obviously.

Never involve yourself with anyone who cannot identify himself by the agreed password or personal letter with known handwriting. Remember that provocateurs often can have knowledge of secret things and try to 'bluff' with them. Avoid as much as possible being known as a zealous patriot. Be careful in expressing your opinion—especially around Germans or members of National Samling—even if you know you are right!

If your contact man is arrested and you believe it involves your work in the organization, go into hiding. Do not remain at home or in the office. Find a natural reason for being away, like a vacation, sickness or such. First try to determine if the police have inquired about you. If you are not being hunted, consider when you can return. Remember that the one arrested is not always examined right away. If you find you must leave the country, you should get in touch with your contact man. Always take heed of warnings, even if they are anonymous.

Be prepared for the Gestapo coming to inquire about you in the daytime at your office, at night your home. But remember, also, that the Gestapo can come just for general information. If you have a way to escape, use it. Take your arrest with great surprise or great indignation. Do not challenge the police. Know beforehand what you will say at the examination. Be careful what you say to fellow prisoners. They may be informers. The Gestapo works in every country. As a fugitive in other countries be as careful in what you say as you are here at home.

Have faith in the Home Front and our ultimate victory over the German occupiers and their armies. This war will be won by you and people like you through patience, dedication, vigilance, selfless sacrifice, and unwavering resistance towards the enemy in everything that we do. Our victory and day of reckoning over our German oppressors and their Quisling collaborators will come. And it will come soon.

Seize the moment, seize the day! All for Norway!

When Dagmar looked up, she felt tears come to her eyes. "I can give you my answer now," she said, feeling a surge of patriotism. "I want to join."

"Are you sure? It is always best to carefully consider important decisions. After all, you are but a girl."

Her eyes narrowed. "I am a nineteen-year-old woman, and I told you I want to join. I have made my decision and it will not change. I want to join you and your *Militær Organisasjon*."

"Just because it says 'Home Front' at the top of the page does not mean you are being recruited by Milorg."

"I am inclined to disagree under the present circumstances."

"Why is that?"

"Because I realize now where I've seen you before."

"What? You recognize me?"

"When I first saw you following me, I knew I had seen you before, but I couldn't remember where. But now I know where it was."

"Where?"

"It was at the Grand Hotel when I was working. I saw you in the lobby with Jens Christian Hauge, the lawyer and chief of Milorg."

His eyebrows flew up. "You know about Hauge? But how could you—?"

"Because I'm observant," she cut him off. "That's why I will make a good spy."

"Well, you're certainly modest, too."

"The other staff members and I didn't know who you were at the time. But the bellman knew who Hauge was. He was just an up-and-coming lawyer back then, as I remember. It was only later that I learned that he had taken over as the head of Milorg."

He seemed to appraise her in a new light. "You are a clever girl. Maybe too clever for your own good."

"I'll take that as a compliment. When is my first assignment? I want to get started."

"Chomping at the bit, are we? You will be contacted. Don't worry, it won't be long."

"Who will be my contact? You?"

"I don't know. But I am your control officer. It could be me that contacts you, or it could be someone else. It depends on how careful and trustworthy you are."

"I hope it is you," she said. "I actually *do* like you."

"It's not important that you like me. It only matters whether you trust me."

"Yes, of course." She felt a little jolt of electricity course through her body, like when she took her first kiss that sunny summer day four years ago back in Eidsvoll. Since the war had begun, she had been hoping for an opportunity such as this—something with a hint of danger, excitement, and intrigue—and now it had fallen in her lap. She couldn't believe she was about to enter the furtive world of the "underground" and take part in espionage on behalf of her beloved country. In some strange way, it seemed as if she had been waiting for this moment her whole life. *Has this been my destiny all along?* she wondered, staring out at the smoke cloud above Victoria Terrasse, starting to drift off in the dusky sky.

Then she looked back at Ishmael. He was First Lieutenant Peder Olav Gleditsch—but for the rest of the war and her entire life she would never know his real name, something she would come to seriously regret.

"We have big plans for you, Dagmar Lahlum," he said. "Big plans. Together, we are going to bring the Germans to their knees."

"I can't wait," she said. "I can't wait to do just that."

CHAPTER 8

GESTAPO HEADQUARTERS
VICTORIA TERRASSE

SEPTEMBER 28, 1942

"GOSSIP IS A NATIONAL WEAKNESS IN NORWAY. In fact, it is one of our best allies in the fight against the Resistance. That's why you are going to tell me everything I want to know in the next five minutes, or I am afraid that I will be forced to make things extremely unpleasant for you. To avoid such unpleasantness, all you have to do is pretend you are sharing the latest gossip with a friend. That should be quite easy and enjoyable for you. What do you say?"

To underscore his gentlemanly nature, SS-*Obersturmführer* Siegfried Fehmer smiled at his prisoner with exquisite politeness and cordial grace before topping it all off with a chivalrous bow of his head. Not surprisingly, his handcuffed prisoner sitting barefoot and shirtless on a stool in Interrogation Cell 3 on the third floor of Victoria Terrasse didn't seem to be taken in by his charm. The Osvald Group saboteur Hans-Peter Thorsen was too busy calculating his chances of survival. Like so many of those that had come before him, the young man was only too aware of the heinous tortures awaiting him at Gestapo headquarters.

"What's that, Thorsen? I can't hear you. And believe me, here at Victoria Terrasse that is not a good thing. We encourage our guests to be as forthcoming as possible."

His prisoner looked at him with a combination of hatred, trepidation, and disbelief, but was still unable to bring himself to speak. Thorsen then looked at SS Lieutenants Hoeler and Bernhard standing next to Fehmer, and then at Fehmer's huge German shepherd tied to a leash in the corner of the room, sizing up the danger they posed. The two officers stared back at the prisoner in stony silence, as did well-trained Wolfie, who had been Fehmer's loyal four-legged companion since the beginning of the Occupation. They all looked poised for their commander to unleash them in attack.

When the prisoner looked back at him, Fehmer gave an ingratiating smile. He knew he looked dapper yet menacing in his gray-green SS officer's uniform with the *Sicherheitsdienst* badges and peaked cap bearing a *Heer*-style eagle together with an SS-Totenkopf. His 1939 Walther PPK 7.65-mm SS officer's pistol in the Death's Head holster at his hip rounded out his attire nicely. Normally, the much-feared officer wore Norwegian clothing, the better to blend in and infiltrate the local population, but not today. Today, he wore his neatly pressed SS uniform.

"I'm going to ask you some very important questions," Fehmer continued in the tone of a maître d' at a gentlemen's club. "I will start with the simple and move on to the more complex. As long as you answer my questions honestly, you can return promptly to your prison cell at Møllergata 19 and enjoy a nice, warm bowl of flavorless soup. Are you ready, my friend?"

The prisoner squinted up at him defiantly and said nothing. Breaking him was going to be a challenge, Fehmer could tell. The communists were always the most fanatical and toughest to crack during interrogation.

"You really must speak up. If you don't, this is going to be difficult for you, I can assure you."

He nodded towards a work table containing neatly arranged stainless-steel surgical instruments, truncheons, three wooden clubs taped with blood-stained cloth, a blindfold, a gag, a coil of binding rope, and a hand mirror. In the corner was a small oven with two sets of copper wires, which during interrogation were heated until red-hot and inserted beneath fingernails. Surveying the implements of torture before him, the prisoner's face turned a shade whiter.

Despite the terrifying tools, Fehmer smiled reassuringly. He often began with the soft approach, talking in a silky smooth and mollifying voice to put his victims at ease. He liked to give his prisoners a chance to tell the truth up front and avoid "enhanced interrogation techniques." Half the time, they would promptly blubber everything he needed to know without a hand being lifted against them. But the other half the time, well, that was a different story.

"Let's start with this, my friend. Do you know who I am?"

"Yes."

"Good. Then you realize you're going to have to talk. There is no avoiding it if you want to walk out of here under your own power. You can avoid needless suffering by telling me and my colleagues what we need to know. Let's start with what information we already have in our possession. The first is your name: Hans-Peter Thorsen. As we told you when we first took you into custody, we know who you are. We intercepted a wireless transmission and you have been positively identified by my team on two previous occasions. We also know the name of your Resistance cell. You are a member of the Osvald Group, which makes you a Bolshevik and a—"

"I am not a member of the Osvald Group. And I am not a communist."

Fehmer feigned a look of surprise. "Did you just interrupt me?"

"I'm not with the Resistance nor am I a communist. You have mistaken me for someone else."

"You're saying that *I'm* mistaken?"

"No, I mean, yes. You...you have been misinformed."

"Misinformed? Now you're saying I am *misinformed*?"

"Yes, Captain Fehmer. I am not with the Resistance. I am but a simple carpenter."

"And I am not actually a captain, only a first lieutenant whose bosses have buried me in the work of three captains. So, it appears that we both may not be what we seem."

The young man just stared at him, unsure what to make of him. But there was steel in his face; he was a tough Norwegian sailor and demolition expert, not a carpenter, Fehmer already knew. The Osvald Group recruited heavily from sailors, dockworkers, and industrial laborers working in and around Oslo Harbor and the other major ports, and Fehmer had informants on the payroll that had identified Thorsen as a saboteur within the group. The prisoner obviously believed he would be less suspicious if he was a carpenter instead of a sailor since sailors were so closely linked with the Resistance and King Haakon's government-in-exile in London.

At that moment, Wolfie bared his teeth at the prisoner and gave a low growl.

"It appears, Comrade Thorsen, that Wolfie is a bit skeptical of your truthfulness. And quite honestly, so am I. Is that not a sailor's tattoo on your left arm?"

"No, it's just a regular tattoo."

"Really? A nautical image of the North Star? I could swear it is what sailors wear for protection at sea. By wearing the compass rose, doesn't that help you find your way home?"

"I wouldn't know about that. Like I said, I'm just a carpenter."

"Well, I'm afraid I don't believe you." He looked at the SS officer to his immediate left. "Lieutenant Hoeler, the blindfold if you please."

"*Jawohl, Obersturmführer.*"

The prisoner wriggled uncomfortably on his stool, his handcuffs jingling. "Blindfold? Why do we need a blindfold?"

"I'm afraid you have forced my hand, Comrade Thorsen. I warned you to tell the truth."

"But I have been telling the truth."

"No, you haven't. Which is why, regrettably, my fellow interrogation officers and I are going to have to resort to more persuasive tactics. I'm sure as a well-trained operative with the Osvald Group you understand the necessity of such methods."

Lieutenant Hoeler stepped forward with the blindfold and a sadistic smile.

"Wait, wait. I don't...I don't know anything."

"Actually, you know quite a lot."

He paused a moment for dramatic effect, heightening the tension as the blindfold was strapped tightly around the prisoner's head, covering his eyes. The Norwegian's head jerked left and right like a bird, and Fehmer saw that already the man's fear was almost unbearable. With the blindfold, every blow would come as a terrible shock and the dreadful anticipation between blows would be agonizing. For many prisoners, it was worse than the actual physical torture.

"Do you want to know how I know you know quite a lot? Because I have discovered that you were involved in last month's attack on the Stapo office. You remember August 21? You should because you were there." He was referring to the headquarters office of the *Statspolitiet*, the National Socialist armed police force. The Stapo was staffed by Norwegian law enforcement officials modeled after the Nazi German pattern and operated independently of the ordinary Norwegian police.

"But I wasn't there. I am telling the truth."

"We have two confirmed sources that place you at the scene of the crime: Hans-Peter Thorsen, late twenties, sailor and demolition expert, swarthy complexion, blue eyes, tall, walks with a slight limp from a firefight along the Swedish border a year ago. That's you, comrade. And you and at least five other members of the *Osvald Gruppen* were there at Stapo headquarters last month. Now we want to know the names of those present and verify whether your group's leader, Commander Asbjørn Sunde, led the operation. If you tell us right now, no harm will come to you. I also want to make you aware of the fifty-thousand-kroner reward being offered for information leading to the capture of Commander Sunde. You could be a rich man, Comrade Thorsen. You just have to be like the rest of your countrymen and indulge in a little gossip."

The prisoner said nothing. Fehmer could see his mind working: *How much can I lie and get away with it? What minor information should I give up to make it appear as if I am cooperating? How long will I be able to hold out?*

"I don't know anything. As I told you, I am not with the Resistance."

Fehmer felt a little twitch. It irked him when his prisoners felt the need to test the boundaries of their physical and moral courage. It was always pointless. The only remaining question was whether to pound the prisoner into submission by attacking every inch of his body—or to restrict the blows to his shins, knees, elbows, and other hard parts without striking the face or risking harming vital organs. That way, the young communist could be interrogated indefinitely while under extreme agony without dislocating his jaw or damaging the brain, which could prevent obtaining any useful information and result in his accidental death.

Fehmer quickly decided on the more brutal approach.

He signaled Hoeler, who was eager to dispense with the preamble and launch into sanguinary action. The lieutenant stepped forward with his rubber-covered truncheon and delivered several vicious blows to Thorsen's nose, drawing a cascade of blood. He followed up with a stiff blow to each knee, the left arm, and the back of the head. Fehmer wasn't sure, but he thought he heard something crack when the arm was struck. The blindfolded Norwegian screamed in agony and Wolfie barked loudly. Fehmer raised his right arm and the dog stopped barking instantly.

The Gestapo officer waited for the screams to subside before addressing his victim once again. Thorsen's head continued to dart left and right like a bird, as he tried to determine which direction the next blow would come from, so he could brace himself for the impact.

"Comrade Thorsen," said Fehmer in a soothing voice. "It is time for you to avoid further needless suffering. Who were your brothers-in-arms in the Stapo attack last month? Just give me their names and answer a few more questions and this will all be over."

"I don't know what you're talking about," the young man said defiantly.

Fehmer nodded towards Hoeler. This time the interrogation officer hit the victim in the face so hard that he fell off the stool. As he flailed about on the floor, Hoeler and Bernhard kicked him several times in the ribs. When the beating was finished, Thorsen just lay there on the floor, groaning like a wounded bear. Wolfie barked until Fehmer again raised his hand in an abrupt motion, silencing the German shepherd.

After calmly waiting a minute for the noise to subside, Fehmer signaled Hoeler and Bernhard to set the prisoner back onto the stool and remove the blindfold. Sometimes, it was useful to put it on and take it off repeatedly to throw a prisoner off balance during at interrogation. That way you could see the look in a man's eyes and tell whether he was lying or close to breaking. With the blindfold removed, Thorsen looked up at the three Germans with a combination of raw hatred and abject terror. Fehmer shook his head at the senselessness of further resistance.

"Now look what you've done, Comrade Thorsen. You must look at yourself in the mirror and ask yourself if your recalcitrance is a wise choice."

He grabbed the hand mirror from the table and held it in front of the prisoner.

"You were a handsome young man when you first stepped into this cell. But that is no longer a Clark Gable face. It already looks like raw steak and we have only just begun. It is going to get a lot worse if you continue this tough-guy charade. Now, was the head of your Osvald Group, Asbjørn Sunde, there during the raid or not? Did he lead the attack?"

"I don't know what you're talking about. What raid?"

At Fehmer's silent command, SS Lieutenant Bernhard picked up one of the heavy clubs taped with bloodied cloth and swung it several times like a baseball bat, striking the prisoner repeatedly in the ribs. Then Hoeler swooped in again and sat on top of him, bent one of his legs back, and twisted the toes of both of his shoeless feet.

The Norwegian screamed in terror.

"You are going to tell me the names, or at least the code names, of the men that attacked the police station, as well as the names of all other persons in your Resistance network. And you are going to tell me everything you know about Commander Sunde."

"I am not in the Resistance, damn you!"

Fehmer motioned Bernhard. The pockmarked lieutenant stepped forward and smashed him in the ribs several times with the club.

"You know Sunde and the men in your cell quite well, no doubt. Like you, they are mostly sailors and dockworkers. They are your comrades in arms. You know their names, code names, and addresses. I need you to give them to me."

The prisoner moaned in pain and did not respond.

Growing impatient, Hoeler and Bernhard twisted his big and little toes on each foot until they broke. Then they propped him back up onto the stool. Crippled and in agony, the victim was now unable to control his bowels. Urine poured down his pant leg and puddled onto the floor.

"Good heavens, that smells terrible, Comrade Thorsen," said Fehmer, wrinkling his nose in disapproval. "Please promise me you will refrain from pissing yourself further. I'm afraid this affront to the olfactory senses is most distressing for me and my associates. Now let's continue the interrogation, shall we?"

The communist saboteur squinted up at him with hate and disbelief in his eyes.

"You have the wrong man. I wasn't at any Stapo raid."

"Where can we find Sunde? How do you make contact with him?"

The prisoner said nothing.

Hoeler smacked him in the nose with the truncheon again, drawing another spray of blood.

"I need the names of your Resistance fighters and I need them now."

Thorsen remained silent.

Again, Fehmer motioned Hoeler and Bernhard. This time the Gestapo lieutenants delivered hard blows to his shins and ribs with the truncheon and club. The blows made sickening thudding noises and the victim screamed in agony. This time, Wolfie panted excitedly but did not bark.

Now Fehmer spoke in a gentle, soothing voice. "I know that hurt badly. Just remember, only you can make the pain stop. Now tell me the names of the men with you on the raid."

"There were none. I was not there."

"What is Sunde's code name?"

"I don't know what you're talking about."

"Where is the location of your hideout?"

"I am not who you think I am. You have the wrong man."

"Where did you get the Mauser pistol we found you with? Did you kill a German officer?"

"I found the weapon on the street. I was going to return it to the authorities."

"What are you doing in Oslo? What is your mission here with the Osvald Group?"

"I am a simple carpenter. I don't know anything about the Osvald Group."

"Liar!"

He drove his fist into Thorsen's stomach, knocking the wind out of him. Hoeler and Bernhard followed up with several blows to the legs and ribs. The prisoner fell off the stool and passed out unconscious on the floor. They threw a pail of water on him and he came to again. He looked up groggily at his tormentors; one of his eyes was swollen shut and his face was misshapen and distorted like an Edvard Munch painting. The two interrogators pounded him in the stomach with their weapons. Thorsen again slumped in the chair and lost consciousness. They revived him with another pail of water. But he still refused to talk, so Hoeler sat on him, bent back his legs, and broke his remaining unbroken toes one by one. When he still didn't talk, Fehmer and Bernhard twisted his arms and kicked him in the face and all over his body. He passed out again and was revived with a splash of water and propped back up on the stool.

Fehmer stood above him. The prisoner, he could tell, was very close to breaking.

"It is time for you to stop this foolishness and tell us what we need to know. We know you were there, Comrade Thorsen, so the only thing left is for you to give us the details. The pain will stop as soon as you tell us what we need to know."

"I request a...a doctor."

"I'm sorry, but you are in no position to request anything."

Pretending that he was going to step away, he turned and delivered a savage blow to the prisoner's jaw, cleaving away skin and opening up a new gash on his cheek that poured with fresh blood. He then stepped back and looked over the prisoner from head to toe, wondering how much more the man could possibly take. Thorsen's nose and left cheek were badly lacerated and bled profusely. All of his toes were broken, and his left foot was swollen and looked like a lump of meat. A number of ribs had been broken and his body was blue, yellow, and red all over where it wasn't obscured from blood. His jaw had been smashed by repeated blows, and the wounds were still bleeding. The knee and the ankle of one leg were already so swollen that the leg looked like a caveman's wooden club.

There can't possibly be any more fight left in him.

But it took another dozen savage blows to the victim's already-injured areas followed by a pail of water to revive him after he passed out before Fehmer's hunch was confirmed.

"Please stop, I'll tell you what you want to know! Just don't strike me again!" begged Thorsen through a mouthful of blood.

At last, the Resistance fighter's voice was filled with resignation. "A wise decision, Comrade Thorsen. A wise decision indeed."

"Sunde was there. He led the raid."

"What was the purpose of the raid? Why was it ordered?"

"In response to a failed operation."

"A failed operation?"

"Involving Dr. Hans Eng," he responded, referring to the prominent Nazi collaborator who served as the private physician for Vidkun Quisling and his family, and as the chief physician for the *Nasjonal Samling's* Department of Public Health and the Bredtveit concentration camp.

"What was the operation involving Dr. Eng?"

"We had planned to assassinate him on August 20. But Eng didn't show up where he was supposed to. Commander Sunde led the attack on Stapo the next day. He was angry that we didn't get Eng and wanted to make a statement."

"The raid was all about the doctor?"

"Yes, he has been on our target list since last March."

"Now that your mission has failed, do you anticipate that the *Osvald Gruppen* will make other attempts on his life?"

"Of course, he is a Nazi collaborator and a pig." He grimaced in pain. "Look at what you bastards have done to me! I won't be able to walk for a month, damn you!"

At the insult, Hoeler and Bernhard stepped forward to deliver more face and body blows, but Fehmer held up a hand to call them off.

"Please watch your tongue, Comrade Thorsen. I will not be able to hold back my officers a second time." He smiled politely. "Who was behind the February 2 bombing of the *Østbanehallen* in protest of the inauguration of Minister-President Quisling? Was it only the Osvald Group, or did you get support from Milorg? Are the two groups collaborating?"

"No, that was all us. Milorg refuses to take part in sabotage operations. They want us communists to do their dirty work for them." He groaned again. "Now that's all I can tell you because that's all I know…and…and I need a damned doctor."

"No, we are just getting started, Comrade Thorsen. I need to know who else was involved in the Stapo attack and how I can track them down."

"Why should I tell you anything? You're just going to put me before a firing squad."

"Most likely you will get the wall, but you can still avoid further needless pain and suffering. That is worth something. And who knows, you might get lucky and your life may be spared."

"In Bredtveit or Grini?" he said, referring to Norway's two most infamous Nazi prisons. "I doubt it." He groaned again. "I want a doctor, or I am not going to say anything more."

Hoeler and Bernhard laughed dismissively. Fehmer just smiled, as if his prisoner was a child with a fanciful imagination. "I'm afraid we cannot allow doctors to visit our prisoners until they have given us the information we seek. Now what is the main theater of operations of the Osvald Group? Is it Buskerud or Oslo, and is that where Sunde has his base of operations?"

Thorsen said nothing.

Bernhard stepped forward and drove the cloth-covered club into the prisoner's balls, eliciting a howl of pain and a series of canine barks from Wolfie in the corner.

"I need the names of your comrades in the group. You know their names, code names, and addresses. I need you to give me this information."

Again, the prisoner said nothing.

This time both Hoeler and Bernhard pounded him in the ribs with their weapons. Thorsen lost consciousness again and fell off the stool. They threw a pail of water on him and he came to again. He glowered up at them balefully, and Fehmer realized the tough communist had somehow gotten a second wind. Why was he clinging to this ill-advised course of action? Didn't he know that he would cave in and tell everything in the end?

"I want to go to my cell. You have broken both my ankles, my toes, and my nose."

Fehmer frowned down at him. "You were doing so well, Comrade Thorsen. Why do you want to screw it up and force us to beat you senseless again?"

"I will not give up my fellow patriots. I shouldn't have said a word before. Now I regret it."

So that was why he was so stubborn: he felt guilty for having let down his comrades. Fehmer couldn't help but be moved by the young man. He had withstood the torture nobly, and far more courageously than most Norwegians.

"Honorable in concept but not very practical given the circumstances, my Bolshevik friend. In time, you will answer my questions. Everyone talks in the end."

"Not me. I have told you all I am going to tell you, you Nazi fuck." He suddenly looked defiant despite his many wounds and broken bones. "I shouldn't have talked in the first place. I was weak. But I didn't tell you anything of value, or that you probably didn't know already. We'll get Dr. Eng one of these days, regardless of what I've told you. And if we don't, the Allies will hang him when the war is over, as they will all collaborators and war criminals."

Fehmer felt his anger rising and Wolfie began to snarl. "Do you want me to sic my dog on you, because it seems as if you are deliberately trying to provoke me?"

A knock sounded at the door and the desk sergeant's face poked in. "*Obersturmführer*, I am sorry to interrupt, but there is someone here to see you."

"Send them away! Can't you see I'm busy?"

"But it is Fräulein Breien, sir."

He felt his rage dissipate instantly. "Annemarie is here? This very minute?"

"You instructed me to notify you immediately upon her arrival to Victoria Terrasse. Well, sir, she's here."

"Yes Sergeant, I know what I told you."

"She is waiting, *Obersturmführer*, and she said it is most urgent."

"In that case, please escort her to my office and have her wait for me, Sergeant."

52

"*Jawohl, Obersturmführer,*" and he was gone.

Fehmer felt like a schoolboy on a first date. He picked up the hand mirror and examined himself. Despite the severe torture he and his men had just administered, he still looked dapper in his officer's uniform. But there was a blood spatter on his lapel bearing his SS insignia.

Do I dare let Annemarie see my like this? What would she think of me if she saw the blood?

Thorsen snorted derisively. "You Nazi fuck. You don't even know which you like more: torturing people or playing Casanova. I almost pity you, Fehmer, you bastard!"

At the insult, Hoeler and Bernhard stepped aggressively towards the prisoner and Wolfie gave a menacing snarl, but Fehmer waved them off. After all, the prisoner was right: he *was* conflicted. Deep down, he hated himself for being a brute. But he hated himself even more for his brutality when he was in the presence of the sweet, gentle, and beautiful Annemarie Breien.

He looked into the hateful eyes of his bloody and battered adversary. He couldn't help but feel admiration. The man was a tough nut to crack and an observant amateur psychologist: he deserved a brief respite.

He pulled a Blue Master cigarette manufactured by J. L. Tiedemanns, Norway's largest tobacco company, from his pack, lit it, and handed it to the prisoner. "Let him enjoy a cigarette and have a one-hour break. Then we'll get back to it," he said to his two subordinates.

"Yes, sir," said Hoeler.

Now Fehmer drew close to the prisoner. "You are a brave man, Comrade Thorsen. But I feel it only fair to warn you about one thing."

Thorsen scowled at him defiantly and said nothing. Fehmer couldn't help but feel pity for him to go along with his admiration.

"Upon my return, we will be using the heated wires." He nodded towards the oven and sets of copper wires in the corner of the room for burning under the fingernails, a torture technique that for some reason worked exceedingly well with the Norwegians. "We'll see how long you hold out after stage-three interrogation."

The young man tried to present a mask of courage but faltered. The wires always did that to the prisoners. "You'll never break me! I won't tell you anything more, I promise you that!"

"Oh, I think you will," said Fehmer, smiling pleasantly. "In fact, by the time we are finished with you, you will be singing like a canary. But for the time being, please do enjoy your cigarette. You have most assuredly earned it."

CHAPTER 9

GESTAPO HEADQUARTERS
VICTORIA TERRASSE

SEPTEMBER 28, 1942

"I HOPE I DIDN'T KEEP YOU WAITING TOO LONG, ANNEMARIE," he said in lightly German-accented Norwegian as the desk sergeant closed the door behind him. In the lavatory on the way up to his fourth-floor office, he had scrubbed the lapel of his SS uniform to remove the blood stain but to no avail. He could only hope that his female visitor wouldn't spot it.

"Oh no, I've only been waiting a few minutes," she replied.

He noted that she still looked a touch nervous in his presence, despite the fact they had met on several occasions during the summer. All the same she looked radiant, an exquisite specimen of Nordic beauty. He walked up to her, bowed formally, clicked his jet-black boots together lightly so as not to startle her, and took a seat behind his spacious desk.

"It's nice to see you again." He was not making small talk; he truly meant it.

"Thank you. It's good to see you again too, Lieutenant."

From her body language, he could tell that wasn't quite true, which disappointed him though he tried not to let it show on his face. He leaned back in his high-backed black leather chair bearing the violent emblem of the *Parteiadler* of the Third Reich.

"As I'm sure you've guessed, I'm here again about my father. Do you have any news for me?"

He smiled graciously. "As a matter of fact, I do. I have arranged for the release of your father from Grini Prison. I just signed the release papers an hour ago and was about to call you when I was momentarily detained."

Her hand flew to her mouth. "Oh my God, thank you!" She was up from her chair in a flash, reaching across his desk with both hands. "Thank you so much, Lieutenant!"

"Please, you must call me Siegfried. How many times have I told you now?"

"Too many, I know! But thank you, thank you!"

Looking into her grateful eyes, he couldn't believe the power he wielded. He took her hands in his, felt her gentle womanly touch, and knew he had done the right thing. Roald Breien had been facing a death sentence, but over the past several months Fehmer had intervened and managed to save his life on behalf of his daughter. It had been a tall order, but he had pulled it off. He still wasn't certain why he had done it. Having the sentence dropped went against his better judgment as well as official police procedure. But it was done now and, looking into twenty-seven-year-old Annemarie Breien's eyes, he knew he had done the right thing.

"He will be released into your care tomorrow," he said. "I will call you later today or tomorrow to tell you what time to pick him up."

There were tears in her eyes. "Thank you so much. This means the world to me and my mother."

"I am glad that it has worked out for you," he said, and he meant it.

"You are a good man. I mean…what I mean to say is you have good in you, Siegfried, despite what people say."

It was a backhanded compliment at best and the words stung him. But through rigorous self-discipline honed from years as a lawyer before the war, he didn't let his emotions show on his face. "I don't know if that was an insult or a compliment, but I suppose I will have to take it."

"Oh, I'm sorry—I didn't mean it like that. Thank you, Siegfried. Thank you for the goodness in your heart."

"You are quite welcome. I knew I had to come through for you."

"You did?"

"Yes, since that first day I set eyes on you last spring, I knew you would not take no for an answer."

Her blue eyes lit up with the gentle glow of recollection and she gave a little chuckle. "I was bold, even I have to admit."

"You were more than bold. You stormed past several armed guards right into my office. It's a wonder you weren't shot."

"He's my father—I had to do it."

"No, you are a very brave woman—and a very lucky one. As Frederick the Great said, 'I have no need in my army for officers who lack luck.' Well, Annemarie, you would have made a fine rittmeister in Old Fritz's cavalry."

She smiled bashfully. "And you haven't done too badly yourself. Here you have pulled off a miracle by saving my father. It's quite remarkable."

"I almost don't believe it myself, but here we are."

"To think, if I hadn't run past those guards it would never have happened. My heart was beating so fast I thought I would have a heart attack."

And my heart was beating fast as well. But for a different reason.

He reached across his desk and gently touched her hand. She let their fingers linger together a moment before pulling her hand politely away.

"So why have you freed my father, Siegfried? You must tell me the real reason. Why have you done the good and just thing?"

He smiled disarmingly. "You know why. You are a very convincing woman."

"Or perhaps you just want to keep tabs on my father and that's why you have released him. Perhaps your Gestapo men in the trench coats will now follow him around Oslo and see who he associates with once he is out of prison. Perhaps your motives are not as altruistic as they appear, Lieutenant Fehmer."

"And perhaps I am merely dazzled by your audacity *and* your beauty."

"I'm afraid flattery will not work with me."

"Well then, that could pose a problem. It is the only weapon I have in my arsenal."

She looked away. He realized, too late, that he had come across too strong and had crossed the line into overt flirtation. They fell into an uncomfortable silence for almost a full minute before he cleared his throat to speak.

"As I have said, I was very impressed that you were even able to get past the guards that day. You were a desperate woman and were not to be dissuaded from your mission. I knew then how much you loved your father. Once again, I have to tell you: he is very fortunate to have a daughter such as yourself looking out for his welfare."

"Well, he will be my mother Nancy's responsibility when he is released. I've done enough."

"Indeed, you have."

"I knew that he would be sentenced to death if the allegations against him were proved. But my father is not and has never been with the Resistance. He just happened to have associated with some people who were, which is a common and forgivable mistake."

Fehmer suspected otherwise. It was rumored, though not proved, that Roald Breien was the number one or two in the Milorg Upper Buskerud Cell of the Resistance. But Fehmer wasn't about to tell Annemarie that. He wanted to bask in the glory of being *Fehmer the Merciful*. The truth was he had feelings for her, feelings he couldn't deny. In fact, he often fantasized about the two of them lying naked together and whispering sweet musings in each other's ear. But of course, that was never going to happen. After all, he was a Gestapo officer and she was a Norwegian with possible ties to the Home Front that he was firmly committed to destroying. An intimate relationship between them would be an impossible fairy tale.

He reached across the desk and gently took her hand in his. He wanted so much for her to, if not actually love him, then at least like and respect him as a human being and not fear him. On his prisoners he often enjoyed seeing fear, for fear was the close cousin of respect. But on the face of Annemarie Breien, he never wanted to see fear. He wanted her sweet, soft face to show love and admiration.

"I had the best time this summer taking walks with you through the park and discussing your views of the world," he said to her in a gentle, soothing voice. "I know these are trying times for both our countries, and even being seen with me has put a strain on you with your husband and your friends. But I have to tell you, I have enjoyed our brief time together very much, Annemarie. And I am pleased that, in some small way, I have helped you and your family."

"Well, we can spend more time together if you continue to do the right thing and release my innocent countrymen from prison. How about that?"

"The key word in that sentence is, of course, *innocent*. Without that, I can be of little use to you."

It was a lie, and he knew it; after all, he had just freed her father from Grini even though there was a distinct possibility that Roald Breien was a senior operative in Milorg. They looked at one another. Her eyes were bright and idealistic, brimming with hope for the future, and he remembered back to when he used to feel that way. He was only thirty-one and already he felt old. It was the damned war, he knew. It had aged him prematurely.

"I do believe there are more good deeds in store for you, Siegfried. I believe in you, even if most of my countrymen do not. Especially now that I've seen with my own eyes what you're capable of."

"Another backhanded compliment, but I will take it," he said, not knowing what else to say. He couldn't help but feel the lonesomeness inside. He didn't want to be the Big Bad Wolf in this country that he dearly loved; Norway was a big part of who he had come to be. But his job required him to police those who resisted—often using harsh methods.

He smiled at her and she smiled back. With the release of her father and show of goodwill on his part, this was a good day for them both. For a moment, her eyes lit up with something close to genuine affection and that brought Fehmer a feeling of warmth, but also longing. He took in her exquisite blue eyes, her perfectly symmetrical face, her silky blonde hair, and most of all, her sweetness. She was perfect in every way, the woman of his dreams—and yet he would never have her. With their two countries embroiled in war, they were an ocean apart. It made him feel sad, in an achingly desperate way.

She rose from her chair, signaling that the meeting was over. He wished she could stay longer but tried not to let the disappointment show on his face.

She held out her hand, as if they had just concluded a business transaction. "Thank you so much, Siegfried. This...what you have done...well, it means the world to me. Because of you, my mother and I and my siblings will soon be reunited with my father. How can I ever repay you?"

"You don't need to repay me," he said. "As you said, it is the right thing to do. That is enough in this terrible time of war."

They shook hands. Her touch was tentative, and for some reason it bothered him. In fact, the entire handshaking business seemed wrong given how much he cared for her. It made him sad to think that all they would ever share was a silly professional handshake like they were doing right now.

"Well, thank you again," she said, and he showed her out.

Two minutes later, he watched from his fourth-floor window as she exited the building and began walking down the street. He studied her gait: gracefully smooth strides, perfectly coordinated yet sexy, like the prance of an exquisite racehorse. A smile came to his lips. He had romanced many women here in Norway since he had left his wife Anni Wille behind in Germany, but Annemarie Breien was exceptional even by his lofty standards. She was unique. He knew that she was playing him to get what she wanted, but she was still a genuinely kind and caring person—as well as quite ravishing. But what he liked most was her sweet, gentle nature. It made him feel ashamed for the brutal tortures he administered to her fellow Norwegians in the cold, soundproofed interrogation rooms of Victoria Terrasse.

After walking a hundred feet in the direction of the Royal Palace, she looked up at his fourth-floor window and their eyes met. She smiled and waved up at him. At first, he hesitated to respond because he felt ridiculous. But then, as if under the force of a spell, he returned a smile, and his hand passed back and forth across the window, as if it had a will of its own. He couldn't believe it, but the sensation was delightful.

Looking down at her, he thought to himself: *How could I possibly feel this wonderful? I must be dreaming.*

CHAPTER 10

"WE'RE CALLING IT OPERATION NIGHTCAP," proclaimed Lieutenant Colonel Thomas Argyll Robertson, the thirty-two-year-old chief of the B1A counterintelligence section of British Military Intelligence Section 5. MI5, as it was known in abbreviated form, was the British Security Service responsible for domestic counterespionage. Robertson was seated at his cluttered desk piled high with case files, memorandums, dossiers, and the latest issues of *The Times*, including today's edition. He wore his trademark McKenzie tartan trews of the Seaforth Highlanders, or "Passion Pants" as his colleagues jokingly referred to them. These same colleagues unanimously agreed that such attire was curiously conspicuous for a man running one of the most secret intelligence operations in the world. The man listening attentively in the leather chair opposite Robertson was nearly twenty years his senior and something of an *éminence gris*: Major Sir John Cecil Masterman, distinguished Oxford don, cricket lover, and chairman of the Double Cross Committee that ran and controlled Robertson's handpicked German double agents living in England.

"It appears that Agent Fritz will soon be going on an extended holiday to our little island and we plan on catching him before he can do any damage," Robertson continued with a gleam in his aquamarine eyes. "As you know, for the past six months our German friend has been undergoing sabotage, communications, and logistical training at the Abwehr Nantes Spy School in Villa de la Bretonnière in Occupied France. Well, based on our most recent intercepts, it now appears likely that he will be paying us a visit sooner rather than later. I wanted to go over with you the trap we're laying for him, Major, before our meeting at 0900. Quite frankly, it's going to be dicey. That's why I wanted to give you the details before we meet with the full Committee."

"Yes, of course, Tar. What have you got from Most Secret Sources?" Tar was the nickname Thomas Argyll Robertson's MI5 colleagues had affectionately given him on account of his initials; and Most Secret Sources was the official name of the Ultra top-secret radio intercept system British intelligence had at its disposal, since the Allies had cracked the German Enigma code in 1940 and were able to read all German radio traffic at Bletchley Park, the location of British decoding efforts in Europe. The Government Code and Cypher School was hidden deep in the Buckinghamshire countryside, monitoring and decoding all German military radio communications as if reading the enemy's mail.

"Based on the most recent intercepts, we've narrowed the drop zones Fritz could possibly use to three: Mundford, North Norfolk, and the Cambrian Mountains. The last we regard as the most probable. We've sent warnings to our security service liaison officers at all three districts."

"What's the latest intelligence on our man?"

"We believe he's under thirty, around six feet tall, nationality British. He speaks English, French, and German, the latter two languages fluently. He is a trained wireless operator. Upon arrival, he may use the name Chapman. That may be his real name, but we're not sure."

"Anything else?"

"It's possible that he may be supplied with means of committing suicide with poison tablets. On his arrest, we have therefore recommended to the authorities that he be immediately searched, detained pending inquiries, and sent here to London under police escort."

"Yes, I can see our interceptors at Bletchley have been busy monitoring and decoding Fritz's latest radio traffic. I don't know how we could ever expect to win the bloody war without them. Now what about our man's mission? Do we know yet what the devil he's up to?"

"Not yet, unfortunately."

"No possible leads from Most Secret Sources?"

"I'm afraid we know only the broad outlines of his mission. But we have several other details on our mystery man."

"Such as?"

"We have his complete dental records and the names on his false identification cards. And we even know the approximate length of his hair."

"His hair?"

"He just had it cut. It's quite short."

"Jolly good. Anything else?"

"We know his password is Joli Albert."

"Joli Albert? What does it mean?"

"We haven't the foggiest. We're still deciphering it."

"This is all well and good, Colonel, but how do you plan on catching the clever bugger?"

"Quite frankly, even with Ultra, our chances are slim. We've rejected a full police dragnet with roadblocks and house-to-house searches."

"Why?"

"Too many possibilities of leakage and we don't want to risk the press sniffing around. If Fritz is alerted that we're looking for him, and is somehow able to escape our net, he may be able to relay that to the Germans. They would realize that we're able to read their communications."

"Yes, I see. Most Secret Sources must be protected at all costs."

"We're considering having a 'flying column' of Field Security Police on stand-by to mobilize under short notice to the drop zone to avoid involving local police. But we're afraid that they would just end up finding out anyway and raise a snit. Plus, we don't think it will actually work."

"Well, what have you decided upon?"

"Nothing yet. We think that the best approach might be some combination of multiple traps."

"Yes, I quite agree. It would appear we're also going to need a dab of luck."

"More than a dab, I should think."

Robertson rose from his chair and went to the window. A light drizzle had begun. He watched the civilians walking down St. James Street, passing a sandbagged doorway and a partially filled bomb crater on the sidewalk just to the west of a scorched building, a remnant of the Blitz. Did these people have any idea that the Germans were about to send over a spy that could change the outcome of the war if he wasn't caught? This operative was not like the other bumbling fools the Abwehr had airdropped into Britain but that had been swiftly apprehended. He was a well-trained agent and saboteur with expertise in explosives and radio transmission. But what made him most dangerous was that he was English and could seamlessly blend in. That was the best camouflage a spy could possibly have. And now, this clever German agent was about to be airdropped by the Luftwaffe into any one of three remote, sparsely populated areas, each up to twelve miles in diameter. They might as well be looking for a needle in a haystack.

God help us all if we don't catch the bloody bastard.

"What's vexing you, Tar?" Masterman—a former Oxford professor and erudite man of letters who, in 1933, had written a Sherlock Holmesian murder mystery novel entitled *An Oxford Tragedy*—could tell the difference between when the colonel was deeply vexed versus only mildly troubled.

Robertson stared a moment at his Glengarry cap hanging from his hat-and-coat rack before answering. "Our man is going to be tough to catch, Major. That's what worries me." He went to his desk, plucked up a decoded message sent from the Abwehr station at Nantes to the Abwehr headquarters in Paris, and handed it to Masterman, who proceeded to read it aloud.

"'Dear France,'" recited Masterman. "'Your friend Bobby the Pig grows fatter every day. He is gorging now like a king, roars like a lion and shits like an elephant. Fritz.' This is one of our man's recent transmissions?"

"It's over a month old, in fact. He's much better now. In fact, he's the Germans best man."

"He's quite a vulgar fellow, isn't he?"

"Yes, but what's more revealing is he's bloody fearless. He's a thrill seeker who just doesn't give a damn. He lives for the rush he gets through subterfuge and cunning. That's what our psychological profilers believe. These kind of men, Sir John, are the most dangerous—and the hardest to track down. We may have rolled up every German spy that has set foot on our soil during the last two years, but this one is quite different. He vexes me."

"Yes, I can what you mean. He isn't like the others, is he?"

"No, he's not."

"Once you know our man's airborne, what's the plan?"

"Operation Nightcap will be officially mobilized. Dick White will be contacted at his private telephone number in London, and regional liaison officers and Fighter Command will be placed on high alert. An intelligence officer stationed at Fighter Command will track all incoming air traffic, and if an enemy aircraft is spotted that appears to be heading for one of the three drop zone areas, he will alert the night-duty-officer at MI5. The duty-officer will then contact the chief constable in the area with instructions to scour the countryside, but discreetly."

"What if the plane is shot down?"

"Our man will be equipped with a parachute, so we expect he would bail out and we would pick him up. If, however, the spy somehow manages to land undetected, the plan is to have the police comb the area working alongside our team. In that case, we'll want them to check the boarding houses and hotels in the area."

"It's going to be tough to keep things quiet with the locals."

"All participants in Nightcap have been given strict instructions to conduct the manhunt as unobtrusively as possible. Under no circumstances will the public learn that we are searching for an enemy spy who has parachuted into our midst. We're going to say we're looking for an army deserter."

Masterman chuckled. "You think the police will actually believe that?"

"Do you have a better idea?"

"Not yet, but I'm sure we'll discuss such options in our meeting." He glanced at his watch. "Speaking of which, it's ten 'til, Tar. Shouldn't we be heading over?"

"Oh yes, the meeting." Robertson looked at his own watch. "We should get going."

The weekly meeting of the Double Cross Committee at the MI5 offices at St. James Street was held every Thursday to discuss the status of the German double-agent system run by Robertson. Within the last four months, it had been confirmed through Most Secret Sources that all German agents in England were under British control, which meant that they were either in prison, had been executed, or were acting double agents willingly serving the Allied cause. During the weekly meetings, Robertson, Masterman, and their team explored new deception operations and plotted how to pass the most usefully damaging information to the enemy through the recruited German double agents. In addition to its MI5 representatives, the Double Cross Committee members included members of Navy, Army, and Air Intelligence as well as MI6—the Secret Intelligence Service, or SIS—responsible for gathering intelligence outside Britain.

"Don't worry, Tar," said Masterman to reassure him. "We'll get our man."

"I wish I shared your optimism. To be quite honest, I place our odds at catching Agent Fritz before he can make a radio transmission back to Germany at forty-percent."

"Forty-percent? That's all?"

"This man, who may call himself Chapman, is no amateur. In fact, he's rather strordnary."

"Yes, I can see he is."

"If we don't catch him, he could blow Ultra sky high. You know where we'd be then, don't you, Sir John?"

"Indeed, I do. Back on the beaches of Dunkirk in a bloody mess."

CHAPTER 11

CAFÈ SETERSTUA
DRONNING MAUDS GATE 10

NOVEMBER 24, 1942

ANNEMARIE BREIEN looked anxiously around the café filled with SS officers and police before once again meeting her father's gaze. At sixty years old, Captain Roald Breien was the District Manager for Milorg in Upper Buskerud and a key figure in the Resistance, as were Annemarie's brother Roald Jr. also with Milorg, her sister Nancy with Polish forces on the continent, and her brother Oscar with the Norwegian Army stationed in Britain. Though she relished the fact that Café Seterstua was a front for the Resistance right under the very nose of the Germans, she still felt nervous coming here to the Wolf's Lair. Though most Germans couldn't speak or understand Norwegian, particularly when it was spoken in a fast-clipped whisper at a nearby table, she dreaded the prospect of being overheard and hauled at gunpoint down the street to Gestapo headquarters.

"You look well, Father," she said to begin their meeting. "Far better than you looked at Grini when I visited you there two weeks ago."

"I still don't know how you managed to get me out."

"Lieutenant Siegfried Fehmer of the Gestapo is the one responsible for your release."

"Don't pretend that he is a saint, Annemarie. That bastard has tortured and killed people."

"Is that true? He claims that he hasn't tortured or killed anyone."

"The man is trouble. And now you owe him, and he is going to want to collect on his debt."

"I know he's dangerous, but I believe he has goodness in his heart."

"What he does is in direct violation of the Hague and Geneva Conventions. Isn't that enough? My God, you act as though he's a semi-respectable human being with some minor character flaws. That bastard is a monster."

"That so-called monster is the man that freed you—as well as several of your friends and colleagues—from Grini Prison. What is it, seven people in addition to you so far? If I were in your shoes, I might be inclined to show a little gratitude."

"What would you have me do, bow before him and give him praise like the Lord Almighty?"

"No, but you can at least acknowledge what he's done. He didn't have to release you, or the others for that matter. He could have kept you all in prison."

"Yes, I appreciate my change in circumstances, but it is Fehmer who put me there in the first place. So please stop giving him the credit for my release."

"I'm sorry but I can't do that. He's the one who did it and deserves the credit. As I said, he could have said no, but he didn't. And that is the reason I wanted to talk to you."

The room quieted for a moment, and they glanced cautiously around the café to make sure no one was listening. There were at least a dozen uniformed German officers sitting at the tables: eating, drinking, talking, smoking, laughing, telling bawdy jokes. She was relieved that none of them seemed to show the least bit of interest in her or her father. They would have been stunned to learn that Café Seterstua was a Home Front stronghold in the middle of the most Nazified portion of Oslo—which was precisely why Resistance members like herself and her father came here. One block from Gestapo headquarters was the least expected place in all of Oslo for members of the underground to plot against the Germans.

"My plan is to further develop my relationship with Fehmer to secure the release of even more prisoners. I believe I have an opportunity here."

Her father shook his head disapprovingly. "I don't think that's a good idea. The man is as dangerous as a jackal. If he catches you, he'll kill you."

"He won't catch me. And who better to work with to secure the release of Norwegian patriots as well as our friends and cohorts than the officer who effectively runs the Gestapo?"

"But he is only a lieutenant."

"His authority far exceeds his title. He happens to be the right-hand man to SS-Colonel Heinrich Fehlis, the overall head of the German Security Services, including the Gestapo, Kripo criminal police, and the SD. I have it on good word from inside the Gestapo that Fehmer is Fehlis's golden boy."

"It sounds like you've thought this out."

"I have. But the other reason I wanted to talk to you was because of the information I found out today from Fehmer."

"What is it?"

"Tomorrow morning, the Norwegian police and Hird are going to round up the remaining Jews in Oslo and ship them to concentration camps in Germany." The Hird was the uniformed Norwegian Nazi paramilitary organization within Quisling's fascist party *Nasjonal Samling*, modelled the same way as the German *Sturmabteilungen*.

"There's going to be another raid?"

"Yes, I'm afraid so." The roundup of all of Norway's male Jews had been attempted a month earlier on October 26. Now Quisling and his henchman Jonas Lie, the NS minister of police, and their Norwegian Nazi Hirdsmen supporters were carrying out a *razzia* of those not ensnared in the first raid. Annemarie was hoping her father would be able to relay the message to the Milorg regional commanders in time to warn the remaining Jews to hide.

"When will the police and Hirdsmen strike?"

"Tomorrow morning before dawn is the word I received from Fehmer."

"Why would he tell you this information?"

"Because he trusts me."

"Come now, that's not the only reason."

"All right, he must also suspect I have access to the highest levels of the Home Front."

"He's using you to get at the Resistance?"

63

"I'm not one-hundred-percent sure what his motives are. He may be trying to hedge his bets in the event the war goes badly for Germany and negotiations are required."

"Or more likely, he wants you under his control. In either case, he's obviously using you to find out more about the underground."

"And I am manipulating him to ensure the release of our countrymen from prison. So, we both are gaining something from the other. In times of war, is that really so remarkable?"

"I suppose not. Who's in charge of the *razzia*?"

"A Norwegian police officer called Knut Roed is the one who has planned the raid. Fehmer told me that Roed will have one hundred taxis and three hundred Hirdsmen at his disposal. The Norwegian police will be divided into approximately fifty groups, each charged with rounding up ten Jews each. You must warn the district commanders so that they can warn the Jews."

"I will get the word out. Hopefully, many will be able to make their way to Sweden." He looked at his watch then back at her. "Thank you for the information. I can see now why you want to keep in close contact with Fehmer. But I would be remiss in my duty as your father if I didn't warn you that you are playing a most dangerous game."

She glanced around the room again. A table of SS officers burst with uproarious laughter. That was the thing about the Germans: they were loud and obnoxious, like bad-mannered uncles that drank too much, took over your home, and refused to leave at Christmas time.

"It's not a game, Father," she said in a low voice. "It's called saving lives."

"I fully acknowledge that it is a worthy cause. But I just wonder what you are going to do when Fehmer wants more than just your friendship."

"I can handle myself. I am twenty-seven-years old."

"I know you can handle yourself, and I am very proud of you. More than proud, for I owe you my life. But promise me that you won't become romantically involved with that Nazi bastard. It would break my heart if you two…you know what I mean."

"Don't worry, that will never happen. Fehmer is nothing but a means to an end to me."

"What does Kjell think about this?"

"This has nothing to do with my husband."

"I disagree. I think it has everything to do with your husband."

"Kjell supports me. He knows how important my work is to the Resistance."

"Yes well, right now the Resistance as you call it is on the ropes. In the last six months, Fehlis and his bloodhound Fehmer have practically wiped us out."

"I know, Father, and I am sorry."

"Feeling sorry for ourselves isn't going to change anything. We have to get smarter and be more careful. This year has been a catastrophe. Between Fehmer and that damned Henry Rinnan and his legion of Norwegian agent provocateurs, the Nazis and their supporters have rolled up most of our Milorg units in Stavanger, Sunnfjord, Bergen, and Oslo. There have been hundreds of arrests and dozens of executions."

"And yet here we are sitting in a café one block from Gestapo headquarters plotting against the Germans. That is precisely why we are going to win this war and beat Hitler. We are better than the Nazis."

"Spoken like a true patriot." He looked around the café for prying eyes and, seeing none, he reached out and took her by the hand. "Still, this is not a game," he said. "You are and will always be my baby girl. I could not bear the thought of anything happening to you."

She squeezed his hand in return. "And I can't bear the thought of anything happening to you and our countrymen. Which is why, despite the risk, I must carry on with my work of getting prisoners released."

"All right, but for God's sake, be careful. I don't know what your mother and I would do if we lost you. You are the best of the both of us."

CHAPTER 12

LE BOURGET AIRFIELD, OCCUPIED FRANCE, AND CAMBRIDGESHIRE, ENGLAND

DECEMBER 16-17, 1942

AT SEVEN MINUTES PAST ELEVEN P.M., they received a hand signal from the pilot that the plane was ready for take-off. Eddie Chapman and his German control officer, Stephan von Gröning—known to him still only as Dr. Stephan Graumann—tossed aside their half-smoked Gauloises onto the tarmac and stamped the cigarettes out. They then walked with a Luftwaffe colonel whose name Chapman did not know to the waiting Focke-Wulf 189 Eagle Owl. The three-seat tactical reconnaissance aircraft specially adapted for parachuting was sleek, black, twin-engined, nearly thirty feet long, and brandished mounted machine guns on each side. Chapman hoped like hell they wouldn't be forced to use the weapons once they were airborne.

As they strode towards the plane, an ear-splitting roar filled their ears from the Junkers 88 Schnellbombers that would escort them across the Channel for the cover bombing mission over Cambridge. The air was redolent of burned petrol and exhaust fumes. Chapman's legs felt heavy and awkward as they crossed the tarmac apron. He was wearing a jump suit over his civilian clothes, heavy kneepads, and landing boots; and strapped to his back was a cumbersome parachute and bulky kit bag carrying everything that a German spy might possibly need in enemy territory—and several items that he most likely would not.

He was anxious and wished he could have one last swig of cognac from the rittmeister's silver flask. He felt the same nervous anticipation that he had often experienced during pre-war safecracking jobs. At the foot of the aircraft steps, both the Luftwaffe colonel and Graumann shook hands with him, wishing him good luck.

"As soon as I receive your first message, Fritzchen," said the German spymaster, wearing a three-piece pin-striped suit, "I promise to break out a bottle of champagne with the boys at La Bretonnière and celebrate."

"Here's to success then," said Chapman, raising an imaginary glass.

"We shall be waiting for your return, the colonel and me. We shall definitely be waiting."

"Cheerio, old man. When my mission is complete, we'll sing Lili Marlene badly together once again."

"I cannot wait, Fritzchen. Good luck and Godspeed, as the British like to say."

Chapman chuckled nervously and squeezed through the cockpit hatch with his heavy parachute pack. The pilot—a rangy *oberleutnant* with an Iron Cross at his throat named Fritz Schlichting—instructed him to kneel over the airplane floor's jump hatch. He crammed into the small, improvised alcove and faced the rear of the plane. The wireless operator, who doubled as the gunner, was already seated at the rear, and a foot away from him was the machine gun itself. *Uberleutnant* Karl Ischinger, the navigator and commander, scrambled in behind him as he began checking the hinge of the escape hatch door as well as his oxygen supply and the communications link. Six inches from Chapman's head were instruments and more were squeezed into the space to his left. To his right was ammunition, which he prayed would not be hit by British nightfighters or flak.

Five minutes later, he heard the pilot ask loudly through the headset, "*Können sie mich hören?*" Can you hear me?

"*Jawohl,*" he answered back.

"*Gut! Gemütliche Reise!*" Well! Comfortable journey!

The engines revved. Three minutes later, at precisely 11:25 p.m., the Focke-Wulf took off from Le Bourget into the darkness and they were airborne. The plane headed out across the coast of France and north towards the hook of Holland in an arced approach across the North Sea and English Channel that would swing in as far from London as possible. Lying flat on his stomach, Chapman couldn't see anything that was happening in the nose of the plane where the pilot and navigator sat; the sole illumination was a tiny flashlight held by the wireless operator. As the plane banked, Chapman caught glimpses of the receding lights of Occupied France through a crack in the door hinge.

The mechanical roar of the Fw 189's engines dampened the voices of the pilot and navigator as they talked to one another through their radio headsets. But over the engine noise, Chapman could hear them every so often discussing their altitude and speed. From time to time, the navigator would write something on a small piece of paper and hand it over his head to the pilot. In the inky darkness below there were occasional pinpricks of light. Soon, he smelled sea air and could make out reflections on water and knew they were over the North Sea.

He thought of his younger brother, Winston. He was a sailor in the merchant marine and Chapman had not corresponded or heard news of him for more than a year. Suddenly, he missed him and hoped he would not come under attack from the German U-boats prowling the Atlantic and North Sea. It was obviously going to be a long and cruel war and many people would die horrible deaths. He hoped he and his brother wouldn't be among the casualties. Then he thought of his old girlfriend Freda Stevenson, whom he had run out on back in 1939 just before he had fled to Jersey in the Channel Islands; and Betty Farmer, the platinum blonde he had been dating when he had to jump out of a window at the Hotel de la Plage in Jersey to escape from the police. He wondered if his two former lovers ever thought about him.

The aircraft climbed higher. He started to feel the cold and his legs began to cramp up in the confined space. Soon, the cockpit was freezing despite the meager warmth from a heater. The wireless man indicated that Chapman should strap on his oxygen mask. A few minutes later, he felt warm fluid trickling down his chin. He realized he had failed to strap the mask tightly enough and blood was seeping from his nose. He readjusted the mask and the bleeding stopped.

The plane flew on. As they approached the British coast, Chapman overheard the pilot talking to the navigator and realized that their signals had been blocked by British jamming somewhere over the North Sea. The pilot was apparently using radio beams to grapple their way to the designated drop zone. After correcting his course slightly, *Oberleutnant* Schlichting seemed to be on track. A few minutes later, Chapman felt his ears pop as the Focke-Wulf dipped its cruising altitude from twenty thousand feet to just a few thousand feet to avoid British radar and allow the pilot to see the coastline. Soon thereafter, the plane banked sharply to the left and began a zigzagging flight pattern to avoid searchlights and coastal antiaircraft batteries. To ensure that British air defenses and shore batteries could not detect a pattern, German pilots seldom flew the same route over Great Britain, or in other countries in Axis-occupied Europe.

Chapman inhaled a deep breath of air to settle his nerves. Far to the south was a ring of searchlights surrounding London. As they crossed over the English coast north of Skegness, he saw searchlights slicing through the sky and colored balls floating upwards. It wasn't until he heard the rumble of explosions and the plane shook that he realized the firework display was enemy flak. To his surprise, Schlichting and his crew seemed unfazed by the explosions in the sky all around them. Far from being nervous or apprehensive, they were laughing and joking as if on a joyride.

He felt a tap on his head. He turned to make out the wireless operator splaying out the fingers of both hands: ten minutes. He fastened his helmet and tied his parachute cord to a bolt overhead. Another tap would be his cue to remove the oxygen mask for landing. But he soon became aware of more frantic signals. At first, he couldn't understand what was happening. It seemed the crew had forgotten to tie the lash line of the parachute to automatically pull it open when he dropped away. In another few moments, he realized with a mixture of fear and shock, he would have pulled the lever and fallen to his death.

Once the problem was resolved, the plane seemed to spiral down, the engines in a fighting scream, and then rose again. Passing over the Cambridgeshire fens, the Focke-Wulf performed a strange figure-of-eight dance in the sky. Suddenly, the pilot's voice came over the intercom.

"*Achtung! Achtung! Nachtjäger!*"

It was a British nightfighter. The Focke-Wulf yawed violently as the pilot headed for the nearest cloud bank. Feeling a flare of excitement, Chapman took another deep breath to steady his nerves. The roar of the two Argus As 410 engines was ear-piercing as a pocket of air turbulence jostled the plane.

"Karl, Fritz has to go!" the pilot said to his navigator, *Uberleutnant* Ischinger. "I don't know where the hell we are, but I have to take evasive action with that damned Tommy on our tail! Fritz has to go now!"

"All right, all right!" cried Chapman, able to hear him over the sound of the twin roaring engines. In desperation, he tore off his oxygen mask, rose to his knees, and pulled hard on the dispatch lever. The trapdoor vanished beneath him and he started to drop. But instead of plummeting downward toward earth, he was jerked back and held suspended in the open hole with his head down. To his horror, he was stuck on the underside of the plane because of his bulky pack. Jammed in by the weight of his equipment, he couldn't pull free. The air from the slipstream rushed past him in a torrent, flapping his clothing like a hurricane. Facing away from the direction of flight, and with the turbulence crackling his ears, he felt a lurching in his stomach followed by a wave of nausea.

Dangling helplessly, he yelled out to the wireless operator. "Help! Help! I can't fucking get out!" he screamed in German.

Above him, the pilot turned around and shouted to the wireless operator. "For God's sake, push him out!"

He felt a good hard kick to the small of his back from the boot of the wireless operator. In the next instant, he broke free and was falling freely towards *terra firma*. As he somersaulted through the darkened sky, he could make out the swastika tail of the Focke-Wulf. Then he became aware of noise closing in on them: a British nightfighter was firing at the plane. For a terrible moment, he was convinced it was heading directly towards him. Would it pulverize him in midair? As he watched the plane screaming towards him in horrified fascination, he couldn't believe he was about to suffer the indignity of being killed after having come so close to making it home. But the Focke-Wulf banked right and the British fighter followed in pursuit.

Hearing the rustle of silk, he peered up to see his chute obediently flutter open and then he disappeared into the inky darkness. The blast of air hit his face like a freight train and the parachute harness jerked savagely upon his shoulders, but then he was floating and it was utterly quiet and peaceful. He continued to float downwards, congealing occasionally from the darkness as the light of the moon and stars caught him in silhouette during his descent. He was vaguely aware that blood was again dripping off his chin.

In the far distance, he saw searchlights flickering in the darkness. Below, he heard the wail of a siren signaling the all-clear. For a strange moment, he wondered if he was staring down at Occupied France beneath his dangling boots and not Great Britain. Could this be another of Doktor Graumann's tests? He drifted down through the windless night, towards a spot in the darkness below. He seemed to be floating and the clouds far below him looked like waves. Suddenly, another darkly paranoid thought struck him: what if he had been dropped by accident over the sea? Moments later, he was engulfed in the shadowy darkness below the clouds. He was unable to make out anything below as the countryside was shrouded in darkness.

As he closed in on *terra firma*, he felt his heart racing in anticipation of the landing. Able to discern the silhouette of a rooftop at the edge of his night vision, he was taken by surprise when he unexpectedly touched down with a jolt in a ploughed field. He hit the ground with full force, and before he could brace himself he had toppled over onto his back and was staring up at the stars. He smelled celery. Had he parachuted into a celery field? A minute later, he was out of his parachute harness and looking at his watch. It was quarter past two.

Scanning the area, he went in search of the house over which he had sailed. It turned out to be an abandoned cottage. He still had no idea he was at least twenty miles from his designated drop zone. He tried to retrace his steps but got lost and it took him fifteen minutes to relocate his discarded parachute. He took off his jump suit, removed any tell-tale signs that he had fallen from the sky, and buried the suit along with his chute and heavy jump boots in mud close by a stream.

By now, his eyes had adapted to the velvety darkness. The only sounds were the distant flak and the low buzz of the receding remnants of the air raid. There was not a house light anywhere that he could see. The landscape was barren except for the abandoned house.

He wondered again if it was all part of the German deception plan, especially since the weather seemed warmer than he had remembered nighttime in the middle of an English winter. His conversation with Graumann after his practice night drop over Nantes the previous summer continued to weigh heavily on his mind. Had they dropped him over occupied territory to test whether he would go ahead with his mission?

Having no idea where he was, he started walking through the muddy celery field. A few minutes later, he spotted a stone farmhouse. He stumbled through puddles of water and mud towards the silhouetted structure, groping through the darkness with his flashlight. Eventually, he climbed over a wall and shined his light through the front door. He could make out a coat rack, an umbrella stand, and stairs. But what gave him relief and made him realize that this was not all some sort of trick was the telephone on a side table and, next to it, a British telephone book.

Now that he knew he was on British soil, he shined his flashlight in through the window and rapped on the door urgently.

A minute later an elderly country woman appeared in her dressing gown and peered out of the window at him. "Who is it?" she demanded.

"A British airman," he replied. "I'm sorry, but I've had an accident." He again looked at his watch: it was now 3:30 a.m.

She opened the door and looked him over, noticing the mud and blood on his face. "One can't be too careful in wartime. Where's your plane?"

He gestured vaguely at the surrounding countryside. "Across the fields," he said. "I came down by parachute and my nose bled from the altitude."

"I thought I heard a Jerry."

"Yes, that would be a cover plane for ours."

Her sleepy-eyed husband came up behind her with a lamp. "I don't expect he'll rob and kill us, Martha. Invite the lad in for a cup of tea."

Chapman stepped inside, was given a cup of tea, and then asked if he could use the phone to call the local constable. An hour later, after he had eaten four slices of bread and drank four cups of tea, Sergeants Vail and Hutchings of the Ely Police Department arrived in a police car with two constables. With a disarming grin, he politely introduced himself, shook hands with them, reached into his pocket, and pulled out his loaded Colt revolver and spare cylinder.

"I expect the first things you'll want are these," he said pleasantly. He handed the weapon to Sergeant Vail along with the loaded cylinder.

"Where did you come from, young man?" the police sergeant asked him.

"All the way from France. I would very much like to get in touch with the British Secret Service."

"The Secret Service? You don't say?"

"Aye, Sergeant. I'm afraid the unbelievable story I have to tell is for their ears only."

CHAPTER 13

CAMP 020 INTERROGATION CENTER
SOUTHWEST LONDON, ENGLAND

DECEMBER 17-18, 1942

THE VICTORIAN MANSION known as Latchmere House in Ham Common was Great Britain's top-secret interrogation and incarceration center for suspected spies, subversives, and enemy aliens. Eight days before Christmas at precisely 9:30 a.m. it was as quiet as a mausoleum. But then again, it was deathly silent here every day—and very much by design. What lurked behind the secluded walls, surrounded by three rows of barbed-wire fencing, was a furtive world that would make even the most Blitz-hardened British citizen howl in protest. For here, in the secret MI5 installation code-named Camp 020, where British officers from the First World War had once convalesced to overcome shell shock, was a torture chamber that rivaled the Tower of London.

The difference was the torture was primarily psychological.

Within the sprawling mansion were 92 block cells with hidden microphones, a punishment room known chillingly as Cell 13, and interrogation rooms where wartime enemies of His Majesty the King were mercilessly grilled until "broken" into telling the truth by any means necessary—short of outright physical torture. The prisoners were isolated in solitary confinement and were not allowed to speak to one another. Guards wore lightweight tennis shoes to muffle the sound of their footsteps. Pipes were buried within masonry to prevent prisoners from tapping Morse code to one another. Food was kept bland, and cigarettes were not allowed. Sleep deprivation and the hooding of inmates were commonly used tactics, particularly in the first few days of incarceration when the enemy was most vulnerable to confessing, changing allegiances, and being "turned" into a double agent.

The man in charge of the *breaking* was Lieutenant Colonel Robin "Tin Eye" Stephens, the commandant of Camp 020. Quite appropriately, he regarded himself as a master of the interrogative arts, for no one could break and turn a German spy like Tin Eye. His colorful nickname came from the steel-rimmed monocle he screwed into his right eye, which reportedly he wore even when he slept and made him as terrifying as a Gestapo chief. He was of sturdy build and ruddy complexion and he wore a neatly creased Nepalese Gurkha military uniform along with his gleaming monocle. Most of all, he was a living, breathing dichotomy.

Stephens hated all things German with religious-like fervor, and yet, he was half-German himself. The object of interrogation, he routinely instructed his staff of officers, was simple: "Truth in the shortest possible time." And yet, he stood steadfast in his mantra—drilled into all his officers—to never inflict physical pain on his charges, and he had a superb record of breaking even the most hardened Nazi spies without raising so much as a finger. He spoke seven different languages fluently and had commanded a regiment of Ghurkas, the elite Nepalese troops of the

British Empire Army, yet he was a raging xenophobe and stodgy imperialist. A frustrated writer, he was outspoken and cruel in his criticism of others, yet he had a natural, comical way with prose and could be quite charming when far removed from an interrogation cell.

Tin Eye succeeded in breaking the enemy by calmly and deliberately peeling away his resistance, extracting vital information without appearing to do so, frightening him to death through psychological gamesmanship as the occasion called for it, and, in the end, coming full circle and winning over the prisoner's trust. Once broken, those precious few who were highly placed enough within the Abwehr to warrant special consideration, willing to spy for England, and were not sent to the gallows or imprisoned were delivered as double agents to MI5's Tar Robertson. Once in Robertson and Section B1A's hands, a new convert's job was to feed false intelligence to the Germans. Tin Eye had worked closely with Robertson since the early days of the war and was an integral part of the Double Cross Spy System that was actively deceiving Hitler and his Nazi war machine.

The clever system employed by MI5 had been, virtually from the war's outset, successful in overwhelming its German intelligence opponent, the Abwehr, by catching all its spies traveling to England and running a select few as supportive British double agents. For the past two years, Robertson and his Double Cross team had been misleading Hitler about Allied intentions in the battlegrounds of North Africa, Greece, and the Balkans, as well as in the occupied countries of Europe and neutral Spain, Portugal, Switzerland, and Sweden. Robertson had deftly handled a widely disparate collection of double agents delivered by Tin Eye—among them playboys, criminals, and drunks with inspired code names like Snow, Tricycle, and Garbo—to bring military success to the Allied cause. But the outcome of the war depended on feeding the Germans false information and deceiving them for as long as possible to win ultimate victory.

To do that, Robertson needed new potential recruits to be double agents.

The question in Colonel Tin Eye Stephens' mind at precisely 9:30 a.m. on December 17, 1942, was whether one Edward Arnold "Eddie" Chapman would fit the bill—or swing from the gallows as so many foreign agents before him had done.

ψψψ

Chapman felt the hairs on the back of his neck bristle as he stared across the table of Interrogation Room 3 at the fierce-looking officer with the monocle, and then at his two stony-faced subordinates. "No chivalry, no gossip, no cigarettes. Your life as you know it is over," the man with the monocle had chillingly greeted him *auf Deutsch* upon his arrival to the dreary building in Ham Common. He was the camp commandant, and Chapman had overheard one of the staff officers in the hallway refer to him in a hushed voice as "Tin Eye." Since his arrival to the camp, he had been strip-searched twice, poked and probed by a man purporting to be a doctor, photographed, thrown in cold concrete cell with two frayed woolen blankets, and fed barely edible food while awaiting what would no doubt be several days of harsh interrogation. He had not been allowed even a wink of sleep or any interaction with the other prisoners. Clearly, his British captors were already trying to break him by reinforcing to him the hopelessness of his position—and they were succeeding.

Tin Eye looked at him as though he had trodden in something unpleasant, then consulted a buff-colored folder. "Your name is Chapman, is it?" he barked.

They stared at one another. It was a matter of honor for Chapman not to show fear, though he was trembling inside. "That's right," he responded cautiously.

"That is the correct name, is it? You're not lying to me?"

"That's right, sir. Yes, I mean no, I am not lying."

"Well then, I shall start off by saying that it is definitely to your credit that you promptly informed the authorities that you had been dropped from a German airplane. It is because of this that you may be of potential value. Do you see?"

"Yes, sir. Quite."

Tin Eye's eyes narrowed beneath his monocle. "I'm not saying this in any sense of a threat, but you must remember that you are in a British Secret Service prison and it's our job in wartime to make sure that we get the whole story from you and that it is completely checked."

"I understand. That's why I am going to tell you everything, starting from the beginning."

"That's good because I happen to believe that a prisoner in war should be at the point of a bayonet, but that, of course, is figuratively speaking. In my camp, Mr. Chapman, violence is taboo, for not only does it produce answers aimed to please, it lowers the standard of information. That's why, unlike the murderous Gestapo to whom your insolent German handlers serve, we never strike a man. In the first place, it is an act of cowardice. In the second, it reeks of stupidity. A beaten prisoner will lie to avoid further physical punishment and everything he says thereafter will be based on a false premise. Do you understand, lad?"

He gulped. "Yes…yes, I do."

"Good, let's have your story. But I'm warning you up front, me and my colleagues will have to see for ourselves whether everything checks out. And we do not suffer liars. Do you see?"

Chapman gulped a second time. "Yes, sir."

"Very good. Now get to it. And remember, we'll be here for as long as it takes to get it right."

For the next forty-eight hours, Chapman told them his story. He was interrogated relentlessly with only brief intermissions, and during that time he told them everything that came to his mind. His recollections of his checkered past as a professional criminal in England and as an Abwehr spy in Occupied France and Nazi Germany poured out of him. Tin Eye and his MI5 officers worked in shifts, late into the night. He was grilled with countless questions about his army career, his criminal past, and his family, friends, and associates while his interrogators took copious notes. They asked the more important questions over and over and in slightly different ways throughout the two days, making him feel as though he was being cross-examined by a clever barrister. Colonel Stephens and Captains Short and Goodacre, the latter two whose names were never revealed to him, dissected the minutiae of his life story in exhausting detail. Meanwhile, unbeknownst to Chapman, in a separate room at Camp 020, a rotating team of expertly trained stenographers recorded every word of the interrogations conducted by the rotating team of inquisitors. It was standard operating procedure to prepare a final transcript of every interrogation session.

He recounted his dismissal from the Coldstream Guards and his criminal past forging checks and robbing safes along with his various early stints in prison and narrow escapes from the police. He described in detail his time in captivity with his friend Faramus on the island of Jersey and in Romainville under the Germans; his recruitment by Dr. Graumann and the Abwehr; his espionage training in Nantes and Berlin; and his harrowing parachute drop into a muddy celery field north of Cambridge. Without reservation, he told his three interrogators about the codes and sabotage techniques he had learned, the secret writing techniques with invisible ink, and the many passwords, code words, and wireless frequencies his German handlers had taught him. In the course of the forty-eight hours, he gave more than fifty descriptions of separate individuals, from his aristocratic friend and spymaster Graumann to the rabid Nazi Thomas, from fellow German operatives Wojch, Schmidt, and the hideous man from Angers with the gold teeth to Odette the cook. He described the flak emplacements at Nantes, the location of the Paris Abwehr headquarters, and the price of black-market butter. He described the Breton nationalists, the treacherous Gaullists, and the countless other suspicious characters and operatives that had passed through Nantes. He explained how he had secretly spied on his German handlers for four months and written up what he had discovered during his training, information that he knew would be useful to British intelligence—only to destroy the revealing document at the last second for fear of exposure.

What seemed to him to be trivial appeared to be important to his interrogators, with detail after detail being verified and cross-checked against his previous answers. How had he been taken to Villa de la Bretonnière? How many guards? What were their names? Where had he met them? And then his travels around the Reich. Where did the equipment come from? On and on they went, his only relief coming when they took him back to his cell for a short break so they could confer in private.

After all the interminable questions were asked well into the second night, he was physically exhausted. He had spilled his guts to his new British overlords, gushing forth in a torrent on the past decade of his life and his training as a German spy in stunning detail, surprising even himself by how much information was stored in his brain. He held nothing back. Towards the end, Tin Eye returned once again to the details of his mission. Chapman retold the monocle-clad officer and his two associates how he had been sent to England to blow up the de Havilland aircraft factory by breaking his way in and planting explosives.

"Sounds like a pretty hazardous undertaking," said Tin Eye. "It seems odd that your German handlers didn't tell you how difficult the job would be. Aren't you surprised that they would withhold that from you?"

"It is no cock-up, sir. They did give me quite a bit of training in sabotage."

"How long did they give you to complete the operation again?"

"Two and a half months. As I said, I was to break my way in."

"You are rather a favorite of the Huns, aren't you? But do they trust you?"

"No question."

"They think rather highly of you? They believe that you can get in anywhere and do virtually anything, you, their well-trained German spy?"

"Yes, I believe they think I can make a difference in the war."

"Well then, back to this two-and-a-half-month period. The Germans want the factory blown up within that time frame, is that it? They are counting on it?"

"Yes. As I said before, it is the top priority of my mission."

"These Mosquito bombers seem to be really worrying them."

"Yes, the Germans want them taken off production. Göring is apparently obsessed."

"Suppose you did blow up the plant, what were your instructions for afterwards, to try and make your way back into France again?"

"The Germans are supposed to arrange to bring me back by U-boat."

"I see." From the table, the colonel picked up a wad of paper bills. The bills were wrapped with a heavy rubber band, like the kind used at banks. "What is this band here around your money? Have you had a look at it?"

He saw that the band was labeled BERLIN in upper case letters. He couldn't believe his eyes. "Well, that's rather strange."

"It's an ordinary bank band, I suppose?"

"That's the fault of Thomas," said Chapman.

"Lieutenant Walter Thomas? Dr. Graumann's second-in-command, the one with the British ancestry who attended Southampton College and enjoys English folk dancing? That Thomas?"

He nodded. "The lieutenant was told to check my money and make sure there was no reference to France or Germany in any of my equipment. I was to have only English items in my possession. But in all the excitement he must have forgotten to take the rubber band off."

"You can see here that it says BERLIN in big, bold letters."

He felt a jolt of anger at Thomas for his lapse. "Yes, I can see. It was given to me like that.'

"You said earlier that you had made notes which might be of use to us...notes on your German handlers and time spent in France during your training. You said you had to destroy them because you were being searched. Who searched you?"

"Lieutenant Thomas."

"Thomas again?"

"Yes, as I told you before he was my control officer in addition to Graumann. When he frisked me, he said that he just wanted to make sure I didn't have French tickets or anything else in my clothes that might identify I had been in France."

"And yet this man who was supposed to be looking out for you frisks you and leaves a German band on your currency? You do realize that his incompetence may have cost you your life."

Chapman felt a surge of anger, feeling a sense of betrayal. "That was a bad mistake on his part, especially since he was warned by Dr. Graumann to make sure everything was in order."

"Yes, well, it's a good thing he's not in the British intelligence service. We tend not to make the kind of mistakes that get our operatives sent to the firing wall."

He felt his ire go up a notch. He hadn't thought of it that way, but it was clear that the Germans, and especially Thomas, had blundered badly. Or was Tin Eye trying to subtly turn him against his German handlers by undermining his faith in their competence? He looked at the chubby, good-natured officer with the owlish face.

"How long do I have to remain in this prison?" he asked Captain Short, who during the interrogation had mostly played good cop to Tin Eye's bad.

"We're not sure yet. That's being decided day-to-day. You see, we want to know if it was your honest intention, when you wrote the commandant in Jersey volunteering to spy on behalf of Germany, to get back to England and work for British intelligence."

"Yes, that was my intention. I've taken quite a lot of risks getting information which I believe is of value. And then there are several other important things which we haven't talked about that I can disclose to prove my worth."

"Yes, that is all well and good," sniffed Tin Eye. "But how do we know you're telling the truth?"

He couldn't help but feel irritated at the colonel's gruff tone. "Although one does not expect gratitude from one's own country, it would be helpful to draw your attention to a few facts. For thirteen months now, I have been under German rule."

"Yes, yes, we know."

"During this time, even when undergoing detention, I was treated fairly. I made many friends, people that I respect and believe came to respect me—unfortunately for them and for me. Dr. Graumann is a good man and a loyal officer to his country who is not fighting for Hitler, but for the honor of Germany. He always treated me with the utmost respect, like one soldier to another. But despite that, I set out from the first day to try to mass together a series of facts, places, and dates concerning the German organization, which I think would be a formidable task even for one of your trained experts. From the start I was very much handicapped, my knowledge of German and French was at best adequate. These are, of course, the two languages most essential for this work. I studied French until I mastered it, even learning the slang. I now read it as fluently as English. Then, sir, for nine months I listened to every conversation I could hear. I opened many drawers containing documents marked top secret—*geheim*. I bored very small holes from the bathroom to the room of Dr. Graumann, a man very much my friend, so I could eavesdrop."

"Isn't this the same Dr. Graumann who said to Thomas that you wouldn't dare turn yourself in to British intelligence or the police because they would lock you up for twenty years?"

"Yes, and as I told you before, it made me angry when he said it."

"Of course, it did. It was plain blackmail." Tin Eye's expression beneath his monocle was one of mock outrage. "Now why are you really helping us, Eddie? Why do you want to offer your services to British intelligence?"

"Perhaps, Commandant, we're talking about patriotism."

"Patriotism. Really?"

"I know it's hard to believe coming from me, a safecracker and German spy. I laugh a little cynically when I think of it sometimes. But there it is. I suppose I have had a bout over my soul and my country won. Why I can't explain. I wish like bloody hell there had been no war, and a part of me wishes I had never started this affair. To spy and cheat on one's friends…well, let's just say it's not nice. In fact, it's dirty. However, as I'm the one who decided to jump into the fray of espionage, I must follow through with it. Don't think I ask anything for this. I don't. But I do have to say that it seems very strange to be working for two different governments— one offering me the chance of money, success and a career, the other a cold prison cell."

"If you are telling the truth, then it would seem you have given us an astonishingly detailed picture of German espionage methods in Occupied France. But it still all hinges on whether you are being aboveboard with us, doesn't it?"

"Now look here. I've not only given you a great deal of useful intelligence, I've told you how you can best use it."

"Oh, you're telling us how to do or jobs, are you?"

"No. I mean, yes. Surely by acting on the information I've given you, you and your colleagues can now easily break the Abwehr code and intercept messages between the various German intelligence units in France, Berlin, and perhaps elsewhere."

They just looked at him in stony-faced silence.

"I don't know what else to tell you blokes. My mind is a frenzied mass of names, formulas, descriptions, places, times, and information on explosions, radio telegraphy, and parachute jumping. Everything's jumbled in my head. Believe me, I'm doing the best I can to help you. But I'm just exhausted. We've been at it for two full days now and I'm at my wits end, I tell you."

"Yes, but what makes you tick, Eddie. Are you truly a patriotic rogue who wants to help his country? Or is there something else that motivates you?"

"Well, I suppose there is one other thing that drives me: my friend Faramus."

"Yes, what about him?"

"He is a hostage for my good behavior."

"For your good behavior in France, or here?"

"Here. He's being used as a kind of lever to ensure I perform the de Havilland job and my other spy work. If I can convince them that I'm doing all they ask of me, then Faramus might yet be spared."

At this, Tin Eye paused to jot down notes before declaring, "Using your friend Faramus as insurance…why there's yet another threat by your good Dr. Graumann."

Chapman said nothing, but he felt anger boiling up inside him. It was true the good doktor was manipulating him, but Tin Eye was still exaggerating the threat to make him doubt his German handlers. All the same, it was obvious Graumann didn't fully trust him and was trying to control him. Furthermore, the Germans wouldn't hesitate to kill Faramus—and him, too, when he returned to France—if they suspected the least bit of treachery.

He couldn't help but feel torn. Torn between his genuine affection for the old man—and the urgent need to betray him. Torn between the desire to save his own skin and that of Faramus. Torn between self-interest and some greater good, which he still didn't fully understand. Torn between his loyalty to his friend and his duty to his country. He was in turmoil. But the whole situation would be immeasurably worse if he didn't make contact via radio soon to his German handlers. The window of opportunity was closing.

"As I've made clear to you, it is important that I establish radio contact with the Boche at the earliest possible moment," he said, using coarse language that he believed might help persuade Tin Eye that he was on the English side. "Dr. Graumann stressed this particular point. He said he would know I was under English control if I took a long time to establish contact after my airdrop into Great Britain. He is a smart man and I would not underestimate him."

"Yes, we are aware that today is supposed to be the day of your transmission."

"British red tape. Dr. Graumann said it would rear its ugly head if I was under control. He was quite clear about that."

Tin Eye scowled. "Yes, we understand timing is critical. But we must make sure you're not lying or holding something back. Well, are you, Agent Fritz?"

"I've told you everything I know."

"We'll soon see about that." The colonel stood up, signaling that he was again leaving the room and allowing his subordinates to carry on the questioning. "Just remember that no spy, however clever and resourceful, can withstand relentless interrogation. Non-stop questioning in a controlled environment will wear down even the strongest constitution in the end. You do understand that?"

"Yes, Commandant, I do."

"Then you can also see that we are in a bit of a quandary. If contact with your German handlers is delayed, then Dr. Graumann might very well suspect something has gone wrong. But if we allow you to respond without being certain you are playing straight with us, or you actively pull a trick during the transmission, the results could be catastrophic for us both. I believe, Mr. Chapman, we have to bring you and your motives into sharper focus."

Tin Eye then left the room. As the door closed behind him, all Chapman could think was, *What the bloody hell have I gotten myself into?*

CHAPTER 14

"WE HAVE CHOSEN THE NAME OF AGENT ZIGZAG for Chapman. What do you think, Colonel Stephens? Does the code name meet your approval?"

Tar Robertson underscored the announcement with a smile. Though the chief of Section B1A claimed the selection of a code name was a joint decision by his team, he always picked the monikers of his Double Cross agents, and typically with a wink of amusement. The Welsh double agent Arthur Graham Owens he had code-named Snow based upon a partial anagram of his last name. Upon the Danish-born Wulf Schmidt he had bestowed the code name Tate because he thought he looked like the comedian Harry Tate. The bacchanalian Yugoslavian playboy Dusko Popov was dubbed Tricycle for his predilection for ménage à trois sex. The name Robertson selected for Eddie Chapman was a tongue-in-cheek acknowledgement of Agent Zigzag's colorful and complicated criminal and romantic history. The man liked to zig and zag.

To Robertson's surprise, the normally stoic Tin Eye liked the code name, too. "I must say it is rather apt," responded the Camp 020 commandant with a rare smile. His glass monocle, rigid military bearing, and neatly creased Nepalese Gurkha uniform contrasted sharply with Robertson's easygoing, ruling-class manner and tartan-trousered Seaforth Highlanders' uniform. "The question now is what we're going to do with him."

"We are moving forward on several fronts in that regard," said Robertson. "But of course, I'd like to hear your thoughts on the matter. I was impressed with your report on the interrogations and wanted to go over some of the details on our new agent. We have big plans for Zigzag."

"The whole interrogation team agrees that Chapman should be used for Double Cross purposes. We believe it should be full speed ahead for a fake bombing operation at the de Havilland plant and the secondary operations the Germans have designated. And then, once his work is completed, we believe he should be sent back to France to join a party of saboteurs already in training to be sent to America for a really big job."

There's no way we're going to send him to America, thought Robertson. *Zigzag is too valuable, and I don't want him wasted by that imbecile Hoover at the FBI. The bastard almost blew Tricycle.*

"Whatever is ultimately decided by your branch," continued Tin Eye, "we believe Chapman should be used to the fullest extent. It's clear he genuinely wants to work for us against the Germans. By his courage and resourcefulness, he is ideally fitted to be one of our top Double Cross agents."

"I agree. But there is a risk in sending him back into France or America. He might be exposed by the Germans, or he might confess to them. He might even change sides again."

"That's true, but the potential benefits of having a spy at the heart of the German Secret Service, I believe, outweigh the dangers. Over the past four days alone, he has given us invaluable information on the Abwehr. We now have a very detailed picture of German espionage methods, particularly at the Nantes Dienststelle. Piece by piece, we have been able to put names to the dozens of German and French operatives that Chapman came into contact with. We haven't identified all of the key players yet, mind you, but we *are* getting close."

"From your report, though, I was surprised at how successfully the Germans kept him in the dark over the identities of his comrades. On no occasion was anyone's real name given to him."

"Yes, that's true. During one interrogation, Captain Short even casually dropped the name 'von Gröning' into the conversation, but our lad showed no visible reaction. He only knows the spymaster as Dr. Graumann. By the way, has Zigzag established radio contact with him yet?"

"Yes, here are the latest communications." He opened a leatherbound folder and withdrew a sheet of wireless transmissions and intercepts from Bletchley Park showing yesterday's and today's faked correspondence between Chapman and his German control officer. The piece of paper read:

Chapman: FFFFF HAVE ARRIVED. AM WELL WITH FRIENDS. OK. HI HU HA.
Von Gröning: THANKS FOR MESSAGE. WISH GOOD RESULTS. OK.

"*FFFFF* and *Hi Hu Ha*?" remarked Tin Eye.

"FFFFF is his control sign to show he is operating of his own free will," explained Robertson.

"And Hi Hu Ha?"

"Zigzag's laughing sign-off. It's a telltale fingerprint that lets the Jerries know they're dealing with the genuine article."

"What's the next step then?"

"Why the de Havilland job of course. It's going to be our biggest deception yet."

"You really think you can pull it off? I understand that to sustain von Gröning's faith in Fritz, some sort of demonstration of his agent's skills and loyalty will be required sooner rather than later. But we are talking about the simulated bombing of an airplane factory."

"It's going to be a challenge, there's no doubt about it. But Major Masterman is most insistent that we do all we can to arrange a speedy and spectacular explosion of some kind."

"The major is quite the showman. I don't suppose he gave you his usual cricket analogy?"

"Of course, he did. And he wants the fake sabotage to be so widely reported in the press that there's no doubt of its authenticity. In fact, he wants it on the front page of the *Times*, Graumann's British newspaper of choice. Sir John even wants to allow German reconnaissance planes to be allowed to photograph the sham explosion—only from twenty-thousand feet and above, of course."

"That's quite an undertaking. I presume you'll have Zigzag visit the plant?"

"Most definitely. A double agent should, as far as possible, live the life the enemy believes he is living. Major Masterman calls it the principle of verisimilitude: the imperative necessity of making the agent experience all that he professes to have done. It is far easier, under interrogation, to tell part of the truth than to sustain a latticework of pure lies. If Z is going to pretend to have blown up the de Havilland factory, then by Jove, he must go and case the joint, precisely as he would if he were genuinely bent on sabotage."

"The plant is in Hatfield, right?"

"Only a ten-mile journey by bus. We'll probably have him visit the plant several times until he's familiar with it. To be honest, that's the least of my worries."

"What's your main concern?"

"How he'll hold up while in England. All of our doubles give us headaches now and again."

"Our preliminary psychological profile from Dr. Reardon indicates that Chapman's motives are—despite his personal affection for von Gröning—his hatred for the Hun coupled with a sense of adventure. There is no woman in the case and no bargain for rehabilitation. He is driven primarily by his personal courage and the thrill of espionage, but the quirky bastard also seems to have a streak of patriotism in him."

"Our biggest worry is that his past will catch up with him. If he's allowed to waltz around London unattended, he'll surely be picked up by the police. He's due for a stretch of twenty years, so if that happens we're going to have some serious explaining to do with the authorities. Or even worse, he might link up with his former criminal gang and return to his old ways."

"Yes, but if he's kept under guard at Camp 020, he will no doubt go sour and might attempt a break. That's why I believe the only way to operate him safely would be to place him at half-liberty, under surveillance but not in prison. Keep him under control in a quiet, country place."

"I quite agree. Camp 020 is no place to run a double agent. If Zigzag is to be effective, he must be kept happy, and that is going to require creature comforts at least comparable to those of La Bretonnière."

"Personally, I think von Gröning and his team pampered him. They pandered to his vanity, granted him almost total freedom, and treated him like one of the boys."

"To compete with that, we're going to have to roll out the red carpet too. Now that we've found a double agent of inestimable value, we don't want to do anything to bugger things up."

"The quality of his equipment shows that the Germans value him highly too. The cash he brought with him is genuine British currency, not the forged stuff that the Abwehr has often palmed off on lesser agents. The match heads were impregnated with quinine to ensure high quality secret writing. The brown pill he was carrying on his person was potassium cyanide, which is instantaneously lethal. His wireless set is from an actual British SOE agent."

"Since he's so valuable to both sides, we're going to have to keep an extra close eye on him."

"Have you given thought as to who his control officer will be?"

"I've assigned Captain Reed. And I was thinking of having Corporals Backwell and Tooth from our Field Security team keep an eye on him as well as see to his needs. There is no reason to doubt Z's loyalty to his country, so they will act only as chaperones to keep him out of trouble and ensure that he's entertained."

"All the same, you'll have to make sure that he's never left alone, day or night. And he should not communicate with anyone, use the telephone, or send letters."

"I'll set the team up in one of our safe houses in North London. The success of the operation will depend upon absolute secrecy. He'll be equipped with a special card with a photograph indicating that he's performing special duties for the War Office. That way he can produce the card if he's ever challenged by officials."

"There's no doubt he has provided and can continue to provide us with valuable intelligence. His powers of observation are remarkable, and he has been truthful in whatever he has told us. But he does appear to be a bit of a blabbermouth. You will have to watch for that too."

"That's a good point. I do trust him, however. Major Masterman doesn't but I do."

"What does the major say?"

"He is skeptical that a criminal such as Chapman could possibly understand the concept of complete honesty."

At that, Tin Eye gave a chuckle and readjusted his monocle. "Even I have more faith in the bastard than that. His resilience after four solid days of cross-examination was nothing short of astonishing. If there's one thing he has convinced me of, it's that if the tables were turned, he won't crack under the pressure when he returns to Occupied Europe."

"But he is conflicted, which makes him vulnerable. You said so in your report."

"It's due to his affection for von Gröning. But you have to admit he is in a rather peculiar position. Here he is a wanted man by the British police but offering—no make that pleading—to work with us to bring down the Boche. If Chapman is to be believed, he has offered to work for the Germans solely as a means of escape, and upon parachuting into a celery field he has willingly and patriotically put himself at the disposal of the British Secret Service to work against them, including against a spymaster that he admires and regards as a father figure. I'm afraid fiction doesn't get any more outlandish and yet it's all true."

"On the one hand, he genuinely wants to please us, get out of prison, and help his country; on the other, he wants to save his friend Faramus and not bring any harm to his mentor and father figure von Gröning."

Tin Eye nodded and assumed an introspective pose. "I've always regarded most enemy spies as rabble, their treachery not matched by their courage," he said. "But Chapman is different. He is, in fact, our most fascinating case to date."

"Why is that do you think?"

"Unlike all the captured agents we have brought into Double Cross before, he has not displayed even a whiff of fear. The bloke is as brave as a bloody lion. Either that or he craves the excitement."

"You're actually moved by him, aren't you? I would never have mistaken you for a sentimentalist, Colonel."

"I'm bloody hell not and you know it. But during my last interrogation of the young man, I couldn't help but wonder what manner of human being is the spy? Is he patriotic, brave? Is he of the underworld, a subject of blackmail? Is he just a mercenary? Spies who work for money alone are few, but they are dangerous. For a convicted felon, Agent Zigzag is strangely uninterested in money. He seems genuinely patriotic. I suppose that's what took me most by surprise."

"I agree he is a very brave man, but he is also a narcissist. At the end of the day, what he may want most of all is to be the star in his own movie: the Eddie Chapman Story."

"If that's the case, you and I must keep our fingers crossed that he wins the award for best actor."

Robertson chuckled. "It is rather strordnary. If our newest Double Cross recruit can stage-manage the next act with enough flair, he just might be our biggest star yet."

"One can only hope," said Tin Eye, squinting through his monocle. "One can only bloody hope."

CHAPTER 15

"NO, FRITZ WILL NOT BE PICKED UP BY U-BOAT. I have read your report, Rittmeister, and I must say I am skeptical. If your agent succeeded in blowing up the Mosquito bomber factory in Hatfield as you claim, then that would make him our very best. Personally, I find that rather hard to believe."

Von Gröning stared across the desk at the querulous face of Colonel Alexander Waag. It was a pity he had to deal with bureaucratic Nazi shits like the chief of the Paris Abwehrstelle. "But he is not ours, *Herr Oberst*," he replied, allowing himself a little smile. "He belongs to *me* and *me alone*, as specified in our contract. However, you are right about one thing."

"What is that?"

"Agent Fritz is truly the very best. In fact, he is a natural born intelligence operative."

"He also happens to be a known criminal and habitual liar. I don't trust him."

"Yes, but do you trust anyone, Colonel?"

"Our job is to *not* trust, Rittmeister. Is it necessary for me to remind you of that yet again?"

They fell into a bitter silence. He and the colonel had been at loggerheads the past two months, since Chapman had been airdropped into Britain, and today appeared to be no different. The two senior intelligence officers squabbled over personnel, training methods, expenditures, and field counterespionage protocols—and sometimes even about the damned weather. Von Gröning found the colonel magisterial and inflexible, as he did many of the National Socialist Party members he was forced to take uninspired orders from within the Abwehr in Occupied France. But what he disliked most of all was being engaged in a battle of wills he could not win. The reason was simple enough: Waag happened to be a nephew of the wife of Admiral Canaris, the head of the German intelligence service and one of only a handful of officers with direct access to Hitler.

"I believe the facts of the case and the conclusions I have reached are inescapable," said von Gröning, continuing to press his case. "Reconnaissance aircraft confirm that two large bombs exploded inside the factory's power plant stations. Our aerial photos have confirmed the damage in two places. The British newspapers have also confirmed that the factory was hit."

"Newspapers? I didn't see anything about newspapers in your report."

"We just received the news today." He withdrew a sheet of paper with a decrypted message. "It came to us from the diplomatic pouch to Madrid. The story appeared in the Monday February 1 morning edition of the *Daily Express*."

"Not the London *Times*?"

"No."

"Read it to me."

"The headline reads, 'Factory Explosion' and below it says, 'Investigations are being made into the cause of an explosion at a factory on the outskirts of London. It is understood that the damage was slight and there was no loss of life.'"

"That's it? That's all it says?"

"To me, the short length of the newspaper report is most revealing. It implies that there's more to the story and that the newspaper is downplaying the damage and has deliberately left out important details."

"What did the afternoon edition say?"

"There's no mention of the factory explosion in the second edition."

"None at all?"

"No, Colonel. But as I said, the extensive bomb damage was evident in our reconnaissance flights over the Hatfield area."

Waag still looked unconvinced. "Let me see your wireless communications with Agent Fritz."

He withdrew several sheets of paper from his leather foldover case and laid them out in order on the desk so that they could read them together. The first wireless message from Chapman to the Nantes Dienststelle alerted von Gröning of the success of the operation, using his call-in sign FFFFF to indicate that he was safe and not under British control, while the subsequent correspondence dealt with the agent's return to Occupied France. They read them over.

Agent Fritz: FFFFF WALTER BLOWN IN TWO PLACES.

Von Gröning: CONGRATULATIONS ON GOOD RESULT OF WALTER. PLEASE SEND INFO ON NEWSPAPER REPORTS. WILL DO ALL WE CAN ARRANGE YOUR RETURN. STATE PROPOSITIONS.

Agent Fritz: FFFFF PICK UP BY SUBMARINE OR SPEEDBOAT. WILL FIND SUITABLE POINT ON COAST. TRYING TO GET SHIPS PAPERS. SEE BACK PAGE EXPRESS FEB 1.

Von Gröning: IMPOSSIBLE PICK YOU UP BY SUBMARINE. USE NORMAL RETURN ROUTE.

When they were finished reading, Waag looked at him appraisingly, "So your plan is for Fritz to return by ship through Lisbon?"

"Yes. It is the safest route."

"And you actually think he can book passage and make it safely to neutral Portugal without alerting the British or Portuguese authorities?"

"It is risky, of course, but it is still the least risky mode of transport."

"Despite the fact that we are in the middle of a war and your agent has but a second-rate identity card, is of fighting age, and has no plausible business cover that he can use? If I wasn't mistaken, I would say that you are trying to actively discourage your man and keep him in Britain."

"That is not the case. Traveling by ship to Lisbon has the added advantage of letting us see how determined and resourceful Agent Fritz is."

"He may very well interpret our refusal to send a U-boat as evidence that we are reluctant to pay him the money he is owed for successfully carrying out the de Havilland operation."

"I would say that is likely."

"What would be the most inconspicuous way for him to get to Lisbon?"

"He will have to pose as an ordinary crewman aboard a British merchant vessel. Which means that he will have to look and behave like a seaman."

"Can he do it?"

"I don't know. But if anyone can pull it off, it is Fritzchen."

"You certainly think highly of him."

"Why shouldn't I? Look at the job he just pulled off."

"I believe you are too close to him. Maybe you should let me handle him as *my* personal operative."

"A minute ago, you thought he might have been turned by the British and the bombing was a hoax—and now you want to steal him away from me and make him your own agent?"

"You're too emotionally invested in this man to be objective. And that affects your judgment. As does your excessive consumption of wine and spirits."

"What?"

"You know precisely what I'm talking about. You are a drunk and it is affecting your job performance."

It took all his self-control to stem back his anger. He glanced down at his hands; they were shaking. *God, do I need a drink right now,* he thought desperately. "Why are you doing this, Colonel? Is this some sort of game?"

"I assure you this is no game. This is your own doing. Your drinking is out of control and you are a disgrace to the uniform."

"I know what you're up to, and I'm telling you right now you'll never get away with it. Fritz is my agent, Colonel, and you're not going to manufacture some trumped-up charge to steal him from me and make him your personal operative. We Germans all drink too much, at least on occasion. That's what soldiers do to blow off steam."

"You don't talk to me that way, you insolent cur! I am your superior officer!"

"Then act like one. You're not going to steal away the man I have trained to be Germany's top spy. Agent Fritz belongs to me and no one else."

"You watch your tongue. Or I will write you up for insubordination and have you shipped off to the Eastern Front. I can do it, you know."

"You would sink that low just to get him for yourself, wouldn't you?"

Waag said nothing, neither agreeing with nor denying the charge.

"You're a bastard, Colonel, if you would stoop to such measures for your own self-promotion."

"Get out of my office!"

"Gladly, but just remember, *Herr Oberst*, the contract that Fritzchen signed is between me and him personally, not with the German government."

Waag just scowled at him.

He studied the little weasel a moment. God, did he loathe these treacherous Nazi fucks like Waag. He hated them for their rigid orthodoxy and unfaltering submission to authority, but what he hated even more was their ruthlessness. They had no shame and would literally climb on the backs of others to get to the top. They were small-minded, backstabbing little men, and he despised them even as he wanted Germany to win the war. As he continued to meet the gaze of the colonel, a light went off in his brain.

"Now I know why you pretended to doubt the factory bombing. You are jealous of me."

"I am nothing of the sort."

"It's because of your jealousy that you want Fritz for yourself. You're only pretending to be worried that he might have been turned by the British and the whole bombing operation is a hoax."

Waag was up and on his feet, his face red with anger. "That is preposterous!"

"No, I can see it in your eyes. You want Fritz as your own agent, so you can look good before your superiors. But as I've told you, he won't work for you—he'll only work for me."

"We'll just have to see about that, won't we?"

Waag gave a gloating smile, but von Gröning was undaunted. Even though the colonel was his boss, he wasn't intimidated by the little shit. At the same time, though, he knew if he allowed the bad blood between them to escalate further his job would likely be in jeopardy. He decided to try a different approach.

"Admiral Canaris would never approve of such conduct, *Herr Oberst*. You do understand, don't you?"

"I wouldn't be so sure about that," said Waag coolly. "I wouldn't be so sure about that at all."

CHAPTER 16

47 STENSGATA, OSLO

FEBRUARY 3, 1943

AT HALF PAST SIX P.M., Dagmar Lahlum left her flat at 15 Frydenlundsgate and headed northwest on Ullevaalsveien. She was going to deliver a message and five forged passports to a Milorg contact at Ullevaal Hospital whom she knew only by code name. It was only a twenty-minute walk and, though it was below freezing and snow covered the streets and sidewalks, she was confident she could make it back before the eight o'clock curfew. She usually performed her courier assignments right before or after work, but she had been forced to put in an extra two hours today filling in for her male boss, who had left early. A lazy *Nasjonal Samling* Party member that she despised, he often took advantage of her by making her fill in for him during his absences. He knew that as a poor girl from Eidsvoll, she wouldn't dare challenge him and risk losing her job as a hotel receptionist. With the Occupation, many had no work at all, and food and resources were increasingly scarce as *Reichskommissar* Terboven and his toady Quisling squeezed more and more out of the Norwegian people.

She followed Ullevaalsveien to Sognsveien and then continued north towards the hospital, rounding several large piles of plowed snow and a dead dog that was frozen stiff as a board. There were a few people out on the streets, and she saw several shoveling their walks, but the city was quiet even for a week night. She had a printed pass to make it through checkpoints, but she would not need to use it until she reached the hospital, which was guarded by German soldiers.

Milorg courier operations were run by a system of cutouts with code names, and no runner knew another operative's real name except in emergency situations. Although she didn't know any of her underground contacts by name, she was able to transmit information and deliver articles of importance by arriving at her designated meeting place at a precise time and reciting a simple phrase or giving a code name. Her code name was *Danser* because she dreamed of one day being a dancer and model, and she was taking classes in both on Tuesday and Thursday nights. The code name of the operative she was supposed to meet was *Rudolf*.

For her courier assignments, she usually walked to the drop location, though in summer she sometimes rode her bicycle. Within Oslo, Ullevaal Hospital had come to occupy an especially important position in the resisting nation's underground activities, and she had made the trip here on several prior occasions. On the fourth floor was the prison ward, which had replaced the dermatology department and become the central treatment area of loyal Norwegians injured in sabotage efforts or in other confrontations with the Gestapo, as well as those transferred in from Oslo jails. It was here that the doctors on the ward became a conduit between the patients and the Home Front as well as functioned as operatives in the transport network of refugees and Resistance fighters to Sweden. Underground contacts regularly delivered false passports to hospital staff members to aid Norwegian fugitives in their flight. Dagmar had been told that the doctors, nurses, and administrators hid the life-giving documents in the infectious disease wards since the Nazis were terrified of such diseases and would rarely search the affected areas.

When she turned right onto Stensgata, she thought she heard a sound behind her. As she had been trained to do, she looked around for signs of surveillance without appearing to do so. To her relief, she saw nothing suspicious…and yet she still couldn't help but feel a presence. Was someone following her? If not, why did she feel like she was being stalked? Or was it in her mind?

She continued walking northeast towards the hospital. Next to the street soared huge oak and elm trees, blotting out the thumbnail moon and stars overhead. She was not afraid of walking at night in this part of the city. Though she detested the occupiers, she had little to fear from the ordinary German soldier. Only the Gestapo and nazified Norwegian police struck fear into her heart, for she had been told they were capable of anything.

At ten paces, she thought she heard the crunch of snow underfoot. A wave of alarm rang through her whole body. She scanned the trees to her right, like a deer picking up the slightest sound. Again, she wondered if she was being followed. She still felt a vague presence that was disconcerting.

She continued along the sidewalk running alongside Stensgata. Two policemen approached her from the north. Sensing danger, she lowered her gaze as they approached and prayed that they would not stop and question her, or even worse find some cause to frisk her. After all, she had five forged passports stashed in her undergarments. But the two policemen walked past her without incident, probably concluding that she worked at the hospital and was arriving for the night shift.

She walked at a brisk pace along the sidewalk. Dappled moonlight trickled through the leafy branches of the overhanging trees. But the trees made her feel hemmed in, threatened. Why did she feel like she was being followed? She kept a vigilant eye out, feeling increasingly unsettled.

As she reached the intersection with Kirkeveien, she paused a moment to scan the well-lit street. There were more people now that she was on a major thoroughfare: shift workers in coveralls returning from a hard day's labor under the Occupation; a pair of fishmongers walking exhaustedly along the sidewalk; an old woman and teenage boy carrying loaves of bread; a pack of young university-age men and women scurrying nervously up the street; and another pair of policemen carefully watching the university students.

Her body stiffened at the sight of the police: they were as bad as the damned Nazis.

All of sudden, from three different directions, a civilian car and small fleet of military vehicles came driving up and pulled to a quiet halt outside the flat at 47 Stensgata. The lead car was a midnight blue Opel Admiral Cabriolet, and from the front passenger seat stepped a tall German officer wearing an SS uniform. Even with only the illumination of the streetlight, she could see that he was a strikingly handsome and charismatic-looking man, with a chiseled jaw, blue eyes like winter ice, thin but muscular frame, and a shock of cornsilk-blond hair sneaking out from beneath his peaked officer's cap. He could have been the type specimen for Himmler's depraved *Lebensborn* "experimental child" program—the Nazi baby-farm scheme to genetically engineer perfect Germans by mating male and female specimens believed to possess the purest Aryan blood. She had never seen him before, but clearly, he was an officer of importance and man to be reckoned with.

He instantly began issuing orders to the soldiers pouring noiselessly out of the convoy of light Volkswagen *Kübelwagens* and heavier troop trucks. Without raising his voice, he quickly posted men around the perimeter of the apartment building before proceeding with a sizable contingent to the front door. The small army of men moved swiftly into position, as if the unit had performed surprise hit-and-run raids on many prior occasions and was well-practiced in the art of such stealthy operations. Within a matter of seconds, more than twenty heavily armed German soldiers had assembled into standard raid formation and set up a perimeter around the building. The only sounds were a few softly uttered commands, the chuff of soldiers' boots on snow and ice, and the click of their metallic pistols and light submachine guns.

Initially taken by surprise but now on high alert, Dagmar Lahlum—at this stage of the war a nineteen-year-old Norwegian spy and Milorg operative—pulled into the shadows, watched, and waited to see who the Germans would take into custody.

CHAPTER 17

47 STENSGATA

FEBRUARY 3, 1943

SIEGFRIED FEHMER—recently promoted to SS-*Hauptsturmführer*—felt a ripple of anticipation as his assault team moved into final position. As always when out on a raid, he carried a loaded 1939 Walther PPK 7.65-mm SS officer's pistol in the Death's Head holster at his hip, and a Mauser Hahn Selbstspanner in his right boot as a backup piece. Though as a Sipo departmental head he spent most of his time behind a desk, he enjoyed being out in the field, taking part in arrests, and the rush of the occasional skirmish against a worthy Norwegian enemy. The thirty-two-year old truly loved the thrill of the hunt and was zealously dedicated to the performance of his job as a senior police investigator and counterintelligence officer. He believed in the Third Reich and the Fatherland and was ready to carry out orders unquestioningly and to the best of his ability.

Drawing a deep breath, he looked a final time at his two SS-*Obersturmführer* subordinates Hoeler and Bernhard of *Abteilung IV* then at his soldiers in their *feldgrau*, black boots, and steel helmets. His assault team had crept into final position with the stealth of a wolf pack and would have total surprise on their side. Anticipation gripped the frigid night, the face of each and every soldier one of focused concentration as vapor plumes blew quietly from mouths from the winter chill. The team edged forward, with Walther, Luger, and Mauser sidearms in the hands of the officers and *Karabiner 98 kurz* bolt-action carbines and *Maschinenpistole* 40 light submachine guns for the non-coms and enlisted men.

This was it. The time had come.

In a matter of seconds, he would have his man in custody. He remembered back to when he had had Max Manus in his mitts, but by some miracle the plucky Oslo Gang saboteur had gotten away. Fehmer had always regretted not recapturing him when the opportunity had presented itself. But tonight, he would get his man. There was no way Tor Hatledal, senior operative of the Resistance group XU, was going to escape from his clutches. The apartment building was surrounded, all possible escape routes sealed off. And beyond the door lay the unsuspecting quarry.

Never one to lead from the rear, Fehmer withdrew his Walther from his holster, opened the front door of the apartment building, stepped inside, and walked carefully up the staircase to the second floor. The rush in his gut grew stronger. He felt supremely confident; he had reconnoitered the apartment complex twice before and knew his prey.

When he reached the second-floor, he stood frozen a long moment studying the layout. He went over the series of maneuvers required to accomplish his objective. A gramophone record droned in a nearby apartment, but that was the only sound. He waited a few seconds until he was certain the coast was clear.

Then he started down the hallway towards Apartment 214.

But the creaky old floorboards squeaked. The sound was scarcely audible, but to Fehmer it sounded like a deafening roar. He glanced back at Lieutenant Hoeler. For both men and the troopers snaking down the staircase behind them, every muscle froze.

He kept his eyes fixed on the corridor. The long, narrow hallway was poorly lit and smelled of cigarettes, grilled salt cod, and something Fehmer couldn't put a finger on. To his relief, no one came out of their rooms.

He started off again. The floorboards squeaked again, but this time he ignored the sound and strode quickly but noiselessly down the wooden floor of the hallway. He felt his heart calling out to him in a turbulent rhythm.

When he reached the room, he stopped and gently touched the doorknob.

Locked—too bad.

He waited a moment for the rest of the team to come up behind him. The overhead light covering this section of the hallway was out, probably on purpose by Hatledal and his Resistance fighters. As Fehmer made a hand signal to Hoeler, a woman stepped out of a nearby apartment carrying a bundle of folded laundry. A sergeant cupped his hand over her mouth and quietly whisked her back into her apartment down the hallway.

Fehmer shook his head. *Scheisse*, that was close. He turned around, raised his Walther in a two-handed grip, and gave the signal. He felt his blood pumping and his breathing accelerated.

This was it—the moment of truth.

Fehmer smiled inwardly. *We've got you, Tor my friend—there's no way out. Unless you can fly, of course.*

He lowered the barrel of his pistol and shot off the lock. Then, without a split-second's hesitation, he drove his shoulder into the door and charged into the room, with Lieutenant Hoeler and a dozen German troops behind him.

The penetration was swift, the surprise total. One of the partisans, a half-Swede named Forsberg, was seated on a couch by the kitchen and in chairs to his right were three other men, two of whom Fehmer recognized and one he didn't. Two of them had guns within reach. He covered them with his Walther as his men swept into the room. But where was Hatledal?

"Gestapo, don't move!" he shouted in crisp Norwegian over the shuffling of boots.

"Fuck!" a surprised voice cried out.

"Put your hands above your head and get down on the floor! *Gjør det nå!*"

Three of the Norwegians surrendered instantly as ten guns trained on them. But Hatledal was not among them. Where the hell was he?

And then Fehmer saw him next to the kitchen window.

"Don't move!" he commanded, and it was only then that he spotted the hand grenade. In a fluid motion, the Norwegian Resistance fighter pulled the pin.

"*Granate!*" screamed Fehmer in German, but he was too late.

With surprising calm and accuracy, Hatledal tossed the compact metal hand grenade underhanded like a bowling ball at the feet of the Germans swarming into the room and away from his comrades in the interior of the apartment. Fehmer's policemen couldn't scramble fast enough to get out of way but met with a stroke of luck as the grenade rolled into the hallway.

"Get down!" Fehmer opened fire on Hatledal as he dashed towards the kitchen and in the opposite direction of the grenade, which he regarded as his best survival option given the close quarters of the room.

He caught Hatledal in the arm. But then the Resistance operative surprised him by jumping out the second-story window. He broke right through the glass, shattering it as he dove out and into a snow bank. Fehmer couldn't believe his eyes: it was the same desperate maneuver that elusive bastard Max Manus had performed two years earlier when he had jumped out of his Oslo apartment window to evade capture but had instead been severely injured.

The grenade exploded. Luckily, the hallway took the brunt of the blast, but Fehmer saw a spout of floorboards fly upwards and two of his men blown apart. The one closest to the grenade had his guts blasted from his body and spattered against the wall like spaghetti.

"Jesus Christ! See to those men!" He then motioned towards the Norwegians. "And get those bastards into handcuffs!"

"*Jawohl, Hauptsturmführer!*"

He rushed to the window.

"Halt!" he cried in Norwegian, but to his surprise, Hatledal was already well on his way to escaping. After jumping out the window, he had landed in a huge conical-shaped snow pile that had accumulated from snow sliding off the rooftop, and then he had schussed down the mountain of snow like a skier in the opposite direction from the troops posted outside. A copse of thick pine trees loomed across the street and it appeared that the Norwegian was making a dash for them. Fehmer realized Hatledal must have scouted out the escape route beforehand.

He opened fire with his Walther from the shattered window. Missing, he yelled out to his men to stop Hatledal. They opened fire too, but not before the Norwegian had withdrawn a pistol of his own and shot down the closest German, taking him by surprise as he rounded the north side of the apartment building. Then, as Fehmer fired again and missed, he saw Hatledal take another bullet. He and the two remaining Sipo men fired at him again as he stumbled across the street, but none of the bullets found their target.

It was then Fehmer saw a figure emerge from the woods and pull Hatledal into the trees across Stensgata.

What the hell?

He and his men fired at the two receding figures as they ducked into the trees.

Cursing again, he jumped through the broken window onto the snow pile, slid down the mountain, and gave chase along with three of his men posted outside. They quickly reached the trees and searched the area.

But Hatledal and his mysterious savior had vanished.

CHAPTER 18

47 STENSGATA

FEBRUARY 3, 1943

"YOU GO THAT WAY—I'LL TRY AND HIDE IN THERE!"

Dagmar quickly scrutinized the wounded man as he pointed northward across Kirkeveien then towards the thick pine forest to the east. His breathing was labored, and from his mouth and nostrils he exhaled a heavy vapor trail in the cold winter air. She could tell that he was losing blood fast: his face had already turned pale.

"You'll never make it. I need to help you," she said.

"No. You need to get as far away from me as possible."

"But I can't just leave you. You're badly hurt."

"They'll kill you, damnit! Now go!"

"But I can't leave you behind to the Gestapo. They'll torture and kill you."

He didn't reply as they heard distinct crunching sounds. The Germans had regrouped and were coming their way, and there were more of them now. They both froze. The man aimed his pistol in the direction of the noises. The thick woods were blanketed in dark shadow, with only faint smears of illumination bleeding in from the streetlight. They paused to carefully listen.

"It's too late for me—you must save yourself," said the wounded man. "I will draw them to the south and you go north. Isn't that where you were headed?"

"Yes, I was going to the hospital." She covered her mouth, realizing she shouldn't have said that. As a Milorg operative, she was not to give any information to or trust anyone, for everyone cracked eventually under Gestapo interrogation and torture. But the man was no longer listening. His gaze was on the trees to the west. He clutched his pistol in a two-handed grip and started walking south.

"Get going now and good luck," he said. "I'll see you, one day, hopefully in a better place."

She nodded and headed to the north through the trees. For a minute, there was no sound and all was calm. Then, with a suddenness that took her by surprise, she heard running footsteps.

"Quick, he's getting away!" a voice cried in Norwegian, a voice she knew belonged to the Gestapo officer she had seen and heard yelling from the broken apartment window.

Feeling her body seized with adrenaline, she darted in the opposite direction.

After a dozen paces, the sound of running feet picked up to her left. She ran as hard and fast as her legs would carry her, ripping through underbrush, stumbling, banging into trees, recovering, running on, her breaths coming in gasps. And then, up ahead, she could make out faint smudges of light where the woods ended and the street began.

She heard an exchange of gunfire and several shouting voices behind her. Had they caught the man? A moment later, more shouting voices erupted, this time from the west, and she came under fire. The enemy let loose with a concentrated fusillade, the white-hot bullets cutting down branches and limbs with a retching crash and carving into an icy snowbank.

She took cover behind a thick-trunked tree and the firing stopped. The woods were suddenly all quiet and bathed in blackness. Only faint smudges of light trickled into the forest from the streetlamps along Kirkeveien.

She paused to carefully listen.

It was still all quiet. But she couldn't help but feel she was being stalked. Did she dare cross the street and make a mad dash for the hospital?

She forced herself to control her breathing.

She was startled by the sound of another gunshot followed by a burst from a submachine gun. Then all was quiet again.

My God, she thought with horror. *Have the Germans murdered him?*

She looked left, right, then back across the street to the hospital. It was only a hundred meters.

Should I make a run for it?

And then she heard a footfall in the snow and turned to see something. At first, it was only a little blur at the edge of her vision, but then she realized it was human. Not more than thirty feet away, a male figure with a beaked cap poked out from behind a tree and then slowly eased back from the light into the oblivion of the forest. The figure was tall and lean yet of sturdy build, and he clutched a pistol in his right hand.

It was the German officer. But why wasn't he shooting?

You've got to make a run for it, Dagmar! she told herself. *Go Now!*

But somehow her feet wouldn't budge.

The German officer emerged from the shadows. The moon poking through the tree cover caught him momentarily. One-half of his face basked in the glow of the fluted light, while the other remained masked in darkness. *One half good, the other half evil,* she thought, mesmerized by the officer as he walked towards her. Thirty feet, twenty feet, ten feet—it was too late for her to run.

He stepped up to her. A cloud passed in front of the moon, throwing his face into complete darkness. At that moment he gave a little smile.

It was like a sign from above. Or more likely from hell.

She stepped from behind the tree, surrendering herself. The fake passports were sewn into the lining of her heavy jacket and she could only hope the Germans wouldn't find them if, or more likely when, they searched her.

"I thought you were a woman," he said pleasantly in Norwegian, though he kept his pistol trained on her chest. "What is your name?"

She was not about to lie; she had come across the Gestapo raid and the escaping man quite by accident and would try and bluff her way out of her predicament. "Dagmar," she replied.

"Dagmar what?"

"Dagmar Lahlum."

"Well, Frøken Lahlum, what are you doing out here?"

"I was on my way to the hospital to visit a friend."

"The hospital. Are you sure your true destination wasn't 47 Stensgata?"

"I don't know that man. I just heard the shooting and helped him. Is he dead?"

"Very. He happens to have been a member of the underground and a common criminal. On the streets of Oslo, that is not a person you should be helping."

"What was his name?"

"Tor Hatledal. Ring a bell?"

"No, I told you I don't know him. But you didn't need to shoot him."

"I respectfully disagree since he was shooting at us," he said, as his armed troops came clomping up through the shin-deep snow behind him. "But at least it is over."

"Yes, it is over, and I must be on my way. I need to visit my friend at the hospital so that I can make it back home before curfew."

"I'm afraid that will be impossible."

"Why? I have done nothing wrong. All I did was pull a man who was being shot at into the woods. I thought you were armed criminals breaking into an apartment. That's why I took cover. I heard shouting and an explosion and then I saw a man running towards me and heard more shouting. I broke no laws."

"But you do understand German?"

"Yes, I speak German."

"If you heard shouting in German, you should have immediately stopped that criminal in his tracks and called out for help."

"I heard no shouting in German. I only heard you and you speak Norwegian. Quite well, in fact."

"I still need you to come with me so that I can take your sworn statement."

"Go with you? But I need to go to the hospital."

"Who are you visiting there?"

"My friend Kristin Larsen."

"What is wrong with her?"

"She has typhus. She is in the infectious disease ward."

He wrinkled his nose. "Typhus. Your friend might be better left alone."

"What kind of person would I be if I didn't visit a sick girlfriend?"

"I see your point, but I'm afraid it will be impossible tonight. As I have said, we will need to take your statement at Gestapo headquarters. You were a witness to a crime. But don't worry, if you are truly innocent as you say then I will make sure that you are quite comfortable over the next few hours when my trained officers and I interrogate you."

"Interrogate me?"

"I'm afraid so." The officer clicked his boots together like a courtly gentleman, knocking the snow off. "But as I said, don't worry. You will get to share my hospitality in my comfortable office. Have you ever been to our headquarters at Victoria Terrasse?"

She gave an involuntary shudder. "No," she said, struggling not to let the fear show in her voice or on her face.

"Well then, I will be more than happy to give you the full tour. However, I have to warn you not to even think of lying to me."

"Or else what?"

He nodded towards the woods. "Or I'm afraid you will end up like that poor gentlemen."

CHAPTER 19

HER FIRST STOP at the dreaded Nazi police headquarters with the life-size painting of the Führer in the lobby was a small, nondescript reception room on the third floor. Here she anxiously awaited her captor's next move while a pair of sullen-faced armed guards watched her intently and made sure she felt uncomfortable. She waited for over an hour as one junior Sipo officer after another filed into the room, took a cigarette, pointed towards her, and whispered furtively to the two guards posted at the door. Dagmar knew what they were doing. This was the initial psychological pressure meant to soften her up for the interrogation that would follow. After fifteen more minutes of waiting, the door swung open again and a pockmarked German soldier clicked his heels together smartly and commanded her to come with him.

"*Kommen sie mit,*" he snapped, as if summoning a dog.

Reminding herself to stay calm, she rose to her feet and followed him through the open doorway, down a long hallway, up one flight of stairs, and to a spacious corner office. Seated behind the desk was the still-nameless officer from the raid—except he was no longer wearing a stiff gray SS uniform, black peaked cap, and boots but rather a fashionable, double-breasted, navy-blue suit and dress shoes. When he looked up at her from his pile of paperwork, she couldn't help but shiver with excitement at the sight of him, but mostly she felt fear. He was as handsome and cultivated-looking as a man could be, German or not, and sitting there in his chair he seemed larger-than-life, like a portrait of some famous historical figure. She found him captivating yet at the same time utterly terrifying, as if she had unexpectedly stumbled across a huge male lion on an African savanna. There was intelligence and charisma behind those wintry blue eyes. He looked at her as if he could read her thoughts; she told herself that she was just letting fear get the better of her and reminded herself to remain calm and talk slowly to drag out the questioning while giving up no useful information.

She wanted to know his name.

"Please sit down, Frøken Lahlum," he said in the tone of a gracious host.

She licked her lips as the door closed behind her and she made her way to the chair in front of his desk. There she took her seat, keeping a wary eye on him.

"I apologize for keeping you waiting, but I had many matters to attend to this evening. There is no rest for the Gestapo here in Occupied Norway, I'm afraid."

He smiled, again like a courteous host at a cocktail party, as he pulled out a pen and a black notebook with a blood-red swastika on the cover. She involuntarily shrank back in her seat, saying nothing in reply.

"So," he began affably, "how long have you been with the Resistance?"

She pretended not to appear taken aback. "I am not with the Resistance."

"Come now, Dagmar…by the way, may I call you Dagmar?"

"If it suits you."

"It does. Lovely name, I must say."

"I'm glad you like it. May I ask your name?"

"Of course. I apologize for not introducing myself when we first met, but sometimes I find it useful to withhold my name until I have successfully completed the interrogation process. I am Captain Fehmer—Captain Siegfried Fehmer."

"Interrogation? Is that what this is?"

"I'm afraid so. I must confess it is hard to believe you are not with the Home Front. It seems that every Norwegian these days *claims* to be with the underground resisting us evil Nazis, fighting us tooth and nail. So, if you are not with the Resistance, it would appear that you are the rare exception."

"I can assure you I am not with the Home Front."

"You are extremely attractive. I know I would have recruited you right from the start if I was in the underground. You could disarm a whole army."

She didn't know what to say to that and felt herself blush. The man was charming yet frightening—and he damn well knew it. In fact, that appeared to be his special talent: using a perfect combination of charm and menace in order to coax information out of those unfortunate enough to be subjected to his interrogation. She could feel her heart rate pick up as she realized she was in the hands of a qualified professional police investigator as well as a master of the dark arts. This was a man who relished the authority he possessed and enjoyed intimidating people. And yet, she couldn't help but notice there might be a softer, gentler side to the loathsome Nazi, and she suspected that most women found him quite attractive. Just not her.

"I'm sorry if I have made you uncomfortable," he said after a moment, watching her closely, like a psychologist studying a patient. "So why don't you tell me, in detail, how your evening unfolded, let's say, from five p.m. until you were brought here? The sooner you tell me the full story, the sooner you can be out of here. And leave nothing out. Every detail is important, as I'm sure you know."

She told him her concocted hospital visit story. She had rehearsed it in her head a dozen times en route to Victoria Terrasse and while sitting in the waiting area, going over and over it until she had it just right. But she was still nervous and fumbled a few times, adding more precise detail than she should have. Though she had received rudimentary espionage training from her Milorg handlers, she was still just a simple courier, and this was the first time she had been detained and interrogated by the police. She was a good liar—she had extensive practice from growing up in Eidsvoll, learning how to get what she wanted out of her parents and other authority figures—but this was much bigger than anything before. It took a full twenty minutes with Fehmer stopping her occasionally to ask questions, but she made it through relatively unscathed. Though young, she was a natural spy and she knew it.

When she was finished, Fehmer said, "I've got to be honest with you, your story sounds far-fetched. You expect me to believe that you were just passing through the neighborhood on the way to Ullevaal Hospital, when you helped this criminal who was shot while trying to escape from the authorities? I'm sorry but I'm not buying it, Dagmar."

"It doesn't sound far-fetched to me because it's the truth."

"And you just decided to pull this bleeding stranger into the trees because you are a Good Samaritan? Is that it?"

"Yes. I am telling you the truth."

"So, let me get this straight. You assumed this man running away from the police was a law-abiding citizen? I find that hard to believe."

"I thought criminals were shooting at him, not the other way around. I also felt sorry for him."

"Because you are a woman?"

"Yes." Her Milorg control officer Ishmael and other contacts she knew in the Resistance were always telling her to use her femininity to dupe the Germans. Being a courier was one of the most dangerous jobs an underground operative like her could perform, for if she was caught with material on her person she could not explain it away, so she needed to take advantage of any trick that would give her an edge over her enemies. Her gender was her greatest advantage. Most Germans, even those in the Gestapo, had a traditional view of women and their capabilities in the war effort. They assumed that woman couldn't possibly be actively engaged in underground activities other than sheltering Resistance members, which Dagmar knew was absurd. Women in the Norwegian Resistance had developed countless ways to use their gender to outwit and escape German control and intimidation, and she was living proof of it.

"You're telling me you helped this man that you had never laid eyes on before because you are a woman and you felt sorry for him? Is that it?"

"When I saw him limping across the street, wounded and bleeding, I had to help him. I'm sorry, but I had a moment of weakness."

He looked at her for a long moment before jotting down notes in his little black book. She thought: *Damnit, he doesn't believe me. He is obviously not as gullible as the rest of his countrymen. Is he going to send me to the basement where the truly unspeakable torture takes place?*

"You know what will happen to you if I think you've been lying to me?" he said, as if reading her thoughts.

She suppressed a gulp. "But I'm not lying to you."

"I will have to send you to the Oslo City Jail at Møllergata 19. After you have stayed with us here for a few nights, of course."

"A few nights? I will not stay in this rathole a single night."

"That depends on whether you are telling me the truth or not."

"I told you, I am not lying to you."

"You've seen Møllergata many times, I'm sure. The prison gates overlook a large square, and before the war it was filled during the day with the carts of street merchants and flower vendors. Across the open square used to be a block of stores and a splendid arcade near the opera theater. Now that is all gone and there is only the prison and the lonely cries of the prisoners inside. Is that where you want to go?"

Now that he was openly threatening her, she realized there was a menacing quality to him to go along with his good looks and silvery tongue. "No, of course I don't want to go to Møllergata."

"Then start telling the truth. What were you doing hiding out in the trees?"

"I wasn't hiding out. As I told you, I was on my way to the hospital. When I heard the shooting and voices, I ducked into the woods. I was scared."

"Who were you visiting at the hospital?"

"I already told you that. My friend Kristin Larsen."

"My men are checking on that as we speak. You had better hope that they find Kristin Larsen in the infectious disease ward as you say."

She tried to appear unaffected by the news, but it was impossible not to show some strain. There was indeed a Kristin Larsen in the ward—the woman was part of her cover—but they didn't know one another. Her real friend's name was Mary Larsen, but she and Kristin were from different families. Dagmar could only hope the doctors would cover for her and would not allow the Germans in to see the sick woman, though she suspected Fehmer was merely bluffing. The Germans were deeply fearful of contracting infectious diseases like typhus and were unlikely to visit any hospital ward that specifically handled such afflictions.

"Where did you learn to speak German?" he then asked her.

"Growing up in Eidsvoll, many people spoke it. It is my second language. Where did you learn to speak Norwegian?"

"I have lived here now for nearly three years. I love Norway and have learned the language because we Germans have a kinship with your country. We are both Aryans and are meant to rule the world."

"I don't like to talk politics. We will just argue and you will probably pull out a gun. That is how you Germans tend to solve disputes."

"What, do you deny it is the destiny of the great Aryan nations like Germany and Norway to rule the post-war world?"

"Let's just say I wouldn't believe everything Herr Goebbels tells you."

He smiled. "That was funny." He then frowned. "But I don't think the Führer or *Reichskommissar* Terboven would enjoy your sense of humor."

"Then I apologize," she said in perfect German.

Speaking *auf Deutsch* had changed the dynamic, she saw at once. Her inquisitor's face showed approval. No doubt he was not used to his charges speaking to him in fluent German, or his interrogations spiced up by attempted humor, especially coming from a woman.

"Usually when a Norwegian speaks German as well as you do, it means he is a spy, a traitor, or both."

"The most important word in that sentence is the word *he*. I am but a simple working woman whose only mistake was to go out tonight to visit a sick friend. The words spy and traitor do not apply to me or anyone I know."

"I'm sorry, but that still remains to be seen. Just know that, if you are with the underground, I will discover it and you will end up talking in the end. Everyone does—even tough battle-hardened soldiers far more stubborn than you. The only question is how long you can last before I break you and you tell me what I want to know. Now, tell me what partisan cell you are from?"

She feigned a look of surprise.

"Come on, just tell me. If you don't, I may have to send you to one of our enhanced interrogation cells. You've heard about them, haven't you? I believe most of Oslo has by this stage of the war."

She tried to look unfazed, but she couldn't help a little grimace at the thought of the tortures awaiting her if he suspected she was lying. From those that had managed to be released from Møllergata and Grini Prison, she had heard that the Gestapo interrogators at Victoria Terrasse most often extracted confessions through pure savagery. The torture techniques of choice were dunking victims in freezing cold water, brass knuckles, bright lights, sticking pins through the penis, blowtorches, heated coils under the fingernails, and pulling out mustache hairs by means of screws and steel bars. The Torquemadas of Victoria Terrasse were also known to stomp on the torsos of prisoners and to lock them in dark cells for weeks on end; and Dagmar had heard that some prisoners had chosen to take their own lives by jumping out windows rather than betray what they knew.

Fehmer said, "I would appreciate it if you would tell me the names and code names of everyone working in your Resistance network."

The words were spoken like a university administrator posing a simple admission question. She shook her head, as if she didn't understand.

"I know you know the men from the apartment at 47 Stensgata. But we have already rolled up that group. Now I want to know, Dagmar, who you know."

"I don't know what you're talking about."

"What is the name of your Resistance cell? Is it Milorg or XU? Or perhaps something outside the city?"

She said nothing, continuing to play dumb.

Now he smiled and spoke in a soothing voice. She shuddered. When the Nazis talked sweetly to you, Ishmael had told her, it was time to worry. "You control your fate," he said. "If you tell the truth, no harm will come to you—or your family."

She tensed involuntarily. "My family? What do you mean my family?"

"Why your family in Eidsvoll. I have one of my men looking in on them right now. Just as a precautionary measure, of course. As long as you're telling me the truth, you have nothing to worry about, I can assure you. You have my promise that they will be safe."

My God, he might hurt my family? For a moment, she thought she would faint. She had always known that being a spy might lead to frightening moments like this, but she was still rendered speechless. Her heart thundered in her chest, and she wondered if it was possible for it to explode.

"Are you all right, Frøken Lahlum? Why if I didn't know better, I would say that you had seen a ghost."

Now she could see the cruelty in his eyes, the flame of anger at the edges of his icy blue pupils. And then, as his head inched closer across the table, she caught a whiff of schnapps mingled with bratwurst on his breath. She felt an overwhelming wave of revulsion, but mostly she felt a deep and abiding fear.

"What is your code name?"

She stared back at him with incomprehension. "I don't know what you're talking about. Spies have code names and I am no spy."

"What is the name of your cell?"

"I already told you, I don't know what you're talking about."

"What are you doing in Oslo? What is your mission here?"

"I work at a hotel as a receptionist and take night classes in modeling. I had no intention of languishing up north and came to Oslo just before war broke out. You can check up on it if you want but it is the truth."

"Do you know how to operate a radio?"

"No, of course not."

"Please stop this foolishness. Who is your main contact in the Home Front?"

She said nothing, giving another look of stunned puzzlement.

"Who is your control officer? Was it Tor Hatledal of 47 Stensgata?"

"I don't have a control officer."

"Are you saying you operate on your own?"

"No, I am not with the underground."

"Come now, you must have a control officer. Is he a cutout that you have never met? Do you only know him by a code name?"

"As I've already told you, I don't know what you're talking about."

"Do you or your underground associates have a radio?"

"No, of course not. It is illegal to own a radio unless you are an NS member and I am not a member."

"Why not? Don't you admire your nation's leader, Minister-President Quisling?"

"As I said, I don't get into politics. That's why I am not an NS Party member."

At that moment, a senior officer knocked on the door and entered the room. Dagmar felt a clinch in her gut as she recognized SS-Lieutenant Colonel Heinrich Fehlis, the overall head of the German Security Services, including the Gestapo, Kripo, and SD. He went to the chair to the left of the desk and calmly sat down as if he was a simple businessman late for an appointment. The thirty-six-year-old officer had a lantern jaw, thin bloodless lips, and a dueling scar on his left cheek that looked like a hissing red snake when he became angry, which reportedly wasn't very often. He held extraordinary power over life and death in Norway, and Dagmar and her Milorg comrades-in-arms had learned the hard way that he was not shy in using it. Since the beginning of the war, he had ordered the execution of dozens of Norwegian Resistance and British Special Operations Executive operatives that had stood in his way. In September 1941, following a city-wide workers' strike protesting the strict rationing of milk, hundreds were arrested and Fehlis had ordered the execution of the two strike leaders. Dagmar knew that Milorg and the other Resistance organizations would only be too glad to see the Nazi bastard gunned down on the street for his war crimes, though the German reprisals would be swift, violent, and out of all proportion to the death of a single man.

"Please continue, Captain—I didn't mean to interrupt," said Fehlis in German, and Dagmar could only hope that he didn't recognize her. On Ishmael's order, she had shadowed the Nazi colonel only a month earlier to document his daily routine, and she prayed he wouldn't remember her. To her relief, his beady black eyes showed not a flicker of recognition.

"I was just informing Fraulein Lahlum here of the penalties for treason against the Reich," said Fehmer. "She claims that she is not with the Resistance."

Fehlis feigned a look of surprise. "Really? After attempting to hide an armed member of the underground in the woods?"

Dagmar shook her head vehemently. "I wasn't hiding anyone. I didn't know who was shooting at him and merely helped him into the trees. If I had known it was the Gestapo chasing after him, I likely would not have helped him."

Fehlis's eyes narrowed on her. "Likely?"

"All right, I *wouldn't* have helped him."

Fehmer shook his head. "I'm sorry, sir, she's just not cooperating. Which means I'm going to have to keep her here overnight."

She felt her head spin again. "Overnight? You have no right to keep me overnight! I have done nothing wrong!"

"Believe me, young lady, we have every right to keep you here as long as we see fit," said Fehlis, the dueling scar on his cheek twitching ever so slightly. "You aided and abetted a known criminal. In most cases, the penalty for that alone would be death. But obviously, *Hauptsturmführer* Fehmer here is graciously giving you the opportunity to come clean of your own accord. We treat people firmly but fairly here at Victoria Terrasse."

"But I didn't know who these men were, or what the shooting was about."

Fehmer shook his head. "I'm afraid that's no excuse. A jury would most likely still find you guilty."

Irked by their condescending and threatening tone, she shook her head. "You need to understand something. I am not with the Home Front and I made a simple mistake." She clamped her arms about her chest defiantly. "Furthermore, I don't belong here and will answer no further questions. And that is final."

"Well then," said the bloodless-lipped Fehlis, rising from his chair. "I hope you enjoy our overnight lodgings. I must say, though, that many of our guests find them somewhat uncomfortable."

He started for the door.

She tried to conceal her horror at the prospect of imprisonment, even for a single night, but at the same time she hadn't been broken. She had kept her wits about her, stuck to her story, and was still very much in the game. "You're not really going to keep me here tonight?" she appealed to Fehmer. "How am I going to get to my job tomorrow? If I can't go to work, then I can't help the German war effort. You do realize that, don't you?"

"I'm afraid you have given us no choice but to keep you overnight. We are in search of answers, and without them, we cannot be as kind and generous to our Norwegian friends as we would like. I'm sorry, but that is the way it is."

Dagmar felt her body slump. Having never been incarcerated, the thought of a cold prison cell terrified her.

"Sleep well tonight," said the senior officer Fehlis, looking back harshly from the open door. "And let's hope that you are more forthcoming tomorrow."

"Yes, one can only hope," said Fehmer, looking at her gravely. "For you and your family's sake."

CHAPTER 20

"WELL DONE, EDDIE—WELL DONE INDEED," said Colonel Tar Robertson ebulliently to his new number one Double Cross agent. "All indications are that the Germans have fallen for the fake sabotage operation at de Havilland hook, line, and sinker. Honestly, I don't know how we could have duped them any better. All thanks to you."

"That is cause for celebration," said Chapman. They clinked glasses and sipped their sparkling white wine the colonel had brought with him to toast the occasion. They were sitting in the parlor of the safe house. Chapman's two MI5 babysitters, Backwell and Tooth, busied themselves in the kitchen while his girlfriend Freda had taken their baby, Diane, out for a walk around the neighborhood again. After two weeks of working as a double agent, Zigzag had insisted upon being reunited with Freda, whom he didn't know had borne his child shortly after the beginning of the war. For security reasons, MI5 had been reluctant to allow Chapman to reunite with his former lover, but in the end, Robertson had allowed it to ensure that his moody prized agent had someone close to him to preoccupy his time and keep him away from his criminal mates in the Soho underworld. The nondescript house they shared along with the MI5 men was located on a quiet street in the unremarkable North London borough of Hendon. To a nosy neighbor or constable, Number 35 would have been suspicious: the blackout curtains were always drawn, a large aerial sprouted up from the back roof, and men in trench coats and bowler hats came and went at odd hours of the day and night.

Robertson again smiled at his charge; though the two men could not have been farther apart in social background, Robertson had taken a special liking to the young spy. He particularly enjoyed being regaled with stories of Chapman's villainous exploits as a London safecracker before the war.

"If I might ask," inquired Chapman, "how did they pull off the deception at Hatfield?"

"To be perfectly honest, it was rather simple: they piled up brick, rubble, bent iron, lumps of concrete, and splintered wood all around the substation courtyard to simulate the bogus blast."

"And that was enough to fool the Germans?"

"Indeed, it was. From the side, one of the buildings looked as though it had been struck with a giant mallet, while the dummy transformers lay smashed among the debris. Apparently, the fake damage was so convincing that the boiler-room operator arrived at the factory office in a state of panic, shouting out to his fellow employees that the building had been struck by a bomb. The whole picture was very convincing. Aerial photographs taken from above two thousand feet showed considerable devastation without creating suspicion."

"That's good to hear, Colonel. I am glad to be of service to His Majesty."

"Quite honestly, I believe the honor is MI5's, though some of my more pretentious colleagues wouldn't agree given your *colorful* past."

"Major Masterman doesn't like me, I know. I suppose I won't receive a Christmas card from him."

"Sir John looks down his nose upon anyone who doesn't have a peerage—which includes me as well, old boy. Seriously, you needn't worry about whether people like you, Eddie. It's the job that matters most. I consider you to be a brave man, and that's why I've come here to thank you personally. Especially since you're prepared to go back to France and carry on working for us."

"You know me, sir. I like to keep busy and be on the razor's edge."

"Of the many spies that have passed through Camp 020, very few can be considered genuinely stouthearted. You, my friend, have been the bravest so far."

Chapman smiled with obvious pride, and Robertson was happy for him. It was true the young man may have once been a criminal, but he was performing inestimable service for his country now. "Thank you, sir. Your coming here means a great deal to me. By chance, can you brief me on my new mission?"

"Yes, I can give you a preliminary rundown. But first off, how do you think Freda will take your leaving…I mean once the departure day draws near?"

"She's accepted my explanation without question." Chapman had been coached by his MI5 handlers to tell Freda that he had escaped from the Jersey prison, and that in return the police had dropped all charges against him provided he join the army and was posted overseas. "I just want to make sure she and Diane will be provided for when I'm gone."

"Don't worry, we've seen to it. She will receive a monthly stipend for the duration of your service with us."

"Then that's all that can be done. But I must confess, I will miss her and the baby. I have in the past month become something of a father. I never expected such a thing in all my life."

"Ronnie tells me you're quite the doting papa." Robertson was referring to Captain Ronnie Reed, Chapman's assigned B1A counterintelligence section case officer. He knew that the two of them had become rather chummy during the past month and that Chapman confided in him. "He says you and young Diane are quite close, which I think is wonderful."

"She's adorable. I do love her so."

"As I said, we'll take good care of both mother and daughter when you leave."

"What will I do for training?"

"The first step is for you to learn your cover story of the de Havilland operation frontwards and backwards. Once you have it down, you will return to Occupied France as a long-term counterintelligence agent with the principal aim of acquiring information about the Abwehr."

"Jolly good, I'm definitely up to it. Having Freda and the baby here has been wonderful, but I am ready for a new mission. How will I get back to Occupied France?"

"The Germans have refused to send a U-boat, so you will have to return by ship through Lisbon, make contact with the Abwehr, and then proceed to wherever they send you. It may not be Occupied France, though after your time in Nantes I would expect them to send you there again for training for your next sabotage operation. Or, should I say, fake sabotage operation."

"I will be taking a boat then?"

"Yes, you will pose as a seaman."

"That's going to be interesting. I am no squib."

"It's funny you should say that. Operation Damp Squib is the name Major Masterman and I have come up with for your triumphant return to Dr. Graumann and the Abwehr."

"What will I do upon my return to the Germans, after they interrogate me, that is?"

"For now, your focus is getting through the German debriefing unscathed. It's not going to be a picnic by any means. They will, of course, toast and fete you while at the same time subjecting you to thorough interrogation to determine if you are telling the truth. They will go over your story over and over, trying to trip you up without appearing to do so, plying you with drink and bonhomie to loosen your tongue. Consistency on your part while being somewhat vague will be your chief protection. Once the Germans are confident you haven't been turned and you have met their approval, they will no doubt prepare you for a return mission to England. You should accept any mission they offer you and then contact Allied intelligence as the opportunity arises."

"Will I be given a wireless?"

"We can't take the chance. A radio adds to the potential for exposure. Nor will you be put in contact with British agents operating in France. Linkups to Resistance cells are too risky."

"But I assume arrangements can be made for me to pass on messages?"

"Yes, but you should not attempt to communicate with us unless you have in your possession critical information of the highest urgency and contact can be safely re-established."

"I will continue then to spy on the Germans, so you can track their personnel and activities?"

"Yes, that is how you can help us most. Quite frankly, I am not at all keen for you to take any action in France that might get you into trouble with the German authorities, and I am most anxious for you not to undertake any act of sabotage or assassination."

"I take it you didn't think much of my plan to assassinate Hitler."

"Actually, Major Masterman and I were quite impressed with your bravery and initiative, but I'm afraid it's rather out of the question."

"Didn't our own PM say that the greatest risk in war is taking no risk at all?"

"Yes, Churchill did say that. But I don't think he was referring to the assassination of the Führer. I'm afraid my bosses have nixed it. In fact, all references to such an undertaking have been purged from the official file."

"I would have loved to get a chance to pull it off. To see the look on Hitler's face just before the bomb went off. Now that would have been priceless. And for me, what a way to go."

"We have big enough plans for you without assassinating *der Führer*, Eddie. And thankfully, we don't need you to give up your own life to take down Hitler and his loathsome Reich."

They fell into silence, quietly sipping their wine. After a moment, Chapman raised a question that he said had been vexing him since his conversation with Lord Rothschild about explosives and the fake de Havilland sabotage operation.

"If I return to Britain with an accomplice—let's say Leo, Wojch, or one of the other lower-level German operatives whom I actually like—then presumably I would be expected to hand them over to the police on arrival."

"Would that pose a problem for you?"

"Yes, I believe it would. Knowing that if I turned them in they would likely be sentenced to death, I'm not sure I could do that. I have never betrayed an accomplice yet."

Robertson looked at him sympathetically, appreciating the double agent's dilemma. Clearly, Chapman had taken a shine not just to von Gröning, but many of the other Germans at the Abwehr Nantes spy school during his training. "Although such a circumstance would be a matter for the law, we would take every possible step to see that your wishes were granted."

"You're telling men I won't be forced to deliver my friends to the hangman?"

"Indeed not."

"When I return to France, what will my cover story be?"

"It will be as near to the truth as possible so that if you are cross-examined in detail by the Germans, you need only tell the truth. Truths and half-truths make good lies."

"It will be good to be back under cover. With danger in the air I tend to feel more alive."

"Yes, I'm learning to understand that about you, Eddie."

They took another sip of wine and laughed. But the danger a double agent faced was no laughing matter, Robertson knew. Sending Z back into Occupied France to spy on the Germans was fraught with peril. Having thoroughly studied the enemy's interrogation techniques, Robertson knew what the young spy would be facing. He had put together a checklist of ways to withstand the pressure: always speak slowly, which enables hesitation to be covered up when necessary; be generally vague and unobservant; give the impression of being surprised or outraged when aggressively confronted; and feign drunkenness or tiredness long before they actually occur. Chapman might well face physical torture, drugs, or anesthetic, Robertson had warned him, but German interrogators generally preferred to get results by causing mental breakdown. Their techniques included making the witness feel uncertain, uncomfortable, ridiculous, or embarrassed. Sometimes, they would strip a man naked or dress him in women's underwear to throw him off balance. Other times, they would make him stand facing a wall, or make him sit on a three-legged chair so that it took constant effort to maintain his balance.

"How many interrogators do you think I'll face?"

"Probably two."

"Blow hot-blow cold?"

"Most likely. One aggressive, one sympathetic. The most important thing for you to remember is to stick to your cover story at all times, and never tell an unnecessary lie."

"That's sound advice."

"We're going to go over it and over it until it becomes second-nature. You're going to know your cover story better than you know your real life."

"Yes, but if I fall into the hands of the Gestapo, and they choose to disbelieve me, they will break me eventually."

"Yes, most likely."

"And then they will kill me."

"That does seem to be their modus operandi."

"Then I'd better make sure they believe me. When will I return to France?"

"Six weeks. It will take that long to prepare you. It's the starring role of a lifetime—the de Havilland job was just the opening act."

"So, I'm an actor now, is that it?"

"You shouldn't act so surprised. You're friends with the screenwriter Terence Young, and you've hobnobbed with film directors and producers. But in this case, Eddie, I do believe you are the star in your own biography."

"What's the name of it?"

"How about *Eddie Chapman: Behind Enemy Lines*?"

"I rather like that."

Robertson gave a paternal smile. "I knew you would, Eddie. You're a narcissist at heart—but I am quite fond of you."

CHAPTER 21

MAXIM'S RESTAURANT AND
PARIS ABWEHRSTELLE AT HÔTEL LUTETIA
45 BOULEVARD RASPAIL, OCCUPIED FRANCE

MARCH 2, 1943

AS RITTMEISTER STEPHAN VON GRÖNING stumbled out of Maxim's into the Parisian sunlight, he was grateful he had his own personal chauffeur and didn't have to get behind the wheel of his Mercedes. The head of Abwehr Nantes spy school had drunk two full bottles of sauvignon blanc to go along with his overpriced lunch of braised Albert sole in vermouth and langoustine. Two full bottles. Though he typically drank prodigious quantities of liquor without showing any effects, today he was tipsy. His driver Leo Kreusch—a young Abwehr operative wearing civilian clothes and an impressively broken nose from a previous life as a pugilist—was waiting out front for him with the car. When Leo opened the rear door for him, von Gröning thanked him and slipped inside the plush Mercedes. Sinking into the leather upholstery, he began singing the familiar strains of *Lili Marlene* to himself, which was something he often did, drunk or sober. The song about a lovesick German soldier always stirred something deep inside him, making him long for his halcyon days growing up in Bremen.

"Go fast, Leo. I feel like driving fast through the streets of Paris today."

"Yes, Doktor. You want fast—I'll give it to you."

The young chauffeur with the broken boxer's nose proceeded to navigate the car dangerously through the winding streets of the City of Lights. It was a splendid afternoon and von Gröning rolled down his rear car window and let the wind blow through his hair. They took the Rue Royale to Place de la Concorde, raced across the bridge, rumbled down the Boulevard Saint-Germain, and veered to the right onto Boulevard Raspail before turning left onto Place Alphonse Déville and parking on the street. The drive took them less than five minutes. Along the way, the only occurrence of note was a handful of SS troops beating two middle-aged Frenchman on the street with their rifle butts. Von Gröning shook his head in disgust and muttered, "Damned bastards!" to Leo, who quietly voiced his agreement.

Though the rittmeister was a veteran in the German intelligence service, he hated the SS and considered them a breed apart. But he loathed Hitler, Himmler, Goebbels, and Göring even more. In his view, the maniac Führer and his overzealous disciples were *destroying* his beloved Fatherland and its people for their demented Thousand Year Reich. Hitler was not and had never been the savior of Germany. Indeed, to von Gröning it was the other way around: Germany had to be saved from Hitler. The war was most certainly not lost, but the tide had turned against the Reich with the defeat at Stalingrad on the Eastern Front and the recent Allied victories in North Africa. With German victory now a remote possibility, what was needed now was a negotiated peace on favorable terms without the intrusion of Hitler and his Nazi stooges, who would not give up until the last bullet was fired or they had committed suicide. But von Gröning kept these types of views to himself and a select coterie of his peers and subordinates with similar political views.

He had always been the furthest thing from a rabid Nazi. In fact, as a member of the German elite, he had never been comfortable with National Socialism or Hitler and his brown-shirted thugs, not even when they first rose to power in the late 1920s. Like many from the upper classes, he had used the Abwehr purely as a means to a pleasant existence far away from the heavy fighting without ever believing at all in Nazism. In his eyes, Hitler was not just a fool, but a very dangerous man. The Bohemian corporal—the disparaging sobriquet Field Marshal Gerd von Rundstedt called the Reich leader—had always posed a threat to the aristocratic families of Germany like the von Grönings; and the head of the Nantes Abwehrstelle would never support anyone that posed a threat to his world of titled opulence. But now Hitler posed grave risk to all Germans. Now the future of the entire German people, rich and poor alike, was being threatened by the Austrian's excessive militarism. What would happen to his beloved country, von Gröning often wondered, when the bombs stopped falling and the armies put down their weapons? Would Germany turn into a nation of uneducated paupers and farmers? Would it fall so low as to become a second-rate power like Italy, Romania, or Hungary?

What disgusted him most about Hitler, though, was what he was doing to the Jews. In the past year, von Gröning had heard from reliable sources within the Abwehr about Himmler's mobile SS death squads—*Einsatzgruppen* they were called. But now he had learned that an even more heinous and far-reaching program of terror and murder was in effect. Now there were large-scale death camps. Though he had known since last summer that when Jews were shipped to the east they never returned, a month ago was the first time he had seen an official SS document on the systematic "Final Solution" taking place in Poland. He was glad that he was far removed from the ongoing horrors transpiring in the occupied countries. He thought the physical destruction of European Jewry was not only morally reprehensible, but a damned waste of time and resources when there was a hard-fought war to be won. But he wasn't the one in charge of making such decisions. All he could do was position himself to serve his country far away from such inhumanity.

It seemed unbelievable to him that the Jews were being subjected to complete genocide in the east. In the intercepted SS order, he had learned of the horrible sufferings and mass killings of men, women, and children at a place in Upper Silesia Oswiecim in Poland. The SS called it Auschwitz. There was said to be a sign in German at the gate that read *Arbeit Macht Frei*—Work Sets You Free—which von Gröning found revolting given that the camp was not a place of work at all but rather a site of systematic industrialized mass killing on a scale never seen before in the annals of civilization. He had never felt the animosity towards the Jews of Europe that so many of his countrymen experienced, and he felt fortunate to be here in Occupied France as far away as possible from the front lines and atrocities he knew were taking place in Poland and Russia. All the same, he knew he was tainted because he fought in Hitler's army.

Once they parked, von Gröning paused to look up at the elegant six-story Hôtel Lutetia before passing through the guard checkpoint at the main entrance and taking the elevator to the fifth floor. In Paris on a routine counterintelligence matter, von

Gröning was working out of the Paris Abwehrstelle for a couple of days. The illustrious hotel had been requisitioned by the German intelligence service to house, feed, and entertain the officers in command of the occupation forces following the French government's evacuation of Paris in June 1940. When he reached the office on the fifth floor that he was temporarily using, an aide poked his head in.

"The colonel wants to see you," the young lieutenant said without preamble.

Von Gröning winced. The last thing he wanted after a fine meal and two bottles of wine was to have to deal with his nemesis Colonel Waag. "I am sorry, but I am quite busy with—"

"He said right now." He looked at his watch. "Where have you been the past two hours? The colonel has been looking for you."

"It just so happens I was at lunch. Now what is this about?"

"All I know is you are to report to the colonel immediately."

"Very well then, let's go."

They walked down the hallway to a bank of elevators, took a lift to the sixth floor, and navigated their way down two more hallways until they reached his boss's office. A secretary checked him in and then he was admitted. He found Colonel Alexander Waag, chief of the Paris Abwehrstelle, sitting behind his desk shuffling through paperwork. When he looked up, von Gröning could see that he was in trouble again. Damnit, he had thought their discord was behind them, but clearly, he was wrong. He suddenly felt an overwhelming sense of gloom, as if he knew, in some ineffable way, that he was about to undergo a dramatic change in fortune.

"Please sit down, Rittmeister."

Maintaining a mask of his usual upper-class calm, he walked to the chair in front of Waag's desk as the door closed behind him with a plangent thud. Von Gröning couldn't help a little shudder.

"I'm afraid you have given me no choice but to have you reassigned to your old unit. Your work as head of the Nantes Abwehrstelle is finished and you are relieved of command."

For a moment, von Gröning struggled to breathe. But one would not have known that by looking at his carefully-composed face. Though he was still inebriated from wine, his sharp mind was already churning forward at a furious pace, trying to calculate his next move. Removal from his post was positively out of the question when he had the top secret-agent in the German intelligence service working under his control and making life difficult for the Allies. There had to be a way out of this.

"You have no cause to relieve me. My work in France to date has been exemplary. And I am not just talking about Agent Fritz and his recent coup at the de Havilland factory. All of my operatives have borne fruit."

"You're wasting your breath. The decision to relieve you of command has already been made. The sole reason I have summoned you here is to notify you of your new orders."

He withdrew a sheet of paper with the official Abwehr seal and handed it to him. Von Gröning's throat went dry as he read over his new orders posting him to the Eastern Front, signed by Canaris himself. Why had he not seen this coming? How could he have so badly underestimated the authority wielded by Waag? He felt his whole face, already red from drink, turn a shade redder, but he struggled mightily to maintain his composure. The von Grönings had been showing aplomb under difficult circumstances for centuries, and despite this most cruel setback, he would not allow the family honor to be tarnished.

"So, you pulled it off, Alexander. I don't know how you convinced your uncle the admiral to sign this travesty of a document, but you did."

"Actually, it was quite easy. You're a lazy, drunken lout of limited competence. It's about time the Abwehr got rid of you."

It took great effort to restrain his anger. "Don't think for one second you're going to get away with this shameful ploy to steal Fritz from me under the guise of my alcohol consumption," he said firmly but without rancor.

"As they say here in Paris, it is a *fait accompli*. The orders are official."

He scanned the orders to see if there was any way out, but he saw nothing. He was to report to Berlin immediately, where he would be then transferred to the Russian hinterland, precisely where the orders did not say. Being posted on the Eastern Front was what every German soldier dreaded like the plague for one simple reason: the fighting there was brutal, with both sides flouting the accords of the Hague Convention of 1907 and Geneva Convention of 1929. The acts of cruelty directed against enemy troops, prisoners, and civilians stooped to levels of savagery not seen since the Spanish Inquisition. Von Gröning and other high-ranking intelligence officers were well-briefed on the excesses of both the German and Big Red Armies in the Eastern theater. The Wehrmacht and SS had wiped out scores of villages during their advance through Russia, and Jews and other minorities were regularly rounded up and shot or poisoned in Himmler's mobile gassing vans. Other cities were looted or starved into submission, and both sides gave no quarter and expected none in return. The war in the East was the closest thing to hell on earth ever experienced by mankind, even worse than the trenches of the Great War, von Gröning had been informed in intelligence briefs and by those who had by some miracle managed to be reassigned to France or other occupied countries in the West. And now eastward into the maw was where he was headed. It brought back memories of *Heart of Darkness*, the strange novella he had read by Polish-British novelist Joseph Conrad about a doomed voyage up the Congo River into the heart of Africa, where supposedly civilized European men had been reduced to savages.

Von Gröning looked at the colonel and shook his head in disgust. "I may be a weak man in many ways and drink too much, but I would never sink so low as to banish one of my subordinate officers to the Russian Front so I could take over his prized agent. You, sir, are a skunk of the first order. Your uncle would be ashamed if he knew what you were up to."

"This has nothing to do with Admiral Canaris! Get out of my office—and I don't ever want to see you again!"

He rose from his seat. "It is you not me, Colonel, who disgraces the uniform. But in the end, it won't matter."

"Why is that?"

"I already told you. When my boy Fritzchen returns to Occupied France, he won't work for you—he'll only work for me."

"What?"

"You heard me." Von Gröning gave a fatalistic smile. "Even lazy, drunken louts have their day. And my time is coming when Chapman sets foot again on French soil."

"I doubt you will survive that long in Russia, but you can always hope for the best," said Waag, lighting up a vile French Gauloises cigarette with a smirk on his face. "Good day, Rittmeister. Forgive me if I don't see you out."

CHAPTER 22

CAFÈ SETERSTUA
DRONNING MAUDS GATE 10

MARCH 21, 1943

ANNEMARIE BREIEN—unofficial covert Milorg operative—surveyed the café, looking for prying eyes, someone familiar or threatening among the crowd of mostly German officers. Seeing no one suspicious or intrusively watchful, she turned her attention to the bland menu just as one of the owner's two daughters who served as waitresses came by her table. She informed the girl that her father would be joining her shortly, ordered a cup of coffee, and the two smiled conspiratorially at one another. Two inconspicuous Norwegian patriots, working clandestinely on behalf of the Resistance and exchanging a furtive glance. The girl walked off.

Annemarie glanced at her wristwatch. It was twelve minutes after noon and her father was late. She wondered where he could be and hoped he hadn't been arrested again by the Gestapo. It had taken her nearly six months to secure his release from Fehmer the first time, and he most likely would not be granted a second chance at freedom. She looked at her watch again: only a minute had passed but it felt like hours.

Where could he be?

She looked around the room again. One of the Germans, a young lieutenant in an SS uniform, was staring at her. She pretended not to see him and looked away. She didn't want to do anything to encourage him to get up and come over to her table. Being alone as a female in Occupied Norway was a dangerous situation; often the Germans thought it an open invitation for social interaction—or, worse, something more.

She breathed a sigh of relief as her father stepped into the café. Roald Breien made a quick but thorough survey of the café before walking over to her table.

"Hello, Father. Is everything all right?" she said in a quiet voice, careful to keep just below the level at which the closest Germans could hear her if they were listening closely.

"I had to get a new ration card for me and your mother. It took forever."

She nodded. She knew how difficult it was to put food on the table these days. Since mid-1942, virtually all goods had been placed under rationing in Occupied Norway. Foodstuffs were allocated in specific quantities. To purchase goods such as bread, sugar, potatoes, and coffee, people had to use rationing cards specifying the amount of each good they were entitled to buy during the month in question. Meats, milk, canned goods, sweets, and most vegetables, for which deliveries were virtually impossible to predict, were rarely available at all. Osloans often had to queue in line for half a day in the hope of getting hold of their rations and were sometimes still turned away with nothing when supplies ran out.

The waitress brought her coffee and they ordered their lunch: salt herring and potatoes, a meal that was becoming all too familiar for most Norwegians as the German occupiers had staked a claim to just about everything else.

"I have news for you, Father. That's why I wanted to meet."

"From Fehmer?"

"Yes, he has kept me abreast of the Gestapo's ongoing pursuit of the Vemork saboteurs."

Named Operation Gunnerside, the sabotage had been conducted on February 28 by a group of Norwegian commandos trained by the British Special Operations Executive. Dropped by parachute from England, the nine-man team successfully placed explosive charges on the heavy-water electrolysis chambers at the lightly-guarded Norsk Hydro Plant in Vemork, located one hundred miles east of Oslo. The Allied mission was a success, resulting in the destruction of the entire inventory of heavy water produced thus far during the German Occupation, over one thousand pounds worth, along with equipment critical to operation of the electrolysis chambers. But unfortunately, the explosion had not irreparably crippled the plant. Fehmer had told her that production would most likely be resumed within a few months and now the plant would be heavily guarded. In response to the attack, thousands of Wehrmacht infantrymen, hundreds of German and Norwegian police, Gestapo investigators, and SS shock troops, and dozens of elite *Jagdkommando* platoons—nearly 8,000 men in total—were unleashed upon the Hardanervidda plateau where the raiders were believed to have established their base of operations. The enemy was supported by locals who knew the surrounding countryside and roving aerial patrols of Fi-156 Storch spotter planes. Despite their vast resources, the Germans had thus far come up empty-handed at tracking down the saboteurs or anyone that had aided them.

"I don't understand how you manage to get all this information from Fehmer and convince him to free members of the Home Front."

"I am a magician just like you, Father."

"Please don't tell me you're giving him sexual favors?"

She couldn't help but feel hurt that she would say such a thing and felt her face blush. Then she leaned in close. "How dare you talk to me like that when I have rescued you and so many others of our countrymen from prison," she said stiffly. "Now listen up and don't interrupt me because I have important news for you."

"All right, I am sorry. As a Home Front leader, I should know better than to ask a fellow operative how she obtains her intelligence. I know what you're doing is invaluable to the Resistance."

"Thank you, Father. Apology accepted. Now what I wanted to tell you is that the Germans have not called off the search. Tomorrow, they will be sending in fresh reinforcements. Trains and buses will be streaming into the Vemork area from Oslo. Fehlis is intent on redoubling the German efforts, particularly immediately north of Rjukan and around Lake Mös. It may seem as if things have quieted down on the Vidda and that it is safe to return to the area for those that haven't made their way to Sweden, but that is not the case."

"Fehmer told you this?"

"No, but I saw the order. Some things he tells me, often to get my opinion, other things I see at his desk or he shows me to gain my trust."

"My God, it seems he is playing both sides."

"Quite possibly he is. But he also doesn't want to harm the innocent. That is why he has released more than a dozen people to date. I have claimed to him that they are low-level figures not worthy of imprisonment."

"When in fact many of those he has released are key figures in Milorg and the other Resistance groups. Like me. I don't know how you are getting away with this. All I can say is you are a clever girl and I am proud of you."

"Thank you," she replied as his coffee arrived.

He took a sip of the dark roast; there was no cream or sugar available. "I would still like to know what Fehmer's game is," he said to her once the waitress was gone.

"Eventually, I'll find out. But for now, I think we should content ourselves with the fact that I have an in with him. He confides in me and is willing to help me."

"Just promise me you'll never sleep with him."

"Is that what you are most worried about?"

"It bothers me. In fact, it would bother a lot of people. Already there is talk, Annemarie."

"Talk is cheap. I actually get people released from prison."

"I realize that and applaud your efforts, but I am still uncomfortable with you working so closely with Fehmer. He is a dangerous man. Surely, you've heard what he has done under *Nacht und Nebel*? He has knowingly sent dozens to their deaths in the German camps."

Her father was referring to *Night and Fog*, the code name given to a decree of December 7, 1941, issued by Hitler and signed by Field Marshall Wilhelm Keitel, Chief of the German Armed Forces High Command, or *Oberkommando der Wehrmacht*. The OKW decree directed that persons in occupied territories engaging in activities intended to undermine the security of German troops were, upon capture, to be brought to Germany "by night and fog" for trial by special courts, thus circumventing military procedure and various conventions governing the treatment of prisoners. Once convicted, the accused were sent to forced labor or concentration camps in which their chances of survival were minimal, which Fehmer no doubt knew. The code name stemmed from Germany's most acclaimed poet and playwright, Johann Wolfgang von Goethe, who used the phrase to describe clandestine actions often concealed by fog and the darkness of night.

"I can handle myself, Father. You know that. And besides, if I don't remain close to Fehmer and continue to take the risks I am taking, I can't get him to release people from prison."

"What does Kjell say?"

"You leave my husband out of it."

"But surely he must not be pleased with how much time you spend with that Nazi bastard."

"You stay out of my marriage. My husband is my responsibility, not yours." She sighed impatiently. "Are you going to act on this important intelligence I have given you today, or should I take this to Hauge?"

"No, I will take care of it. Is there anything else?"

"Yes, the order I saw says that the Germans are going to scour the countryside, searching for every farmhouse and cabin for the fugitives or their supporters. They are particularly on the lookout for illegal weapons, explosives, radios, newspapers, and other contraband."

"Which means that many of our regular operatives hiding out in the mountains and woods around the lakes in the area will be vulnerable."

"Yes, and that is why I called you."

"What else did the written order say?"

"Travel in the Vidda is banned and a six o'clock curfew has been imposed. Anyone found wandering in the area will be arrested immediately. Any homes or dwellings known to have provided shelter to the saboteurs or for Resistance purposes will be immediately burned to the ground. Anyone in violation of the new restrictions will be shot without warning. Apparently, they will be hitting the area south and west of Lake Mös hard."

"You have done well, my daughter. You are truly making a difference in this war and I want you to know, again, that I am proud of you."

"I can feel the inevitable *but* coming."

He smiled guiltily. "But please be careful. The truth is Hauge wants you to continue this association with Fehmer for as long as possible. But Hauge is not your father—I am. I worry for you, and so does your mother."

"Well, I have to do this. If I could save a dozen more of our countrymen in exchange for my own life, I would gladly do it."

"I know you would. But please promise me you will be careful. There's no telling what a man like Fehmer is capable of."

"I have more control over him than you think, Father. And he is also a better man than you think. He actually puts a high premium on human life—as long as it does not conflict with his role as a criminal investigator. When his back is against the wall and his superiors are demanding not only answers but confessions and arrests, that is when he becomes the blind instrument of Nazi oppression. And that, Father, is when I hate him."

"And what if there was an order to kill him?"

"An order to kill him? Is anything like that planned?"

"No, but it has been discussed. It shouldn't be any secret to you that Milorg would love to see him dead. And Fehlis too. If something like that were to materialize, could you get close to him?"

"No, I would never do that."

"Why not?"

"Because, Father, I am in the business of saving lives, not taking them away."

With that, their meals of salt herring and boiled potatoes arrived and they quietly ate. All the while Annemarie Breien wondered if perhaps, one day, she would change her mind and drive the nail in the coffin of Siegfried Wolfgang Fehmer.

CHAPTER 23

MI5 HEADQUARTERS
58 ST. JAMES STREET

MARCH 21, 1943

TAR ROBERTSON COULDN'T BELIEVE WHAT HE WAS HEARING. The secret plan to return Agent Fritz/Zigzag to his Abwehr handlers involved having him pose as a crewman on the merchant ship *The City of Lancaster*, sailing out of Liverpool for Lisbon, and then jumping ship when it docked in Portugal. According to the latest Bletchley Park Ultra intercepts, the double agent had succeeded in his mission—but upon making contact with the Germans at their Lisbon embassy, he had shockingly agreed to attempt to blow up the ship with a bomb disguised as a lump of coal to be placed in the coal bunker. Robertson could only surmise that this was in response to a request from Lord Rothschild and MI5's explosives and anti-sabotage section that he obtain examples of German explosive devices. But there was an even graver possibility—and that was that Chapman was a traitor to his country and willing to blow up a British ship on behalf of Nazi Germany.

"Are you telling me, gentlemen," he posed to Major Masterman and Captain Ronnie Reed, "that Z has been in Lisbon only two days, and already he's offered to sink the ship that brought him there on behalf of the bloody Nazis? Is that what you're telling me?"

"If the latest batch of wireless intercepts is to be believed then that is indeed where we find ourselves," said Masterman. The scholarly Oxford don, mystery writer, cricket enthusiast, and talented sportsman who had played tennis at Wimbledon and field hockey for England had harbored his doubts about and looked down upon Eddie Chapman since the beginning, regarding him as an "enterprising and practical criminal" rather than an invaluable intelligence operative working on behalf of Great Britain. But Robertson knew Sir John had also come to admire the former safecracker for his bravery.

"I still don't believe he would turn on us," said Ronnie Reed.

Robertson found it hard to believe, too, as he regarded the young captain for a moment from across his desk. But they could not afford to take any chances. Robertson knew that as Agent Zigzag's primary control officer, Reed understood him the best and he trusted his opinion. In addition to interrogating Chapman, Reed had spent countless hours in casual conversation with the former safecracker the past two months at the Crespigny Road safe house and had come to respect his talents as a spy. All the same, all they had to go by at this point was the intercepted German wireless communications.

"Who did he meet with in Lisbon?" asked Robertson.

"We don't know," said Reed. "We can't tell from the Bletchley intercept."

"Well, who do we think it is?"

"In all likelihood, he was passed up the food chain," replied Reed. "And that chain ends with Major Ludovico von Kartshoff."

"As in the head of the Lisbon Abwehr station?"

"Yes, it's quite possible Z met with von Kartshoff himself. The man is fluent in German, English, Spanish, and Portuguese."

"Lisbon," said Masterman, with a spy novelist's gleam in his eye. "A boiling cauldron of espionage, awash with refugees, smugglers, spies, hustlers, arms dealers, deserters, profiteers, and prostitutes. Definitely Eddie Chapman's kind of town."

"That goes without saying," said Robertson. "But what the bloody hell is he up to?"

"I don't know the answer to that, but we can all agree that Lisbon is dangerous. It's become an international clearing ground, a busy ant heap of spies and agents, where political and military secrets and information—true and false, but mainly false—are bought and sold like a marketplace. And now, in this cauldron, we want to divine whether Zigzag is with us or against us."

"We can't afford for this to turn into a cock-up or Churchill will have our heads," said Robertson, shaking his head in dismay again. "Hope for the best, but plan for the worst—that's what I always say. What we know for certain is that the Abwehr station in Lisbon sent a top-secret message to Admiral Canaris notifying him that Agent Fritz was in a position to sabotage the *City of Lancaster* with a coal bomb."

Masterman lit his pipe. "And in that transmission, the enemy requested authorization to proceed from Canaris himself since it contravened the established policy of the Abwehr not to undertake sabotage in or from neutral Portugal. To make matters worse, the same message described the precise route to Lisbon taken by the *Lancaster*; and how many ships had been sunk in the attack on the convoy. So regardless of where Zigzag's loyalty lies, we've got a problem."

"I understand that the information could only have come from Chapman," said Reed. "But I still don't believe he has double-crossed us and is working on behalf of the Germans."

"Perhaps you don't know him as well as you think," said Masterman. "He is a rather dodgy fellow."

"At the very least, he has told the Germans more about the convoy than he should have," said Robertson. "In the process, he has put us in an awkward position."

"And the worst case is we failed to turn him and he is, in fact, treacherously working for the other side," said Masterman. "I suppose that's what we all love about the intelligence business. No shortage of excitement, is there?"

"Yes, but unfortunately this isn't a game of cricket, Sir John. Not only are lives at stake, but our whole Double Cross spy system. I hate not being in control."

"In times like these, don't we all?"

"Well, what do you propose we do, Colonel?" asked Reed.

"We're going to put together a detailed action plan, and it will have the three following components. First, we must protect the ship and its crew. Whether or not Z is bluffing the Germans or not, we cannot allow loss of life or damage to come to the *Lancaster*. Second, we must protect Ultra and Most Secret Sources at all costs. Double Cross and reading the enemy's radio traffic without the Germans knowing it is at the very heart of Allied intelligence efforts and must remain secret. Finally, we cannot interrupt the mission unless we know with a high level of certainty that Chapman is indeed double-crossing us. Are we agreed, gentlemen?"

"Agreed," said Masterman.

"Yes, sir," said Captain Ronnie Reed. "But I still can't believe that Chapman would turn traitor on us. I have to wonder if he was forced or instructed by the Germans to carry out the sabotage, or if it was his own idea."

"I've always said he's an enterprising and practical criminal," said Masterman. "I suspect that he concocted the plan himself—for better or worse."

"Whatever view we all have of Zigzag's character and patriotism," said Robertson, "we cannot run the risk of taking it for granted that he would not, in fact, commit this act of sabotage."

A knock sounded on the door and a young officer poked his head in. "Colonel, I believe you're going to want to hear this. We have new information concerning Agent Zigzag."

Robertson sat upright in his chair. "Yes, what is it, Lieutenant?"

"Berlin has given the green light for the proposed sabotage of the *City of Lancaster*. The order came from Canaris himself. We're having Bletchley double check it, but I thought you should know." He handed him a sheet of yellow paper with the Ultra decryption of the Abwehr transmission. "There's something else, sir."

"Something else?"

"MI6 has also read the cable, and they are not pleased by the present state of affairs. They're proposing to use their own people in Lisbon to neutralize Zigzag."

"Oh dear, that's just what we need right now—meddling from our sister service," grumbled Masterman.

Robertson shook his head incredulously: could the situation become any worse? He had suspected MI6 would get their fingers into this mess sooner rather than later, but he was still surprised at how quickly they had become involved. Since the war had begun, the two rival British intelligence services, MI5 and MI6, had been in competition with one another and didn't always cooperate. While the task of MI5 was to control counterespionage in the United Kingdom and throughout the British Empire, and MI6's charter was to operate in all areas outside British territory, in actual practice the intelligence gathering and dissemination activities of the two agencies often overlapped, causing inevitable friction. It was in these circumstances that relations between the two competing British intelligence services were most strained. The men who ran the internal espionage branch did not appreciate their rivals from the external security branch that ran overseas operatives encroaching on their patch—and vice versa.

"I'll have to telephone Stewart and Ewen and tell them to call off their dogs," said Robertson after a moment's reflection. He was referring to Major General Sir Stewart Graham Menzies, Chief of MI6, and Lieutenant Commander Ewen Montagu, the naval intelligence officer on the Double Cross Committee.

"What makes you think Menzies will listen to you?" asked Masterman.

"He probably won't but we have to try." He looked at Reed. "The *Lancaster* is not due to leave port for a few days, correct?"

"Yes, sir."

"Well, since Zigzag is planning to jump ship just before she sets sail, we have plenty of time to intercept him and the coal bomb. I'm going to instruct MI6 to wait. It's the prudent course of action."

"And when the time comes, who's going to do the intercepting?" asked Masterman.

Robertson looked at Agent Zigzag's control officer. "Why Ronnie here of course. He's acquainted with all the relevant facts. Moreover, the ship's master and Z both know Ronnie and it will, therefore, be easier for him to approach them with less chance of arousing German suspicion than anyone else."

"MI6 will still have their own man there to take Chapman out if it's discovered he has been turned by the Germans," said Masterman. "We will have to move quickly."

Robertson nodded in agreement. He felt better now that they had worked out a plan of action and all that was left was to implement it. "Ronnie, I'm going to need you to fly to Lisbon posthaste. Once there, you must quickly locate Zigzag and interrogate him. Unless he volunteers information about the sabotage plot, freely and without prompting, you're going to have to arrest him at gunpoint and bring him back in handcuffs."

"I shall of course do my duty, sir, but I still don't believe Chapman has gone rogue. Also, don't you think he will be a bit surprised to see me?"

"Indeed, he will. But there's no reason for him to deduce that we're able to read the Germans' cables. He doesn't know about Ultra and our ability to intercept Abwehr messages. Though he may be surprised to see you, it would still be quite natural for us to send you to Lisbon to make sure he's in play and to ascertain if he's made contact with the Germans. It will be as if we are looking out for his safety and the integrity of the operation."

"Looks like you're in for a bit of excitement, Captain Reed," said Masterman. "Are you up to it?"

"Yes, Major, I am. But I must confess that I am something of a novice at this type of spycraft. After all, I'm just a simple radio ham. I only joined MI5 because I liked to play with wireless sets. To think that I may have to bring a known criminal back to London from a neutral country by the point of a gun…well, sir, it boggles the mind. But, of course, I shall do my duty."

"Inexperienced though you may be, Ronnie, buggering this up is not an option— and that's a bloody order," said Robertson, only half-joking.

"Don't worry, gentlemen, I promise to keep the British end up. When do I leave?"

"The day after tomorrow," said Tar. "We've got to get your paperwork in order. You'll take the two o'clock BOAC Whitchurch-to-Lisbon."

"Very good, sir. Now let's just hope the Luftwaffe doesn't shoot the plane down before I touch down in Lisbon and take Z into custody."

CHAPTER 24

WITH UNUSUAL CARE, Eddie Chapman made his way up the gangplank of the *City of Lancaster*. In the rucksack strapped to his back were two large coal bombs, given to him by the Germans shortly after he had made contact with them upon his arrival in the Portuguese capital. He had been told by his Abwehr handler—a cosmopolitan young operative wearing horn-rimmed spectacles who spoke excellent English and called himself Baumann—that the bombs would only explode when exposed to heat, but he was taking no chances. He walked carefully up the gangplank, like a trapeze artist on a high wire.

He was keeping his fingers crossed not only that the bombs wouldn't detonate, but that he could pull off the ambitious plan that he and the ship's master, Irish Captain Kearon, had concocted to fool the Germans and help Chapman further demonstrate his loyalty as an Abwehr operative. It was a plan fraught with peril—which was precisely the kind of danger the mysterious man recorded in the ship's logbook as assistant steward Hugh Anson thrived on.

The coal bombs constructed by the Germans were impressive and made to look precisely like natural Welsh coal. They consisted of two irregular black lumps approximately six inches square that were indistinguishable in terms of shape, weight, and texture from bituminous coal unearthed from Wales. Rather than drill out existing pieces of coal and to pack in more explosives, Baumann's engineers had ingeniously taken a canister of explosive with a fuse attached and molded a plastic covering around it, which had been painted and covered in coal dust. The only clue to the lethal contents was a small borehole, the diameter of a pencil, drilled into one of the faces on each of the coal lumps.

Once on board, Chapman stashed the rucksack in his locker, thus completing the first part of the plan Captain Kearon and he had worked out the evening before, which was to smuggle the explosive device safely on board the ship. Now it was time for the second part of the plan: once he had brought the bombs on board and was prepared to leave the ship for good, he was to start a fight. This would allow the captain to punish him while providing the cover story that seaman Anson must have jumped ship to avoid another prison sentence in England. Throughout the lengthy journey from Liverpool to Lisbon, Chapman had, at the captain's request, been pretending to be an unruly sort. Getting into a scrap at the end of the journey would reinforce his cover story as a "bad egg," as Kearon called it, as well as help explain his disappearance once he had handed over the coal bombs to the captain and jumped ship tomorrow morning. That was the third phase of the plan. His Abwehr handler Baumann had confirmed that once he jumped ship, all the necessary paperwork was ready to smuggle him out of the country, including a new passport with a photograph taken in Lisbon two days earlier when the *City of Lancaster* had first docked in port.

When he had safely tucked away the bomb-filled rucksack, he went to the berth of a hulking gunner named Dermot O'Connor, who lay dozing on his bunk. After taking a deep breath to summon his nerves, he punched the Irishman hard in the nose, instantly waking him up. O'Conner had been identified by Chapman as the crew member most likely to be goaded into a brawl without suspecting a setup— and he did not disappoint. In a flash, he was up and off the bunk, his ham-like fists ready to inflict considerable damage.

Chapman lunged at the brawny Irishman.

And was dealt a jarring blow to his mouth that sent him reeling to the floor next to the bunk. He shook it off and started to his feet, taking a vicious punch to the ribs. Falling back down, he felt another punch hammer the side of his face, then ducked another before leaping to his feet and, to his own astonishment, landing a punch to O'Conner's bulky midriff. But the blow only seemed to enrage the Irishman.

What in bloody hell have I got myself into? wondered Chapman as a crowd of seamen gathered around the two brawlers, roaring their approval and placing bets. Chapman licked the blood from his split lip; it tasted metallic, iron-like. Squinting at his adversary, he wished he had selected a less formidable opponent.

The Irishman came at him again, his massive fists clenched. This time he brought Chapman down with a loud thud by tackling him to the floor and smashing his elbow into his face, drawing blood from his left nostril and making him see stars. Through the pinpoints, Chapman could make out the Irishman's gritted teeth, the gleam of animal rage in his eyes. He knew he was in for a savage beating if he didn't get up and off the floor. Squirming free by twisting his body, he was somehow able to pull free from the clutches of the bigger man and rise to his feet.

Chapman then drove his fist into his adversary's stomach but received two stunningly quick punches in return. That's when he grabbed a half-empty bottle of whiskey from a nearby bunk and clobbered O'Connor over the head. The big man wobbled dizzily and fell to one knee before shaking off the blow, grabbing him by the lapels, and headbutting him. Chapman was again knocked to the floor. But before collapsing, he recovered his senses enough to reach out again with the half-empty whiskey bottle and whack O'Connor in the head.

But once again, the blow seemed to have little effect on the hulking Irishman. He drove forward with a right-handed blow that grazed Chapman's chin, then connected with a pair of jabs and a roundhouse right that drew not just audible grunts, but a cascade of blood. Then for good measure, he headbutted him again in the face. Chapman collapsed in a heap to the floor.

This time he was unable to get up.

At that moment, Captain Kearon and a pair of his men stormed in to break up the fight. "All right, all right! That's enough, you stupid blokes!" growled the ship's master, acting out his part with aplomb.

The next thing Chapman knew he and his opponent were dragged off to the sick bay. Bleeding from his nose and mouth, he shouted to the Irishman, "You've violated the Queensberry rules, you bastard! That's not the way a gentleman fights!"

"Oh, shut up, Anson!" snorted the captain, loudly so the whole crew could hear.

A half hour later, both men were patched up. Chapman looked at his face in the mirror. It was a terrible mess. He had a swollen eye which was rapidly discoloring, one of his teeth had been knocked out, and his nose had been hit so hard it was still dribbling blood. He complained again to Kearon that it had been an unfair fight.

The captain pretended to have none of it. "I've had enough of your insolence, the both of you! You are hereby docked a day's pay! Let this be a lesson to you!"

"A day's pay?" protested Chapman. "But you have no right!"

"That's enough out of you, Anson. You're in serious trouble."

"Is that so?"

"Yes, by thunder. But at least you've met a better man at last."

"I have done no such thing. After I beat him by the Marquis of Queensberry rules, he head-butted me in the face. The men on this ship are hooligans."

"Are you the only decent one on board then?"

"Why yes!"

"Well, that's a load of codswallop! You are hereby confined to quarters!"

"That's fine by me!" bristled Chapman, but inside he was suppressing a smile at their fine performance.

ψψψ

Despite the severe pain on his battered face, the next morning Chapman, still dutifully pretending to be assistant steward Hugh Anson, was up at the crack of dawn to deliver Captain Kearon his early morning tea. Rapping on the door, he was told to enter. He slipped inside the cabin carrying a tray in one hand and his rucksack filled with ten pounds of high explosives in the other.

"Good God!" gasped Captain Kearon from his bed as Chapman closed the door behind him. "You've actually brought the bombs to my quarters?"

"I'm not sure why you're surprised, Captain. I told you yesterday that I was going to try and smuggle them on board for transport back home."

"Aye, but I didn't think you'd bring them here. What's to prevent them from going off?"

"I've been told they are one-hundred-percent safe unless heated."

Kearon crawled out of his bunk in his long johns, stifled a yawn, and ran a hand through his tangled, iron-red beard flecked with gray. If he had been carrying a trident, he would have been the spitting image of Neptune. "I don't trust the damned Huns—not a single bloody one of them. I don't want those bombs in my cabin."

"I understand your sentiments, Captain, but you're going to have to trust me. I told the Germans that I would sabotage the *Lancaster* and the enemy has agreed to let me do it. So, I must hand over the bombs to you, and you will in turn give them to the British authorities."

He held out the rucksack. Kearon looked at it warily, making no move to take it.

"Captain, you must take these bombs off my hands. You know from Captain Reed that I am a double agent. I am performing a vital secret mission on behalf of the British government, and you are responsible for me while on board. You are a key part of this operation and a link in the chain with British intelligence."

"I know that. But that doesn't mean I have to agree to take those bloody bombs aboard me ship."

"If I don't hand them over to you, what else am I to do with them?"

"I don't know. But if I take them, I will have to weigh anchor immediately and head back to Liverpool. If those bombs go off, they would blow the bottom out of the boilers. That would be enough to disable the vessel and kill half my crew."

"No, I'm afraid you can't make sail back to England, not yet. Any deviation from your current route to Spain will attract the Germans' suspicion. And as I told you, the bombs pose no risk as long as they are not placed near a heat source, such as a coal furnace or oven."

The captain stroked his beard. "All right, I'll take them and hand them over to the authorities when the proper time comes." Taking the rucksack from him, he set it down on the floor next to his safe, leaned down, and unlocked the safe with a key fastened about his neck. From the safe, he withdrew a large bulky envelope, tied with string, sealed with a blue seal, and stamped *OHMS*, which stood for *On His Majesty's Service*. The package had been locked in the captain's safe since departing from Liverpool and was to be handed to assistant steward Anson prior to his jumping ship in Lisbon. Inside the special MI5 package put together by Ronnie Reed was Chapman's Colt .45 revolver with a spare loaded chamber, 50 one-pound notes, and a ration book and clothing book made out in the name of Hugh Anson. There were also press clippings describing an explosion at a factory in North London that would be used along with the other materials to lend authenticity to Agent Fritz's espionage activities in Britain on behalf of the Reich over the past four months.

Chapman took the articles from him and the captain carefully placed the coal bombs in the safe, shut the door, and turned the lock. Chapman stuffed the papers and money in his rucksack and handed the revolver back to Kearon.

"Consider this a little present since I've been such a hard case aboard your ship."

"Oh, you haven't been a hard case, lad. It's been a thrill to have a genuine spy aboard the *Lancaster*. You've performed your role admirably."

"Thank you, Captain."

"No, thank you, lad. In return for your parting gift, let me give you the address of my sister-in-law, Doris Neal, in case you encounter any trouble during your stay here in Portugal. She lives north along the coast. The name of the town is Porto." He withdrew a sheet of paper and a pencil and started to scribble down the address.

"No, no, don't write it down. If the German's find a note on me, they'll kill me. Just tell it to me and I'll remember it."

"Very well. As I said my sister-in-law is Miss Doris Neal. She resides at 1308 Avenida da Republica, Vila Nova de Gaia, in Porto."

Chapman repeated the address out loud so he would remember it. "I've got it. Thank you."

"Doris will help you if you need it. Godspeed, lad."

"Good luck to you too, Captain."

After they shook hands, Chapman quietly stole away from the ship and disappeared into the misty Portuguese dawn, completely unaware that MI6 had posted an agent to watch the vessel and stand by for orders to seize and, if necessary, liquidate him.

CHAPTER 25

"SO, GENTLEMEN, IT APPEARS Z has been playing straight with us all along. I have now received several telegrams from Captain Reed in Lisbon that confirm Chapman has pulled off the impossible. I must confess that on Monday and Tuesday, I still had my doubts, but not after learning the details of Ronnie's debriefing with Captain Kearon."

"What did the captain say?" asked Masterman.

Robertson looked at the latest telegram. "He said that Chapman behaved magnificently and that his plot to sabotage the ship was nothing but a ruse to obtain the bombs. He further said that the two lumps of exploding coal have been handed over to Ronnie."

"It was a ruse to fool the Germans all along then," said Colonel Tin Eye Stephens. "And here we thought he was a traitor trying to plant a bomb on one of His Majesty's ships. We would have had to search through tons of coal in the ship's bunkers to locate the devices."

"Tragedy narrowly averted," said Masterman, who then added a cricket analogy, as he so often did when describing the tradecraft of MI5's Double Cross operatives. "I have to give our lad his due. He's had some good innings."

Smiling, Robertson pictured Chapman. *The rapscallion's certainly capable of thinking on his feet; he must feel on top of the world right now.* "Zigzag said to Captain Kearon that the coal was high explosive, which is why it was to be given to Ronnie. He then suggested that MI5 stage some sort of fake explosion on board to send up his prestige with the Germans."

"Chapman proposed that? Why he's even more cunning than I thought," observed Masterman.

"Captain Kearon also described how it was he and Z together who agreed that the ship's compass course and the German U-boat attack on the convoy en route to Lisbon could be reported to the Nazis without endangering British shipping. He also said that Chapman started a brawl with an Irish gunner named O'Conner for the sake of his cover story. In short, gentlemen, he went above and beyond the call of duty."

"As far as I am concerned, the lad has not only proven his loyalty," said Tin Eye, "but we now have two intact bombs of a type we have never seen before."

"Strordnary," agreed Masterman. "Lord Rothschild—alias Mr. Fisher to Z—is ecstatic beyond belief with the prospect of studying the Germans' newest explosive devices."

That drew a chuckle from Robertson. "I almost feel guilty for doubting where Chapman's loyalties lie. As Captain Kearon said, he acted his part superbly. He lived up to his reputation as a jail-bird most realistically.'"

"Frankly, I'm not surprised," said Tin Eye. "The whole operation is typical of the risks the lad has been prepared to undertake on our behalf. He offered to carry out a sabotage mission knowing that when the *Lancaster* did not sink at sea, he would be suspected of double-dealing, with possibly fatal results to himself. Yet he took the chance. He believed the value to us of getting examples of the devices used by the Germans justified the risk to himself. All in all, a most brilliant show."

Now it was Masterman's turn to laugh. "Why Colonel Stephens, you talk of him as if he is the great illusionist Jasper Maskelyne himself."

"I'm telling you, he deserves credit. Twice now he has pulled off major deceptions for us. I must say, the young chap has won me over."

Robertson smiled. "And that is no small feat. In any case, I'm glad it has all worked out."

The three senior intelligence officers nodded and fell into a momentary silence. The last seventy-two hours had been anxious and taxing on them all, and they felt a sense of overwhelming relief. From Ronnie Reed's communications, it was clear that Agent Zigzag and Captain Kearon had acted out their roles with great derring-do and the entire Double Cross Committee would be jubilant when they heard the news. Now the question for Robertson moving forward was what to do with the coal bombs and where would Zigzag go next from Lisbon? He would, of course, be monitored through Most Secret Sources, but German radio intercepts alone could only provide at best an incomplete picture and he would now be at the mercy of the Germans with no one to throw him a lifeline. If they interrogated him and somehow, despite his countless hours of mock questioning at Crespigny Road, he cracked under the strain, they would torture him until he told them what they wanted to know. And then they would kill him.

Robertson cleared his throat, resuming the conversation. "One of the more pressing issues now is what we're going to do about MI6."

"They believe we've been encroaching upon their turf?" asked Tin Eye.

"I would call that an understatement. They flatly refuse to contemplate staging a fake sabotage of the *Lancaster* in Lisbon or anywhere else in the Mediterranean."

"Did they give a reason?"

"They said it would be politically complicated."

"What are we going to do with the bombs?" asked Masterman.

"Lord Rothschild instructed that they not be brought back on a commercial flight. If there is an acid-fuse trigger, he said there's no telling what even a slight change in air pressure might do to the internal workings. He said the bomb had been primed by someone else and he had no idea when it was set to explode. Therefore, he said for that reason alone, the piece of coal should be photographed, x-rayed, placed in a heavy iron box padded with cork, sent to Gibraltar on the next British vessel, and from there delivered to Mr. Fisher in Whitehall."

"Mr. Fisher is it? Lord Rothschild certainly enjoys playing cloak and dagger games, doesn't he?" said Tin Eye.

"He certainly does. In Gibraltar, the package is to be picked up by an MI5 agent who will say, 'I come from Ronnie.'"

"Now that is cloak and dagger," said Masterman.

"Lord Rothschild was insistent on one other point as well."

"What's that?" asked Tin Eye.

"The bombs should be delivered intact and should under no circumstances be sawn in half."

"Sawn in half?" said Tin Eye. "Only a grown-up child with too much money like Lord Rothschild could imagine that anyone would want to take a saw to a lump of coal packed with high explosive."

They all laughed.

"But if all we do is bring the coal bombs back to study them, won't the Germans want to know how and, more importantly, why the *City of Lancaster* has not been blown up?" wondered Masterman aloud once the laughter had died down.

"Yes, that would appear to be a problem," agreed Tin Eye.

"Indeed," said Masterman. "I believe the Germans will be anxious to discover if the act of sabotage actually takes place and will follow the progress of the ship with great interest."

"That's why, Sir John, our next step will be to develop an elaborate deception plan for why the bomb didn't go off, since MI6 won't allow us to even consider faking an explosion on board the ship."

"I quite agree," said Tin Eye, squinting through his monocle. "If the coal is not found, there must either be an explosion or Zigzag is blown."

Masterman nodded. "Well then, our scientific cloak-and-dagger expert Lord Rothschild will just have to come up with a deception plan, won't he?"

"Yes, he most certainly will," said Robertson. "And he'd better hurry. The Germans are going to be asking Z a lot of hard questions when they interrogate him in the coming weeks."

"He won't crack," said Tin Eye. "Our lad is made of sterner stuff than the Germans. Much sterner stuff."

"Yes, but he no longer has von Gröning looking out for him," said Robertson. "At least with the old man, he had someone whose professional success was tied to him."

"What the bloody hell are you talking about?" snapped Tin Eye. "What's happened to von Gröning?"

Robertson looked at him. "You didn't know? We recently decrypted an intercept that says he's been shipped off to the Russian Front."

"Great Scott—you're telling me Zigzag is all alone out there?"

"Alone, yes. But as you say, our lad is made of sterner stuff."

CHAPTER 26

STARING ACROSS THE MUDDY FIELD at the German patrol framed against the distant tree line, von Gröning thought back to his last massed cavalry charge during the Great War.

The year was 1916. He was an *oberleutnant* in the legendary *Königin Olga*—the White Dragoons, the most elite cavalry regiment in the imperial army. The mad dash across gently rolling French farmland on the Western Front came back to him like it happened yesterday. He remembered the snorting and thundering hooves of the horses, the quirts slapping the muscled rumps, the wild screaming of his fellow cavalrymen, the feathered helmets bobbing in the saddle, the feeling of invincibility charging on horseback, and finally the deadly crackle of reality as the British machine guns opened fire. The bulk of his regiment was wiped out in a matter of seconds. But by some miracle, he managed to survive despite his grievous wounds and was awarded the Iron Cross, Second Class, for bravery on the field of battle.

Until he had witnessed firsthand the slaughter of that day, war had appeared something of a romantic undertaking and the world had seemed full of promise and adventure. God, how young and naïve he had been, he thought, as he stared across his newest killing field, this time on the Eastern Front. Looking at the line of skirmishers in the distance through his Zeiss binoculars, he couldn't help but feel old and tired, like a spent warhorse. He was only forty-four years of age, but with his heavy drinking and the atrocities he had witnessed in the last few weeks alone he felt much older.

He couldn't believe that he had sunk so low as to be banished to the wretched Russian Front. Out here on the wind-ravaged steppes, the slaughter, inhumanity, and gross stupidity were even worse than during the trench warfare of the Great War. The ongoing battles on *die Ostfront*, he knew, constituted the largest confrontation between two armies in military history. But more importantly, war in the East was characterized by unprecedented ferocity, wholesale destruction, mass deportations, and immense loss of life due to the combined effects of combat, starvation, exposure, disease, and massacres. Even if he hadn't witnessed the mind-numbing carnage with his own eyes until recently, von Gröning had heard the horrific tales for two years now. And now, regrettably, he was here: in the place of the recently launched extermination camps as well as Himmler's roaming *Einsatzgruppen* death squads, the ghettos, and the pogroms. The East was central to the Hitler's Final Solution for the Jews—and Von Gröning hated himself for being forced to rejoin his old unit, *Heeresgruppe Mitte*, and thereby be a party to the madness. He should be in Occupied France not in this hellhole surrounded by war criminals. Over the past two weeks, he had been interrogating captured Russian soldiers and partisans in the advance outposts outside Smolensk, and he had witnessed more than his fair share of murder and brutality.

He withdrew a silver flask and took a stiff drink, letting the fiery liquor sit in his mouth before letting it slide down his throat. It was *kirschwasser*, a colorless fruit brandy with a subtle cherry flavor and hint of almond. He felt better instantly, but even though he numbed himself with alcohol, it couldn't deaden the pain of having been banished to the Eastern Front in disgrace and having to wordlessly bear witness to endless carnage and cruelty. He knew he shouldn't have pushed Waag as far as he had. He shouldn't have quarreled with the head of the Paris Branch on policy issues nor should he have insisted that Agent Fritz be picked up from Britain by U-boat. Waag had used his fondness for drink as an excuse to strip him of his post in Nantes and order him to rejoin his old unit in Russia.

He took another drink, briefly fingered the Iron Cross at his throat, and peered again at the German skirmish line advancing towards the forest.

It was then a pack of Soviet T-34 tanks plowed through the trees and opened fire.

"Take cover! Take cover!" he shouted down the line.

He felt a giant swoosh as a pair of projectiles zoomed past his ears. Then the earth shook, an eruption of loamy sand spewed up from the ground in two places, and German soldiers screamed in terror as they were pulverized by the blasts and mowed down by machine-gun fire. When von Gröning next looked up, he saw an apparition that was as ghostly as it was grisly. A Wehrmacht-helmeted head had been blown completely off with nothing remaining but an upper torso and pair of legs leaning against a string of concertina wire.

He shook his head in dismay: the poor bastard had taken a direct hit. It reminded him of the Headless Horseman from *The Legend of Sleepy Hollow*. His former British wife had insisted he read the book when they were vacationing in Davos shortly after their wedding.

Now Soviet BA-20 light armored vehicles came bursting through the trees on his right flank and opened up with machine-gun fire. Between the tanks and armored cars, he and his men were quickly pinned down along a set of railroad tracks and the thick forest. Despite the protection afforded by the cinder brow of the rail embankment, several more soldiers from his unit were killed by the lethal blasts. He and the other men from his advanced element hunkered down and returned fire. But they were no match for tanks and armored vehicles.

"Fall back!" he cried.

"No, there is no falling back!" a stentorian voice countered. Looking to his right, von Gröning saw that the voice belonged to a Wehrmacht major. He didn't recognize the officer, but he had only been back in his old unit for a short time and was still learning the names of the men. At least the bastard didn't outrank him.

"They have tanks, you fool! We're no match for them!" he snapped. Then to the rest of the outfit. "Fall back! Fall back!"

"No, you swine! We must remain here and fight!" shouted the recalcitrant major.

The man withdrew his pistol. But to their mutual surprise, a pair of German Tiger tanks and several armored vehicles came racing up from the rear, like cavalry arriving in the nick of time. The soldiers cheered. The mere cough of a German

Mark VI Tiger engine was enough to send Russian tank crew members racing for cover, and the Tigers quickly took aim on the pack of Russian tanks. With its 76.2 mm high-velocity tank gun, the Soviet T-34 possessed an unprecedented combination of firepower, mobility, protection, and ruggedness—but tank-for-tank it was no match for the Tiger, which was a beast from the Book of Revelation. With an 88-mm cannon and 100-mm thick frontal armor, the 60-ton Mark VI Tiger was superior to every other tank in the war possessed by either the Allies or Germans. Neither the American Sherman, with its 75-mm gun, or the vaunted Russian T-34 was a match for Hitler's weapon of choice for blitzkrieg.

Once the Tigers moved their turrets into position, they unloaded with their dreaded 88-mm guns. Within seconds, they had destroyed three of the T-34s and six of the Russians' light armored vehicles. That was enough for the enemy, and they quickly withdrew from the field, content with having inflicted dozens of casualties in the surprise attack.

Again, the soldiers cheered. This time, they waved their hats and helmets and tossed them in the air. But the stubborn major wasn't celebrating along with them. He was instantly in von Gröning's face, his mouth spewing saliva.

"I am bringing you up on charges, you coward!" he shrieked.

"It is over!" countered the anti-Nazi spymaster. "What you and I think doesn't matter! The tanks have decided the battle!"

"I'm still preferring charges against you, Rittmeister!" He had a little black book out in a flash and was writing in it. "What is your full name and Soldbuch number?"

"Get out of my fucking face!"

As if on cue, an open-topped *Kübelwagen* bearing a driver and a junior intelligence officer that he recognized named Kessel came racing up from the rear and ground to a halt. The officer jumped out of the car, strode quickly towards him, clicked his heels together, and gave the standard Wehrmacht—as opposed to the official Hitler—salute.

"Rittmeister, I am to take you back to headquarters immediately," he said. "There is an important telegram waiting for you."

The insolent major stepped forward. "You can take me back, too. I am bringing this officer up on charges."

"No, my orders are to bring Rittmeister von Gröning back to headquarters and no one else."

Von Gröning smiled. "You heard him, Major. Out of our way."

"This is not the end of this!"

"Oh, I think it is." He quickly followed young Lieutenant Kessel to the *Kübelwagen* and they drove off. When they had made it halfway back to headquarters, they were stopped at a checkpoint and von Gröning was given additional orders, this time directly from his commanding officer, who had spotted him at the gate and quickly stepped from his staff car to issue verbal instructions.

"I need you to take care of something for me, Stephan," said the colonel. "It's rather delicate and that's why I need you. I have to meet with General Gersdorff."

Von Gröning knew Gersdorff. Like him, he had come up through the ranks of the cavalry. He was the Army Group Center intelligence liaison with the Abwehr, and was reportedly an anti-Hitlerite well informed about the war crimes against Soviet POWs and the mass murder of Jews by *Einsatzgruppe B*.

"I know the *generalmajor*," said von Gröning. "What has happened?"

"Apparently, there are mass graves in the forest to the south at Katyn."

"Mass graves?"

"They contain the remains of thousands of Polish officers shot by the Russian NKVD back in 1940. We are going now to investigate and that's why I need you to take care of an assignment for me. There is the fear that the Russians will try to blame the atrocity on us."

"I can see why that would be of concern."

"Here are the orders given to me. It involves a Russian Orthodox church. It is in the town of Morosovo, only a few kilometers from here. You are to reopen the church for the townspeople. The Russians closed it down and shot the priest and now you are going to reopen it. The new priest has requested a senior officer be present, so make a good show of yourself. Then you can return to headquarters and pick up your new orders."

He handed him the paperwork.

Von Gröning was confused. "I'm to reopen a church?"

"Yes. As I said, it was closed down by the Russian Army and they killed the priest. But now that we have taken the territory back, we are opening it for the people. They want to attend services again. Once you've reopened it, you can obtain your new orders."

"Do you know what my new orders are?"

"No. All I know is they are top secret and a very high priority, and you are to open them in person. But before you do that, can I count on you to take care of this church matter?"

"Yes, sir. I'll take care of it."

"Good. Stay clear of the SS. They have been killing partisans in large numbers to the south of Morosovo as we straighten our lines. Don't go near them."

"I've been trying to avoid them since the war began. But it is not so easy."

"All I can say then is good luck."

"And good luck to you too, Colonel."

They saluted and parted ways. Fifteen minutes later, Von Gröning reached the small hamlet of Morosovo and located the boarded-up orthodox church. The new priest, dressed in a black cassock with a purple sash, and a crowd of peasants had gathered outside the church and in the streets in anticipation of the reopening of the church. Von Gröning introduced himself and spoke briefly with the priest in his broken Russian, and then under his supervision, Lieutenant Kessel and his driver pried loose the boards sealing off the front entrance and the church doors were thrown open.

The peasants, numbering close to seventy people, flooded inside the church and fell to their knees to pray. Von Gröning stepped inside and took a seat in the rear pew as the church filled up with people. As they paid tribute to God, tears flowed down their faces and many recited prayers and gave thanks to their neighbors. Von Gröning was utterly moved. He was not a religious man by any means, but he could not help but feel deep emotions as he gazed upon the profound piety on the faces of the people. In the midst of a pitiless war, there was hope for the human spirit. He looked at the crinkly faced women and the beaten-down men and the dirty children and he saw the greatness that was instilled in all people: the capacity for love and kindness.

He looked around the church and felt an inspiration in a God that he didn't pray to or understand. The vast interior seemed to dwarf the humanity that found its way inside. The lofty ceiling was vaulted in sturdy wood, the cross-ribs covered in shimmering gold paint. The nave was separated from the sanctuary by a wall of icons with double doors in the center. The icons were Byzantine in style and consisted mostly of small paintings on wood and copper figurines. The stained-glass windows along the walls and behind the altar shone like precious gems, throwing pools of brilliance into the church. He took in the sheer vastness and graceful artistry of the sanctuary; the pained, otherworldly expression of the savior nailed to the holy cross in humble surrender; the multicolored brilliance of the stained-glass windows. Gradually, as he watched the simple peasants kneeling in prayer and showing goodwill towards their neighbors, the holiness of the place took hold inside him. He felt at inner peace with himself, as though he was somehow closer to understanding the mystical power of the universe.

The priest sat down next to him. "Thank you, my son," he said in Russian. "Thank you for your kindness."

There were tears in the old man's eyes.

"I am glad to do it, Father," replied von Gröning in the priest's native tongue. "But now I must be on my way."

"You are a good man," said the priest. "A good man in an ugly war."

"When it's all over, Father, I only hope I will have God's forgiveness. But having fought on behalf of Hitler's Reich, I do not consider that likely," he said, and he left the church, drove back to headquarters, and picked up his telegram.

His fingers were shaking as he opened it. He needed a drink badly.

With great anticipation, he read the message:

DOKTOR. PROCEED OSLO VIA BERLIN.
RNDZ FRITZ GRAUMANN AT AIRPORT. HU HA HU HA.

Von Gröning—alias Dr. Stephan Graumann—looked out the HQ window towards the heavens and smiled. He was headed to Norway. But more importantly, he and Eddie Chapman were about to be reunited and he was back in the spy game.

CHAPTER 27

6A TULLINS GATE, OSLO

APRIL 5, 1943

AS A SENIOR CRIMINAL INVESTIGATOR, Fehmer had made it a point to blend in seamlessly with the indigenous population—the better to do his job catching Norwegian spies and saboteurs. After three years in Oslo, he now spoke Norwegian as well as any Norseman. He frequently wore handsome Norwegian suits, wool sweaters, and cross-country ski knickers. He had befriended many male homegrown NS members who passed on useful counterintelligence information to him. And he routinely took Norwegian women to bed. In fact, he had slept with so many members of the opposite sex that he had acquired a reputation as a Lothario not only among his German compatriots but the very Osloans who had grown to hate him and wanted to kill him. After all, it was one thing to hunt down their Resistance fighters—but it was quite another to deflower their women with unmitigated relish.

The truth was that he liked having sex with Norwegian women—and they liked having sex with him. But there was only one fair maiden for whom he felt true love, and that was Annemarie Breien, a woman who was still, despite his strong feelings for her, nothing more than a reluctant ally. He knew perfectly well she was using him to free her own people from prison, but he still held out the hope that one day they would be something more. She was not a woman that he wanted for pleasure— she meant far more to him than that. Instead, she was the girl of his dreams. She was the girl that, if Germany and Norway had not been at war, he would gladly marry and be devoted to for the rest of his life. She was brave, intelligent, and caring and he knew he would be lucky to have her as his own.

In fact, he often daydreamed of being in her arms and kissing her sweet, soft lips.

But he wasn't thinking about her now as he took in the big blue eyes, buxom chest, and silky-smooth skin of the young *fräulein* approaching his bed. He was thinking more lascivious thoughts. She wore a lacy black brassiere, G-string, garter, and black fishnet stockings reminiscent of the cabarets of Berlin when he had first been stationed there. He felt his heart rate click up a notch as she sashayed her way towards him. She was a ripe one and he was truly going to enjoy the bounties of her splendid Norwegian body.

How many women had he bedded since Fehlis had brought him to Norway as a young *obersturmführer* in late April 1940? It had to be at least thirty—and every one of them strikingly beautiful.

Siegfried Fehmer had a way with women.

The *fräulein* gave a clever smile as she climbed onto the bed and nuzzled up close to him. They kissed and he gently rubbed her moist area with his hand. Her name was Gerda and she was a work of art—in an intoxicating, desperate way. He could smell her sweet, hot breath on his face and neck and he could feel her warm

fingers in his hair. Her full Norwegian lips brushed up against the skin of his neck, driving him wild with desire.

After passionately kissing for several minutes, she lay on her stomach near the edge of the bed and arched her rear end upward, the cabaret G-string dividing her smooth, sculpted buttocks with perfect symmetry. He felt overwhelmed with lust, but he didn't want to be too greedy and rush things.

He knew how to please a woman and that drawing out the foreplay was what made the final denouement so exquisite. He could feel his heart rapping against his chest as he climbed up behind her without entering and just gently rubbed himself against her while gently stroking her back. She let out a moan and he rubbed a little harder.

"You have to put it in me," she said, breathing heavily. "God, you have to put it in me."

"I do believe you're ready for me," he said, and he grabbed her hips and slipped inside gently from behind.

"Oh my God," she gasped, and he pushed in softly but firmly all the way, filling her up with his manhood.

Now he was filled with an overwhelming feeling of lust as they began to move in a gentle rhythm. He was entranced. His latest conquest Gerda that he had met at the Ritz Hotel bar seemed to know everything there was to know about pleasure.

Soon, he and his partner spasmed and moaned while endorphins shot through their bodies and made them feel fine in a dangerous way. Finally, the event reached its climax and there were two quivering, shrieking bodies on the edge of the bed.

When the event was consummated, he turned her over and softly licked one of her hard nipples. Then they sat upright. He reached for the bottle of wine and a pair of handblown glasses next to the bed. He poured them each a glass and they sat in bed French kissing, drinking, debating whether it would snow tomorrow or not as the weather forecasters predicted.

Fehmer knew what they had just performed was not lovemaking, but mischievous indulgence. It had little to do with romance, which was the way he wanted to keep it with Gerda. He would make love to her twice more tonight, and he would no doubt see her again for she was ripe as a melon, but he would sleep with other women as well. That was just the way he operated here in Occupied Norway.

He enjoyed the breaks from police work and from his lonely thoughts of his wife Anni Wille that he had been forced to leave behind in Germany. Here in the land of the Norseman, he got to act out his role as one of Oslo's foremost Lotharios. He liked bringing perfect specimens of Aryan and Nordic beauty to his well-furnished apartment at 6a Tullinsgata and making passionate, and sometimes just downright dirty, love to them.

But what he liked most of all was reality for him was other people's most exotic fantasies.

There was just one problem: in the face of every woman he made love to, he saw the face of Annemarie Breien. And he knew there was only one way to remedy the situation: he had to find a way to make her love him.

CHAPTER 28

FORNEBU AIRPORT AND
VON GRÖNING FLAT, 8 GRØNNEGATE, OSLO

APRIL 6, 1943

LOOKING OUT THE PASSENGER WINDOW of the small Lufthansa airliner, Eddie Chapman marveled at the spectacular beauty of the Norwegian coastline. Spread before him were rocky hills with snow still clinging to their crests and glacially-scoured fjords, carrying in their still waters the reflections of endless conifer forests. For a moment, he forgot about the war. Then he saw the German U-boat pens, reservoirs, and guard outposts flanking the majestic Oslo Fjord—and he remembered why he was here. He was a British spy trying to penetrate the secrets of the German foreign intelligence service and help his country win the bloody war.

Today had been a long journey and he was relieved that the plane had not come under attack from Allied fighters. After embarking from Berlin's Tempelhof Airport early that morning, the flight had taken Chapman to Copenhagen for refueling before making the final leg across the North Sea in a direct beeline towards the Norwegian capital. Without a sufficient heater, the plane was cold; although bundled up, the double agent had shivered incessantly along with the other sixteen passengers throughout the flight. After a horseshoe-shaped descent that gave Chapman a fluttery stomach, the Lufthansa touched down at Oslo's Fornebu Airport, seized three years earlier by Göring's Luftwaffe. It was 5:23 p.m.

After deboarding, he scooped up his valise from the luggage man and took the walkway to the German customs and passport control along with the other passengers. Here he handed a pimply-faced official the papers the Abwehr agent in Berlin had given him: a Reich passport in the name of Fritz Graumann and a military pass—*Ausweis*—which identified him as an *oberleutnant* domiciled in Berlin but born to German parents living in New York. A moment later, he was waved through customs and made out a familiar face in the crowd.

It was Doktor Graumann—wearing his bulky military greatcoat and gleaming Iron Cross at his throat. He was accompanied by a rotund, ruddy-faced man in a naval uniform. Chapman was genuinely moved to see his old friend and drinking companion, whom he looked upon as a father figure. To his surprise, his fondness for the old man was undimmed by the months he had spent betraying him, and he intended to continue the deception here in Occupied Norway.

"Thank God you are back, Fritz!" cried von Gröning.

"It's great to see you again, Doktor!"

They hugged one other like reunited family members. Chapman felt a rush of emotions, a combination of excitement to be joined again with a trusted colleague but at the same time a deep-seated fear of being exposed as a traitor. He had to remind himself that even though he was reunited with a man he respected, the German was still his enemy and, ultimately, a means to an end.

They pulled away for a moment and looked one another in the eye. They had been apart now for five months, since December of the previous year, and in that time, it appeared as if Graumann had aged several years. At the age of forty-four, the German spymaster had begun to look like an old man. His hair was streaked with gray not only at the temples, but all over his head, and it wasn't a handsome, dignified, silvery gray but the drab color of a wharf rat. His skin was sallow and drooping, and his eyes were puffy and bloodshot from drink and lack of sleep. Most noticeably, he had become pulpy and bloated from lack of exercise. Of course, he had never been the blond, strapping, blue-eyed model of Aryan perfection, but even so he had slipped dramatically these past few months as the Big Red Army pushed westward and American and British tanks rolled towards Tunis, poised to take North Africa. No doubt his hands still shook until stilled by the first drink of the morning. And yet…and yet, there was still something noble about the man. The descendant of Bremen courtiers was somehow larger-than-life standing there in his military greatcoat with his Iron Cross dangling from his throat. Despite how badly he had aged, he still gave off an aura of chivalry, intellectual rigor, and dissipated hauteur that was utterly unique. Chapman found that he was still enthralled by his great mentor.

"This is *Kapitän* Johnny Holst," said von Gröning in his upper crust, German-accented English, introducing the chubby, balding figure in the naval uniform standing next to him.

"It appears our man *over there* has returned. Welcome to the Land of the Midnight Sun," said the affable Holst in execrable English.

"Thank you. After what I've been through, I'm looking forward to a little rest and relaxation."

"And you shall have it, Agent Fritzchen, my good friend. Don't you worry about that," said von Gröning. "How was your flight?"

"Not bad. The plane stopped over to refuel in Copenhagen."

"And your food? Tell me you were taken care of."

"I was indeed. Now I know why you Germans refer to Denmark as the Promised Land. During the layover, I feasted on bacon, eggs, and cheese and followed this up with several pastries with cream. I must say it was most delightful."

"Wonderful. Johnny, be a good boy and take his valise, will you?"

"Yes, of course." He took the small suitcase from Chapman.

"Thanks, mate," said Eddie with a smile. He could already tell that he and Johnny would get along just fine. The jovial seaman looked like a man every bit as fond of drink and a carousing nightlife as the man he and Chapman worked for.

"Follow me," said von Gröning. He led them to a silver Opel Admiral Cabriolet and they climbed inside. Tired from his journey, Eddie stretched out like a cat in the plush back seat with his controller. With Johnny Holst behind the wheel, they began driving from the airport along Drammensveien towards the heart of the city, following the verdant coastline.

"You've most definitely earned a well-deserved holiday," said von Gröning with a pleasant smile. "But before we can do that, I'm afraid you will have to be interrogated one last time. Once you have done that, I will prepare a full, definitive report for Berlin and then you can enjoy yourself. The report is just a formality."

Chapman knew that wasn't true as he stared out the car window at the Bygdøy peninsula on the western side of Oslo. But he gave an understanding nod as if he had expected no less. As far as he could tell, the Germans genuinely believed he had blown up the Mosquito factory outside London and placed a pair of coal bombs aboard the *City of Lancaster*; and there was no doubt that von Gröning was enthusiastic about his success. But a final verdict still needed to be handed down at the very highest levels. Knowing this, Chapman presented a mask of indifference, but inside he couldn't help but dread having to endure yet more questioning. After two and a half weeks of friendly but persistent grilling in Paris and Berlin by a dozen different Abwehr agents—some that he knew from his training period at the Nantes Stelle, others that were new to him—he was worn out. The last thing he wanted was to be interrogated again, knowing that all it took was one little mistake, one little inconsistency, to expose that he was a charlatan.

"I apologize for everything you had to go through to get here. It's the fault of that bastard Colonel Waag. He wanted you to be his personal operative, and when I told him you would never accept that, he shipped me off to the Eastern Front."

"Yes, I didn't like him at all."

"Well, you don't have to worry about him anymore. He is out of the picture and now you shall receive the one hundred thousand reichsmarks I promised you."

"Actually, it was one hundred fifty thousand reichsmarks."

"Ah, yes, I almost forgot. One hundred and fifty it was."

"Walter was there to witness it, remember? By the way, where are he and the other members of the Nantes team?"

"Walter is in Berlin. But he will be coming to Norway shortly to resume his duties as your personal escort around the city. Along with Johnny here of course, who will be more than happy to take you sailing and show you the nightlife."

Inwardly, Chapman groaned. Walter Praetorius, the young Nazi with the passion for English country dancing whom he knew as Walter Thomas, was such a humorless, by-the-book martinet that he sucked all the fun out of life. Chapman secretly prayed that he would be watched by Johnny Holst instead of Thomas, but it was more likely that he would be under the day-to-day control of both men.

Von Gröning's expression turned to one of gratitude. "I have to thank you for saving my life, Fritzchen. If you hadn't insisted on being reunited with me, I would still be freezing my ass off on the Russian Front."

"Was it bad?"

"Words cannot describe the things I saw."

"Can you tell me about it?"

"No, I can never talk about what I witnessed in that hell on earth. Except for the day when I saw peasants praying in a church. That was a wonderful day."

"Don't tell me, you're now a religious man?"

"No, I'm not that hypocritical. But when I saw the look on those people's faces when their church was reopened after being shut down by the godless communists, I know there is a benevolent God up there somewhere. I just wish he would end this bloodbath."

"Don't we all," said Chapman. "But until then I must spy for you."

The old gentleman smiled. "You are our man, Fritzchen. That's why I'm hosting a nice reception party for you at my flat this evening."

"Really? A party *pour moi?*"

"Oh, yes. Everyone is going to be there. Molli Stirl, Peter Hiller, and Max. You're going to love Max. He's a garrulous Pole with long matted hair, flashy jewelry, and always a good joke on his lips."

"Molli is quite lovely," said Johnny Holst in his broken English from the front seat. "Peter and I fight over her charms."

"They most certainly do," agreed von Gröning good-naturedly.

"Well, you know me, Herr Doktor. I always enjoy the company of a pretty woman."

"Yes, Fritzchen. You are quite the Casanova."

Sharing a bawdy laugh, they soon left the coastline and drove up Parkveien. The historic street had been built with the name Big Parkvei as part of the residential neighborhood behind the Royal Palace in the 1840s. From Parkveien, they headed southeast parallel to the expansive royal gardens until they reached Karl Johans gate and skirted the south entrance to the Palace. Military-uniformed Hirdsmen were posted as guards along the perimeter. Five minutes later, they reached von Gröning's comfortable flat at 8 Grønnegate.

Ten minutes after that, the old man opened a bottle of Norwegian aquavit to celebrate his prized agent's safe passage to the Land of the Midnight Sun; the stunning Molli Stirl arrived followed quickly by the other two guests; and the party began.

But all Eddie Chapman could think about was that tomorrow he would be interrogated by the old man, a true professional who knew him intimately. With that daunting prospect hanging over his head, he decided to drink himself into a stupor.

CHAPTER 29

DESPITE HIS AND CHAPMAN'S MASSIVE HANGOVERS, von Gröning started the interrogation promptly at nine o'clock the next morning. After going over some preliminaries, he asked his protégé to give a full recounting of his adventures in England and aboard the *City of Lancaster*, reminding him to be as detailed as possible and to leave nothing out. The Abwehr's approach was to make an agent tell his story over and over to uncover inconsistences that could lead to the kinds of probing questions an operative would never be able to answer if he was lying. The attractive Molli Stirl, the head secretary of the Oslo Abwehr station, was on hand to record and transcribe every word of the proceedings.

When the first run-through was over, von Gröning lit up a Dunhill cigarette and exhaled a puff of blueish smoke without saying a word, pretending to still be digesting the story he had just heard. He wanted to keep his subject slightly off balance by being friendly and mildly threatening at the same time. That was the way to get at the truth.

He didn't want the truth for truth's sake. Now that he had been liberated from the cold winds and bloody killing fields of Mother Russia, he wanted to know the truth for a different reason: to get the story right for Berlin. For his own fate was bound up with the success of Chapman. Within the Abwehr's decentralized structure, he controlled his own network of spies—with only Canaris at the top of the food chain to pass judgment on him. But that was only as long as his agents were productive and successful. Otherwise, he would again be out of a job or a candidate for the Front. Therefore, at a minimum he needed Chapman to be at least perceived as truthful and successful by his higher-ups, who had yet to render a final verdict regarding Agent Fritz.

He knew it was the central flaw of the German foreign intelligence service. But there was still no way around it. In the Abwehr, each control officer promoted his own spy to the point where he might suppress his own suspicions and insist on the loyalty and efficiency of an operative despite massive evidence to the contrary. Even when an operative was useless, or worse, acting as a double agent, the spymaster was often unwilling to admit the failure, on the assumption, logical but disastrous, that it was better for selfish reasons to have corrupt or disloyal agents than to have no agents at all. Von Gröning knew this was how the system worked and there was no way around it.

Thus, his own self-interest, indeed his own personal safety, was bound up with the man with the two gold teeth, salt-and-pepper suit, and wicked hangover sitting across from him. He hated being in such a weak and co-dependent position, but that was how he found himself. He didn't want to be banished again to Russia, which meant he had to get the story right so that Berlin would sign off on it, formally decreeing the man seated across from him a hero of the Reich and paying him the money they owed him for his services abroad.

ψψψ

"That's an incredible story, Fritz. But is that really how you pulled off the de Havilland job? It just seems so unbelievable. I think you'd better go through it again because I can hardly believe that's the way it happened."

Chapman winced inwardly but tried not to let it show on his face. After having spent months learning the details of his cover, he thought the description he had given was believable. But as he stared into the heavily-lidded eyes of his controller, he felt some doubt.

Does the old man believe me or not? he wondered. *Could he already be on to me?*

"All right, I'll go through it again," he said agreeably, though all he wanted was for the questioning to be done and over. "As I told you before, after arriving in London I left messages at various clubs for Jimmy Hunt from the old Jelly Gang. Jimmy was the one person I had to have to pull off the job."

"How did you find him again?"

"Eventually he got my message and set up a meeting. We met in a pub."

"How did he greet you?"

"He said, 'Hello, bastard-face.' That was his standard greeting."

"Where was he living at the time?"

"Sackville Street near Piccadilly. But he reckoned that this bolthole wasn't safe since the police had been chasing him. He was about to rent a house in Hendon and he said it was all right for me to live with him there."

"Where was the rental property located?"

"Beaufort Road."

"When did you two begin planning the sabotage operation?"

"We spent two or three evenings plotting it out once we had settled into his new place. He was pretending to run an electrical business based in a North Kensington mews house."

"So, you're telling me he just accepted you with open arms after three years of being away?"

"More or less. Jimmy was keen to join in with sabotage activities. Like me, he's always enjoyed living on the edge."

"When did you go to the de Havilland plant?"

"Early January. We went up there together to reconnoiter the place. That's when we discovered that the factory's main power house was too brightly lit for any act of sabotage. People were in and out of there the whole time."

"What did you do?"

"We came up with the backup plan to destroy the transformers."

"The transformers?"

"As I told you before, by taking them out we could bring production to a halt by destroying the electrical output of the whole factory."

"How were you able to get petrol when there is serious rationing?"

"With his legitimate work as an electrical contractor, Jimmy had access to petrol. But he was even better at forging petrol coupons."

"Where and when did you get the gelignite to blow the factory?"

Chapman cautioned himself to slow down a bit, as Tar Robertson had warned him to do when under interrogation. The key, the senior British officer had said, was to speak slowly to draw things out and to not be too specific with dates, times, or technical details. "A few nights after we visited Hatfield, we went to a quarry in Sevenoaks. There we found several hundred sticks of gelignite and a couple hundred detonators."

"And what happened next?"

"We made up a wristwatch detonator for two separate bombs, which were wired into attaché cases."

"And how did you pull off the sabotage?"

"On the day we did it, we got there around 6 p.m. By then, it was dark and a new shift had just come on duty. We climbed over the perimeter fence in overalls posing as employees. A few minutes later, we parted company and I made my way to one of the transformer houses, jumped the wall, and entered without being noticed. With a fuse already set, I left a case under one transformer while Jimmy did the same at the other. We then went back to the car, drove two miles from the factory, stopped the engine, and waited for the bombs to go off."

"You heard two explosions?"

"Aye."

Puffing on his cigarette, von Gröning pushed a pad of paper and a pencil towards him. "Draw the bombing locations at the plant for me. I want to see the layout."

Chapman hesitated. "What?"

"Draw where you and Jimmy placed your bombs on a map and explain to me how the explosions took place. I don't understand why you deviated from the plan and blew up different power sources from those we had agreed upon."

Keeping his face and body language nonchalant, Chapman quickly sketched out the actual transformer locations that he and Ronnie Reed had observed during their inspection of the facility. "There, that's how I remember the layout," he said.

"You said that you and Jimmy heard the explosions and saw the sky light up twice, but how do you know for sure the damage the bombs caused when you were some distance away by that time?"

"Three days after the bombing, I gatecrashed a staff dance for a contractor to de Havilland's at a local pub in Hendon. At the party, I discovered from talking to a woman that the main Hatfield factory was in an awful state. She said the local authorities and company were trying to hush it up."

Von Gröning stamped out his cigarette in the ashtray. "With regard to your explosives' case, where were the batteries again?"

"The batteries were taped with adhesive inside the case with drawing pins on the right-hand side of the case."

"Right hand side? But earlier you said you had taped the batteries on the left. Which is it?"

Aware that he made a mistake, he felt suddenly hot. "I meant the left-hand side."

"It was the left-hand side then? You're sure?"

"Yes."

"Very good." He looked at Molli. "Please make a note of that. The batteries were taped on the *left-hand* side of the case."

"Yes, Rittmeister."

Von Gröning continued on with the questioning for three more hours before breaking for lunch. They were back at it for four more hours in the afternoon. From his experiences in Nantes, Chapman knew that Graumann was a formidable inquisitor, but even he was impressed at how cleverly the German probed for the truth and exposed it, as if peeling away the layers of an onion. Several times he felt as though he had been caught in a lie, but then he would somehow manage to extricate himself. Behind the heavy lids, the burly spymaster appeared to be half asleep at times, but then he would slip in a question under Chapman's guard that would leave him scrambling. The interrogation process was meticulously thorough and continued for two weeks with every word typed up by Molli Stirl.

But Chapman noticed something different about the way he was being questioned compared to his interrogations in Portugal, Spain, France, and Berlin. The old man wanted him to get the story right. When Chapman contradicted himself or made an error of chronology or fact, the spymaster would calmly lead him back and iron out the inconsistency before resuming the interview. It was obvious the old man was on his side. He could tell that he wanted him to succeed not just for his agent's sake, but also for his own. In Nantes, Chapman had been dependent on the German's goodwill, eager for his praise, and flattered by his attention. The roles had not quite been reversed, but they were more equal.

Chapman needed the old man to believe him, and the spymaster needed Chapman to succeed. Together, they had forged a tacit complicity. At times during the interrogation, Chapman felt as though Graumann was grateful towards him, without whom he might still be wading through the blood and gore of the Eastern Front. But it went deeper than that: the old man was now reliant on him, and that, Zigzag reflected, was his best security. During his time away in Britain, Graumann's stock had plummeted, but now that he had returned the old man's status in the Abwehr was restored. Chapman was more than just another spy: he was a career investment, the golden goose who had made and continued to make Graumann in the German Secret Service.

And now they both knew it.

ψψψ

Von Gröning installed Chapman at the Forbunds Hotel. The spacious, comfortable, wood-built lodging in the Oslo city center had been commandeered by the Abwehr and Luftwaffe at the beginning of the war. To ensure his prized agent was kept happy, he handed over five hundred kroner as spending money and told him he could have more when he required it. The balance of the payment, he told his protégé, would be paid when the report had been written up, taken to Berlin, and approved by his superiors.

CHAPTER 30

"THREE OF OUR OPERATIVES were caught yesterday by Fehmer. He's imprisoned them at Møllergata 19 and no doubt they will soon talk. No one can withstand torture indefinitely."

Dagmar looked around the café then back at First Lieutenant Peder Olav Gleditsch, her Milorg control officer she knew only by the code name Ishmael. Like others in the Home Front, Ishmael considered Café Seterstua one of the safest places to rendezvous, for the arrogant Germans would never believe that the Resistance would dare hold meetings directly under their noses. And yet, Dagmar had the oddest feeling they were being watched. She subtly scanned to the left and right at the nearby tables, towards the front door, and in the direction of the kitchen, but there was no one watching them. The four German officers at the table against the wall appeared to be ensconced in their own conversation; the man two tables away was busy reading a copy of *Fritt Folk*, the official Norwegian newspaper of the NS; and the patrons at the four other occupied tables were pitching hungrily into their dinners while chattering contentedly amongst themselves.

Seeing nothing out of the ordinary, she returned her gaze to her control officer and cutout here in Oslo. He looked disconsolate delivering the news of yet another setback in the Resistance movement. But even worse, his eyes were red, bleary, and ringed with black circles from lack of sleep; he was as skinny as a steel rail; and he had a nasty cut on his chin, from whom or what she did not know. Did he get into a scrap with a German and narrowly escape? Whatever had happened to him, he looked terrible. He seemed to have aged a year since the last time she had seen him a mere fortnight ago.

The stress of being hunted under the German Occupation was not only taking a toll on him, but everyone else in the Home Front, including herself. The Gestapo was cracking down on the Resistance with increasing ruthlessness and brutality, under the orders of Terboven, Fehlis, and their bloodhound Fehmer, who was leaving no stone unturned in search of those who dared to resist the occupiers. The whole city was on edge and it showed on the faces of the people on the streets.

She spoke in a quiet voice so they could not be overheard. "Does this mean that you and I have to go into hiding?" she asked.

"No, we are not connected with the prisoners in any way. But there are many who have been forced to go underground and several more who have been sent to Sweden. The damned Germans are uncovering our network faster than we can replace our operatives."

"God, I hate them," she said, glancing at the four Sipo officers at the table against the wall without appearing to do so. "What can we do?"

"That's why I wanted to meet with you. I want to take it to the Germans and hit them where they least expect it."

Dagmar felt a little jolt of excitement. "Are you talking about sabotage?"

"No, I am talking about an undercover operation."

"An undercover operation? What do you mean?"

"I am talking about laying a honey trap."

She felt her body tense with outrage. "Not a chance! I am not going to spread my legs for these bastards to get information!"

He looked at her sharply. She covered her mouth and looked around the room, knowing she shouldn't have raised her voice like that. Luckily, only the owner of the café and his daughter who was waiting on them seemed to have noticed, and they were with the Resistance, or at least that's what Dagmar suspected. They, too, shot her a look of disapproval before returning to their tasks behind the counter. Fortunately, her minor outburst had occurred at precisely the same moment as the German officers at a nearby table, who were already irritatingly loud and obnoxious, had roared with laughter at a joke.

"That was out of line," Ishmael scolded her in a firm but quiet voice.

"I know it was. I'm sorry," she said.

"Just stay under control and listen to me. We are losing the spy game and need new approaches to obtain information."

"I'm not going to sleep with fucking Germans."

"I'm not asking you to do that. Just hear me out."

He paused a moment as a plate of *klippfisk* and *smorbor* containing little open-faced sandwiches of salted cod and salmon on flatbread and slivers of pickled herring flew past on a tray carried by a waiter, who had just stepped out of the kitchen. Dagmar felt her stomach growl at the prospect of food; she hadn't had anything to eat all day but a little *gamalost* and *knekkebrød*—a hard, crumbly, brownish-yellow aged cheese on crisp bread that had been standard Norwegian fare since the Vikings. The mouthwatering sandwiches were promptly delivered to the Germans.

"All we need from you is to hang around the nightclubs, flirt a little bit, and be a fly on the wall. No one gives out classified intelligence information like drunk German officers. Your courier work has been superb, but we need to ramp up our efforts. You are a beautiful young woman, Dagmar. Every German officer in this city that comes into contact with you is going to…"

She looked at him sternly. "Going to what?"

"Want to be with you."

"You mean want to sleep with me."

"I didn't say that."

"You didn't have to. It's what you meant to say."

"We need this, Dagmar. If you handle this right, you could be more important to the war effort than ten infantry divisions."

"It sounds like Mata Hari."

"Yes, but she was working for the Germans. You're on the good side."

"You're asking me to go into the lion's den. ·If they discover what I'm up to, they'll kill me."

"Look around you. You are already in the lion's den. Every day that we continue the underground fight, we put our lives on the line. We are at war."

"Yes, and meanwhile most of the men of this country do nothing but tromp back and forth in the woods pretending to be real soldiers. When will Milorg actually put up a fight and kill Germans?"

"You know when."

"When the Allies gain a foothold on the continent, take the major ports, and Norway is cut off from the enemy."

"Precisely. You sound like a general, Dagmar. In the meantime, all we can do is train for the day when liberation is near and we can kill Germans at a ratio of one to one instead of suffering reprisals of ten or a hundred to one."

"I still think we should be fighting."

"Well, not everyone is as stubborn and defiant as you. Or as brave. That is why I am asking you to venture into the lion's den and see what kinds of secrets you can discover. You speak German reasonably well and you are an absolute knockout. By the way, how are your modeling classes going?"

"I quit."

"Why did you quit?"

"Why do you think? The war," she said with a frustrated sigh.

"That's too bad. I'm sure that one day you will make a very fine model. When this bloody mess is over with."

"By then, I'll probably be too old and wrinkled."

He smiled. "You're only twenty. We'll have won this war by your twenty-second birthday, mark my words."

"Now you're just trying to flatter me."

"We need this, Dagmar. We need to get closer to the damned Germans."

They paused a moment as the waitress came by and replenished their cups with steaming, dark-black *kokekaffe*. "No more outbursts," warned the teenage girl. "Unless you want the Gestapo to storm in here and place you under arrest."

"I'm sorry," said Dagmar guiltily. "It won't happen again."

"It had better not, or you will not be allowed back. That's *Hauptsharführer* Etling himself over there."

As the waitress walked off, Dagmar glanced at the four officers and recognized Etling among them. She had seen him before on several occasions. The master sergeant was the head of the Gestapo motor transport division that was used to patrol the city and make arrests. Fehlis, Fehmer, and Etling were all dangerous SS men that she knew she should stay clear of if she wanted to live through the war.

"All right, since you want me to venture into the lion's den, what establishments of depravity do you want me to troll for your Nazi brutes?"

"I think you know the answer to your own question."

"The Ritz."

"I was also thinking of the Löwenbräu."

Dagmar winced with disgust and more than a little apprehension. The Ritz Hotel and Löwenbräu Restaurant were the drinking playgrounds and eateries reserved exclusively for the German occupiers and their Norwegian collaborators. Located in the exclusive Skillebekk neighborhood, the Ritz was a classical-fronted, cream-colored building with wrought-iron balconies and a polished mahogany bar that had once been the exclusive province of Oslo's blue bloods. Now, like its more egalitarian counterpart the Löwenbräu, it served as the relaxing retreat for a different kind of elite. Every night at both establishments, officers of the SS, Gestapo, and Abwehr mingled with legionnaires from the pro-Nazi Viking Regiment, members of the Quisling government, and Nordic women willing to share a bed with them for the right price or just to have a good time.

"You're asking me to pretend to be a German tart?" she said in disbelief.

"Solely to gather information."

"But you want me to act like a whore."

He held up his hands. "Stop it, you're raising your voice again."

She felt her face reddening. What kind of men were these Home Front officers that they assumed she would be willing to be treated as a sex object? Damn them!

"I'll raise my voice whenever I want when you ask me to pretend to be a *tyskertøs*. But I am not, nor will I ever be, a German's whore."

In her anger, the words had come out louder than she had intended. Ishmael was looking around the room. Dagmar glanced at the other tables, but luckily no one seemed to be eavesdropping on their conversation or interested in them. The husky-voiced German officers were so loud that they dampened out the other voices. And yet, once again she couldn't help a feeling of being watched. To assess the danger, she made a second discrete pass, scanning every table for signs of prying eyes, but the only person who seemed to be looking at them was the man with the newspaper.

Damnit, had he been watching and listening this whole time. My God, was he Gestapo? She forced herself to maintain her poise. Being a spy was the most stressful thing she had ever been party to in her entire life.

"I am going to have to think about this," she said. "If I go through with it, I will be a branded woman. I love my country, but I don't know that I want to do that."

His expression was one of sympathy, but it was still hard and pragmatic. "I know it won't be easy, but you will be doing Norway a great service."

"And in the process, I'll be branded a *tyskertøs*, perhaps for my whole life. During times of war, people don't tend to forget these types of things."

"If anyone can overcome the odds, it is you. You are a strong woman, Dagmar Lahlum."

"Maybe I am, maybe I'm not. But you are asking me to risk not death, but my honor as a human being and my pride as a patriot. So, like I said, I'm going to have to think about this."

"Very well," he said. "You let me know when you've made up your mind."

"I will."

With the practiced calm of an experienced operative, she rose from her seat. It was then she noticed SS-*Hauptsharführer* Axel Etling studying her. Her heart skipped a beat. But she told herself to just act naturally and pretend not to notice him watching her, as she had trained herself to do. Taking a deep breath to collect herself, she went to the front door, stepped out of the café, and walked briskly down the street in the opposite direction of Gestapo headquarters before Etling or anyone else had a chance to stop and question her.

CHAPTER 31

AS HE WENT TO OPEN the front door for Eddie Chapman, von Gröning debated telling him the truth about his recent trip to Berlin. After spending two solid weeks interrogating his coveted agent, he had boarded a Lufthansa a week ago for the German capital with the final version of the Brit's story, neatly typed up by Molli Stir, in his briefcase. There, he presented his findings to a panel headed by Canaris himself. The meeting, held at Abwehr headquarters at 76/78 Tirpitzufer, did not go well. In fact, the final verdict of the meeting had come within a hair's breadth of approving the liquidation of Agent Fritz. It had been so close that von Gröning was sure he was going to be banished again to the Eastern Front.

The former safecracker's fate—which the German spymaster knew now went hand in hand with his own—had been vigorously debated for five straight days. One faction of the German Secret Service, headed by von Gröning, wanted Fritz rewarded while another pressed for his extermination. Von Gröning argued that his prized agent had performed the only successful sabotage ever carried out by the sabotage branch of the Paris Abwehr. His most outspoken opponent was Lieutenant Colonel von Eschwege, the officer newly appointed to head the Paris station. Von Eschwege argued that von Gröning's coveted spy was either controlled by the British or a fraud. Far from carrying out a successful mission, the colonel claimed, when Chapman went to England he did nothing, and lied about his activities. In von Gröning's view, von Eschwege was out to make a name for himself as the new head of the station and didn't want to give any credit to his predecessors.

Luckily, after the fifth day of the back-and-forth debate, Canaris rendered a ruling on the case: the war was no longer in the Reich's favor, German intelligence needed a success story, and there was no hard evidence to prove that Chapman was double-dealing. On the contrary, there was plenty of evidence, including English newspaper reports, to back up his account. In Canaris's eyes, Chapman had shown exemplary bravery in the service of Germany and should be rewarded, congratulated, pampered—and closely watched. And so, von Gröning had returned to Oslo relieved not to have to return to Russia and beaming with pleasure.

He opened the front door for his guest. "Come in, Fritzchen, come in." Smiling effusively, he waved at the idling car bearing Chapman's two handlers that were dropping him off: Walter Praetorius and Johnny Holst. Holst gave a nod and the car drove off.

"Good to see you, Herr Doktor," said Chapman, stepping inside the apartment. "How was your trip to Berlin?"

"Splendid, splendid," answered von Gröning, deciding not to tell the agent how close he had come to being selected for termination. "Come, let's have a drink. I have good news for you."

He went to a side table and quickly poured them each a glass of aquavit. They sat down in his front parlor room. Chapman looked at him with a combination of anticipation and vague amusement.

"So, my friend Fritzchen, my superiors in Berlin have decided to award you the sum of one hundred ten thousand reichsmarks: one hundred thousand for your good work in England, and an additional ten thousand for the plot to sabotage the *City of Lancaster*. Even though the ship was not actually blown up, they have agreed to give you a bonus. Well, what do you say?"

The room went totally silent as Chapman made no response.

"Did you hear what I said? This is a great honor. The higher-ups have decided to award you one hundred ten thousand marks."

Still nothing.

Finally, Chapman spoke: "It is not enough. You yourself promised me one hundred fifty thousand marks for the work at de Havilland, and in Madrid and Paris they said I was to be given a bonus for the ship sabotage and the reports."

Von Gröning looked at him, unable to believe what he was hearing. Was his prized agent in fact pleased with the offer but only pretending to be offended and unwilling to accept the remuneration?

"One hundred ten thousand is still a lot of money."

"Not for the risks I took."

"Are you telling me you will not accept the money unless it is the full amount?"

"No, I suppose I'll accept it. But it is less than we agreed upon."

My God, if he only knew how close he came to being put before a firing squad. With this kind of bravado, he must be telling the truth. "If I didn't know you as well as I do, I would say you sound very insincere. But I know that is not the kind of man you are."

"All right, I'll take the money. But I want to be paid in notes."

"I'm afraid that will be impossible."

"Then how will I be paid?"

"I will hold your money in credit at the Oslo Abwehr headquarters. You will be able to draw on it when necessary." He was about to add, "This way you will be less tempted to abscond with the cash" but he held his tongue.

"So now you're my spymaster and my private broker, is that it?"

"Whenever you want money, I will take it from the account and hand it over. You will also receive a monthly wage of four hundred kroner."

"Four hundred kroner. All right, that sounds better."

Von Gröning reached for a pen and the two agreements on the table sitting next to a small leather case and handed them to the agent. "Please sign both copies."

Chapman did so. Von Gröning countersigned and dated the two sheets and handed him a copy for his records. Setting down his own copy, he then reached for the little leather case, rose solemnly to his feet, stood erectly to full height, and handed the case to his protégé.

"What's this, a present?"

"Go ahead and open it," said von Gröning with formal military bearing.

Slowly, Chapman opened the box. It contained an Iron Cross, First Class—the highest symbol of bravery and enduring symbol of Nazi iconography. Von Gröning reached inside, carefully removed the medal along with its red, white, and black ribbon, and handed it to him.

"It was sent to our *Dienststelle* to be awarded to the member who had shown the most outstanding zeal, bravery, and success in the past year. After consultation with the chiefs in Berlin, you are the unanimous choice!"

That wasn't true, of course, but the high praise appeared to have the appropriate effect on his protégé as Chapman stared at the medal in amazement.

"Do you know the history of the Iron Cross?" He touched his own Second Class medal at his throat.

"No, I'm afraid I don't."

"It was first awarded in 1813 to Prussian troops during the Napoleonic Wars and was later revived by the Kaiser in the First World War, which as you know was when Hitler and I both won ours. Now, in the present conflict, it serves as the greatest symbol of courage. All across Germany, children and adults alike collect the postcards of the most famous recipients and place them in books and posters."

"But I am a British citizen."

He smiled. "Ironic isn't it?"

"Yes, it most certainly is." And with that, they picked up their glasses and drank a toast.

ψψψ

As they retook their seats, Eddie Chapman thought to himself wryly: *Not bad, Oberleutnant Fritz Graumann! Now you have one hundred ten thousand reichsmarks and the Iron Cross! If you stay with this mob long enough, you might end up a Reichsmarschall!*

"Is there something that amuses you?"

Astonished and privately amused at receiving such an award when he was a British double agent actively working against Nazi Germany, he had to suppress the urge to smile. "No, Doktor, I was just thinking of how grateful I am for your return. I would not have won this award if not for you."

"It would seem then that we have both earned plaudits. No doubt I would still be freezing my ass off in Russia and getting shot at by godless Bolsheviks if not for you."

"We have both been very fortunate. So now that you are back, what are your plans for me?"

"For the time being, you don't have to do anything. Just enjoy yourself."

"That sounds good to me."

"You are free to explore the countryside. Go yachting and bathing."

"That's it? I'm on one big happy holiday here in Norway?"

"Well, not quite. You will need to brush up on your Morse. I will also have a photographer teach you photography."

"Who is the photographer?"

"A man named Rotkagel. He is the former manager of a Leica factory. He will issue you your own camera and film."

"I should like to take some pictures. Such a beautiful country."

"Yes, but be forewarned, the Norwegians can be chilly sometimes."

"Yes, I have noticed that. They call it *Is Fronten*—the Ice Front."

"You've experienced it firsthand?"

"I have indeed."

The truth was the Ice Front—Norwegian society's collective cold shoulder intended to freeze out the German occupiers by publicly ignoring and slighting them—had already chilled him on several occasions since his arrival to Oslo three weeks earlier. He regarded the Norwegians as a truly brave, patriotic people for their refusal to accept the Nazi "New Order," but their cold stares still aggravated him since he was on their side. Early in the war, the paper clip, an ingenious Norwegian invention, was worn by many as a symbol of unity against the German occupiers and it was quickly banned. Now the acts of passive resistance were performed purely to alienate those in power, both German and Norwegian. German soldiers and intelligence officers were scorned in public in subtle rather than explicit ways so as to not risk severe reprisal. Waiters in restaurants would frequently serve their countrymen first, and Norse citizens would cross the street to avoid eye contact with a German and speak only in their native tongue even though many spoke the language of the invaders. On buses and trams, Osloans would refuse to sit next to German soldiers, even when the conveyance was packed with commuters, a form of passive disobedience so galling to the occupiers that it became illegal to stand on a bus or tram if a seat was available. In a similar vein, NS members and Norwegians who lent assistance to, or socialized with, the occupying powers were branded collaborators and openly shunned by former friends, neighbors, and family. The Germans and those who collaborated with them were rarely openly reproached in public, but they were ostracized. For Chapman, the scornful stares of the Norwegians made him feel on edge.

"Don't worry about the Ice Front, Fritz. Soon you will be too busy having fun to even notice it. With regard to your new posting here in Norway, you will also be counted on to serve as an expert consultant on sabotage matters from time to time to our visiting dignitaries. You will give advice and tell of your exploits as the man who has already been *over there* for us."

"Will I have the freedom to come and go as I please?"

"Not quite. You will still need to have Johnny or Walter with you, at least for the time being."

"I should have known."

"I think you are making it out to be worse than it is. Our jobs are on the line. We would be remiss as intelligence officers if we trusted you unconditionally, don't you think?"

"Yes, that is true."

"And is it not also true that you get along fairly well with both Lieutenant Thomas and Sergeant Holst?"

"That's something I wanted to talk to you about. I'm okay with Johnny, but Walter is driving me crazy. Isn't there some way you can get rid of him?"

"I'm afraid I can't. You know I find him no less annoying than you, but Berlin has specifically ordered him to be present not only at the debriefing but during your acclimation period here in Norway."

"But every day I have to listen to him spouting his Nazi propaganda and practicing his dancing steps. In my room at the Forbunds, he dances endlessly and rages on about how much he wants to kill the Reds, as if he's deliberately trying to irritate me. I think he has a hero complex."

"I'm afraid there's nothing I can do about him. Until you win over his full trust, you two are stuck together."

"Well, at least I have Johnny. He has a sense of humor."

"Yes, you must count your blessings. Be thankful you have him—and me. As it turns out, you will be going sailing with Johnny on a regular basis this summer. It will get you ready for your next adventure."

"Are you trying to tell me something?"

"Only that your next mission could involve some seamanship. I'm afraid that's all I can tell you at present."

Even though you owe me your very life for rescuing you from Russia, he thought, though he refrained from voicing his opinion. It didn't matter. In the three weeks he had been here in Norway, Johnny Holst had proven to be a decent daytime companion and a damned good nighttime drinking partner at the Ritz and Löwenbräu.

"Johnny will be at your disposal to teach you yachting whenever you need him."

"I'm not much of a sailor."

"Yes, but you can learn."

"From Johnny?"

"Yes."

"He's a wireless instructor."

"He is more than that, I can assure you. But yes, he is a wireless instructor first and foremost, though from what I have heard he is available to go sailing or drinking at a moment's notice, postponing classes whenever he feels so inclined. Is that not something that appeals to you?"

"In fact, it is. Now I realize that Johnny is one hell of a seaman, but are you truly giving me my freedom or is this a ruse?"

"You just received the Iron Cross. What do you think?"

"I like Johnny, but why does he have the shakes?"

"It's called acute delirium tremens. It's a disease. He's a drunk, as you know, and suffers from serious alcohol withdrawal. But he's the best you're going to get so you'd better keep on good terms with him. Unless, of course, you want our mutual friend Walter Thomas to be your babysitter day and night."

"All right, I get the bloody picture."

"Learning how to sail, then, will be a top priority, at least starting out. But you will also need to practice photography and get your wireless skills back in order. Johnny will teach you."

"I would love to learn to sail. I'm sure I could become quite good at it if you give me my own boat."

"You want your own boat?"

"Very much so."

"Very well, then you shall have it."

Chapman had made the request half-jokingly. But to his surprise, instead of dismissing the idea out of hand, Graumann promptly pulled a wad of cash from his wallet and handed it to him.

"Johnny will take you tomorrow to buy you a fine little yawl that will be perfect for sailing up and down the fjords. Have fun."

Chapman smiled gratefully. "Thank you, Herr Doktor—I will become a sailor yet. But just to make sure, you're not toying with me, are you?"

"Now why would I do that? I just awarded you the Iron Cross and gave you three thousand kroner to buy yourself a fine little yawl. I want you to enjoy yourself in the land of the Norsemen."

Chapman knew that his personal gratification was certainly not Graumann's top priority. But what was important to him was that his agent remained in good standing and continued to demonstrate his loyalty by preparing for his next mission. The truth, Chapman knew, was that Graumann didn't fully trust him, and neither did the other German military and intelligence figures here in Oslo. The friendly but vigilant Johnny Holst and the insufferable Walter Thomas were under strict orders to keep an eye on him, the German officers who came and went at the Forbunds seemed mildly suspicious and incommunicative, and the Abwehr officials he had met thus far never divulged their real names. Yes, Graumann promised him complete freedom, but Chapman knew that he was essentially under house arrest. He had been here three weeks already and he had yet to step into the wireless training center or cross the threshold of Abwehr headquarters, a large block of flats at Klingenberggate. The old man had instructed him to relax and not to work, except when it came to learning to sail and brushing up on his wireless—and yet Chapman could tell that his enforced leisure wasn't so much a reward as a security precaution and clever technique to keep him at arm's length.

"At the same time," continued von Gröning, "I want you to carry a pistol at all times, report promptly to me if you have been followed, and be vigilant about never being photographed."

"What, you think there are British agents keeping an eye on me?"

"Of course, there are, Fritz. Are you naïve? And not only are they watching you, they may try to target you."

"So not only am I being watched by you and your German friends, but I've got to worry about the British?"

"And the Norwegians. Don't forget, they are everywhere too."

"That's certainly reassuring. Who may I ask then are my friends?"

"I am your friend, Fritzchen.'

"As long as I am of value to you. And then what?"

Von Gröning gave the faintest of smiles. "Just be a good boy and you have nothing to worry about. Nothing to worry about at all."

CHAPTER 32

KARL JOHANS GATE, OSLO

APRIL 29, 1943

THE SPRING SNOWSTORM that struck predawn left a patchy white veneer across the Norwegian capital. Though the thermometer had dipped into the twenties several hours earlier, the sun was already poking through the gray-rimmed clouds hovering above the Nazi-occupied Royal Palace to the west. The temperature was climbing steadily into the upper forties and the snow on the streets was turning to slush.

Holding the leash to his beloved and impeccably-trained German shepherd, Siegfried Fehmer looked dreamily at his companion Annemarie Breien. She had visited him at Victoria Terrasse an hour earlier to thank him for recently releasing the dentist Knut Reidar Bergwitz-Larsen on her behalf and to implore him to release several more prisoners from Grini and Akershus. Unbeknownst to Fehmer, Bergwitz-Larsen was not merely one of the usual suspected dissidents taken into custody and locked up by the Gestapo, he was a Milorg captain and Breien's chief contact with the Home Front. He was in communication with key executives in Milorg through Else Endresen, who in turn reported to Jens Christian Hauge, and was instrumental in helping smuggle Milorg operatives who had come under suspicion into neutral Sweden. But Fehmer did not know this.

Unaware that Bergwitz-Larsen was a key figure in the Resistance, Fehmer had, after a lengthy back-and-forth, acceded to Breien's request to release more Norwegian prisoners from incarceration. His concern was not so much that those he let go might have ties to the underground but that his immediate superior, Hellmuth Reinhard, or the overall head of the German Secret Service in Norway, Fehlis, would not approve of his actions and relieve him of duty. Which is why he didn't inform them of the releases, preferring to keep them a secret. Though he had significant latitude as the lead criminal investigator in Norway, he knew that neither Reinhard or Fehlis would not take too kindly to his releasing Home Front operatives who might pose a danger to German soldiers. But Fehmer considered it important to show acts of good faith towards the Norwegian people, to build alliances in the event of a German defeat, and to show that he was not a monster, though he still maintained harsh interrogation methods for those he was convinced were guilty. But mostly he released prisoners to please Annemarie, whom he was growing increasingly fond of and spending more time with, though they were not lovers and their relationship was still primarily a humanitarian one.

To consecrate his alliance with her, he asked if she would take a stroll with him with Wolfie, whom he needed to take on his daily walk. At first, she had resisted—she didn't want to be mistaken for a collaborator and subjected to ostracism from her countrymen—but eventually he talked her into it. Now that the spring day had turned into a sunny one, they could both use a breath of fresh air under blue skies.

When he wasn't solving crimes, coaxing beautiful Norwegian women not named Annemarie back to his bedchambers, or trying to break Resistance operatives,

Fehmer liked taking pleasant strolls with Wolfie. But mostly, he wanted to be alone with the woman he suspected he was falling deeper and deeper in love with as the occupation of Norway dragged on, a woman to whom he still had not yet revealed the full extent of his feelings. He wanted desperately to tell Annemarie how much he cared for her, but he hadn't yet summoned the nerve. Deep down, it pained him that she was betrothed to another and that they would never be able to be together like they were in his dreams. Not only were they both married, but their countries were at war and he could put her in jeopardy. A professional or humanitarian association with a German was allowable in Occupied Norway; a romantic relationship was not unless one wanted to be subjected to the full brunt of the Ice Front.

Today Annemarie was a sight to behold. Her silky blonde hair was perched along her slender shoulders and her well-sculpted face carried a hint of a smile. They walked up Roald Amundsen gate, named for the illustrious Norwegian polar explorer, and then along Stortingsgata before turning into Eidsvoll Park. The park benches had been cleared of snow and they sat down bundled up in their heavy Norwegian jackets with Wolfie at their feet. It was rare to see Fehmer in his SS uniform these days; he wore Norse attire virtually all the time now, the better to keep comfortable as well as to blend in and perform his job as a police detective.

Suddenly, he noticed that Annemarie had stiffened.

"What is it?" he asked her.

She tried to shield her face with her hand. "It's nothing."

"I can tell that's not true. What's going on?"

She continued veiling her face. "There's someone over there I know."

He looked up to see a brawny man in a heavy overcoat and fedora. He had come to a stop in the middle of the square and was frowning at them disapprovingly. Fehmer felt like telling the Norwegian to go fuck himself, but he didn't want to make a scene or upset Annemarie, whose affections he strongly desired.

"So, he's seen you on a park bench with the big bad wolf. Big deal."

"The Ice Front is a big deal to me. I don't like it."

He found the sullen, insolent loathing Osloans held for him and his fellow Germans and those that supported the occupying forces intensely annoying. "How well do you know him?"

"He works at my husband's law firm. But he recognizes you too. Most people do in this town. You know that, don't you?"

"Yes, but he is being rude."

"This is his country, not yours." She sighed worriedly as she leaned down and pet Wolfie, whose company she enjoyed too. "I knew this was a bad idea. Now he's going to tell my husband."

Fehmer had never met Kjell Langballe and wondered what he was like. He had checked into his background and compiled a dossier on him, as he had done on many lawyers in Oslo since lawyers tended to have ties to the Home Front, but he hadn't found anything suspicious. Langballe was a successful young professional who was married to the woman that Fehmer was in love with but could not have. That was the only threat he posed. Fehmer had put him briefly under surveillance several months earlier after discovering that he knew the lawyer Jens Christian Hauge, the chief of Milorg. Fehmer had, of course, never told Annemarie about his subterfuge.

Now he looked at her apologetically, wishing he hadn't upset her. "I thought you had already told your husband about me and the work you're trying to accomplish."

"I did. And he's not happy about it."

"But surely he supports prisoner releases."

"Yes, but he doesn't like me associating with you. In fact, it makes him angry— especially when he drinks."

"I am sorry. In helping you, I have never meant to put your marriage in jeopardy. I only wanted to do the right thing."

"I know you did."

Fehmer looked again at the man staring at them. He glared back at him and, after a moment, the man moved off. *Mein Gott,* he thought, *the Norwegians are getting more brazen every day now that the war has turned in the Allies' favor.* He hated the Ice Front, but it was an undeniable fact of life here is Norway. The Norwegian people refused to be bullied into National Socialism—and he couldn't help but admire them for their proud but subtle defiance in an effort to maintain their dignity in the face of a superior adversary. There was only a minority of active Resistance members in the country, but every day a large percentage of the population engaged in individual acts of passive resistance: public slights that were so commonplace yet insignificant as to not be considered illegal. *Is Fruten* was Norwegian society's psychological warfare against the occupiers and those that supported them without drawing draconian reprisals—and Fehmer had seen with his own eyes that it worked. He knew the best solution to the problem was to ignore the Norwegians right back and pretend that they didn't exist. Two could play at that game.

"I'm sorry that we cannot just spend a few minutes alone together quietly talking," he said, feeling suddenly guilty in making her come on a walk with him. "This war is hard on us both."

"I would say it is a lot harder on me and my countrymen."

"Yes, that is true. But there is no reason that Germany and Norway shouldn't be united as one. We are similar people with a similar history when you come right down to it."

"Nazism will never take root here and you know it. The NS is dying."

"I didn't come here to get into a political debate with you."

"How can we not? Our countries are at war."

"I am genuinely sorry. I just wanted to take a walk with you and…and get away from the war, if only for a few minutes."

"I'm afraid we can't get away from the war. Not when your own Minister of Propaganda Goebbels declared only a few months ago, 'If the Norwegians will not learn to love us, they shall at least learn to fear us.' Everyone has heard the quote. It was in the papers."

"Not in any paper I read."

"Yes, well, we get our news from different sources."

"You know that such talk is dangerous in these perilous times.'

"Now you sound like Herr Goebbels himself."

Wolfie stiffened and gave a low growl, as if the dog, too, didn't like where the conversation was heading. "Please, let's stop," Fehmer said. "You know that I care about you and want to help you, so why do we argue like a pair of schoolchildren. I am going to release the men you've requested. I gave you my word and I intend to keep it."

She seemed to recover her equanimity. "Yes, I know that, Siegfried. You have been true to your word."

"But?"

"But I have heard the stories of what goes on at Victoria Terrasse."

He felt himself tighten defensively. "What you have heard are exaggerations. We have very strict guidelines for prisoner interrogations at Gestapo headquarters and we follow them to the letter. I should know because I drafted them myself. As you know, before the war I was a lawyer like your husband."

"Yes, I know that in your own eyes you don't see yourself as a cruel man, merely an enforcer of the law. But me and my countrymen see it differently. Especially when I have heard that you have even sicced Wolfie here on prisoners. Tell me, Siegfried, is it true?"

The pair of women seated at the next park bench gave them a cold stare and got up and left their seats. Fehmer felt their eyes pierce him and Annemarie like daggers. He felt like putting them under arrest. *That would show them who is boss in this country.* But with an effort, he restrained himself.

"I can't be here like this," she said, rising to her feet. "I must leave."

He got up and bowed cordially, hoping his chivalry and grace under fire would make her think differently of him. "I'm sorry," he said. "I just wanted to take a pleasant walk with you."

"It's not your fault. I know you meant well."

He took her gently by the hand. "I would never do anything to hurt you, or anyone that you love. You know that, don't you?" He detested himself for the note of desperation in his voice.

"I know you wouldn't. I know you have goodness in your heart. You didn't have to release Larsen, but you did. And now he is safe and sound with his family. But the torture, Siegfried—that is the devil in you that you must purge from your soul. You must stop the torture. That is your only hope if you do not want to be considered a war criminal when this conflict is over."

"It is not as simple as that and you know it. The men that we subject to enhanced interrogation are terrorists, Bolsheviks, and common criminals. More importantly, every single one of them is guilty and lying to us."

"How can you be so sure? There has to be a better way, Siegfried—there just has to be. But I do acknowledge all those you have released. As I said, there is goodness in your heart. That is the reason I remain your friend."

In that instant, he realized that his primary motivation in releasing the prisoners was to win her approval. *Do you not understand that I am madly in love with you?* he thought to himself, feeling the longing inside him swelling like the sea.

"I'll see you soon, I hope," he said.

"Yes, but the next time it will have to be in private. We cannot be seen together in public ever again."

CHAPTER 33

SITTING AT THE POLISHED MAHOGANY BAR with Johnny Holst, Chapman looked around the Ritz. In addition to his Abwehr colleagues, all the usual suspects were here tonight: Wehrmacht and SS officers mingled with members of the Norwegian Viking Regiment, *Nasjonal Samling* office holders, and pro-Nazi Norwegian police detectives and businessmen, several of the latter of which he had been told were making a handsome profit off the war. After a moment, he saw a young woman at a nearby table roll her head back and laugh like Marlene Dietrich. She was sitting with another young woman in the corner of the bar room. She even looked a little like the legendary actress, he thought—except that she was much younger, far more beautiful, and obviously Norwegian.

Gently, he elbowed his handler. "Hey, Johnny, take a look at that *fräulein* in the corner. My God, she's gorgeous."

Holst turned. "You're right, she's a looker all right," the German agreed.

"Don't even think about it, Johnny. She's mine."

"That's suits me. She has a friend."

He continued to study the young woman, planning his next move. Luckily, she was engrossed in conversation and hadn't seen him observing her yet. Unlike the uniformly dowdy Germans, Norwegian women were naturally elegant and attractive, but this woman was far above the standard fare. She had luminous skin, big bedroom eyes, and straw-colored hair. She wore a low-cut, fashionably risqué dress and high heels. As if on cue, she reached inside her handbag, pulled out a Craven "A" cigarette from a pack, and inserted it into a long ebony holder in a fluid motion that brought a smile to Chapman's lips because it was pure Dietrich.

"There's my signal, Johnny Boy—that young lady needs a light," he said, and he was up and out of his chair at the mahogany bar with his silver Zippo clasped tightly in his right hand. "Don't come over until I've established a beachhead. I'll signal you."

"You've got it, Fritz."

He dashed across the room, praying that some Jerry lout wouldn't get to her first. To his surprise, he accomplished his goal. He snapped open the lighter with a pop, leaned like a cavalier across the table, and offered her a light.

"*Bitte schön*," he said with his best gentlemanly smile.

"*Nein*," she snapped back, and then to make sure there was no doubt in his mind where she stood, she shook her head, flashed him a look of acid disdain, and lit her own fancy Craven "A" cork-tipped Virginia cigarette with her own silver lighter.

Undaunted and chuckling good-naturedly, he drew up a chair, withdrew a gold monogrammed cigarette case, pulled out his own cigarette, and lit it. "I'm not German and I promise I won't bite," he said, still maintaining the charming smile that had worked on most women, including Freda Stevenson and Betty Farmer.

The woman continued to glare at him. Seeing her up close, he realized that he had underestimated how beautiful she was. She had sweetly delicate features, large eyes with almost colorless pupils, and the kind of figure that made full-grown men weak in the knees. But so far, she wasn't succumbing to his charms and now her friend was looking nervous.

The woman blew a cloud of smoke into his face.

He smiled. "Thank you very much for that. They say Craven 'A' smoke wipes away wrinkles."

"Does it now?" she said sharply.

"But before you do it again, I think you should know something."

She rolled her eyes. "What's that?"

"I'm French."

She looked genuinely surprised. "You're French?"

"Absolutely," he lied. "I'm a French journalist writing an article for a Paris newspaper."

With dramatic flourish, he repeated the words in French, making sure to sound as authentic as possible. And then, for good measure, he smiled again, this time a little cockily.

"That changes things a bit, doesn't it?" he said.

"I don't know," she came back with aplomb. "Ask me in five minutes."

ψψψ

Though she had survived the opening act and felt herself relax, Dagmar Lahlum still felt tense and out-of-place here at the Ritz Hotel Bar. She could tell her friend Mary Larsen—whom she had coaxed into coming here to help with her cover story and was not with the Resistance—was uncomfortable too. The truth was neither of them wanted to be here with scores of Nazis and NS sycophants prowling around. But Dagmar had accepted Ishmael's challenge and agreed to enter the lion's den, and she had convinced her unwitting friend to come with her for company. There was no going back now.

All the same, she wondered what she had gotten herself into. Who was this suave foreigner with a gold monogrammed cigarette case and expensive wristwatch? She could only pray that it wouldn't end badly for her and she would be exposed as a spy. She also felt guilty for using Mary in her clandestine operations without telling her what she was up to. Mary Larsen didn't even know that her best friend was an active Resistance operative.

"So," she said to Chapman, both speaking in French and occasionally English now. "You're doing a report on our country. What do you want to know?"

"I want to know if Norwegian women are indeed the prettiest women in the world. Because judging by you two, I would have say that the answer is affirmative."

"Oh, now you're pulling out all the stops, aren't you?"

"Actually, I've only just begun. My next step is to ply you with more drinks. But first you must tell me your names."

She hesitated.

"Don't worry, I won't bite. Remember, I'm a Frenchman. The first thing out of our mouths is, 'I surrender!' and "Mon Dieu, you have burned my Crêpe Suzette!'"

She couldn't help but giggle.

"All right, my name is Dagmar."

"Last name."

"I'm withholding that for now. And this is my friend Mary."

"Enchanted to make your acquaintance."

Dagmar took a puff of her cigarette from her ivory mouthpiece. "And what is your name?"

"Fritz Graumann."

"That is a German name, not French."

"Not if you're from Alsace-Lorraine. Now what would you like to drink?"

"I'll have another Løiten Linje aquavit. It seems to be taking the edge off."

"Thank goodness for that. And you, Mary?"

"I'll have the same, thank you."

He waved down a waiter and placed the order. Then he smiled devilishly and told them a pair of bawdy jokes that made them laugh. Slowly, Dagmar felt herself loosening up. She decided that he was telling the truth about not being German but lying about being French. His accent was good, but it wasn't quite French. She wondered why he would lie. She also wondered whether he was an important enough intelligence target to satisfy her control officer. Did he have any information that would be of value to the Allied war effort, or was he just a nobody out looking for a good time?

She looked at him pointedly. "Where are you really from? If you are indeed French, your accent is not one I have heard before."

"As I said I'm from Alsace. It's a rural part of the country with its own unique dialect. It is also a place where not much happens."

"Sounds like Eidsvoll where I grew up. Nothing of significance has happened there since the Norwegian Constitution was signed in 1814."

At that moment, the man that Fritz had been sitting with at the bar appeared at the table.

"Ah, this is my friend Johnny. He's a sailor. Johnny, this is Dagmar and Mary."

"Pleased to make your acquaintance, ladies," said Holst with a wide grin, and he pulled up the chair next to Mary and started flirting with her in Norwegian.

Dagmar studied him a moment as she and Chapman resumed their conversation in French and English. He was burly and had a round, happy face lined with the pink, veiny skin of a heavy drinker. She noticed straight away that he had a German accent. Which meant that while Fritz may not have been German, he was associating with Germans. By the looks of him, Johnny appeared to be an officer of some kind. She filed away the face and the name along with those of the man she was now speaking with. Ishmael would want to know the details and every little snippet of her conversations with these men. Though it was still early, she was beginning to get the feeling they were somehow important and not quite what they seemed. She suspected they had a connection to German intelligence but were not SS. SS men had a certain way about them, an ingrained militancy, lack of humor, and aura of violence that made you instinctively fear them. In contrast, Fritz and Johnny may have been dangerous, but she did not feel danger in their presence.

Soon, the waiter brought their drinks and the four of them drank a toast together before returning to their separate conversations. Eventually, Dagmar confided that she had in late March celebrated her twentieth birthday, was a model and dressmaker, and that, like most of her fellow Norwegians, she resented the German occupiers for what they were doing to Norway. Since he was supposedly French, she contended that he should understand her displeasure towards the Occupation. He claimed he did understand and sympathized with Norway's plight. Then, after the third round of drinks, he popped the question to her while Johnny and Mary were ensconced in conversation.

"If you wouldn't consider it too forward of me, I'd like to take you out to dinner this evening. What do you say?"

"I'd have to say no. I don't know you well enough yet."

He looked deflated. "Why? I thought we were having a swell time."

"We are, but I still don't know you."

She pulled another Craven A from her handbag and he lit it for her. "You're not just a good-time girl—that I can most certainly tell. But I don't see why you won't have dinner with me. Johnny here is a nice enough fellow, but I'm afraid he's something of a bore compared to you."

"Hey, what's that you're saying about me?"

"Hush up, Johnny, and go back to fawning over Sweet Mary there."

"Now that I can do!" he roared good-naturedly, tossing back his lager.

They all had a good laugh. Dagmar looked into Eddie Chapman's eyes. When he smiled, they lit up just a little. What should she do? She had succeeded in entering the lion's den and had managed to entice a man who, at the very least, had a connection to the German military or intelligence in some manner, for though Johnny no doubt knew his way around a boat and spoke Norwegian and Danish well based on his conversation with Mary, he was no Norwegian seaman. So why was she so resistant to having dinner with Fritz? Was she frightened? Or was it that she thought it was beneath her? Or was her deep and abiding fear that people might label her as a *tyskertøs?*

"Come now, Dagmar, you must have dinner with me. I've never had a woman spurn my advances like this and I'm afraid you might destroy my self-esteem altogether. Indeed, I might never recover."

She hated to admit it, but there was something endearing about him. He was trying awfully hard to be funny and she couldn't begrudge him that. Most men were only nice when they wanted something—usually food, money, or sex—and their selfish motives were always transparent. But Fritz seemed different.

"I know there's a war going on," he persisted, "but in my humble view that should never stop two young people from having a pleasant dinner together."

She kept her expression blank, neither rejecting nor accepting him. But she could feel her resolve weakening before him. "What do you want from me?"

He laughed, a mirthful bellow that carried across the bar room, and in that moment, she knew she sort of liked him. *He's definitely not like most men.* "To be honest, I find you terribly attractive, plus I've never met a woman so impervious to my charms."

"Have you charmed a lot of women?"

"Two before you."

"I don't believe that for a minute."

"Come on, you've got to have dinner with me. Otherwise, I'll have to go beat up one of those Viking Regiment Supermen to prove myself to you."

Dagmar couldn't help but chuckle. She found a mixture of emotions vying for space inside her: guilt at being here in an establishment that catered to the enemy; rapture that a man who actually seemed pleasant had taken an interest in her; fear at the idea of being exposed as a spy; and an even greater fear of her fellow Norwegians mistaking her for a collaborator when she was in fact an underground operative. She couldn't help but feel that there was something special about Fritz, something beyond his good looks and sense of humor. There was a boyish charm about him and, though she hated to admit it, she felt a connection, a spark.

"You really must have dinner with me. You want to know why?"

"Why?"

"Because I'm a charity case. Now what do you say to that?"

She realized what was bothering her: she was most afraid of how her fellow Norwegians would perceive her if she was out and about with a man who consorted with Germans. *Then what are you doing here?* she asked herself. *This is precisely what you have been assigned to do. This is your mission.*

"Please, Dagmar, do I have to get down on my knees and beg? Will you have dinner with me?"

"Not tonight I'm afraid."

"How about tomorrow night?"

"No."

"You're playing hard to get, aren't you? Well, how about Monday night?"

She shook her head.

"Then it has to be Tuesday. I promise to make it the time of your life."

He underscored this with a winsome smile.

"I don't know...I..." She swiped a hand across her face in exasperation, like the host of a party scrambling around at the last minute to prepare for guests. "Okay, I suppose I'll do it. Good heavens, you are most persistent."

"Persistence is my middle name, *mademoiselle.*"

"Oh, so you two are going on a date? How delightful," quipped Johnny Holst, who had broken off his conversation with Mary Larsen for a moment as she had stood up to go to the powder room. "Now where are you going to take her?"

"Why the Engebret Café, of course."

Dagmar was stunned. "The Engebret! But that is the finest restaurant in all of Oslo!"

"Yes, I know," said Eddie Chapman with a devilish smile. "But as my dear mother used to say, nothing is too good for a Norwegian girl on a first date."

"Your mother never said that!"

"You're right, she didn't, but she should have!" And with that, they all had another good laugh.

CHAPTER 34

ENGEBRET CAFÉ, OSLO

MAY 4, 1943

AS HE GAZED AT DAGMAR LAHLUM, Eddie Chapman was certain that she had the most beautiful eyes he had ever seen. "Tell me about yourself," he said in English. "I want to know everything about you."

"But you are an enemy invader and I don't trust you," she replied. "How can I possibly tell you my life's story when you may have me thrown in jail?"

Though her tone was playful, he sensed an underlying tension and fear in her, something private and alert. In that way, she was like him, he realized. "Come now, I told you I am a French journalist doing an article on Norway. I just want to know what makes you and your country tick."

"For a Frenchman, you sure have a funny accent."

"And for a Norwegian, I must say yours is exquisite."

"Does charm always work for you?"

"Yes, but apparently not with you. But at least I did get you to go out with me tonight."

"You wouldn't take no for an answer."

"Now that is the truth."

He pulled out two Craven "A" cigarettes from his pack laying on the table and handed her one. She inserted the cigarette in her four-inch-long, carved, ebony, wooden cigarette holder and he lit it for her, then lit his own. They puffed for a moment before blowing swirls of blue smoke towards the ceiling.

"All right, I'll tell you about myself," she said. "But then you have to tell me something about yourself. And it has to be the truth. Do you promise?"

"Yes, I promise. But I still get to go first. Now where were you born?"

"I was born in Serumsand, but I grew up in Eidsvoll."

"The north country. You told me that nothing ever happened in Eidsvoll since your Constitution was signed."

"You have a good memory."

"Surprisingly enough, even after a few drinks." He looked up as their waiter appeared. "Oh, what perfect timing. Two cognacs, *s'il vous plait*." And then in formal Norwegian, he added. "*Tusen takk*." Thank you very much.

The waiter scrutinized them a moment, trying to determine whether they were patriots, occupiers, collaborators, or something in between. Then, still not quite sure, he nodded to himself and walked off.

"He doesn't know what to make of us," said Dagmar conspiratorially. "He knows I'm Norwegian, but he's confused about you. To tell you the truth, I am too."

"You know that I make you laugh."

"Yes, I do know that."

As she said the words, she smiled, her big brown eyes lit up like precious gemstones, and Chapman thought to himself, *I could get used to a smile like that.* They both laughed and took a moment to look over their mouthwatering menus.

"Tell me about growing up in Eidsvoll," he said, peering over the top of his menu. What did your father do?"

"I regret to say that I am the daughter of a shoemaker."

"That's an honest trade. You shouldn't regret it." And then he thought: *If you only knew what I did for a living before the war.*

"I didn't mean to say it like that," she said, "but the truth is I had a hard childhood. There was hardly any money for me or my mother, or my much-older sister and two step-brothers."

"I'm sorry to hear that. I had a hard time growing up too."

"It was so bad my father struggled just to put food on the table. These were during the crisis years in the 1920s and 1930s. That's why, to save money, I learned to mend and sew my own clothes."

"You are a skilled seamstress then?"

"Yes, I love to sew. But I also work as a hotel receptionist."

"I hate poverty. It is hard on families, especially children." He sighed reflectively. A part of him wanted to open up to her about his past, as she was doing with him, but he knew he couldn't. Telling her the truth about his life growing up back in England, his wild adventures as a safecracker with the Jelly Gang, or his thus far colorful career as a British double agent could very well get himself killed. "When did you move to Oslo?"

"Just a few weeks before the German invasion. In the spring of 1940."

He took a pull from his Craven, blew out a cloud of smoke, and glanced at the cigarette appreciatively. "You must have been awfully young then. How old were you?"

"I was seventeen. I was desperate to get out of Eidsvoll."

"Why is that?"

"I was dissatisfied with my family's situation."

"I can understand that."

"I was a hot-headed and opinionated teenager. I was resentful of being so poor and I'm afraid I blamed my father. It was unfair of me. I know that now, but when I was seventeen I only thought about myself. I was a selfish girl. Now there is a world war going on and I know better."

"You were a teenager. We were all like that once. War makes people grow up fast."

"It most certainly does. How old are you?"

"Twenty-seven, I think."

"You think?"

"Okay, twenty-eight. It just sounds so old compared to you I didn't want to say it."

"You are a curious fellow, aren't you Fritz Graumann?"

"Yes, I'm a bit of an odd duck. Now tell me about your teenage transgressions. I always love a good story of youthful angst and turmoil. After all, I went through it too."

164

"In all honesty, the neighbors and local gossips thought I was far too attractive and snooty for their respectable town. They were just as glad to see me go as I was to leave them behind. Norwegians are terrible gossipers. Absolutely terrible."

"So, one day you just packed up and moved to Oslo?"

"My aunt lives here. She used to send me the latest fashion magazines. I came here with dreams of making a name for myself in the high-end fashion and modeling world."

"But then the war started."

"Yes. I've been working as a hotel receptionist and seamstress ever since, although I just quit my receptionist job so I'm sewing full time now. So much for my dreams, eh?"

"You'll get your chance someday. You're a bright and beautiful young girl."

"Flattery just might get you somewhere with me. But you have to tell me one thing. Is Fritz your real name?"

"I'm afraid I'm going to have to leave that to your imagination, my dear. Where, may I ask, do you live here in Oslo?"

"You're not supposed to ask girls questions like that on a first date."

"Who do you think I am, Jack the Ripper?"

"No, I think you're funny. But I also know that you have had a lot of women."

"Have I now? How can you tell?"

"Your confidence. You're a charmer but also a bit of a narcissist."

"That's an awfully big word. I'm not sure I know what it means."

"Oh, yes you do. You're a clever man and well read. A girl can tell, you know. Particularly when we were waiting for our table and you were quoting Chaucer and Victor Hugo."

"Yes well, I guess you're onto me then. I've tried to be a semi-educated man and lead a life of abstinence."

"I certainly doubt that."

"All right, enough ribaldry. Where do you live?"

"I have a tiny flat in Frydenlundsgate."

"What do you like to do in your spare time?"

"I like to read books about art and poetry and paint clothing designs. I've also been taking modeling classes at night on and off for the past three years."

"When I first saw you, I thought you looked like a model. I must say, you are most beautiful and adorable. And I also must say I appreciate your opening up to me. I have to say I am having a delightful time flirting with you."

She blushed, and he thought, *I could get used to that too.* "Yes, it has been wonderful so far, but you have to admit it has been one-sided. You have told me hardly anything about yourself. But now it's your turn to open up to me."

At that moment, the waiter reappeared with their cognacs and asked if they were ready to order. With the prompt service, Chapman realized the waiter must have decided that they were not Germans or German-sympathizers. Either that or he needed the money and was looking for a good tip. Chapman opted for the Lutefisk served with boiled potatoes, mashed peas, and bacon; Dagmar the Norwegian lamb with the fresh mushrooms and asparagus. Chapman noted that the prices were exorbitant given the German-enforced food shortages of the Occupation, but he didn't mind; he had just earned himself 110,000 kroner for two fake sabotage operations. Snapping his leather-bound menu shut with a resounding flourish, he raised his glass of cognac in a toast as the waiter moved off and once again they were alone.

"Here's to us, Dagmar," he said with a smile.

"Yes, here's to us."

She giggled and they each took a sip. Chapman let the warm liquor trickle down his throat. He was glad that she seemed to be loosening up. But more importantly, he knew he was becoming infatuated with her. She was young, vibrant, and gorgeous. And yet, he couldn't help but feel that she was holding something back. Despite her candid description of growing up, she seemed to have a secretive quality about her. She seemed to see through his ruse as well: she obviously wasn't convinced he was a Frenchman.

"As I said before, now it's your turn. Tell me about yourself," she said to him.

"Yes, I did promise, didn't I? I suppose I should start out with an admission."

"An admission? Are you saying you've been lying to me?"

"Let's just say I've been less than forthcoming."

"The intrigue grows."

"Indeed. The truth is I'm not actually a French journalist. I'm a German, born and raised in the United States."

"Does that mean you're fighting for the Germans?"

"No, it doesn't mean that at all. Indeed, you needn't worry. But I'm afraid I can't tell you any more than that."

"That's it, after I told you my whole childhood story? You must tell me something more about yourself."

"All of Europe is embroiled in war. It is not safe to talk about many subjects—particularly not on first dates."

"Well, you can at least tell me who your favorite author is."

"Why H.G. Wells, of course."

"H.G. Wells, the Brit?"

"The father of science fiction along with Jules Verne."

"Why I love his books too. They've been translated into Norwegian, you know."

"No, I didn't know that, but I am glad of it. He is one of the greatest men of our age."

"I didn't know he was still alive."

"Oh yes, he lives in England."

"That's where you're from, isn't it?"

"No, it's not. I told you I am German but have lived in America."

"I have to be honest—I don't believe you're German-American."

"You're saying you don't believe me?"

"Yes. And as you'll soon find out, I'm right most of the time."

"That's going to make things interesting," he said. "Because I happen to be too."

CHAPTER 35

MAY 4, 1943

AFTER DINNER they walked down Kongens gate, named in 1624 by King Christian IV, who had embroiled Scandinavia in countless wars and renamed Oslo as *Christiania* after himself, a name adopted until 1925. As they approached a second cross street, a black Mercedes-Benz bearing two miniature Nazi flags and several drunken, singing officers roared down the street, took the corner sharply, and nearly bowled them over before racing towards the wharf. Eddie Chapman— whom Dagmar still knew only as Fritz Graumann—hurled a string of curses at the receding vehicle but to no effect. Shaking their heads, they walked on.

The night air was cool but not frigid. Overhead puffy clouds drifted past a thumbnail moon. Commuting workers, most finished for the day but others beginning their dreary night shifts, shuffled past in steady streams, most with their heads down. The German Occupation hung over every citizen like a wood axe, with police terror, snooping neighbors, and critical shortages of food as the ever-present realities of daily life. Terboven, Quisling, and their band of thieves and cutthroats had sucked the happiness and beauty out of the city and it showed on the faces of the people. From Kongens gate, they headed for the tram loading station, took the streetcar to the Drammensveien stop next to the Palace Park, and then proceeded north on foot towards her apartment at 15 Frydenlundsgate. The Germans rigidly controlled the tramways in Oslo, printing tickets and signs with Nazi emblems on them, which nettled Dagmar.

But what nettled her even more was the Ice Front. When she and Fritz sat down in their seats in the tram, several of the *trikk* riders moved to the back of the electrical carriage to give them the cold shoulder. Being the patriot that she was, the last thing she wanted was her fellow Norwegians openly shunning or glaring disapprovingly at her, regardless of who she was with. In that dreadful moment, she realized that her date stood out like a sore thumb. He had been pegged as a German, collaborator, or unwanted foreigner of some kind by his clothing and accent, and she was guilty by association. It infuriated her to be thought of as a quisling.

When they reached Parkveien and exited the tram, she vented her frustration. "I still don't understand where you developed such an unusual accent. You are obviously not German-American. So why don't you just tell me where you're really from?"

"Why are you angry with me?"

"You saw what happened on the tram. Would you call that fun?"

"It's not my fault. Those people were being rude."

"That may be. But it would help if you just told me where you're really from and what you're doing here in Oslo. I don't appreciate that kind of abuse from my own countrymen. So where are you from?"

He came to a halt. She looked at him closely, trying to read him, but his face was inscrutable. And yet, she had the feeling he wanted to tell her something.

"What are you not telling me? You can't keep who you are from me forever. Not if you want to see me again."

At that moment, a convoy of heavy, black-canvas-topped trucks filled with German soldiers raced past them. One of the vehicles struck a rut, nearly splashing them with water. When the trucks passed, he looked at her and smiled.

"Okay, you can't blame me for that."

"You're just trying to change the subject."

"No, I just want you to understand when there's a war going on, sometimes it's best to keep some things to oneself. It makes for a greater life expectancy."

"Now that I can agree with."

They walked on. The breeze picked up, chasing through the trees, and Dagmar found the night suddenly cold. They took a slight left onto Pilestredet and then turned right onto Dalsbergstien.

It was then she saw a disturbing sight. The SS had encircled a house and a Norwegian family was being led out onto a street and into a truck under armed guard. A middle-aged husband and wife, their two teenage sons, and three daughters were being herded towards the truck with snarling and barking German shepherds pulling on their leashes and frightening them to death. The soldiers prodded them along with submachine guns, jabbing the family members like pecking roosters. In front of the house, a senior SS officer that she didn't recognize stepped from an idling Volvo PV53 and barked out orders to one of the soldiers standing in front of the vehicle, his harsh guttural voice slicing through the night like a knife. The SS officer's jet-black uniform and jackboots gleamed in the light of the streetlamp, and his skull-and-crossbones insignia leered belligerently from his lapel.

"What's going on? Are they rounding up Jews?" asked Chapman.

"No, I don't think so," she said. "There are no Norwegian police. During the Jewish roundup last fall, there were some German SS officers, but it was handled mostly by the Stapo. They're said to be even crueler than the Germans."

"I can see now why you hate them so. And the Germans, too."

"By the look on your face, you don't look as though you approve either."

"Yes well, for the time being why don't you keep that to yourself. As I told you, there's a war going on and we don't want to be hauled before a firing squad."

"My lips are sealed."

"I don't understand why they're taking the whole family. What do you think they've done?"

"They must be connected with the underground somehow. They probably handed out a few pamphlets and now they'll be locked away in prison for the duration of the war."

"For handing out pamphlets?"

"We Norwegians have been locked away for far less."

"My God, I had no idea it was this bad."

"These days being caught with a radio gets you sent to Grini."

"Radios have been banned?"

"It's not just radios. Everything has been banned. Curfew is set at 8 o'clock, we can't travel outside of certain zones without a special identity card or pass, and nothing is published in Norway without the Nazi censor's stamp of approval."

"That seems excessive."

"It's actually much worse. New schoolbooks have been printed to teach students that Hitler is Norway's savior and that the well-known 'Heil' salute is an ancient Norwegian tradition dating back to the Vikings. Strict rationing of coal, gas, food, milk, and clothing has left families scraping by. Some have been reduced to making shoes from fish skins and clothes from old newspapers. But if that's not bad enough, the Germans take whatever they want for themselves, from the finest cuts of meat to the best houses and hotel rooms."

"I've seen what you're describing in the few weeks I've been here. But you've got plenty of Jøssings pushing back."

She acknowledged this with a nod. Jøssing was the general term applied to Norwegian patriots and opponents of the Nazi "New Order." The opposites of quislings, they supported the Home Front and Allies, desired a return of the prewar regime, and promoted the idea of Norwegian independence in accordance with Norway's Constitution. Dagmar was proud to be one of them.

"Yes, there are some who fight back by organizing protests, strikes, sabotage, and even assassinations, but most either support the Nazis, do what they're told, or passively resist. There are not as many Jøssings as the Germans would have us believe."

They continued to study the scene. After a moment, she saw him look away. Was it shame or regret on his face, she couldn't tell?

Suddenly, a pair of beefy SS guards motioned aggressively and started to approach them. "Hey, what are you looking at?" one of them shouted.

"Nothing, we're just on our way home," replied Chapman in German, and he took Dagmar by the arm.

"Well then, get lost! *Schnell!*"

They walked away quickly. When they had gone fifty feet, Chapman said, "You're absolutely right. It appears it's not safe in this town for either of us."

"I told you," said Dagmar.

They kept up a brisk pace, with vapor on their breath in the suddenly chilly air. Soon, they made the turn onto Frydenlundsgate and he held her hand. She didn't resist. She knew even if he was involved somehow with German intelligence or the military that he wasn't anything like the SS men they had just seen; he was clearly different somehow and she doubted whether he was even German as he claimed. Yet what was he doing here in Oslo? And what was he doing accompanied by Germans at a bar frequented by Nazis and quislings? The same, of course, could be asked of her—and she couldn't help but wonder if he was a spy not for the Germans but the Allies. It would explain why his English and French seemed to be better than his German and why his French accent was so peculiar.

When they reached her apartment, still holding hands, she found herself wishing the night didn't have to end. Fritz was almost too good to be true. Whether he truly was her sworn enemy working for the Germans—he was still funny, smart, and considerate. But more importantly, he had empathy. She had seen it in his eyes when the family was being arrested by the SS. When she had looked into his eyes, she had seen disapproval and sadness and deep feeling. She had not peered into the eyes of an enemy—she had seen an ally and sympathetic soul. And she had seen vulnerability.

She knew she was falling for him, and he for her.

Which made it all so confusing. She wasn't supposed to fall for her target; she was supposed to use him to obtain information.

When they reached the doorstep to her apartment, he politely asked, "May I kiss you goodnight?"

"If you don't I shall be disappointed."

He leaned in close and their lips softly touched. As she kissed him back, she wanted desperately to pull him inside and make love to him. She had not been with a man for some time and wanted to feel the passion and whirlwind of emotions. Then afterwards, she wanted to lie around lazily, talking and caressing. But she didn't know him well enough yet and it would be best not to rush things. She decided not to ask him upstairs.

"It's been a strange but wonderful night," she said to him. "So many things have happened. Do you think this war will ever end?"

"I hope not if it means I can be with you."

He kissed her again and she felt warm all over. "Can we get together tomorrow?" he asked. "I would love to take you sailing. I just bought a lovely little Swedish yawl and Johnny's teaching me to sail. What do you say? Or do you have to work?"

"As I told you, I don't work at the hotel any longer. I'm sewing full time these days, so I have my own hours. I would love to go sailing, as long as you don't drown me, of course."

"I promise I won't. I'll swing by at ten." He kissed her softly on the lips once more.

"Goodnight, Fritz. If that is in fact your real name."

"Goodnight, Dagmar, if that is truly yours." And with that, he gave a devilish wink and she thought to herself, *I could get used to a wink like that.*

CHAPTER 36

"WHAT THE BLOODY HELL HAS HAPPENED TO ZIGZAG?"

Tar Robertson stared across his desk at an anxious Sir John Masterman and shook his head grimly. He didn't know the answer. All he knew was the Germans had fallen for the *City of Lancaster* ruse and then Eddie Chapman had disappeared from the airwaves and not been heard from since. When the ship put in at the Rothesay docks on April 25, a small army of British Field Security Police clambered aboard, rummaged through the coal bunkers in full sight of the crew, and after several hours of feigned searching located what was whispered to be two lumps of coal packed with explosives. Every member of the crew was promptly interrogated. The emphasis of the questioning was on the voyage to Lisbon and the disappearance of the suspicious assistant steward Hugh Anson. Then, to spur the rumor-spreading, the gossipy sailors were instructed not to breathe a word to anyone.

Within a week, rumors had spread from the seamiest bars of Europe all the way to the German High Command in Berlin and the White House in Washington, D.C. about how a top German spy had tried to sabotage a British ship. Why even Churchill himself was showing considerable interest in the case. And then, quite suddenly, Britain's most important agent and the star of the Double Cross spy system, celebrated by the Germans as their top operative, vanished from Abwehr wireless traffic altogether. His fate was still unknown.

"We had a brief surge of hope when Most Secret Sources reported that the Lisbon Abwehr station was asked to provide a cover address for Fritz at Berlin's request," explained Robertson. "But the request was never followed up and there has been no further mention of our man."

Masterman scratched his cleanly shaved chin. "But where could he have gone, if not Nantes, Paris, or Berlin?"

"We don't know. Every day, the radio listeners and codebreakers at Bletchley are continuing to scour the airwaves for any trace of him. But we haven't heard a peep in more than a month."

"But we do know the Germans bought the *Lancaster* deception."

"Yes, but still there's been no mention of Fritz's whereabouts."

"A dead end then?"

"Not only has there been nothing from Chapman himself, but there's been no indication from Most Secret Sources that Fritz is still operative. Furthermore, there have been no sightings reported by our network of SOE spies spread throughout Occupied France."

"And not a single message from Zigzag himself?"

"Nothing. But as you know, we've instructed him not to make any wireless transmissions unless he has critical information and is certain he can do it without raising an alarm."

"It looks, then, as though we have to face the very real possibility that Zigzag has been compromised and may very well be in mortal danger."

"It would appear so, Sir John."

They fell into a momentary silence. Robertson picked up a worn, red first-class cricket ball on his desk and ran his index finger along the slightly raised, sewn seam. Though he was not in the league of Masterman as a cricketer, they were both avid cricket players and loved to talk about memorable contests, legendary strikers and batsmen, and glorious summer days with hearty shouts of "Owzat!" and murmurs of "well-bowled" and genteel hand-clapping from the gallery.

Masterman was staring out the window in the direction of St. James Park, probably reminiscing about stumped strikers, downed wickets, and run outs. "There's been nothing from Most Secret Sources on von Gröning's whereabouts either?" he asked after a moment of contemplation.

Robertson shook his head. "The Nantes Dienststelle appears to have been shut down, and von Gröning's name no longer appears in Abwehr wireless traffic."

"Strordnarily bad luck. I suppose all we can do is make sure our radio operators continue scanning the airwaves for any word from our man."

"That's it then."

"I just spoke with Dick White—who had just got off the phone with Duff Cooper," said Masterman, referring to the former minister of information now supervising covert operations, who was an intimate of Churchill's. "Duff has discussed the Zigzag case at some length with the P.M. Winston has made it clear that he wants to be informed if Zigzag resurfaces. As you know, he's taken quite an interest in the case since we handed over the case file to him. He wants to be kept abreast of any further developments."

"Yes well, the P.M. does love his spy games. I just wish he understood that to us it's not a bloody game."

"Yes, quite."

"I just hope Chapman hasn't been broken under interrogation."

"You think the failure to blow up the *City of Lancaster* has brought him under suspicion, despite our charade at the Rothesay docks three weeks ago?"

"Or perhaps he has been betrayed by a British mole."

"Are you feeling guilty? Perhaps if we had done a better job with his interrogation training, he wouldn't be in the position he may be in now."

Robertson pondered a moment before answering. He was not a sentimental man, but the possibility that Zigzag could be undergoing torture at this moment made him feel deeply uneasy. The truth was he had come to admire the former safecracker and considered him the bravest of his Double Cross agents, followed closely by Dusko Popov, the Yugoslavian playboy code-named Tricycle.

"In preparation for his cover story, we made it as near to the truth as possible. If cross-examined in detail, he was trained to, for the most part, rehash the truth. We gave him a detailed checklist of ways to withstand pressure under interrogation and prepped him for more than a month. We taught him all the tricks and we rehearsed them in multiple dry runs. And once he had made it through the training, he was the best that any of my team members has ever seen. The truth is, as a former criminal, the lad is a natural born liar."

"Yes, but what if they've been subjecting him to extreme physical torture, or they've been using drugs or anesthetic on him?"

Robertson shook his head. "The Germans prefer to break their prisoners by psychological means. Their preferred methods are to strip subjects naked, dress them in women's clothes, make them stand facing a wall, or force them to sit on a three-legged chair, which I am reliably told is inordinately difficult."

"He needs to stick to his cover story, and never tell an unnecessary lie."

"Yes, but even then, his exhaustive training may not be enough to save him. If he falls into the hands of the Gestapo and they choose not to believe him, they'll break him eventually. No one can withstand torture indefinitely. And then they'll put a bullet in his brain."

They fell into a bleak silence. Robertson thought of his wife Joan. *What would she think of me sitting in an office talking about torture and murder as if they are items on a menu?* Feeling a flash of guilt, he sincerely hoped he had prepared Chapman well enough that he hadn't come under suspicion by the Germans. But with no word from either von Gröning or Zigzag, the situation did not look good. All the same, he tried to put a positive spin on it.

"Our codebreakers at Bletchley were able to follow Chapman's route from Lisbon north to Paris, and from there to Berlin, before we lost contact. And we have picked up one other important detail."

Masterman raised a brow. "What is that?"

"He was issued two different passports."

"He was?"

"Yes, so we know the Germans bought his story initially. In one he posed as a Norwegian, the other as a German."

"Interesting."

"The first passport issued in Lisbon was a Norwegian passport in the name of Olaf Christiansson, describing him as a seaman, born in Oslo. The second was issued in Berlin in the name of Fritz Graumann."

"Von Gröning's code name."

"Yes, but there's still no sign of the German spymaster. He disappeared without a trace over two months ago."

"But the name Graumann is again in play. 'Tis a good sign, don't you think?"

"Or we could be grasping at straws."

"Yes, but our lad is an exceedingly resourceful and cunning sort. Who knows, by now he may have convinced the Huns to award him the Iron Cross."

Robertson couldn't help but crack a smile. "Come now, Sir John, he's good— but he's not that bloody good."

"I wouldn't count him out. As I've said many times, our little crook Eddie is a most cunning devil."

The two clubby gentlemen spymasters chuckled in agreement, and a secretary brought them their afternoon tea.

CHAPTER 37

OSLO FJORD AND LANGØYENE ISLAND

MAY 25, 1943

WITH A FULL WIND IN THE CANVAS AND HIS HAND AT THE HELM, Eddie Chapman maneuvered the Swedish yawl across the shimmering water of the Oslo Fjord. During the past seven weeks, he had been trained by Herr Rotkagel in photography, had again become proficient at wireless transmissions, consulted on matters of sabotage with high-ranking German military figures, and eventually gained sufficient trust from his German handlers that he was no longer required to have Johnny Holst or Walter Thomas as his constant chaperones. But the thing that he enjoyed most was sailing with his newfound love Dagmar Lahlum.

This was the fourth time he had taken her aboard his sailboat. The small cabin was ideal for navigating the local fjords and he was a good enough helmsman that he could manage the yawl on his own. In addition to training him in wireless, Johnny Holst had spent three solid weeks teaching him how to sail before allowing him out alone. On his third solo, Chapman had nearly drowned when he put out from the mooring into the choppy waters of the Oslo Fjord against Holst's advice and lost his sails in a storm. He was towed back to harbor, but instead of being mocked for his foolishness, the narrow escape only seemed to enhance his stock among his German handlers. Soon thereafter, Holst and Thomas no longer dogged his every step and he was frequently allowed to be alone with his Norwegian beauty.

It was a splendid day. He looked at Dagmar and smiled. The sun caught her smooth, oval face and she reached out and gently touched his hand gripping the helm. Then she gave him a soft peck on the cheek. The war seemed far, far away. Splotchy altocumulus clouds formed a heavenly backdrop to the glacially-carved islands in the middle of the fjord, and higher up wispy cirrus floated across the light blue sky like little slivers of cake. The sailboat knifed through the water, gently pitching and rolling. He loved the salty spray of the sea on his face and feel of Dagmar in his arms.

Though the war seemed distant out here during another lazy day on the fjords, he still maintained a high degree of vigilance concerning his surroundings. Every day, he continued to quietly and patiently record in his mind his observations of the German Occupation. In the process, he mentally filled out the detailed questionnaire MI5 had prepared for him prior to his departure on the *City of Lancaster*. He recorded the locations of possible RAF targets, ammunition dumps, the huge tanks where the Luftwaffe stored petrol on the Ekeberg isthmus, and the harbors where the U-boats docked and refueled. He memorized the faces of the officials he met, the addresses of key German administration buildings, and the names of the informers and collaborators who milled around the bars. In a month and a half, he was already well on his way to drawing a mental map of the German military and intelligence services in and around the Norwegian capital.

His thoughts were interrupted by his lover. "What are you thinking about?"

"He smiled. "You," he said.

"Really? Because it looked like you were thinking about something else."

His smile widened. "All right, you've caught me red-handed. I was thinking about making love to you in the woods on that little island right over there and then going for a swim."

She kissed his cheek. "That sounds delightful."

He pointed. "I'll pull into that little cove."

When she kissed him again, he felt a little out of breath.

ψψψ

Dagmar lay next to Chapman on a blanket spread out on a thin carpet of pine needles, tingling as their naked bodies touched. The woods were dark and foreboding and she couldn't help but feel a trickle of trepidation, with the huge vertical trunks and overhead canopy of jutting limbs swamping out the light and blanketing the woods in a sepulchral stillness. But it was also peaceful, and it seemed to her as if the war didn't exist at all. Indeed, when she was alone sailing with her beloved Fritz, it was as if it had never existed and there was only love and beauty in the world instead of terror, treachery, and death.

She moved her body so that she was astride him. Their lips touched softly. She felt desire flowing through her veins, and her head swam with euphoria.

"Oh, Fritz," she whispered in his ear.

They rolled over for a moment so that she was on top and then they changed positions again and his tongue reached inside her mouth, softly, and she kissed him back. He began stroking her hair and rubbing against her. She felt a delightful shudder of excitement take hold of her entire body, but it was the emotional connection that truly gripped her. She knew she was tapping into something sacrosanct, something only true lovers felt, a sense of profound intimacy.

She would *remember* this moment.

She had had lovers before since traveling to Oslo at the age of seventeen, but she had never experienced passion with a grown man like this before. She was experimenting with sexuality for the first time and swept up in the adventure of pure discovery—indeed every day of the past three weeks had been a new romantic adventure.

She kissed his mouth, nibbling his lips gently. A moment later, when he entered her, it was like a perfect dream. Everything about it felt right, natural.

As they began to move together in a gentle rhythm, she took more and more pleasure in his body, in his kisses and caresses and thrusts.

Her body was responding with a passion she didn't know she possessed.

She moved with him in a gentle rhythm. His hands squeezed her swelling nipples, and she gasped with delight.

She wondered if it were possible to go insane with pleasure.

He kissed her on the lips tenderly and she slid her tongue deep into his mouth, clasping his tight buttocks and pulling him deeper inside her. She moaned softly between kisses; she could tell the sound of her voice excited him all the more.

As the pace quickened, the air filled with desperation. She felt herself letting loose with excitement, coming as never before. She sensed that he too was about to let go of his seed.

"Look into my eyes," she gasped, pulling him still deeper.

He pulled his head up and his eyes locked onto hers. "I'm looking, I'm looking!"

She stared at him mesmerically, her eyes as wide as pebbles as the climax came. They held each other's gaze as their bodies shook fitfully and she felt his warmth flowing inside her. Then suddenly tears streamed from her eyes.

"Are you all right?" he asked, worriedly. "Did I hurt you?"

"No," she cried.

"Are you upset? What...what happened?"

"I'm overwhelmed. I'm overwhelmed with joy."

"I love you, Dagmar," he said, like a poet. "I love you as much as a man can love a woman."

ψψψ

Afterwards, they lay there on the blanket—hugging, kissing, nibbling, stroking, and chatting—before getting dressed again and deciding that it was time for them both to relieve themselves. She stepped behind a granite outcrop, and he headed towards a clump of trees to the south. When she reached the outcrop, she felt along its cool rough surface for a few feet then pulled down her skirt, squatted, and began relieving herself. A few seconds in she thought she heard a sound to her right, in the opposite direction from where Fritz had gone. She told herself it was nothing, but she couldn't escape the feeling that someone was out there and they were being watched. She quickly tamped herself dry with some loose paper she had in her pocket, refastened her skirt, and stepped back out into the open. She could see Fritz in the dark shadows of the forest on the other side of the blanket, still pissing, and stepped quickly towards him, bumping into an unseen sapling and fighting the panic as she almost went down.

"Are you all right?" he asked as she came stumbling up, her heart racing wildly.

"I thought I heard something."

"Really, I don't see anyone. What's the name of this island?"

"Langøyene."

There was the sound of a snapping twig. She looked at him. "Tell me you heard that?"

"No, what was it?"

"Are you hard of hearing?"

"No, honestly, I didn't hear it."

"I know I heard something." She strained for sound and scanned the woods, but she heard nothing and saw no unusual movement, nothing out of place. She took a deep breath to steel herself, suppressing a lance of fear. Again, she had the uncanny feeling they were being watched.

"It's probably nothing," he said. "Just a squirrel or rabbit. Let's get back to the boat. We can have a little drink to celebrate our lovemaking."

"We've been making love two or three times a day practically every day for the past three weeks."

"I know, but I am so in love with you."

He pulled her close and kissed her. Then they picked up the blanket and started back to the sailboat. But before they had gone five paces, Dagmar heard the noises again and this time Chapman heard them too. They halted in their tracks. Whatever it was, it didn't sound like a small animal.

"Hello?" he called out in Norwegian, his voice unnaturally loud in the quiet woods. "Who is it?"

There was no answer.

"Somebody there?" asked Dagmar, trying to act casual despite the thumping inside her chest.

They peered into the stands of pine trees, blanketed in dark shadow. There was nothing more than faint smears of light coming through the roof of the forest. They paused to carefully listen. Again, Dagmar's instinct told her they were being watched.

"I feel like we're Hansel and Gretel in the Black Forest," said Chapman. "Let's get out of here."

They started walking again, this time at a brisk pace. They walked ten feet, twenty feet, without incident and then, quite distinctly, Dagmar heard a crunching of brush behind them. This time there was no mistaking: they were footsteps. But were they animal or human?

She stopped abruptly and wheeled around, yanking Chapman by the arm and halting him too. The woods stretched empty behind them, bathed in a pool of faint eerie light.

"Who's there?" she demanded, her voice louder this time and carrying a note of anger.

Chapman reached into his belt and jerked out his pistol. "I've got a gun!" he cried, his voice sounding more desperate than threatening.

"You have a gun?" she asked incredulously.

"As you can plainly see. Unfortunately, I've never fired it, but I am a good shot."

"Well, that's reassuring."

They called out again, but again there was no response.

They waited but there was nothing but the low gurgle of the waves lapping against the rocky island's coast. Still, she couldn't rid herself of the nagging feeling they were being stalked. It was as if someone was deliberately masking the sound of his footsteps by keeping in rhythm with theirs. She fought against the instinct to run and reminded herself that there was no reason to panic, not until they knew what they were up against.

And then, suddenly, her worst fears were realized. Not more than fifty feet behind them, a dark form poked out from behind a tree and then shrank back from the light into the oblivion of the forest.

She looked at Chapman and saw that he had seen it too. "That can't be good," he said. "Let's get out of here!"

He grabbed her by the hand and they turned and ran like jackrabbits.

The sound of running feet quickly picked up behind them and Dagmar felt her whole body seized with panic. Were they being chased down! They ran as hard and fast as their legs would carry them, ripping through underbrush, stumbling, banging into trees, recovering, running on, their breaths coming in terrified gasps. Up ahead, Dagmar could make out faint smudges of light where the woods ended and the beach and glittering waters of the cove began.

They broke through the clearing at a full run and sprinted to the yawl, where they snatched up the starboard line and waited for their pursuer to show himself. Chapman kept his pistol pointed at the tree line, but still nothing happened. A full minute passed, then two.

She looked at him. "Who do you think it was?"

"I don't know. It doesn't appear anyone lives on the island."

"You don't think they were watching us when we were..."

"I don't know. Wait, there's someone coming."

She could hear the sound now too. It was growing louder.

"Who do you think it is? Do you think it's the Germans?"

He kept his gun on the trees. "I don't know, but maybe we should pull anchor."

There was a crash of underbrush.

They waited but nothing happened.

And then they saw a pair of white-tailed deer, a buck and a doe, trotting out of the woods and across the clearing north of the beach.

They looked at one another and smiled. "Maybe they were making love in the woods before us and we interrupted them," he said.

She nuzzled up next to him. "Look at them. They don't even know there's a war going on."

"Today neither do I."

"Me neither," she said.

They kissed again, opened a bottle of cognac, and sailed back to Oslo Harbor in each other's arms, with afternoon sunlight on their faces and the mainsail and mizzen snapping brightly in the breeze.

CHAPTER 38

"WHAT'S HIS NAME?"

Dagmar didn't answer at first. Instead, she watched as Ishmael pulled aside the blackout curtain and checked the street below. It was after the 8 p.m. curfew, the time when the Gestapo did their dirty work, and they were both tense and anxious. Unable to meet at their usual rendezvous point, her control officer had chosen a vacant apartment that months earlier had belonged to a Jewish family. The unfortunate family had been arrested by the Norwegian police in February, shipped to Germany aboard the *Gotenland*, and then transported by rail to Auschwitz, where they were promptly exterminated by incineration. Now Dagmar and her control officer stood in the empty apartment where a happy family had once lived just one block south of her tiny flat at 15 Frydenlundsgate. All that remained of their existence was a single threadbare couch, a chair, and a scratched table that now bore a triumvirate of wax candles.

She cleared her throat. "His name is Fritz Graumann."

Ishmael wrinkled his nose disapprovingly. "Fritz. So he's German?"

"I don't think so."

He stepped away from the window and sat down in the battered wooden chair across from her on the couch. "What do you mean you don't think so?"

"I don't believe he's German. He says he's German-American. At first, he told me he was a French journalist, and then when we went out to dinner he said he was born in Germany but grew up in America. He speaks French, German, and English quite well, but his accent is strange. If I had to guess, I would say he is not German, French, or American."

"British?"

"That's what his accent would suggest. English seems to be his first language."

"Is Fritz his real name?"

"No, I don't think so. He intimated as much."

"Where is he living?"

"He's staying at the Forbunds."

"Then he must be working for the Germans in some capacity. That's where the Luftwaffe and Abwehr officers are billeted. How often have you been seeing him?"

She hesitated, uncomfortable with the personal tone the debriefing was taking. "Every other day at least. Some weeks more."

"Are you sleeping with him?"

She felt herself blush. "I'm afraid that's none of your business."

"I'm afraid it's very much my business. I'm your control officer. When I ask a question, I expect it to be answered."

She said nothing. He stared at her, boring through her like a drill bit.

"Don't tell me you've fallen for the bastard?"

She felt herself reddening.

"You have fallen for him. Don't you know that in situations like these, you've got to keep some emotional distance. It's the only way to keep your head clear. Now how many times have you had sex with him?"

She jumped out her chair. "Now that is definitely none of your business!"

"Quiet!" he whispered sternly. "Do you want to alert the whole apartment building!"

She lowered her voice. "Then don't ask me questions like that."

"I'll ask whatever questions I like. As I said, I'm your control officer. Now how many times have you had sex with him?"

She sat back down. "I don't know, maybe twenty times."

"Twenty times! My God, what are you, rabbits?"

Dagmar felt her face flush with anger. "I told you I don't like these questions."

"You'd better get used to it because I've got a lot more. Now I'm not trying to poke fun at you, I'm just surprised is all. He must be quite the Teutonic knight in shining armor."

"I told you he's not German. But he does spend a lot of time with Germans."

"You've met them?"

"Yes."

"How many and what are their names?"

"I only know two of them and I only know their first names. One is named Johnny, the other Walter."

"Tell me about them."

"They are his escorts here in Oslo. Johnny is the easygoing sailor and heavy drinker. I think he's German, but he won't tell me. He speaks Norwegian and Danish quite well, but his English is atrocious. Walter, I believe too, is German, but he speaks English very well, so it is hard to tell. He is a martinet with no sense of humor and likes English country dancing."

"English country dancing?"

"Yes, he was showing us the steps. Once on the boat and once in the lobby of the Forbunds when Fritz and I came downstairs to be picked up by our two chaperones. Apparently, he does it all the time. He's obsessed with it."

"Crazy fucking Germans. When you're with Fritz, are Johnny and Walter always with you—aside, of course, from when you're sleeping together?"

"I would prefer it if we didn't talk about our sexual arrangement. You are making me uncomfortable."

"All right, I'll try. Why do you say these men are chaperones?"

"It's just the feeling I get. Even though they're friendly, they seem to be keeping an eye on Fritz. Sometimes only one of them comes with us. It is not always two. But lately, they don't come along with us at all and we are alone together."

"Are you saying that this Johnny and Walter are allowing you to spend time alone together because Fritz has passed some sort of loyalty test?"

"Yes, that's the feeling I get. It has been this way for the past two weeks. We went sailing twice last week and three times this week all alone, and we walk through town and go out to dinner without anyone. But like I said, it wasn't that way in the beginning. Early on, Johnny and Walter were keeping their eyes on us. Or at least that's the way it seemed."

"Interesting. Is this Fritz some sort of seaman?"

"No, he just learned how to sail. In the beginning, Johnny sailed the boat and he taught Fritz. But now Fritz knows how to handle the yawl quite well. He made it through a bad storm on one of his first solo attempts. He lost his sails and had to be towed back to shore by a fisherman, but he survived the ordeal. That seems to have raised his stock with the Germans because they have let him alone ever since."

"Have you met anyone else?"

"Yes, there are two others. One is an older man, and the other is a pretty young woman. The paunchy older man is said to be a Belgian journalist, but I think that's a lie. Neither he nor the others have offered a name so there is an element of mystery regarding this man. But he does speak English quite well. Fritz calls him the 'old man,' with obvious affection I might add."

"And the young woman?"

"Her name is Molli. I don't know her last name. She is definitely German."

"Are these the only people you've come into contact with?"

"So far."

"Where do you see them mostly?"

"We go to the Ritz and Löwenbräu almost exclusively. Molli I met in town."

"What do you make of this Fritz? Do you think he's a spy?"

"I don't know for sure, but he is secretive. I suspect he's working for the Germans, but he's definitely not a Nazi. He doesn't believe in Hitler's New Order."

"What makes you say that?"

"Just the way he acts. I have not been shy about telling him I am anti-Quisling and that I am opposed to the German Occupation. When we talk about it, he seems sympathetic to our plight here in Norway. He's even made fun of the SS."

"It could be an act."

"No, it's no act. I have heard him do it on several occasions. Whatever he is, he is not a hardened Nazi."

"And you don't believe he's German-American as he claims?"

"No, I don't."

"Then what is he doing here in Oslo?"

"That I don't know. Not yet anyway. But he does have a lot of money."

"He does?"

"Yes. He has taken me out for fancy dinners on several occasions and he won't let me pay for anything. Plus, he buys me things."

"Jewelry? Clothing?"

"Things. I'm not going to tell you more than that. This is my life too, you know."

"It was your life. Now you belong to Milorg."

"If that's the case then I want protection."

"Protection? What do you mean protection?"

"When the war is over, I'm not going to be labeled a *tyskertøs*. Already people on the streets look at me sharply when Fritz and I are together. They call me a Nazi's tart behind my back, and I don't like it. I'm worried that I'll be branded a collaborator. I am a Resistance operative just like you and those who bear weapons in EXE, Milorg, and the SOE. I am a patriot, the same as you, and want assurances that my role in the Home Front has been documented. Right now, I only have you to vouch for me. But if something happens to you where does that leave me?"

He scoffed. "Nothing's going to happen to me."

"You don't know that. I want protection, or I'm not working for Milorg anymore."

"You don't understand. After the Gestapo nearly wiped us out last year, we have instituted new security protocols. All our deep-cover operatives like you are cutouts. None of you know anyone's real name to ensure that you give the Nazis nothing if you are caught. As a cutout, you cannot be linked to other agents."

"When the war is over, I don't want to be arrested as a suspected collaborator and brought before a war crimes tribunal. If you're telling me you're the only one who knows I am a Milorg operative, then I have no lifeline."

"You don't have to worry about that. Nothing is going to happen to me."

"That's not the point. If something does, who's going to clear me of wrongdoing and restore my good name? Who?"

"Look, for security reasons, we can't have lists, letters, and such. That is just the type of loose-end thing we did early in the war and it's why Fehlis, Fehmer, and their henchmen rolled us up and nearly destroyed us last year. Those days are done—we are organized now."

"That's not good enough for me. I don't want my obituary or my epitaph to read: 'She was a German collaborator and mistress to a Nazi spy.' I deserve better than that and you know it."

"It's going to have to be good enough for you, because that directive comes straight from our new head of Milorg himself."

"Jens Christian Hauge?"

He nodded. "For those deep-cover operatives not in our military network, their security officer is the only one that knows who they are. This is to protect you, Dagmar. If you don't know anyone, you have nothing to divulge. For our male military personnel, we have a different network system in place. It's an early warning system. Contact cards have been prepared for each Milorg military unit member which lists all other Milorg men the individual knows. If he is arrested, the security officer for his unit has the responsibility of warning all contacts on the arrested man's card. It is unrealistic to ask a captured member to withstand torture during interrogation indefinitely, so Hauge has devised a system whereby those caught are to maintain silence for twenty-four hours if they can. By then, it is hoped, all those listed on his contact card will be on their way to Sweden and the Gestapo will come up empty when they set out to make arrests. This is the overall system we have devised and there are no exceptions."

"I understand that you have to have tight security. But I don't like being out on a limb like this."

"Don't worry, nothing is going to happen to me. You just keep up your relationship with this Fritz fellow. I have a feeling you'll soon have intelligence that will bear fruit. You just have to hang in there and not worry so much."

"That's easy for you to say," she felt like telling him. But instead she kept silent and the clandestine meeting ended with her stomach still twisted in knots.

CHAPTER 39

LÖWENBRÄU RESTAURANT, OSLO

JUNE 17, 1943

GAZING INTO HIS LOVER'S CAPTIVATING EYES, Eddie Chapman ached to tell Dagmar Lahlum the truth. *I am a British double agent—I'm only pretending to work on behalf of the Germans and am in fact bringing them great harm!* he longed to confide in her. But he held back from untangling his tangle of lies, knowing that here in Occupied Norway telling the truth could get them both liquidated.

They were watching a bawdy cabaret on the stage below. A large glass partition ran the full length of the restaurant, and he was sneaking occasional peeks at her shimmering reflection in the glass. There were no Wehrmacht troops or officers in this particular room; the only soldiers allowed in this exclusive setting were SS and Abwehr officers, and here they could get anything they wanted, including attractive luxury items like tins of lobster, bottles of champagne, and nylon stockings that no Norwegian could find except on the black market. There was no need to ask for anything: it was all free.

Chapman remembered back to the first time he had brought Dagmar to the Löwenbräu. When a cluck of Gestapo officers wearing jackboots, gleaming SS insignia, and Death's Head holsters bearing Lugers and Mausers had pranced in, she had gasped with shock. "Don't worry about them," he had told her. "Carry on eating." But he had seen the revulsion on her face at the sight of the imperious bastards, and he would never forget it. Unfortunately, he and his newfound love had no choice but to dine at the Ritz or Löwenbräu, the only two unambiguously pro-German establishments in town, because Dagmar refused to accompany him to restaurants used by Norwegians.

When the opening act of the show was finished and a break was announced, he bought a bottle of champagne for the two of them and for Johnny Holst, who had showed up fifteen minutes earlier and was already tipsy. Filling their crystal flutes, he made a toast to the end of the war without claiming victory for either side and they tossed back the bubbly. It was then that they heard an inebriated Viking Regiment officer talking obnoxiously loud at the adjacent table.

Chapman had heard word of the vaunted SS fighting unit. Indeed, all of Norway had. But to most people from the Land of the Midnight Sun, they were Nazi traitors to their country, quislings to be shunned and avoided at all costs. The Norwegian legion had been deployed by Hitler on the Eastern Front to wipe out "partisans," a code phrase widely understood to mean Jews, Communist Party activists, and other "undesirables." The tall, blond lieutenant proceeded to tell a joke.

"'One day, a Norwegian secretary from Oslo told her doctor she was pregnant by a German soldier,' he began, his voice so loud it carried throughout the room.

"'And where is the father?' the doctor asked the young Norwegian tart."

"'I don't know,' the dim-witted but fine-figured girl replied. 'He's gone away.'"

"'Gone away?' sniffed the doctor. 'Don't you know his name?'"

"Well, when he left I think he said *Auf Wiedersehen*."

He laughed drunkenly, and his friends roared along with him and banged their hands hard on the table, like pounding gavels.

Chapman looked at Dagmar and could see she was hurt and irritated. The whole point of the story was to make fun of *tyskertøs,* something she clearly did not consider herself. During the past three weeks of their courtship, she had been subtly ridiculed by her fellow Norwegians on several occasions. He had heard the scathing whispers behind her back that she was a "German's tart," and she had endured cold stares and unflattering jokes at her expense. On the street, Osloans would stare at the two of them walking together and holding hands, a Norwegian girl and a suspected German, and she would turn red with embarrassment. Furthermore, the town gossips noted sourly how she smoked black-market American cigarettes and sported an expensive new wardrobe. Because Chapman had bought her the latest fashions and lavished her with gifts, everyone erroneously assumed she was pro-German. The rule was if you had money, you must be collaborating. But unbeknownst to her, the only collaborating she was doing was with a British double agent. Seeing firsthand how much the persistent sniping from her own countrymen aggravated her, he sympathized with her growing hurt and embarrassment and bristled on her behalf.

"I'm sorry you had to hear that," he said. "We can leave if you like."

But she wasn't listening. She was glaring at the SS Viking Regiment officer, who in return was looking at her with salacious condescension.

"What are you looking at, fräulein! If you want, I'll show you a good time! A real good time!"

His comrades burst into laughter and again banged their hands on the table. Egged on by them, the drunk lieutenant made a lewd face and started making moaning sounds.

"I know how to make fast girls like you scream in delight!"

Looking at his flapping mouth and Dagmar's reddening face, Chapman erupted with violent fury. He knew, in the microsecond before his fist landed hard on the young officer's nose, that he and Dagmar should have just left the restaurant, but animal impulse overtook him. The first punch caught the Norwegian Nazi straight in the jaw, the second and third in his nose and stomach. Drunk and caught off guard, the bastard was instantly flat on his back. Chapman fell on top of him like a pouncing lion and within a matter of seconds, he had him pinned to the floor of the restaurant and was beating the glue out of him.

"Oh, shit!" he heard Johnny Holst cry out. "Come on now, Fritz! Stop it!"

But he couldn't stop, or maybe he didn't want to stop, as his fists struck satisfying blow after blow. For the first time in his life, he felt like a lethal killing machine. It scared him, but it also made him feel deliciously alive. Like some sort of ancient Viking warrior.

And then, he felt arms clasping him, trying to yank him off. But he was in such a state of fury that it took more than a minute for Holst and two of the Viking Regiment legionnaires to dislodge him. He stood there restrained by three pairs of arms, fuming and puffing and red-faced, sweat pouring down his face as the fallen blond-haired, blue-eyed *Übermensch* at his feet moaned and greedily sucked in air.

The young Nazi had not seen Eddie Chapman coming. Blood gushed from his obviously broken nose in a crimson torrent.

"I'm going to report you for this!" the SS legionnaire shrieked, blood spewing from his flapping mouth. "You're a dead man!"

"Fuck you, you Nazi prick!" fired back Chapman, and he grabbed Dagmar and led her out of the restaurant with a stunned Johnny Holst acting as a rear guard.

CHAPTER 40

GESTAPO HEADQUARTERS
VICTORIA TERRASSE

JUNE 19, 1943

WHEN VON GRÖNING looked up at the Gestapo headquarters at Victoria Terrasse, he was reminded of the foreboding castle in American filmmaker Orson Welles's *Citizen Kane*. It wasn't the three separate, white, four-story administrative buildings with the slate rooftops that gave him pause, rather the blood-red Nazi flags fluttering in the breeze against the violent backdrop of an ominous cumulus-laden sky. The giant black swastikas on red backgrounds and roiling storm clouds bearing down from above gave him an intense feeling of claustrophobia, which was intensified by the howling wind and scratching sound of the branches of the trees.

He had dreaded coming here all morning, but he had been summoned—and he thought he knew the reason why. The SS considered him a traitor to the Reich, or at least found him to be insufficiently loyal, and he was being sent back to the Russian Front. Most likely, Fehlis or his minions wanted to question him to uncover the extent of his guilt. He should have known his luck here in Norway wouldn't last. Praetorius must have written up a report and ratted him out to the Gestapo. Damn the little Nazi and his English country dance steps!

He gave one last look at the façade of Victoria Terrasse. He knew that for many Norwegians, the threat to life and freedom began here, but he had never expected to be in their shoes. On the third and fourth floors, a fortunate few endured no more than rigorous questioning, reinforced with threats of violence, before being released with ominous warnings. More commonly, victims were beaten and tortured as the first step of a harrowing experience that led to further imprisonment or even to execution. The most common victims of the repression were suspected members of the Resistance movement: editors, printers, and distributors of underground publications; possessors of prohibited radios or newspapers; couriers and saboteurs; union leaders; noncooperating civil servants; teachers; clergymen; and university professors.

Any individual aiding, or suspected of abetting, escaping Norwegian or Jewish fugitives or any family member, friend, or contact of anyone under suspicion of committing crimes against the Germans was subject to the Gestapo's "routine" interrogation. "Routine," von Gröning knew, included every method Victoria Terrasse's squad of torturers could conceive to extract information from reluctant captives. From his Abwehr contacts in the city, he had learned that most of the questioning was led by Criminal Counselor Siegfried Fehmer, Fehlis's right-hand man. Though, like Fehlis and Fehmer, von Gröning was a senior officer in the German intelligence service, he had as much desire to meet either of these two men as he did a leper.

Feeling butterflies in his stomach, he stepped up the sandbagged front entrance of the Victorian building located just across Drammensveien from the grounds of the Royal Palace. Since he was wearing his officer's uniform, he was waved inside immediately by the two guards standing sentinel at this outermost security checkpoint. From there, he made his way through the front door, across a spacious marble-floored lobby, and to a security check-in desk at the bottom of the stairs. Two neatly dressed Gestapo officers manned the desk.

"Papers!" the one on the left snapped.

Removing them from his pocket, he handed them over one at a time. First, his *Soldbuch zugleich Personalausweiss*—the official pocket-sized booklet carried by every enlisted man and officer in the German intelligence service, navy, infantry, and air force. The Germany Military *Soldbuch* was a condensed personnel file with data such as birth date, height, weight, parental information, vaccinations, eye examinations, but also information about rank, military training, units, transfers, duties, and promotions. His rank was listed as rittmeister in the cavalry, his profession as senior civil servant to disguise that he was in fact a spy, and his awards showed that he had received the Iron Cross, Second Class, for gallantry in the Great War. Next, he withdrew his passport, or *Dienstpass*, that was issued in 1940 and was full of visas and port of entry stamps including Poland, Denmark, Belgium, Denmark, and Norway along with several German Border Police stamps.

The officer examining his documents made a big, cumbersome show of cross-checking the identifications. With bland officiality, he eventually handed them back to him, and the other officer checked his name off an appointment list.

"You may proceed to Captain Fehmer's office."

Von Gröning slowly climbed the stairs to the fourth floor. Portly and ridiculously out of shape, he was gasping for oxygen by the last step. Stopped briefly at another desk, he was eventually led by an unusually attractive receptionist not to the captain's office, but to a conference room.

He stepped inside, bracing himself for disaster.

And was immediately surprised to see not only Fehmer but his lantern-jawed superior and the supreme chief of the entire SS apparatus in Occupied Norway: SS-*Oberführer* Heinrich Fehlis. He gulped mightily. His situation was even worse than he had imagined.

To his surprise, the two officers rose from their seats and shook his hand while a secretary brought him a coffee. He took his seat, his hands trembling slightly. *God, did he need a drink!* It was Fehlis who spoke first.

"Rittmeister, I know your time is precious, so I will get right to the point."

He held his breath.

"An incident occurred last night at the Löwenbräu. A member of the Viking Regiment was apparently assaulted by a spy working for you. The man goes by the name Fritz Graumann. It is our understanding that he is responsible for the sabotage of the de Havilland plant in England and is working under your control. Is this true?"

For a moment, von Gröning was confused. Here he had thought he had been summoned to Gestapo headquarters because his loyalty to the Führer had been called into question, but instead the summons was about Chapman. He breathed a sigh of relief, though he warned himself not to count his chickens before they hatched. The situation could turn badly in a heartbeat here at Gestapo headquarters.

"I'm afraid that is confidential information, Colonel."

"Oh, cut the bullshit, Rittmeister. We have not called you here to chastise you."

Von Gröning looked at Fehmer, who looked like a German shepherd ready to bite. "You could have fooled me. But of course, I am not an SD man."

"Yes well, there is a reason we have not involved your boss," Fehlis went on, referring to *Kapitän-zur-See* Reimar von Bonin, the chief of the Abwehr in Occupied Norway. A portrait of the seaman himself, with piercing blue eyes, bald head, and weak chin, hung in the lounge of Abwehr headquarters at 8 Klingenberggate. "Our interest in this situation is purely to make sure that we don't have a double agent working under our noses here in Norway."

"Why would you suspect he's a double agent?"

Now for the first time Fehmer spoke. "Because of what Graumann said last night after he struck the soldier. I am told from reliable sources his exact words were, 'Fuck you, you Nazi prick!' We have heard the word on this man from Berlin and know that he is a high-level agent. What concerns us is that he may be working against not only you but us as well."

"I can assure you that he is working *for* all of us. Agent Fritz has conducted the only successful sabotage operation ever accomplished in England. In fact, he was just awarded the Iron Cross for his inestimable services to the Reich."

Fehlis and Fehmer looked at one another: they hadn't expected that.

Von Gröning decided to make the most of his temporary advantage. "You didn't know that my supposed double agent is a hero of Germany and a favorite of *der Führer*? Are you telling me that Berlin didn't fully brief you?"

"No, we were not aware that he was awarded the Iron Cross," said Fehlis. "But that hardly makes a difference. Our goal is to make sure that he doesn't perform any sabotage here in Norway."

"Why would he? He's working for us against the Allies."

"But he's British," pointed out Fehmer. "Which calls his loyalty into question."

"Maybe for you, but not for me. He blew up the factory that manufactures Mosquitoes and planted a pair of coal bombs on a British ship. The explosive devices were later discovered by the authorities, but that is beside the point. Not one of our spies has accomplished what he has overseas. Which is precisely why, gentlemen, he was awarded the Iron Cross. It is quite an honor, as you know."

He fingered the medal at his throat, a military decoration which neither of them carried.

Fehlis said, "There are many in Berlin who question whether your super-agent, Herr Graumann, has done any of the things you say he has. There are even those who say he should be eliminated. They claim that your Agent Fritz is either controlled by the British or a total fraud. Far from carrying out missions on behalf of the Reich, they forcefully maintain that your prized agent did absolutely nothing when he went to Britain and has lied about his activities all along."

"You're talking about von Eschwege and his cronies. Well, I can tell you that the newly appointed head of Paris station is a fool."

"A fool you say?"

"He believes that nothing that took place before his tenure is any good—and that makes him not only a fool but plain wrong. There is nothing to prove that Chapman has been dealing from the bottom of the deck, and in fact, there's plenty of evidence from English newspapers and the reports from seamen in Portugal, Spain, and Vichy France to back up his account of everything that's happened. The man has shown exemplary bravery in the service of Germany."

Fehmer stroked his chin thoughtfully; something about the delicate action hinted at suppressed violence to von Gröning, but he wasn't sure why. "We acknowledge your position, but we still maintain ours. You must prove to us that this man is telling the truth and that we don't have a wolf wearing sheep's clothing in our midst. Our job here in Norway is to ensure the security of our troops and administrators—and we are not convinced this man does not pose a risk."

"Are you threatening me?"

Fehlis held up his hands in an assuaging gesture. "We are all German soldiers here, Rittmeister. We are not threatening anyone, and we understand the importance of your spy to the war effort. All we are telling you is to make sure your house is in order."

"Or else what?"

"Or else we'll do it for you," said Fehmer. "And that is a personal guarantee from me."

CHAPTER 41

VON GRÖNING FLAT, 8 GRØNNEGATE

JUNE 20, 1943

THE INSTANT CHAPMAN STEPPED INSIDE THE FLAT he knew he was in trouble. Seated in the drawing room was a tall, gray-haired man in an expensive-looking English suit, who was obviously here to question him. Word of his outburst at the Löwenbräu must have reached the old man and his superiors at the Oslo Abwehrstelle, and the rittmeister had either decided or been forced to bring in some sort of expert to assess his loyalty to the Reich. Chapman wished he hadn't lost his temper and beat the tar out of the insolent Viking Regiment legionnaire. But it had filled him with volcanic rage when the bastard called Dagmar a tart. He knew how much it hurt her to be called such names and to have her fellow Norwegians give her the cold shoulder.

As von Gröning closed the front door, the man stood up from his seat and made his way towards them. "Greetings, Agent Fritz. My name is Doctor Konig," he said in excellent English with an American accent. "Please sit down and let's have a talk."

Chapman looked at his handler, feeling the usual butterflies in his stomach that he felt before being interrogated but reminding himself to appear confident and relaxed.

"He just has a few questions," said von Gröning with his characteristic smile and understatement. "I'll be in the other room."

The spymaster left them. Turning to face his adversary, Chapman presented a mask of calm as he and Konig took their seats in the drawing room. He took a moment to size up the good doktor and collect himself in preparation for the questioning, which he could tell was not going to be easy despite his extensive training and hands-on experience in duplicity. There was something in Konig's clinically cold manner and intense hawk-like gaze that he found deeply unnerving, as if the man could peer into his soul. He suspected the German was some sort of army psychologist.

"Where could you leave a valuable package safely in London?" Konig began without preamble.

Chapman tried his best not to look surprised at the suddenness of the questioning. "Why the Eagle Club in Soho, of course."

"Who would you leave it with?"

He thought for a second; he needed to come up with a name the Germans could never trace. "Milly Blackwood," he lied through a poker face. Milly had indeed once been the owner of the Eagle Club, but she was dead. Safely dead.

"Where would you conceal a secret message for another agent?"

This one he had practiced with Ronnie Reed back in London. "In a telephone booth or a public lavatory."

"Where did you leave your wireless?"

"I buried it in a garden near a large tree at a house in London."

Konig looked at him long and hard. "I am running an agent who will shortly be going to England on a mission. This agent might need the wireless."

Suddenly, Chapman felt a wave of desperation. Herr Konig had cleverly set him up for a trap. The wireless set that had been airdropped along with him in December 1942 was stashed away in an equipment room in Whitehall, and he had no way of contacting MI5 to arrange for it to be buried. He could give an invented address for the hiding place, but if the Germans did send an agent to find it and turned up nothing, his entire story would unravel. His British handlers had not anticipated this flaw in his story. Even the old man had missed it. Or had he chosen to overlook it? Was Konig bluffing about sending an agent into Britain? Did Chapman dare counterbluff? He decided to play the part of the aggrieved operative.

"I won't allow another agent to use my radio. I expect one day to be sent back to England."

The German squinted at him.

"It's bloody unfair to make me give up my radio when I will need it for my own mission."

The gray-haired interrogator continued to eye him coldly. Chapman knew he had been caught off-guard and was grasping at straws: the Abwehr could easily find him another transmitter.

Konig continued the interrogation. Chapman clung steadfast to the story he had rehearsed a hundred times back at the MI5 safe house at 35 Crespigny Road. With the German's withering stare grating on his nerves, he sought occasional refuge by slowing down the pace and staring off as if intrigued by the two reproduced oil paintings on the wall. Von Gröning had told him that the famous originals were by the 19th-century German Romantic landscape painter Caspar David Friedrich, and that Hitler—a failed painter of mediocre talent—had worshiped Friedrich's patriotic work. Both paintings showed allegorical landscapes and contemplative figures silhouetted against night skies, morning mists, barren trees, and Gothic ruins. Chapman was not much of an art aficionado, but he knew enough to know that he much preferred Italian Renaissance and Dutch masters, as well as the later French Impressionists, than Friedrich's paintings celebrating Germanic culture, customs, and mythology. When he looked at the paintings, Chapman couldn't help but see the face of the Führer.

After a full hour of questioning, Konig drove him to a quiet restaurant, where they ate dinner and drank cognac while the hawk-faced interrogator continued to probe for signs of disloyalty. Once again, Konig asked him the details of where he had hidden his radio transmitter and requested a safe contact and address—and again Chapman proffered the name Milly Blackworth at the Eagle Club on Gerard Street, whom he knew had passed away years earlier. Chapman got drunk, but not nearly as drunk as he appeared. By the end of the evening, they were both slurring their words, Konig seemed less suspicious, and Chapman believed he had hoodwinked the enemy. He knew the Abwehr's approach. Even if they trusted him, they still made it a point to question operatives repeatedly about the same details. In his view, they seemed to work on the principle that a double agent would always remember the truth but never be able to repeat lies convincingly.

At eleven p.m., they staggered to their feet to leave. It was then Konig dropped a bombshell.

Fixing him with a hostile stare, he pronounced accusingly, "You are not absolutely sincere."

Chapman held the stare for a second, and then grinned: "I know I am not," he replied, maintaining a cloak of ambiguity. "Do you expect me to be?"

With the question left unanswered, the German delivered him to Forbunds Hotel and drove off into the night, leaving him to wonder if his fate had been sealed and he would be selected for termination.

CHAPTER 42

LÖWENBRÄU RESTAURANT, OSLO

JUNE 24, 1943

FOUR DAYS LATER, Chapman stared expectantly at the front door from the mahogany bar of the Löwenbräu. Still no sign of Dagmar. He looked at his watch for the tenth time. Quarter after seven p.m. She was only fifteen minutes late, but it was not like her to be tardy for a date. *Where could she be?* he wondered. *Has something happened to her?*

He looked around the room. Tonight, the restaurant was filled with the usual crowd of Abwehr and SS officers, Norwegian Nazi political hacks and war profiteers, and Viking Regiment legionnaires. He didn't recognize anyone except *Hauptsharführer* Axel Etling, the head of the Gestapo motor transport division. He was eating dinner at a nearby table with several other SS officers. Etling was responsible for sending out the vehicles used to arrest suspected saboteurs and anti-Nazi Norwegian military and police officers. Chapman had dined with him on more than one occasion and found him a sufficiently agreeable fellow, though he still cautiously regarded him as a Nazi thug and man to keep his eye on within the Gestapo hierarchy.

Looking at Etling and his entourage in their neatly-pressed Gestapo uniforms, he couldn't help but wonder if he was being watched. But they seemed oblivious to his presence. Was there someone else in the room keeping him under surveillance? The morning after his encounter with Doktor Konig, Graumann had told him that the interview had been successful and that his inquisitor was quite satisfied with the answers and information he had received. The spymaster had been in a buoyant mood and concluded breezily with, "You passed the test." But Chapman couldn't help but wonder if the old man was giving him false reassurance and he was still not yet out of the woods. For some reason, he had the uncanny feeling he was being watched by the Germans.

"May I sit here?" he heard a voice politely inquire in German.

Deep in his thoughts, he nearly jumped up from his seat. Quickly recovering his composure, he looked up to see a flashily dressed woman of around forty-five pointing to the chair next to him.

"Yes, by all means." He, too, spoke *auf Deutsch*, and helped her into her chair. "I'm just waiting for my girlfriend."

"I am Anne."

"Fritz Graumann."

They shook hands. She ordered a schnapps and they made small talk for a moment before she said, "You have a most unusual accent. Where are you from?"

"I was born in Germany but raised in America."

"Oh, America," she said enthusiastically, switching now to English, which she spoke perfectly. "You must love Clark Gable."

"Yes, he's a good actor. I loved *Gone with the Wind.*"

"I just love Hollywood films. So much more fun to watch than those drab Goebbels propaganda films."

Chapman said nothing. He felt his red-flag alerts registering. Something about this woman didn't feel right.

"I'm Norwegian, but I have to admit back in 1940 and '41 I used to believe in the Reich. But not anymore. No, Herr Graumann, not after what they've done here in Norway during this Occupation. There's never enough food, we Norwegians no longer have any rights, and the German soldiers goose-step their way up and down the streets like they own the city. Frankly, I'm sick and tired of it. What do you think?"

He shrugged. "I don't have an opinion on the matter. I just want to get through the war."

"Oh, come now. You're telling me that you think it's fair that the Germans take the best fish, cuts of meat, and vegetables as well as all the milk while we have strict rationing of not only food but coal, gas, and clothing? Some people have been reduced to making shoes from fish skins and clothes from old newspapers."

He nodded in understanding but said nothing.

"Why the Germans have requisitioned the best hotels, apartments, houses, and government buildings for themselves. Victoria Terrasse has been desecrated by the Gestapo, and Terboven and his henchmen have overtaken the parliament building in the heart of the city and thrown up the Nazi flag. Doesn't this bother you?"

"There's a war going on. War is hard on the people on both sides."

"That's all you have to say? They've removed judges, clergy, administrators, journalists, policemen, and teachers by the thousands, claiming they are not loyal to the New Order, and replaced them with quislings. Don't you think that's wrong?"

He said nothing and sipped his drink. The woman was becoming annoying and had to be some sort of agent provocateur, testing his loyalties and trying to trap him into criticizing German policy. He told himself not to say anything further. Then again, was it possible she was a genuine member of the Resistance?

"Would you like to have dinner with me?" she asked.

"No, as I said before, I am waiting for my date."

"Some other time perhaps."

"Perhaps," he said ambiguously.

It was then she downed her cocktail, her face turned cold, and she showed her true colors. "I think you are an English spy," she spat.

Her delivery was loud enough to be heard at the nearby tables and several heads turned, including Etling's. Steeling himself, Chapman feigned a look of shock. "What did you just say?"

"You heard me. You are a British spy and are only pretending to be an Abwehr agent. Furthermore, Fritz Graumann is no doubt a made-up name."

Now he gave a look of outrage. "I told you I am a German who lived in America. And that is all I have told you."

"You are a liar! You are a British double agent!"

Now the whole room was looking at them. Chapman made sure to keep his emotions in check by maintaining a neutral expression, as he had been trained to do. The woman—whom he would soon learn was a Norwegian agent provocateur working for Fehmer's Gestapo named Frau Arne—shuffled off to the table next to *Hauptsharführer* Etling where several SS officers were sitting. After tossing back his drink, Chapman watched in mute horror as she talked animatedly to the other uniformed SS men, who every so often cast cold glances in his direction.

Deciding that it would be best to ignore them, he ordered another cognac from the bartender. Then he looked at his watch again. Where the hell was Dagmar? Why was she taking so bloody long? Had something happened to her? God, he hoped she was all right.

His cognac came. He downed it in three large gulps. Then, to his further dismay, he saw Etling rise from his chair and start over towards him.

Oh, bloody hell! This is it—I'm done for!

"Good evening, Graumann," said the master sergeant as he slid onto the seat next to him. "I hear you have been causing trouble."

He pretended ignorance. "How is that?"

"Well, Frau Arne here says she is going to report you to my bureau on suspicion of being a British spy. What do you have to say to that?"

Frau Arne—so that was her real name. He felt his heart thumping in his chest. Was this really it for him? Had he buggered the whole thing up? Fearing for his life, he produced his most disarming smile. "A British spy? Well then, I would have to say that she certainly has a vivid imagination. I would venture she's been watching too many Hollywood pictures."

Etling just looked at him, his eyes narrow. And then he took the double agent completely by surprise by tilting his head back and exploding with laughter.

"You, a British spy! Our man who's been over there for us and successfully blew up the Mosquito factory! Now that is rich!"

"I'll say!" said Chapman, feeling a wave of relief.

"What is rich?" he then heard a female voice say. He turned to see Dagmar.

"Oh, your boyfriend here has just been accused by that hatchet-faced woman over there of being a British spy!" cried Etling drunkenly, tipping his head towards the glowering Frau Arne at the table next to his. "Isn't that the most ridiculous story you've ever heard?"

Chapman's and Dagmar's eyes met. There was something knowing in her big chestnut eyes, as if she was seeing him clearly for the first time. "Our friend Fritz a British spy?" she posed rhetorically. "Why, it's almost inconceivable."

"Yes, that's what I said! I can't even begin to express my indignation at such a slanderous accusation being leveled against him!" roared Etling, and he slapped Chapman heartily on the back. "Now get out of here, you two. Go home, have a drink, and make passionate love. Maybe when you're finished, the war will be over!"

"If only we could be so lucky, Axel," said Chapman.

And with that, he took Dagmar on his arm and they left the Löwenbräu. Tomorrow, he would have to tell Graumann about Frau Arne. The old man would know what to do with her.

CHAPTER 43

GESTAPO HEADQUARTERS
VICTORIA TERRASSE

JULY 5, 1943

"YOU MUST STOP THE TORTURE, SIEGFRIED. If you don't, the Norwegian people will curse your name for a thousand years. Is that how you want to be remembered?"

The words stung, but Fehmer tried not to let the hurt and anger show on his face as he gazed into the earnest blue eyes of Annemarie Breien. He realized in that moment that he would do anything to win her love and affection. She spoke in such a gentle yet persuasive tone that, once again, a part of him couldn't help but feel like a barbarian for all the cruel punishment he had meted out to her countrymen during the past three years of the Occupation. But the other part of him, the pragmatic and compliant side that had sworn an oath to the Führer, reminded himself that what he was doing was necessary. The enemy combatants he brought in for questioning and shipped off to prison were criminals, saboteurs, and terrorists—not soldiers wearing uniforms. They had to be aggressively interrogated and, if the situation demanded it, sufficiently motivated through physical punishment to come clean with the truth. Only by extracting the truth from them could he properly protect the state, maintain law and order, and send a message to the Resistance. They were enemies of the Reich trying to overthrow the New Order—and they had to be stopped in their tracks.

"We do not torture prisoners," he replied in a clinical voice. "It is true that on occasion we are compelled to subject them to enhanced interrogation. But we do not torture them."

"Oh, don't play games with me, Siegfried. Everyone has heard the stories of what goes on here."

"And have they also heard the stories of the twenty-seven men I have released on your behalf? Have you told your fine Norwegian friends of my compassionate deeds, or is it easier for you to label me a Nazi brute and leave it at that to make yourself look good?"

"You know I have praised your efforts to those close to me. But the truth of the matter is you have mistreated and locked away far more men than you have set free."

He decided to try and turn the tables on her. "Maybe I should stop then. If my deeds have no value, then what is the point?"

Her face flashed alarm. "No, no, please don't do that," she pleaded.

"Why not? If I am of no use, why should I continue with the releases at all? Perhaps you and I shouldn't see each other anymore. If your visits don't bear any tangible fruit, what's the point?"

She jumped up from her chair. "This work is too important! You can't do this!"

He realized he had regained the upper hand and he had her right where he wanted her—and yet, at the same time, he couldn't help but feel guilty for manipulating her. *Do you know how much I care for you, Annemarie? Do you have any idea?*

"I didn't mean to upset you," she said, leaning across his desk and apologetically touching his hand. "I came here to talk to you, not to argue."

"Good, then I want you to know the truth." He reached into his desk drawer, withdrew a document, and handed it to her. "These are the special provisions under which physical force can be used here in Norway. I wrote them myself. Would you care to read them to me?"

"I...I'm not sure I—"

"Please just read them. Then you will understand that this is a complex legal matter with no simple solution. We here at Gestapo headquarters are not monsters. We are not like the SS, you know."

She looked scared. He hated himself for eliciting fear when he cared for her. She took a moment to look over the top sheet before clearing her throat to speak.

"It says here that the following criteria must be fulfilled prior to using enhanced interrogation on a prisoner. First, it should be perfectly clear that the accused in question has committed serious unlawful acts."

"That is Criteria Number One. And what are the others?"

"It says that they must also be allowed to give only the information desired relative to important unlawful activities affecting German military interests."

"Good."

"Third, it states that full confidence cannot be placed in statements by 'trustees' even if such 'trustees' have hitherto acted in a way to inspire absolute confidence."

"Number Four?"

"Before any exception can be made to said prohibition against the use of physical force every other means of interrogation must have proven to be a failure."

"And the last one, Number Five?"

"The decision to use force on accused persons rests exclusively with the official directly in charge of the case as he is in the best position to determine if a suspect is lying or not."

"Very good. So, as you can see, we strenuously adhere to the rule of law here at Victoria Terrasse by following guidelines that I myself have developed."

"Guidelines are not the same as laws."

"No, but in times of war, they are the best that can be done."

"Well then, Siegfried, you and I must agree to disagree. I'm afraid that is the best I can do."

"I appreciate your honesty. At the same time, however, I hope you can appreciate my position as a criminal investigator."

She said nothing. The conversation was fast becoming uncomfortable, and he didn't want it to escalate into an argument or for them to part ways on a sour note. He smiled with cordial grace, hoping he could reclaim the situation with his charm.

"What can I help you with today, Annemarie? I know you didn't come here to lecture me on my lack of moral scruples."

"I'm sorry. I didn't mean to upset you."

"You haven't upset me. We have a difference of opinion—nothing more. Now what can I do to help you? That is why you have come here to my evil lair, isn't it?"

She bowed her head in submission and he loathed himself for making her feel the necessity of bowing before him. *Damnit, can't you see that I am human and have feelings too? Do you think that I like playing the role of the Big Bad Wolf?*

"Today, I have but one request," she said.

"And what is that?"

"I want you to release a friend of mine. He also happens to be an important figure here in Norway."

"A man of distinction, is he?"

"Yes."

"What's his name?"

"Sigurd Evensmo."

"The communist partisan? That's the man you want released? You've got to be joking."

"I am not joking, and he is not a communist. Sigurd merely supports labor rights."

"Tell that to my two bosses. They regard the man as dangerous."

"Your *Oberführer* Fehlis and Head of the Gestapo Hellmuth Reinhard don't have to know. You don't have to tell them."

"I haven't been telling them about *any* of the releases I have been undertaking on your behalf. But if I keep doing it, they most certainly will find out. Do you understand the risks I am already taking to help you? Do you, Annemarie?"

Her face softened. "Yes, I appreciate all you have done, but Sigurd Evensmo is not dangerous. He is a journalist and playwright not a labor leader, though he speaks out on behalf of the rights of the common worker. He is being held in Grini Prison and his prisoner number is 1747-2755. Please, can you help me secure his release?"

"Even if I wanted to, I don't see how it can be done."

"Why not?"

"Because Evensmo was sentenced for being active with the Resistance not just dabbling in illegal newspaper activities."

"He was not active with the Resistance. He just wrote articles."

"Perhaps, but *Bulletinen* is still an illegal paper and he is still a criminal. That's why he went into hiding and tried to flee Norway. But he was caught. And you want me to release this criminal?"

"He is not a criminal, he is a writer. Before the war, he wrote a play called *Konflikt*. It was a masterpiece. And he didn't write for an underground paper until you Germans invaded in April 1940 and occupied our country. He wrote for *Arbeiderbladet*, which was shut down as a newspaper by the Nazi authorities. *Nasjonal Samling* evicted *Arbeiderbladet* from its premises and began using it as headquarters for its party organ *Fritt Folk*. Where was he supposed to go to write? *Arbeiderbladet's* printing press was also stolen by *Fritt Folk*. How was he to continue his work?"

"When you write newspaper articles criticizing the New Order, you are going to be put out of business. It is as simple as that."

"Sigurd Evensmo is not a threat to Nazi Germany. The man is brilliant and that is why I want you to release him."

"I am sorry. You're asking the impossible."

"If he isn't removed from Grini, he will die. Do you want to be responsible for his death?"

"Don't try and pin this on me. I wasn't the one who arrested him."

"But you can save him, just as you have saved my father and more than a score of others. You hold the power of life and death in your hands, Siegfried. All I'm asking is for you to do what is right. I know you have to deal harshly with spies and saboteurs, but we are talking about a well-known journalist, playwright, and creative human being not a threat to the Reich."

"Unfortunately, Fehlis and Reinhard do not see it that way."

"But we already agreed that you will not tell them."

"We agreed to nothing. You tried to put words in my mouth. If they ever found out what I am doing, they would ship *me* off to Grini."

"Please, I implore you to release Evensmo. I fear for his life in that prison."

"We are at war, Annemarie. You are asking me to perform the impossible."

"All I ask is that you try. Can you at least promise me you will do that?"

"Yes," he said. "I promise I will try." He allowed his eyes to narrow slightly in warning. "But if I were you, I wouldn't expect much. If you do, your heart may very well be broken."

CHAPTER 44

KARL JOHANS GATE, OSLO

JULY 10, 1943

"HOW WAS YOUR TRIP TO BERLIN?" asked Dagmar as she and Eddie Chapman—who still had not revealed his real name to her despite their torrid love affair—walked hand in hand from the National Theater Square onto Karl Johans gate with a resplendent summer sun on their shoulders.

He flashed her a devilish look that made her smile. "You know I can't tell you that. At least not until I'm in your arms on my boat with the waves lapping gently against the hull."

"You're a naughty boy with a one-track mind, aren't you?"

"Around you I am, my love. You bring out the beast in me, I'm afraid."

"Like your creatures on the island of Doctor Moreau?"

"Quite. One look at you and I want to ravage you. But to be perfectly honest, what man wouldn't? You are quite ravishing."

They stopped along the sidewalk north of the theater and laughed. That's when she noticed that people were looking at them disapprovingly. She felt her whole body deflate like a balloon, going from elation to embarrassment in an instant. It was the same way she had felt on the tram earlier in the day. When a few blocks from the harbor they had first stepped onto the conveyance, several people had stood up when they suspected her lover was German and made a point of sitting on another bench. Publicly shunned and humiliated, she had crimsoned with shame.

She did it again now.

"I'm sorry," he said, seeing that she was blushing. "It's such a lovely day—I had hoped we could enjoy it without being abused by your countrymen."

"We should only be so lucky," she said, trying to present a stiff upper lip but hurting inside. As before on the tram, she felt as if a knife had been stuck in her heart at being seeing with a "despicable Nazi" even though she already knew in her heart that Fritz Graumann was the furthest thing from a rabid Nazi. In fact, she felt certain that he didn't have a lick of German blood in his veins, though she had yet to tell him this. After their incredible lovemaking last night, she wanted desperately to come clean and confess to him that she was a spy for the Allied cause and that she suspected he was too. But she knew that taking such a risk could get them both killed.

"Let's keep moving," she said. "It's all we can do."

"Yes, let's go."

They quickened their pace, crossing Universitetsgata and racing past the storefronts like children in search of candy.

"Which is your favorite H.G. Wells book?" she asked after a minute.

"It would have to be *The Time Machine*."

"That's my favorite too," she said.

"Something about Wells's utopian socialism appeals to me. I've seen some cruel things in my life, and sometimes I wonder if the author's vision of the world is the answer to what ails us. Take this war, for instance. If we were more like the gentle Eloi and less like the Morlocks, we wouldn't be in this world-wide mess we're in now."

"I agree. And I would say that if anyone is the Morlocks, it is Hitler and his Nazis. I hate them, and I must say that you don't seem to be too fond of them either."

He gave no reply and they kept walking. Despite his silence, she sensed that he wanted to come clean with her just as she did with him. She could feel it in the air that they both had secrets and wanted to reveal their true nature.

After two blocks, they stopped at a store window next to the Grand Café used by the Nazis to display anti-Allied propaganda. Usually the posters in the window took the form of a giant cartoon. Today, the main poster showed Churchill and Roosevelt as two monstrous airplanes dropped bombs on German churches and hospitals, while women in Britain jitterbugged and drank cocktails. Next to the main poster were several other propaganda posters. One was designed to recruit Norwegian collaborators into the Waffen SS. It showed a steel-helmeted Norseman with a shield bearing a swastika and read *Kjemp for Norge*—Norwegians, Fight for Norway! Another was a Norwegian SS ski-troop recruiting poster for volunteers to fight for Hitler that read *Den Norske Skijegerbataljon*. Dagmar had heard that Hitler was both surprised and infuriated by Norway's refusal to bow to Nazi might and send her sons to fight for the Reich. Though Quisling had been trying to institute compulsory military service and raise volunteers for the now-faltering German war effort following the defeat at Stalingrad in February, the Norwegian people had stoutly resisted, and no military draft had been put into effect. The Germans desperately needed manpower on the battlefields and in the war factories, but they were getting little help from Norway except the SS Viking Regiment.

Chapman pointed to the poster of Churchill and Roosevelt with the airplanes bombing German churches and schools while English women jitterbugged and tossed back cocktails. "I must admit Herr Goebbels is a clever propagandist. But in this case, I think the poster does the German cause more harm than good. Allied pilots are most certainly not targeting churches and schools, though they are no doubt hitting some by accident."

"We are lucky there is seldom any bombing here. The situation in Norway has been bad during the Occupation, but not been as bad as elsewhere. We have had food, clothing, and petrol shortages, but we have been spared the horrors that poor Poland and France have suffered."

"That is true. But I am growing sick and tired of salt fish."

They walked on to the Parliament Building at 22 Karl Johans gate. The yellow brick and light-gray granite *Stortingsbygningen* that combined several architectural styles, including inspirations from France and Italy, had been taken over by the *Reichskommissar* and his Nazi administrators. A triumphant banner draped over the front entrance boasted *DEUTSCHLAND SIEGT AN ALLEN FRONTEN*— GERMANS WIN ON EVERY FRONTLINE.

Dagmar shook her head in disgust. "*Deutschland liegt an allen fronten,*" she said subversively.

Chapman chuckled. "The Germans *lie* on every frontline," he said, getting the inside joke that by substituting the single letter "l" for "s" in "siegt" the entire meaning of the banner was transformed from a German boast to an incisive Norwegian barb.

Retracing their steps on Akersgata, they turned right onto Karl Johans gate and walked two blocks before Dagmar halted them in front of a tobacconist.

"Wait here," she said. "I won't be but five minutes."

He gave a look of surprise. "What, you've run out of cigarettes?"

"No, I just need to see a friend for a moment. Can you please just wait?"

He leaned forward and kissed her. "For you, I can wait an eternity."

"That's what I like to hear."

She gave him another peck on the cheek before ducking into the tobacco shop. She quickly scanned the store. A middle-aged husband and wife stood behind the counter tending to a single male customer. After making eye contact with the husband, Dagmar walked up and down the aisles pretending to shop until the customer at the counter had purchased his tobacco and left the store. When the coast was clear, she stepped up to the counter and looked at the man and woman.

"Hello, you may call me *Danser*. Ishmael sends his regards."

"The midnight sun shines bright in Tromsø this time of year," said the woman.

"Indeed, but not for quislings," pronounced Dagmar.

With the passwords exchanged, they all relaxed. The man leaned forward and whispered excitedly, "I have great news! The Allies have invaded Sicily! Generals Patton and Montgomery are leading their men into battle and are reportedly gaining a foothold on the island as we speak! The BBC is calling it the largest amphibious attack of the war! They say it will open the way for the invasion of Italy and a second Allied front!"

She felt the excitement shoot through her body. "My God, that is wonderful news! The taking back of the continent has begun! A part of me thought this day would never come!"

"We just found out," said the woman. "When the Germans eventually announce it, they will lie about the invasion and say they expected it all along. But the truth is, they never saw it coming."

"Everyone was saying Greece or Sardinia."

"The Allies fooled us all," said the man. "We are going to win this war now. After Stalingrad, North Africa, and now Kursk and Sicily, the Germans are spread too thin. They will not be able to recover the offensive."

"This is a turning point," said Dagmar, beaming.

"Yes, my child, we are at a turning point," said the woman. "Thanks to brave souls like you." She made a "V" for victory sign, made famous by Churchill and later appropriated unsuccessfully by Goebbels and his Nazi propaganda machine.

Dagmar made the sign in return. "I will relay the news," she said as a new customer entered the store.

"It is time for you to go," said the man, eyeing the newcomer cautiously before apparently deciding that he posed no threat. "Tell everyone you trust the good news. All for Norway!"

"Yes, all for Norway!" She left the shop, feeling positively giddy. She was excited not only by the news but that she was contributing to the war effort just like the Allied soldiers on the battlefields. As she stepped into the sunlight, she felt as if she was not just a twenty-year-old girl but a part of the powerful sweep of history.

"What is it? What's going on?" Chapman asked her straight away, seeing how excited she was. He looked at her hands. "You didn't buy any cigarettes?"

She took him by the elbow and they started down the street. "No, I didn't go in there for tobacco. I went in there for information."

"Information?"

"The Americans and British have invaded Sicily! They're pushing inland from the beaches as we speak!"

"Good heavens! But wait a second—how did you find this out? The news of the invasion has not been broadcast on Norwegian radio."

She gave him a knowing look as they crossed a side street.

"I see. You could only have obtained such information through the underground."

"I must say you are awfully perceptive. I would also like to say that you appear every bit as exhilarated by the news as I am. Aren't you, Mr. German-American?"

He smiled guiltily but again didn't respond directly. "Okay, enough with the games. Who told you?"

"I can't tell you that."

"I'm not asking you to reveal the names of any of your contacts."

"I should hope not!"

"Just tell me if the information came through the patriotic Norwegian Jøssings or some other group?"

"I can't tell you that. You're going to have to draw your own conclusions."

"I already have, Miss Jøssing. And I think we both can agree that you're playing a most dangerous game."

"And you're not?"

"I regret to say I cannot answer that question so as not to risk your and my personal safety. But I will say this. Since the night we met at the Ritz Bar, I have often wondered who caught whose eye."

"I have wondered the same thing, Herr Graumann. I have wondered the very same thing."

And with that she gave him a happy kiss on the lips.

CHAPTER 45

THE EXPLOSION ROCKED THE HOTEL.

Chapman looked at Dagmar, saw the alarm on her face. Was the Forbunds under attack?

He dashed to his first-floor window and threw it open. A large and comfortable wood-built hotel in the Oslo city center, the Forbunds had been commandeered by the Abwehr and the Luftwaffe early on during the Occupation and was, thus, a target of the Norwegian Resistance. Chapman and Dagmar had been enjoying a cup of early evening tea after making love in his room when the explosion had sent a shudder through the hotel.

Suddenly, a cry of *Fire!* resounded through the corridors.

Peering out the window, he quickly saw that the top floor was in flames. The blaze leapt from the window of a room like a demon and appeared to be engulfing the two apartments on either side. To make matters worse, the Germans had opened the windows to let out the smoke, but all this did was further fan the flames.

He and Dagmar watched the scene, certain that the fire was going to spread and quickly consume the entire hotel. Chapman shook his head in dismay but was relieved that he hadn't been the target. He knew it had to be an act of sabotage since the hotel was occupied exclusively by German military and intelligence officers. The Luftwaffe even had a reserved suite where films were developed for the Information and News Section of their intelligence branch. The large hotels in Oslo did not escape the attention of the saboteurs, Chapman knew; the Norwegians could not sink them like the ships in Oslo Harbor, but they could burn them to the ground.

"Looks like your Norwegian friends don't much like the hotel's clientele," he said.

"It would appear so," agreed Dagmar, staring up at raging inferno.

Now they heard shouting voices inside the hotel, and down below on the street passersby stood gawking and German officers began scrambling out the front door. While Dagmar continued staring out the window, he quickly checked the hallway. Panic-stricken German officers rushed past him, some fully dressed in neatly pressed military uniforms, others disheveled or only half-dressed. The hallways and staircases were filling up fast with smoke.

He looked at his watch. It was two minutes after five o'clock.

"We need to leave. I'll grab my things."

"Here, let me help you," she said.

They stuffed his few belongings into a suitcase and clattered down the staircase to join the throng in the street. Several German officers were shouting orders, but Chapman noticed that no one was obeying them. Fire bells clanged, and telephone bells rang, while outside, more and more Norwegians gathered along Tullins gate.

Many were grinning triumphantly at the German loss, but an equal number were NS, or at least non-committal, and they weren't. He and Dagmar stared up along with the rest of the crowd as the top floor of the hotel blazed. By now, the flames were pouring through several windows, the gray smoke billowing up towards a periwinkle blue summer sky. Norwegian onlookers continued to gather as German officers poured out the front door in the confusion, many out of uniform.

Suddenly, there was another tremendous explosion. A second window blasted open in a fiery flash of orange. The flames surged out of the broken window and a cascade of glass shards showered the street below along with an eruption of black smoke. Standing there clutching a pair of suitcases, Chapman felt a wave of searing airborne heat on his face. A third explosion followed the second, as five rooms on the top floor merged as one behind an expanding wall of fire. The people in the crowd were occasionally forced to cover their heads as glass and burning timber rained down on them from above.

After a long delay, the Norwegian fire brigade arrived on the scene amid cheers and laughter from the assembled throng. Slowly and deliberately, the firemen mounted their ladders and fixed their hoses. Chapman could see that they were plainly in no hurry. Inside the hotel and around the perimeter, the Germans fumed at the delay.

Finally, once the hoses and ladders were all properly positioned, they began spraying water everywhere—everywhere except the fire that is. Now the mostly Norwegian crowd jeered and cheered. Chapman thought the scene worthy of a Marx brothers' script as he watched the firemen complete their leisurely work.

Dagmar touched his arm. "There's someone I need to see. I'll be back in a minute."

"What do you mean someone?"

"You have to trust me. I'll be right back."

She disappeared into the crowd.

What the bloody hell is she up to? he wondered. *Is she trying to figure out who is behind the fire? Or is it possible she has something to do with it?*

Though surprised by her odd behavior, he returned his attention to the blaze. Flames poured from half of the upstairs windows, rumbling like a storm. He couldn't help but conclude that the hotel would have been better off if the fire brigade had not arrived at all as water was squirted into the rooms, on the roads, on the rooftops without having any observable effect on the fire.

And then suddenly the Gestapo arrived. An Opel Admiral Cabriolet bearing a driver and officer pulled up to the curb south of the entrance along with several SS troop transports. From the lead Opel stepped a tall, blond, blue-eyed officer who flashed a Sipo badge to a senior uniformed Luftwaffe officer. The plainclothed Gestapo officer was dressed in a finely-tailored Norwegian suit and could have been the poster child for the Super Aryan *Lebensborn* program. He immediately began barking out orders to the SS troops disgorging from the fleet of heavy trucks lined up behind him. Chapman had never seen the officer before but made a mental note of him for Tar Robertson. Under the Gestapo officer's vigilant direction, the blaze was quickly brought under control with several blasting hoses. The crowd booed their disapproval.

It was at that moment Dagmar returned.

"Where did you go?" he asked. "The Gestapo is here, and I was worried about you."

"I had to see someone."

"Who?"

"I can't tell you that. But I can tell you who is behind the fire."

"Who is it?"

"It is the work of the British."

"The Special Operations Executive has struck in Oslo again?"

"I didn't say it was the SOE, just that the British were behind it. But I suspect you're right."

Chapman nodded. The Special Operations Executive was the British government agency set up to promote resistance activities in the occupied countries of Europe. SOE's job was to foment sabotage, subversion, and resistance, a goal that its creators hoped would disrupt and eventually help destroy the Nazi war machine. Churchill, an enthusiastic champion of the unconventional commando outfit, dubbed the SOE "the Ministry of Ungentlemanly Warfare" and instructed its first chief to "set Europe ablaze." Thus far in Norway, the most successful action undertaken by the SOE had been the series of heavy-water raids conducted upon the Vemork Hydrogen Production Plant in Telemark. Five months earlier, in February 1943, a team of SOE-trained Norwegian commandos had succeeded in destroying the heavy-water production facility. Other SOE-directed actions conducted by home-grown, British-trained Resistance operatives—like Max Manus and Gunnar Sønsteby whose inspiring exploits were legendary among Norwegians—included the sabotage of ships, trains, and railways.

They continued to stare up in awe at the conflagration. Thick black smoke billowed up from the dying building as fire hoses continued to dampen the flames. Ten minutes later, the fire was close to extinguished, but the Forbunds Hotel was in ruins and it appeared as if a goodly portion of the building had been demolished to put out the fire. Chapman could see that scores of rooms had succumbed to the flames, while an equal number appeared to have remained unscathed by the fire but had been ruined by water. His bedroom on the first floor was so flooded that it was uninhabitable. Water had seeped through ceilings and walls like Niagara Falls and come in through the windows. But he knew the chief damage had been to the prestige of the German conquerors. They had been made to look like fools, and many of the Oslo onlookers he saw to his left and right would return home that night feeling deeply gratified.

Suddenly, he felt Dagmar squeezing his hand.

"We have to go! We have to go!" she whispered urgently.

"Why? This is just getting interesting."

"That Gestapo officer is staring at us." She tipped her head towards the tall, blond officer in the finely-tailored suit. "He is making me uncomfortable."

He studied the German, who he realized was making a very conscious effort to blend in with the local Oslo population. He could have easily passed for a Norwegian.

"Do you know who he is?" he asked her.

"Yes, that is Siegfried Fehmer. He is the Gestapo's lead investigator of the Resistance here in Oslo. They call him the Commissar."

"The Commissar?"

"He is lethal."

"What is the name of his department, do you know?"

"Why would you want to know that?"

"Whether friend or foe, it's always good to know who to watch out for."

"He is a *hauptsturmführer* and *kriminalrat* in the *Sicherheitspolizei Abteilung IV* at Victoria Terrasse. Believe me, you don't want to spend the night there. Come on, we need to go. It is not safe to be here—for either of us."

Chapman continued to study the man as he parted his way through the crowd, finding him intriguing. He wanted to know more about him. MI5 would be very interested in knowing more about the chief investigator of the Resistance in Oslo.

He felt a firm tug on his hand. "Please," said Dagmar, her face now showing visible concern. "The man is trouble. He will cause us no small amount of grief."

"You actually know him?"

"Yes, he interrogated me some time ago. All I was doing was walking on the street minding my business when the Gestapo raided a house near the hospital. I made the mistake of pulling a wounded man into the trees when he was escaping. Fehmer questioned me for several hours then held me overnight to threaten me. It was before I met you."

He couldn't help but feel she wasn't telling him the whole story.

"We really need to go. I don't want him to see me here. Wait, where did he go?"

Turning, he searched the crowd but couldn't see Fehmer anymore either. "I don't bloody know. He's gone."

"He's like a ghost. Come on, let's go—I don't like this."

"Well, well, well, if it isn't my old friend Dagmar Lahlum."

Chapman looked up to see the Gestapo captain smiling belligerently. His heart literally skipped a beat and, for a moment, he was breathless. How did the clever bastard move through the crowd so quickly?

"Why is it that you always make a grand entrance during critical times?" Fehmer continued, still smirking. "Why if I didn't know better, I would have to say you were with the underground."

Chapman was taken aback by Fehmer's effrontery, but not by his accusation. All the same, he didn't like the man's silky-smooth style and insinuating manner. There was also something salacious about the way he looked at Dagmar that made the Brit's skin boil.

"Now look here, *Hauptsturmführer*. I am with the Wehrmacht, this is my hotel, and this young Norwegian lady is with me. You had better treat us accordingly." He quickly withdrew his Wehrmacht pass, showed it to him, and thrust it back in his pocket, as if no further explanation was required.

"Yes, Herr Graumann," said Fehmer unctuously, "we meet at last."

"We meet at last? You know who I am?"

"Yes, I'm afraid your reputation has preceded you." His eyes narrowed. "You look angry. I hope you're not going to punch me in the face like you did that

Norwegian officer from the Viking Regiment. I should warn you—that would be a mistake."

"I don't like being threatened. And neither does my friend Dagmar here."

"Let's go," she whispered urgently in his ear. "This will only lead to trouble."

"What did she just say?"

"She said she would prefer more pleasant company. We're leaving now. My room has been flooded and I will now have to make alternative living arrangements."

The Nazi smiled like a reptile. Again, Chapman felt his heart skip a beat. There was an air of charming menace to the Gestapo officer that was unnerving.

"You are free to go, Herr Graumann," said Fehmer. "I wish you good luck in your search for new lodgings."

"*Danke, Hauptsturmführer.* I didn't mean to be argumentative when we're fighting on the same side."

Fehmer's smile widened, as if he was about to tell an inside joke. "We'll have to see about that. Whether we're fighting on the same side, that is."

"Are you threatening me?"

"Of course not. But I am keeping an eye on you." He shifted his gaze to Dagmar. "Or rather, I should say, I am keeping an eye on you both. Because the truth is I don't trust you."

CHAPTER 46

CENTRAL CABINET WAR ROOM
KING CHARLES STREET, LONDON

JULY 13, 1943

WEARING HIS CUSTOMARY GLENGARRY CAP with tartan facing and the trousers of his beloved Seaforth Highlanders, Robertson stared across the conference table at Sir Winston Churchill. The two men were alone in the cavernous briefing room that was more aptly described as a bomb shelter. The underground warren of war rooms situated beneath Whitehall on the west bank of the Thames served as the nerve center of the British war effort, providing a safe meeting place for the Prime Minister and various spymasters in the Secret Service, Army, and Royal Navy and Air Force with whom he worked. Since the Blitz, when wave after wave of German bombers had blasted London with high explosives and incendiaries, the subterranean labyrinth of conference rooms, map rooms, communications rooms, and working bedrooms were the very picture of British order and calm amid the tempestuous storm of the ongoing war aboveground.

"Prime Minister," Robertson began the briefing in his mellifluous Scottish brogue, "one year ago, me and my colleagues at B1A Branch made the then-startling claim that we, not Wilhelm Canaris and the Abwehr, controlled the German espionage network here in Great Britain. In a formal memorandum to the Twenty Committee that you were copied on, we contended that the only network of agents possessed by the Germans in this country was that which was under our control. Since last summer, our large-scale Double Cross deception operations and wireless intercepts from Most Secret Sources at Bletchley have irrefutably verified this. We have—on a number of occasions—succeeded in making Hitler and his generals believe precisely what we want them to believe. In short, Prime Minister, the Combined General Staff in this country have, in our MI5 double agents, a powerful means of controlling the *Oberkommando der Wehrmacht* in every occupied and neutral country in Europe. But at the same time, as we prepare for the invasion of Occupied France and our biggest deception yet, we are still vulnerable. In fact, sir, we have an Achilles Heel."

Here he paused to let his words sink in, given that Churchill was known to be excessively obsessed with, and often meddlesome about, intelligence matters. But the Prime Minister said nothing and continued to puff on his seven-inch-long, Cuban "Pepin" Fernandez Rodriguez cigar in silence. Over his portly five-foot eight-inch frame, he wore his trademark black morning coat with waistcoat and striped trousers, and a spotted bow tie. The skin beneath his eyes drooped like a wilted flower, and he was pulpy from lack of exercise and excessive drink. But with his ruddy complexion, keen twinkling eyes, and dapper parliamentary attire, he looked every inch the powerful statesman who had inspired millions during the Battle of Britain and led his country to victory over Rommel and von Arnim in North Africa.

All in all, the British Bulldog looked exquisitely vigorous and defiant—like a man who knew the tide of war had turned and was poised to win a great Allied victory.

"And what is this Achilles Heel, Colonel Robertson," he said, glancing appreciatively at his cigar as he blew out a puff of grayish-blue smoke.

"The misleading information that we feed the Germans via our double agents is bolstered by an intricate system involving several other agents, so that over the past year, the agents are not acting independently but are part of an interrelated web of deception. The interconnected nature of Double Cross is precisely what lends it credibility in the eyes of the Germans—but is also the very thing that makes us vulnerable to discovery. As the Abwehr itself has observed, 'If one pearl is false, the whole string is false.'"

"Yes, I see. All it takes is a single mistake or betrayal to reveal to the Germans that not one, not a few, not even most, but all their agents are false. In that case, rather than us shaping German war operations, Hitler would know exactly what falsehoods we're trying to foist upon him and change his plans accordingly."

"Quite so, Prime Minister."

"In fact, the mistake or betrayal doesn't even have to come from the agent—it could come from within MI5, MI6, or SOE."

"You are correct, sir. Once a spy has top-level security clearance and virtually unlimited access to military and non-military installations, he is free to gather, synthesize, and analyze all kinds of important data into a meaningful picture."

"Do you believe there's a mole or an unaccounted-for spy that has slipped through our net?"

"No, sir, fortunately we are confident that is not the case. But it is true that all that's needed to bring down the whole house of cards, thus exposing Double Cross, is one resourceful, motivated, and plucky spy with access to classified secrets. If one of our doubles is really a triple agent, then far from unveiling a war-changing new weapon, he could be leading us and our allies towards disaster."

"I see your predicament, Colonel."

"It is impossible to be certain in such cases whether the Germans are fooling us, or we are fooling them. However, I should point out that Gisela Ashley, BIA's expert on the German mentality, insists that while the Nazis are very good double-crossers, they lack the patience and guile to set up a carefully and cleverly worked out system of deception."

"How many double agents do you have working for you now?"

He withdrew from his briefcase two copies of the new monthly B1A Twenty Committee Report and handed a copy to the Prime Minister. "That is your copy, Prime Minister. If you could please turn to page two, you will see that in all, a total of one hundred twenty-six enemy spies have fallen into our hands. Of these, twenty-four have been found suitable and are currently being used as Double Cross agents. In addition, twelve real and seven imaginary persons have been foisted upon the enemy as Double Cross spies. Another thirteen spies have been executed. Our operatives are no longer an exotic sideshow; they have been fully integrated into military operations under the direction of Colonel Bevan. As you have seen in the past several reports, the stars of our motley crew of spies are Garbo, Zigzag, Mutt and Jeff, Tricycle, Brutus, and Bronx. Several of them were recently used for our Sicily deception, Operation Mincemeat, which is described on page four."

"Ah, yes. Quite a stroke of genius, that," exclaimed Churchill, and he turned to page four and read the description of the operation. Like the deception for the Operation Torch landings in North Africa in late 1942, Operation Mincemeat was conducted to deceive the Germans about where the actual Allied attack would take place in Southern Europe and, thus, force Hitler to spread his forces and divert manpower out of the planned theater of operations. The plan had been audacious but breathtakingly simple. A dead body was floated ashore in Spain carrying forged documents indicating an Allied landing in Greece and Sardinia rather than Sicily. In response, the Germans moved large numbers of troops and air power out of Sicily to the Aegean and Sardinia. The wireless intercepts of the past three days since the attack revealed that Hitler's general staff had swallowed Mincemeat whole and the invasion of Sicily on July 10 had come as a total surprise.

"Now tell me about these operatives of yours? Are you still having trouble controlling them?"

"Unfortunately, yes. As Major Masterman says, every one of our agents is inclined to be vain, moody, and introspective, at least at times. That's why managing this band of invaluable misfits is daunting to say the least."

"Yes, I don't know how you and the major pull it off."

"Since last summer, one of our top operatives managed to get himself arrested, another was in the throes of a spectacular marital bust-up before we stepped in, a third was demanding women, chocolates, and silk shirts while living the life of a pampered prince, still another begged us for more money while offering services to MI6. Handling all these disparate individuals in such a high-stakes game is quite stressful, and there is no doubt that the constant need to monitor, cajole, flatter, and build up our roster is taking its toll. But it is all worth it since we are actively fooling Jerry at every turn to help win the war."

Churchill's eyes glittered as he puffed his cigar. "I can only imagine the difficulties with which you and your team have to deal with. All the scripting, clearing, and synchronizing of the streams of information to be put across to the other side boggles the imagination."

"Yes, it is taxing, but we're getting quite good at it."

"Tell me how you go about it. I'm dying to know the details."

"Well first, Colonel Stephens, Major Masterman, and I must decide up front if we can trust them, what their motives are, and where their loyalties lie. Even this first step isn't easy."

"I can imagine."

"Then if they pass the initial test, we have to assign them a case officer and find them somewhere to live, to write their secret letters, and tap out their messages with an MI5 operator at their elbow. After that, we have to get them identity cards, ration books, petrol coupons, money, housekeepers, real jobs or plausible cover stories, while all the while keeping a discreet eye on their love lives, how much they drink, what they gossip about in pubs, and any signs of depression or second thoughts. Then, once we have done all that, we still have to create, clear, and coordinate the agents' responses to the Abwehr's instructions and queries, making sure not only that each piece of the deception jigsaw does not have some operational or strategic risk, but fits with the deceptions around it. Whatever is reported by the agents and the growing number of their fictional sub-agents must be events which they themselves have witnessed. This means driving them as far afield as Scotland, the major port cities, the industrial Midlands, and the West Country—unless they can plausibly claim to have seen them for themselves in their normal jobs or to have heard about them from some loose-lipped but well-placed contact. These ruses do not merely include troop sightings, bomb damage reports, or even faked sabotage attempts. We create sophisticated rumors that supposedly emanate from senior government and military officials or other spies."

"Great Scott, that is quite a lot to keep abreast of."

"But that's not all, sir. The decrypts provided by Most Secret Sources must be read and re-read with care and suspicion, crosschecked and collated, to see how the stories are being received, and how the Abwehr is assessing its agents and their material, and what plans are being concocted for new arrivals. Hardly less complex is devising schemes to enable the Abwehr to send money into Britain for their supposed agents without knowing they are doing so under our control. Once all that is taken care of, we still must cope every day with our doubles' tantrums, qualms, the strained relationships some of them have with their national governments-in-exile in London, and their domestic travails."

"Strordnary, strordnary indeed. I don't envy you, Colonel Robertson. But I can tell you that what you are doing is of tremendous service to our country in this epic struggle against tyranny."

"Thank you, sir. As I said, it's all worth it if we can continue to dupe the Germans. And one day, I hope our roster of spies can somehow manage to deceive them into making some large and disastrous mistake."

"Oh, you will have your chance, Colonel. During the cross-channel invasion of Occupied France. President Roosevelt and General Marshall are most insistent that it happen next year."

"We are ready and looking forward to it, Prime Minister. Our team of cricketers has stepped up to the crease and begun piling in the runs rather nicely. We have built up a team of trusted agents and are in a strong position to make the Germans believe whatever we wish. That is the most important thing I wanted to convey to you for today's briefing."

Churchill's eyes twinkled; it was obvious that he fascinated by the black art of deception, in the proud tradition of Sun Tzu. "Tangle within tangle, plot and counter-plot, ruse and treachery, cross and double-cross—all these you and your brilliant team have interwoven in many a texture so intricate as to be incredible and yet true."

"Well spoken, sir. Perhaps you should be one of our agents."

He puffed his cigar indulgently. "I would delight in such an undertaking, I can assure you. But my overexuberance and inability to keep a secret would no doubt bring a Gestapo garrote about my neck in the time it takes one of your agents to tap out a false message to his Abwehr control officer." He chortled a laugh and blew out a cloud of smoke. "In any case, we must not strike at Hitler's *Festung Europa* until we are absolutely certain of success based on Most Secret Sources. And I'm sure that when the invasion comes, your Agent Zigzag will play a prominent role."

"I don't see how. We haven't heard a peep from him in over two months."

"What? But he's one of our top agents."

"He most certainly is, but I'm afraid we've lost all contact with him."

"Good Lord, do you think he's been found out?"

"We don't know. But that would be my guess. Then again he is very resourceful."

"Please let me know as soon as you hear anything. I would hate for us to lose our star batsman for the championship round."

"Believe me, Prime Minister, I would too."

CHAPTER 47

FROM THE EDGE OF THE TREES, Dagmar and Chapman stared breathlessly at the official residence of the Norwegian Nazi leader Vidkun Quisling. She knew that they shouldn't be here and could very well end up being shot on sight for snooping around as spies, but she was more than up to the challenge. All the same, her heart was rapping against her chest and she could feel sweat on her brow. Trespassing on the hated Minister-President's property was not something one did every day.

They had set sail earlier that afternoon, untying the little Swedish yawl from its mooring, slipping out under the shadow of Akershus Fortress that had for centuries protected Oslo from enemy attack, and tacking west along the coastline. With Chapman at the tiller, they sailed past the Aker shipyards towards the Bygdøy peninsula, where a mere mile from the harbor they proceeded to drop anchor and wade onto a small pebble beach, empty except for a pair of deserted fishing huts. From there, the pair climbed through a patch of dense woodland and found a path leading to the hilltop, on which stood a resplendent stone villa ringed with concertina wire and bearing guard posts, a machine-gun nest, and armed sentries.

Since 1941, the current Minister-President had taken up residence in the sprawling stone mansion just outside the city. Originally named Villa Grande, it was built by a WWI industrialist before becoming state property. Quisling renamed it Gimlé, after the place where the gods reside after the apocalypse in Old Norse mythology. The Bygdøy peninsula was Norway's most exclusive preserve, a gated enclave divided into a series of estates, and Gimlé now served as Quisling's private fortress and administrative headquarters. The villa provided magnificent views overlooking the fjord and the city and was surrounded by a lush green park. It was said that Quisling packed the spacious mansion with his antiques, books, art treasures, and all his secrets. At the bottom of the garden, a speedboat was kept moored in constant readiness for a quick getaway across the water.

"Let's take a closer look," whispered Chapman.

They crept up the slope to a thicker stand of trees skirting the sprawling estate. Now they were near enough the machine-gun tower guarding the gated entrance to hear voices. Beyond the gated checkpoint, an avenue of lime trees led to the large stone mansion. Dagmar made a mental note of the estimated height of the barbed-wire fences and counted the armed guards at the gate and tower.

It was then she thought she heard footsteps coming up from behind. Then, to her surprise, the voices and footsteps stopped.

"Did you hear that?" she whispered as they stared at the Hirdsmen guarding the estate. They were armed with German Mausers.

"No, what was it?"

"I thought I heard footsteps, but then they stopped."

"Are you sure it wasn't just your imagination?"

She scanned the dark, forbidding forest but saw nothing. "No, I definitely heard something."

"Let's stay quiet," he said. "Hopefully, it's just a squirrel or rabbit."

They stared up at the massive stone mansion, once home to a Norwegian millionaire and now Quisling's private fortress. Dagmar thought of the legend of Gimlé, the great hall in Norse mythology where righteous souls dwelled for eternity. In her eyes, the traitor Quisling was no Norwegian, and she wished he hadn't invoked the ancient Viking legend as the name of his home. She studied the armed guards. She felt a lance of fear watching them smoking and talking with their submachine guns slung over their shoulders before the backdrop of the huge spooky mansion. In that moment, the great hall seemed as if it were haunted by old Viking ghosts.

"I shouldn't have brought you here," he whispered, as if reading her mind. "It's too dangerous."

"I told you I wanted to come."

"Yes well, now we're leaving."

They headed back through the woods the way they had come, skirting the eastern edge of the estate until they neared the edge of a clearing. The voices of the guards receded until they were only a murmur in the breeze.

But then Dagmar thought she heard a sound again. This time Chapman heard it too. He came to a halt and pulled her into a clump of trees. They listened closely, ears pricked in the direction of the noise, but they saw nothing. Maybe they had surprised some deer like they had on Langøyene Island six weeks earlier. Or maybe they were being stalked by Quisling's guards.

The noise sounded again.

Was it a snapping twig? Whatever it was, the sound came from the north at a ninety-degree compass angle from the mansion.

"Did you hear that?" she asked him.

"Unfortunately, yes," he replied.

He crouched low in the brush and motioned her to do the same. She strained her ears and scanned the mansion and the woods beyond. But she heard nothing and saw nothing out of the ordinary. She took a deep breath to steel herself, suppressing a faint miasma of fear. They were not imagining the noises. What they had heard was real and someone was out there. But she felt an even stronger presence than that: she felt like they were being stalked.

"It's probably nothing," he said after a minute had passed without incident. But she soon realized that he was merely reassuring her because he removed his Luger pistol.

"Is that really necessary?" she asked him, alarmed that he thought he might need his gun.

"Best to be prepared. I have my German identification, so I doubt anyone will seriously question us out here in the woods away from the mansion. But a gun sends a strong message."

"That bastard Quisling shouldn't be allowed to live there. When the war is over, they're going to hang him. Even if they don't, that traitor and his wife Maria won't be living at Gimlé."

"You certainly seem confident of Allied victory," he said.

"With what's happening at Sicily and Kursk, how could I not be? The Germans are having to fight on two fronts now while keeping troops stationed all over Occupied Europe. Spreading themselves too thin will be their downfall."

"I'll believe that when I see Hitler waving a white flag. Until then, we'd better buckle up for a long, bloody war."

They waited to see if the sounds returned, but there was nothing. He motioned her forward and they started moving again down the footpath that cut through the lush peninsula. She felt her body relax. It was a relief to have someone sharing the danger with her; as a courier, she was often on her own with incriminating information or items on her person, which made her nervous.

Once again, she wondered if Fritz was a spy. Why else would he be sneaking around Quisling's compound? But it was just as much his cat-like body language. His movements were wary, deliberate, and confident like an operative in action. His eyes were also watchful, and she couldn't help but think that he had been specially trained for subterfuge.

When they reached the edge of the clearing, they stopped to study the boat. It was still anchored offshore with no one having boarded it. She felt a wave of relief.

"She's ready and waiting. Come on, let's go," he said, and they dashed across the beach, splashed through the water, and boarded the yawl.

Once on board, he opened a bottle of cognac, poured them each a glass, and they set sail to the west, scudding through the waves. After ten minutes and two glasses of the soothingly fiery liquor, he handed over the helm to her while he pulled out a sketch book and drew a map of the Quisling estate and its defenses. He didn't even try to hide it from her.

She was tempted to ask him why he was drawing a map of the Norwegian Nazi Minister-President's estate, but she already knew the answer. Fritz Graumann was obviously a spy, and it was no longer plausible that he was doing it on behalf of the Germans, whom she believed he was only pretending to work for. On their frequent sailing journeys through Oslo Fjord, he was always closely studying the German ammunition dumps and fuel storage terminals, as well as U-boat docking and refueling pens along the coast, as if making detailed mental notes and maps.

Closing his sketch book, he took the tiller from her again and gave her a kiss on the cheek. She kissed him back on the lips.

"I must say that was exciting," she said, her cheeks flush with youthful vibrance.

He smiled. "It was, wasn't it? But I shouldn't have taken you there. If we would have been caught by the guards, they would have put us on meat hooks. I couldn't bear the thought of anything bad happening to you."

They kissed again. When they parted, he looked at her with the most loving and sincere eyes she had ever seen.

"What is it?" she asked him.

"I have to tell you something—something important." He tossed back another glass of cognac, fortifying himself for what he was about to say with liquid courage. "But first I want to make love to you."

"Oh, you do, do you?"

"Yes, I do. Are you game?"

"I believe you know the answer to that question."

He smiled that winsome, devilish smile that reminded her of a naughty schoolboy she had known back in Eidsvoll, a boy so charming that it was impossible to become angry at him. "Further down the coast, we'll set anchor and I'll tell you everything."

"*Everything?*"

"Yes, my love, *everything*. And believe me, it's a very long and interesting story."

CHAPTER 48

OSLO FJORD

JULY 14, 1943

AFTER SETTING ANCHOR IN A TUCKED-AWAY COVE, they made love in the woods next to the beach like reckless teenagers. For Chapman, the world spun in a pleasant way, as if he were on a merry-go-round. He arched his back and kissed Dagmar's lips as she slid back and forth on top of him. He kissed her repeatedly on her hard, slippery nipples as they continued to thrust in unison. Her womanly scent was sweet and thick. His arms reached out, clasped her shapely bottom, and pulled her down on top of him so that he was plunging upward, deeper. Soon, a churning euphoric sensation seized hold of his lower stomach as he was about to let go with his seed. And then it happened. They moaned with delight in unison and came simultaneously together as never before, all the pent-up emotion and excitement of the day released in an exquisite burst of passion.

Afterwards, as was their summer custom, they went for a naked swim in the fjord before climbing back aboard the little yawl, drying themselves off, putting their clothes back on, and pouring themselves a cognac. It was a perfect summer afternoon, and as the sky turned to dusk he took her in his arms and wanted desperately to tell her the truth about who he was and why he was here in Oslo. He had wanted to untangle his true feelings and come clean about his real identity for more than a month now—and deep inside he had sensed that she had wanted to do the same—but he had held out. That is, until now, because he swore to himself that this time he was going to go through with it. Out here on the idyllic fjord, in the arms of this remarkable young woman that he had fallen hopelessly in love with, after the illicit thrill of sneaking up for a close-up peek at the traitor Quisling's fortress, under the unmistakable influence of drink—he knew it was time to open up his heart and soul to his beloved. It was a monstrous roll of the dice, but he was determined to do it. He loved her that much.

He took her by the hand. "Dagmar, my love," he began, feeling deep and powerful emotions the likes of which he wasn't sure he had ever felt before this day. "I cannot bear to lie to you anymore."

"Lie to me? What do you mean?"

"As you have no doubt suspected for some time now, I am not a French journalist or an American born in Germany. I am, in fact, a British double agent."

He paused a moment to allow her to say something, but she didn't so he forged on.

"The Germans thinks I am a loyal German spy when I am actually out to royally screw them. In fact, they want me to return to Britain on a mission in the not-too-distant future. There, I've said it. I've told you the truth and am putting my very life in your hands. What do you have to say?"

Still, she did not speak. In the excruciating silence, he slammed back another glass of cognac, as if to underscore what he had just said. Though he had an almost inhuman tolerance for alcohol, he was mildly drunk from the four full glasses of liquor he had imbibed, and now there was no turning back as the cat was out of the bag.

"I know how hard it has been on you to be with me," he continued, feeling a great unburdening in his chest. "You are taunted daily with whispers of being a Nazi's whore and are ostracized by your own people when you are, in fact, a Norwegian patriot of the highest order. I know how much you despise the Germans, and I hate to see you so distraught at the ill treatment you receive from your countrymen. I also know you have links to the Resistance and are the furthest thing from a *tyskertøs*, and that I risk losing you if I continue to pretend to be a German. Bloody hell, this is not easy for me. What I mean to say is, I love you, Dagmar, and holding on to you is more important to me than anything else in the world. This war is a soul killer—but loving you these past few months has brought me more happiness than I have known my entire life. I have never felt more alive. I love you, Dagmar. I love you and that's why I'm telling you all this. I can't stand the thought of losing you."

At that moment, the fading sun caught her smooth, oval face and he could see the tears in her eyes. They were tears of love but also relief. She, too, appeared to feel some sort of unburdening and newfound freedom in his admission. She fell into his arms and they kissed, the sudden catharsis of the moment overwhelming them both. After a moment, they pulled away and she reached out and gently touched his face.

"I love you too," she said softly. "You are handsome, kind, and generous—but most of all, I love you for making me laugh. During this terrible war, laughter is as precious as gold. But I must also tell you that I am not surprised at all that you are a British spy."

"I knew you had questions about me, but I didn't think I was *that* bad an actor."

"You weren't. It's your accent. I have suspected that you are British and not American all along as your accent is curious. I knew for certain you couldn't be German. Germans don't have a sense of humor, not like yours anyway."

"I like to ham it up, I can't deny that. And since I'm in full disclosure mode here, my real name isn't Fritz Graumann. It's Eddie Chapman."

"Eddie Chapman—that is very British." They laughed and sipped their cognacs. "I must say," she then said, "how relieved I am to know the real you. It makes it easier for me to be honest with you about my own situation."

"You mean that you are working for the Norwegian Resistance? I already know that. I'm not bloody daft, you know."

"Sometimes you are. But that's just another thing that's lovable about you."

"You have been giving me hints for weeks, Dagmar. I wouldn't be much of a spy if I didn't recognize that you were desperate to tell me the truth too, now would I?"

"I should have been more careful, I suppose."

"Not really. We both knew early on that neither of us was what we seemed. We just didn't know exactly what we were."

"Yes, in fact I have trusted you since almost the beginning."

"Really. Then perhaps today isn't as much of a confession as I thought."

"I suspected you were working secretly for the Allies even though you were pretending to be German. There was just something about you that was too kind and funny to be German."

"Let's hope my handlers aren't as clever as you."

"They seem to trust you. What are their full names, by the way? I only know their first names and those may be aliases, right?"

"I believe so. The Belgian journalist you know simply as Stephan is, in fact, Stephan Graumann and Walter and Johnny's last names are Thomas and Holst. Their surnames are most likely aliases, but I don't know for sure."

"At least I can love you now without shame. You must be wondering why I allowed myself to be picked up by a man posing as a German officer. Well, now I can tell you why. Initially, I did it because I thought you might have information useful to the Resistance. But then I got to know you, and that's when I realized that you were a kind person and not what you were pretending to be. Plus, there was always the accent."

"Well, I can say without reservation that I'm glad you gave me a chance."

"I'm wondering what kind of work you do for the British?"

"I'm afraid I can't tell you that. Knowing about the Germans here in Oslo is one thing, because that is something that even an ordinary Norwegian would want to know with the Reich occupying the country. But when it comes to my work for British intelligence, you really should know as little as possible. That's why I need you to swear to me, right here and now, that you will keep quiet about what I am telling you here today. We live in desperate times. The reality is that if you let slip to the Germans that I have double-crossed them, it could have disastrous consequences. Not only would it let the Abwehr know that one of their trusted agents is deceiving them, and not only would they swiftly and mercilessly interrogate, torture, and kill me, but it could call into question the reliability of their other agents abroad that are secretly working for the British."

"I swear before you to silence. I will take your being a British spy with me to my grave."

"Really? You'd do that for me?"

"If it's important for your safety and the war effort, absolutely."

"That's my girl," he said, and he kissed her and poured them both another drink. "I was also meaning to tell you that I have moved into a new flat. A house actually. I was hoping you might join me and live there. I have plenty of money for the both of us and have fallen hopelessly in love with you, as you know. What do you say?"

"Where is it?"

"In Grafsin," he replied, referring to the quiet suburb north of Oslo. "The address is Kapellveien 15."

She shook her head. "I'm sorry, but I can't live with you."

"Why the bloody hell not? I love you and want to take care of you!"

"It's already hard enough on me with people thinking I'm on friendly terms with the Germans. But if were to live in the same house with a known sympathizer and suspected Abwehr operative, they would crucify me. I just can't do that."

"Oh, they can piss off. I've got plenty of money and you will no longer have to pay rent for your apartment. The Germans have been paying me unusually well for deceiving them, I must say."

"You've already been lavishing me with too many gifts. I don't need you to pay for my housing too."

"But why wouldn't I? I'm madly in love with you."

"I know you are, and I feel the same way about you, but it just can't work. I'm already under enough strain as it is. I don't want my countrymen to spurn me even more as a kept woman."

"Oh, come on. If we live together, we can spy together. You could be of real service to me and the war effort as a British subagent."

"Are you recruiting me, unofficially, into the British Secret Service?"

"I most certainly am. I'm telling you, you could be of real use. Graumann likes you. If you were able to be alone with him and get him to talk freely, you could find out information useful to the Allied cause. You could also help gather information on the other members of the Oslo Abwehrstelle."

"And what happens when you go off on your new mission?"

"I'd still remain in contact with you. It's the perfect setup: you and I, spies working and living together underneath the noses of the Germans."

"I must admit it sounds exciting. But I am growing weary of the Ice Front—and if I move in with you it will only get worse."

"I will take care of you and we will ignore them together. What does it matter to you what other people think when you know you are a true Jøssing working for the Resistance? I admire you for what you do. Though exactly what it is you do still escapes me."

"Just as it is dangerous for you to tell me who you are working for and what you do, it is dangerous for me to disclose my secrets to you. But suffice to say I am a courier for Milorg."

"You are much more than a courier, I can tell you that. Say, wait a minute, how do I know you weren't laying the honey trap that first night I met you at the Ritz? I must say yours was the best Marlene Dietrich impression I had ever seen. Smoking those Craven A's and dressed to kill."

"I looked nothing like Dietrich. I was scared to death."

"But how do I know I can trust you? Perhaps it is you who are the German spy?"

"You really think that I was planted by the Germans at the Ritz as a honey trap?"

"In our line of work, one can never be too careful."

"You've got an overactive imagination. You're right that I am a spy—but on behalf of Norway not Germany."

"So, like me you have a control officer?"

"Remember what we've both said about need-to-know. It's not just an operational protocol, it saves lives. I believe it's in our best interests for both of our lips to remain sealed."

"I wouldn't have it any other way. Which is also why I have a little test for you."

"What, you really don't trust me?"

"I've taken a wild gamble here today and put my life in your hands, so let's just say some additional insurance will help me sleep better at night."

"All right, what is the test?"

"Do you know the location of the Abwehr headquarters office here in Oslo?"

"No."

"That is as I figured. It is a carefully guarded secret and even I'm not even allowed inside the building, though I know the address. The Germans trust me, but apparently only to a point."

"You want me to find out the address of the Oslo Abwehrstelle, and if I do, that will prove my loyalty to the Allied cause?"

"Aye, me fair lassie. You have two days."

"Two days? I've still got to make ends meet. I have a job, you know."

"Sorry, but I have to give you some sort of time limit."

"All right, but if this is the way you're going to handle it, then you will not be able to make love to me for the full forty-eight hours. Can you wait that long?"

"Bloody hell, I hadn't thought of that. Maybe I should only give you one day."

She poked him in the ribs. "You bastard!"

They laughed, and he raised his glass in a toast. "All right, let the game begin. If you locate the Abwehr headquarters, it will be proof of your commitment. On the other hand, if you fail, well, I suppose I will wind up in a Gestapo prison, or even worse, a corpse."

She raised her cognac. "I suppose that's the risk you'll have to take in not trusting me. Let's just hope it turns out all right and the Germans don't send you to the wall."

"Oh, you naughty girl," he said. "You're actually trying to scare me, aren't you? My God, that makes me desire you even more."

And with that, they clinked glasses, tossed back their cognac, and fell into each other's arms as they stared out at majestic Oslo Fjord and the dusky midsummer evening.

CHAPTER 49

1 FRYDENLUNDSGATE, OSLO

JULY 15, 1943

"YOU MOVED IN TODAY WITH THE NAZI BASTARD. NOW THAT TRULY IS ENTERING THE LION'S DEN."

Dagmar didn't appreciate Ishmael's mocking manner. They were in the Frydenlundsgate meeting place a block south of her old apartment. She had moved in with Eddie Chapman to the German-controlled safe house in Grafsin in the morning. Later, just before dinner, she had told Eddie and his German minders that she had to take a tram into the city to meet her girlfriend Mary Larsen. Instead, she had quickly made her way to Frydenlundsgate to meet in secret with her control officer and relay to him the latest intelligence. For the past twenty-four hours, she had grappled with the decision of whether to disclose to Ishmael that Abwehr Agent Fritz Graumann was a British spy, but in the end had decided to keep the astonishing secret to herself. She could brief Ishmael on her important findings at her new home at Kapellveien 15 without exposing her lover as a double agent. The information was what was most important, not how she managed to come by it.

"He's not a Nazi and I'm in love with him," she said flatly. "He is kind, generous, handsome, and one-hundred-percent not German. But there's no doubt he's working for the Germans in some capacity."

"If he's not German, where is he from?"

"I don't know," she lied. "He still claims to be German-American."

"What's his game?"

"I don't know that either. He's obviously performing some service for the German foreign intelligence service, but he's not German. I've told you his accent is all wrong."

"Do you think it's possible he's a double agent? We've checked up on him and he doesn't appear to be working for the Resistance, but that doesn't mean he's not working for both sides."

"I only know that he works for the Abwehr and is anti-Nazi. But he seems to be here almost on vacation, like he's in between assignments. I mean, we sail alone together and go out to restaurants several times a week. It appears he is free to do whatever he wants. Of course, I'm asking that you keep my relationship with Fritz between you and me."

"Milorg doesn't make private security arrangements with its couriers— especially not when they're sleeping with Nazis."

"Oh, shut up, Ishmael. Sometimes you sound like Herr Goebbels with all your by-the-book procedures. I have a valuable informant that you ordered me to pursue, and yet here you are being a nitpicker."

"All right, what other intelligence do you have for me?"

"I now have the names of his German handlers. The supposed Belgian journalist is a senior Abwehr officer named Stephan Graumann, and his two subordinates that spend the most time with Agent Fritz are Walter Thomas and Johnny Holst. The names are likely at least partly fictitious."

He wrote down the names. "This is useful information. I'll need to cross-check them against our lists. We may have something on them. What else have you got for me?"

"I'll tell you in a moment. But first I need something from you."

"From me?"

"Yes." She still had not found out the location of Abwehr headquarters and wondered whether Ishmael could provide her with such information. The clock was ticking: she had only until tomorrow to tell Chapman where the Oslo Stelle was located. To her surprise, her lover had been watching her closely since his admission of being a British double agent. Once she had moved her belongings into the new house this morning, he had deliberately left her alone in the company of Stephan Graumann, Walter Thomas, and Johnny Holst and then carefully studied her face for any "change of attitude" that might indicate betrayal. She was confident that he had not detected even a flicker of suspicion.

"Where is the Oslo Abwehrstelle?" she asked him. "I don't actually know it's location. It appears to be a well-guarded secret."

"Why do you want to know?"

"Stop acting like my father and tell me where it is."

"It is located at 8 Jilingenberggate. The head of station is a naval officer with four rings on his sleeve. Unfortunately, I can't recall his name at the moment. Who wants to know?"

"Me. You should have told me this before. It's important information."

"You didn't ask until now. Now how do you know this Fritz Graumann isn't a German and a hard-core Nazi?"

"I've already told you why. From his accent, and the things he's said to me about Hitler."

"Or is it because you've fallen for him and you don't want him to be a bad guy?"

"That's a stupid thing to say. As you yourself said, he is working for the Germans in some capacity. But I just don't happen to believe that he's a German spy harmful to our interests here in Norway or the Allied cause. He seems too nice."

"You're only saying that because you're sleeping with him."

"If I didn't know better, I would say you're jealous. Are you angry that I've fallen for a non-Norwegian, as if you have possession over my body? Because if I had to guess, I would have to say that you are treating me as if I am a *tyskertøs*. But you of all people know that I am no such thing, so don't treat me like one. You're the one who coerced me into playing Marlene Dietrich at the Ritz. I was absolutely petrified, you know."

"Yes, but now you have a new boyfriend who passes on useful intelligence information to you on the Abwehr. I was right to send you in there."

"And now I'm living with the asset and two German babysitters. One false move and I'm kaput."

"Let's hope not." He changed the subject. "Your boyfriend Fritz seems to have a lot of money. Is he still lavishing you with gifts?"

"Yes, besides the French perfume he brought with him from Paris, he has bought me several dresses, shoes, jewelry, and of course wonderful meals. The money is plentiful, but not endless, and he's burning through it at an astonishing rate."

"Ah, the things one does for king and country."

"I don't like your sarcastic tone. These Germans could very well end up killing me and you damn well know—"

She stopped right there as the sound of screeching tires came from the street below. They jumped up from the couch and peered out the corner of the blackout curtain. Dagmar couldn't believe her eyes. An army of submachine-gun-wielding SS troops had swooped in on heavy trucks, cordoned off Dalsbergstien between Frydenlundsgate and Schwensens gate, and were conducting an aggressive door-to-door search and arresting people. Parked next to the German convoy was a black Volvo PV53 and a silver surveillance van with a large revolving aerial on the roof. A young captain in a jet-black SS uniform that she didn't recognize stepped from the Volvo and began barking out orders. More German SS troops with rifles began jumping out of the trucks and running towards the entrance to their apartment building overlooking Frydenlundsgate.

"Jesus, it's a roundup!" exclaimed Ishmael. "Normally the Gestapo only makes arrests at night, but it's not even six o'clock."

"They must have intercepted a radio transmission," she said. "Look at that surveillance van. Either that or they've caught someone listening to the BBC."

"They must have triangulated their position."

"Oh shit, there's more of them."

A second fleet of trucks screeched to a halt at the curb three floors below. Dagmar saw *Hauptsharführer* Axel Etling, chief of the Gestapo motor transport, jump from a Holzbrenner "wood burning" Volkswagen that had likely been requisitioned from some unfortunate Norwegian. Armed to the teeth, he and a contingent of SS troops burst through the front door.

"I don't think they're after us, but it doesn't matter. We still have to get the hell out of here," said Ishmael. "But first we have to see if it's clear out back."

Dashing quickly to the apartment's rear bedroom, he pulled back the curtain. Dagmar followed him, and they looked out the window. She didn't see any movement on the street behind them and there was no sign of the Germans, but that didn't mean an SS squad wasn't assembling out of view or waiting in nearby trucks. Unfortunately, part of her view at the rear of the building was obstructed. But from what she could tell, the escape route behind the apartment building was a better option than the street below. Then she saw a throng of young Norwegian men dashing down the street and she knew it was probably their only escape option.

Ishmael realized it too. "We have to go now!" he cried.

Now they could hear shouting voices coming from the staircase along with the sound of knocking on doors, breaking glass, and objects being overturned in the apartments beneath them. The bastards had already swarmed inside in force and were rounding up people. The pounding of the jackboots echoed on the stairs and down the hallway: the Germans were already on the second floor and coming up fast.

They dashed out into the hallway, went to the window, and peered down at the street. A truck screeched to a halt and a squad of square-jawed SS troops leapt out and started chasing a pack of young Norwegians trying to escape.

A cold hand closed over her heart. They were trapped on both sides now. But at least the SS squad was running down the street in the opposite direction from them.

Ishmael quickly opened the window. They climbed down the fire stairs to the street level and ducked into a narrow side street as another Nazi foot patrol raced in from the south. They waited for the Germans to fan out down the street and enter a pair of buildings before starting off again, heading northeast on Collett's gate.

They walked at a brisk but reasonable pace for several blocks, trying to remain inconspicuous since it was still daylight. But it wasn't easy to maintain a mask of calm and blend in when there were few civilians on the streets and the enemy seemed to be everywhere. For Dagmar, it was surreal to see the Norway she dearly loved transformed into such a dangerous place.

They turned right when they reached St. Hanshaugen Park and dashed into the trees, taking refuge among the towering oaks. A German foot patrol came marching past but didn't see them hiding in the shadows among the cover of heavy limbs and leafy green foliage.

Five minutes later, the coast was clear.

"The safe house could be blown. I'll contact you in two weeks in the usual way," said Ishmael. "By then, you should have some more information on your new German roommates."

"They are not my roommates. I'm only living there to save money and be with Fritz."

"Well then, you'd better make the most of it. They are high-level targets," he said sternly, before dashing off to the northeast and leaving her to fend for herself.

CHAPTER 50

TAKING AIM WITH HIS LUGER P08 semi-automatic pistol, Chapman squeezed the trigger twice in rapid succession, like a gunfighter in an American Western. To his surprise, both empty aquavit bottles lined up against the back wall next to the garden exploded under his accurate fire.

"You bastard, you've bested me again!" cried Johnny Holst in disbelief.

"It's not that hard, *Kapitän*. Your hands shake like a bloody earth tremor."

"That's because I'm not drunk yet." He grinned a smile typical of how he looked after three or four drinks but before he had downed a whole bottle. The Hamburgian had once been an excellent marksman, but he could no longer hold a gun straight due to his affliction of delirium tremens.

"You are a fine shot, Fritz, drunk or sober, but so am I," said SS-*Oberleutnant* Walter Thomas, as usual performing his English country dance steps on the back porch. They were wearing civilian clothes and speaking in English. "Here, let me give it a try."

With acrobatic grace, he jumped off the back porch and dashed down a gently inclined hill to where they were shooting. Since moving into the safe house yesterday, following their forced evacuation in the aftermath of the Forbunds Hotel bombing, the three of them had shot at bottles and the occasional incautious wood rat each afternoon in the back yard. Chapman found their new home splendid: it reminded him of an illustration from a Nordic book of fairy tales. The large wooden abode was set back off the road in a large garden surrounded by trees of pears, apples, and plums along with fragrant currant bushes. It had belonged to an affluent middle-class Jewish family that had owned a successful barber and clothing shop. Unbeknownst to Chapman, the husband and his wife were murdered by their Norwegian guides when they had tried to escape to Sweden in late 1942, while their son had been gassed at Auschwitz. The property had been seized by the SS and served as the quarters for German officers before von Gröning had requisitioned it for his staff. Chapman had seen the nameplate on the front door that read "Feltman" and had asked his German handlers what had happened to the family. In response, he was instructed to stop asking so many questions.

Thomas took the pistol from him and proceeded to shoot down a liquor bottle on the first shot. "Ha, you see! Both Fritz and I should be serving on the Eastern Front. We are both superb marksman and could be killing a hundred Reds a day. With us as sharpshooters, it would be like shooting fish in a barrel!"

Chapman shook his head. "No thanks. You want to be a decorated war hero, that's fine by me. But I'm staying put right here on the fjords until I return to spy in England. You go on ahead to Russia, Walter. I can promise you will be a frozen corpse by Christmas."

"That would be one hell of a Christmas present for us both, eh Fritz," teased Holst. "Then we wouldn't have to listen to him yelling, 'Heil Hitler!' or watch him perform his silly dancing every day."

"You heard him, Walter," said Chapman. "I swear you will not rest until gun in hand, you have single-handedly defeated the godless Bolsheviks."

"Better death for one's ideals than sitting here in Norway doing nothing at all," said Thomas.

"Oh, but we are doing something," said Chapman. "I visited the sabotage training center in Grafsin this morning. I'm learning about limpets, magnetic clams, and detonators. You should see these new explosive pellets I'm working with. They come dried in a muslin sleeve. I don't know what the bloody hell I'm supposed to do with all this training when simple gelignite will do, but I am most certainly not standing by doing nothing."

"Yes, but the old man will never let you blow anything up. Johnny here said that he wanted to create some explosions, but Graumann was against it. How can you continue to be an explosives expert if you can't blow anything up?"

"Fritz doesn't have to prove himself," said Holst. "He may not be learning anything new in sabotage, but he is still regarded as an expert."

"Yes, our boy is quite the celebrity. He is often asked to give his advice to our fellow German intelligence officers, regaling them with tales of his exploits in jolly old England. But personally, I think we could all do with less celebrity in the rear echelons and more fighting at the front. I know that's where I should be."

Chapman rolled his eyes and took the Luger back from him. "Walter, you are such a bore," he declared as the telephone inside the safe house rang.

"Heil Hitler!" snapped Thomas, and he dashed the full length of the garden and then dove headfirst through the open porch window to answer it.

It was at that moment Chapman saw the teenage boy who lived next door at Number 13 Kapellveien staring down at them from a second-floor window. He waved at him, but the boy frowned, jerked the blind shut, and disappeared.

"Nosy little bugger," said Holst. "I hope he didn't overhear us."

"I doubt it. The window was closed."

"He could read our lips if he understood English."

"The neighbors already know we're German, Johnny. What are their names anyway?"

"They are the Myhres."

"What's the boy's name?"

"Leife. He's seventeen and lives alone with his parents."

"I presume you had them checked out."

"Yes, of course. What kind of operation do you think we run here?"

A sloppy one, Chapman wanted to say, though he kept his thoughts to himself. *After all, you're the same idiots who gave me the Iron Cross for spying against you.*

They were interrupted by the sound of a car pulling into the driveway. Chapman recognized the sound of the engine: it was von Gröning's Volvo PV 36 Carioca. In 1940, shortly after the German invasion, the luxury car had been requisitioned by the Luftwaffe from a wealthy Norwegian family with anti-fascist political leanings, but it had since been given to the Abwehr spymaster for his personal use. Chapman and Holst went inside to greet him. He instantly made it known that he wanted to talk with his British protégé alone. Holst grabbed something to eat in the kitchen while they made themselves comfortable in the drawing room and Praetorius finished his phone call.

"Fritz, I have here your money." He produced a wad of bills and handed them to Chapman. "Here you go. Five thousand kroner."

The double agent stuffed the bills in his pocket.

"Don't you want to count it?"

"No, I trust you."

"Very good. Please sign for it."

He held out a pair of disbursement agreements and a pen for him to sign the documents. After scratching out his signature, Chapman returned one signed agreement to von Gröning and kept a copy for himself, stuffing it in his pocket with the cash. He was acutely aware that the man he knew as Doktor Stephan Graumann was embezzling money from him, but once again he let it go as he had been doing since his arrival to Occupied Norway. Whenever Chapman asked for a ten or twenty thousand kroner payment due him for the de Havilland and *City of Lancaster* jobs, the control officer only produced half to two-thirds of the requested amount, pocketed the balance for himself, and made him sign a chit in the full amount, which was what was likely being reported to his superiors.

But Chapman had not uttered a word of protest about the skimming. He was content to let his spymaster take a sliver of the pie, for it ensured that Graumann was indebted to him and could be counted on to remain silent if he ever discovered his prized asset was indeed a British double agent. In France, Chapman had regarded the man as his savior and mentor: brilliant, upright, and unassailable. Now he knew the German aristocrat was no aristocrat at all, but rather a somewhat pathetic embezzler who was dependent on him for his success as an Abwehr officer. So far, neither man had spoken of their peculiar relationship, their tacit understanding forming yet another strand in the web of complicity between them. To von Gröning, Chapman had become far more than just another spy: he was a career investment, the man who had "made" him and continued to ensure his survival and financial comfort in the German Secret Service—and they both knew it.

"You should take that fine girlfriend of yours out for dinner, Fritzchen."

"I plan to when she gets here." He glanced at his watch. "She's due any minute now. But before dinner we're going for a stroll."

"It's nice to be in love, isn't it?"

Chapman saw his eyes fill with fond reminiscence of some past love. "Yes, I must say it is. I'm sure you've had many women in your day, old bean."

"Ah yes, but not as many as you, my friend. You have a way with the fräuleins."

"Yes, but in the present case, I have fallen in love. I'm trying to be a good boy."

"You can try, but you still have a wandering eye, Fritzchen. I know you."

"Not anymore. Dagmar is the girl I aim to marry—when the war is over, that is."

"I wish you the greatest happiness. You two make a fine match. Just be careful what you tell her. We wouldn't want her to discover any of our deep, dark secrets, now would we?"

"I didn't know we had any."

"Oh yes, we have many skeletons in the closet. That's why keeping one's political views to oneself and not saying too much is the order of the day. It tends to keep one safe when the wolves are on the prowl, if you catch my meaning." He nodded towards the other room where Praetorius was talking loudly on the phone.

"Indeed, I do catch your meaning." The portly German smiled at his protégé and Chapman smiled back. He genuinely liked and admired the old man, even if he was on the take and his stock in Berlin wasn't what it once had been. He just hoped the money wouldn't run out for either of them. It was not endless, and he was burning through his funds at a rapid rate. The funny thing was that Graumann seemed to encourage his profligate spending habits, and it was for this reason that Chapman hosted extravagant drinking parties, ate out often at the Ritz and Löwenbräu, lavished Dagmar with whatever fineries she desired, and footed the bill on many occasions. Just as he was wise to Graumann's skimming, he knew why the old man quietly supported his prodigal spending ways. Once he had spent his money here in Norway, he would need to go back to work on a new mission to Great Britain. A spy who was flat broke, like a spy deeply in love, could be easily manipulated. It was the same reason Graumann observed his burgeoning relationship with Dagmar with calculated approval. An asset in the throes of passion was an asset who was easier to handle, and Dagmar—of whom von Gröning and the Germans had no suspicion—might serve as a useful bargaining chip. MI5 had made the same calculation over Freda back in London.

"Ah, speak of the devil, here's your true fine love right now," said von Gröning, staring out the window as Dagmar walked up the driveway carrying a sewing and clothing bag. "She really is quite lovely."

"I'm glad you like her. You two seem to get along quite well."

"Like you, Fritzchen, she understands me. And that is no easy matter."

They shared a convivial laugh. Chapman opened the door for Dagmar and the three of them sat down in the drawing room along with Walter Praetorius alias Thomas, who had finished his phone call. They made small talk for a few minutes and were soon joined by Johnny Holst. A fresh bottle of aquavit was opened, and they enjoyed a late afternoon drink together, like one big happy family. Except unbeknownst to von Gröning and his German comrades, two of the family members were Allied spies only posing as German sympathizers.

Throughout the conversation, Chapman studied Dagmar and the others closely. At several points during the past two days, he had deliberately left her alone in the company of Graumann, Thomas, and Holst and then, upon his return, he carefully studied their faces for any change of attitude that might indicate a betrayal. He detected not a flicker of suspicion, and looking closely at the faces again now, he was certain Dagmar was not working for the Germans and that her appearance at the Ritz months ago had not been the opening night of a honey-trap deception. All the same, she wasn't completely out of the woods. She still hadn't told him the address of the Oslo Abwehrstelle and her time was running out.

"Bottoms up, everyone," said Chapman, raising his glass in a toast. "Dagmar and I are going to take a walk before dinner and leave you chaps to your vices."

"Here, here," said von Gröning, rising to his feet.

The group drank their toast and then the old man saw Chapman and Dagmar to the door. "There is nothing like young love," he said with a pleasant twinkle in his eyes. "Have a wonderful walk."

"We will," said Chapman, and he took her by the hand and they walked south on Kapellveien and then headed east on Grefsenveien until they came to a grassy park with a small pond filled with honking geese.

"I found the information you wanted," said Dagmar excitedly. "The Abwehr headquarters is at 8 Jilingenberggate."

"Most impressive."

"That's not all I have. The head of station is a naval officer who is known to wear a full naval uniform with four gold bars on his sleeve. I don't know his name but at least you can now identify him."

"Well done, Agent Lahlum. I can most certainly rest easier now that I know you are faithful to the Allied cause. And for your information, *Kapitän-zur-See* Reimar von Bonin—the bald, blue-eyed chief of the Abwehr here in Occupied Norway— happens to live in a plush home in Munthessgate across from Frogner Park. I have not yet met the man but am told I will be making his acquaintance in the near future."

"Wait, I have more."

"More?"

"The head of the SS at Victoria Terrasse is Colonel Heinrich Fehlis. He is a truly despicable man, responsible for the torture and murder of scores of Norwegians."

"I have not heard of Fehlis. That is useful information."

"So now that you know you can trust me, what have you been doing for the Germans since you arrived here in Norway?"

"Besides the photography, which you already know about? Well, I've been mostly brushing up on my Morse with Johnny and giving lectures on explosives, but they don't seem to be in a hurry to send me back to England. But that is indeed where I am headed once they figure out what to do with me."

"Do you have any idea when you will be leaving?"

"No, it could be a few weeks, or it could be months. But I am definitely going. That's what they told me and Graumann during our trip to Berlin."

"I wish you didn't have to leave, but if what you're going to do can help us win the war, I am one-hundred-percent behind it. Whatever happens, you can count on me."

"You are going to be of great value as a spy. We'll work together as a team. We're quite a love match—now we get the opportunity to work on the same side as spies."

"I can't wait. What will you have me do?"

"You're privy to all sorts of interesting information from your Resistance contacts, so I want you to keep me informed of any intelligence you learn on the enemy through your Jøssing friends. You're also going to enable me to move about more freely and take photographs and make maps of key German intelligence offices, military installations, submarine pens, training centers, and the like. A man taking a photograph of a military installation would arouse suspicion, but what could be more natural than a young man taking snapshots of his Norwegian girlfriend?"

"You want me to help you with your cover? I can do that."

"As I told you before, because Graumann likes you, you should also continue to take every opportunity to be alone with him and get him to talk freely. The same goes for Thomas, Holst, Molli, and any of the other members of the Abwehrstelle. Any and all information gleaned from talking to people may be of value to MI5 upon my return to England. You'll just have to keep your eyes and ears open for any information that might be of use to the British."

"And what about when you leave?"

"We have to take the precaution of agreeing on a plan in case I don't make it or am somehow delayed until after the war. If anyone needs to contact you on my behalf, you must make sure that they greet you up front by calling you by your full name: Dagmar Mohne Hansen Lahlum."

"That will be our codeword?"

"That's it: Dagmar Mohne Hansen Lahlum. Do you think you can remember it?"

Giggling, she poked him in the ribs. "Yes, I think I can remember my own name."

"I know it seems like a game, but we have to remember at all times that our lives are in danger and we are in the middle of a terrible war."

"Yes, but we still have to maintain a sense of humor."

"Indeed, we do. It's the one thing that makes us feel alive."

"That and our love for one another. I love you, Eddie Chapman."

"And I love you Dagmar Mohne Hansen Lahlum. Now that I've said it a third time, I know you'll never forget it."

"Oh, you devil!"

She gently pushed him. Pretending to fall, he cradled her in his arms as they touched down pillow soft on the lush green grass of the park. Her hair was swept back in the cool summer breeze and her cheeks were brilliantly flush like a rose-colored sunset. At their feet, the fading sunlight sparkled off the cobalt-blue surface of the little pond and white-headed geese bobbed and honked contentedly at one another. Beyond the lake, the backdrop of the dense forest north of Oslo rose up like a precious emerald against the pastel skyline. For a moment, he forgot about the war: the bloody Nazis, the fanatical Hitler, the Ice Front, quislings and patriots, and all the madness, secrecy, and killing on a massive scale never seen before in the annals of civilization. There was only a beautiful woman, a rippled Norwegian pond, and a verdant forest rising up against a sparkling summer sky. It was a vast and wondrous country here in the land of the legendary Vikings. It made his head spin in a pleasant way and the war seem far, far away.

He raised an imaginary glass and made a toast. "Here's to us, Dagmar. Here's to the Spies of the Midnight Sun."

"The Spies of the Midnight Sun. I like that," she said as he enveloped her in his scrappy arms and they kissed one another.

In that blissful moment that Eddie Chapman and Dagmar Lahlum would remember for the rest of their natural days, with the orange ball of sun sinking to the west, they both felt as if they would live—and love one another—forever.

CHAPTER 51

NATIONAL THEATER, OSLO

AUGUST 10, 1943

STARING AT THE FLUTTERING NAZI FLAG atop the National Theater, Dagmar wanted to tear the damned thing down. Blood-red swastika banners had been slung from government offices and historic buildings throughout the city for more than three years now, since the beginning of the Occupation; but with the recent victories by the Americans and British at Sicily and the Russians at Kursk, the tide of war was turning, and she was sick and tired of being forced to stomach ever-present emblems of Nazism. They were annoying, like having dirt smeared in one's face by a big, fat bully. A bully who was now vulnerable and losing his once indomitable grip.

Designed by architect Henrik Bull, the *Nationaltheatret* was a resplendent building within the heart of Oslo just off Karl Johans gate. Dagmar studied the ornate façade and handsome columns framing the front entrance before turning her attention to the statue of Norwegian playwright and favorite son Henrik Ibsen standing out front of the theater. Set on a cylindrical stone plinth, the life-size statue depicted the man many regarded as one of Europe's finest playwrights as a stern, bushy-bearded figure with both hands behind his back and wearing a long overcoat. The theater had its first performance on September 1, 1899 and had long been considered the home for Ibsen's plays, with most of his works having been performed there. Dagmar had had the good fortune to attend a play at the theater just before the Germans had marched into the city but had not seen anything since.

As she turned to head back to Karl Johans gate, a young man stopped her in her tracks. She recognized him as the boy who lived next door to the German safe house at Kapellveien 15, where she had been living with Chapman the past month. She had learned that the family's last name was Myhre, but she didn't know the boy's name.

"I've been meaning to talk to you," he said without preamble.

Though taken by surprise at his insistent manner, she smiled politely at him. "You're the boy that lives next door in Number 13. I'm pleased to make your acquaintance, but please tell me you weren't following me."

"No, I wasn't following you," he said stiffly, clearly agitated about something. "And I'm not a boy. I'm seventeen, only a year or two younger than you."

"Yes, you are nearly old enough to fight. That is, if we had an army that was fighting. As for me, I am twenty. Practically an old maid."

He waved a finger at her. "You shouldn't be mixing with those Germans. You are Norwegian—you shouldn't be living with them."

His scolding tone put her on the defensive. "I am not working for them, you know," she said, looking around to make sure no one was close enough to overhear them.

"Then what are you doing staying with them? Are you a kept woman?"

"You should watch your tongue, boy," she snapped at him, feeling herself getting angry. "You have no right to talk disrespectfully to me like that."

"I told you I am not a boy. My name is Leife. Leife Myhre."

"Well, Leife Myhre, you should learn better manners. What are you doing here anyway? Shouldn't you be at home with your mother?"

"I'm not trying to make you angry. I am just warning you. If you keep mixing with those Germans, you know what's going to happen to you. When the war is over, and the Allies have won, people will shave your head and parade you down the street while all of Oslo turns out to shout taunts to your face and hurl stones at you. Is that what you want? Because if you keep up with these German fellows, that is what will become of you."

She looked down guiltily: the boy who lived next door had struck a nerve. But her guilt quickly turned once again to anger. "As I told you before," she said, taking him firmly by the arm, "I am not working for the damned Germans. Do you understand me? I am a patriot—and far more so than you or your parents. And that is a fact."

"Then you shouldn't be living there. Do you know who used to live in that house?"

"No, what does that have to do with anything?"

"It belonged to a Jewish family named Feltman. Joshua and Rachel Feltman and their adopted son Herman. They were good people."

"What happened to them?"

"They were forced to go into hiding. They're probably dead now. Before your friends moved in, a group of German officers lived there. The Feltman's home was requisitioned by the Nazis."

"Well, you can't blame me for that."

"Yes, but I can blame you for mixing with them. They are dangerous, and one day you will pay for being on friendly terms with them."

"No, I will not because I don't work for them. I am not an NS supporter and I hate the Germans as much as you. Probably more."

"The Feltman's were good, hard-working people and didn't deserve to be driven from their home just because they were Jewish. I used to run errands for them on Saturday mornings, and Rachel gave me the best biscuits I've ever tasted. They shouldn't have had their home stolen from them and been forced to hide in the woods like rats. That's what has happened to the Jews, you know, since they were first rounded up last fall."

"I am no part of that and neither are the men who live in Number 15. As I said, I am not working for or helping the Germans in any way. In fact, I am…"

She stopped right there, catching herself. This was a mistake: she shouldn't be talking to this boy at all, and yet she desperately wanted to prove to him that she wasn't German's tart at all and was, in fact, fighting for the Resistance. How stupid she had been to allow herself to get caught up in a pointless debate with a meddlesome boy and let her emotions get the better of her.

"I have to go now," she said, feeling a mixture of embarrassment, defiance, and fear.

"I am sorry if I have upset you. But you had better remember what I've said. When the war is over, if you don't want to be locked away in prison, you will take my advice and leave those damned Germans behind. Get out while you can—that's my advice to you."

"I'll keep that in mind," she said, trying to maintain an air of stoicism. But she felt tears coming to her eyes and was unable to hold them back. Embarrassed, she walked off briskly towards Karl Johans gate, feeling as if she had made a terrible mistake moving in with two Abwehr operatives and a British double agent that everyone in Oslo but she believed was a German spy.

CHAPTER 52

GESTAPO HEADQUARTERS
VICTORIA TERRASSE

AUGUST 28, 1943

WHEN FEHMER saw the blood trickling down the prisoner's gashed skull, he couldn't help but feel a modicum of compassion. After all, he was not a heartless martinet without scruples but rather a decent, law-abiding criminal investigator with a difficult job to perform. That job was the ugly but entirely necessary task of catching, interrogating, and passing judgment upon potential enemies of the Reich. Or at least that's how he perceived the role of himself and the *Geheime Staatspolizei* in Norwegian wartime affairs. He knew that the members of the Resistance who were unfortunate enough to cross paths with him would not agree with his logical criminal prosecutor's assessment. Especially not poor Lars Njølstad, the prisoner bleeding onto the concrete floor before him. But it was not his job to worry about what the Norwegian people thought about him; his foremost priority was to ensure that his beloved Führer and National Socialism were not threatened by partisans and agitators bent on bringing down the New Order here in Occupied Norway.

"Please stop this nonsense, Lars, and tell us what we want to know," he said in an uncommonly genteel voice that matched his finely-tailored Norwegian suit and hand-tooled Nordic leather dress shoes. "You cannot withstand our enhanced interrogation procedures indefinitely. No one can."

The young man—who Fehmer knew had received a law degree just like him and recently graduated from the University of Oslo—said nothing. He had to be in agony, judging by the gaping crack at the top of his head. Fehmer looked at *SS-Obersturmführers* Hoeler and Bernhard, his two particularly sadistic pit bulls who struck even more fear into the prisoners of Victoria Terrasse than he did. They had done severe damage in less than five minutes with those truncheons of theirs. This time they were doing their bloody work in one of the dank, dingy interrogation rooms on the fourth floor, the floor from which several prisoners had jumped to their deaths rather than face further torture at the hands of the Gestapo. The torture room was large and dark, with curtains drawn so that no light could enter. The walls were covered with sound-proof material, and embedded in the ceiling were large lamps, which were regulated during interrogations to have maximum psychological impact. In one corner rested a chair very like a dentist's chair next to a tray of sharp medical instruments. In another was a table with an oven and copper wires that were heated to burn beneath the fingernails of victims and a huge tub of cold water and ice for subjecting the prisoner to the much-feared "water treatment." On one wall loomed a portrait of Hitler, and on the opposite wall one of Himmler—in case a prisoner needed to be reminded to whom they would ultimately have to answer.

"All right, that's it then. I tried to give you a chance, Lars, I really did. But I'm afraid we're going to have to give you the water treatment now."

Though reeling from repeated blows, the prisoner's eyes popped wide open.

"Oh, I can see you don't like that idea. Then please come clean and admit that you are working for the Resistance. Just tell us about your underground activities and contacts. Then the pain and suffering will stop."

Njølstad said nothing.

Fehmer motioned Hoeler and Bernhard.

They jerked the prisoner off his wooden stool, carried him to the corner of the room, and placed him before the huge tub of ice-cold water. His hands were manacled behind his back and his ankles were bound together.

"Nun fahren Sie zum Himmel!" bellowed Hoeler, as if they were about to play a fun children's game. *Now you go to heaven!*

He and Bernhard then seized him by the hair and thrust his head and upper body forcibly beneath the frigid water. As unconsciousness closed in, the prisoner was yanked from the freezing water until he recovered. Then Fehmer questioned him. He knew that Njølstad was merely a low-level courier and illegal newspaper distributor for *Militær Organisasjon,* so he asked him simple questions about Milorg's structure, locations of secret printing presses, his contacts and cutouts, and where he and his fellow operatives stashed their weapons and copies of their underground newspaper. But what the wily police detective really wanted to know was information on an important senior officer in Milorg with the code name Ishmael, a man whose real name he did not yet know but was reported to run a small team of special male and female cutouts in Oslo. When the prisoner refused to answer or was slow or evasive, the process was repeated, again and again, with Fehmer patiently repeating the questions. The torture ended only when Njølstad passed out unconscious from lack of oxygen.

They took a cigarette break and allowed him ten minutes to return to the land of the living before placing him back onto a stool in the middle of the room.

"Lars, so far you have told us very little. This does not bode well for you, I can assure you. In fact, I'm afraid we're going to have to ramp up our enhanced interrogation techniques."

He gave a subtle nod to Hoeler, who proceeded to beat him ferociously with his truncheon. Fehmer and Bernhard both stepped in and delivered repeated blows of their own, Fehmer with his Walther PPK pistol, Bernhard with a huge padded club reminiscent of something the Vikings might have once used on their captives. And then, suddenly they stopped and Fehmer asked in Norwegian, "Do you know Ishmael? What's he like?"

Taken off guard by the unexpected curtailment of violence, the prisoner answered honestly. "Yes, of course I know Ishmael! He is a true son of Norway!"

Fehmer smiled inwardly. He had known he was right all along. He had an instinctive feel for which of his prisoners were telling the truth and those that were lying to him, and in his professional experience, he had never tortured anyone who wasn't ultimately found to be harboring illegal secrets or who wasn't actively working for the Resistance.

"So, you do know Ishmael. Where can we find him? We were hoping to pay him a friendly visit."

Realizing his inadvertent mistake, the man clammed up. "I am not going to give you the satisfaction of speaking another word. Besides, I don't know anything except his code name."

"Oh, I believe you know more than that, my Norwegian friend. I also wager that you'll change your mind."

He gestured towards his two pit bulls. They came in swinging and the thrashing continued for several minutes until Hoeler and Bernhard were out of breath. Fehmer resumed the questioning—issuing threat after threat when his questions remained unanswered. Hoeler kicked the prisoner in the shins with his jackboot and Bernhard struck him so hard with a club that the wind was knocked out of him. Then he fainted once more. Once again, Hoeler threw a bucket of water on him and he came to.

"Lars, you must stop this. We need you to tell us about your responsibilities with Milorg and your work with Ishmael. As someone who knows the law, you are an important man in the organization. I'm sure you will make a great lawyer one day. Just tell us what we want to know so you can have a bright future after the war. What do you say?"

When he didn't respond, Fehmer had his two subordinates take hold of the prisoner's legs, drag him out of the room, and pull him down three flights of stairs to the first floor and then back up again so that his head bumped repeatedly on the hard stairs. By the time they brought him back to the interrogation room, he was deeply bruised, lacerated, and unconscious. Bernhard threw water on him and, after a minute, he regained consciousness.

Fehmer placed two sets of copper wires in the oven along with a metal fireplace poker and turned the temperature up high. "Bring in the other Milorg prisoner, the fishmonger two doors down."

"Nansen?"

"Yes, Bjørn Nansen. We'll see if our friend here changes his tune when he sees what we've got in store for poor Bjørn."

Hoeler and Bernhard left the room and returned two minutes later with the manacled fishmonger, who, like Njølstad, had been subjected to torture on and off for the past twenty-four hours yet yielded virtually no useful information. Once they had set him in a stool directly in front of Njølstad, Hoeler put on a pair of protective gloves, grabbed a one-handed bar clamp, and carefully withdrew one of the red-hot copper wires from the oven.

Fehmer then proceeded with the introductions. "Herr Njølstad, meet Bjørn Nansen. We are going to have a little contest. If you tell us what we want to know, you will both be set free with a bit of cash and mild sentences. All you have to do is confess in the next five minutes. The alternative is…well, it is quite different. You control your fate, gentlemen. Now which is it going to be?"

The two men looked at one another but made no response. Then their expressions stiffened with resolve as they appeared to make some sort of tacit pact to hold out and not give in to torture.

Fehmer shook his head with disappointment. "An unwise decision, I can assure you, gentlemen. But I must admit I do admire your tenacity."

While Bernhard held down Nansen, Hoeler stepped forward and carefully inserted the red-hot wires beneath the fingernails of each of the fingers in his right hand manacled behind his back.

The prisoner screamed.

Fehmer looked at Njølstad to see if he would give in but was met with a stoic expression. It was going to take a lot more than sympathy for a fellow Milorg brother-in-arms to get him to talk. The captain motioned Hoeler to repeat the procedure with the other hand.

He did and, once again, Nansen shrieked in agony.

But still his cohort would not budge.

Now Fehmer went and grabbed the heavy maul with the forged steel head leaning against the wall and handed it to Bernhard.

"I don't believe our friends understand the gravity of the situation," he said to his subordinate. "If you would please, Lieutenant, make them understand."

"My pleasure, *Hauptsturmführer.*"

"Wait, wait!" Nansen and Njølstad protested simultaneously, but their pleas went unheeded as the maul came crashing down on Nansen's right kneecap. Fehmer heard an audible crack, but just to make sure maximum damage had been sustained, he instructed Bernhard to strike the fishmonger again in the same place. The torturer swiftly administered a violent blow and a second cracking sound echoed grotesquely in the room. *Yes, the kneecap is definitely shattered,* Fehmer could tell, as the prisoner screamed in agony. After more than three years of occupation, he and his team of interrogators had perfected their torture regimen to a fine art. Striking hard bony parts and joints like kneecaps, shins, ankles, elbows, shoulders, and ribs rather than the head or soft vital organs was now standard procedure when prisoners dug their heels in and refused to talk. This ensured that a prisoner experienced unbearable agony without endangering his life or hurting him so badly that he was incapable of providing sought-after information.

"Now, gentlemen," Fehmer said after letting the pain subside for a moment. "The time has come for you to talk. You have established that you are brave men, so further resistance is pointless. Now tell me about Ishmael. How can I find him?"

"We don't know anything, damnit!" cried Njølstad, looking worriedly at his comrade. "You have the wrong men!"

Fehmer shook his head disconsolately. "I had held such high hopes for you, Lars. And this is how you treat me and my men?"

Again, he gave a little nod towards Hoeler, who, with a fiendish smile, inserted the hot copper wires beneath the prisoner's fingernails. Then he turned loose Hoeler with his maul again, who as he stepped forward bore a demonic expression on his face and was, quite literally, salivating with excitement. Fehmer had seen the look many times before and knew that the young lieutenant derived a sadistic pleasure in his interrogation work. All Fehmer wanted was for his charges to confess their crimes and name names; he didn't care how he got there. The maul again struck Nansen's kneecap with violent force and he passed out.

"You see what you have done," Fehmer said to Njølstad. "He won't be able to walk for months and you are the one to blame."

"It's not my fault! You're the one who has done this to him!"

"No, Lars, you are the one to blame. Even supporters of the New Order, your so-called quislings, quake with fear when they peer up at our curtained windows. As do the citizens who come here with a clear conscience to obtain a pass or seek permission to visit a relative. These people, on both sides, tremble in their shoes when they pass through our doors. But not you, Lars. You seem to have a death wish. You don't give a damn about yourself or your friend here."

"I can't tell you anything because I don't know anything!"

"I think you do." He motioned towards Hoeler and Bernhard. "Wake him up. It's time to reverse the roles."

They splashed water on Nansen's face, reviving him, and made him watch as this time Bernhard took the maul and smashed Njølstad's kneecap. Fehmer heard the bone shatter and both prisoners screamed in anguish. Fehmer plucked the padded mallet from the table and gently touched the broken kneecaps of both men, eliciting moans of agony. Then he waited a full minute before speaking, letting both prisoners shudder in pain. Njølstad made hardly any sound, bearing the pain stoically, while Nansen begged repeatedly for mercy. Breaking a bone was an especially useful technique during interrogation: once a bone was broken, pressure or additional blows could be inflicted upon the damaged area to ensure excruciating pain for an extended period without resulting in death.

"Are you two finally prepared to answer my questions?" Fehmer then asked.

When they said nothing, he tapped the padded mallet against their broken kneecaps a second time, again drawing moans of agony. It was then Nansen broke.

"All right, I will tell you what you want to know! Just don't hurt us anymore!"

"You promise not to lie to me and to answer my questions?"

"Yes, yes, I'll do whatever you want! Just...just don't hurt us anymore!"

"You bastard!" protested Njølstad. "You can't give in like this!"

The young man groaned in agony and shook his head with resignation. "I'm done, comrade. I'm spent."

"Buck up, damnit! Show some courage!"

"Bjørn here is a practical man, Herr Njølstad," said Fehmer. "I would let him go his own way on this if I were you. But we want to bring you into line as well. Two singing canaries are always better than one. That way we can cross-check your stories and find out about this Ishmael."

He underscored his threat by tapping the mallet against the broken bone again. Njølstad screamed in agony and Nansen again fainted. He was unable to bear the sight of a comrade being brutally tortured in front of him, a common reaction with which Fehmer was familiar. They splashed water on him again and, after a few minutes, he came to. But this time they had placed a blindfold over his eyes and Njølstad had been gagged so that the only sound in the room was his muffled moaning.

"All right, we won't harm your comrade if you come clean with the truth," Fehmer said to Nansen reassuringly. "We will give you money and you will be released from custody. What do you say?"

When he didn't respond, Fehmer realized that he was either too wounded to speak or was having second thoughts. He signaled Hoeler, who gave a sinister smile and stepped forward to deliver another blow with the maul.

"No, no, please," cried the blindfolded Nansen, hearing the approaching footsteps.

But the lieutenant only feinted in his direction and instead delivered a devastating blow to Njølstad's right forearm. Fehmer heard the snap of bone and Njølstad gave a muffled scream through his gag.

Again, Nansen fainted.

Fehmer waited a moment to make sure he was unconscious before commanding, "Wake him up again."

Bernhard picked up a bucket of water from the corner of the room and tossed the water in Nansen's face. After a few seconds, he came to again and began pleading for mercy.

"This will all end when you tell me what I need to know," said Fehmer in a friendly voice, as if he was lecturing a small child. "You control whether it is to be pain or the relief of pain. If you will tell us what we want to know, I promise to fetch you a doctor. He will give you a shot of morphine."

"Please...give it to me now and...and I will tell you everything I know."

"No, I'm afraid I can't do that. You need to tell me what I want to know first."

"I'll tell you everything. Please, please, just stop hitting me and Lars!"

"Oh, so you two do know each other?"

"Yes, we know each other," the young man replied, to the sound of his comrade's muffled protests.

"It is good that we have an understanding." Then to Hoeler. "Remove Herr Njølstad from the room."

"*Jawohl, Hauptsturmführer.*"

When the prisoner had been dragged from the room, Fehmer removed Nansen's blindfold and handcuffs, lit a British Dunhill cigarette, and slid it gently into his mouth. "Now, if you tell me everything I want to know, I will have you taken to the hospital instead of Number 19. Do you understand me?"

"Yes," groaned the young man.

"Very well then, let's start with this. You know Ishmael, don't you? You were telling the truth earlier, weren't you?"

"Yes, I was telling the truth."

Fehmer smiled cordially, as if sharing a smoke with a dinner guest on the back porch. "Well then, my friend, tell me everything you know about our mystery man. By the way, I *do* like his code name. Like many Norwegians, I've always enjoyed Melville's tale of the great white whale and Captain Ahab. Remember how the obsessed bastard vows to chase Moby Dick round the Norway Maelstrom and perdition's flames before he gives him up? I must admit I am a bit like old Ahab when it comes to hunting down Resistance operatives, wouldn't you agree?"

"Yes, I agree. I have read the seafaring tale and you are like the captain," said the fishmonger Nansen. "You are relentless."

"I'll take that as a compliment. *Moby Dick* is a favorite of Doktor Jung's, you know. '*Call me Ishmael*'—I just love the opening line. Now let us finish our friendly discussion so that you may see a physician. Tell me about our friend Ishmael—and leave no detail out."

CHAPTER 53

GESTAPO HEADQUARTERS
VICTORIA TERRASSE

AUGUST 28, 1943

"WHY IS THERE BLOOD ON YOUR SUIT, SIEGFRIED?"

For a moment, Fehmer was too stunned to speak. Annemarie Breien had taken him by surprise by waltzing into his office at 3:47 p.m. as if she was his personal secretary. My God, was that Hamburgian simpleton Wortmann on the first floor no longer checking passes at the front desk and sending people to the fourth floor without questioning them? With embarrassment, Fehmer looked down at the sleeve of his suit; indeed, a pair of blood spatters had stained the green-gray fabric.

"I'm afraid you caught me at an inopportune time. How did you get in here anyway?"

She ignored the question. "Have you been torturing prisoners under interrogation? My God, Siegfried, what's become of you? How can you do this to my people?"

He felt himself flush with shame. He rose quickly from his chair, rounded his desk, and closed his office door so they couldn't be heard by the clerical staff and junior-level officers in the main office, who were listening intently. Then he took her gently by the elbow and sat her in the upholstered leather chair before his spacious, cluttered desk. He thought about lying to her by explaining that he had cut himself shaving, but he knew she would never believe that.

"My job, as you know, is not an easy one, Annemarie. Sometimes, I must obtain information from saboteurs and terrorists using enhanced interrogation methods. There is no other way to get the timely information we need to save lives."

"To save German lives, you mean. Didn't you tell me the last two times we met that you were no longer going to torture people?"

"We don't torture them. We apply pressure. And for your information, in no routine case can it be proved, as far as I know, that an accused person was subjected to enhanced interrogation for information he was unable to give."

"The end justifies the means—is that what you're saying?"

"Look, I don't want to argue with you. Can you please tell me why you are here? As always, I will help you if I can, but I will not be lectured by you. I am not a bad man and don't appreciate being treated like one, especially when I am the one who has ensured the freedom of more than thirty of your family members and friends by arranging for their release from prison."

"I'm sorry, I didn't mean to sound ungrateful. I just think you're better than this." She waved around the room. "You should be a lawyer, not a torturer."

"Like your husband? How is Kjell doing by the way?"

"You know the answer to that question. He doesn't like that I am continuing to meet with you against his wishes, even if it is for a good cause."

"I can understand that. If I were your husband, I wouldn't approve of you meeting another man on a regular basis either. I would probably challenge him to pistols at dawn."

"I thought you Germans preferred sabers."

"That is only Prussians. Besides, I grew up in Latvia."

"Yes, I almost forgot. Your parents are Russian citizens and growing up you belonged to the German minority in Kurland. And then you moved to Moscow before the First World War."

"Is there a point to all this?"

She ignored his protest. "As a boy, you experienced the Russian Revolution at the end of the war first hand. That's when you first began to hate the Bolsheviks. And then, in 1918, you and your parents became German citizens when you and your family moved to Berlin just before the November rebellion."

"Those were perilous times, just like today. Again, I have to ask is there a point to all this?"

"I don't know. Should there be?"

"Why have you come here, Annemarie? If it is to heckle me, you are doing a fine job of it."

"I didn't come here to provoke you. I'm just upset is all." She gave a weary sigh. "You're better than this, Siegfried. You're better than the Nazis."

"Aren't you forgetting that National Socialism is probably the only thing that is going to save Norway?"

"You know that's not true. You have been brainwashed by Hitler's and Goebbels's propaganda."

"Be careful, Annemarie. Treasonous talk can get you sent to Bredtveit Prison."

"Oh, am I to earn the same tragic fate as Gunnar Eilifsen? Is that it?"

"Eilifsen refused an order. That's why he was executed."

The decorated Norwegian police officer had been shot ten days earlier for refusing to arrest three girls who did not show up for forced labor, and Osloans were still upset about the incident.

"He was illegally arrested and murdered, Siegfried. It is as simple as that."

"He was found guilty by a Norwegian special tribunal."

"It was a sham proceeding and you know it. And now, dozens of police officers have been arrested and are being shipped off to concentration camps because they wouldn't sign the NS 'loyalty statement.' Gunnar Eilifsen was a hard-working policeman and a hero—and so are the others who refused to sign the false oath of loyalty to Quisling and Terboven."

Fehmer rose abruptly from his chair. "You cannot talk like this, Annemarie. You know perfectly well it is treason. Now what has gotten you so riled up?"

"How do you know something has riled me up? How do you know that I am not just angry with you for being a brute?"

"Because I care about you, I'm going to pretend I didn't hear that."

He reached across his desk and tried to touch her hand, but she pulled it back out of reach and glared at him.

"What is wrong, Annemarie? Why are you doing this?"

"It's my husband," she admitted. "He says if I don't stop meeting with you he's going to leave me. He said I have to make a choice."

"I don't want to be the cause of your marriage breaking up."

"But the work I'm doing…I mean, the work *we're* doing is too important. You and I are making a difference in people's lives by getting them out of prison. The work must continue at all costs."

"Even at the expense of your marriage?"

"Yes."

"But you love Kjell. He is your husband and you made a vow when you married him. That is not something to be taken lightly."

"Is that why you have slept with half the young women of Oslo? Because of your fealty to your wife Anni?"

"Just because I'm a hypocrite doesn't mean you have to be."

Reaching across his desk, she took him firmly by the hand, her eyes pleading. "I need you to keep doing the right thing, Siegfried: securing the release of the prisoners on the list I gave you. You are making progress, aren't you?"

"I will have two more names on your list set free by the end of next month."

"But that's so far away."

"I'm afraid it's the best I can do. The truth is I may already be under suspicion."

"From who? Fehlis? Reinhard?"

"Reinhard has been asking questions. Thus far, I have been fortunate not to have to answer them, but we both know that luck doesn't last forever."

"But you've provided ample justification for the releases you've authorized. I don't understand how Reinhard would be able to cause a fuss."

"Because he's head of the Gestapo and he doesn't see things the way I do."

"I'm sorry if I've made your situation difficult, but you must find comfort in the fact that, for more than a year now, you have been doing the right thing."

"Doing the right thing could get me sent to the wall for high treason."

"It is worth the risk, Siegfried. You are not like Fehlis or Reinhard—you are better than that. Unlike them, you can be proud of what you are doing."

"Unfortunately, pride has its limits. I have also managed to get two prisoners at Grini out of solitary confinement. They are on your list and are no longer on bread and water."

"Thank you, Siegfried." She reached out and touched his hand. "And what about Sigurd Evensmo?" she asked with reference to the respected young Norwegian journalist and labor supporter.

"I can do nothing for Evensmo. Not yet anyway."

"Well, can you at least promise me to keep trying?"

"I gave you my word, Annemarie. I plan on keeping it. Don't you believe me?"

"Yes, I believe you. Because, unlike most of my countrymen, I believe in the better angels of your nature. Good day to you."

"Good day to you too," he said with feeling. "And be sure to be careful out there. There are many who, in these troubled times, are not nearly as enlightened as me."

"Are you talking about Germans or Norwegians?"

"Both—I am talking about both. Just be careful, Annemarie."

CHAPTER 54

VON GRÖNING FLAT, 8 GRØNNEGATE

SEPTEMBER 7, 1943

STANDING AT THE FRONT DOOR, Stephan von Gröning smiled regally and waved his guest inside his flat. "Welcome, Fritzchen, welcome."

"Good to see you, Doktor," replied Chapman as he stepped inside the well-furnished apartment and into the front hallway.

Von Gröning was truly pleased to see his protégé; they had much to discuss now that he had received the green light from Berlin to once again unleash his star operative upon British soil. Closing the front door, he led him into the drawing room and poured him a cognac. They clinked glasses and sat back in their seats. Having never had a son, the older man felt a special paternal-like affection for the former criminal who had done so much good work on behalf of the Reich.

"I have good news, Fritzchen," he said to begin the meeting, tipping his head towards the contract lying on the table in front of them. Molli Stirl had drafted the document only this morning.

"What kind of good news?" inquired Chapman, glancing cautiously at the sheath of papers.

"Berlin has approved my plan for new sabotage work in England. I have the contract for you to sign."

He picked up the document and handed it to Chapman, who took a minute to read it over while casually sipping his drink.

"Just sign on the dotted line and we can begin your preparations," he said affably, unscrewing the lid of his silver fountain pen.

Chapman continued to peruse the contract, his face eventually scrunching up into an unmistakable frown. Von Gröning felt a twisting sensation in his stomach.

"What is it? What's the matter?"

Chapman carefully set the contract on the table. "It's not good enough. I won't do it."

"But why? What's wrong with it?"

"I don't consider the proposition of sufficient importance."

"But the contract is the same as the first one you signed last year in France. It promises the same financial reward: one hundred fifty thousand kroner. You are going to be a rich man."

"I have plenty of money already."

Von Gröning was up and on his feet. "What the hell are you trying to pull here?"

"Nothing. I just don't need any more money. I have plenty."

"No, you don't. You are burning through your funds at an alarming rate, my prodigal friend."

"Thanks to you and your German friends."

"What are you saying?"

"Whenever you, Johnny, or the others invite me to the Ritz or Löwenbräu, we drink bottle after bottle of cocktails, champagne, and liqueurs and smoke expensive cigars—and most of the time I am left footing the bill. Your plan all along has been to force me to squander all I have earned as rapidly as possible. That way, once my loot is exhausted I will have no choice but to undertake more of your dirty work. Well, I won't do it. Your plan has backfired because I know I still have plenty of money. I've been keeping track of it. I still have eighty thousand kroner coming to me."

It took all von Gröning's effort not to become enraged. He took a deep breath to calm himself down and tossed back his cognac. His protégé's infuriatingly placid demeanor and air of civility made him even angrier.

"Now look here, Fritz," he said, no longer using the affectionate diminutive for his star agent. "Need I point out that without my support, you would still be rotting in Romainville, or even worse, dead."

"Of course, I appreciate what you did for me. But this contract bloody stinks and I refuse to sign it."

"But why?"

"I just told you. The job is too imprecise, and the money is not enough given the risk. But more importantly, sabotage is an unworthy task. There has to be something more dramatic than blowing up some silly factory."

"But factories like the de Havilland Mosquito Plant are precisely why the Allies are winning the war."

"That may be, but the money's still not enough."

"My superiors will not stand for this."

"The only way you're going to get me to go back to England is if you pay me what I deserve."

"And just what exactly is your worth on the open market?"

"I want at least five hundred thousand reichsmarks or fifty thousand pounds."

"They'll never pay that much. What I'm offering you is a fortune."

"I'm not interested in anything less."

For the next five minutes, they argued bitterly. Von Gröning fumed and sputtered, threatening all manner of punishment, until the combination of rage and drink turned his face an alarming scarlet and made the veins stand out on his flabby neck. Catching his reflection in the mirror above the clock, he was shocked by what he saw.

"If you do not get on board, Fritz, I will cut your funds in half. Or maybe I'll just cut you off altogether. We'll see how you like it then, you greedy bastard!"

To the spymaster's dismay, Chapman gave an insolent shrug, clearly not impressed by his threats. "Go ahead. You'll only be chopping off the hand that feeds you. That wouldn't be very smart, now would it?"

"I'll have you thrown in Grini, damn you!"

"You can have me sent back to Romainville for all I care. I will gladly face such a fate rather than be taken advantage of."

"Get out of my flat!"

"With pleasure, old bean."

Chapman tossed back his cognac and left. As von Gröning watched his protégé walk down the driveway, he clenched and unclenched his hands in anger. How could he have allowed himself to be outmaneuvered like this? And then he wondered if Chapman was only pretending to be upset about the money. Was his refusal a ruse to buy time and delay his parting from Dagmar, with whom he had fallen deeply in love? No, the spymaster suspected that wasn't the main reason. Though Chapman was hopelessly infatuated, he was still a swashbuckler who needed danger and adventure if he was to feel completely alive. Dagmar was part of the reason but there was something else going on.

Was Chapman, in fact, a British double agent? In pretending to be rankled at his lack of financial compensation, was he making a play for a more concrete assignment, so he could report something significant to his British spymasters? In the espionage game, von Gröning knew that it was not only important to obtain information on the enemy but to know what information the enemy coveted to discover what he lacked and where he was most vulnerable. But could his top operative truly be a double agent? Were the de Havilland job, the attempted bombing of the *City of Lancaster*, and his training activities here in Norway all a sham? Was the field operative he and Canaris had honored with the Iron Cross a complete fraud?

With sudden realization, he knew that it didn't matter. He could never say a word about his suspicions to his Abwehr superior here in Oslo—von Bonin—or to Berlin. Not unless he wanted to be put before a firing squad, for the spymaster who admitted that the agent to whom he had awarded the Iron Cross was a fraud was a dead man. No, Fritz—the clever bastard—was safe and untouchable. He had been thoroughly vetted by a dozen Abwehr and SS interrogators and that vetting had resulted in him being awarded Germany's highest military honor and feted in Norway. Von Gröning cursed himself for having been fatally compromised by his dependence on Chapman and understood, quite plainly, what had just taken place.

Today had been the defining moment in their relationship and the balance of power had shifted: he needed Eddie Chapman more than Chapman needed him.

And they both knew it.

CHAPTER 55

OSLO

SEPTEMBER 11, 1943

WHEN THE GERMAN CONVOY PASSED, Dagmar smiled into the Leica camera and posed like a fashion model as Chapman snapped photograph after photograph of her. She wore a simple but elegant dress and matching jacket that she had designed and sewn herself, while Chapman was dressed in a Norwegian sweater and a beret set at a rakish angle, as if he were a professional fashion photographer. The backdrop for the pictures had been preselected by Dagmar: a German Luftwaffe supply depot on the Grefsen Skole, located in the Kapellveien northeast of Oslo town center. Though they were here today only to photograph the depot, along with several other key military installations dotting Oslo, they agreed it would make a most inviting target for British Royal Air Force bombers when the proper time came.

As she continued to pose for the photographs and Chapman clicked away, they both studied the German anti-aircraft guns positioned around the perimeter of the main building. The heavy flak cannons were bordered by huge fueling tanks, a pair of dispenser islands, equipment and control sheds, and a small fleet of heavy trucks and *Kübelwagens*. It was amazing how easy it was to sneak in and take photos of top secret installations, and Dagmar knew that she was a vital prop. A young man out alone taking photographs of a military installation would arouse suspicion, but not if he was taking snapshots of his fetching Norwegian girlfriend, one who had a documented history as a fashion model.

"I think we've got enough," said Chapman. "MI5 is going to love these."

She placed her hands on her hips and threw back her head in a sexy pose. "Just one more, Rhett Butler. And then it's off to our next location."

"All right, say omelette!"

"Omelette!"

He clicked one more, she sashayed over and kissed him, and they walked on to their next sensitive military installation. It was a German tank and armored car depot located a mile south in Sandakerveien. Again, they stopped and pretended to be merely a pair of young lovers out taking photographs on a sunny, late-summer Saturday afternoon. This time, Chapman reeled off a half dozen pictures, zeroing in especially upon the neat row of Panzer and StuG IIIs parked on the pavement next to a fueling and storage terminal.

When finished, they walked to the closest *trikk* station and rode the tram into the city. Taking seats in the rear of the half-filled tram and speaking quietly in English, they were fortunately not subjected to the Ice Front by anyone, which had been grating increasingly on their nerves when they went out in public. But the front of the car did clear out and several Osloans did move to the rear of the tram when a pair of German soldiers stepped on board. The passengers refused to sit near either of them. Although Nazi rule had outlawed such cold-shoulder treatment by placing placards on board that read, PASSENGERS WHO DEMONSTRATE AGAINST

THE GERMAN MILITARY OR MEMBERS OF THE NS BY CHANGING PLACES WILL BE EXPELLED AT THE NEAREST STATION, the Norwegians still did it anyway, continuing to treat the occupiers—and the collaborators, or merely *perceived* collaborators, who supported them—with undisguised contempt.

Just south of the Royal Palace, they exited the tram and took their picnic lunch in the park. Dagmar watched as Chapman took playful photographs of children. He snuck up behind a group of toddlers sitting on a bench, focused his camera, and shouted "Boo!" The startled little faces spun round and squealed with delight as he caught them on film. Sauntering back to her triumphantly, he claimed the photograph was the best he had ever taken.

Dagmar could tell he was getting good at photography. Chapman had told her about the professional photographer named Rotkagel, the former manager of a Leica factory, detailed by the Abwehr to teach him photography. He had been issued with his own camera and film and was taught by Rotkagel how to hold and focus the instrument, how to read the light meter, how to ensure high quality pictures without too little or too much sunlight or shadow, and eventually how to photograph documents, charts, and maps. Within a short time, he had become quite proficient.

Today, they had planned to photograph a total of six German military installations and intelligence offices. After their picnic lunch, they turned their attention to the third and fourth targets on their list: the Luftwaffe administrative headquarters located at 1 through 11 Klingenberggate and the *Sicherheitsdienst* headquarters at Victoria Terrasse. During the photographing, the Luftwaffe building appeared rather mundane, but the dreaded, heavily-guarded Gestapo building with the Nazi flags snapping overhead gave them pause, making them look left and right like twitchy birds to see if anyone was watching them.

"This is where Fehlis is based. The place gives me the shivers," said Dagmar after posing nervously for several photographs. "I think we should go."

"No doubt the head of the SS and SD would make an inviting target. I have yet to make his acquaintance."

"Milorg would like nothing more than to target him for assassination. Him and Siegfried Fehmer both. But they are afraid of reprisals."

"What do you know about Fehmer?"

"He's Fehlis's bloodhound. They came to Norway together back in April 1940. Fehmer's only a captain, but he's the lead investigator of the Resistance here in Occupied Norway. They say he has shared the bed of many a Norwegian beauty. He is a handsome devil, I'll admit, but he is an absolute monster. He supposedly can turn from charming to savagely violent in the blink of an eye."

"Dr. Jekyll and Mr. Hyde."

"Yes, that is Fehmer all right."

They stared up at the ghoulish white building with the curtained windows and long rows of patrol cars and two ambulances parked out front.

"A number of prisoners have jumped from the windows on the upper floors rather than submit to further torture at Victoria Terrasse," said Dagmar. "I have been inside only once. After Fehmer took me into custody, I was shoved into a waiting car and driven here. I was scared out of my mind."

"I can imagine."

"When they led me through the main entrance, I remember being unsteady on my feet. I found it difficult to climb up the steps into the guardroom."

"Well, hopefully you'll never see the inside of the building again. We should go. I'm getting the shivers like you just looking at it. Some courage I have, eh?"

He took her by the arm and they walked east to their next location, the Ostbane Station where Wehrmacht and Viking Regiment troops leaving for the Eastern Front entrained at a small station about a half mile east of the *Østbanehallen*. The soldiers stood in rows four deep waiting to board a train. They wore a combination of *feldgrau* and camo, black boots, and steel helmets. Slung from their shoulders were bolt-action rifles and Schmeissers. When Dagmar posed for a photo, the closest troops cheered and waved their long-brimmed caps. Chapman waved at them and clicked off several photographs. But soon a stern-looking officer stomped over and asked them what they were doing. Chapman instantly produced his Wehrmacht *Ausweis* pass and his German-authorized license to carry and operate a film camera, and the officer went skulking back to the station.

Dagmar sighed with relief. "This is getting dangerous. Perhaps we should call it a day."

"No, we've got one more stop."

"I thought it was two."

"It is but I agree we shouldn't press our luck. Let's take a peek at the Signals Communication Center in Ekeberg. Then we can pack it in and have a drink."

"All right." She gave him a peck on the cheek. Though she was uneasy sneaking about and taking snapshots of German installations, she was confident that he knew what he was doing. He had an innate ability to think on his feet and remain calm and composed when under suspicion. He had dispatched the meddling German officer by swiftly producing his passes. She wished she was more like that, but the truth was she was an emotional person and was not always able to conceal her true feelings. It was just the way she was.

They took another *trikk* south, walked a short distance, and soon came upon the Signals Communication Center that Chapman had found out about from an innocent conversation with Johnny Holst. The communications center was used for contacting U-boats by wireless transmission. It was located on the east side of Oslo Harbor in Ekeberg, south of the marine container and ship fueling port at Sørenga. But as Chapman began clicking photographs, they noticed two men approaching from the north side of the center. Dagmar took them for either Gestapo or Norwegian NS detectives: they stood out like sore thumbs in their fedoras and trench coats, and one of them donned a pair of Himmler-like wire-rimmed spectacles.

"Evading questioning once is one thing but doing it twice in a row is pushing it," she whispered to Chapman.

"I agree," he said. "Come on, let's make for those woods. If they catch us, I'll present my pass and official photography license. But I can't let them have my camera or film. They'll see we've been photographing key military installations."

"And if they insist?"

He touched beneath his armpit where his Luger was tucked away in his leather shoulder holster. "I hope I don't have to use it, but this is the reason why I have it.

Graumann told me to keep it on me at all times. He also said to report to him if I felt I was being followed."

"Yes, but in this case we're in Ekeberg taking photographs of a Wehrmacht Signals Communication Center."

"You're right, of course. Let's go."

They started off at a brisk pace, taking a narrow footpath through the trees towards Mosseveien Road that wrapped around the Oslo Fjord in the coastal area of Bekkelaget. They passed through a forest of lime-pine trees and heavily-fractured limestone bedrock with scattered scrub vegetation and large deposits of dragon head, *Filipendula vulgaris*, and wild garlic. As they slipped deeper into the forest, their situation began to seem even more dangerous to Dagmar, especially when she heard voices and footsteps coming from their right on a separate footpath. There were at least two people, maybe more.

"There's someone else. We have to move faster," said Chapman, hearing the sounds to the north too.

"But who are the men in the trench coats? Gestapo?"

"Most likely. Whoever they are, they must have been following us earlier. They probably saw us taking photographs at one or more of the other locations. Now they're going to try and seize our film as evidence and arrest us."

"As you said, we can't let them have the film or camera."

"Don't worry, we won't. Just keep moving."

They increased their pace to a brisk walk on the verge of a light jog. After fifty paces, Dagmar chanced a look over her shoulder. The two men in the trench coats were now bearing down upon them from the east, a hundred feet and closing, but she could only hear, rather than see, the other group that was making crackling sounds as twigs and brush were trampled underfoot. Who knows, maybe it was just a small group of hikers with no connection to the men in the trench coats?

They continued on, taking branching foot trails but continuing to head west towards the fjord. Soon they came to a southwest-facing, sun-exposed outcrop of marlstone and beneath it a steep, talus-ridden slope looking out onto Mosseveien Road and Oslo Fjord beyond. They were forced to pick their way through the outcrop and loose slabs of limestone. When they reached the base of the slope, they looked back nervously for the men following them, but they were no longer there.

Where the hell have they gone?

They looked at one another. The aura of razor's-edge paranoia had been replaced by confused surprise. At that moment, a German transport filled with troops singing *Lili Marlene* raced past along the roadway. She and Chapman quickly crossed Mosseveien and set out on the shoreline footpath that ran along the western edge of the highway in Bekkelaget, walking north.

In the woods above the roadcut on their right, they heard a sudden burst of gunfire. A moment later, the two men in the trench coats emerged from the trees with three university-aged Norwegian prisoners holding their hands above their heads, including one man who had been wounded in the leg and was limping.

"They weren't after us," said Chapman. "They were after those kids."

"Those must have been the other voices we heard. We should help them."

"Not a chance. We can't get mixed up in this."

She knew he was right, but she still felt badly for them. They continued on the footpath, passing a German marine fuel depot on their left. Behind them, the men in the trench coats marched the three prisoners to a car and drove off to the south, which Dagmar found surprising. If they were Gestapo, or even Norwegian undercover police, shouldn't they be taking the prisoners into the city rather than south? Where were they taking them? More importantly, once they got there, what were they going to do with them?

They walked on. Gradually, the sense of danger dissipated, and she felt herself relax. They continued to look vigilantly back over their shoulders for signs of the enemy, but she could tell that the worst had passed. A quarter mile up the trail, Chapman came to a stop and touched her arm.

"Look over there," he said. "It's a pod of killer whales."

He pointed offshore into the shimmering water of the fjord to the cluster of whales surfacing and blowing water from their spouts. Several times in her lifetime, Dagmar had seen a pod of the black-and-white orcas "carousel feeding" just like they were now, and the sight brought a smile to her lips. The whales were working together as a team to bring a school of herring close to the surface, circling around the fish to panic them into a tighter and tighter ball. She and Chapman marveled when the whales began slapping their massive tail flukes through the school to stun and disable their prey, so they could be picked off at leisure.

"Nature may be red in tooth and claw, but that is a beautiful sight," he said. "Those giants are one of the greatest hunters of the sea."

"Yes, they're marvelous. I'm just glad we're not the herring."

"But a few minutes ago, when those bastards were following us, I felt like I was. Didn't you?"

"Yes, I most certainly did. I feel badly for those three kids."

"I do too. But they'll be all right. Those two Gestapo goons could have shot them all, but they didn't. I'm sure they'll be okay."

"Yes, but why did they take them south instead of into Oslo?"

"I don't know but we can't concern ourselves with it. We have enough to worry about ourselves with this roll of film. This is important intelligence and I need to get it to MI5."

"I understand but I still feel badly for those kids. I hate the Germans."

"That makes two of us, luv. That's why we're pulling the wool over their blasted eyes."

They went thoughtfully silent and continued to stare out at the fjord, glimmering in the late afternoon sunlight like a precious diamond, and the feeding killer whales. It was an idyllic scene and soon the frenetic tension of a few minutes earlier melted away. For the first time of the day, Dagmar didn't feel as if someone was following them, lurking in the shadows, or about to arrest them, steal their camera, and seize their incriminating film. In that moment, all her troubles seemed to disappear, and the war felt like it was on another continent. Standing there looking out at the glistening fjord and watching the spectacular orcas with their flapping tails, she felt the transcendent power and beauty of nature.

And she knew in that immaculately clarifying instant that she had never loved—nor would she ever love—another man as she loved her fellow spy Eddie Chapman.

CHAPTER 56

VON GRÖNING FLAT, 8 GRØNNEGATE

SEPTEMBER 15, 1943

"HOW WAS BERLIN?"

Von Gröning smiled his most ingratiating smile, confidant that this time he would win over his protégé and put the ugliness of the past week behind them once and for all. The spymaster had enlisted the aid of the other members of the station—Praetorius, Holst, Molli Stirl, and the other secretaries—but Chapman had held fast. He had not submitted to von Gröning's threat of dire consequences if he refused to sign the contract, insisting that he was after some bigger and better job that paid far more money, and that he couldn't possibly accept anything so vague. After three days, with the deadlock still unbroken, von Gröning had taken the drastic step of cutting off his funds altogether. Chapman responded with an angry letter, saying that if the rittmeister persisted, he was prepared to go back to Romainville and face his fate. By the end of the week, von Gröning knew he had no choice but to submit to the spy's demands. He had flown to Berlin to convince the higher-ups to accede to his intransigent agent's demands.

"Berlin was fine, Fritzchen," he replied pleasantly. "Though I must tell you that the Allied bombing has been stepped up and many buildings have been reduced to rubble. For the first time I can remember, I couldn't help but feel we may lose this war if we don't reclaim the initiative and take bold action. Which is why, my friend, your new mission is so important."

Chapman took a sip of his cognac. "Tell me about it. What are the new terms? I can only assume that Berlin had the good sense to agree to meet my demands."

"Yes, I am confident that you will be quite satisfied this time around."

He picked up the contract lying on the table and handed it to Chapman, who proceeded to read it over while sipping his cognac.

"As you can see, the big shots have earmarked you for an important new espionage mission for which there will be a large cash payment upon its successful completion. You are to find out how the Tommies are winning the war under the sea. We believe the British have developed a submarine-detection system that enables them to track our U-boats from the surface. Your mission is to identify this submarine detector, find out how it works, photograph it, steal it if possible, and then bring it back to Occupied France."

Chapman stopped reading and looked up. "But I don't know anything about U-boat tracking devices."

"Don't worry about that. You will have access to our experts."

"I will definitely need a lot of coaching then."

"You will receive the finest training, and for your services to the Reich you will be paid handsomely."

"Yes, I can see: one hundred thousand reichsmarks."

"And an additional two hundred thousand marks in a currency of your choosing, and your very own Abwehr command in Occupied Europe. As the Americans like to say, that is hitting it out of the park, wouldn't you say?"

"I must say it is most generous. Of course, if I accept I will need access at the highest levels. So, if I understand correctly, the British are sinking German U-boats at a high rate, and Berlin believes this is because of a sophisticated detection device. Do they think it's sonar?"

"We're not sure. What we do know is that during the first three years of the war, our prowling wolf packs ruled the Atlantic, sinking millions of tons of Allied shipping—and now the roles have been reversed and the British are killing us. Our U-boats used to swoop in on convoy routes, and when one U-boat located the prey, the wolf pack would swarm in for a mass attack, send several ships to the sea bottom, and steal away unseen and most often unscathed."

"I've seen them in action. I saw a wolf pack up close six months ago when I sailed on the *City of Lancaster*. Several ships were sunk in a matter of minutes and the U-boats disappeared without a trace before the escorts could counterattack."

"Churchill himself is reported to have said the only thing that has truly frightened him thus far during the war has been our U-boats—and that includes the Battle of Britain when London was being bombed every day during the Blitz. But as I said, lately the balance of power has shifted, and the Allies are the ones on top. Now it is our U-boat fleet, not Allied shipping, that is being decimated. In the last few months alone, over one hundred of our U-boats have been sunk and more than two thousand German sailors killed. That is why your mission is so critical. We need to know how they're doing it, so we can develop appropriate countermeasures."

What neither von Gröning nor Chapman knew was that German U-boats were not being hunted by some sophisticated submarine detection system, but because the Allies had cracked the Enigma code and were tracking, on a daily basis, German U-boats as soon as they left port, thanks to the Most Secret Sources intercepts at Bletchley Park. Instead of being the hunters, the *Kriegsmarine* wolf packs were now the hunted through intercepted radio messages.

"What do you say, Fritzchen? Are we back in business?"

Chapman smiled. "Yes, we are back in business."

"Very good then. Please sign the dotted line to make it official and then I'll open a bottle of champagne to celebrate. It's a Veuve Clicquot '41—for you, I have spared no expense."

"It's a dangerous mission, but somebody has to do it." He scrawled his name on the two sets of contracts that von Gröning had already signed and stuffed one signed copy in his pocket.

The old man smiled. "I'll fetch that bottle." He lifted his corpulent frame from the chair, stepped into the kitchen, and returned a minute later with an open bottle of the famed French champagne and two crystal flutes. After pouring them each a glass, he raised his flute in a toast.

"To my number one spy, the only bastard who truly understands me! And the only person who can match me drink for drink! To you, Fritzchen!"

"And to you, Doktor! The only bastard who truly understands *me*!"

And with that, they drank the whole bottle of champagne then followed up with two full bottles of aquavit and several garbled renditions of German drinking songs before passing out on the couch. Three days later, von Gröning restarted his prized agent's money supply and nothing was ever said again about their week of hell. They were father and son once again.

CHAPTER 57

UNIVERSITY OF OSLO

NOVEMBER 30, 1943

WHEN SHE HEARD the three gunshots, Dagmar pulled Chapman towards the protective cover of a brick wall. She didn't have to time to think about it; she just followed instinct.

"Bloody hell, they're shooting at the poor bastards?" Eddie cried in disbelief.

"No, I think those were just warning shots," she replied. "Look!"

She pointed to a German sergeant with a raised Mauser pistol; thankfully, it was apparent that he was not gunning down the student protesters but engaging in a foolhardy attempt to bring order to the agitated crowd. More than a thousand people—a mixture of University of Oslo undergraduates and graduates, teachers, administrators, civilians, Norwegian police, and German military and law enforcement personnel—were packed into the *Universitetsplassen*, surrounded by Gestapo and Hirdsmen guards. The guards were arresting the students and other protesters, following the fire in the university's Great Hall two days earlier and *Reichskommissar* Terboven's publicly announced closure of the university an hour earlier. Chaos, violence, and martial law now ruled in the Norwegian capital, and Dagmar and Chapman had come to witness it firsthand.

Suddenly, a teenage youth shot past them, chased by several Gestapo guards armed with submachine guns. The crowd cheered when the boy managed to evade them. He dodged in and out of the trees across Karl Johans gate until one of the Germans drew a pistol and threatened to fire, whereupon the youth surrendered.

"The bastards," seethed Dagmar. "They have no right to be closing down the school and hauling away these students like this."

Chapman concurred. "I wish there was something we could do, but they'll just throw us in the slammer."

"They say they're rounding up all the students, sending them to concentration camps in Germany, and that Terboven's reason for the university's closure has nothing to do with the fire. The Germans are just frustrated that the NS has failed in its attempts to implement its Nazification program at the university. The teachers and students have been resistant since day one."

"You can't brainwash people, especially not rebellious teenagers. The Nazis are getting desperate now that they're losing the war.

They pressed forward for a closer look, parting their way carefully through the crowd. When they were even with the *Domus Bibliotheca*, they stopped and watched the pandemonium. More and more bystanders like them were coming on to the scene and the crowd was growing thicker in University Square. Dagmar felt an oppressive feeling of danger and violence in the air, like a powder keg about to explode.

They watched in horror as another half dozen students and a pair of teachers were jerked from the ranks of the encircled protesters, beaten with clubs, and dragged off to waiting canvas-topped trucks. Looking to her left, they then saw a

Gestapo officer through a gap in the crowd smash a knuckle-dustered fist into the face of a student who had failed to understand an order. Blood poured from his facial wound as he was shoved into the heaving crowd. Dagmar was stunned. A moment later, she found herself and Chapman being pushed hard in the back.

"You seem rather too interested in this," a harsh voice shouted into their ears.

They turned around to face a young German corporal, who glared insolently and shoved Chapman again.

"What the hell? Get your bloody hands off me!"

"*Dere mä gå tilbakke!*" the Nazi cried in broken Norwegian. *You must go back!*

"Me and my girlfriend will go where we bloody well please! You have no authority over us!"

"Then you are under arrest!" He pointed his Schmeisser at him.

"Get that thing out of my face, you fucking bastard!"

"I said you are under arrest! Hold up your hands!"

"Fuck you! We refuse!"

"What is going on here?" snapped another voice.

This time, Dagmar and Chapman turned to see a captain, who had come over to investigate.

"This ignorant corporal has just shoved a German officer and his friend in the back," bristled Chapman. Before either of the Germans could protest, he pulled out his *Ausweis* verifying his official position in the Wehrmacht as German Officer Fritz Graumann and handed it over to the captain, who proceeded to examine it closely before snapping it abruptly shut and turning on the corporal.

"You stupid swine!" the senior officer growled at the enlisted man. "The next time you decide to arrest someone, make sure it is a Norwegian and not a Wehrmacht officer! Now get out of my sight!"

"*Jawohl, Hauptmann!*" and he moved off sheepishly.

The captain now addressed them. "I apologize for the ill treatment," he said. "Things have gotten out of hand here today and we are all a little jumpy."

Dagmar decided to probe the German officer for information. "What is going on here? We know the university has been closed because of the fire at the *Universitetets Aula* ceremony hall, but why are the students being dragged away?"

"Our orders are to arrest the male students and bring them in for interrogation to discover the arsonists responsible for the fire. They are most likely communists."

"You don't know that," countered Dagmar. "The fire could have been started by the Germans."

The captain looked at her sharply then at Chapman. "Is this woman with you?"

"Yes, but she happens to be very outspoken."

"Then you had better warn her to watch her tongue." He waved his hand expansively at the scene of chaos all around them. "I'll tell you what's going on here. This situation has been brought about by the Resistance. The university has been a hotbed of underground activity since the beginning of the war. Two years ago, the rector refused to embrace the New Order and he was sent off to a labor camp and replaced with a new man, and just last month the Norwegian police arrested ten faculty members and sixty students and imprisoned them. That is what happens to those who resist. Now if I were you, I would be on my way and not ask any more questions. Now go!"

They shouldered their way back through the crowd. To the north, a gunshot rang out. Dagmar heard a collective shriek of horror and saw people recoiling from the *Universitetsplassen* in panic, running in every direction, staggering, colliding, the pandemonium spreading like a contagion as it moved through the frenzied crowd. She and Chapman were suddenly swept up, ineluctably, in the tidal wave pushing its way towards Karl Johans gate.

It was then Dagmar saw one of her comrades in the Resistance—a University of Oslo student who wrote for an underground newspaper and performed occasional courier runs code-named Dapplegrim—being hustled away by a German sergeant and pair of soldiers.

She tugged on Chapman's heavy wool jacket. "Wait, that young man is a friend of mine! He is a fellow Jøssing with the Home Front! Hurry, we must help him!"

"All right!"

He and Dagmar raced over to the Germans and quickly intervened, just as they were about to throw the young man in a truck.

"Wait!" cried Chapman, once again presenting his Wehrmacht pass. "I need this man released into my custody!"

"Who the hell are you?" snorted the sergeant.

"If you would bother to read, you would see that I am *Oberleutnant* Fritz Graumann and that I outrank you. I'm taking this man with me—he is an important informant."

"I'm afraid that will not be possible. He could be the one who started the fire and tried to burn down the university."

"I tell you he is an informant and is coming with me. I need to talk to him."

"You're too late. We snatched him first."

"This is not a competition. Stand down immediately, or I will have to report you to my present commanding officer, *Kapitän* Reimar von Bonin."

The sergeant stiffened instantly and now closely examined the pass. "Von Bonin? The chief of the Abwehr?"

"One and the same. Now are you going to stand down, or shall I put you both under arrest?"

The German handed back his *Ausweis* and clicked his boots together. "You are free to go," he said. "My apologies for any inconvenience we may have caused you."

"That's a very wise decision, Sergeant. We will be on our way now."

The three of them left the square. As they threaded their way down Karl Johans gate, Dagmar made eye contact with her Home Front cohort, who still seemed bewildered at his sudden change in fortune. They exchanged subversive smiles.

And then she thought to herself: *Well done Eddie, my British guardian angel. Well done indeed.*

CHAPTER 58

TAR ROBERTSON stared out at the large crowd packed into the MI5 briefing auditorium on the HQ's third floor. A moment earlier, the roomful of clubby spymasters from the British "old boy level" had been ensconced in patters and murmurs of gentlemanly conversation, but now, as he cleared his throat at the podium in preparation for his speech, the crowd deferentially hushed. There were perhaps thirty people in the audience, all men, representing members of the Twenty Committee, W Board, and other departments within the British military and intelligence establishment, as well as a cadre of Americans from the Office of Strategic Services, several of whom were for the very first time being brought into the inner circle with regard to Enigma, Most Secret Sources, and Double Cross. His crisply-dressed audience was seated in neatly arranged rows and looked up at him with palpable anticipation.

For Robertson, it was his most important presentation yet during the war.

"Gentlemen, today we are going to discuss our final deception operations for Occupied France and Norway, and the role our Double Cross spies will play in those operations. Most of you are familiar with these plans that have been bandied about for the past month now. Today, we are going to delve into those plans in detail, focusing specifically on how our turned double agents are going to be used to fool the Germans before, during, and after the invasion of Hitler's *Festung Europa*. We have with us today many American friends, several of whom will be hearing about these matters for the first time, so we will be going over some previously covered topics. My apologies to those of you on the Twenty Committee and W Board who are about to be subjected to a bit of redundancy, but we have to ensure that everyone is fully briefed and brought up to speed. I don't think I need to remind you gentlemen that the success or failure of our deception plan may very well decide the outcome of the war."

The room went still and quiet as a cathedral as the audience realized the momentousness of the occasion. This was followed by nods of ascent and murmurs of approval.

"As you all know, BIGOT is the super-secret classification of those with knowledge of the forthcoming Allied invasion of German-occupied Western Europe. That is you, gentlemen. You belong to an exclusive club of a few hundred military officers and high-level government officials privy to the innermost secrets of the invasion, which will eventually include the time and place, deception plans, and order of battle, as well as the operations of our Double Cross agents. For those of you who don't know, the name BIGOT comes from a military stamp "TO GIB" imprinted on the papers of officers traveling to Gibraltar for the invasion of North Africa in November 1942. To confuse the Germans, we simply reversed the letters.

TO GIB—To Gibraltar—became BIGOT—or the BRITISH INVASION OF GERMAN OCCUPIED TERRITORY. We English have always thought of ourselves as rather clever. Now we know for certain that is not actually true."

The room echoed with chortles of laughter, particularly from the Americans, whom Robertson had always found appreciated a good joke.

"For those of you who are visiting our shop for the first time, Double Cross is the code name of MI5's anti-espionage and deception operation for our turned German agents. Every German agent in Britain has been under our control in our Double Cross system. We know this because we can read all German radio traffic through Most Secret Sources, also known as Ultra. In a nutshell, we've cracked their code from a captured Enigma cipher machine. We know what the Jerries are thinking and doing, at all times, because we listen in and see how they take the bait when we send them false or meaningless information. They value their field agents above all else, which is why we have a real opportunity to make them think and do as we want them to."

Again, there were agreeable nods and murmurs all around. Everyone in the room appeared to be eager to manipulate and deceive the Germans in a thrilling high-stakes game that would hopefully tip the scales of war in the Allies favor.

"Operation Fortitude is the code name for the massive operation of deception we're going to foist upon the German High Command. We're going to fool Hitler into believing that our two primary invasion locations are the Pas-de-Calais in France and in Occupied Norway, which *der Führer* considers to be the 'Zone of Destiny' for the Allied offensive. Fortitude is divided into two sub-plans, North and South, with the aim of misleading the Germans as to the location of the imminent invasion. The invasion plans are being developed by SHAEF, the Supreme Headquarters Allied Expeditionary Force. This is the group responsible for planning of the main invasion at Normandy, the follow-up attack in Vichy-controlled Southern France, and the accompanying deceptions at the Pas-de-Calais and Norway. The aim will also be to make the Germans believe that the Normandy landings and the subsequent attack in Southern France are mere diversions, and that the real landings will take place in Pas-de-Calais. That way the German Army will concentrate its troops there during the landings.

"Both Fortitude North and South involve the creation of phantom field armies. Fortitude North is the fake threat to Norway using the fictional British Fourth Army based in Edinburgh. Fortitude South will pose and maintain the threat to the Pas-de-Calais using a fictional American army group near Dover. The operations have been designed to divert Axis attention away from Normandy and, after the invasion, to delay reinforcements by convincing the Germans that the landings are purely a diversionary attack. Now, before we get into the details of Double Cross, are there any questions?"

A senior American OSS officer whose name Robertson didn't know raised his hand.

"Yes?"

"What's the name of the fictional U.S. command?"

"FUSAG: the First United States Army Group. That will be the phantom Army Group we're going to set up in southeastern England. Its purpose will be to draw

Hitler and his generals off the trail of other invasion plans which have been set in motion as part of Bodyguard."

"Will this fictional army have a commander"

"Yes, the decoy army will be commanded by none other than your General George S. Patton—or 'Old Blood and Guts' as your American newspapers delight in calling him. His goal and that of the fictitious FUSAG will be to deceive Jerry into thinking that our crack troops will land in the Pas-de-Calais for the major invasion of Europe instead of Normandy. That way the Germans will hold back twenty or more divisions from Normandy, until, of course, it's too late."

The room went silent as the men around the table mulled over what they had been told thus far. It was a ruse de guerre unprecedented in the history of warfare, and Robertson knew its greatest weakness was its reliance on absolute secrecy. The truth was there were too many damned BIGOTs already here in Great Britain, with more arriving and being brought into the coveted inner circle every day. The more that were in on the grand deception, the harder it would be to control the leaks.

"But if FUSAG is not a real army," asked another OSS officer, "how can such a deception be pulled off?"

"Because we're going to set up a dummy camp that looks and acts just like a real one. We're going to build a vast movie set and employ the use of our Double Cross agents and fake radio traffic to keep the deception alive. Inflatable and wooden tanks, fake trucks and landing craft, and troop camp facades constructed from scaffolding and canvas will be built all along the southeastern coast as part of the deception. Believe it or not, we're even going to allow the Luftwaffe to photograph the camps. Only above thirty-thousand feet, of course, so they can't make out the details. Now if there are no further questions for the time being, let's turn to the roles of our turned German double agents."

He paused to take a sip of water from the glass at the lectern before continuing.

"As most of you know, one of our main deception channels for Bodyguard is via the turned double agents we control here in Britain. In this endeavor, we are not proposing to use all our operatives in this great affair, for we must be vigilant in avoiding risk where avoidance is possible. An agent who, in spite of all our precautions, turns out not to be believed by the enemy, might wreck the whole enterprise, or, even worse, his messages might be read in reverse and the true target of attack be exposed instead of concealed by him. That is why we have decided to cut down the number of operatives to the bare minimum we need to effectively deceive the Germans, while ensuring that the remaining agents are highly regarded, as verified by Most Secret Sources. We want only the best agents in the eyes of the Germans to transmit deception material, while the others will be kept going for subsidiary purposes to raise the stock of the primary agents.

"Before I get into who our top Double Cross agents will be for the deception operations, it must be emphasized that we are continuously assessing and reassessing their reputation with the enemy. This is done in a variety of ways: by a most careful scrutiny of all the questions asked; by tracking the actual payments made to an agent, which provides a measure of an agent's monetary value; by remarks made at interviews in cases where our agents had personal contact; and by the Germans' Enigma wireless decrypts in which one or more Abwehr stations or even Berlin itself praises the agent's work. All this reveals how the agents are regarded on the other side, and in many cases their reputation varies greatly during the course of changing events. Based on a comprehensive analysis and current conditions then, the agents ranked highly by the Germans that we shall use as our top actors in the charade are Agents Garbo, Brutus, and Tricycle. Others who will likely be used in a support role to further validate these operatives include Treasure, Tate, Mullet, Gelatine, Bronx, and possibly Mutt and Jeff. Though the climax of the war has been long in coming, I believe we are all prepared and more than adequately staffed for the final denouement with Hitler and Nazi Germany. We have waited the entire war for this decisive moment—and now it is finally upon us."

Robertson beamed as a round of light applause filled the room. Like the other men, he felt a part of the epic sweep of history. But more importantly, he felt a magnificent euphoria in the certainty of victory. *We are going to pull off this invasion and win this war, by Jove,* he thought triumphantly—*and Double Cross is going to play a big part in it.*

When the applause died down, he cleared his throat to speak. "The star of the show is going to be Juan Pujol García. Agent Garbo, as we call him, is a Catalan who managed to get recruited by German intelligence. The Germans know him as Agent Arabel. He has created a network of more than twenty imaginary subagents, and the Abwehr has been unwittingly paying the British Exchequer large amounts of money regularly, thinking they are funding a network loyal to themselves. The false intelligence he will provide will pinpoint the Pas-de-Calais as the main thrust of the Allied attack and ensure that the Twelfth SS Panzer, Panzer Lehr, and First Panzer Divisions are not available for counterattack in Normandy.

"Our number two is Roman Czerniawski, Agent Brutus. He is a Polish officer who ran an intelligence network for the Allies in Occupied France. Captured by the Germans, he was offered a chance to work for them as a spy. On his arrival in Britain, he subsequently turned himself in to British intelligence and his stock in the eyes of the Germans is second only to Garbo.

"Our third man is Dusko Popov, a Yugoslavian lawyer and playboy code-named Tricycle because he enjoys three in a bed sex. Yes, even you Yanks must agree that my naming conventions for our Double Cross spies are, if nothing else, inspired."

Again, the room chortled with laughter. Robertson thought it a good idea to keep things a bit light, given that they were in the midst of a terrible world war that was killing millions and seldom had time to laugh about anything. It was all part of keeping a stiff upper lip through times of trial and tribulation, as his playful mother, not his martinet of a father, had instilled in him. Soon thereafter another question was asked. Again, it was one of the Americans, this time a uniformed major.

"I've heard, Colonel Robertson, that Popov has some question marks. Is it possible that he might be too risky?"

"I believe you're referring to when Tricycle was sent over to the U.S. in 1941. His job was to work with the FBI as a double agent in rooting out German spies on American soil."

"Yes."

"The truth of the matter is Director Hoover didn't like him."

"Why not?"

"Because unlike your Director Hoover, Popov is a foreigner and likes women instead of men."

The entire room roared with laughter, the red-faced Americans laughing the loudest. Robertson had known he would get a good laugh on that one. There was no love lost between General William J. Donovan and his fledgling U.S. spy agency, the Office of Strategic Services, and J. Edgar Hoover and his imperial and zealously protected Federal Bureau of Investigation. The rivalry between the FBI and OSS was just as nasty as that between MI5 and MI6.

"We always appreciate a good joke at the director's expense, particularly when he's more than three thousand miles away," said the American. "But I must at the same time acknowledge something."

"And what would that be, Major?"

"Director Hoover has taken a special interest in one of your Double Cross agents. The subject is an operative that I am surprised has not been mentioned in your MI5 roster for the forthcoming deception operation."

"Does this operative have a name?"

"Agent Zigzag. I must ask you, Colonel, is there some reason that this highly coveted agent is not on your list?"

"Yes, there is a very good reason."

"What is it?"

"We don't know where the bloody hell he is."

"Excuse me?"

"We lost all communication with Eddie Chapman last April."

"Where was he last heard from?"

"Berlin."

"Berlin?"

"That's the last word we received on his whereabouts from Most Secret Sources."

"You figure he's dead then?"

"He could be. But the truth is we don't know what's happened to him. For all we know, he could be somewhere in Occupied Europe training for a new operation."

"And what are the chances of that?"

"Perhaps fifty-fifty. But if there's one thing we know about Zigzag, he's a survivor."

"All the same, he won't be part of Operation Fortitude?"

"No, he won't. Not unless he gets back here in the coming weeks."

"What do think he's going to do, drop out of the sky?"

"That's exactly how he did it last time. And if he's still alive, that's the way he'll do it again."

CHAPTER 59

KARL JOHANS GATE AND GRAND HOTEL, OSLO

JANUARY 30, 1944

STARING INTO THE FURRIER SHOP WINDOW, Dagmar thought back to just before Christmas when Chapman had bought her the silver fox coat she now wore. She had often admired the beautiful piece of clothing whenever they walked by the store and one day he had bought it for her, along with a pair of fox furs, for the staggering price of nearly twenty thousand kroner. It was an amazingly generous gesture, but at the time she recalled being horrified.

"I can't wear it," she had informed the British spy. "What will people think?"

"Why can't you?" he replied. "It's winter—it's bloody cold."

"But people will talk, and I'm already under suspicion as it is."

"Please, darling, you must take it. I want you to have it because I love you. It's as simple as that."

"But are you sure? It's so expensive."

"Yes, I'm sure. You must accept my gift. If you don't, I'm afraid I'll have to turn you into the Gestapo."

"Well then," she replied with a smile, "I suppose you leave me no choice."

She remembered it like it was yesterday. Once she had accepted the extravagant gift on a particularly frigid Christmas eve, she had worn the fur coat every time she had gone outside and, in the dead cold of winter, it had become her most valued possession.

Stepping away from the window, she continued down the street. She was supposed to meet Chapman at the Grand Hotel for dinner at seven p.m. and, feeling a little blue, had decided to go for a walk down Karl Johans gate. The truth was she had for some time now been feeling sad and lonely. She had important information for her lover she had been putting off. But she could put it off no longer.

There had been so many changes in her life since the birthday bash she and Doktor Graumann had thrown for Eddie on November 16 at their Kapellveien flat— and she was a person who didn't like change. They had had so much fun. Walter Thomas had given Eddie a radio, Johnny Holst an ivory ashtray, and the spymaster Graumann a magnificent van Gogh print. She had baked a cake and took countless photographs of the revelers as souvenirs, and later that night, she and Chapman had made love and climbed into the attic, peeled back the metal sheet that protected the wooden girder next to the chimney stack, and hid the film inside. Together, the two spies had managed to obtain a complete photographic record of the Oslo Abwehr team. Not for a fraction of a second had the high-level German operatives suspected they were being duped by a vague, pretty Norwegian girl who smiled a lot and asked seemingly innocuous questions.

And then, in less than a month, everything had changed. The Germans had shut down the university, rounded up more than a thousand of its students and teachers, and shipped them off to concentration camps inside Nazi Germany. Soon thereafter, the relationship between Doktor Graumann and Walter Thomas, never friendly, had steadily deteriorated and finally Thomas had been granted his wish to return to Germany. The anglicized Teutonic Knight, long convinced of the therapeutic physical and cultural effects of English folk dancing, had somehow persuaded the German authorities of this and was duly appointed dance instructor to the Wehrmacht. Though she and Chapman had always considered Thomas an irritating pedantic and rabid Nazi, they both couldn't help but feel a flicker of regret when he left their cozy little flat at Number 15. And then, a mere week later, Chapman had informed her that he would be leaving in March for Great Britain. His mission on behalf of the *Kriegsmarine* was to unravel the mystery of how and why the British were winning the war in the Atlantic. Finally, in the past month, as the German losses continued to mount and the tide of war turned, she came under suspicion by not only her friends but many in the Norwegian Resistance for which she was fighting. People on the streets were now openly calling her a German's tart and she felt herself increasingly at risk. But that was only part of it. Now there was something else that had happened to her. It was something deep and painful that threatened to shake up her life even more dramatically—and she needed to tell Chapman about it.

She felt tears come to her eyes. She longed to tell her countrymen the truth about where her true sympathies lay and her diligent work on behalf of the Resistance, but she knew for her own protection she could not.

She wondered: *How could I have let my life become so desperate? How could I have allowed my own people to misinterpret me as a tyskertøs when I fight for Milorg?*

She thought of her lover. Their espionage partnership—an alliance, at one remove, between the British Secret Service and the Norwegian underground—wasn't the reason she loved him. She loved him because he had a genuinely good heart, made her laugh, and was full of surprises. For Chapman was an uncommonly kind, generous, and unpredictable man who lived a life that was anything but dull. Yes, that was why she loved her Eddie.

But now, as she stepped into the lobby of the Grand Hotel where she had once worked, she had news for him that was going to change everything.

ψψψ

She found him at the polished mahogany bar, nursing a Scotch. As always, he was all smiles and happy to see her as he leaned forward and kissed her softly on the lips. With an effort, she pushed aside her melancholy. She told herself that she must at least pretend that everything was all right and she was excited to see him. But instead, her heart was filled with dread for what she had to tell him.

"You look lovely darling. Say, wait a minute, what's wrong? Why do you look so glum?"

Is it that obvious? she wondered.

"Come on now, be a good girl. Out with it. I can't make you feel better until I know why you're so blue."

"We need to get a table. I don't want to tell you here at the bar."

"Yes, of course. In the meantime, what will you have to drink? It appears that we could both use one."

"An aquavit will be fine."

He motioned towards the waiter, ordered them a pair of fresh drinks, paid the bill, and then escorted her to an unoccupied booth across from the bar. Meanwhile, she mentally prepared herself for what she had to tell him. She was so torn up inside, she didn't know where to begin.

He took her by the hand. "You can trust me," he said. "I love you and am here for you."

She felt her throat clutter, tears coming on. But with an effort, she held back from crying.

"Please, darling, you must confide in me. I want to help you. What is it? What's troubling you? Have people been bothering you on the streets? Is the Gestapo onto you, or us? Please tell me."

"I'm pregnant," she said.

Though no one at the nearby tables overheard them, the whole bar seemed to come to a standstill. They looked at one another in silence, neither of them sure what to say next.

"But that's not the worst of it," she said. "I can't keep this baby—not when people believe you're a German officer. My friends are asking questions and none of them even knows I am in the Resistance. Everyone but you, my control officer, and a handful of people I know only by code name think I'm a Nazi tart. I can't have my child go through what I've been going through. When this war is over, people are still going to hate the Germans and anyone who associated with them during the war. It will never go away—my child will be tormented his or her entire life when he or she did nothing wrong. That wouldn't be fair."

He held her hands in his. "I am so sorry, Dagmar. It's my fault. I should have been more careful."

"It's no one's fault. It just happened, and now we have to deal with it."

"You really want to have an abortion?"

"I can see no other way out without ruining my life and that of my child once the child is born. People will never understand. We'll forever be known as the German whore and her bastard child. I won't put my child through that. Plus, if I had the baby, that would bring danger to you with your colleagues."

"I don't care about that. I want to do what is best for you and the baby."

"If we bring this baby into the world, it could severely affect your standing with the Abwehr. It could also bring you unwanted attention by the SS. You will never be able to hide it. Word will get out that a British Abwehr agent got a local girl into trouble. Questions will be raised, and we won't be able to control our fate. Both Norwegians and Germans will be unsympathetic. There's no way around it—that's what's going to happen."

"Yes, but an abortion. Are you sure you want to go through with it?"

"We have no choice if we want to remain safe. My country is at war with Nazi Germany. Having this baby is only going to bring all three of us trouble. A lot of my friends are already suspicious, and I am no quisling."

"All right, if you think this is the best approach."

They fell into a somber silence. She took a sip of her aquavit as Chapman tossed back his entire drink and ordered another Scotch from a passing waiter.

"We can't have the procedure done by a Norwegian doctor. If we do, word will get out about you and me. It also happens to be restricted."

"You're saying we would need to get a German doctor?"

"Yes, it's the only way."

"I could talk to Graumann. He might be willing to help us."

She felt tears coming to her eyes but fought them back. "I can't believe it has come to this. I don't want to do this to my poor baby, but I can see no other way. Do you really think Doktor Graumann would help us?"

"Turning to him makes sense. He and I are close, and he is fond of you as well. I'm confident he will be able to help us arrange for a termination."

"I'm sorry about all this. I feel terrible."

"Feel terrible for what? You haven't done anything wrong. These things happen—they're part of life. Don't worry I'm going to take care of you."

"But what's going to happen to me when you leave on your mission in March?"

"Don't fret, I'm going to come back for you and vouch for your important work on behalf of the British Secret Service. Everyone's going to know what you did here in Occupied Norway, and they'll never call you a German's tart again, trust me."

"But what if something happens to you?"

"Nothing's going to happen to me. Let's just deal with one problem at a time, shall we?"

"All right, if you say so."

He took her in an embrace. "That's my girl," he said, gently stroking her hair. "Everything's going to be okay. I'm going to take care of you. When this terrible war is over, I want to come back here and marry you. Then we'll open a wonderful club in Paris, have beautiful children, and live the good life. I love you, Dagmar. I will come back for you and then we'll be together forever."

Looking at him, she could tell he truly meant it. But just because he loved her didn't mean it was going to play out that way. "Come now, Eddie, that's just make-believe."

He shook his head adamantly. "No, it's not, I promise. We're going to get through this tough situation with the pregnancy, make it through the war, and then I'm coming back for you. It's going to all work out, just like in the fairy tales."

"You promise?" she said hopefully. "You promise you'll come back for me following your return to England?"

"I give you my word," he said. "Our life together is going to be like a dream. It's going to be bloody perfect."

CHAPTER 60

VON GRÖNING FLAT, 8 GRØNNEGATE

JANUARY 31, 1944

"BEFORE WE GET DOWN TO BUSINESS, FRITZCHEN, YOU'VE GOT TO SEE THIS PICTURE I RECEIVED FROM THOMAS. IT IS A TRAVESTY!"

Chapman took the photograph from the spymaster and examined it. He had arrived five minutes earlier to talk to von Gröning about Dagmar and they had just poured brandies in the drawing room of the flat. The black-and-white photograph showed *Oberleutnant* Walter Praetorius, appearing dashing in full parade-ground military uniform, giving a sword dance lesson to German troops.

"Can you believe the bastard couldn't find more meaningful work than to prance around the Fatherland giving lessons in sword dances and reels?"

"I must confess I was stunned when you told me he had managed to persuade Berlin to appoint him as dance instructor to the Wehrmacht. All the same, touring Germany instructing soldiers in sword dancing is not a bad way to finish out the war. He could have gotten his wish and been posted on the Eastern Front—and he would probably be dead."

"Berlin's decision to deploy him on the dance floor is yet further proof that the German High Command is in the hands of complete imbeciles. You and I may laugh, Fritzchen, but it is no laughing matter. I cannot conceal my supreme disgust at such stupidity when the Fatherland is in a fight for its very survival."

Chapman again scanned the photo. "At least the old boy looks happy. Remember, you two weren't getting along prior to his departure before Christmas."

"That is true. The poor bastard…he accused me of plotting to keep him here in Oslo to deny him the heroic military future he craved. When he left, I didn't tell you that he was in fact relieved of duty here in Norway. He fell out of favor with our colleagues and was asked by the chief of the Abwehrstelle to return to Berlin."

"Von Bonin asked him to leave?"

"Ordered him is more like it." He sipped his brandy. "Oh well, what's done is done. He was a ruthless Nazi bastard, but I must confess part of me misses him."

Chapman handed back the photograph. "Surprisingly, a part of me does too."

"Well, it's all behind us now. Now tell me about Björnsson and Júlíusson. How are they coming along?"

Chapman took a moment to compose his answer, not wanting to sound overly critical in his response. Since his meeting with von Bonin, he had been courted by both the German Navy and Air Force regarding his forthcoming return mission to England. Both arms of the Reich's military service wanted their part of the operation to have priority, and von Gröning had intervened in the internal dispute and settled the matter by declaring the naval mission regarding the sinking of German U-boats would take precedence over the Luftwaffe's night-fighter radar intelligence-gathering mission. In the weeks since, Chapman had busied himself with giving lectures as a sabotage expert to his German military colleagues and to training new recruits in wireless techniques. Under Holst's direction, he had again become a highly-skilled operator. Six months earlier, he had been kept away from W/T operations as he was still viewed as a potential security risk, but now he was asked to teach telegraphy to two young Icelanders, Hjalti Björnsson and Sigurdur Júlíusson. Thus far during their training, they had proved to be far better at downing drinks at the Löwenbräu and Ritz café than operating wireless sets, both men proving to be more than willing but inexplicably obtuse. It had taken Chapman several weeks of intensive instruction before they had mastered even the rudiments of wireless transmission techniques.

"They are improving daily," he said to von Gröning evasively.

"Yes, but are they ready?"

"No, they're going to need some more work," he admitted. "Let's just say the blokes don't catch on very quickly."

Von Gröning groaned. "Good lord, I can't believe the low caliber of material I get. Sometimes, I wonder if we are deliberately trying to lose this damned war. Now tell me about Dagmar. How is she taking news of your imminent departure?"

He licked his lips, going through quickly in his mind all the things he wanted to say. He didn't want to ask for the old man's help regarding Dagmar's termination of her baby until he had worked out what her future role as a spy would be when he left Norway and returned to England. His foremost priority was to make sure she would be looked after by the spymaster once he had embarked from the country on his new mission.

"She's taking it reasonable well, but she is anxious about what will happen when I'm gone," he said, bringing voice to his thoughts. "That's what I came here to talk to you about."

Von Gröning gave a paternal smile. "Yes, I know. I can tell that you are troubled about what to do about her."

"I love her madly. In fact, when the war is over I aim to return to Norway and marry her. I've never been with anyone like her before and I don't want to lose her."

"Don't worry, my friend, I shall see that she is looked after when you are gone. What did you have in mind?"

He pondered a moment. Since she would be working as an unofficial British secret agent, she had to be paid and be given suitable lodging. Just as he had left instructions for MI5 to look after Freda and his daughter Diane, he had to arrange for Graumann to provide for Dagmar. A part of him couldn't believe what he was going to ask for. Did he truly want to have two different women, under the protection of two different secret services, on opposing sides of the war? It seemed dangerous. But he had to do it for Dagmar, the woman that he truly loved and wanted to spend the rest of his life with.

"I believe she should be paid a monthly allowance of six hundred kroner from my account until further notice."

"Consider it done. Anything else."

"She should also be provided with somewhere to live, preferably closer to the town center."

"I will have Johnny take care of it. What else?"

He needed a moment to think. He was surprised at how swiftly the old man had acceded to his request, but then he realized the answer: as long as his Norwegian lover was under the protection of Graumann and the Abwehr, then Chapman's loyalty would likely be assured. But there was still one more thing. He had to ask the old man to help with the termination of her pregnancy.

"What is it, Fritzchen? What's bothering you? I can see there is something else on your mind."

"It's about Dagmar. Something's come up."

"You got the poor girl in trouble, didn't you?"

"Great Scott, how did you know?"

"I am a good reader of people. How do you think a lazy bastard like me got into the intelligence business?"

"Dagmar's beside herself and we don't know what to do." He took a sip of brandy and followed up by lighting up a potent Blue Master Norwegian cigarette. "Because of me and my association with Germans, she can't have the child, and she's afraid that if she uses a Norwegian doctor to perform the procedure, she will be ostracized by her countrymen even worse than she is now."

"You're asking me if I can arrange for a German doctor to do it?"

"We could really use your help."

"I understand. Just leave it to me and I will see what I can do. But you must understand that what you're asking is technically against the law here in Norway."

"We realize that, and that's one of the reasons we've come to you."

"You did the right thing. Is Dagmar certain she wants to go through with this?"

"She doesn't want to do it, but feels she has no other choice unless she wants to be shunned as a 'kept woman' and 'German's whore' for the rest of her life. A baby would be a visible reminder for the foreseeable future, and she doesn't want to subject the child, or herself, to that kind of abuse. The Norwegians are relentless in their cold-shoulder treatment."

"I've seen the Ice Front first-hand many times. They hate us Germans and those willing to do business with us more and more with every passing day. They know we're losing the war and they are becoming emboldened. Resistance activities are on the rise, especially with the Allies poised to invade the continent."

"You think the invasion could come any day?"

"No, but it will definitely come by late spring or early summer. That's when the English Channel can be safely crossed with hundreds of thousands of troops. But it doesn't matter when the attack comes. All that matters is that when it does, unless the Allies are driven swiftly back into the sea, the war will be lost. Germany cannot defend three separate fronts while keeping over three hundred thousand troops here in Norway."

"Is that how many there are here?"

"Yes. And that is why Hitler is obviously a nincompoop."

"The Führer a nincompoop? I don't believe I've heard you say that before."

Now von Gröning gave a conspiratorial expression and lowered his voice, as if the walls had ears. "Well, I mean it. Did you know that Hitler is no longer in charge of the direction of military operations? It is in the hands of the German general staff, and one no longer reads 'I, Hitler, command thee...' on army orders. Churchill on the other hand—now there's a true leader. I've always admired the man. In fact, I secretly listen to the BBC every night in bed."

"Good thing Thomas is no longer here to check up on you at bedtime. He would have you sent to the Russian Front for such treasonous talk."

"Come now, you can't fool me, Fritzchen. I know where your true loyalties lie. As a man who has been hunted by the police, you may not love England in the same patriotic manner as your old schoolmates back home, and you may spy for Germany for the excitement and the money, but I know from how you have chastised Thomas that you don't really believe in the Reich. And it is just as well as Germany's never going to win this war."

"Herr Terboven and Herr Quisling would say that you have come down with a bad case of defeatism."

"I hate Hitler, Fritzchen. It is the simple truth. He is the cause of everything that ails Germany. I cannot accept that my country conducts the mass murder of European Jewry. It is an abomination. And did I tell you that my sister Dorothea has recently adopted a Jewish girl to save her from the gas chambers? I am an old-fashioned German patriot. I am committed to winning the war, if it is fact an attainable goal, but I am equally determined to oppose the horrors of Nazism. In short, I am not loyal to my Führer—I am loyal to my country."

He underscored how he felt by shaking his head vigorously and then tossing back his brandy.

"Of course, none of what I have said must leave this room, my friend. For if it does, I will swing from the gallows or be put to the wall just as surely as the Allies will invade France before the end of summer."

"Your secret is safe with me, Doktor."

"And yours with me. Tomorrow, I will see what can be done for Dagmar."

"Thank you. Do you have a doctor in mind?"

"As a matter of fact, I do. I believe he will be willing to bend the rules. As I have said, he's not supposed to do anything like this. But he is a friend of mine and will hopefully perform this medical service as a courtesy to me. He may want somebody to assist him during the procedure though."

"Tell him he can count on me. It will also make Dagmar more comfortable if I am at her side."

"Indeed, it will. You should go home now and reassure her. She is hopelessly in love with you, you know."

"And I am hopelessly in love with her. As I've told you, we've made plans for after the war. We're going to set up a club together in Paris. I will be the manager, Dagmar the charming hostess. We would love it if you would join us."

The spymaster chuckled. "I have to admit it sounds wonderful. Such an establishment would, of course, allow me to carry on my espionage activities after the war, perhaps against the Russians."

"It doesn't have to be make-believe. We can make it real."

"And indeed, we should, Fritzchen. Let's have a toast." He poured three fingers of brandy into their snifters and they raised their glasses. "To you, me, and Dagmar. To our life after this terrible war in *la Ville des Lumières*—the City of Lights."

CHAPTER 61

WHEN ANNEMARIE BREIEN stepped into Café Seterstua, she found her father already seated. It was only an hour before curfew and the restaurant was not crowded for dinner, though there were four uniformed SS officers in the corner table.

"I have gotten my hands on another list." Discretely, she handed him four sheets of paper across the table.

"From Fehmer?" asked Roald Breien. When she nodded, he then said, "Good heavens, the contradictory nature of the man ceases to amaze me."

"No, this is more than that. This a gift from God." She watched him as he began reading the Gestapo list over. "As you can see from the two columns on the right, our Nazi friend has, so far, set free forty-one people, and he has agreed to liberate another dozen in the coming months. Forty-one freed and another dozen about to be set free—that's certainly no trifle, Father. And I might add that Captain Fehmer has followed through on his promises and actually set free everyone that he has said he would. You can call him many things, but you cannot call him a liar."

"You can be sure to put a good word in for him at his war crimes' trial. Maybe then they'll shoot him instead of hanging him. That's as much sympathy as you're going to get from me."

"As long as he keeps releasing prisoners and passes along useful intelligence information to me, I don't ask questions. By the way, did you notice some of the new names on the list?"

"Fehmer has agreed to release Sigurd Evensmo. I can hardly believe it."

"I told you I'd come through for Milorg, Father."

"You most certainly have. But until I see Evensmo in the flesh strolling down the streets of Oslo, I am certainly not going to trust the likes of Siegfried Fehmer."

"No doubt. But let's not forget that he is the one who had you released."

"As you have been reminding me for the last year and a half."

They paused as a waitress, one of the owner's two daughters, came by their table. They ordered coffee. The young girl flashed her a conspiratorial smile and returned to the kitchen.

Roald Breien looked at his watch. "Unfortunately, I don't have much time. What other news do you have for me?"

"Fehmer knows that Max Manus and the Oslo Gang are back in operation."

"How the hell does he know that?"

"Because he knows that Manus and his men are the ones that recently sank the German patrol vessel in Oslo Fjord with the 'baby' torpedoes."

"How did he find that out? I don't even know anything about that job."

"The Germans have new radio direction-finder vans. They were brought in a few days ago and are being used to sweep the city and improve the German's triangulation. From a wireless intercept, the Germans know that the Manus attack on the patrol vessel was part of some operation called Operation Bundle."

"My God, how many of these new vans are there?"

"Three, which brings their total to six in the city now. The Germans now have twice the direction-finding and eavesdropping capability they had before."

"The bastards. No wonder three more Milorg men were arrested just two nights ago. The Germans are getting more aggressive every day."

"The war is going badly for them. With their backs against the wall, they are becoming more and more desperate. The Americans and British have taken Anzio and are only thirty miles from Rome, and the Russians are pushing west every day along the Eastern Front. We're lucky the BBC has kept us so well informed. But the Allied victories are coming at a heavy price in the occupied countries."

"With these new radio-detection trucks, the Germans will no doubt catch more of our men."

"I'm afraid so. Fehmer says Haugland is a top priority." She was referring to Knut Haugland, the Norwegian SOE radio man who had parachuted into Norway in the fall of 1943. As part of the Norsk Hydro Plant attack and related sabotage operations, Haugland's mission was to set up a radio network that communicated directly between the SOE and Milorg headquarters. Unfortunately, Fehmer and his Gestapo had captured him in Kongsberg, but the daring commando had managed to escape and subsequently set up shop as a radio operator in Oslo, tracking and reporting on German movements and activities.

"Knut Haugland will never be caught. He is like Max Manus—a veritable Houdini."

"That may be. But with these new radio direction-finder crews working around the clock, no one in the Home Front is safe."

"In any case, you have done Norway a great service. Haugland and many others will be warned. Has Fehmer told you anything else?"

"No, that is it for now. I will contact you if there is anything else."

"There is one other thing I want to talk to you about."

He glanced cautiously around the café to make sure no one was listening before responding. She followed his gaze. The only Germans were the uniformed SS officers seated at the table in the corner; luckily, they seemed engrossed in their conversation. All the same, she felt unnerved at the sight of them with their SS insignia on their lapels and their Lugers and Walthers stuffed into their jet-black Death's Head holsters. At that moment, the waitress brought their coffees. When the young girl walked off, her father leaned across the table and spoke in a low voice.

"Kjell came by to see me," he said.

"My husband came to see you?"

"Yes. He's worried about you."

"Worried about me?"

He blew on his coffee and took a small sip before answering. "Worried about you and Fehmer. He says you are spending an awful lot of time with him these days."

"How do you think I get all this valuable information and all of these people released from prison? By *not* spending time with him."

He took her by the hand, his expression one of genuine fatherly concern. "I'm not trying to meddle in your affairs, Annemarie. I'm just worried about you—and so is your mother."

She pulled away her hand and took a sip of coffee, picturing the face of Nancy Breien. Her mother was the glue that had held their family together since she was a little girl, the woman who had four children and a husband fighting on the side of the Allies and lived every day with the possibility of their death at the hands of the Nazis. In that moment, she knew how hard it must be for her poor mother, the sense of worry that she must endure.

"I cannot stop what I am doing, Father. I must see this through until the end of the war."

"Even if it costs you your marriage?"

"Kjell understands the importance of what—"

"No, he doesn't understand," he cut her off. "That's why he came to see me and your mother."

"He asked you to intervene?"

"No, he did nothing of the sort. As I said, he's worried about this relationship between you and Fehmer. He says that it borders on obsession."

"If I don't work to get these prisoners released, who else is going to do it?"

"I don't know. But are you willing to jeopardize your marriage over it?"

"If I hadn't convinced Fehmer to spare your life, you would have been sentenced to death and sent to the wall. Now that your life is spared, you want me to just give up on others?"

"No, but perhaps you are becoming too close to this man. He is a Gestapo officer, not a teddy bear to be cuddled."

"Are you and my husband worried that I am having sexual relations with Siegfried? Is that it? I am not having sex with him if that is what you're insinuating."

"*Siegfried*—you just called him *Siegfried*. Don't you see? You *are* getting too close to him when you're calling him by his first name. I think you need to take a step back."

"What do you mean?"

"You may not be having sex with him, but you are clearly getting too emotionally involved with this man."

"You think it's clouding my judgment?"

"Only you can answer that question. But sometimes it's best to go about one's business with emotional detachment. You are doing great things for the Resistance and Norway, Annemarie. But you are in a situation with two men—one of whom is your husband, the other the second ranking officer in the Gestapo—that if it persists can only end badly for you."

"I'm sorry, but I'm not giving up on my work. It's too important."

"There's more to it than that, Annemarie. People are starting to talk about you and Fehmer. You've been seen together too many times over the past two years."

"People are talking? People are always talking, Father."

"This is different. They're calling you a *tyskertøs*. Even some of your friends, behind your back. Do you really want to be called such names?"

"I don't care. The work is too important for me to put my own selfish motives ahead of saving people's lives."

"I know what you're doing is the right thing and is very important for the Resistance, and Jens Christian Hauge feels the same way, believe me. But I am talking to you as your father, not as a Milorg captain. It is not worth having your life destroyed over this, Annemarie."

"Lives are at stake. That is the most important thing to me."

"All right, I just hope you know what you're doing. I don't want you to lose everything."

"If I do, it will be on behalf of a worthy cause."

CHAPTER 62

KARL JOHANS GATE

FEBRUARY 13, 1944

HOLDING HANDS, DAGMAR AND EDDIE strolled up Karl Johans gate on a surprisingly mild Saturday afternoon with the temperature in the upper forties. Von Gröning—whom the two still knew only as Doktor Stephan Graumann—had obtained a German doctor to perform the abortion. It was a little boy. The termination had taken place eight days earlier and Chapman had been at her side assisting the physician the entire time, which she had found reassuring. Though she had recuperated physically, she had not recovered emotionally and was still in a fragile state.

She had been deeply conflicted about having the procedure performed in the first place. She loved Chapman and didn't want to end the life that grew inside her. But she could not bear the thought of raising a child who would be forced to bear unspeakable cruelty as the offspring of a *tyskertøs*, nor did she want either her or her child to have to be stigmatized for the rest of their lives. Chapman may have been a British double agent, not a German spy, but the Norwegian people and everyone in Milorg except Ishmael didn't know that. They considered him a Nazi and her a German's whore, which would make their child the butt of endless jokes and physical abuse. Even her friends were shunning her nowadays, for she hadn't disclosed to them that she was a Resistance operative and spy for the British Secret Service. Most likely, they wouldn't believe her anyway.

They passed the furrier shop where two months earlier Chapman had bought her the silver fox coat she now wore. They stopped and peered in the window.

"My, my, look in there. They've put a new coat in the window," observed Chapman. "But it's no match for yours. Then again, that could very well be because of the woman wearing it."

"I still can't believe you bought it for me," she said. "Twenty thousand kroner is way too much for me, or any girl for that matter."

"Is that so? Is that why you haven't taken the coat off since I bought it for you?"

"Yes, it's true I love it. But it is too much."

"Codswallop. Nothing's too much for my beautiful Norwegian girl."

He drew her in close and gave her a kiss. Though she felt a touch melancholic, she couldn't help but smile and feel warm inside. He always knew how to cheer her up when she was blue. She knew it was his special gift: he had a knack for reading people and lifting their spirits when they were down.

"Everything's going to be all right," he reassured her. "Good things happen to good people—and you are a brave and generous person, Dagmar. It's all going to work out for the best. I have a great master plan for us if you're open to it. With everything that's been going on, I didn't want to overburden you. I was going to tell you about it when you were ready."

"Well, I believe I'm ready now."

"Good." He kissed her again and they continued walking up the street. "My scheduled week of departure for my new mission is now the week of March 8. Graumann told me last night."

She felt a wave of sadness but tried not to let it show on her face. She didn't want him to think her weak and vulnerable, even though that's precisely what she was right now after terminating her pregnancy only a week earlier.

"I want you to continue to act as my agent after I'm gone."

"Really?"

"Yes, there's no one else I trust, and you have developed into an exceptional field operative."

"I'm glad you have faith in me."

"The old man will be accompanying me, but you should maintain contact with the other members of the Oslo Abwehrstelle. Johnny, Molli, and the others."

"Yes, I can do that."

"Keep your eyes and ears open for information that might later be of interest. Once I reach London, I will arrange for the British to make contact with you once they feel it is safe. But you should trust nobody that approaches you unless they give you the proper password."

"Dagmar Mohne Hansen Lahlum."

"There can be no exceptions. Don't worry, we're going to go over this all again in detail the day before I leave. I just wanted to give you an initial briefing on how I'd like to proceed, with your approval of course."

She felt a little surge of excitement. "I approve. To be perfectly honest, I'm thrilled you trust me as your agent."

"No, I'm the one who has been lucky to have you. Without you as my cover, do you really think I would have been able to photograph and document the location of every important military and intelligence building in and around the city, including Quisling's compound on the Bygdøy peninsula? And was it not you who photographed Graumann, Johnny Holst, and a dozen members of the Abwehr here in Oslo without drawing suspicion? My God, Dagmar, I couldn't have pulled off any of this without you. And let's not forget that you are the one who told me about Fehlis. I had no idea he was the one in charge at Victoria Terrasse."

"I am happy to help. But the truth is I am going to miss you terribly."

She felt tears come to her eyes. She struggled mightily to hold them back but was unable to do so. They stopped and he held her in his arms, consoling her.

"I'm sorry," she said. "After everything that's happened, I'm afraid I'm a wreck. But you can count on me to follow through and be a good agent."

"I know I can. You're my girl—the best spy a British double agent could have."

"We are the Spies of the Midnight Sun, right? We are a team."

"Yes, we are indeed the Spies of the Midnight Sun and a truly great team. And because you are working as a British agent, I have made arrangements with Graumann that you should be paid."

"Truly?"

"In my absence, you are to be paid a monthly allowance of six hundred kroner from my account until further notice. The old man is also proceeding with arrangements for a place for you to live."

"What?"

"In the past three days, Holst has been on the lookout for suitable accommodations. He has identified a lovely little flat in Tullins gate. It's not far from the Royal Palace, Victoria Terrasse, and the Luftwaffe administration offices."

"Oh dear, I will certainly be in the lion's den, won't I?"

"Let's just say you'll be in a position to gain valuable intelligence. Of course, Graumann has his own reasons for doing this: as long as you're under German protection, my loyalty will be beyond question and I can be controlled. Which means that you will be serving as human collateral and will have to be extremely careful."

"I'm fine with that. As long as I have the chance to spy on the Germans and help my country."

"Yes, but the risks are grave. Just remember, it's not a game. Those bastards, even Johnny and Molli, will kill you if they discover what you're up to."

"I know. I will still also be working for Milorg so I know there will be risks."

"Don't tell me any more than that. If I'm discovered, the last thing I want to do is give your name up under torture. I also need you to swear to secrecy about me being a British agent. That's why I have told you very little about my work for MI5, only what I have done for the Germans, which the enemy already knows about. The less we tell each other the better."

"I swear I will take your secret with me to my grave. I will keep my word."

"I will keep mine as well. I promise to come back for you, one day, and we shall be married."

As he leaned forward to kiss her, they were shoved hard towards the street. "Nazi go home—and take your whore with you!"

Recovering their balance, they looked up to see a young Norwegian man in a wool hat and long overcoat with a challenging look on his face. It was exceedingly rare for Germans, or Hirdsmen and other German sympathizers, to be publicly castigated rather than subjected to the more common cold shoulder of the *Is Fronten*, but confrontations were happening with increased frequency now that the tide of the war had shifted and it was expected that Nazi Germany would go down in defeat.

Chapman glared at the insolent youth. "You bastard, what the bloody hell do you think you're doing?" He stepped forward, his right hand formed into a fist.

"Leave our country, you Nazi fuck! And take your *tyskertøs* with you!"

With a suddenness that caught even her by surprise, Dagmar leapt towards the young, snarling man and yelled, "You have no right! I fight on behalf of Milorg and the British Secret—"

She stopped right there, instantly cupping her hand over her mouth as she saw a nearby uniformed Hirdsman point at her, shout for them to stop in their tracks, and blow his whistle. *My God, what have I done?* she screamed to herself.

"You...you're with Milorg?" the youth gasped in shock.

Again, the Hirdsman blew his whistle and yelled, "Stop, you! Stop!"

The youth turned on a heel and ran in the opposite direction. Suddenly, a blonde woman in her late twenties appeared at their side.

"Quick, follow me!" she cried. "You have to get out of here!"

Dagmar looked at the Hirdsman. He had been joined by one of his uniformed NS comrades and was pointing at them and talking to the young uniformed Nazi.

"Now, we have to go now!" commanded the blonde woman.

Dagmar saw Chapman finger his Luger in his shoulder holster. "No, Eddie, no! Not here!"

"You have a gun?" cried the blonde woman. "Put it away and follow me! Quickly now!"

She pushed them into a crowd of people and then led them in a hurry down the sidewalk. They ran down Karl Johans gate until they came to Kongens gate, named in 1624 by King Christian IV, and then ducked into a tobacco shop. It was the same tobacco shop where Dagmar had learned of the invasion of Sicily. Who was this woman leading them out of trouble? Had she seen the woman before? Did she also work for Milorg?

The woman led her quickly through the shop to the counter. Dagmar's contact, a woman code-named Thelma, was not behind the counter. Instead, an older man was, a man she recognized but whose code name she didn't know. The blonde woman spoke a few quickly whispered words and led them through an opening into the back, out a rear door, and into a small bookstore. With only a few words exchanged with the bookstore's elderly male owner, they were led to an upstairs apartment above the bookstore.

The blonde woman quickly drew the blackout curtains and blew out a sigh of relief. "There, we are safe," she said.

Dagmar looked at Chapman, who was smiling, then back at the woman.

"So, you are with Milorg, and you also work on behalf of the British Secret Service. You do realize that that's not the kind of thing you want to be announcing on the street."

"I lost my temper. The Ice Front is weighing heavily on me. They call us names all the time because they don't know we are Allied patriots and I am growing sick and tired of it. I am sorry."

"You don't have to apologize to me. Just be more careful in the future. Or you won't last long."

"Yes, I know. I'll have to go to Victoria Terrasse again and be grilled by that bastard Fehmer. He kept me there overnight a year ago. I still have nightmares."

"Fehmer? You know Fehmer?"

"I believe all of Oslo does. Why?"

Chapman was looking at their female rescuer closely. "Who are you? Are you with the Resistance?"

"It's best not to talk about such things. You never know when you're going to be interrogated."

"We understand," said Dagmar. "But we would at least like to know who to thank. After all, you saved us back there."

The woman smiled, and Dagmar saw that she had an unusually sweet and trustworthy-looking face. "My name is Annemarie Breien," she said.

"And mine is Dagmar Lahlum. I am pleased to make your acquaintance."

Annemarie now looked at Chapman. "And what is your name?"

"I'm afraid that's top secret, luv. But I do want to thank you for your timely assistance."

CHAPTER 63

"HAVE YOU HEARD THE NEWS?" asked *SS-Oberführer* Heinrich Fehlis as he leaned into Fehmer's office, catching him off guard at his desk.

"No," said his subordinate, pausing from stroking Wolfie. "What has happened?"

"The ferry DF Hydro carrying the supply of heavy water from the Norsk Hydro Plant has been sunk by saboteurs this morning on Lake Tinnsjø. With all the Allied attacks during the past two years on the plant, the heavy water was being transported to Germany for safekeeping. But now it is all lost."

He sat upright in his chair and gently pushed his German shepherd away. "It's all at the bottom of the lake?"

"I'm afraid so."

"How many were killed?"

"Eighteen, including nine of our soldiers."

"And the survivors?"

"Twenty-nine."

"How did the bastards manage to pull it off?"

"We don't have all the details yet, but it appears that the saboteurs somehow managed to board the ferry last night, plant plastic explosives in the bow bilges, and then slip back to shore. They set the timers to blow when the ferry was over the deepest part of the lake, just before reaching the lighthouse at Urdalen. Apparently, the DF Hydro immediately headed for land but the ship's crew didn't have enough time to release all the lifeboats before she sank. She went to the bottom an hour and twenty minutes ago, at 10:30. The farmers from across the lake were soon in their boats and came to the rescue of the crew and passengers."

Fehmer stood up at his desk. "I'm sure it was Milorg behind the attack. We'll catch the bastards. Someone must have seen something."

"You see to it. I just got off the phone with Terboven and Falkenhorst. They are furious and are calling for swift and bold action. I told them that I already had my best man on it."

"I will go straight away to Lake Tinnsjø." Though Fehmer rarely wore his uniform these days, he was in full uniform today and now reached for his peaked cap bearing a *Heer*-style eagle with an *SS-Totenkopf* from his coat rack. After slipping it on his head and adjusting it to a slight angle, he reached for his Death's Head holster that bore his Walther PPK.

"We expect results, Siegfried. That heavy water would have helped us build a nuclear device that I am told could win us the war. Now we are back at square one and our heavy water program is kaput. The Führer is going to be furious and want swift reprisals."

He began fastening his holster about his waist. "I understand, sir."

"No, I don't think you do. I am growing tired of these sabotage operations. A year ago, there was nothing but minor damage. Now these Norwegian gangsters are affecting the very outcome of the war. It has to stop."

"I will proceed to the lake and commence an investigation immediately. I will make this right, *Herr Oberführer.*"

"The Führer's Commando Order is still in effect. All captured commandos are to be shot as spies."

"I don't have to worry about that. My job is just to catch them."

"Yes, and you are quite good at that. But I have also heard rumors that you have a knack for setting prisoners free, too. Please tell me, Captain, that this is just a rumor."

He had no alternative but to lie to his boss but he would make sure it was only a white lie. "It is nothing but a rumor, sir—except in a handful of instances. The low-level prisoners I have on previous occasions released were subsequently tracked by my men and helped us capture more important and higher-ranking members of the underground. Given the success of the operations, I did not feel the need to inform you or Colonel Reinhard."

"I have given you great latitude in your investigations, Siegfried. But I expect results. Please make sure that you keep that in mind, especially when it comes to these home-grown terrorists who have sunk the DF Hydro."

He plucked a leather dog's chew toy from his desk and tossed it to Wolfie, who now sat obediently in the corner of the room. The German shepherd snatched it up and began gnawing on it. "I will catch those responsible, sir. We will intensify our search for Milorg operatives by sending out all of our radio direction-finder crews."

"Very good."

"With the new surveillance vans we have at our disposal, I believe we are getting close to catching their main radio operator."

"Haugland?"

"Yes, sir, he is almost within our grasp."

"Last fall, you had him under arrest and yet he got away."

"I know, sir, but that won't happen again. We're closing in on him and his men and arresting Milorg members every week now. We think they may be using hospitals to send their messages."

"Hospitals?"

"Quite ingenious, though highly unethical. But as we all know, ethics are the first thing thrown out the window in wartime."

Fehlis squinted disapprovingly. His gaunt, hollow-cheeked face was as taut as a drum, lending him the physical appearance of Count Dracula. "Not by the Reich," he bristled.

"Yes, sir." He raised his right arm. "Heil Hitler!"

"Heil Hitler! And more importantly, Captain, catch these criminal gangsters."

"I will do my best."

"No, you must succeed. Now good day and good luck."

"*Danke, Herr Oberführer.* I won't let you down."

CHAPTER 64

AS THE PLANE that would take Eddie Chapman away from her, possibly forever, taxied up to Fornebu terminal, Dagmar told herself not to cry. "Tell me about our wonderful little club in Paris," she said to him, wanting him not to leave and for the moment to last forever. "I want to hear you tell me one more time, so I can picture it in my mind."

He smiled at her as she rested her head gently upon his shoulder. "It's going to have a mahogany bar, great food, and the best cabaret in all of Paris. Of course, it will be on the Left Bank, and you and I will have a lovely apartment up above where we'll live as Picasso, Matisse, and Hemingway once lived."

"*La Rive Gauche*," she said quixotically. "It sounds so romantic."

"It is going to be romantic. In addition to running the best club in all of Paris, we're going to travel and see the world. The French Riviera, the Alps, and the Greek Islands here in Europe. The Orient, Africa, and America for our overseas adventures. And we're going to have several ruddy-cheeked children with splendid Norwegian names like Leif and Sonja and upper-crust English names like Asher and Winston."

"Oh, stop it. You're so silly."

"That covers what we're going to do after the war. Now let's go over one last time what we need to do while this bloody thing still rages on."

"All right, Sir Eddie, I'll endure your lecture one last time."

"When Doktor Graumann and I get on that plane"—he tipped his head towards the spymaster reading a newspaper next to Johnny Holst in front of the flight check-in desk—"you are on your own as my special British agent here in Norway. You are to maintain contact with as many members of the Abwehrstelle as you can, and to keep your eyes and ears open for anything that could prove useful to the Allied war effort."

"Yes, yes, I know. And I am to trust nobody unless they use my full name as the code name: Dagmar Mohne Hansen Lahlum."

"Jolly good, you remember it!"

She jabbed him in the stomach. "Oh, stop it."

He nuzzled up close and kissed her and she kissed him back. "All right, now what else?"

"I have the keys to my new apartment."

"Tullins gate 4a. It's quite a beauty."

"Yes, thankfully I'm only a two-minute car ride from Gestapo headquarters. That way they can arrest me, haul me in for interrogation, and ship me off to a concentration camp in no time at all."

"You know that's not funny."

"What? I thought you appreciated a little gallows humor."

"Only when it comes to me. I couldn't bear the thought of anything happening to you, so I can't joke about you."

"I shouldn't be joking either. My situation is rather precarious. Not only am I with the Norwegian Resistance, I am now employed as an unofficial British agent at the same time I am being maintained by the German Abwehr to the tune of six hundred kroner per month and a nice little flat. If the enemy ever figures out what I'm really up to I'm going to be in serious trouble."

He stroked her hair while, thirty feet away, Graumann looked at them and smiled. "Don't worry, my darling. If anyone can do it, it is you. You and I both— we are survivors."

"That makes me feel better. But we both know that if you're discovered then I, too, will fall under German suspicion. And if Germany loses the war, which is likely, my countrymen will seek reprisals against me for being on supposedly good terms with the enemy."

"That's not going to happen. As I've told you, when the war is won I will arrange for the British to make contact with you. Acting through me, the British authorities will set the record straight and clear your name. You don't have to worry about that. People will know the truth."

"But what if you don't make it back to Norway?"

"All I have to do is get to London and tell my control officers."

The flight was boarding now. People were on their feet, queuing in line with their tickets, and Graumann was motioning them. Holst, her ride to and from the airport, was at his side, and suddenly Dagmar dreaded what it would be like to return to the city alone in the car with him. Without Chapman or Graumann around, would he try something? Suddenly, she felt the oppressive burden of being all by herself in her apartment. It was going to be so lonely with her dear Eddie gone.

Despite her best efforts, her usual Nordic stoicism withered before her and she began to cry. After the emotionally upsetting pregnancy and abortion, and now her lover leaving her behind to fend for herself while she continued to act as a clandestine agent, her world had become perilous.

"I don't want you to leave," she sniffled, gripping his shoulder fiercely.

"I don't want to go either," he said, and she could tell that he, too, was miserable. "But everything's going to be fine."

"I will never tell anyone your secret. I promise to take it with me to my grave to protect you."

"And I promise to come back for you. I have never loved anyone like I love you."

"I know I'm crying, but I'm not afraid. If the Norwegians mock me and call me a German's tart, I will just tell them to mind their own damned business."

"That's my girl."

She wiped away the tears. "Just tell me one last time that you're going to come back for me. It may be the only thing that will sustain me through this terrible war."

"I'm coming back for you, Dagmar. I promise. And when I do, you and I are going to be together forever."

She put her lips to his and they kissed with unbridled passion, the tears pouring from her eyes, and then he reluctantly pulled away and was walking towards Graumann to board the plane for Berlin.

Forever, she thought hopefully. *When he comes back, we're going to be together forever.*

CHAPTER 65

KNUT MAGNE HAUGLAND—code-named Primus—grabbed his radio headset and prepared to send today's three o'clock message from Radio Station Barbette Red to the Norwegian government-in-exile in London. His transmission location was the attic above the Maternity Ward of the National Hospital, where he had been hiding out under the care of Finn Bøe, junior registrar in the Department of Obstetrics and Gynecology. The special transmitter-receiver sitting on the work table was a hand-keyed Morse apparatus, the size of a small suitcase, tuned by quartz to a single pre-set frequency, and powered by batteries that gave it about twenty watts. It would take Agent Primus five minutes to transmit his message to London— and, as always, those five minutes would be inordinately tense and seem like an eternity.

In February 1943, the radio operator with the SOE-trained Linge Company had successfully organized and carried out the raid on the Norsk Hydro Plant at Vemork along with nine other Norwegians. After planting explosives and blowing up the heavy water producing cells, he and several of his comrades-in-arms who had remained in Norway rather than escape to neutral Sweden were hunted for months by thousands of German soldiers. In November 1943, he was captured by Fehmer and the Gestapo, but by a miracle managed to escape. Since his arrival to Oslo following his escape, his task was to train radio operators in the Resistance movement and to set up a direct transmitter link with London. To keep one step ahead of the Gestapo, he had been moving his transmission locations in the city every few days. He had only recently begun using the attic of the Oslo *Rikshospitalet* to send messages to the Norwegian government-in-exile.

Working swiftly yet calmly, he set up his distinctive "call sign," adjusted the transmission frequencies, checked signal strength, and completed several more steps to ensure direct communication between Radio Barbette Red and London, and then sent his encoded message along with his security check on 13,980 kilocycles. The message, reporting on German troop strength and fortifications in and around Oslo, was limited to five hundred letters broken into five message parts of six typewritten lines. Each message took just under a minute to transmit.

Once Primus had obtained "message received" confirmation from London, he signed off and put away his wireless set. It was then he noticed that something wasn't right. The hospital was too quiet. Tucking away his set in its secret compartment beneath the floorboards, he went to the small V-shaped window, pulled back the blackout blind, and looked down at the front entrance of the hospital.

A black Mercedes and six German troop transports had pulled up stealthily to the curb in front of the hospital along with a pair of surveillance vans with revolving aerials on the roof. An officer in a gray-green SS uniform stepped from the Mercedes and began barking out orders. He couldn't believe his eyes: it was Siegfried Fehmer! Damnit, why couldn't someone have killed the bastard? He just wouldn't go away! His eyes grew wider as dozens of German soldiers with rifles and submachine guns began jumping out of the trucks and running towards the various entrances.

Haugland quickly went over his options. It was unlikely that he could bluff his way out of his dire predicament. Though he was dressed in workman's overalls and had with him a spanner and other tools, Fehmer knew who he was and what he looked like. The bloodhound detective was gunning for him and would not mistake him for a maintenance man or electrician. There were, however, a total of six exits in the hospital and, because it was a three-story building, it was possible to jump out the windows on all sides. There were also several large air ducts and shafts as well as multiple back stairs that led to the basement. In short, the hospital was the ideal place for both hiding and escaping. All the same, he still had to get down from the attic and outside without being recognized by Fehmer, or his men who might know what he looked like from police photographs.

Now he could hear the sharp staccato of German voices and heavy boots pounding in the stairwells. The enemy was coming up fast.

He looked down again at Fehmer. Suddenly, he thought of his helper Bøe and his wife Aslaug, who was heavily pregnant. He dreaded the thought that they might be arrested, tortured, and sent to prison for giving him refuge in the hospital. Bøe's apartment was on the second floor of the Department of Obstetrics and Gynecology and Haugland had been sneaking to and from the apartment in his maintenance man's outfit to make his daily transmissions. Bøe's help had included not only the cover apartment and information about the layout of the building; in the beginning, he had also come to the attic to make sure that nobody could hear Haugland transmitting from within the airshaft, and he had learned how to encrypt and decipher telegrams to assist at busy times. Haugland knew that if he was caught, Bøe and his pregnant wife would, in all likelihood, be arrested too. That he could not bear.

Stepping away from the window, he reached for his loaded Colt Model 1911A1 U.S. Army .45-caliber pistol, favored by the British SOE, along with four 7-round detachable box magazines.

Damn, it looks like it's going to be a shootout, he muttered to himself as he stepped to the air shaft. *Oh well, I guess I always wanted to go out like a cowboy in an American Western.*

ψψψ

Fehmer stared up at the dignified red-brick façade and beyond at the prominent chimney of the Maternity Clinic at Stensberggata—and knew that, finally, he had his man.

"Lieutenant Schuttauf, take twenty men inside and make the arrest! Lieutenant Bernhard, with the rest seal off all the exits! I want a machine-gun on every one of them! Now get moving!"

"*Jawohl, Hauptsturmführer!*" and they were off, more than fifty soldiers wearing *feldgrau*, coal-scuttle helmets, and *Gott min Uns* belt buckles, armed to the teeth and rushing in like a swarm of angry hornets. Some even had fixed their bayonets.

Fehmer pulled out a vile *Eckstein* and lit it with an engraved, silver lighter. Normally, he liked to lead from the front, but he wanted to give his men time to locate the transmitter and its operator. He pictured Haugland's face from the last time he had seen the Linge Group saboteur. He had had the son of bitch in his mitts and yet he had gotten away. This time, he would not let that happen. This time he had more than four dozen well-armed men and the building surrounded. He blew out a wisp of bluish-gray smoke. He had already caught two local Milorg radio operators this week, locating them with the D/F vans, but he was after bigger fish.

Haugland was a Resistance big shot and Fehmer wanted him badly. He didn't want the bastard to escape from his clutches again like Max Manus. The experienced SOE operative had been airdropped into his native country to successfully pull off the Norsk Hydro Plant sabotage operation and to establish a radio network with London—but now his time was over. Fehmer knew Haugland was the one transmitting from the hospital because of his distinctive radio signature based on his unmistakable keystrokes and overall technique. To Fehmer's radio interceptor squads, Haugland's telltale "fist" was as unique as fingerprints and would be the thing that led to his arrest.

Suddenly, he heard a muffled gunshot, followed by three more.

His hand reached involuntarily to the holster at his hip, which bore his loaded Walther. In his right boot, he carried his backup piece: a Mauser Hahn Selbstspanner.

A second round of gunfire.

"Jesus Christ, it's coming from the first floor or the basement! Lieutenant Hoeler, you come with me! The rest of you men, stay here and cover every entrance!"

He and the lieutenant dashed into the hospital. As he ran down the hallway, he heard more shots and screaming voices. A sergeant stepped from a stairwell. From the blood stain on his uniform, Fehmer could see that he had been shot on the right side of the stomach. It was a bloody and painful wound, but thankfully not fatal.

"What is happening, Sergeant! Where is Haugland!"

"We chased him through the airshafts and had a shootout at the stairs! He killed two men before getting me, the English-loving swine!"

The sergeant grimaced in pain and crumpled slowly to the floor with Lieutenant Hoeler reaching out and cushioning his fall.

"I'll be all right," said the sergeant. "I just need something to stop the bleeding and lay here for a minute."

"Where is Haugland now?"

"The back stairs leading to the basement is where he's headed. He may be trying to make it to the back yard, where he can jump the fence. If you hurry, you can cut him off." He pointed to the stairwell at the end of the hallway, which troops were tromping down in their heavy boots.

Fehmer signaled a doctor in a white physician's jacket down the branching hallway. "Help this officer now!"

The doctor nodded and stepped forward. Fehmer and Hoeler ran down the hallway, flew down the stairs to the basement, and dashed down a hallway. Up ahead, Fehmer saw a German officer fall through a swinging hospital door and to the clean white floor in a spatter of blood. The soldier with him dragged him behind a wall, smearing a trail of blood across the clean white hospital floor.

"We've got him trapped!" cried Lieutenant Hoeler.

Now Fehmer heard breaking glass.

"Damn, he's made it to a window and is trying to get outside! Hurry!"

He ran down the hallway, burst through the door shoulder first, and came face to face with his Norwegian adversary just as a German soldier emerged far down the adjoining hallway.

Haugland opened fire, dropping the soldier at a distance of thirty yards.

Fehmer pointed his Walther at him and fired, but the shot missed.

Haugland jumped through the broken window and rolled onto the snow-covered lawn behind the hospital.

This time he and Hoeler both fired at the Norwegian, but the shots sailed wide. Fehmer darted to the window and saw Haugland pop in a fresh magazine as he jumped to his feet with the spryness of a panther. Again, the Gestapo man fired, but again his shot missed.

Mein Gott, what is it going to take to hit this bastard?

He and his two comrades in arms let loose again—and this time he saw Haugland stiffen, but only for a fraction of a second. Had they hit him? If they had it was only a grazing wound, for the Norwegian, wearing a pair of dirty one-piece overalls that a janitor might don for work, scaled the nine-foot-tall barbed wire perimeter fence like a monkey, climbed part way down the other side, and then jumped down to the paved road.

"*Scheisse*, we can't let him get away!"

He leaped through the broken window, nicking himself in the arm on a jagged sliver of glass, and ran across the snow-covered lawn. When he reached the barbed wire fence, he couldn't believe his eyes. There was no sign of Haugland and, on the other side of the fence, the ground dropped off precipitously. He estimated the drop-off from ground level to be fifteen feet to the base of the roadcut etched into the granite rock, which meant that Haugland had jumped around twenty feet before disappearing into the thick woods on the other side of the road. How the hell had he made it without breaking a leg?

Hoeler came running up along with the other soldier. "Where did he go?" gasped the lieutenant, unable to believe his eyes.

"Maybe he's right below us, leaning against the rock so we can't see him," said the soldier.

Fehmer shook his head. "No, he's in those woods. See the tracks in the snow."

He pointed. The two men nodded in amazement as dozens of troops began coming up from the hospital.

"Well, don't just stand there, Hoeler! Take a company and go after him!"

"But it's more than a twenty-foot drop."

"Cut the damned fence and jump from there, Lieutenant! And that's an order! If a Norwegian can make it, then by God so can a German! Now see to it!"

ψψψ

To the west, from the edge of the woods, Haugland took off his dirty overalls and watched as Fehmer chewed out his men, cursing and waving his arms and stomping his feet in the snow like an insolent child. Then he took a clump of snow, washed his face, and started off through the woods on foot, moving at a solid clip. Three hours later, as the Gestapo was combing the woods and outlying neighborhoods, a man wearing a Norwegian policeman's uniform and carrying special driving and curfew passes made his way through three separate checkpoints, picked Agent Primus up, and the two drove away quietly to the north.

Leaving Haugland with a grin on his face and the hated Siegfried Fehmer with yet another lost opportunity.

CHAPTER 66

"WE'VE LOCATED ZIGZAG. We don't know where he is at the moment, but we know that in March he was in Occupied Norway preparing for a return mission to England," declared Robin "Tin Eye" Stephens, a ghost of a smile suffused on his ruddy face beneath his gleaming monocle.

Tar Robertson broke into a grin, too, and looked at John Masterman. The chairman of the Double Cross Committee was obviously pleased as well, nodding his head and smiling at the resourcefulness of their plucky double agent.

"Well then, it seems our prodigal son is back on our radar," said Robertson jauntily. "How did you find out, Colonel?"

"Two young Icelanders were arrested three days ago along with a German. They were sent to me at Camp 020, and I spent yesterday interrogating them. I must say they were rather poor material. It took me less than two hours to break them."

"What are their names?"

"Hjalti Björnsson and Sigurdur Júlíusson. The German is one Ernst Christoph Fresnius. I played Fresnius off against his retainers and they sang like canaries."

"Yes, I'm just glad I've never had to be on the receiving end of one of your interrogations," said Masterman.

"Me too," agreed Robertson cheerfully. "Now what precisely was their cover story and mission, Colonel?"

"They claimed to be gathering meteorological information for a German shipping institute. But their real mission was to monitor and report on our troop movements."

"It would appear that the Jerries are still worried about the possible use of Iceland as a base for the continental invasion."

"Quite."

"And what is the connection to Agent Zigzag?" inquired Masterman, taking the words right out of Robertson's mouth.

"To be perfectly honest, the dim-witted Icelanders were beginning to put me asleep during the interrogation," admitted Tin Eye. "And then they began to describe their sabotage training in Oslo. One of their wireless instructors, they recalled, was known as Fritz though they weren't sure of his nationality. They said he spoke German with a pronounced English accent, had two gold teeth on the upper right-hand side of his mouth, wore a pepper-and-salt summer suit, and had, in their recollection, a rather loud and high-pitched voice."

Robertson smiled knowingly. "That's Z all right. I can see how the prisoners' description would get your attention."

Tin Eye nodded and adjusted his monocle. "The two bumbling Icelanders then proceeded to describe how this instructor had been showered with money and had a rather alluring Norwegian girlfriend as his constant companion when he wasn't teaching them wireless communications. He also apparently enjoyed the amenities of a private yacht, which he is said to have used quite frequently as a rendezvous point with his Nordic beauty."

"Oh, good heavens, the inevitable love interest," said Masterman. "Now we know for sure it's Chapman."

Robertson couldn't help a smile: he had been thinking the same thing. But it was the two gold teeth that clinched it for him. The man described by the Icelanders could be no other than Edward Arnold Chapman—infamous safecracker, Lothario, and spy extraordinaire.

"They say that this Fritz not only trained them on wireless techniques, but he gave lectures to senior Abwehr officers on his sabotage of the de Havilland Plant. Can you imagine that, our Agent Zigzag lecturing the bloody Germans on a demolition operation that never actually took place?"

The room shook with jocular laughter at the Germans' expense. Robertson pictured himself telling Tin Eye's story of the bumbling Icelanders to his wife Joan and daughter Belinda, who had said she wanted to be a spymaster like her father when she grew up. How much they would have enjoyed hearing how badly Double Cross and its slew of turned double agents were pulling the wool over the eyes of Hitler and his Nazis? But of course, he could disclose nothing about his clandestine work to his family.

"What do the prisoners know about Fritz's planned operation here in England?" he then asked.

"Nothing. All they heard was a rumor that he would be following after them."

"I take it that we can expect him any day now then."

"It appears so."

"It seems then that our old friend is coming home to dinner," proclaimed Masterman. "Let's just hope he gets here before D-Day. He could add immeasurably to our roster of batsmen," he added, as usual applying a cricket analogy.

"Yes, he could indeed," agreed Robertson. He looked at his watch. "I apologize, gentlemen, but I have to attend a briefing with MI6. It appears that they're once again poking into our affairs." He stood up from his desk.

"Oh, not again," bristled Masterman. "When are they ever going to let up?"

"You know the answer, Sir John. Never. Now what are we going to do with these Icelanders and the German? Should they be used for deception purposes?"

"I believe so," said Tin Eye, squinting through his monocle like a Prussian count. "They may be dim-witted chaps, but we will be able to control them. But I still need to question them further to make sure their loyalties are in alignment with us."

"Very good," said Robertson. "Keep me posted, Colonel, on your progress."

"Yes, sir." He saluted. "It would be quite a coup to have these Icelanders and Z in play right before the invasion. They could tip the scales in our favor."

"Especially Chapman. If he's survived this past year in Norway being feted like a king, then it's only fair to say, gentlemen, he's the bloody best we've got."

"God save the king," said Tin Eye. "Our favorite rogue will soon be here in the flesh—and I must confess I can't wait to see the rascal."

CHAPTER 67

HÔTEL LUTETIA, 45 BOULEVARD RASPAIL
PARIS, OCCUPIED FRANCE

JUNE 25, 1944

"YOUR MISSION, FRITZCHEN, IS QUITE SIMPLE: TO WIN THE WAR FOR GERMANY. NOW DO YOU THINK YOU ARE UP TO IT?"

Though they were mildly intoxicated, Chapman looked at Graumann and could tell that he was only half-joking. Back in mid-March when he had flown with the spymaster to Berlin and saw the capital city had been reduced to rubble, Chapman knew that Germany would lose the war without some truly spectacular breakthrough that could radically alter the conflict. He also knew that, in the eyes of the German High Command, the ace up the sleeve of Hitler's Third Reich was none other than himself—a British double agent who was actively working to undermine Nazi Germany. As always, the sheer irony brought a smile to his lips.

Since his arrival in Paris in late March, he had been in a holding pattern for his mission, anxiously waiting for the continuously bombed and battered Luftwaffe to secure a plane for his airdrop into Britain, which was proving unexpectedly difficult given the Allies overwhelming air superiority. He had received two letters from Dagmar declaring that she was having a good time in Oslo since he had left. This was their agreed-upon code that she was still being paid her monthly allowance of six hundred kroner and was not under suspicion by the Germans. She also noted that she had met a certain *sturmbannführer*, which indicated that she was continuing with her spy work on behalf of Britain by making potentially useful contacts with members of the German Secret Service. Chapman noted that the second letter had been opened, presumably by the SS.

Von Gröning tossed back the last of his Rémy Martin cognac, poured himself a fresh glass, and topped off Chapman's drink before continuing with his briefing. Fading Parisian sunlight trickled through the diaphanous window shades of the mahogany-paneled room. One of the City of Lights' finest hotels, the Hôtel Lutétia had been commandeered by the Abwehr shortly after the French surrender in June 1940. It had recently transitioned into the headquarters of the SS.

Months earlier, in February 1944, the Abwehr was abolished due to Hitler's growing suspicions of anti-Nazi disloyalty in the German intelligence service. Wilhelm Canaris was fired and given the meaningless title of Chief of the Office of Commercial and Economic Warfare. The Reich's global intelligence operations were absorbed into the *Reichssicherheitshauptamt*—Reich Security Main Office—under Himmler's SS, which took over the Abwehr offices like the Hôtel Lutétia while retaining staff not suspected of treachery. With the flick of a pen, von Gröning found himself no longer working for the reasonable Canaris but under the control of *Brigadeführer* and *Generalmajor* Walter Schellenberg, the fanatical chief of the SS foreign intelligence service and police. Since finding out about the change months ago, the spymaster had been in a funk and drinking heavily. For his part, Chapman had done his best to console the old man, buying him for his birthday an engraved ivory statuette as a memento of their stay in Paris.

Von Gröning continued with his briefing on Chapman's long-anticipated mission. "Your top priority will be to obtain details of Britain's U-boat tracking apparatus. Once that objective has been realized, you can move on to your secondary objective."

"To steal the radar-type device used in the Allies' night-fighter aircraft," said Chapman.

"That is correct."

"And what is the third objective?"

"To give detailed reports on the effects of our V-1 missiles, specifically the timing and location of impacts and the resulting damage."

"Yes, of course. That makes sense."

Chapman had not seen a *Vergeltungswaffe* 1, or Vengeance Weapon 1, flying bomb, but he had heard about them from his handler. The missiles represented the Germans' long-feared counterpunch designed for terror bombing of London to turn the tide of the war. The first V-1 had been launched at the city on June 13, one week after D-Day, and was prompted by the successful Allied landings on the beaches of Normandy. Known to the Allies as "buzz bombs" or "doodlebugs" because of the strange intermittent buzzing noise they emitted, Hitler's terrifying weapons of vengeance were fired from ski-ramp-like launch facilities along the Pas-de-Calais and Dutch coasts. Because of the weapons' limited accuracy, the old man wanted him to accurately report where and when the bombs were exploding so their effectiveness could be properly assessed by the German High Command.

"As we both know, the British are pretending that the missiles are having negligible impact. We need you, Fritzchen, to penetrate the fog of British propaganda. We need reliable eyes and ears on the ground. An important part of your mission will be to assess the extent of the destruction caused by the V-1s and to send back details along with weather reports and barometric readings."

"I see. So, I'm to act as a target spotter and damage assessor, to enable the gunners to aim their flying bombs from the launchpads in northern France with greater precision."

"That's right."

"And what else will I do during my mission?"

"You are to locate the various U.S. air bases in Britain and identify which German cities are being targeted by each air base. For this latter assignment, you may need to employ a member of your former Jelly Gang to monitor the bases and report using a second radio."

"You really weren't kidding when you said my mission is to win the war. If I do all these things you've just laid out for me, I will not only win the war for Germany, I would have to be Superman."

"Yes, an *Übermensch*. I believe you are already that, my friend. There's a reason you were awarded the Iron Cross."

Chuckling, they raised their glasses and took a drink of cognac. They both found the Rémy Martin superb. The sheer complexity of his mission, coupled with the startling effects of the massive air bombing campaign that now engulfed not only

Nazi Germany but all her occupied territories, confirmed to Chapman that the Germans were desperate. They were counting on him to achieve the impossible, and it was unlikely that even if he wasn't working for the British he could achieve one of the intelligence objectives Berlin had set out for him. But what Agent Fritz/Zigzag, von· Gröning, and the *Oberkommando der Wehrmacht* issuing them their marching orders didn't know was that Nazi Germany's entire spy network had been turned against them and they didn't have a single active agent in Britain. Several of the fictitious agents the Germans believed they had—especially the doubles the British referred to as Garbo, Brutus, Tricycle, Treasure, and Tate—were held in as high regard as Chapman. But they were performing no service for the Fatherland, and none of them had ever been asked to undertake a mission as fraught with peril as the one Chapman was about to perform. Having attained near-mythical status for his fictitious accomplishments thus far, the British spy was believed to be the trump card that just might be able to, virtually single-handedly, win the war for Germany.

Von Gröning set down his cognac. "Now let's go through your equipment." He pointed down at the table. "As you can see, we have spared no expense and put together for you the finest espionage kit we could provide."

Chapman feasted his eyes, though he knew he wouldn't need any of it: he would promptly be handing it over to MI5 after touching down by parachute on British soil.

"Here we have a miniature Wetzlar camera and a larger Leica camera. The Leica is to be passed on to one of our operatives when you reach London, along with one thousand pounds from your funds. The code name and contact information for this operative will be disclosed to you immediately prior to your departure."

He picked up the small Wetzlar camera and aimed it towards the painting on the wall.

"You also have a Leitz range finder and exposure meter as well as six rolls of film."

"Jolly good." He pretended to snap a photograph then set down the camera.

Smiling approvingly, von Gröning motioned again to the table. "For your radio, we have given you two brand-new sets complete with aerials, headphones, five crystals, and a Bakelite Morse code key."

Chapman feigned delight as he examined the set. "Oh yes, this is a beauty. I won't have any transmission problems this time."

"For self-defence, you have been issued a Colt revolver with seven rounds."

"If I have to use that I'm done for. And what is this?" He picked up an aluminum vial and began inspecting it.

"Be careful with that. It contains white liquid and several pills."

"Poison?"

"Yes. I am told the effects are nearly instantaneous. It could prove useful should anything go wrong."

He nodded, suppressing the urge to smile. *If I get caught, I'm not going to bloody kill myself! Why would I, old bean, when I'm a British fucking spy?*

"And now the pièce de résistance." The spymaster now opened the bulky canvas bag on the table and began pulling out worn manila envelopes. "There is over six thousand pounds in here, containing notes from Great Britain of various denominations."

Chapman plucked one of the envelopes from the table and opened it. Six thousand pounds was more money than he had seen since the smash-and-grab raids with the Jelly Gang in the 1930s before the war. "I can tell Berlin really does believe I can win the war single-handedly."

"Yes, we have great faith in your abilities, Fritzchen. I also have here two fake letters to prove your bona fides. One is addressed to Mr. James Hunt of St. Luke's Mews, London. The other is signed by your former girlfriend Betty Farmer and filled with harmless chatter."

"Well, you can't say I won't be prepared this time."

He stuffed the money envelope back in the bag, zipped it up, picked up his cognac, sat back in his chair like a prince, and raised his glass in a toast.

"Here's to the mission, old boy. May it be a rousing success."

They clinked glasses and tossed back the liquor.

"Oh, I almost forgot—there is one last thing," said von Gröning. "Are you going to keep the same code and sign off we discussed in Berlin?"

"It's good that you mention that. Yes, my radio code will remain a double transposition operation type as I have used before, only based this time on the code word ANTICHURCHDISESTABLISHMENTARIANISM."

"You're sure you don't want to make life easier for your W/T receivers?"

"No, I'm rather partial to this code."

"What about your control signal?" he asked, referring to the word or phrase that would indicate he was not under British control and operating freely.

"My free messages will always contain the word DAGMAR. These will be the equivalent of the FFFFF sign I used during the de Havilland operation."

"Very well, I will duly inform Paris and Berlin. If the message does not include the word *Dagmar*, Agent Fritz is operating under British control."

Chapman raised his glass again. "Let's have a final toast. Here's to Dagmar and to the mission's success."

"To Dagmar and the mission!" echoed von Gröning.

Chapman smiled and the two men—spy and spymaster—slammed back the fiery liquor. He had put considerable thought into his control signal: DAGMAR was a coded warning and thinly veiled threat to his German handlers.

If anything should happen to Dagmar, then all bets are off and Nazi Germany is on its bloody own!

CHAPTER 68

STANDING WITH THE OLD MAN next to the flight tower at the edge of the
tarmac, Chapman studied the pilot, his flight crew, and the mechanics as they made
their final preparations for air-dropping him once again into his homeland. He wore
blue flight coveralls with money belts draped over his shoulders. After all the delays,
he couldn't believe he was finally about to depart for his mission as he gazed upon
the sleek Junkers 88. In the last three and a half months, he had gone from Oslo to
Berlin to Paris to Belgium and now to Holland—but only tonight was the mission
truly about to become a reality. Despite the butterflies in his stomach, he felt much
better trained and prepared for this second go-round.

After his experiences during his first parachute drop into the Cambridgeshire in
December of '42, Chapman was thankful that one of the flight mechanics had done
some last-minute work on the trap door. He had inspected the man's handiwork
closely, not wanting to re-enact the tricky experience of being stuck in the hole when
he made his drop. The bomber pilot and his crewmen were all young men, nineteen
or twenty at most, and one of them had told him in the mess that he was to go on
leave as soon as the airdrop was completed. The old man had assured him that,
although the crew was young, it had been trained extensively in night flying.

On the drive over from the mess hall, von Gröning had also informed his prized
agent that his flight had been timed to coincide with a massive Luftwaffe air raid
upon London. The ensuing confusion would reportedly help mask the airdrop. But
in truth no such air raid was planned. Despite the spymaster's reassuring words, the
Junkers bomber was on its own and would not be concealed amidst a larger raid.
The reason was simple: with the Luftwaffe decimated and with the Allies'
overwhelming air superiority and strong anti-aircraft defenses, the German air force
was incapable of even mounting let alone surviving such a raid. Though Chapman
had no idea the old man was lying to him to make him feel better, his biggest fear
was still that his German plane would be shot out of the sky before it reached the
shores of England.

The pilot was now signaling them. "Looks like they're ready for take-off,
Fritzchen."

They stepped towards the Junkers. As they neared, the crew stood at attention
and saluted Chapman. One of the young men then stepped forward to strap him into
his parachute.

Von Gröning leaned in close. "Remember, my friend, to send your first message
three days after landing. We will want to know that you're safe."

"I will. Under control signal DAGMAR."

"Yes, of course. Good luck, Fritzchen, and Godspeed."

The two men embraced. Chapman felt a wellspring of emotion; the old man had long been his mentor, drinking partner, and trusted friend—and he was going to miss him. Having never had much of a relationship with his seafaring, marine-engineer father, the man he had known for the past two years as Doktor Stephan Graumann had been more of a father to him than Ralph Chapman ever had.

"I'm going to miss you, old man," he said. "Almost but not quite as much as I miss Dagmar."

"I can't say I blame you. I possess not even a tenth of the beauty that she does. Now off you go and be sure to establish contact within three days."

"Don't worry I will."

The engines roared as the pilot turned the ignition switch and flames from the exhaust flickered in the bright airfield lights. The two men gave one final handshake and then von Gröning shouted in German, "*Glück, viel Glück!*" over the noise. Good luck, good luck!

Three minutes later, shortly before midnight, the bomber took off and climbed into the dark night sky. As it flew north, Chapman was dimly aware of the recognition lights on the wings, which signaled to the German flak gunners on whose side they belonged. Soon, they were switched off and the Junkers banked left and began crossing the North Sea, flying so low to avoid radar detection that the plane nearly shaved the tops of the rolling waves. The flight was rough as the pilot seemed to purposefully swerve, dive, and swoop like a bird. Chapman suspected he was using lighthouses along the coast of England as beacons.

As the Junkers neared Great Britain, it banked left and flew parallel to the coast, keeping out of the direct light of the rising moon. As they drew closer to the British shore batteries, Chapman couldn't help but notice the extreme nervousness of the young crewmen.

Suddenly, he caught sight of searchlights waving frantically. *My God, there must be hundreds of them. How the hell are we going to get through now?*

A moment later the Junkers came under attack from nightfighters and antiaircraft batteries. The engines screamed as the pilot took evasive action, spiraling up to four thousand feet, and then plunging back down again. Chapman's stomach rolled with every twist. His guts lurched again as flak thudded near the aircraft's tail. Now he began to feel nauseated, especially when he saw a nightfighter pass no more than a hundred feet from their tail.

The jumpmaster shouted out the order to prepare to jump as they neared Six Mile Bottom in the Cambridge fens. "Action stations! We are almost over target!"

Feeling a flare of excitement, Chapman took another deep breath to steady his nerves and hold back from vomiting. The roar of the Junkers 88's engines was ear-piercing as a pocket of air turbulence jostled the bomber. He felt a powerful churning in his stomach, his heart pounding, as he made his final preparations to leap off into the blackness.

A green light flashed and the jumpmaster shouted, "Go! Go! Go!"

Just as he pulled the escape lever, the plane jolted from an explosion of nearby flak. Protecting his face from the instrument panel in front of him, he tumbled awkwardly out of the hatch into the darkness and was hit instantly by the slipstream. Even wearing his helmet, the blast of air struck his face like a freight train and the parachute harness jerked savagely upon his shoulders. He felt his stomach drop faster than the rest of him and then, before he knew it, his parachute was open. Buffeted by the strong wind, he drifted to earth for more than ten minutes, clutching desperately to his large suitcase filled with radio and photographic equipment, swinging in the empty sky like a pendulum in a vast clock.

But all the motion of the last ten minutes was too much for his stomach. Leaning over the side of his harness, he spewed the remains of his banquet luncheon at the Hôtel Lutétia all over the Cambridgeshire.

Despite his queasy stomach, it was a perfect night for a parachute drop. Just after three a.m., in midsummer's twilight, there were a few wisps of cloud. The descent was much less painful this time around, but the landing was far worse. When he was within landing distance, a gust of wind carried him past a clump of trees, over a hedge, and into the middle of a narrow country road between Cambridge and Newmarket. Swinging wildly in the wind, he was unable to properly cushion his fall and hit the ground unexpectedly hard, knocking himself out. For fifteen minutes, he lay stunned on the ground before staggering to his feet. A sharp pain shot through his lower back and he realized that he must have badly bruised his spine.

Shaking off the pain, he cut loose his pack, took off his boots, and replaced them with comfortable shoes. Then he wrapped his overalls, boots, gloves, kneepads, belt, and entrenching tool into the parachute, and hid the bundle under a hedge. He was about to make his way down the country lane when he became aware of footsteps somewhere behind him. Soon, he realized that there were torches flickering in the distance. A line of searchers, walking methodically through the fields, were slowly but surely making their way towards him. Determined to evade them and make his own contact with MI5, he crawled away on his stomach and managed to avoid the search party by hiding under a hedge. After waiting for the group to pass, he staggered a quarter of a mile down the road. He was in terrible pain from the injury to his back and thoroughly soaked from pre-dawn dew.

Why were they were waiting for me? he wondered. *Did they know I was coming?*

He soon came upon a row of houses in a quiet village. He breathed a sigh of relief as he knocked on the door of the nearest cottage.

Almost immediately, a window opened above him and a woman's head appeared. "What do you want?" she shouted down to him.

Still dazed, he tried to explain to her that he had just made a forced landing, but the words came out awkwardly. "I'm a British flyer who's had an accident. Could I use the telephone?"

She took one look at his civilian clothes and cried, "Go away, you wicked man!" Then she slammed the window shut.

Great Scott, I should have remained in Norway with Dagmar instead of coming back to this Godforsaken country!

Carrying his suitcases with his transmitter, two cameras, and six thousand British pounds of various denominations, he set off as fast as his wobbly legs would carry him, fearful of a shotgun blast in the back. This was not the welcome he had been hoping for. Walking down the lane, he came across another household which seemed to already be awake. He steeled himself for another try.

This time, the reception was more cordial. The farmer who answered the door was up and getting ready to head out to his fields. His bleary-eyed family welcomed Chapman inside, offered him a cup of tea, and allowed him to telephone the nearest police station. To his surprise, he managed to get through to the dozy-sounding night-duty officer, who began, with plodding precision, to take down his name, date and place of birth, and other unimportant details. When Chapman impatiently instructed the man to contact his chief constable immediately and explain that a British double agent had landed and that he wanted to be picked up, the officer replied, "Don't be silly—go to bed."

"That's exactly what they told me before!" cried Chapman through gritted teeth. "Ring up your station in Wisbech! They'll remember me from last time!"

When the officer refused, Chapman made the call himself. A vaguely familiar voice answered.

"About two years ago," said Chapman without preamble, "were you on duty when a British parachuter arrived in the early hours of the morning?"

"Yes, that was me," said the voice with a note of pride.

"Well, it's me again. Do you think you could pick me up?"

Two and a half hours later, Chapman found himself back at Camp 020, saluting crisply before Colonel Robin Stephens. Tin Eye looked as intimidating as always with his neatly creased Nepalese Gurkha military uniform and gleaming monocle, but in the sleepy early morning hours of June 28, 1944, there was something decidedly different about the man. He was smiling almost affectionately.

"Colonel Stephens, it's good to see you again, sir. I have quite a lot of valuable intelligence for you."

"Yes, of course you do. We've been expecting you, Agent Zigzag, and I must confess that we are all most eager to hear your story."

CHAPTER 69

"I UNDERSTAND YOU AND COLONEL STEPHENS had an interesting chat early this morning," said Tar Robertson with a welcoming smile. He and Chapman were having lunch in a discrete corner booth of London's elegantly appointed, cherrywood-paneled club for British military officers overlooking Green Park. "A little different from your first meeting with old Tin Eye, wasn't it?"

"It most certainly was. I was exhausted and my back was killing me—I only lasted an hour before I fell asleep at the table."

"I also take it you are finding your Hill Street lodgings in Mayfair satisfactory?"

"Yes, Colonel, I most certainly am."

Robertson held up his glass of sherry. "Well, we're all glad to have you back with us, Eddie," he said, and he meant it. "Here's to a job well done and to your glorious return."

"Here, here," echoed Ronnie Reed, Agent Zigzag's affable, blue-collar control officer who had done the most to train him as a double agent prior to his departure on the *City of Lancaster* more than a year earlier. "I have to say that I am particularly delighted to see you once again—and roaring like a lion."

They tossed back their glasses of sherry. Robertson waved down their waiter to pour them another and to order lunch. The creator of Double Cross opted for the codfish pie with English peas and fennel, while Chapman ordered the roast leg of salt marsh lamb with rosemary jus and Reed the Lincolnshire suckling pig with apple and black pudding. On the heels of the success of the Normandy landings, and thanks to American largesse with so many Yanks with ample money to spend in England, rations had improved across the board and select establishments were serving traditional English cuisine, though in smaller portions.

When the waiter walked off, Robertson said, "Now tell us about your new mission, Eddie. What is Jerry counting on you to do for him this time?"

"As I told Colonel Stephens earlier this morning at Ham, they want five things. The first is to procure photographs or plans of the British gear for spotting submarines."

"That's their highest priority?"

"Yes, I met with several *Kriegsmarine* experts when I was in Norway and they believe Britain has special devices for tracking and sinking their U-boats."

"What is the second priority?"

"To ascertain details of the radio location system employed for the detection of planes, particularly as fitted to nightfighters."

Robertson looked at Ronnie Reed. "Interesting."

"Task three is to report on damage caused by these flying bombs that are wreaking havoc upon London. I'm supposed to gauge the efficiency of the so-called

V-1 buzzbombs—or 'doodlebugs' as I understand people are calling them—and help in pinpointing their aim, reporting when and where the missiles land. As part of my spying, I'm supposed to obtain barometric pressure readings or reports to help the Germans direct V-1's at their targets more effectively."

"What's the fourth objective of your mission?"

"To locate the American air force stations. The Germans believe that certain aerodromes deal with the bombing of specific towns in Germany. The Führer, it seems, is livid about the bombing, and when I was in Berlin, I could see why. The city resembled the ruins of Pompeii and no effort was being made to even dig bodies out from the rubble."

"And number five?" asked Ronnie Reed, writing down notes.

"To get information about a new wireless frequency. The Germans believe we have developed a new frequency to disrupt their V-1 weapons."

Robertson was surprised at the sheer magnitude and complexity of Chapman's mission on behalf of the Germans. It showed just how desperate they were now that the Allies had taken the beaches of Normandy and the Germans had to fight along three separate fronts—France, Italy, and Western Russia—while still managing to maintain their iron grip on the occupied territories.

"Now that you've told us about your new mission," he then said to his star agent, "why don't you tell us about your adventures overseas. Later this afternoon, you're scheduled to have a full psychological evaluation with Dr. Dearden and another chat with Colonel Stephens, so you can just give us the highlights. But Ronnie and I are anxious to hear about your recent exploits."

For the second time in two years, the former safecracker unburdened himself to his British spymasters. Robertson and Tin Eye had already spoken at length and agreed upon a friendly approach this time around, as if their debriefing sessions were not interrogations at all but rather a reunion of old and dear friends. In fact, instructions had already been circulated to all MI5 officers connected with the case stating that Agent Zigzag should be greeted as a returned friend and conquering hero who was in no way under suspicion. This time around, Robertson noted that Chapman's recollections did not consist of an incoherent jumble of partially remembered facts he had brought from the Nantes Abwehrstelle, but the detailed, precise, minutely memorized dossier of a trained agent. In fact, Chapman's recollections were so detailed that he was able to answer virtually all the questions laid out by Reed in the original questionnaire. Robertson found the sheer volume of high-level intelligence Zigzag was able to provide in his debriefing extraordinary.

As they tucked into their sumptuous lunch and imbibed fine sherry, Chapman recounted his exploits during the past sixteen months and the increasingly vulnerable state of Hitler's Reich. He told them about the design characteristics of the V-1 and other German weapons. He described the people he had met, the places he had seen, and the various sensitive military installations he had identified as potential bombing targets, including the location of the SS, Luftwaffe, and Abwehr headquarters in Oslo as well as the tank depots, the U-Boat signals center, air supply bases, naval yards, flak defenses, and even the traitor Vidkun Quisling's mansion on the Bygdøy peninsula. He told them how Goebbels's propaganda had persuaded the Germans that London was in shambles from V-1 attacks when that obviously wasn't true. He described how the morale of the German Navy was particularly low owing to the British U-boat detection and tracking devices that remained a mystery to the *Kriegsmarine*. He described how petrol was particularly short in Germany and how several German cities were in ruins. Unlike his first airdrop into England, his observations this time around were precise and chronologically accurate, presenting a detailed portrait of Nazi Germany at home and in the occupied territories. At the end of the debriefing, he produced an undeveloped roll of film with photos of senior Abwehr officials, and a scrap of rice paper on which he had written the crystal frequencies used by the Oslo Abwehrstelle for radio traffic as well as the codeword *PRESSEMOTTAGELSETRONDHEIMSVEIEN*.

At first, Robertson was inclined to believe that his prized double agent was stretching the truth, or at least embellishing his role to some extent, but as the top-secret information poured out of Zigzag, his initial skepticism evaporated. Most of all, he was struck at what an outstanding spy the former criminal had become during the past year. The man and his exploits were worthy of a Masterman spy novel.

"Well, I must say, Eddie, that is one fantastic adventure story," declared Robertson as the postprandial drinks were served. "I feel as though I'm talking to Robinson Crusoe himself."

"I second that," said Ronnie Reed. "Now we're really going to stick it to the Jerries."

"I'm looking forward to it," said Chapman. "I would imagine that you will want to get me started right away on some sort of deception."

Robertson could see that Zigzag was genuinely anxious to get to work. "That's exactly what we're going to do, but first we are going to have to spend a few more days debriefing you. You've already told us a great deal, but we're going to need to get every word of it down. It's also going to take us some time to digest everything. It is rather remarkable."

"Yes, at times I almost don't believe it myself."

"Well, you've done your country a great service, Eddie," said Reed. "But now you can make an even greater difference. Our foremost priority at present is these blasted doodlebugs. We believe you could help trick the Germans into changing their firing coordinates, so the bombs hit outside of densely populated areas."

"Yes, I believe I can be of great service in that regard. But first, I had better witness one of these devices with me own eyes. Here I am supposed to be an expert yet I haven't even observed one."

"Don't worry," said Robertson. "You will soon enough."

As if on cue, an air raid siren sounded. Robertson looked at Chapman and Reed. "I don't bloody believe it."

They went over to a large window overlooking the park along with a dozen other diners. In a matter of seconds, they could see approaching in the distance one of Hitler's vengeance weapons. The missile streaked across the sky like a comet. On several occasions, Robertson had experienced the eerie sound of a doodlebug coming to the end of its flight when it delivered its explosive payload—and, as with most Londoners, it never failed to strike terror in his heart. Within seconds, the V-1's engine chugged to a halt and there was a terrible silence, seemingly interminable. And then the explosion sounded, the concussion of the blast vibrating the window.

"There now, Eddie," said Robertson grimly. "You have your wish."

"The sound just before the explosion. Why it was like the grim reaper himself."

"Unfortunately, that's just the opening act. There will be ten more today coming from the same damned place that one was fired from. And believe me, I'm not over-egging the pudding."

They returned to their table and glasses of sherry, glummer than before.

Robertson said, "You're going to have quite a spate of work to do, Eddie, if we're going to stop those bloody things."

"Yes, I know, sir. But I must say I am rather looking forward to it."

CHAPTER 70

STARING INTO FEHMER'S GLACIER-BLUE EYES, Annemarie Breien felt her skin crawl. The man repulsed her and yet…and yet, there was something powerful and magnetic about him, and she could not deny that a part of her cared for him. It was indisputable that considerable goodness resided inside him. The other day during their walk along the harbor, he had held her hand and kissed her on the cheek, and for a moment, she had wanted to kiss him back—on the lips. But she had caught herself, and later she had felt ashamed. What would her husband think? Despite being a hardened Nazi, Fehmer was a strikingly handsome man, and in her presence, chivalrous, gentle, and considerate. But she knew what he did to her countrymen and it sickened her. She detested herself for her increasingly intimate feelings towards him and knew she was playing a dangerous game.

Remember, he is but a means to an end, she reminded herself. *You have gotten close to him solely to spare the lives of Norwegians and to destroy the Nazis.*

"You look wonderful today, Annemarie," said Fehmer with a sincere smile from behind his paper-cluttered desk.

"Thank you," she said bashfully.

"I enjoyed our stroll this past Saturday so very much. For an hour or two at least, it seemed as if there was no war going on at all."

"I know, I felt like that too," she admitted, and again she felt ashamed for her emotions.

"You know that I love Norway. I wish our two countries were not at odds with one another. Honestly, I do."

"I realize that," she said. "But to prove it to others, you must stop being so cruel to my people. Everyone knows what goes on here—and only you and Fehlis can stop it."

"Then you must tell your countrymen to stop sabotaging us. It takes two sides to achieve peace." He sighed wearily. "But I know you didn't come here to argue. As usual, we will have to agree to disagree as politely and humanely as possible, and not talk about politics."

"I agree. That's why I have come here to ask another favor of—"

She stopped right there as SS Lieutenants Hoeler and Bernhard flew into the room, taking her and Fehmer both by surprise. "Sorry to interrupt, *Hauptsturmführer*," barked Bernhard in German, "but we have important news."

Fehmer looked angry at the interruption. "Well, what is it?"

Bernhard shot a glance at Annemarie then stepped forward to the edge of the desk and spoke into Fehmer's ear. Though he tried to speak quietly, his voice was unusually loud and she overheard the German words for "radio direction-finder," "transmitter," "summer house," and "Flaskebekk," which was all she needed to deduce what was going on. With their direction-finding vans, the Germans had located a transmitter in a summerhouse on Flaskebekk at Nesodden. She hadn't overheard the name of the radio station, its precise location, or who and how many Norwegian agents manned the station, but she knew enough to warn Milorg. No doubt Fehmer would order an immediate large-scale raid of the radio transmitter site.

Which meant she had to hurry. But she couldn't be in too much of rush to leave, or she would draw suspicion.

When Bernhard was finished with his briefing, he and Fehmer looked at her appraisingly. She gave her most innocent smile and pretended not to have heard a word of what was said by the careless, loud-voiced lieutenant. Luckily, the two men seemed to believe her. Though she and Fehmer spoke Norwegian when together, she was fluent in German from having lived in the country and in Switzerland and he knew it. But he seemed convinced that she had not overheard anything, or perhaps he didn't care. They were spending so much time together these days that he may have considered her loyalty beyond question.

He looked at her politely and spoke in flawless Norwegian: "I am sorry, but something has come up. We are going to have to continue this meeting another time."

"What is it? Is it something bad?" she asked in her native tongue, still feigning complete innocence.

"I'm afraid that must remain confidential as it is of a military nature."

"I understand," she said. "When will I see you again?"

He stood up from his chair. "Soon. I will call upon you soon. Perhaps we could have dinner together."

"I would like that," she said with a sincere-looking smile, playing out the act to the fullest.

Bernhard and Hoeler exchanged knowing glances at one another, as if she were nothing but a Norwegian tart sharing the bed with their senior commander and receiving favored treatment and luxury items in return, like the hundreds of other willing *tyskertøs* who had sold their souls to the occupiers. She recoiled at their sneering contempt, but she knew she had to keep her wits about her and not look offended if she was to take advantage of the intelligence she had just gathered.

Fehmer rounded his desk and spoke in a soft, gentlemanly voice. "Thank you for your understanding, Annemarie. I will make it up to you, I promise."

Believe me, you're making it up to me ten-fold right now, she wanted to say, and she left the room. When she stepped out the front door of Victoria Terrasse onto the street, she felt her heart racing. She had to warn her Milorg contact—Knut Bergwitz-Larsen whom she had convinced Fehmer to set free from prison in spring 1943— quickly.

There was not a moment to lose and she only hoped she wasn't too late.

CHAPTER 71

AS THE ASSAULT TEAM reached the edge of the trees, Fehmer called a final halt and studied the Norwegian summer cottage a final time. He had with him a full company of SS troops, and they stood in the shadows of the woods like stalking hyenas, peering into the windows of the small wood-frame home. All the shades were drawn closed and he couldn't see anyone, and there was no car in the driveway with which to make an escape. The question was whether the radio operators were here now, for the last transmission had been hours ago.

And then he heard—or thought he heard—a sound coming from inside the house? Or was it outside?

He scanned the windows for signs of movement and, seeing nothing unusual, scanned the dark woods that enveloped the home. The massive pine trees blotted out the light and blanketed the lush woods in a deathly stillness. It was the perfect setting for an assault—but it was also the perfect place for a counter-ambush.

For an instant, he wondered if other Milorg members besides the radio operators might be lurking in the shadows and this had all been a set-up. But there was no sign of any interlopers, save for a doe and her fawn nibbling grass in the field bordering the property.

But what about the noises inside the house? Were they his imagination?

He turned to his men and ordered a final weapons check. They snicked off safeties, inspected chambers, and counted magazines as quietly as mice. Fehmer checked his Walther PPK 7.65-mm SS officer's pistol and his Mauser Hahn Selbstspanner backup piece tucked into in his right boot. As he did so, he watched the deer and her fawn. He and his men were downwind of the animals and the deer had not noticed them. The sight of the peaceful creatures made him long for home, and for a moment he felt sad and lonely. He wondered if he would ever make it back to Germany. Did he even want to return home? With all the Allied bombing and millions of dead amid the rubble, and with the Russians pounding away from the east and the Americans and British from the south in Italy and west at Normandy, creeping closer to Berlin every day, would there be anything to return to?

He looked towards the sky. It was gray and overcast, the air leaden with moisture. They were not far from the fjord and the salty scent of the sea filled the air.

He broke the SS company up into three teams and issued orders.

"According to our intelligence, the Corncrake radio transmission station is manned by a pair of Norwegian agents named Leif Karlsen and Ivar Wagle, and possibly one or two others. Lieutenant Hoeler, you will lead Eagle Team around the north side of the house and come in from the rear. Lieutenant Stehr, you and your men will come with me and Wolf Team and attack from the front. Lieutenant

Bernhard, you and Fox Team will form a perimeter along the edge of the woods to the south in case they try to escape in that direction. Once my team enters the house and locates the enemy, I will give them one—I repeat, one—chance to throw down their weapons and surrender. If they do not, Lieutenant Stehr and I will provide heavy sustaining fire, while Hoeler and Eagle Team locate and engage the targets and Lieutenant Bernhard and Fox Team keep them from escaping. Hopefully, if we bring enough firepower to bear, they will give themselves up without a fight."

The men looked at him with beady eyes in the not-quite darkness of the forest, their faces an odd palette of blood red and soot black in the tree-filtered light. The SS raid troops looked like they were itching for a brawl.

He continued: "If Karlsen and Wagle are here, it is critical that we take them alive, if possible. We want to be able to interrogate them about other Milorg cutouts and their communications with the British SOE. This is it, men. Stay low, keep moving, maintain a hot suppressing fire, and, no matter how bad it gets, don't be pulled into a goddamned cross-fire. When you hear Fox Team break down the front door, we will hit them from both sides. The objective is to take them by surprise with overwhelming numbers and arrest them without loss of life. I repeat, I don't want to lose anyone so don't be sloppy."

Here he paused. "Any questions?"

No one spoke.

"All right, let's move!"

They dashed through the clearing to a second set of trees flanking the western edge of the summer house, the officers clutching Luger and Walther pistols, the enlisted men *Karabiner 98 kurz* bolt-action carbines and *Maschinenpistole* 40 light submachine guns. From there, they broke up into their three designated groups. Standing with Fox Team at the front door, Fehmer waited a moment for Hoeler and Eagle Team to get into position at the back. The house was still; not a peep could be heard. He looked at his waterproof SS wristwatch and counted down the seconds to penetration.

It was then he heard a noise.

Was it a snapping twig? Whatever it was, the sound came from outside the house at a sixty-degree compass angle from Eagle Team. He looked at his third-in-command, Lieutenant Stehr.

"Did you hear that?"

"No, what was it?"

"I thought I heard something." He strained his ears and scanned the two houses next door and the woods beyond. But he heard nothing and saw no unusual movement, nothing out of the ordinary. He took a deep breath to steel himself. Were they perhaps stumbling into a trap?

He heard another noise. Now he knew he hadn't imagined it the first time. What he had heard was real and someone was out there.

"It's probably nothing," said Stehr. "But then again, it could be the big bad wolf." He pointed to the dark, forbidding forest all around them.

Fehmer shot the lieutenant a withering glare. This was no time to joke around, not when they were likely about to engage in a gun battle. Somehow, this raid felt different, and Fehmer couldn't help but feel blood was about to flow. Perhaps it was because the war wasn't going well for Germany and Resistance forces everywhere had become more aggressive since the Allies had taken Normandy and Rome a month earlier.

Now he heard a definite crunching sound. This time Stehr and several members of Wolf Team heard the noise too. Everyone froze in their tracks, aiming their pistols and rifles towards the trees. The thick woods were blanketed in dark shadow at the edge of the lighting, with only faint smears bleeding into the forest. Fehmer paused to carefully listen.

Again, his instincts told him they were being watched.

He looked at Stehr; with his gaze focused intently on the trees and clutching his Luger in a two-handed grip, he was no longer making jokes.

For a moment, there was no sound and all was calm. Then, with a suddenness that took everyone by surprise, Fehmer heard a thumping sound to their right, followed by a tearing through brush. This time there was no mistaking the source: running footsteps. And then he heard voices coming from inside the house.

He quickly ordered three men to follow in pursuit and two others to bash down the front door, then he and Stehr charged inside the house with ten SS troops.

The world all around him instantly exploded with gunfire.

He flattened himself down onto the floor, rolled, and let loose with answering fire. The bullets hurled into the walls with terrifying force, causing prodigious destruction. The lethal burst came from deep in the interior of the house. He could tell instantly by the sound that it was a Sten submachine gun favored by the Norwegian Resistance and British Special Operations Executive. The Sten was designed to use the 9x19 mm Parabellum Luger cartridge, which was also used by the Germans, and it was also deliberately designed to fit German 9 mm magazines from the MP-38 and MP-40, so that Allied Special Operations and Resistance operatives could use captured German ammunition and equipment if needed.

From a kneeling position, he delivered a fierce suppressing fire as his team charged into the front parlor behind him, while Lieutenant Hoeler and Eagle team hit the enemy from the rear of the house. Bullets continued to whine and snarl overhead, dislodging splintery shards of wood, lathe, and plaster.

He slid to his right. The storm of lead continued.

He let loose with another blast of cover fire as Hoeler and his men did the same, pushing in from the front door. The air quickly turned thick with gun smoke. His warm pistol felt supple and reassuring in his hands. He was answered by another blast of enemy fire. His team fell back towards him, crouching and firing as they retreated, crab-like.

The shooting slackened for a moment on both sides. Listening closely, he heard shuffling feet and voices speaking in Norwegian. Were they retreating or moving into offensive position?

He took the opportunity to call out to the enemy in their native tongue, commanding them to surrender. The response was a series of obscene, defiant curses and more bursts of gunfire from the Stens.

He let loose with another round of suppressing fire, leapt to his feet, and charged. Once again on the offensive, he and his men quickly drove their way down the hallway that led from the front parlor into the main part of the cottage. When they reached a second room, they fanned out.

But the enemy had disappeared.

He looked around the room. Where the hell had they gone?

And then he heard voices again followed by breaking glass.

They were making an escape from the house!

"They're outside!" he cried. "Quick, follow me!"

They dashed back to the front door, darted outside, and came under fire instantly from three sturdy-looking Norwegians in their mid- to late-twenties wearing civilian dress. He and Stehr opened fire along with their men and there was another ear-rattling exchange of gunfire between the two parties as the Norwegians made a mad dash for the woods, firing a rear-guard-action spray of bullets behind them as they ran. He heard a grunt and Stehr fell to the ground, blood bubbling through his fingers as he clutched his throat.

"*Scheisse*, I'm hit," he gurgled.

Fehmer commanded a soldier to stay with him and apply pressure to the wound, and then he led the remainder of Wolf Team towards the woods. But they hadn't gone three steps before Lieutenant Bernhard and Fox Team, which had formed a perimeter along the edge of the woods, opened fire. They swiftly drove the Norwegians directly towards Wolf Team.

One of the enemy went down but the other two sprinted towards him, their Stens letting loose with a blistering fire, which Fehmer and his SS squad returned.

Another Norwegian was hit. Then the sergeant standing next to Fehmer went down.

He opened fire with his Walther on the last Norwegian, who was screaming at the top of his lungs as he rushed towards Fehmer, but he missed. Suddenly, his hat was knocked off and he felt himself driven backwards by a gunshot, followed quickly by a burning sensation along his scalp line near the top of his skull.

My God, I've been hit in the head!

It seemed to be only a grazing wound, but head wounds bled like crazy and his was no exception as crimson fluid flowed down his cheek in a torrent. He suddenly became lightheaded and fell to the grass next to the wounded sergeant, who was groaning and cursing. Another SS trooper went down. Fehmer felt a searing pain in his head as the world around him erupted in a confused melee, and he realized his head wound was worse than he had thought. Bodies flew past in a blur. Bursts of automatic weapons fire echoed across the woodscape. Primitive-sounding screams and grunts added to the orchestra of violence as the lone remaining Norwegian sent a spray of bullets into Wolf Team.

Despite his bullet wound, Fehmer rose to his feet to carry on the fight. He felt lightheaded but still capable of leading his men. Somehow, the remaining Milorg operative had managed to take cover in a clump of trees next to the house, pop in a fresh magazine, and was holding his attackers at bay, at least for the time being. Sighting the man's exposed torso and head, Fehmer swung up his pistol, pointed it, and squeezed the trigger. He saw the agent's face register astonishment as a little red blot appeared at his unprotected neck. He squeezed the trigger two more times and the man staggered and fell to the ground.

But as he fell, he was able to pull the pin of a hand grenade and throw it at his attackers. Fehmer and his team dove for cover, but the desperate throw was surprisingly accurate and they were unable to get out of the way. This time he felt a pair of sharp sensations along his temple and upper arm from the grenade shrapnel. *Mein Gott, I have been hit again?* Falling to his knees, he lost his hearing for a moment before being blasted with sound from all directions: voices screaming and shouting, feet running towards him, wounded men groaning.

He tried to get to his feet but failed.

Feeling overcome by great weariness, he squeezed his hand against his head and body to clamp shut the flow of blood. Again, he tried to climb to his feet. This time he collapsed onto the wet grass, unable to move.

The battle was now over.

He lay there sprawled in the grass, blood pouring from two head wounds and an arm wound. The world seemed unusually peaceful as he stared up at the cobalt-colored sky, thinking about how beautiful Norway was in July and how much he would like to take Annemarie on a stroll in the country holding hands with her.

Then he heard, or thought he heard, her voice. "Hold on, Captain! You're going to make it—just hold on!"

But then he realized it wasn't her at all but rather Bernhard. "Lieutenant Bernhard, is that you?" he croaked, struggling to bring his subordinate into focus. Now he noticed that Hoeler was standing next to him. Their faces were fuzzy, like in a dream.

"Yes, Captain, it is I," replied Bernhard. "Just hang in there."

"Don't even think about dying on us," said Hoeler.

"They're all dead, aren't they? We have no one to interrogate."

"No, there's one still alive," said Bernhard. "But he's in bad shape. And we've lost Stehr."

"Stehr's dead?"

"Yes, he's gone. The main thing is you're going to be okay. But you must hang in there."

"I'll do my best," he said, but he could feel himself getting weaker by the second. And then his vision went blurry again. He felt a sensation of moving. Were they carrying him inside the house? Then he lost consciousness for a short time before coming back. Now they were moving down a hallway. He looked up at the faces but this time they were all hazy and unfamiliar. He heard a radio crackle and had a fluttery feeling of rapid descent, like he was on a diving small-engine aircraft.

Then everything started to slowly go black, the world to slip away.

He knew then that he wasn't going to make it.

CHAPTER 72

TAR ROBERTSON looked across the conference table at Tin Eye. "Based on your interrogations, Colonel," he said to begin the meeting, "do we have any reason to doubt Zigzag's loyalty? For five days now, he's been undertaking a rather massive deception with the Germans regarding the landing sites of these doodlebugs, and we want to make sure that you are comfortable with us continuing to use him for Double Cross purposes."

The colonel took a moment to adjust his silver monocle, smooth his Ghurka uniform, and sit upright in his chair before responding. Since June 13, some seven hundred German V-1 bombs had landed on London. The Germans seemed to be aiming for the Charing Cross area, but the mean point of impact was calculated to be Dulwich Station in South London. Chapman's instructions from his German handlers were to monitor the bomb damage, and since July 1, he had been sending von Gröning deliberately inaccurate reports misrepresenting the location, timing, and damage inflicted by the bombs. Since the impacts were tending to cluster near Dulwich, MI5's goal was to use Zigzag and the other doubles to persuade the Germans to decrease the range of their V-1 weapons. By convincing them that they were consistently overshooting, British intelligence was tricking them into correcting their targeting and sending the bombs to thinly populated locations in Southeast London and the fields of Kent rather than crowded Northwest London.

Thanks to Chapman, the deception was already proving to be enormously successful. Agent Zigzag's false information campaign was forcing the Germans to correct their aim and reduce the average range of the destructive weapons terrorizing London. To further bolster his credibility with his German handlers, Robertson was also having him provide daily weather reports with barometric readings, but with slight errors introduced to further fool the enemy. Most Secret Sources had already confirmed that the bomb reports were being accepted by the German High Command, and the German bombs continued to fall short of North London and in the southern suburbs and countryside. Here they still killed and destroyed, to be sure, but on a far lesser scale.

Now Tin Eye spoke: "Well, I have to say first off that Chapman has done a bang-up job. He has survived who knows how many tests. He has proven himself able to match their best shooters and drinkers without giving the show away, and to lead a life as hard as any of his Nazi cohorts."

"Why if I'm not mistaken, Colonel Stephens, you seem to admire him. And here I thought he was the three things you despise most: a double-crossing spy, a rake, and a moral degenerate."

"He is, of course, all of those things. But I must confess I am deeply impressed, even moved, by this strange young man for his courage in the face of the enemy.

Yet there is something more to the story than that, for Chapman has faced the searching inquiries of the German Secret Service with infinite skill and resource. He has rendered and may still render his country great service. For that, in return, Chapman deserves well of his country and a pardon for his crimes."

"I quite agree. That's why I've circulated a general instruction to all MI5 officers connected with the case stating that Zigzag should be greeted as a long-lost friend. But I wanted to hear your final word on the matter now that you've had the opportunity to question him on several occasions."

"In that case, there are two aspects of Z's story that trouble me."

"The first?"

"His continuing loyalty to von Gröning."

"And the second?"

"His relationship with his Norwegian lover, Dagmar Lahlum."

"Yes, Ronnie and I weren't altogether keen on the new dalliance either. But let's talk about Doktor Graumann first. What concerns you about him?"

"The potential problem as I see it is that Zigzag's friendship with von Gröning definitely grew stronger during their second go-around together in Norway and France. It must always be borne in mind that he has had a very close connection with the man and holds him in high regard."

"You're concerned that his loyalty to us and his native country might be tempered by his affection for his German spymaster?"

Stephens nodded. "He regards von Gröning as being anti-Nazi and liberal in his outlook, and he's always quick to defend him. He insists that he is a very able man, cautious and resourceful, but has been handicapped by the poor material in the way of personnel at his disposal. Zigzag even recently pointed out that the spymaster's sister has adopted a Jewish child."

"Interesting. Do you believe her motives to be altruistic, or is she hedging her bets in preparation for Germany's inevitable defeat?"

"I think von Gröning and his sister are genuine anti-Nazis. But Nazi Germany is not defeated yet, and we must consider the possibility that Z and his German spymaster might be in league together. There's always been something unknowable and fickle in Chapman's makeup. He's a difficult subject and a certain percentage of his loyalty is still for Jerry. One cannot escape the thought that, had Germany been winning the war, he could quite easily have stayed abroad. In England, he has no social standing, but in Nazi Germany and the occupied countries he is accepted. Among Nazi thugs, mind you, but still accepted and even feted."

"So, it would seem you are not entirely satisfied with his loyalty."

"It is not easy to judge the workings of Chapman's mind. He is bound to make comparisons between his life of luxury among the Germans, where he is almost a law unto himself, and his treatment here, where he still has the law to fear because of his criminal past."

"That's what Len Burt said. He's the head of Special Branch and the senior police officer liaising with us. On the basis of Zigzag's past record, he remains convinced that he is a man without scruples who will blackmail anyone if he thinks it worth his while. Burt says he would sell out to the opposition if he believed there was something to be gained from it."

"In that case, it appears that there is but one course of action. Chapman will have to be watched at all times, and his relationship with von Gröning will have to be further probed."

"At the same time, he will need to continue to be handled with kid gloves and treated like a prince. We may not be able to match the munificence of his Nazis handlers, but we can surely try. Although we cannot supply him with champagne and filet mignon, these are the sorts of things with which we must compete. Frankly, I'm more concerned about his relationship with Dagmar Lahlum."

He removed a photograph from his folder on the table and pushed it across to Tin Eye, who proceeded to look it over.

"Ah yes, the inevitable girlfriend. I must say she is quite lovely. But in confiding in this untested woman, Zigzag has blundered badly. It goes without saying that as a double, or perhaps even triple agent, she could betray him at any moment with disastrous consequences."

"That's my feeling as well. If von Gröning ever realizes that he has been double-crossed, any information Chapman has sent to Germany will then be interpreted, rightly, as the opposite of the truth."

"Chapman would then provide real, not false, intelligence to the enemy, and von Gröning will go back and review the record in detail. But it is unlikely that he would admit his mistake of taking Chapman in as his top spy to his superiors in Berlin. They will incarcerate him—or banish him to a meaningless post as they have done with Canaris."

"What's your feeling about Dagmar's loyalty?"

"Chapman certainly insists, loudly and repeatedly, that she is not only loyal to him, but a skilled spy in her own right. He also says that she is vigorously anti-German."

"Do you believe him?"

"Yes, but I still believe she poses a risk."

"What did he say about her under interrogation?"

"He described how he wooed her, and how he had debated with himself for months before telling her the truth about being a British spy. He claims she is not a fast girl. He's also quite certain that she was not planted by the Germans when he first met her at the Ritz in Oslo."

"What was his evidence?"

Tin Eye pushed the photograph of Dagmar Lahlum back across the table, pulled away his monocle, rubbed his eyes, and placed the glinting piece back into its proper place over his right eye. "He claims that if she had betrayed him to the Germans, he would have at once observed a change of attitude of the Germans towards him. He further states that if von Gröning and his team had suspected Dagmar, or himself, they would not have agreed to provide her with a free apartment and a monthly stipend."

Robertson examined the photograph, noting the high cheekbones, smooth skin, and large intelligent eyes. There was a good reason she was an aspiring fashion model as well as a spy. "So, what you're saying is Dagmar has his complete confidence."

"Yes, and he can't stop talking about what a brilliant field operative she is. It's clear that he is smitten with her far more than his usual liaisons."

"That's just what is so troubling for us as his handlers. The unofficial introduction of this girl into the service of the British government has added an unexpected and unwelcome complication."

"Without question. We also have to wonder if he's even capable of an objective opinion when it comes to her. Like I said, he's anxious to talk about her at every opportunity. Without fail, he returned to the subject again and again during our recent interrogations. He insists that he's made a promise to ensure her financial position and clear her name after the war."

"That's going to prove difficult. As we both know, our service operates under strict secrecy, and even you and I won't be able to breathe a word to anyone of what we did during the war."

"All the same, Zigzag says that one of his principal objectives after the war is to reinstate her with her compatriots by asserting that she actively double-crossed the Germans. He is quite adamant about it and is angry about the way she's been treated by her own people."

"There's no question his passion is genuine, but none of us has forgotten about Freda," said Robertson, picturing in his mind Freda Stevenson, Chapman's former lover and mother of his child who was still being supported by MI5 along with Chapman's young daughter Diane. "As I recall, there was supposed to be some sort of understanding, of which Zigzag has by now doubtless repented, that if he ever came back he would marry Freda."

"That's not going to happen. He's too in love with Dagmar."

"Do we know for sure that she's working for the Norwegian Resistance?"

"He provided considerable evidence."

"What exactly?"

"He described how she knew about the Sicily landings before it had been publicly broadcast and about the bombing of the Forbunds Hotel right after the incident. He claims the only way she would have had access to such high-level information is if she was working for the Norwegian underground, specifically Milorg. There's also no question that she assisted his spying activities when it came to reconnaissance of key German military and intelligence installations and von Gröning and his Oslo Dienststelle. He had the photographs to back it up."

"She still poses a risk. Our intelligence services are in regular contact with Milorg, but we've had some issues with the organization. We regard them as inefficient and unwieldy—and especially prone to leaks. We're worried that since Dagmar's part of Milorg, she may have told her people about Zigzag's real identity."

"Yes, I can see how this could turn into a full-fledged cock-up. As genuine as she appears to be, she is still working for one secret organization, in league with another, and being paid by a third. From our point of view, the young lady has too many suitors for comfort."

"It is rather complicated. Nonetheless, I still believe that Chapman has demonstrated his loyalty repeatedly and need not further prove himself."

"My faith in Z is undimmed, too, Tar. But to protect Double Cross we must be cautious."

Robertson gave a nod, but said nothing, prompting Tin Eye to continue.

"I do not wish to be held wanting in admiration of a brave man any more than you do, but we have to face the facts. In England, Chapman is a wanted criminal. In Germany, he is admired and treated royally by the German Secret Service. It is not unnatural, therefore, that he has come to dislike the English in many respects and to admire the Jerries. Indeed, there is more than admiration, there is a genuine affection for Graumann. His present ambition is to settle down with Dagmar in Paris at the end of the war. Where do the loyalties of Chapman lie? Personally, I think they are in fine balance."

Nodding in affirmation, Robertson looked down at the photograph again and wondered aloud: "Who are you truly, Dagmar, and what the bloody hell are we going to do about you?"

CHAPTER 73

DAGMAR STARED OUT THE THIRD-FLOOR WINDOW of Ullevaal Hospital. Below on Kirkeveien Street, a German patrol was stopping people and inspecting their papers at a checkpoint, including hospital staff coming on for the night shift. It was past six p.m. and a hazy orangish ball hovered in the western sky, towards Great Britain where she knew her lover Eddie Chapman must have made it by now. She had taken the tram and walked up the Ullevaalsveien to deliver two messages and a half dozen forged passports to a Milorg contact who worked in the Department of Ophthalmology, and now she was pondering what route to take for the return trip home with less than an hour until curfew.

Though hospitals were one of the Norwegian Resistance's favored safe havens for transmitting and receiving information, temporarily hiding people, and delivering critical resources such as false documents, the Germans had been cracking down on the institutions in the past six months. Several radio transmitters had been seized by the Gestapo in the past two months alone. Some Osloans believed there were serious ethical problems involved in using hospitals on behalf of the Resistance, but Dagmar disagreed. In her view, the normal rules didn't apply since the Nazis were such a brutal and unethical adversary. The success of the partisan struggle had to be balanced against the normal rules of warfare and concerns for society. The situation was extreme, and Milorg and the other groups comprising the underground movement routinely made use of hospitals. Doctors and nurses in the cancer wards, ophthalmology, obstetrics, and gynecology departments, bacteriological laboratories, and institutes of forensic medicine regularly risked their lives on behalf of the Resistance.

Staring out the window at the German soldiers, Dagmar longed for her beloved Eddie. She hadn't felt safe since he had left four and a half months earlier. She didn't want to lose him and prayed that he would come back for her after the war. She imagined their life together living along *La Rive Gauche*, the south side of the Seine and artistic center of the city where many of the famous writers and artists who had once called Paris home, including Hemingway, Picasso, and Matisse, had lived. They would open their wonderful club together, have beautiful children, and live a grand post-war life knowing they had fought the good fight, albeit clandestinely, for their countries.

She couldn't bear the thought of losing him. At this point in the war, her memories of their days sailing Oslo Fjord and making love in the woods and swimming in the ocean were the only things that sustained her. In his absence, her love for him had only grown stronger, and she knew that she would never love anyone the way she loved her Eddie. But just as important in these perilous times, he had made her feel safe. She was still under the protection of the Abwehr, who provided her with an apartment and allowed her to continue to draw on a portion of

Chapman's salary, but with the war going badly for Germany and the Gestapo cracking down with increasing violence and brutality in reprisal, she didn't feel entirely safe. Making her situation more precarious, she still had her own people to contend with, Osloans who continued to presumptively assume she was a Nazi tart under the protection of the occupiers. It pained her that she could tell no one she was a true patriot.

"Dagmar Lahlum, what a surprise it is to see you here."

She recognized the silky-smooth voice instantly: Fehmer! She felt a sudden shortness of breath and didn't want to turn around. *How could I have let myself get caught like this?* She shouldn't have been daydreaming and staring out the window, and now she would have to bluff her way out of the situation.

Slowly and despite her trepidation, she turned around.

She quickly realized he was in no position to do her any harm. Heavily bandaged about the head and arm and supported on one arm by a nurse, he was a patient in the hospital walking down the hallway to get some exercise. She remembered hearing from Ishmael that he had been critically wounded during a raid on a Milorg radio site in Flaskebekk three weeks earlier.

She looked him in the eye, her heart thundering in her chest.

"It is me, Captain Fehmer. Don't you remember me?"

"Of course, I remember you," she said blandly. "Everyone knows who you are."

He looked at her appraisingly. She tried to think of an excuse to leave the hospital immediately and be free of him but was unable to come up with anything. Her brain had become muddled out of fear.

"What happened to you?" she asked.

"I was shot by one of your Norwegian comrades."

She looked at the young nurse assisting him, whose face showed visible fear. "My friends don't shoot people. Like me, they are law-abiding citizens."

He smiled knowingly. "Are you sure about that?"

"Yes, I am sure."

"What are you doing at the hospital? Are you visiting someone?"

"I was. Now I am leaving."

"Was it your friend Kristin Larsen perhaps?"

"You have a good memory, Herr Fehmer."

"As I recall she had typhus and was undergoing treatment in the infectious disease ward. But the ward is on the second floor not the third."

He was a clever bastard, and she couldn't believe her bad luck. Of all the hospitals in Oslo, Fehmer had to be sent to Ullevaal Hospital to recover from his gunshot wounds. But then she realized it made complete sense. It was the closest hospital to Gestapo headquarters, and even closer to the Tullins gate neighborhood where many German intelligence officers were housed.

"I wasn't visiting my friend Mary," she replied firmly but reasonably. "I was visiting someone else. And now I'm afraid this interrogation is over. I must be going, and you must get back to your room. If your healing process should be lengthened even a minute on my account, I would never forgive myself."

"Yes, Captain, we should take you back to your room now," agreed the nurse, coming quickly to her aid. "The doctor doesn't want you pushing yourself too hard."

"Yes, we mustn't disobey the doctor," he said sarcastically. "Until we meet again then, Frøken Lahlum."

His liquid blue eyes gazed at her intently, and for a moment she found it hard to breathe. "I wish you a speedy recovery," she said, struggling to keep her wits about her.

"I know you don't really mean that, but it is nice of you to pretend," he said with a gracious smile. "I bid you goodnight and a safe return home. It is not long until curfew."

"Yes, I am aware of that," she said. "Goodbye."

She turned on a heel and walked briskly down the hallway, wanting to get away from him as fast as possible. When she had gone ten feet, he called out to her.

"Frøken Lahlum, one more thing!"

Though she warned herself not to turn around, she did. "Yes, Captain?"

"Who were you visiting here at the hospital?"

She gave an involuntary start. "I'm afraid it's a confidential matter involving a priest. I'm sure you understand," she said, and she turned around and made her way quickly towards the staircase that led to the first floor before he could get another word in. As she pushed her way through the door and started for the stairs, she bumped into a blonde woman in her late twenties, nearly knocking her down.

"Good heavens, I am so sorry," she gasped.

Recognition registered on the attractive woman's face. "Dagmar, is that you?"

At first, Dagmar couldn't recall her name, but then she remembered. "Annemarie Breien," she said with relief. "What brings you to the hospital?"

The young woman looked down the staircase and then an adjoining hallway, making sure no one was within earshot. Dagmar followed her cautious eyes. Down the corridor, a pair of white-sheeted gurneys bearing two young unconscious civilians flew past and into an adjoining hallway. They were covered with blood, and Dagmar wondered if they had been attacked by the Germans or merely suffered some unfortunate accident. Emergency room technicians and doctors and nurses in clinical white hurried past before disappearing around the corner.

"I am visiting someone," replied Breien once she had confirmed the coast was clear and no one could hear them.

"Who?" asked Dagmar. "A friend or family member?"

"Oh, it's just an acquaintance."

She seemed embarrassed, and Dagmar wondered who the "acquaintance" was. Was it possible that the person she was visiting was German and she was ashamed? And then the thought struck her: *My God, it couldn't be Fehmer, could it?*

She drew closer and spoke in a whisper. "Thank you for helping me and my friend last spring. If not for you, I might not be alive today."

Annemarie smiled, and when her gentle blue eyes lit up Dagmar realized she was even more beautiful than she had previously thought. "It was the least I could do."

"Well, it meant a lot to the both of us."

"How is your British friend?"

"I don't know. I haven't seen him for several months. Are you still with Milorg?"

She looked around again. "We shouldn't talk about things that can get us locked up."

"Of course, you're right. But you already know that I work for Milorg and that I was with a British operative, so at least from my end the damage has already been done. I was working directly for British intelligence and it was very exciting, but now I am just a lowly courier again. The surprising thing is people think I am working for the Germans."

"Because of your friend?"

"Yes. As I said, he is gone now. I shouldn't say any more than that in case we fall into enemy hands."

"You're right, of course. But it's nice to know others are risking their lives working in secrecy for the Home Front. The people on the streets think that I, too, am a Nazi sympathizer. Sometimes the burden is too much to bear."

"I know exactly what you mean. To be falsely labeled a *tyskertøs* is worse than demeaning."

"Unfortunately, it is the cross we must bear." She leaned forward and touched her wrist gently. "But we must continue to fight the good fight even if we are treated as outcasts by our own countrymen. One day, people will know what we've done on behalf of Norway. Eventually, the Germans will be driven out and we can tell people what we did. At that time, they'll give us the credit we deserve."

"I hope you're right. But I must confess I have my doubts."

"Don't worry, it will work out for the best. Norway won't let us down."

"The reason people have branded you like me…is it…is it because of the acquaintance you are visiting here in the hospital?"

A look of surprise. "How did you know?"

"Just an educated guess. You seemed embarrassed because of who you were visiting."

She looked around nervously.

"Is it Siegfried Fehmer? I just saw him in the hallway."

Now she blushed. "I just use him to get information," she said defensively. "There's nothing going on between us."

Dagmar could tell there was more to it than that. "I'm the last person with whom you have to justify yourself, Annemarie. I, more than anyone else, can appreciate what you're doing on behalf of the Resistance. One cannot get close to the enemy and betray him by studying him from a distance."

"He was shot in a raid three weeks ago in Flaskebekk. That's why he's in the hospital."

"I heard about it."

At that moment, a pair of SS guards appeared down the hospital corridor. The two women tensed reflexively. "We'd better be going," said Annemarie Breien. She reached out again and took Dagmar's hands in her own. "Good luck to you, Dagmar. It will work out for us both, don't you worry. One day people will know what we've done, and instead of being ridiculed on the streets, we will be celebrated, at least by our friends and families. Just you wait and see."

"When it's all over, I hope to see you again. And if by chance our paths don't cross again, I want to say it has been an honor knowing you, if only briefly."

"No, the honor is mine. You are a brave woman."

"But not as brave as you who has gotten close to Fehmer. Whatever happens, good luck to you—and be careful."

"The same to you, my friend."

They tipped their heads and went in opposite directions. Dagmar hoped that Annemarie was right about the future.

But she had her doubts.

ψψψ

When she entered his hospital room, Fehmer felt his entire body fill with joy. The sight of her was like a magnificent sunset or breath of freshly cut roses, and he knew he was hopelessly in love with her. But would he ever have her as his own?

"Annemarie," he said with emotion. "You don't know how pleased I am to see you." It was the fifth time she had visited him at Ullevaal Hospital, and the second time this week, but it seemed like it had been an eternity since her last visit. Though he was growing stronger every day from his gunshot wounds, he was still at least two or three weeks away from being released. Now he knew why badly wounded soldiers took so long to be sent back to the front. Recovery from bullet wounds was a painfully slow process, especially when you were shot in a critical area such as the head as he had been.

She pulled up a chair next to the bed. "Siegfried, I must say you look much more vigorous than my last visit. You are healing fast."

He smiled, feeling a great warmth inside just being near her. "You are just saying that. I look like hell warmed over."

"No, you're getting better. Soon you will be on your feet full-time."

"Yes, but I still won't be allowed back at work any time soon." In fact, his boss Fehlis had said early on that, due to the nature of his wounds, he most likely wouldn't be allowed to return to his post full-time for two months. But based upon the progress he was making so far, Fehmer was confident that he would be ahead of schedule.

"Here, I brought you a little present," she said, reaching into her pocket and pulling out a chocolate bar.

He smiled approvingly. "Dutch chocolate. What a pleasant surprise. But it must have cost you a fortune."

"No, a friend gave it to me for doing her a favor."

She handed it to him, and he opened the wrapper and took a bite. "Oh my, this is magnificent. You must share it with me." He handed it to her.

"All right, just a little."

She took a bite and he watched her. *Do you have any idea how much I love you? Any idea at all how much I would give up just to be with you for the rest of my life?*

"I can't stay long," she said, instantly dashing the feeling of euphoria surging through his body at her soothing presence beside his bed. "I just wanted to check in and make sure you were doing all right."

"I will release more prisoners," he blurted. "You don't even have to ask. I will see that it is done."

He reached out and took her hand in his, and she looked at him with something approaching genuine affection.

"You have already released more than sixty," she said. "What will Colonel Fehlis think if he should find out?"

"He won't find out. He hasn't yet and there's no reason that he will do so in the future."

"But if he did, that will be the end of our arrangement."

"Arrangement? Is that what we have—an arrangement?"

"I didn't mean it like that."

"Then how did you mean it?"

"I meant only that we have been doing important humanitarian work together arranging for prisoner releases and it would be a shame for it to end prematurely."

"Don't you want me to set more Sigurd Evensmos free?"

She reached out and gently touched his hands; they were warm. A part of her was strangely aroused—and yet another part was intensely repulsed. *What are you doing, Annemarie? If your father and brothers combating the Nazis could see you now?*

"Of course, I want you to free more people," she said, rubbing the soft skin above his thumb. "But I just don't want you to get caught for overstepping your authority."

"Don't worry, I won't get caught. You know I would do anything for you."

She looked away with embarrassment. "You shouldn't talk like that. Getting romantically involved can only lead to trouble."

He gripped her hand tighter. "We belong together, Annemarie. If there was no war going on, we would make the perfect couple."

She gently pulled her hand away. "But there is a war going on, and that's precisely why we can never be a couple even if we wanted to. But even more importantly, I am a married woman."

"But you don't love Kjell. Not anymore, after the way he has treated you. He doesn't even acknowledge the important work you are doing to liberate your countrymen. Has he ever once thanked you for your efforts? No, because he doesn't care about you enough to recognize you for the important work you do. What kind of husband does that, Annemarie, tell me?"

"Stop it," she snapped. "Leave Kjell out of this."

"How can I when I love you?"

She felt her heart lurch in her chest and her body froze.

"It's true, Annemarie. I've fallen terribly in love with you."

She shook her head. "Don't you dare say that! It can never work and you know it!"

"I don't care because I love you. In fact, I have loved you since the first day I set eyes upon you when you burst into my office to plead for your father's freedom."

She jumped up from her chair, feeling tears coming to her eyes. "Stop it! Don't say that!"

"But it's the truth!"

"No, it's not!" she said. "Don't say you love me—because it can never be!"

CHAPTER 74

STARING OUT THE WINDOW OF HIS FLAT in West London, Eddie Chapman felt like a prisoner. He missed Dagmar terribly—and the old man as well. He couldn't believe the irony of his situation: the bloody Germans treated him better than his own damned countrymen.

In his heart, he knew it wasn't that black-and-white but all the same he felt deeply dispirited since his return to England. Although he was continuing to aid the war effort, he was becoming bored with his fake radio transmissions to his Abwehr handlers. The lack of romance and adventure in his home country compared to exciting Norway and France was staggering, but most of all he missed the easy companionship of Dagmar and Graumann, who had lavished him with money and let him do as he pleased. He was also tired of having to be chaperoned around the city by his British handlers and severely restricted regarding the company he kept.

In late July, the V-1 deception program that had fooled the Germans into thinking they were overfiring Central London and forced them to reduce the average range of their buzz bombs was suspended by MI5 because the London newspapers began accurately reporting the locations of the bombing sites, potentially threatening the deception and, thus, risking the exposure of Double Cross. Unfortunately, that left Chapman with little to do until a new deception operation could be worked out in detail and put into action. But the primary cause of his distress was not boredom but rather his insufferable new B1A counterintelligence section case officer. Major Michael Ryde had recently taken over for the likeable Ronnie Reed, who had been promoted and was now posted with the American invasion force in France as an intelligence liaison officer.

Chapman loathed Ryde from the moment he met him. The son and grandson of chartered surveyors, the case officer was a bombastic, moralizing, and humorless bureaucrat who did things inflexibly by the book and drank to excess. Except for his enjoyment of wine and spirits, he was the opposite of the agent under his control in every respect—and he and Chapman were at odds with one another from the very start. Eddie couldn't believe his bad luck. But what struck him most of all was the irony of it all: he had to betray Graumann, his closest friend, out of duty towards his country, but the man who should have been his foremost advocate regarded him as a lowly criminal. Like many of the clubby MI5 officers, including the pretentious John Masterman, Ryde looked down with sneering contempt upon Chapman's disreputable past and working-class upbringing. Furthermore, he didn't believe the agent deserved to be feted for his accomplishments as a spy. But Ryde took it a step further: he wanted to shut Zigzag down as a double agent. To do that, he had to make Chapman look bad before Tar Robertson.

Eddie continued staring out the window, thinking back to those halcyon days sailing his little Swedish yawl and making love to Dagmar on Oslo Fjord. God, what he would do to be in her loving arms again. And then, just as he imagined himself kissing her soft lips, Ryde drove up to the safe house. Chapman gritted his teeth as he watched the bastard get out of his car and stride pompously up the walkway. He was a tall and handsome man, and when not deep into his cups had a certain charm, but Chapman knew him for what he truly was: a preening, class-conscious prick who looked down his nose upon anyone who was not born into his station. Chapman stepped quickly towards the front door to confront him.

"I'm going out tonight," he said the instant the door opened. "I should be back in a few hours, but if I'm not don't bother to wait up."

Ryde frowned like a Puritan. "No, you're not. You're not going anywhere."

"I'm bloody hell not staying here. If you won't drive me, I'll walk. I need more money too."

The control officer looked at him incredulously. "You've already spent what we gave you?"

"It was a pittance and you know it."

"Perhaps, but we know what you've been up to. You have plenty of money."

"What's that supposed to mean?"

Ryde smiled knowingly, the edges of his mouth curved upwards like a crocodile. They stepped away from the front door and into the parlor. "Last Friday, you skipped an appointment to transmit information to the Germans because you were at the dog races."

"So what?"

"We know that you fixed the races, Eddie."

"I didn't fix anything. I just made money on the bet."

"Stop lying. We know you've been up to no good and making quite large sums of money by backing the winners of races which have been fixed. Why you act as if we don't know what goes on at White City."

Knowing he was in trouble, Chapman tried to figure a way out of the mess he had created. He had disclosed too much to Ryde's slightly more tolerable MI5 associates, Wilson and Reisen. The White City track in West London had always been a mecca for the criminal fraternity, and while horse racing had been eliminated in wartime, dog racing flourished. The tracks acted as a magnet for black market activities, including race fixing, money laundering, and the bartering of stolen identity cards and petrol coupons.

"I am not directly involved in the race fixing," he pointed out. "You're making a mountain out of a mole hill."

Again, Ryde smiled his crocodilian smile. "Oh, so you did nothing wrong, is that it?"

"You know perfectly well that I am becoming bored and restless—and yet you do nothing to allow me to fight for my country."

"Fight for your country? What you have done is most certainly not fighting, old sport."

"I have done more than you. While I have been behind enemy lines and sending messages to deceive the enemy, you have been sitting behind a desk all day. Oh, and getting drunk at night."

Ryde's face reddened. Chapman wished he hadn't been quite so cruel, but the condescending bloke deserved it.

"MI5 has long feared you would become a problem," grumbled the starchy case officer. "Well, it now appears as if our fears have been proved correct. Now that your overseas adventures have dried up, you have, quite literally, gone to the dogs."

"Because I am bored to death. I am a field operative not a keyboard puncher. I need a new assignment with a whiff of excitement."

"Field operative? When it's all said and done, you're nothing but a lowly criminal. Why you can't even walk the city's streets alone in case you're arrested."

"It's not my fault Scotland Yard has a long memory."

"Oh, but it is. Once a criminal, always a criminal."

Feeling a bristling anger inside, he had to remind himself to control his temper. He desperately wanted to punch the prissy bastard in the nose. But he would be locked away for a very long time if he raised a hand against him.

"Maybe I should just quit the intelligence business."

"You know what will happen then: you'll just end up back in prison. Look at you. You've already returned to the tracks and fallen back in with the wrong crowd."

"Why doesn't MI5 just send me back to France? I could help comb out any German underground movement which may have been left behind."

"That's out of the question. Colonel Robertson wants you here in Britain feeding lies to the enemy. Needless to say, I don't share his enthusiasm for your espionage skills."

"But I don't want to be here anymore. I'm madly in love with Dagmar and want to spend the rest of my life with her."

"Is that so? Why just the other day, you were telling me how anxious you were to write Freda and tell her you were back in London. And what about your daughter Diane?"

"Freda was a mistake and I haven't been a father to Diane in a year and a half. Dagmar is my true love. She's going to be in my autobiography."

"Autobiography? We've already been through this, Eddie. You know perfectly well that it is quite impossible for you to disclose your activities on behalf of British intelligence during the war."

"I don't care about your petty rules. I want to write up an account while it's still fresh."

"I warn you not to do any such thing—unless, of course, you want to go to prison."

"I promise to confine my reminiscences to my old criminal activities. Would that suffice?"

"No, it would not. And you know Colonel Robertson will agree with me. And he'll also agree with me about your betting on the dog races."

"What do you care about betting on the bloody races?"

"Taking advantage of other people's dirty work to fleece the bookmakers cannot be regarded as a desirable occupation under any circumstances. MI5 has a reputation, you know."

"I've got to do something, damnit. I'm bored to death cooped up in this fucking safe house with you looking over my shoulder every minute."

"We always knew that if you got bored, you would turn your tortuous mind to working out schemes for making more money, which will undoubtedly bring you to the notice of the police. But this profiteering off fixed dog races is a new low. It will be embarrassing if you were to be arrested whilst in our care. Doesn't that bother you, or do you have no scruples whatsoever?"

"You're a disgrace. You should have my back and yet all you care about is destroying me. Why you're not even half the man Doktor Graumann is despite the fact you are British and he is our country's sworn enemy."

"How dare you talk to me that way!"

"Oh, shut up! I'm going out drinking and getting away from the likes of you. And tomorrow, I want a meeting with Colonel Robertson. And if he won't see me, then I'll make contact with the French or Americans to offer my services as an agent!"

"You wouldn't dare!"

"Oh, yes I would. Now shut your gob and set up the meeting with the colonel!"

CHAPTER 75

"WELCOME, EDDIE," said Tar Robertson, ignoring the agitated expression on his prized double agent's face. "I'm so glad you could join me for lunch." He stood up and waved him courteously to a chair.

"Thank you, Colonel," replied Chapman as he took his seat, and Robertson knew he had disarmed him with charm. The best way to win over Zigzag, he had learned from experience, was to cater to his vanity. The lad carried a chip on his shoulder from his humble upbringing: treating him as a man of privilege above his actual station had proved the surest way to win his affection and trust, as Robertson suspected his opposite number von Gröning realized as well. He poured him a glass of sauvignon blanc. For their second meeting at the sumptuously appointed Naval and Military Club, their lunch table was next to a window overlooking luxuriant Green Park. Seated around them were plainclothed and uniformed British military and intelligence officers from various branches of service along with a smattering of high-ranking Americans with beige ties neatly tucked into their olive-brown dress jackets. To put his guest at ease, Robertson tried to begin with a bit of small talk, but Chapman was too seething with resentment against his new MI5 case officer to engage in meaningless chit-chat for more than a couple of minutes.

"Ryde has to go," he declared, his high-pitched voice more strident than usual. "He is not handling the case properly, and I can no longer work with the man."

Robertson held up his hands in a mollifying gesture. "Now just hold on, Eddie. The major is a fine officer and I'm sure we can work out a solution that is satisfactory for all parties. Tell me specifically what is troubling you."

"First off, I believe more ought to be done to exploit my case, and if it can't then it should be closed down and I should be released from service. Secondly and most importantly, the major is a condescending snob, a prig, and he treats me like a child—and I'm bloody sick of it."

He realized that Chapman was angrier than he had anticipated, and that the agent's personal appraisal of Ryde was spot on, though he wasn't about to tell the lad that. There were two sides to every story and the story that Ryde had put forward earlier in the week claimed that Agent Zigzag was the intransigent and insufferable one. They had met in person in Robertson's office where Ryde had made it clear that he regarded his new working-class ward as a vulgar recidivist criminal, an encumbrance, and an embarrassment and danger to the British Secret Service due to his illicit past and what would likely prove to be an unlawful future. The major had flatly called for terminating the Zigzag case and tossing Edward Arnold Chapman onto the street without even a pat on the back, despite the risks he had taken on behalf of his country. Robertson thought that was extreme.

Ryde claimed Chapman was "most discontented" as well as costly to maintain, mercurial, disreputable, and, most importantly, an untrustworthy rogue who would gladly pass top-secret information to the Germans if they paid him enough for it. He complained that he was engaging in illicit dog racing, had been keeping "the bad company of some professional pugilist with whom he has been hitting the high spots," and was "always in the company of beautiful women"—as if the latter were a crime and not the desire of most men in the Western hemisphere. He had ended the meeting by saying that "the Zigzag case must be closed down at the earliest possible moment." Neither Roberson nor John Masterman agreed with Ryde's gloomy assessment and he was swiftly brought into line by both superiors, who recognized their star agent's immense value to the clandestine war effort.

"I know the major is a first-class prick, Eddie, but we're a tad short-handed here in London with every able-bodied man in France fighting the Jerries."

"Ryde is gunning for me. He's collecting as much ammunition as he can and plans to use it against me to undermine my credibility and shut me down."

"That's rather paranoid, don't you think?" *Or is it?* he wondered as they perused their menus. "The question is what your future plans are?"

"I wish I knew. I just know that it doesn't feel right anymore. It feels like you all are against me."

"I'm not against you and you know it. In fact, I've gone out on a limb for you on several occasions."

"I know you have and I appreciate it. I'm just restless is all."

He gave a sympathetic nod. "Of course, you are," he said. "It's not easy to perform the rather humdrum business of tapping a key at our instructions when you are a man of action and raw adventure."

"I couldn't have said it better myself."

"Seriously though, Eddie, what do you want to do with yourself? You must have some ideas."

At that moment, a white-jacketed waiter arrived to refill their crystal wine glasses and take their orders. Robertson opted for the Parmesan- and herb-breaded plaice fillets with lemon mayonnaise and a main course of smoked Salmon Wellington, while Chapman ordered a duel appetizer of British Lion egg and cress and tuna mayonnaise with rocket to go along with a main dish of Coronation chicken. The waiter commended them on their excellent choices and sauntered off with white linen napkin in hand.

"I believe," said Chapman in response, "that I have narrowed it down to three options. The first would be to set up a wonderful club in Paris with Dagmar."

"And the second and third options?"

"To run a pub here in London or work for MI5 after the war."

"Work for MI5? You can't be serious?"

"You cheeky bastard. Why you sound as skeptical as that pompous ass Ryde."

"Come on, you know I didn't mean it like that, Eddie. I just think that a free spirit like you has better things to do than be a buttoned-down bureaucrat. After the war, I doubt that even I will stay on at MI5."

"Is that a jest, sir? Why I thought you were a spit-polished secret service bloke through and through."

"No, Major Masterman is, but not me. And neither are you. Your sense of iconoclastic freedom is what makes you you, Eddie—and you bloody well know it."

"I suppose you're right. All the same, I don't know what I want to do going forward. I just know that I can't stand Major Ryde."

Robertson took a delicate sip of wine and gently daubed his damp upper lip with his white linen napkin. "Just let me and Major Masterman deal with him. The most important thing right now is that the Germans continue to trust you as one of their top agents. That's why Graumann recently sent you a message asking you to suggest a method for delivering a camera and money to a fellow German spy living in London. But he didn't just stop there. He also instructed you to find a suitable person who could monitor bomber formations at airfields in East Anglia."

"Is that what you want me to do?"

"No. Unfortunately, the Air Ministry vetoed any deception operation for fear of exposure. Which is why we're going to have you stall."

"What am I going to say?"

"That you're still searching for a recruit."

"Why?"

"Because the professional colleagues you need for the operation are in prison or otherwise unavailable."

"Sounds reasonable."

"There are many things you can do to help the war effort, Eddie."

"Such as?"

"Such as helping the Allies when they get to Paris in identifying German intelligence officers and agents posing as civilian war refugees."

"I could be useful in such a role, and I could reconnect with Dagmar in Paris."

"Yes, there is that prospect too." It was apparent to Robertson that, unlike during Chapman's first go-around, the state of the war effort had changed dramatically and so, too, had Zigzag's role in the conflict. In the last few months of the fighting, the double agent would have a less critical role to perform, though he would still have an opportunity to make a difference. To all intents and purposes, he and the other doubles would be increasingly sidelined in the coming months as Double Cross wound down and became of less strategic importance.

"Maybe I should just quit," blurted Chapman, taking Robertson by surprise.

"I would rather you didn't do that. We need you, Eddie."

"Do you though? Because it seems as if at this point in the war I might be more useful to the Americans, or even the French."

"I'm afraid that's out of the question."

"Why? I could offer my services to the Yanks or French as an agent. I could be of great value to them and reunite with Dagmar in Paris, and after the war we could open our club together."

"Churchill won't allow you to work for our competitors."

"I thought they were our allies."

"They are but only as long as the war lasts."

"But if I returned to France, I could help comb out any German underground movement which may have been left behind."

"That is something we can look into going forward. But for the time being, you're too valuable as a double agent in Britain feeding lies to the enemy."

"Maybe I should just open a club in the West End or a hotel in the South End. But surely you and your colleagues don't want any MI5 money—or any of the finances given to me by the Germans—to be used for such an enterprise."

"You're right, we don't. But that doesn't mean we wouldn't help you start up a legitimate enterprise. After all, you've done your country a great service."

"Thank you, that's good to hear."

"As far as I'm concerned, you have not only served your purpose as an intelligence operative, you have performed an extremely good and brave job. From that standpoint, perhaps it would be best if the case was to shut down and we give you a substantial sum of money."

"How substantial?"

"Something in the neighborhood of five thousand pounds."

"That's less than the Germans have given me."

"I know, but it's still a small fortune, enough that you could make a new life for yourself with Freda and Diane."

"If I did it, it would be with Dagmar."

"Well then, with Dagmar. I would get the payment approved with Brigadier Harker, and Freda and Diane would still continue to be taken care of per our previous agreement."

"I'll have to think about it."

"Yes, of course," and they fell into silence. Robertson realized that MI5's original assessment of Chapman's character had been spot-on. He had an unquenchable thirst for adventure and whenever things slowed down, he became intolerably bored and inevitably drifted back into criminal enterprise. That was why he was making bets on rigged dog races. The funny thing was only in the last two weeks could he even walk the streets of London alone in case he was arrested, for he was still wanted by Scotland Yard. Under British constitutional law no citizen could be pardoned for a crime unless he was already tried and convicted, so MI5 had simply implemented a behind-the-scenes campaign on behalf of their coveted agent. Scotland Yard and other police forces around Great Britain that might want to prosecute Agent Zigzag were quietly informed through Special Branch that the home secretary "desired that no such proceedings should be brought" and that "no action should be taken against him without prior consultation with MI5." This was, in essence, a full pardon for his past crimes, although Chapman was not informed that his slate had been wiped clean. The threat of prosecution remained a useful leash for Robertson and MI5 to control the double agent.

"I suppose I'm not all too keen to stop being a spy just yet," admitted Chapman after tossing back the remainder of his sauvignon blanc. "Isn't there an operation in which I could be useful?"

"As a matter of fact, there is. And just like before, it's top secret."

Zigzag's face lit up. "Tell me about it."

"As you know, the Germans are still very concerned about the vulnerability of their U-boats. We were rather hoping you might be willing to exploit those fears by relaying false classified information on their submarine devices."

"Go on."

"The idea is that you could dispatch messages to Graumann and the Abwehr that you have located a factory in the north of England where a new submarine detection device is being manufactured. You would claim that you were unable to obtain the device itself because the factory is in continual active operation, but you were able to steal documents and photographs from an office in the building."

"I could transcribe the documents and relay the descriptions by wireless, and I could send photographs via Lisbon."

"Precisely. The key is to play to German fears. As Graumann informed you during your time in France, the *Kriegsmarine* is alarmed by the rising U-boat toll in the Atlantic, North Sea, and Mediterranean. They believe that we have developed a new secret anti-submarine weapon that is destroying their U-boats in large numbers. You could be instrumental in the deception."

"What are you going to call the operation?"

"We were thinking of Operation Squid. What do you think?"

"I like it."

"So do I." Robertson smiled approvingly. He was only telling the double agent part of the story, of course. While the Germans believed some new and unprecedented anti-submarine tracking technology was the cause of the increased U-boat kills, the Germans were, as usual, wrong. The increased sinking of U-boats from Hamburg to Dover to Crete was due primarily to the Mark XXIV sea mine and the successful routine interception and decoding of U-boat signals using Ultra. As Robertson well knew, the most important British weapon in the underwater war was still the ability to pick up and read German U-boat radio traffic. However, if the Germans believed there was some other new and powerful underwater weapon in use, that fear should be encouraged and expanded—and Eddie Chapman alias Agent Fritz could be instrumental in that deception. In fact, British destroyers, frigates, and corvettes had recently been fitted with a device called a "Hedgehog," a mortar bomb that exploded on contact with a submarine. Most Secret Sources revealed that German intelligence had found out about the Hedgehog through careless talk by merchant seamen. Since the enemy already knew something about the weapons, the Royal Navy believed a great deal of misinformation could be loaded onto a little real information. By making the unimposing Hedgehog appear to be a beast of terrifying ferocity, Naval Intelligence hoped further to erode German morale and make the U-boat fleet wary of attacking convoys. Most importantly, if U-boat commanders feared that the British had a rocket-propelled device that could hunt them at the bottom of the ocean, then they would be less likely to dive deep. Nearer the surface they were easier to destroy.

"What do you say, Eddie? Are you game for a new deception?"

"Why I believe I am, Colonel."

"Good. Then we are back in the game."

"Yes, sir, we are back in the game."

And with that, the waiter appeared with Robertson's Parmesan and herb breaded plaice fillets and Chapman's British Lion egg and cress and tuna mayonnaise with rocket. To seal the deal and toast the occasion, the colonel ordered another bottle of sauvignon blanc.

CHAPTER 76

LANGBALLE-BREIEN APARTMENT, OSLO

AUGUST 29, 1944

"I'M LEAVING YOU, ANNEMARIE. I've packed a bag and will collect the rest of my belongings later this week. I'm moving out."

She had just returned to her apartment and her husband was sitting on the couch. His cheeks were rose-colored, and she could tell he had been drinking. Like many Norwegians, he had been doing it more and more as the war wore on. They had been arguing for over a year now about her peculiar relationship with Fehmer and she had known for some time that this sad and contentious day would come. But still she was surprised. He was finally following through with his threat to leave her and it appeared they would now be separated.

"I can't stand you being with that Nazi bastard any longer. Everyone we know is talking about you two and I'm sick and tired of it."

"I know you are and I'm sorry," she said, wanting to calm him down since he was drunk. A man who had been drinking was hard to reason with and posed a physical danger, and Kjell Langballe was no exception.

"You've humiliated me, goddamn you!" he blurted, and it was then she realized the true cause of his hurt.

She edged closer to him on the couch, presenting an expression of sympathy. "But I love you and you know how important the work I do is for the Resistance."

"I know your work is important, but I don't care anymore. The Allies have taken Paris and the war will soon be over. People are calling you Fehmer's whore and I can't take it anymore."

She tried to take him by the hand, but he pushed her away. His face was now tomato-red, and she realized he had probably drank much more than she thought. "You know that's a lie," she said, still hoping to calm him down. "You're my husband and I love you."

"Do you deny that you have feelings for him?"

Do I? she wondered, but she realized she already knew the answer—and it scared her. All the same, she wanted to deny it to herself. "It is you I have married and love, Kjell. Captain Fehmer is a means to an end, nothing more."

"*Captain* Fehmer? You act like he's an honorable military officer when he's a fucking Gestapo torturer and murdering son of a bitch! Captain? Seriously?"

"He's freed over sixty Norwegian prisoners, many of whom are major contributors to the Home Front. Do you not think that is worth something?"

"Have you been fucking him? Is that how you've convinced him to do this?"

It took great effort for her not to slap her husband for the slurred insult. "I'm not going to talk to you when you're like this."

"You'll talk to me when I say, woman."

"You're drunk. You don't know what you're saying."

She rose from the couch and went and sat in the chair to gain some much-needed distance between them.

"Yes, I'm drunk, and I'm going to get a whole lot drunker." He pulled a concealed bottle of aquavit from beneath his jacket resting on the couch.

She frowned. "You've been walking around town drinking from a bottle like a common drunk? What, you had to do it to screw up your courage to finally confront me so you're going to drink a whole bottle of liquor? Is that it?"

He glowered at her for a long moment before tossing back his head and taking a hefty gulp from the bottle. Then he smacked his lips, aggressively. For the first time, she realized she might be in danger. They had had arguments before, but not like this, and especially not when he was this drunk. He had been simmering for more than a year now and his anger was pouring out of him like a busted dam.

"*Tyskertøs.* I can't believe I would ever hear that word used to describe my own fucking wife."

"I have not done anything with that…that man. I am no adulterer."

"But you have cozied up to him—and that's all that matters. My God, you've even visited him at the hospital as if you're his own personal nurse."

"Yes, I have visited him at the hospital several times, but I have not cozied up to him, I promise you."

"Are you saying that you haven't kissed him or held hands with him? Are you saying that you have not had any sexual relations with him, or encouraged him in any way?"

She felt herself stiffen reflexively. "I…it's not…I mean we haven't…" She was unable to finish the words and realized that she had faltered badly.

"Jesus Christ, you have fucked him!"

"No, I haven't. We…I mean we held hands and…and we kissed…but that was just once and I…I felt terrible afterwards. You've got to believe me, Kjell."

"You're telling me you haven't spread your legs for him?"

"I have not had sex with him, I promise you. Nor would I ever."

"But you've led him on by holding hands and kissing him. You and that Nazi fuck have had sexual relations. Goddamn you, I should have left you two summers ago when this all started!"

"How do you think I get so much valuable information for Milorg and all of these people released from prison? By not spending time and ingratiating myself with him? It's all for the war effort, damnit!"

He tossed back another slug of the liquor, setting the bottle down on the table. "No, it's not. You have fucking feelings for him."

She wanted to rise up in her own defense, but she was unable to say anything. She knew he was right: she did have feelings for Fehmer.

Damn him! Damn the Nazi bastard for making me feel all confused!

"Your parents don't approve of what you're doing any more than I do, you know," Kjell Langballe then snarled.

"Yes, I know you've been speaking with them. But what you say isn't true. They support what I am doing for the war effort. My father, brother, and several extended family members would still be in prison if not for the work I'm doing with that man you so despise. You know, he doesn't have to set anyone free—and yet he does. Don't you see, there is good in him after all."

"He's just manipulating you to get information. By falsely posing as a humanitarian, he is stealthily infiltrating the Home Front."

"But I'm not giving him information. I'm getting it from him. I warned Milorg twice that Fehmer was planning a raid on Radio Corncrake on Nesodden, but nothing was done."

"There wasn't enough time."

"That's not my fault. I informed my contact as soon as I learned of the raid."

"I wish Fehmer had been killed instead of wounded. Then we would no longer be in this mess." He snatched the bottle from the table and tossed back another blast. "I've got to go. I can't stand to look at your fucking face anymore."

She started to cry, feeling deeply ashamed. But she was not going to quit the work she was doing on behalf of the Resistance. It was too damned important, and her husband had shown his true colors today. He may have once loved her, but he didn't now. The only thing he seemed to care about was whether she had slept with Fehmer or not. He was more worried about his own reputation and being humiliated than he was about preserving their marriage or saving human lives.

He took another swig and staggered to his feet. "I should beat the shit out of you, you little fucking whore!"

For a moment, she said nothing as the tears poured from her eyes and onto her white blouse. Then she said quietly, "I'm sorry that's how you feel. But I'm not giving up the fight."

"Then fuck you!" He slammed back the last of the aquavit and threw the empty bottle against the wall, shattering the glass into a hundred little pieces. He then picked up his bag and went to the door, turning around when he reached it. "I'll pick up the rest of my things on Saturday. Make sure you're not within a hundred yards of this apartment, or I'll fucking strangle you!"

When he left, slamming the door behind him, she put her hands to her face and wept.

CHAPTER 77

BREMEN, GERMANY

AUGUST 30, 1944

AS HE DROVE ACROSS THE TANNIN-COLORED WESER, von Gröning was stunned at the punishment inflicted by the Allies on his beautiful city. He had managed to scrounge up an old, bullet-ridden Mercedes-Benz W31 three-axle staff car, though no driver was available, and was navigating along General Ludendorff Street with his younger sister Dorothea and her adopted Jewish daughter, Alice. In the Middle Ages, the historic town in Northwestern Germany had been a major trading center and was enclosed by a solid protective wall; now it was reduced to a wilderness of devastation of bomb-razed buildings and endless piles of rubble. As the German spymaster drove, he only wished that his family's historic mansion at Am Wall 113 had managed to escape the latest round of bombardment and was still standing.

The city of Bremen had been thrashed beneath the shadows of British bombs since May 1940. The British nighttime bombing raids—later joined with those of the U.S. 8th Air Force in daytime raids—grew increasingly frequent and devastating in subsequent years. In the last year alone, thousands of German civilians had been killed and wounded by the hundreds of roaring Wellingtons, Lancasters, Stirlings, and Halifaxes that descended upon the city like swooping vultures. Von Gröning had heard about the damage to his home town, and he had seen Berlin transformed from a beautiful city to a concrete wasteland, but he and Dorothea had yet to see with their own eyes what fate had befallen the place where they grew up. The Focke-Wulf factory, AG Weser U-boat construction yard, Kunsthalle Bremen art museum, local gasworks, and city's merchant-navy college were among the badly damaged buildings they had seen thus far during their visit to the beleaguered city.

As they left the bridge and entered his old neighborhood, his sister gazed out from the passenger seat and said, "*Das sind die Ruinen von Pompeii.*" Those are the ruins of Pompeii.

"*Traurig,*" was all he could say. Sad.

They drove north towards the Am Wall, one of the oldest and most historic residential and commercial streets in Bremen. A flood of pleasant childhood memories flooded through his brain, images that were wholly incompatible with the devastation he saw all around him. From the exhaustion on the faces of the citizens on the street and the appalling wreckage of the city, the conclusion was inescapable: Germany was facing certain defeat in the war, and the aftermath would be even worse than the ignominy following the Great War a generation earlier, when he had returned home with his Iron Cross as a young cavalry officer. He noticed that some houses were standing and quietly prayed that somehow the von Gröning family home—that great five-story symbol of aristocratic eminence where he and Dorothea had been raised by their father Heinrich and mother Helene—had not been flattened by Allied bombers.

And then they turned the corner onto Am Wall and saw that their worst fears were confirmed. The mansion had been leveled to the ground as if a giant had stomped in and squashed it underfoot, leaving only a ruined pile of rubble. Although he had considered it unlikely that the old family home would still be standing, he was nonetheless surprised. Luckily, no lives had been lost during the bombing of the house: the cook, chauffeur, valet, gardener, maids, and other servants had been laid off before the invasion of France. All the same, it was a pitiful sight and his sister began to cry. The gilded carriage had been stolen, the family cars commandeered by the Nazis, and now the family had suffered the humiliation of the destruction of their once-resplendent home. Further down the block, he could see hunched-over men, women, and children picking through the wreckage of the other beveled houses.

"We'd better poke around and see if there's anything of value," he said, though he knew that was unlikely.

They stepped from the car and began combing through the splintered wood and rubble. Now little Alice was crying too, and von Gröning couldn't help but be struck by the irony. The Allies had bombed the home where the young Jewish girl might have been able to live. As they rummaged through the wasteland, he soon realized that he had lost everything. Months earlier, he had converted much of his money into articles of value—assets that could be moved easily in the unpredictable aftermath of defeat—and stashed them in the attic of the mansion. But it was all to no avail and he had lost everything: his pictures, antiques, china, silver, and other valuable *objets d'art*—all the remains of his great inheritance—had been stored in the attic and were now obliterated.

"There's nothing left," said his sister in disbelief, echoing his thoughts. "They've destroyed everything."

He shook his head sadly, saying nothing.

"Hitler's responsible for this—the bastard," she cursed in an enraged whisper, so her daughter couldn't hear. "I wish he had been killed in that bomb in July."

"That makes two of us. But unfortunately, the plot failed."

The assassination attempt had happened six weeks ago on July 20, and the aftermath of the failed bombing orchestrated by Colonel Claus von Stauffenberg's and the German Military Resistance had proved to have a deleterious ripple effect upon von Gröning and other liberal, anti-Hitler officers like him. Stauffenberg had planted a bomb in an attaché case in a conference room at the Wolf's Lair, the Führer's command post for the Eastern Front near the East Prussian town of Rastenburg. The device exploded against the heavy leg of an oak table, which shielded the Nazi leader from the full force of the blast. Von Gröning knew that Chapman, an expert with explosives, would never have made such a fundamental mistake. More than five thousand members of the German military and intelligence services had thus far been arrested in the aftermath of the failed plot, including Admiral Wilhelm Canaris and his deputy, General Hans Oster. Most had been tried, convicted of treason, and hung, but Canaris and several other high-ranking figures were being held until more incriminating evidence could be gathered or they could be used as bargaining chips for the inevitable reckoning with Nazi Germany by the Allies at war's end. Von Gröning had not been implicated in the plot, but as a wealthy and progressive Abwehr officer of the old school with anti-Nazi views, he knew that he had been, and probably still was, under suspicion.

"I hate Hitler," Dorothea said to him. "Look what he has done to our country."

Tears poured from her eyes and she pulled Alice close and hugged her. For a moment, they both just clutched one other fiercely and cried. He just shook his head and stared to the north at the bomb-cratered landscape and incinerated trees next to the canal. The once-verdant field and forest had turned into a pockmarked, blackened world devoid of life. Or hope. Looking to the west up Am Wall Street, he saw only a single four-story building standing in the neighborhood. It looked like a little island in a sea of rubble.

The sight of the single standing home made him feel sad and lonely inside, and he wondered if Germany would ever become whole again. Did he even want to return home after the war, or should he go to Britain or America? More importantly, would the Allies even take him? With all the Allied bombing, millions of dead amid the rubble, and Nazis still in post-war administrative power because they would be needed to make the trains run on time, what would there be to return to? Von Stauffenberg and the German Resistance had tried to kill Hitler, but they had failed miserably. Was there not someone out there who could successfully rescue the Fatherland from the maniac Führer who was destroying the country and its people for his demented Thousand Year Reich? Was there no way to get rid of Hitler?

They picked through the rubble for nearly an hour before calling it quits. The only item of value he was able to recover was a singed silver plate engraved with the names of his fallen comrades in the White Dragoons. He had loved fighting and drinking with those brave young men during the Great War, but he had seen far too many of them die. And now he was stuck in a second world war that was still killing millions even though Allied victory was no longer in doubt. It sickened him.

They started for the car. As they were about to climb back in, they saw a column of SS *polizeiregiment* troops, more than a hundred men, goose-stepping down the street. Nearly all of them were old men in their forties or older, and as they marched they were singing *Hupf, Mein Mädel*—Skip, My Lassie—a sappy ditty that front-line soldiers had enjoyed singing since the invasion of Poland. Von Gröning found the song insufferably annoying.

He, Dorothea, and her daughter just stared at them, almost incomprehensibly. The clap of more than one hundred fifty boots echoed on the battered pavement and carried up the wide street. The *polizeiregiment* troops, marching three abreast, wheeled right onto General Ludendorff Street. They were singing at the top of their lungs, their chests pushed forward like crowing roosters. Von Gröning looked into his sister's eyes and saw hate, then he looked at young Alice and saw mortal fear in the little girl's eyes. She clung to her adoptive mother's skirt. Looking back at the soldiers, he realized that he hated and feared them too. In his eyes, they were Nazi monsters not human beings. He studied them closely as they marched in lockstep, singing in unison, and he wished he had a machine-gun and could mow them all down. The SS troops filled the entire street, tramping rhythmically, and then they disappeared around the corner out of sight.

"We should get out of here," he said. "There is nothing left for us here."

"When the war is over, will there be any hope left for the Fatherland?" asked Dorothea rhetorically, staring out at the blackened, bomb-scorched woods and grass next the canal.

"I don't know. All I know is the war is lost."

"All this madness has led to is our ruin. It has all been for nothing but the destruction of our country." His sister looked at him with a devastated look on her face, her lower lip trembling with emotion as she clutched her Jewish daughter's hand. There were tears in her eyes.

"Then we'll have to pick up the pieces and make a better world for Alice," he said.

And with that, they climbed back into the car and left.

CHAPTER 78

DAGMAR WAS SOUND ASLEEP, in the midst of a strange dream, when the external sound registered in her unconscious mind. It didn't even sound real, which is why she thought it was part of her dream. But then she thought she knew what it was: the sound of jiggling keys outside the door of her apartment at Tullins gate 4a. Or was it a set of lock picks?

The sound wasn't particularly loud or obtrusive, but it was enough to awaken her from her slumber. Opening her eyes, she listened for a moment half-consciously, hoping the noise would stop so she could roll over and go back to sleep. She remained silent and motionless, casting an ear towards the front door, trying to separate out the noise from the sound of the wind outside her apartment.

Then she heard a light chuff of shoes across creaking floorboards and the sound of a key—or, again, was it a lock pick—and she knew she was in serious trouble.

Someone was breaking into the apartment! Was it the Gestapo?

Crawling quietly from her bed, she slipped on a robe hanging from the nearby chair and reached for a precious stone of amethyst on the table. It wasn't much of a weapon, but it would have to do.

She moved stealthily to the wall next to the door, gripping the violet chunk of decorative rock like a paper weight. There it was again, a soft footfall. Every sense was suddenly acute.

The noise outside the door stopped.

She waited for what seemed like an eternity. But there was nothing.

Then she heard the floorboards creak again and the sound of something scraping and being lifted. Something heavy.

She stepped up next to the door, clasping the stone in her right hand. Carefully, she slid her hand along the bumpy wall, feeling for the light switch.

It was then she saw the door slowly start to open.

Her entire body froze as a tremor of fear lanced through her. Who the hell was it? Could it be that terrifying Nazi bastard Siegfried Fehmer?

The door inched open a crack. Then some more, slowly.

She felt a taut knot of muscle squeezing her chest.

A shadow of a figure fell across the open doorway.

Pressing herself against the wall so she could jump out at the last second, she hoped to take the intruder by surprise. She felt her heart palpitating in her chest, threatening to explode, and she thought of her beloved Eddie. She wished he was here to protect her. She glanced down at the block of amethyst, felt the solid heft of it in her hands. It wasn't a bad weapon, but she still wished she had something heavier.

Summoning her courage, she edged closer to the slowly opening door, the rock gripped tightly in her right hand.

She raised the weapon to strike.

Suddenly, the light turned on and she was momentarily blinded.

Then she heard a loud whisper.

"Goddamnit, were you going to hit me?" It was Ishmael. He quickly closed the door behind him.

"What the hell are you doing here?" she fired back.

"Shush, you must speak in a quiet voice. I am sorry if I scared you, but I had to talk to you. My cell has been infiltrated and I had to warn you."

She lowered her voice but not its urgency. "That entitles you to break into my apartment? There are SS all over this neighborhood. How did you get in anyway?"

"Lock pick. I am an expert."

"You could have just knocked."

"No, that would wake too many people, and I didn't know if you were here. I'm afraid I have to hide out here for the night."

They stepped into the living room. She led him to a stuffed couch and they sat down. He looked around the small but handsomely furnished room.

"I can see the Germans have been taking good care of you. You have some new furniture."

"I am their insurance for their spy whom they have no idea is a British double agent. That's why they treat me well. They gave him the Iron Cross for a reason."

"How much are they paying you these days?"

"Still six hundred kroner per month. It's taken from Fritz's share per his agreement with Graumann."

"That's not bad. Are you ever going to tell me your boyfriend's real name?"

"No, as I've told you a dozen times already, I promised him I would keep it a secret. To be honest, I have told you too much already."

"As your control officer, I'd say that's debatable. Have you had word from him?"

"No, I have not. But I believe by now he has made it to England." She looked at him. "Why are you here? This can't be the best place to hide out and you could get me in trouble."

"You are wrong. This is the best place to hide out for the simple reason that is right under the Germans' noses. That's why Graumann put you up here: this is the Nazi part of the city."

"Yes well, I don't feel very safe with you here."

"I'll be gone by morning."

"Are you on the run?"

"As a matter of fact, I am."

"Then you didn't plan on coming here."

"Let's just say I happened to be in the neighborhood."

"Five hours after curfew."

"I'm afraid so. Tell me more what you've been up to. It's been three weeks since our last meeting. You need to bring me up to date because I'm going to have to go underground for a while. Unlike you, I am not under the protection of the Abwehr."

"You act as though I am not at risk. If the Germans ever found out that I am a Milorg operative, they will send me to a forced labor camp in Northern Norway. That's why I am considering taking on a new job that will protect me."

"Protect you?"

"Yes, through my German contacts I have met this driver. He lives in my building and his name is Iredi."

"Iredi?"

"SS-*Oberscharführer* Otto Paul Iredi. He works as the driver for Fehlis."

"The chief of the *Sicherheitspolizei*—now that is a big fish. Good heavens, how have you managed to infiltrate Fehlis's circle?"

"By luck and circumstance. Sergeant Iredi is in Sipo *Abteilung II D3*, the administrative department for the raid truck fleets that have been hitting the radio transmission stations. I know him."

"So Iredi has access to Fehlis?"

"Not only is he his personal driver, but he works in his office and is a source of information on the man. He knows his daily routines and has access to documents and other kinds of information that could be useful."

Ishmael looked at her thoughtfully. "Fehlis is Milorg's top assassination target along with Fehmer and Terboven. This Iredi is unquestionably an important connection. But does he trust you?"

"Yes, in fact, he has proposed that I work for Sipo. He says he can get me a job."

"In what department?"

"Letter censorship at the main post office here in Oslo. I would read and check letters coming from Sweden to Norway. Many Norwegian women work in the letter censorship department."

"Yes, I'm quite aware of that."

"I was going to ask you if I should take the job to aid in the Resistance effort. I haven't decided on it yet."

"When did Iredi talk to you about it?"

"A couple of days ago. He said there might be an opening in the near future and that he could help get me the job."

"You certainly are getting cozy with these Germans."

"Fuck you. You know perfectly well how much I hate these bastards. What I do in this war I have done for Norway, and I provided cover for Eddie that allowed him to gather ten times the intelligence that he would have been able to gather on his own. We photographed more than a dozen military installations, offices, and U-boat pens together with me posing as his Norwegian girlfriend, so don't treat me like a schoolgirl from Eidsvoll."

"But you are a schoolgirl from Eidsvoll."

"Not anymore I'm not. I'm a trained spy and just as clever as you."

He nodded grudgingly. "All right, you should take the job. It sounds promising. You could be a fly on the wall and have access to important communications."

"And who am I to report to if you have to close down your cell and seek refuge in Sweden?"

"I don't know yet. But someone will get in touch with you."

"I certainly hope they don't pick my lock and sneak in at night."

"Don't worry, they won't. No one can pick a lock like me."

"Except for my British friend."

"You were in love with him, weren't you?"

"I still am. We're going to get married and open a club together in Paris after the war."

"You'd better hope he survives then."

"As I told you, I believe he's safely back in Britain by now. But enough about him. The question is what's going to happen to me?"

"What do you mean?"

"You and Eddie have been my only contacts who know I've been working for the Norwegian Resistance and British intelligence the past three years. If something happens to you two, who's going to vouch for me when the war is over? Right now, virtually everyone I know thinks I'm a Nazi's tart, even my friend Mary Larsen. I have sworn secrecy to you and to Fritz, and you two are the only ones who know I'm with the Home Front and supported British intelligence."

"Don't worry, I've got you covered."

"But if something happens to you, who will know that I am a Milorg operative? You are on the run from the Germans. If you are arrested or killed, who is going to vouch for me?"

"I told you I would take care of it. Now where am I going to sleep?"

"Here on the couch."

"All right then. Please get me a pillow and…" He left the words hanging.

"And what?"

"And don't worry. Everything will work out."

"You promise?"

"Yes, I promise," he said, but inside Dagmar wasn't so sure. If she took the Sipo job, she would once again be getting in deep with the Germans and create even more doubt amongst her countrymen.

And it scared the hell out of her.

CHAPTER 79

6A TULLINS GATE, OSLO

SEPTEMBER 12, 1944

"THANK YOU FOR RELEASING THREE MORE PRISONERS, SIEGFRIED. You are making a genuine difference in people's lives."

Fehmer reached out and touched Annemarie Breien's smooth cheek. They were sitting on his sumptuously furnished couch in his apartment not far from Gestapo headquarters. "I told you I would do it. You didn't believe me, did you?"

"Of course, I did. You may be the sworn enemy of Norway, but you have never gone back on your word. It was a good and noble thing you did today."

She leaned forward and kissed him. He knew it was merely a reward for his good behavior, but he still felt his head swimming with euphoria and kissed her back. Her lips were warm and soft and moist. *I did it partly as a gesture of good faith, Annemarie, but mostly I did because I am madly in love with you. Do you have any idea how much I love you?*

She pulled away gently and looked him in the eyes. "Do you want to…?" She left the words unfinished, but he knew what she meant. The look on her face made his blood turn warm and his body thrill with excitement.

But she wasn't like Gerda and his other conquests. With her, he wanted to be gentle and loving and play the part of the gentleman not the Lothario.

"Are you sure?" he asked.

"Yes," she said. "But in the bedroom."

"Of course," he said, and he escorted her to the room. As they quietly undressed, he pictured them in the heat of passion and felt himself growing hard at the thought of the squeaking bed and her moaning voice. The sight of her exquisite, perfectly lubricious body cast a spell over him. He had been waiting for this moment for two years now and couldn't believe it was finally about to happen. He would be on top and her nubile, young body would bend to him and take him in and then they would arch and thrust in unison and swim together in the ecstasy of an orgasm.

He set his clothes on the chair and peered out the window. The three-quarters moon radiated a restrained brilliance—like a freshly burnished silver candlestick. She climbed under the covers and he turned to join her. As he slipped in next to her, he caught his reflection in the mirror as the light of the silvery moon caught him momentarily. One-half of his face basked in the glow of the fluted light, while the other remained masked in darkness. It was as if one half of him was good, the other half evil.

So be it, he thought with quiet resignation. *That's what I am.*

They began to kiss passionately. Again, he couldn't believe it was about the happen. He had been fantasizing about making love to her for so long it seemed unfathomable that it was finally happening. Her lips tasted as sweet as honey.

After a moment, he slid beneath her so that she was on top.

They continued to kiss and he fondled and sucked her breasts before slipping inside. As they began to move together as one, the world began to spin in a pleasant way and he felt like he was a little boy back in Berlin on a merry-go-round. He arched his back and kissed her lips as she slid back and forth on top of him. A churning euphoric sensation took hold of his lower stomach. He kissed her on her hard, slippery nipple as they continued to thrust in unison. Her womanly scent was fresh and scented, like a field of Norwegian summer wildflowers from the Dovre and Jotunheimen mountains. His arms reached out and clasped her smooth bottom. He pulled her to him, plunging upward, deeper. She let out a moan and he could feel himself about to let go.

He thought: *I want to come with you; it's always best that way.*

He had waited two years for this. Two long years.

ψψψ

As their lips softly touched, Annemarie felt desire flowing through her veins. But she also felt fear. By making love with Siegfried, she had opened a door into a new and potentially dangerous world and it frightened her. At the same time, her head swam with euphoria.

"Oh, Siegfried," she whispered in his ear.

He rolled her over so that he was on top. His tongue reached inside her mouth, softly, and she kissed him back. She felt a delightful shudder of excitement take hold of her entire body, but with it came the sense of danger, of doing something that was taboo. What would her family, friends, and fellow members of the Resistance think of her now?

She knew the answer: they would be shocked and revolted and call her a *tyskertøs.*

She felt a sudden wave of confusion and her body tightened reflexively. At the same time, she felt an emotional connection that gripped her. The man making love to her may have been a rabid Nazi, but there was some good in him and she knew that he cared deeply about her. Despite her conflicted feelings, she knew she was tapping into something sacrosanct, something only true lovers felt.

He does love me. But still, you shouldn't be doing this.

She kissed his mouth, nibbling his lips gently. A moment later, when he thrust deeper, it was like a perfect dream. Everything about it felt right, natural.

And yet she still felt terribly guilty.

You shouldn't be doing this, Annemarie. You shouldn't be doing this.

But he was a generous lover and she put the thought out of her mind. As they began to move together in a gentle rhythm, she took more and more pleasure in his body, in his kisses and caresses and thrusts.

Her body was responding with a passion she thought she no longer possessed. Her separated husband Kjell had certainly never made love to her with this much passion. She was resurrecting glorious emotions that she had never known she possessed.

He thrust back and forth knowingly, in a gentle rhythm. His mouth suckled her swelling nipples, and she gasped with delight.

She wondered if it were possible to go insane with pleasure.

He kissed her on the lips tenderly and she slid her tongue deep into his mouth, clasping his tight buttocks and pulling him deeper inside her. She moaned softly between kisses; she could tell the sound of her voice deeply aroused him.

As the pace quickened, the air filled with desperation. She felt herself letting loose with excitement, coming as never before. She sensed that he too was about to let go of his seed.

"Look into my eyes," she gasped, pulling him still deeper.

He pulled his head up and his eyes locked onto hers. "I'm looking, I'm looking!"

She stared at him mesmerically, her eyes as wide as pebbles as the climax came. They held each other's gaze as their bodies shook fitfully and she felt his warmth flowing inside her. Then suddenly tears streamed from her eyes.

"What happened?" he asked, worriedly. "Did I hurt you?"

"No!" she cried.

"Are you upset? What...what has happened?"

"I'm overwhelmed. I'm overwhelmed with joy."

"Then why are you crying?"

"Because I hate myself."

"Hate yourself? But I don't understand."

"I hate myself for what I've done because you are the enemy and we can never be, Siegfried. We can never be and you and I both know it. I am sorry, but it is the truth."

CHAPTER 80

CRADLING A WHISKEY, Chapman stared drunkenly out his bedroom window at yet another bleak London skyline, his mind once again harkening back to sunny summer days making love to Dagmar and sailing Oslo Fjord with her on his little yawl. The year of intimacy with his Norwegian beauty had been the best year of his life, and he couldn't help but wonder if he would ever find such joy again. Would he and Dagmar ever make their dream come true by getting married, moving to Paris, and opening their club? Or was it all just an impossible fantasy?

He was still on full German pay with his living expenses paid for by the British, but he was miserable. After the romance and heart-thumping danger of his earlier clandestine days of the war, the naval deceptions involving the fictitious Hedgehog anti-submarine device that the Germans seemed to be buying hook, line, and sinker seemed terribly tame. Even more bored and restless than during the summer, he was spending an increasing amount of his time with his hard-drinking criminal friends, a half dozen of whom were sprawled in his sitting room in a drunken stupor, including his old safecracking mate Jimmy Hunt from the Jelly Gang, who had recently been released from prison. He was hosting a party and they had been drinking heavily for the past four hours straight, but the prodigious alcohol he had consumed only served to darken his mood and make his future seem even more precarious.

Michael Ryde was sucking the life out of him. To make matters worse, he knew that the control officer looked down his nose at him and was actively trying to undermine him before Tar Robertson and John Masterman. Ryde was obsessed with his close relationship to Graumann, and the other day at the safe house, after Chapman had transmitted his morning message to Germany, the major had deftly steered the conversation towards the doktor. Then, over the next few minutes, he had bombarded him with questions while trying to act nonchalant, as if he was simply making conversation. At first, Chapman hadn't any sort of ruse. But he quickly realized that Ryde thought he was withholding information about his relationship with the German spymaster and was probing for something he could use to hang him.

"Do you think Dr. Graumann and the Germans ever had any suspicion that you were being worked under control?" Ryde had begun innocently, and then, before Chapman could answer, he continued, as if thinking aloud: "If Graumann did suspect this, it is unlikely that he would reveal his suspicions as it is in his own personal interest to keep the case going as long as possible."

"You're quite right," Chapman confirmed without hesitation. "Graumann is my best security."

"What do you mean?" asked Ryde, leading him along.

"He has made a great deal of money out of the case. For example, when I ask for six thousand pounds, he probably draws twelve thousand and pockets the change."

It was at that moment Chapman realized what Ryde was up to. He cursed himself for his lapse in judgment and swiftly changed the subject. But from Ryde's smarmy expression he could tell it was too late and the damage was done. If he and Graumann were in league embezzling money from their Abwehr superiors, he could see Ryde's mind working, then it was likely that Chapman had confided that he was working for the British. If so, then the German spymaster, for reasons of greed and ambition, was betraying his own country with an agent he knew to be false. This evidence of financial collusion, Ryde was no doubt thinking, increased the chance that Agent Fritz-Zigzag had revealed his true identity as a British double agent. Even if it was unlikely that Graumann would report the betrayal to his superiors, since his own fate was on the line, it was still a serious breach of security protocol and proof that Chapman was a liar, or at least a withholder of information. Furthermore, if he had revealed his true identity to Dagmar and Graumann, who else might he have let in on the secret? Ryde was a prig and a pompous ass, but he was still a cunning and ruthless spy with the intuitive ability to detect a lie, and Chapman knew he had been caught red-handed.

Tossing back the last of his whiskey, he grabbed the pack of American Camel cigarettes sitting on his dresser and rejoined his inebriated mates back in the sitting room. As he turned to walk back in the room, he heard a burst of bawdy laughter from Jimmy Hunt, whom Chapman had christened "the prince of all safe breakers." A cool, self-possessed, and determined character when he was sober, he had been a key figure in Chapman's early criminal career as a safecracker and done three years for a post-office job and safe breaking. Later Hunt, while in prison, had played a crucial role in his second career as a spy by serving as one of his imaginary criminal contacts that had helped him pull off the de Havilland deception. Chapman walked into the room. Sitting and standing all around Hunt were a dozen characters from Chapman's felonious past and increasingly dubious present, including the pugilistic brawler George Walker, a hard-drinking journalist named Frank Owens, and several members of the Soho underworld that MI5 would no doubt consider "undesirables." The room was so loud from jabbering and laughter that it was hard to hear.

"All right, quiet down you cocksuckers, I'm telling a bloody joke," cried the boxer George Walker. He waited a moment for people to stop talking before continuing. "How do you tell British and American planes from the bloody Germans?"

"I don't know, tell us, Georgie!" cried Chapman gleefully.

"When a green plane flies overhead, it's British. When there's a silver plane streaking across the sky, it's American. And when there's no aircraft at all, it's the bloody fucking Luftwaffe!"

"Here, here, Georgie!" the gang of underworld figures roared.

"Okay, now it's my turn," said the jobby journalist Frank Owens. "Hitler, Göring, and Goebbels are standing atop the Berlin radio tower. Hitler says he wants to do something to put a smile on the faces of the German people. So Göring and Goebbels say at the same time: 'Good idea. Why don't you bloody jump?'"

Again, the room exploded with drunken laughter. Eddie and Owens clinked glasses and downed the contents.

"You shouldn't laugh too hard though," added Owens after belching loudly. "I heard that a German factory worker was executed for telling that one."

"What?" cried one the revelers. "Just for telling a bloody fucking joke?"

"I heard that too," said Chapman. "All right, gents, now it's my turn. I met an RAF pilot the other day at a bar."

"What bar?" asked Walker.

"I can't tell you that, Georgie, or else you might go there and embarrass me!"

They all laughed and drank some more.

Chapman continued, "So this pilot sits down on the stool next to me and he says, 'The skies are clear of German aircraft over England now, but not so over France and Germany. In fact, the situation is really tough.'"

"I said to him, 'Is that so, mate? I didn't know that.'"

"'Aye,' he says. 'The Germans still have a strong air force on the continent. Why just the other day I was protecting the bombers and suddenly, out of the clouds, these Fokkers appeared.'"

Owens and several others giggled.

"'I looked up, and right above me was one of them. I aimed at him and shot him down. They were swarming. I immediately realized that there were several other Fokkers behind me, coming at me with their guns blazing.'"

More laughter.

"'Now I think I should point out to you,' the pilot continued, 'that *Fokker* is the name of the German-Dutch aircraft company that makes the bloody planes. Did you know that?'"

"I said to him, 'Yes, I did.'"

"And he said, 'But of course that's beside the point.'"

"I asked him why."

"He said, 'Because these Fokkers were flying Messerschmitts!'"

The room erupted with laughter, backslapping, and clinking glasses. The noise lasted for several seconds before terminating abruptly. Chapman followed the gaze of Owens and several others to the front door and saw Ryde's MI5 deputy, an officer named Reisen, standing awkwardly inside the room in front of the door. *Oh shit!* thought Chapman as he realized that the junior case officer had come to the safe house to pick him up and drive him to Hendon to make his scheduled late afternoon radio transmission. Unfortunately, the lad had stumbled upon a scene of debauchery. But Chapman wasn't going to allow the little shit to ruin the festive occasion. Reisen's intrusion had already made the room uncomfortably silent.

Chapman smiled at him cordially. "Can I get you a drink, Lieutenant?" he asked.

"No thank you," said Reisen, his eyes gazing around the room and taking in the inebriated faces disapprovingly.

It was then the words Chapman later realized had sealed his fate with MI5 were spoken in a drunken slur.

"I suppose you have come to take Eddie away on a job," said his old Jelly Gang cohort Jimmy Hunt with a knowing grin.

The room turned so quiet Chapman could have heard a pin drop. He winced inside but said nothing.

"No, I just popped in for a visit," said Reisen innocently.

But Chapman could tell he was trying to cover up his astonishment with a cheerful, noncommittal reply. Reisen knew perfectly well that Hunt was referring to his friend's other career as a spy. And Chapman knew instantly that to MI5, the implication of Hunt's remark was clear: Agent Zigzag had violated his agreement with British Intelligence by disclosing that he had been working for the British Secret Service in the war effort. Chapman shook his head in dismay; he knew he had failed miserably. He had held his state secrets close for five years, but now, it seemed, he had blabbered unforgivingly. This time he had not brought a potentially useful Norwegian Resistance operative into his confidence, which though risky was at least excusable, he had spilled the beans to a newly liberated, extremely drunk convict, and in so doing he had served up his own head on a platter.

He looked at Reisen. The junior case officer wisely did not say anything in the presence of Jimmy Hunt and the others, but Chapman knew it didn't matter. The damage was done. By his expression alone, it was obvious that he had no doubt that Jimmy Hunt knew the nature of Chapman's work. Eddie cursed his bad luck: he had been overconfident, flush with cash, and telling colorful stories of his espionage activities to his hard-drinking underworld friends—and now it had come back to bite him.

You've really cocked it up now, he thought, picturing the face of the vindictive Ryde when Reisen delivered him the incriminating news. *Now the bastard will move in for the kill as if you are an enemy spy. May God help you.*

CHAPTER 81

MI5 HEADQUARTERS
58 ST. JAMES STREET

OCTOBER 24, 1944

WEARING HIS GLENGARRY CAP and Seaforth Highlanders' trousers, Robertson stared across the conference table at the humorless, priggish face of Michael Ryde. He knew that the major had been putting together a damning case against Eddie Chapman, and he wondered if there was anything he could do to stop it.

He was quite aware of the double agent's flaws and eccentricities, but he still believed him to be a critical resource in the war effort, as did many others on the Double Cross committee and Churchill himself. As he had put forward in a recent internal memorandum, he believed Chapman had "done an extremely good and brave job" and a "very considerable service for his country," and "that the best thing to do with the case was to shut it down and pay Zigzag off by giving him a fairly substantial sum of money." But now, it appeared as if circumstances might preclude an amicable ending to the relationship, though he reserved final say regarding Zigzag's termination along with John Masterman.

Seated at the conference table with them were Lieutenant Commander Ewen Montagu, the naval intelligence officer on the Double Cross Committee and orchestrator of the recent Hedgehog deceptions under Operation Squid; and John Marriott, a former London solicitor who had served as an MI5 lawyer and Robertson's deputy during the war. The honorable Ewen Montagu, RNVR, was the son of a Jewish banking magnate, a graduate of Harvard and Trinity College in Cambridge, one of the best fly fisherman in Britain, and worked alongside talented spymaster Ian Fleming in Room 39 of the Admiralty. Today, Robertson and Montagu would decide the fate of Chapman with input from the bean counter Ryde and the MI5 lawyer Marriott.

He nodded towards Ryde. "Very well, Major, you may proceed," he said.

"Yes, sir. As you gentlemen are aware, I have long suspected that Zigzag had no regard whatever for the necessity of observing complete silence regarding his connection with us here at MI5. Lieutenant Reisen recently called at the flat to take him out to Hendon for a transmission. On this occasion, Reisen found a number of undesirables in the flat, one of whom was Jimmy Hunt, who was already known to him. Upon his arrival, Hunt immediately said to him, 'I suppose you have come to take Eddie away on a job.' Reisen naturally did not pursue the remark in the presence of so many criminal types, but he felt quite certain that Hunt knew the nature of the job to which he referred."

"So, you're saying that Zigzag disclosed to Hunt that he was working for British intelligence? Is there further evidence he actually did this, or is this reference to 'a job' all you have?"

"That's it, Colonel, but in and of itself it is quite damaging."

"That remains to be seen. Go on."

"There's also the matter of Graumann. Zigzag has always spoken of him in the highest terms and has expressed something akin to affection for the 'old man' as he calls him. In a recent conversation with Zigzag, we touched on the subject of the security of the case and as to whether the Germans have any suspicion that he is being worked under control. When I remarked to him that, even if Graumann did suspect this, it was unlikely that he would reveal his suspicions as it is in his own personal interests to keep the case going as long as possible, he agreed without a moment's hesitation, and added that of course Graumann was his best security. When I asked him what he meant by that, he said the German spymaster has made a great deal of money out of the case."

"You're saying that Graumann is embezzling money."

"Quite so. As an example, when Zigzag asks for six thousand kroner, Graumann draws twelve thousand and pockets the change."

"Oh dear," said the lawyer Marriott. "That's certainly the definition of embezzlement."

"I agree," said Robertson. "But what's this got to do with Z's indiscretion?"

"I'm getting to that, sir. At the time of our conversation, it was my impression that Zigzag knew perfectly well what was in my mind but wasn't going to admit it, and my earlier suspicions were proven correct."

"Earlier suspicions?"

"I believe Zigzag has not only revealed his true identity to his Norwegian girlfriend Dagmar Lahlum and to Jimmy Hunt, but very likely to Graumann himself. If it's true that Graumann is aware of Zigzag's position in this country, it is very unlikely that anyone other than Graumann knows and there is probably little danger to us at the present. However, it may show that Zigzag withheld from us this very important piece of information and it is against our principles to run a case with anyone who is found not to be absolutely open with us."

That was not quite true, Robertson knew from experience. Most of the Double Cross agents under MI5's control were difficult to work with. No doubt many of them had revealed that they were working for the British Secret Service to friends and lovers, or at least secretly engaged in the support of the war effort. It was true Chapman had cocked things up by confiding in Dagmar Lahlum, but he had done so to bring her under his control as a valuable agent. Unfortunately, MI5 was still uncertain of her role in the Norwegian Resistance. Robertson had made a request to the Special Operations Executive Command Center to see if they could find anything in their records about her, but they had no word on her activities with Milorg, which suggested she was under deep cover.

Ryde superciliously pressed on: "As we discussed in September, sir, there have been several other instances of inexcusable negligence on Zigzag's part. He has been overheard boasting of his espionage activities in a Kensington pub with his criminal rabble."

Marriott rolled his eyes. "To his friends, that's just Eddie being Eddie. They're more likely to dismiss his colorful stories as Walter Mitty-esque fantasies than they are to believe him."

"I think not, and there is more. I myself have on different occasions seen Zigzag walk up to a Norwegian and address him in Norwegian. I have seen him in the company of highly undesirable characters, speaking to a German Jewess in German, a Frenchman in French. Even worse, I have heard him discussing with a man with a known criminal record conditions in Paris in such a way that it must have been apparent that he has been there within the last few months."

"Yes, yes, we saw your memo, Major," said Robertson. "But are you sure you're not doing all this just to spite Chapman? It goes without saying that these accusations have validity and the lad must be sternly dealt with, but are you doing this purely because you don't approve of him and want his case shut down? Because that's an insufficient reason, Major."

Ryde stiffened in his chair, but he said nothing to either refute or support what his superior had said.

For the first time, Montagu spoke. "What else do you have, Major? Because I must say from the naval perspective, the Operation Squid deception has been a resounding success. We haven't discovered yet precisely how the German *Kriegsmarine* has utilized the Hedgehog information, but we know from Most Secret Sources that the deception has succeeded in breeding maximum anxiety among German U-boat commanders and has been keeping them close to the surface. Thanks to Zigzag, the operation has been a triumph."

Ryde remained unimpressed. "But I very much doubt there is any substantial chance of the special photographs of the anti-submarine devices reaching Berlin. Which means that unless the Admiralty wants to carry on the case, I am convinced that we ought to close it down and part company with Zigzag as soon as possible without giving him any financial bonus."

Robertson looked at the major incredulously. "Are you saying you want to fire him and not give him a penny for what he's done for his country? You're quite serious?"

"I feel strongly that under the present circumstances it will be exceedingly difficult to justify the continuation of the Zigzag case. In my view, his irresponsible actions over the course of the past two months provide a first-class excuse for closing the case with him in the wrong and for the administration of a very firm rebuke. It should be made clear to him that he has broken the most elementary security rules and has had a complete disregard for the security of his own position and our interest in the case. In these circumstances, it seems to me that we should dismiss him, explaining that he has broken his side of the bargain and that from now on he need expect no assistance from us in any trouble he may find himself going forward."

"You don't think that's bit harsh and reactionary?"

"No, I don't. Having seen this immoral brigand up close these past two months, these recent revelations of his irresponsibility do not surprise me. As I've said previously, it increases my suspicion that he has told his beloved German master of his connection with us in this country."

"You still have no proof he disclosed anything to Graumann," pointed out Marriott the lawyer.

SAMUEL MARQUIS

"No, but it must be considered likely given his disclosures that he confided in Dagmar Lahlum and Jimmy Hunt." He continued his denunciation with a flourish. "In any case, we must consider all of Zigzag's improprieties, and if we do, the conclusion is inescapable: he has broken the most elementary security rules and can no longer be trusted. Not only has he confided in at least two, and most probably three, unauthorized individuals, he has attempted to extract money from MI5, knowingly gambled in illegally-fixed dog races, and kept the company of professional criminals and other undesirables. He has threatened to work for rival secret service agencies in the Americans and French, and he is costing us a small fortune to maintain his lifestyle of champagne and loose women. Even leaving aside his fealty to Graumann, who clearly has a vested interest in his success, the Germans have been shown on occasion to be uncertain of their spy's loyalty with the connection to Brutus, and the speech in the House of Commons by Duncan Sandys may have eroded his credibility anyway. But most finally, and fatally, he has bragged to a known criminal about his work for the British Secret Service. And for that alone, he has to go."

Robertson shook his head. "No, he has to go when he is no longer of any use in deception operations that will help us win the bloody war."

"Yes, sir, point taken. But in my view, the only reason not to give Chapman the axe is if the Admiralty still wants to keep him active. Commander Montagu will have to decide whether in light of the inflammable situation caused by Zigzag's indiscretions to his very doubtful friends, he wishes us to continue this aspect of the case further."

Robertson looked at Montagu. "What are your thoughts, Ewen?"

"Well, as I said previously, Z has done a bang-up job for us, not just with Operation Squid but with his earlier operations. But at the same time, I would have to concede that at this point any benefit which might accrue from the delivery of the Hedgehog photographs to Lisbon is small."

"Are you saying you agree with Major Ryde that the Zigzag case should be shut down?"

Montagu took a moment to assemble the precise words. "I'm saying that if the Double Cross Committee decides to shut down the case, the Admiralty does not attach sufficient importance to the photographs to keep the case running. However, having said that, it should be noted that Operation Squid is still ongoing, and other deception opportunities not apparent to us now may become desirable in the future."

Robertson pondered a moment before looking at Ryde. "If we were to shut down Z, then as far the Germans are concerned he is notionally away contacting the courier for the Lisbon drop. Should he never reappear on the air again, the assumption would be that he has been arrested whilst attempting to make contact. Is that correct?"

"Precisely," said Ryde. "And furthermore, I strongly advise against continuing the Zigzag traffic with Germany without Chapman himself. Any attempt to impersonate his radio technique would pose, I believe, a considerable risk due to his distinctive style. The case should simply be shut down in a clean break, leaving the Germans to believe that Chapman has been caught."

Faced with Ryde's incriminating dossier gathered over the past two months, Robertson realized he had little choice but to agree and would now have to put a recommendation for dismissal from MI5 before the Double Cross Committee. The Admiralty would most likely acquiesce but with reluctance since Operation Squid was still under way. He stroked his chin and gave a heavy sigh. "Well then, I suppose that if the Admiralty rates the value of the case to be low, we have no choice but to shut it down. Major Cussen will have to visit Z for the final closure."

Ryde gave a gloating smile. "It's quite the right thing to do, sir, and Major Cussen will have to explain his position to Zigzag as forcibly as possible. One thing that must be made perfectly clear is that he can expect no assistance from us in any future trouble in which he may find himself. I should also be opposed to paying Zigzag any more money, for once we do this we lay ourselves open to further approaches, and the value of taking advantage of this opportunity to close the case with Zigzag in the wrong will be lost. Instead, we can now say to him that he can expect no further assistance from us either financial or legal, we have obtained for him from the police a clean sheet, he has had a large sum of money which he never would have obtained without our assistance, and he has now let us down badly and should be thankful we are not going to lock him up."

Robertson shook his head sarcastically. "That's all? Is there nothing else, Major?"

"As a matter of fact, there is. He must understand that he must now stand on his own feet and that all those officers who have had any association with him—including me, Reisen, Horsfall, and others—have received strict instructions that any approach Zigzag may attempt to make to them is to be reported to this office. Should he attempt to make any such approach, we will consider whether he should not be interned or otherwise *disposed* of."

"He's already been pardoned for the outstanding crimes he is alleged to have committed," said Marriott. "Any police with an interest in prosecuting Z will continue to be informed through Special Branch that the home secretary desires that no such proceedings should be brought."

"A pardon in effect, if not in name," observed Montagu.

Robertson nodded. "No action is to be taken against him without prior consultation with us."

"Are we going to tell him that his slate has been wiped clean?" asked Marriott.

"No," replied Robertson. "I love the lad like a son, but he doesn't know how to keep his bloody mouth shut. And he's still probably intending to write his memoirs or sell his services to the Americans or French, which for obvious reasons we can't allow. No, the threat of prosecution remains a useful leash for our Eddie."

Ryde frowned. "He's not *my* Eddie."

Robertson shot him a look. "I believe you've made that abundantly clear, Major." He looked around the table. "Does anyone else have any further questions or concerns?"

Ryde cleared his throat. "Yes, sir. What's the next step?"

"I am going to put the matter before the Double Cross Committee. I suspect the Committee will concur with my decision and Zigzag will be dropped for lack of security on the part of the agent. Unfortunately, it appears his successes have gone to his head and he cannot stop talking about them. For that reason and that reason alone, it has become necessary to terminate his case. I want to add also that I do so with grave regret as Z has performed inestimable service on behalf of his country. My God, he's even won Tin Eye over and that, gentlemen, is no small feat."

"I quite agree," said Ewen Montagu.

"If the Committee concurs with your decision, sir, who's going to tell Zigzag?" asked Ryde.

"Chomping at the bit, are we, Major?"

"He poses a clear and present danger to national security, sir. So, who shall deliver the news?"

Robertson hesitated, thinking back to when he had first met the impetuous, colorful, courageous, and surprisingly patriotic Edward Arnold Chapman. He couldn't believe their time together was coming to an end. The lad had faced the formidable Tin Eye Stephens, Walther Praetorius, von Gröning, Frau Arne, and a host of other fearsome interrogators in Portugal, Spain, Berlin, France, and Norway who would have him tortured and killed in an instant if they had suspected he was double-dealing. Through his resourcefulness and instinctive gifts at deception he had survived these inquisitions by countless highly trained officers and agent provocateurs from the British Secret Service, the Abwehr, and SS—and not one of them had been able to trip him up or come remotely close to breaking him. Instead, it was one of his own countrymen, the sniveling Michael Ryde, a fastidious yet meaningless bean counter of Whitehall, who had brought his legendary spy career to a premature end. Robertson could only shake his head at the irony. He hated to see his prized double agent go out in such an unfairly wretched fashion, but Zigzag's tongue was loose and he was proving a handful to properly maintain.

"If the Committee votes for his removal, you should be the one to tell him, Major," said the colonel. "After all, you're the one that stuck the knife in his back."

Ryde's eyes glimmered with malice. "Very well, sir. I am looking forward to it."

"I know you are, Major, and that's what worries me. Be professional and let him down easy—and that's a bloody order."

CHAPTER 82

IT WAS THE INGRATIATING SMILE that tipped Chapman off that something wasn't right. Michael Ryde almost never smiled—and only then when the heavy drinker was intoxicated. The man was an utterly humorless sourpuss with no concept of having fun. And yet, here he was smiling happily, asking Chapman about how his day was going and making lighthearted jokes. His actions were totally out of character, and yet Chapman couldn't put a finger on what might be happening. He only knew that something was off kilter.

Ryde had driven to the Hill Street Flat with Leonard Burt, the head of Special Branch and senior police officer liaising with MI5, who along with Ryde and Reisen had kept an eye on Chapman the past few months. Unlike his sour relationship with Ryde, Chapman got along well with Burt, though he was unaware that his frequent babysitter had confided to his superiors that he was "quite convinced that Zigzag is a man without scruples who will blackmail anyone if he thinks it worth his while and will not stop even at selling out to the opposition if he thinks there is anything to be gained out of it."

After a few minutes, Ryde said, "Oh, we were having so much fun, I almost forgot. Colonel Robertson wants you to sign this document."

Chapman was a touch surprised, but he still didn't sense a trap. He looked at Burt, but his expression revealed nothing. "What is it?" he asked his case officer.

"Oh, it's nothing, just the standard agreement back at the shop that we all have to sign." He handed the sheaf of papers to him with a piece of yellow tape affixed to the page he was supposed to sign.

Chapman took a moment to examine the cover sheet and text beneath the heading. "The Official Secrets Act. You want me to sign this?"

"All employees and contractors of the British Secret Service are required to do so. It was recently discovered that you hadn't signed your copy, and the colonel needs you to sign it to ensure that you've agreed to adhere to the same national security protocols as the rest of us. It's just a formality."

Now he realized why Ryde was being so ingratiating: the case officer was worried that he might not agree to sign the act and make his terms of service official. But that was nonsense: he had no problem signing the document. He quickly read over the agreement. The language was dry and orderly, written no doubt by a team of government lawyers, but nothing seemed out of the ordinary. As an agent working on behalf of the British Secret Service, he was simply agreeing that he was "subject to the provisions of the act" and that he understood that he would be "guilty of an offence if without lawful authority he disclosed any information, document, or other article relating to British security or intelligence." There was nothing remarkable about the document; it was a standard non-disclosure agreement that would have been required to be signed by anyone working in espionage for either side during the war.

"Here's a pen for you to sign." Ryde handed it to him.

He signed the signature block just above where it read: "I understand that any disclosure by me, whether during or after the present war, of facts relating to the undertaking upon which I have been engaged will be an offense punishable by imprisonment for a term not exceeding two years or a fine or both." When he was finished, he handed the pen and signed document back to the case officer. Ryde, in turn, handed it to Burt for his counter-signature. Once it was signed, he carefully tucked the agreement in his foldover leather case.

"So, is that all then or am I to make a radio transmission today?" Chapman asked his case officer.

It was then Ryde's expression changed, and Chapman knew that not only was something not right, but he was in serious trouble. He looked at Burt sitting in his chair and saw that he, too, had undergone a change.

"No, Eddie," said Ryde sarcastically with quiet rage in his eyes, "we're not going to make you send a message to your Nazi stooges today—because you're fired!"

"Fired? What do you mean fired? On whose authority?"

"Colonel Robertson's, Major Masterman's, and mine—that's bloody hell who!"

His expression was as venomous as a snake's, and Chapman saw at once that Ryde had fantasized about this moment for more than two months now. He looked at Burt again, but the liaison officer looked away guiltily. While Ryde was gloating and vindictive, Burt was ashamed of the way their charge was being treated, although he likely agreed with the decision to terminate Agent Zigzag's services.

But Chapman wasn't about to go out without a fight. "Are you drunk, Michael, because your face is as red as a bloody tomato?"

"Don't you dare talk to me like that, you lowly criminal. It's Major Ryde to you, and you're through, finished, kaput. I just thank God I don't have to set eyes upon you again."

"What am I supposed to have done that I have been sacked by MI5?"

"You have failed to follow the most elementary security protocols by blabbering about your espionage work to practically every Tom, Dick, and Harry. You have had no regard whatsoever for the necessity of observing silence regarding your connection with us, and for that it has become necessary to terminate your case."

"You're talking about the incident last week with Jimmy?"

"No, you imbecile, I'm talking about all the people you have disclosed sensitive information to: your Norwegian tart Dagmar, Dr. Graumann, Jimmy Hunt, and your other criminal friends on the streets and in the pubs. Why half of Kensington knows the exaggerated exploits of Eddie Chapman the super spy."

"Don't call Dagmar a tart, or I'll box your bloody ears off."

"Go ahead and try! Then you'll be right back in prison where you belong!"

Chapman realized he had grossly underestimated what a vile human being and petty bureaucrat Michael Ryde truly was. He looked again at Burt for help, but he wasn't going to have anything to do with a debate.

"You should see yourself, Major. You are a pompous ass and vindictive little shit if there ever was one. If I had had any inkling you were such a tortured soul, I would have quit this business months ago."

"Shut up and get out! You have brought this upon yourself! Your lack of judgment in security matters is staggering!"

"That may be, but you are also jealous of me."

"What? That's ridiculous!"

"You've always envied me for the women I hang around with in the clubs. You hate that they're attracted to me and consider me fun to be with. Why I'll bet you've never even taken a beautiful woman to bed, have you?"

He looked at Burt, who was suppressing a smile. *Ha,* thought, Chapman—*he knows it's true!*

Ryde was apoplectic with barely suppressed rage. "Stop this nonsense and get out! You should be thankful we are not locking you up and throwing away the key!"

"So first you gag me and then you sack me. That's why you were attempting to be so uncharacteristically pleasant before I signed your bloody Official Secrets Act. It was a setup job all along."

"You should know—you're the criminal. Now pack your things." He looked at his watch. "You have exactly five minutes to gather your belongings."

Now Burt was no longer smiling. "Come on, Eddie. You have to go. Those are the orders from the top, and we're just the messengers. Please collect your effects and let's not make a scene."

Ryde nodded belligerently. "You are to vacate these premises and never come back, never demand anything else of the intelligence services, and never work as a spy again. And you cannot under any circumstances make contact with the French or American governments to offer your services as an agent."

"I warned you about that, Eddie," Burt reminded him. "Because of your obligations under the Official Secrets Act, it will be impossible for you to disclose any of your wartime activities for a long time. I also advised you that if you disclose any facts relating to your criminal past, you will no doubt render yourself subject to action, if not by the police then by some of the parties whose goods you have stolen."

"You and I have already been through this, Leonard. I realize publication will be impossible, but I still feel inclined to set down my recollections while they're still fresh. I did my part for my country—far more than either of you and behind enemy lines—and it should be properly documented." He didn't care about MI5 threats of reprisal if he revealed his story; he knew that one day his story would be told despite the agreement he had signed. Ryde, Burt, and their superiors had obviously suspected that he might cause trouble in this regard after he had blithely informed them that he was penning an autobiography, but until Jimmy Hunt had blown his case wide open they had been hesitant to sack him. But no doubt Ryde had been plotting his downfall since mid-summer.

"We are warning you," snarled Ryde, "that if you dare breathe another word about what you have done during the war, you will be prosecuted to the full extent of the law. It is as simple as that and nothing more needs to be said."

"Yes, I think you and Mr. Burt here have made that quite clear."

"You must also understand that you will now have to stand on your own two feet. If you should make any approach, we, the security office, will be forced to arrest you. Now go and quickly pack your things, or I shall throw you out into the street with nothing at all. Go!"

God, did he want to punch the priggish bastard. But he knew that would just play into Ryde's hands. The man was a monster even in victory and Chapman saw no reason he should sink to his level. He looked at Burt: he was firm in his resolve but not vindictive, and he also seemed a touch guilty. The two of them had been on friendly terms and ending things this way was an ugly business.

Without saying another word, he went into his room to pack. He had risked his life for his country and provided invaluable intelligence that had contributed directly to the Allied war effort. In doing so, he had penetrated the upper echelons of the German foreign intelligence apparatus and helped disrupt V-weapon attacks on Central London. Even now, German intelligence officers were poring over documents he had furnished describing a nonexistent anti-submarine weapon. He had extracted more than seven thousand British pounds worth of currency from his German handlers while at the same time taking grave risks that none of his control officers—from Tar Robertson on down to Lieutenant Reisen—had taken during the war. And he had done all this while costing the British government virtually nothing.

His Achilles Heel, he knew, was his loose tongue, vanity, and restlessness. These were the things that had always gotten him into trouble. But with the exception of Robertson, with whom he had gotten along famously, what his MI5 controllers really objected to was his criminal past and working-class background. In their eyes, he was not the kind of person they wanted to see hailed as a conquering hero. He was not and never could be a member of their *club*.

As he began packing his suitcase, he felt angry at his mistreatment, but at the same time he felt a sense of relief. The reality of his current predicament was that he was no longer under the thumb of either the British or German intelligence services. Instead, he was a free man at last. True, he was being tossed out like dirty bathwater, but he had his freedom and the knowledge that he had done as much as any of his countrymen to help win the war and thwart Nazi Germany. He had also come out far ahead of where he had started the conflagration: he had been granted an informal pardon from his native country while at the same time being treated like a prince, given a significant sum of money, and rewarded with the Iron Cross from his country's top enemy. MI5 had threatened dire reprisals if he revealed his story, but he knew that one day it would be told. All the same, despite his sense of relief at obtaining his freedom from the British government, he still found it hard to believe that his case was closed and that, at the age of thirty, his career as a swashbuckling secret agent was over.

He would just have to make the best of a bad situation. With the war soon to be won by the Allies and most Englishmen away in foreign lands fighting Germans and Japanese, he was in position to capitalize on new moneymaking schemes. And, of course, there was still Dagmar. But when Nazi Germany finally surrendered, would MI5 even allow him to go to Norway and track her down?

Damnit, I hadn't thought of that, he reflected gloomily, shaking his head at the unfairness of it all. *The bastards are never going to let me go, are they?*

CHAPTER 83

GESTAPO HEADQUARTERS
VICTORIA TERRASSE

MAY 8, 1945

AT EIGHT MINUTES PAST MIDNIGHT, Fehmer stared down at the steady stream of soldiers moving through the city under a brilliant full moon. He stood on the balcony with Annemarie Breien and Wolfie. For the past two hours, since the announcement of the German surrender at ten p.m., they had been serving as intermediaries between the Norwegian Resistance and Occupation authorities to help ensure a bloodless transition from German to Allied hands.

Fehmer had been working the phones lines to give assurances that the remaining Norwegian prisoners at Akershus Fortress would not be shot in a final act of vengeful madness, while Breien was acting as a mediator between the Home Front and German authorities to prevent further bloodshed. During the past twenty-four hours, security had been loosened in Victoria Terrasse so contacts between German and Norwegian civil and administrative authorities and Milorg leaders could be made and ensure that the country could function when German rule ended. While these negotiations were taking place, on every floor of Victoria Terrasse incriminating documents were being burned to leave no trace of the German atrocities perpetrated during the five-year-long German Occupation.

Down below, the streets were teaming with marching footsoldiers and a hodgepodge of conveyances: official military trucks, half-tracks, and motorcycles jostled for road space with requisitioned civilian automobiles, many adapted for wood-burning. Most of the Wehrmacht and SS rank and file and officers had been out on the town in the clubs and brothels when the news of the surrender had broken, and they were returning to their military barracks for what was expected to be an official capitulation ceremony later today. But there were also SS men that Fehmer knew had no intention of returning to their barracks and apartments, except to gather their loot and civilian or Wehrmacht clothing to disguise themselves. Then they would quietly steal from town and either make a dash for the Swedish border, as those from the Norwegian underground had been doing throughout the war; or try and pass themselves off as German soldiers.

It was these men that Fehmer now watched closely. He had worked side by side with them for years and knew many of them well. If caught, they could expect to be dealt with harshly in Norway during the inevitable post-war criminal proceedings. He couldn't help but see them as rats abandoning a sinking ship—yet he knew he would have no choice but to join them by tomorrow's first light if he wanted to save his own skin. His superior Fehlis had already issued him and other SS officers enlisted men's uniforms so they could be concealed among the mass of more than three hundred thousand German soldiers that would be handing over their firearms when the official Document of Surrender was signed tomorrow or the day after. Thankfully, there was still time to make his escape; while the official surrender to the Allied Commission would be tomorrow, the formal surrender of arms might take two to three days.

Gazing down at the chaotic scene, he shook his head in dismay. Defeat clung to the air like a burial shroud, and it sickened him to see his countrymen appear so weak and puny. Many of the men were bleary-eyed, unshaven, and unkempt, and most were strangely quiet. There was none of the usual singing or any attempt at military formation. Having been ordered to stand down by General Franz Böhme, who had taken over in January from von Falkenhorst as commander-in-chief of German forces in Norway, they wanted nothing more than to make it safely back to their barracks or to evade capture and make their escape. He shook his head at the thought that the *kameraden* before him had in April 1940 represented the spearhead of one of the most powerful armies in the history of warfare, and now they looked like a pack of skulking dogs. How many of them, he wondered, still believed in the promise of Hitler's Thousand-Year Reich?

"They don't look so fierce any more, do they?" observed Annemarie Breien, as if reading his mind. They had stopped being lovers several months ago but had remained frequent companions to maintain the link between the Occupation authorities and Home Front and enable Breien to ensure the continued release of Norwegian political prisoners.

"No, they don't," he admitted as he leaned down to pet Wolfie. "We have failed in our mission to bring National Socialism to the world, and now our country will be in ruins for decades."

"It is Hitler that has brought Germany to ruin. Not the Allies."

"Yet, strangely enough, it is only in the past week that I have come to realize this."

"I am sorry for the future you and your countrymen will face. But I would be remiss if I didn't point out that it can hardly be worse than what we Norwegians have had to endure for the past five years."

"I know. We have done you and your people a grave injustice."

"You also did some good, Siegfried. You saved more than eighty of my countrymen from Grini and the other prison camps. You could have simply obeyed your orders from Fehlis and not done anything—and yet you took grave risk to free many of my people. You can be proud of that, at least, and for making sure there are no last-minute reprisals against political prisoners held at Akershus."

"When I see my defeated army down there, I'm afraid that is little consolation."

"You should be happy the war is over. The most important thing is that smiles will soon be returning to the faces of the children on both sides."

"Yes, that is a good thing. This war has been too great a cost for everyone. I am sorry...I am sorry for everything."

"I know you are," she said, and he could tell that she meant it.

They fell into silence as they continued to watch the activity below on the street. Up until a few days ago, Terboven and other leaders of the German Occupation force had been considering plans to make Norway the last bastion of the Third Reich and sanctuary for German leaders. But following Hitler's suicide in his bunker on April 30, the Führer's successor, Admiral Karl Dönitz, summoned Terboven and the man who would soon replace him, General Böhme, to a meeting in Flensburg, where they were ordered to follow the High Command's instructions. Upon their return to Norway, Dönitz dismissed Terboven from his post as *reichskommissar* and transferred his powers to Böhme, who proceeded to issue a directive to his commanders via a radio broadcast in which he declared that German forces in Norway would follow the strictest standards of military discipline and avoid hostilities with the Allied Army and Norwegian Resistance.

The declaration quickly led to the immediate and full deployment of Milorg as more than forty thousand armed Norwegians, the only Allied armed force on hand, were summoned to occupy the Royal Palace, Oslo's main police station, and other public buildings—but not the Gestapo headquarters at Victoria Terrasse. Through Annemarie's Breien's Milorg contacts, Fehmer had learned that the Home Front's main task was to protect Norwegian property and lives until the British arrived, while steering clear of the SS to avoid bloodshed. To his credit, Böhme had seen the futility of continued fighting and adopted the same peaceful stance as his Norwegian adversaries, for whom the order of the day from the Resistance leadership was to promote dignity, calmness, and discipline until the official Allied liberation force arrived.

Though Nazi Germany had been defeated, the Norwegian authorities wanted to avoid provoking the occupying German Army in any way, since it remained a potent 350,000-man-strong fighting machine that had never lost a battle on Norwegian soil and had maintained a firm grip on the country for five straight years. The Norwegians had everything to lose in an open fight with an enemy that had close to ten fully trained and equipped soldiers to every Milorg field operative. The instruction to the nation, including Milorg, during the past week had been quite simple: keep a low profile, show discipline, don't provoke the enemy, and wait for the arrival of the Allies. But for the Norwegians and the Germans both, the strain of waiting since the announcement of Hitler's death and capture of Berlin by the Allies had been almost unbearable.

With the Allied Commission having not yet reached Oslo for the official signing of the surrender document, the Home Front was the only Allied authority in Norway. From his boss Fehlis, Fehmer had learned that Milorg Chief Jens Christian Hauge had persuaded Böhme and the German High Command that the Home Front posed no threat to German troops and was the only guarantee of law and order during the transition period from German to Allied control. Fehmer had also learned that Hauge was unable to persuade Böhme to give up control of the Norwegian State Broadcasting radio station in Oslo until the Allied Commission arrived, but he did convince the general to allow an interim newspaper with no political affiliation, the *Oslo Pressen*, to be published. The resumed printing of newspapers that had been suppressed during the German Occupation was an essential requirement of returning Norway to a free democracy, and it was agreed that the paper would make the announcement of the German surrender and Norwegian liberation from the Home Front leadership in the morning.

They stepped from the balcony and returned to making their phone calls. Like Hauge and Böhme, they still had much work to do to facilitate negotiations between the occupiers and the Home Front and to help promote a smooth and bloodless handover of power to the Allies. Fehmer's foremost priority was to make sure that there were no further executions of Norwegian political prisoners and that his fellow SS troops and officers would not be gunned down on the streets when they surrendered their arms tomorrow or the next day when the official Allied military force arrived. Breien relayed Fehmer's messages to the Milorg leadership and worked with the spokesmen of the daily papers on how the Germans were conducting themselves and to make sure the news would be presented responsibly in the critical period of transition. By five a.m., they were both exhausted and decided to call it a night. After Annemarie called her cousin and asked him to come fetch her in his car, they returned to the balcony and gazed out at the first streaks of pre-dawn light.

"This is the last time I will see you, Annemarie," he said to her.

"Are you going to try and hide or make a run for it? You won't get away, you know."

"I honestly don't know what I'm going to do," he lied, knowing full well that the first thing he would do when he returned to his apartment was put on his recently acquired *feldgrau* Wehrmacht private's uniform and make for the Swedish border. All the same, he hated himself for lying to the greatest love he had ever known and would probably ever know.

"I know you're lying to me, Siegfried. I just wish you would surrender and atone for your sins. As I said, there's no chance you will get away. As you are aware, tens of thousands of armed Milorg soldiers have been dispatched to scour the country for war criminals and collaborators. They will find you."

He was taken aback by her forthrightness and intuition. "You are quite right, I shouldn't lie to you. And that's why I am going to ask a favor of you."

"A favor?"

"Yes. Will you take Wolfie for me? He has done nothing wrong and deserves to be loved, and you...you are the only person I can trust."

"Me?"

"You may not remember, but I was in love with you once. In fact, I have to say that for a short time last fall, we shared something special."

"I am sorry but that was a mistake."

"No, it wasn't. I was madly in love with you. In fact, I still am."

"Don't say that. Not now when we are so close."

"So close to the end you mean? For you it is a day of victory. For me, it is an ignominious defeat. But our comeuppance has been a long time coming. Five years now. We were one of the most powerful armies in history, but it's over. The Reich is finished."

Her hand reached out and touched his softly; he felt goosebumps like when he was a little boy in Bolshevik Russia. "I didn't mean to rub it in," she said to him. "You know that I care for you...or at least a part of you."

"But you could never love me for what I am."

"No, I could never love you as a woman should love a man. That would be impossible."

"I am sorry that I have let you down. But will you take Wolfie for me?"

"Yes, I will look after your dog. I know how much you love him."

"I have never loved him a hundredth of how much I love you."

"You know we can never be together."

"I know, but it still makes me sad. You mean everything to me." He glanced reflectively at his office door. "I remember the day you burst through that door. Your hair was swept back from the wind and your face flush with color. You were the most beautiful thing I had ever seen in my entire life. I was in love with you from the moment I laid eyes upon you."

"Stop it, Siegfried. You know it can never be. The war is over and now it is time for the healing. And the accounting."

"For both of us, it would seem."

She shot him a look. "What's that supposed to mean?"

"You know perfectly well what it means. Your countrymen have seen you come and go at Victoria Terrasse now for four straight years. Do you think when the accounting is done, they will let you off scot free?"

Her head dipped ruefully. "No, I don't suppose they will."

"That's right, my former love. Though it pains me to say this, they have been calling you a 'German's tart' for quite some time now, and your future may very well be as precarious as mine."

She licked her lips. "I know what I have done on behalf of my country, and that is enough for me."

"Is it? When they shave your head, spit upon you, and lock you away in prison as if you were Vidkun Quisling himself, will the honor of what you have done be enough to sustain you then?"

"No, of course not," she said quietly.

He reached out and touched her cheek; it was warm and soft, and he felt himself longing for her love. "I am sorry," he said. "I didn't mean to be cruel. It's just that everything has been turned around."

"What do you mean?"

"On the one hand, my conscience is pure regarding my service to the Reich even though Hitler has taken his life and Germany has capitulated. But on the other, I feel a terrible shame for the things I have done on behalf of my Führer."

"Do you consider yourself a war criminal?"

"No, I don't. Not any more than Max Manus and his Oslo Gang that took the lives of innocents during the course of their sabotage actions."

"But surely, you are not comparing yourself to a national hero like Max Manus?"

"Absolutely, I am. I may have been tough on your people but in the end, I freed more than eighty of them. And many of them I knew all along played at least some role in the Resistance."

"You knew all along?"

"Of course, I did."

"Then why did you do it?"

"Because I was in love with you and wanted to please you."

"Surely that's not the only reason."

"All right, I suppose I also wanted a pipeline to the Home Front, and you gave that to me. But the foremost reason was always you, Annemarie."

She shook her head sadly. "I still don't understand how a man could be so sweet, caring, and generous—and yet so cruel, violent, and primitive."

"All men have good in them, and all men have evil. It is only the relative proportions that differ."

She took a deep breath of the cool, early morning air. "It would appear so."

"I don't consider myself a war criminal for the simple reason that my good works have far outweighed the effects of torture and the transfer of prisoners to German prison camps."

"You mean death camps."

"I have cared about Norwegian life and property all along and you know it, Annemarie. I love Norway. That's why I learned the language and customs and fell in love with a Norwegian girl."

"You mean many Norwegian girls. I know of your reputation."

"It is true I have had many women. But as I have said to you many times, no one can hold a candle to you."

"You ruined my marriage, you know. Kjell and I are still separated."

"That was your doing, not mine. You are the one who insisted on bailing out every political prisoner in the land. I mean come on, Sigurd Evensmo? I knew from the moment he was arrested that he was working for the Resistance."

"Then why did you set him free?"

"You know why: because you cast a spell over me and I couldn't say no to you."

"You act as if I am some sort of a magician."

"You are. Your combination of sweetness and beauty is a form of witchcraft."

"I know you are a smart man and that you freed many prisoners and helped improve conditions for many others by removing several of the most prominent Gestapo torturers, but you still lack cultural enlightenment. You do understand that, don't you?"

"Don't you think that is a bit harsh?"

"No, I don't. Furthermore, it is this lack of enlightenment that has made you an easy prey to Nazism and given you a more primitive form of morality than most people are accustomed to. But what I want to know is have you changed?"

"What do you mean?"

"Do you still believe that National Socialism is the answer?"

"No, obviously not. In the last week alone, I have come to have serious doubts about Hitler and Nazism."

"How has it felt for you personally?"

"Sometimes, I feel as if I have been falling and falling, past everything I have believed in and fought for, and I have no idea where I will land. I am sorry...sorry for this war and all the pain and suffering it has brought along with it. I hope that one day you can forgive me."

"I already forgive you. But my countrymen won't forgive you or Nazi Germany for a very long time, I'm afraid."

She looked so kind and gentle that he was suddenly overtaken with an impulse. He took her in his arms and kissed her on the lips. He felt a warm and desperate feeling envelope him, but also a crushing sadness as he knew that after tonight he would likely never see her again.

"I am sorry," he said. "But I just had to do that to remember you by."

"Oh, Siegfried," she said, and he could tell a part of her still cared about him, "why do you have to be two different people: one good, the other evil. It boggles the mind."

She leaned forward and kissed him on the cheek, a little peck that a younger sister or mother might give but certainly not a lover. And yet…and yet there were tears in her eyes.

"I know you still care about me, Annemarie. You can't hide your true feelings, especially not from the head of the German police here in Norway."

"I do care about you, Siegfried. But I care far more for Norway."

"I know you do," he said, feeling a wave of melancholy. "And that is precisely why I must go now."

"I hope you change your mind and turn yourself in," she said.

He touched her warm cheek again. "Please take good care of Wolfie."

"I will," she said.

"I hope you have a wonderful life. You deserve it," he said.

"Goodbye, Siegfried. Wherever you go and whatever happens, you know you will have to pay for your sins."

"I know," he said. "In this lifetime and the next."

CHAPTER 84

TULLINS GATE, OSLO

MAY 19, 1945

AT THE CORNER OF TULLINS GATE AND ST. OLAV'S GATE, an old hag sliced in from Dagmar's left and spit in her face. At the last second, she had looked up from the crosswalk and spotted the old woman—red-faced, puffing, and stomping towards her—but she was unable to get out of the way in time.

"Leave our city, you German's whore!" the old hag snarled, wagging a belligerent finger at her.

Dagmar recognized the plump, crinkly-faced woman from the neighborhood but didn't know her by name. The woman had seen her two or three times with SS-*Oberscharführer* Otto Iredi, Fehlis's personal driver, who had lived in the apartment building Dr. Graumann had put her up in when Eddie had left and had helped her get the Sipo job. For an instant, she was too stunned to move or utter a word. Then she saw the hostile and suspicious stares of the people around her waiting to cross the street and she was gripped with a sudden primal urge to flee. Wiping the spittle from her face, she dashed across the street, weaving dangerously through the traffic. Twice drivers were forced to break hard to avoid hitting her, and they leaned on their horns and cursed her for her carelessness.

When she reached the other side, the old hag and two young men standing next to her yelled at her to stop. But she didn't stop, not until she had made it safely back to her apartment, short of breath and heart racing uncontrollably.

As soon as she closed the door behind her and fastened the lock, tears erupted from her eyes. For the past three years, she had risked her life as a spy working on behalf of the Norwegian Resistance and British Secret Service and this is how she was treated? Since January, when the Allies had entered Germany, her control officer Ishmael had been reported killed, and she had been told to keep a low profile and abstain from further contact with Milorg, she had known that with the defeat of Hitler and the Axis Powers she would likely be accused of fraternizing with the enemy, and possibly accused of treason, since there was no one to vouch for her wartime contributions. Although she had thus far managed to avoid arrest, every day was still torture. She dreaded walking the streets for fear that someone would recognize her and report her to the authorities. Since the German surrender ten days ago, she had been verbally and physically harassed on countless occasions on the streets, and the situation was growing worse every day. Even her friends weren't talking to her anymore. She felt like her beloved country had lost its mind.

At the same time, she was surprised that she hadn't been arrested like the thousands of Norwegians being pulled from the streets and locked in prison every day. Thus far, more than twenty thousand people had reportedly been arrested and brought before police interrogators for questioning. Dagmar had learned that Milorg had joined with a special Norwegian police unit that had been trained in Sweden, and the combined police force was now combing the city in search of collaborators and war criminals. The Milorg men—most of whom, unlike her, had not been within spitting distance of actual German military units or intelligence operatives during the war—marched about self-importantly arresting suspected collaborators, wearing armbands and makeshift uniforms of knee-pants and jackets. But how many innocents were swept up in the widely cast net of hasty retribution? Dagmar wondered. Most people on the streets and the editorial pages of the post-war newspapers like *Dagbladet* were demanding harsh penalties for alleged traitors and firing squads without trial for war criminals. It was a witch hunt, and she knew it was only going to get worse.

Wiping away her tears, she looked at her hands: they were shaking. She went into the kitchen, pulled a bottle of aquavit from the cupboard, poured herself a glass, and took a gulp. The strong fennel-flavored liquor burned her throat at first but then filled her with soothing warmth, like sitting next to a winter hearth. She had been drinking more heavily during the past six months of the war, and even more since the German capitulation last week. It was all she could do to cope.

With her glass in hand, she went to the window and stared out onto the street below. Thankfully, there was no sign of the old hag or the two young men. Though the woman lived somewhere nearby, Dagmar hoped she didn't know where she lived even if the woman was aware of her association with Iredi. She lifted her head towards the sky. Thick thunderheads consumed the foreground above the apartments along Tullins gate, and in the far distance, a purple haze of shower threw a giant curtain above the city. She couldn't escape a feeling of impending doom.

Her thoughts turned to Eddie. She wondered if there was some way she could get in contact with him, or if he would ever come back to her as promised. She remembered back to the sparkle in his eye when he told a joke or bought her a present, and she realized in that moment that she would never get over him or have another lover like him. She hoped desperately that he hadn't moved on with his life or forgotten how meaningful their relationship was. She thought of their times together sailing on the fjord, making love in the woods, and swimming in the cold saltwater. Those were the most precious moments of her life, those times of loving intimacy when it seemed as if there was no war going on at all. She felt a tide of emotion wash over her; this was the way she wanted to remember their relationship.

She felt tears coming to her eyes, a powerful sense of loss. Was it possible that she had already lived the best moments of her life and would never feel such joy again? She stared out the window, tears pouring from her eyes. There wasn't a damned thing she could do to stop them.

It was then she heard a hard knock on the door, followed by an explosion as a half dozen uniformed policeman battered down her door and stormed into her apartment. Ripping off both the chain and lock, they poured into the room like a pack of ravenous wild dogs. She wanted to scream but her shock was so great no words came out. She couldn't help but see the uniformed men as no different from Fehmer and a pack of his Gestapo agents, or a swarm of angry NS Hirdsmen.

Jumping back involuntarily, she found her voice. "What are you doing?"

The red-faced officer out front looked at her severely. "Dagmar Lahlum, I have a warrant for your arrest!" He held up the warrant and flashed a badge. "Put your hands above your head and get on the floor!"

"But I have done nothing wrong!" she protested.

The officer snarled, "Shut the fuck up and do as I say! You are under arrest!"

The next thing she knew she was knocked viciously to the floor and handcuffed. As she was being roughly handled, she felt as though her countrymen had gone stark raving mad and she was the only sane person left.

"What am I being charged with, damn you?" she demanded.

The senior officer glared at her balefully. "Treason—under the General Civil Penal Code, Paragraph 86."

"Treason? But I am no collaborator and have always been sympathetic to the Resistance. In fact, I am part of it."

"You're a liar. You are no such thing and have collaborated with the German occupation of the country. We have proof of your working at Sipo and it clearly states it on the arrest warrant."

"It is true I worked for Sipo, but I also worked for the—"

"Shut your mouth, you German's whore, and come with us!"

"I am not a whore, you brute!"

"Like hell you're not!" He smiled maliciously. "Oh, we know all about you, Dagmar Lahlum. You've been spreading your legs for the Huns—with great relish from what I hear."

Unable to believe what she was hearing, she looked at the other policemen but they just shook their heads disapprovingly and sneered condescendingly at her. She felt her face crimson with embarrassment, and it took all her self-control not to break down and cry. "Where are you taking me?" she asked, trying to remain strong though she just wanted to curl up into a ball. How had her life turned so suddenly into a nightmare?

"Bredtveit Prison."

She was stunned. From 1941, the Nazi collaborationist party *Nasjonal Samling* had used Bredtveit as a political prison but now that the war was over it was being used to incarcerate women awaiting trial for collaboration. It seemed unthinkable that she was to be consigned to such an obscenely unjust fate after all she had done for her country.

"Prison? I'm going to prison?" Though she had known for months that such a grim accounting might be in her future, it was still hard for her to believe it was actually happening.

"That's where we put collaborators, you know. Don't say another word or I'll be forced to stuff a gag in your goddamned mouth. It makes me sick to even look at you after what you've done."

One of the other officers shook his head in mock disbelief. "Spreading your legs for those Nazis. That's something our soon-to-return king is not likely to forgive."

"He's right, it's not," said the one in charge. "Now let's move!"

He jerked her by the wrist and muscled her towards the door along with one of the other policemen. When they reached the police roundup truck on the street, the old hag was standing there with a triumphant look on her face.

"Now you go to prison where you belong, you Nazi whore!"

Once again, she spit in her face—and the policemen did nothing.

CHAPTER 85

SITTING ON THE STEEL BENCH of her dirty, stench-ridden, crowded holding cell, Dagmar wondered how many years she would be imprisoned for faithfully serving her country. It all seemed like a bad nightmare—and yet since Eddie had left Norway, Ishmael had been killed, and Milorg had essentially dropped her she had suspected that when the Germans were defeated her situation would turn out like this. Now her worst fears had been realized: no one was there to speak on her behalf and she was marked as a traitor. After a month of being held against her will as a prisoner, she was close to giving up all hope of going on to live the life she and Eddie had dreamed about.

She glanced around her ten-foot by ten-foot cell that she shared with five other female inmates. Like her, they were among the tens of thousands suspected of providing assistance to the enemy. They were not shackled with leg and wrist irons but the conditions in the prison were deplorable nonetheless. A doctor had been on hand to inspect her when she had first arrived at Bredtveit, but that was a month ago and since that time she had been crammed together with the other five women in a stifling hot cell with insect-infested mattresses, little in the way of light or comfort, and only rats for company. They were kept under close watch and were allowed outside to stretch their legs for no more than an hour per day. Their diet consisted of salt fish, soup, bread, margarine, and occasional rancid reindeer, cow meat, or sausage. Since her arrival to the prison, Dagmar had lost eleven pounds.

She went to the window and peered through the iron bars at the sentries. Armed with machine guns, they stood in the guard towers at either end of the barracks. She found it ironic that many of them were from Milorg just like her—yet during the war most had performed nothing but training activities and had not seen any action against the Germans. While she had risked her life as a courier and spy against the Oslo Abwehrstelle, they had traipsed about the woods marching and training with fake rifles, waiting for the Americans and British to do their fighting. She had been in the enemy's lair spying on the Germans for most of the war, carrying messages and falsified documents on behalf of the Home Front—and yet she was the one imprisoned for treason? How could she have allowed it to come to this? She had seen it coming so why hadn't she done more to protect herself?

She realized she already knew the answer: she had put too much faith in Eddie.

She heard a footfall outside the cell in the corridor followed by the jingle of a set of keys and the sound of the jail door opening. Two guards stepped into the cell. The older one, a sour-faced man with the pinched chin of Joseph Goebbels but with blond hair and blue eyes, instructed her to follow them. They escorted her to a spartan interrogation room with a scratched brown table, metal folding chairs, and out-of-place pictures on the walls showing icy fjords and snowy mountain peaks. Seated at the table were two men who gazed at her accusingly as she walked in.

"Sit down," the older of the two men commanded gruffly. He was ugly as sin, with a crush of fissures and pock marks lining his face and a nose that looked like it had been broken several times. He was dressed in the same drab policemen's uniform as his comrades except his was pinned with a pair of medals. She wondered what he had done to deserve them when, for the past five years, the vast majority of Norwegian policemen had done the bidding of Terboven's totalitarian police state and Quisling's puppet government. He ran a fat hand through his brilliantined hair, which was flipped over the top of his head, like a mop, in a futile attempt to cover his bald spot. The younger interrogator was blond, lantern-jawed, and in his early-thirties, with ballooning biceps his neatly pressed police uniform failed to conceal.

Dagmar fought back the urge to scowl at them as she took her seat. She distrusted police under any circumstances, but in the current environment of mindless paranoia and retribution, she was terrified to death.

"State your full name and date of birth please," said the older one in charge, Pock Face, to begin the interrogation as he looked over her file in front of him.

"Dagmar Mohne Hansen Lahlum. I was born on March 10, 1923 in Sørumsand."

He then proceeded to ask her a series of preliminary questions about when she first came to Oslo and a full list of her jobs during the German Occupation before getting to the crux of the interrogation. He finished up by describing the nature of the crime for which she was being detained: treason through the aiding and abetting of Norway's military enemy Nazi Germany as promulgated in Paragraph 86 of the General Civil Penal Code, specifically by "establishing, joining, taking an active part in or giving significant economic support to a party or an organization which operates for the benefit of the enemy."

When he was finished with his opening remarks, Pock Face posed his first question like a cross-examining attorney, "When did you first begin collaborating with the enemy?"

She met his accusing stare without flinching. "I've never collaborated with the enemy."

"Are you denying that you worked for the *Sicherheitspolizei* in letter censorship since November of last year until the German surrender?"

"No, I do not deny working at Sipo. But I only did it because I was warned that if I did not have a job I would be sent to a prison camp in the north. I was out of work for part of last fall and needed to find work."

"Who told you this?"

"Otto Iredi."

"Who is this Iredi?"

"Sergeant Otto Paul Iredi. He is…I mean, was…Colonel Fehlis's personal driver."

"SS-*Oberführer* Heinrich Fehlis, the Chief of the German Security Service?"

"That is correct. Iredi was his military driver. The sergeant lived in my apartment building and helped get me the Sipo job. I took the job so I wouldn't be shipped north to a forced labor camp. You have to believe me because it's the truth."

The two policemen said nothing, staring at her through slitted crocodile eyes. Everything about them was unsympathetic, suspicious, quietly hostile. They were not here to discover the truth but to even the score, she could already tell.

Pock Face resumed the questioning: "What were you doing fraternizing with the enemy, and an SS man to boot? That, in itself, is treason."

"I was not helping the enemy. I was hurting him. I worked for the Resist—"

"Just tell us about this Iredi."

"I didn't know him very well."

"And his rank was sergeant?"

"Yes. He was the *kriminalangestellter* in Sipo *Abteilung II D3*, the administrative department for the SS vehicle fleet."

"Were you romantically involved with this Iredi?"

"No. He came to my apartment a couple times but that was it. I despise Germans and have never been a member of the NS."

"Then why were you inviting them up to your apartment?" When she scowled at him and didn't answer, he looked over his notes and began a new line of questioning. "It is my understanding that you had an affair with a German intelligence officer in the Abwehr."

"No...I mean yes...actually no—"

"No, yes, which is it?"

"The answer is yes I had an affair with an intelligence officer, but he wasn't German—he was British."

"British, you say? Is that so?" He looked at his younger colleague, who appeared equally skeptical.

"Yes, he was a British double agent."

"A British double agent? How do you know?"

"Because he told me so and I saw him spying on the Germans. Many times."

"But you believed he was German?"

"I could tell early on that he was only pretending to be a German officer. He actually said he was a French writer but intimated he was working for the Germans."

"Intimated?"

"Well, at first it wasn't clear exactly who he was working for. But he was in the company of Germans, there was no question about that."

Now Pock Face spoke with mock courtesy. "And what was Mr. Wonderful's name? Do you remember it by chance, or was the relationship rather brief?"

"Don't talk to me like that. I am not a loose woman."

"That's not what your neighbors say. They refer to you as, and I quote, a 'German's tart' and a 'Jerry bag.' More than half a dozen people have come forward and reported on you and your German gentleman friend—and not one of them has a kind thing to say. So I'll call you, Frau Lahlum, whatever I damn well please and you will answer my questions. Do you understand?"

She hated to back down from such a bully, but she had no choice. "Yes, I understand. But as I told you he is not German, he is British. That's what I later found out."

For the first time, the younger inquisitor, Blondie, spoke. "And what was his name? You never got to that part."

"Eddie, his real name was Eddie. But he went by Fritz Graumann. That was his cover name for his German handlers."

"Where did you and this Eddie—I mean Fritz—meet?" asked Blondie.

"It was by accident. I was there at the Ritz with my friend Mary Larsen."

Now Pock Face took control again. "The Ritz was a Nazi club, frequented by members of German intelligence and the SS and NS. When did you meet there?"

"April 1943. He asked me if I spoke French, but my French isn't very good, so we spoke in German."

"Your German is good then?"

"It is far better than my French."

"So, this Eddie code-named Fritz spoke German and French?"

"And English. That was his first language."

"How do you know?"

"It was obvious because we spoke it together. He also told me it was his first language once we had been together for a while and he felt he could trust me."

"So, you started a whirlwind romance that night, is that it?"

"No, it started a few days later. He was very persistent."

"And then what happened?"

"We began spending a lot of time together, going sailing and out for dinner and drinks. We spent a lot of time at the Ritz and Löwenbräu. As I said, he was a British double agent pulling the wool over the eyes of the Germans. He lived with two of them. I don't know what they did exactly, but they were most certainly spies with the Abwehr. I think they were his trainers and chaperones. He confided in me that he was a British spy working against German intelligence one day when we were out on his little yawl sailing. I had felt all along that he was British, so I wasn't surprised. His German accent never seemed quite right."

"You're telling us this British secret agent fell in love with you and told you all about his operations?"

"No, he actually never told me about his work. He just told me he was a British spy and that we were working for the same side. He told me not to tell anyone or he could get in trouble with the Germans. He said they would kill him if they knew he was a British spy. He also said he could get in trouble with his British handlers back in London if I ever told anyone."

"So why are you telling us now?"

"You know why: because the danger has passed now that the war is over, and I have been wrongfully accused and should be released."

Now Blondie spoke up again. "I presume the British can back up your story?"

"That's what Eddie said. He said at the end of the war I should go before the British authorities, tell them who I am, and Eddie would clear my name."

"If that's the case, why haven't you gone to the British?" asked Pock Face.

"To be honest, I don't know where to find them."

He made a note in his file. She could tell they didn't believe what she was saying, and felt her life slipping away. He looked at her and she still saw not a hint of sympathy in his pock-marked face. When he glanced at his watch, she realized he just wanted to wrap up the interrogation so he could move on to the hundreds—perhaps thousands—of other treason cases that were on his plate. She felt a lump of despair clog her throat. She was just one case among tens of thousands of cases and would never get a fair shot at justice. But even worse, she was already blacklisted not only for having had a relationship with a known German intelligence officer, which made her an unpardonable and reviled *tyskertøs*, but in working for Sipo she had supported the SS, the most repressive arm of Hitler's Nazi police state. Together, these two strikes made her a traitor in the eyes of the overworked police—and her patriotic work on behalf of Milorg and British intelligence could never offset that even if they believed her. The despairing thought tore her up inside, and it was only with great effort that she was able to stifle tears.

Pock Face's harsh, stentorian voice snapped her back to reality. "Describe the work you did for Sipo?"

"As I said before, I only took the job because I was desperate and didn't want to be shipped to a labor—"

"Yes, yes, we know. Just tell us about it."

"Well, I...I read letters that came from Sweden to Norway and censored them in accordance with the guidelines provided to me."

"Provided to you? You mean by the SS? The Nazis?"

"Yes. But it was just a job to make ends meet."

"Did this Eddie tell you it was all right to take the job?"

"Yes...yes, he did. He said he would clear my name after the war."

"Where is Eddie, or Fritz, now do you think?"

"I have no idea. I sent a letter to him in Occupied France in the summer of 1944 and then I lost all contact with him."

"What was he doing in France?"

"Preparing to return to Great Britain. That's what he told me before he left, that he was returning home to again fool the Germans about a deception operation. He didn't tell me any more than that."

Blondie scratched his lantern jaw. "One thing puzzles me. Why would you be willing to work for Sipo if you are a loyal Norwegian? The threat of being sent up north doesn't seem to be enough, at least not in my reckoning. Is there something you're not telling us?"

Should she tell them about her work for Milorg? But what difference would it make when her control officer Ishmael was long gone? She wondered if he had been killed by the Gestapo or Norwegian Nazi police. The Milorg case officer that had contacted her back in January to notify her of Ishmael's death had only said that he had been killed while trying to escape from the police.

"No, I have told you everything," she said. "My sympathies have always been with my country and the Resistance. I request to speak with the British authorities as they represent the best chance for me to clear my name."

"I wouldn't count on that if I were you. You've been mixing with some very unsavory characters."

She crossed her arms protectively about her chest. "All the same, I want to talk to the British."

"All right," he said. "We'll notify them."

He snapped his case file shut perfunctorily. The bureaucrat had check off his little box and thereby absolved himself from further investigation because the case could be passed on to another legal body.

"Well, I suppose that's it then," he said, washing his hands of the matter. "It's in the hands of the Brits."

CHAPTER 86

FOR ANNEMARIE BREIEN, TOO, life was like a bad dream as she was escorted down the hallway towards the interrogation room at Akershus. On June 3, under the orders of the British, she had been imprisoned at Norway's historic fortress that had resisted foreign invaders for seven centuries. She was being held in custody pending trial as if she was a criminal no different from her country's most notorious traitor, Vidkun Quisling; its most sought-after Gestapo officer, Siegfried Fehmer; and its vilest home-grown infiltrator of the underground, Henry Rinnan, the head of the independent Gestapo unit *Sonderabteilung Lola* responsible for the arrest of more than a thousand people in the Resistance and British SOE, torturing hundreds of prisoners, and the death of more than a hundred people. For Breien, it seemed unthinkable that she was locked up in the same place where, for three years, she had trudged carrying packages and suitcases bearing food and clothing for prisoners and delivered illegal communications to undermine the Germans.

During times of reflection, like when she was confined to her cramped cell, it seemed like she had been cursed to live out someone else's life. Someone who was a true traitor to Norway, a real collaborator like the many policemen, NS bureaucrats, business owners, and factory workers who had done the Germans' bidding throughout the war and personally profited from it, or at least had never lifted a finger against the enemy. She was not one of those traitors and yet she was being treated worse than them. Why? She knew the reason even if the judges and police would not come out and say it at her forthcoming trial: she had spent considerable time with and been intimate with a high-ranking German officer. That was the one and only crime she was guilty of—and that, in itself, was no criminal offense. But it was because of this perceived breech of proper moral conduct in the face of her countrymen that her work on behalf of Milorg did not matter. All that mattered was that she had become uncomfortably close to an SS captain, and the fact that it had been done for the singular purpose of freeing her countrymen meant nothing. In the minds of the police and country at large, the ends did not justify the means and she was considered guilty.

When she reached the waiting room outside the suite of interrogation rooms, she was told curtly by a Milorg guard with peach-fuzz on his chin and an armband to sit and wait until her name was called. She did as instructed, taking a seat in a metal folding chair across the room from where two armed guards were posted. Cold industrial lights glinted down from above in the sterile waiting area. She looked around the room. There were a dozen other women waiting to be interrogated, some of them talking in low, discreet voices. Though she couldn't help but feel sympathy for them, she knew that most of them weren't like her at all and that she didn't belong here with them. And yet here she was against her will—arrested, booked, and soon-to-be tried like a common criminal.

For several minutes, she stared off despondently into space. Then a door to one of the interrogation rooms opened and a woman and two uniformed British officers stepped out. They spoke a moment with one of the guards. Something about the woman looked familiar. After a moment, Annemarie was able to place her, though the young woman was wearing a stark prison uniform, her hair was cropped short, and she appeared to have lost a dozen pounds since the last time Annemarie had seen her. When the group was finished speaking, the woman was escorted to a seat and instructed to wait. The seat next to the woman was empty and Annemarie rose from her chair and went up to her.

"Dagmar, is that you?" she said in a quiet voice so as not to arouse suspicion amongst the guards. "What on earth are you doing here?" Now that she was up close, Annemarie could see that she had been crying.

"Annemarie, it is good to see you. I...I just wish it was under better circumstances."

"Why? What has happened?"

Dagmar sighed wearily. "I was brought here today from Bredtveit Prison to meet with the British." She tipped her head towards the interrogation room where she and the two officers had just stepped out of. "I was hoping they would be able to vouch for the work I did for them but...but it looks like...they...don't know anything and aren't willing to..." She suddenly burst into tears, leaving the words unfinished.

Annemarie hugged her. "I am so sorry, Dagmar," she said consolingly.

"They weren't able to vouch for me at all," she finished through a pair of sniffles.

"What did they say exactly?"

Dagmar gently pulled away and wiped the tears from her eyes with her hands. Annemarie wished she had a handkerchief to offer her, but she didn't have one. "They said they have no record of my Eddie."

"The British agent I met?"

"Yes. They said they have no record of any such person working for British intelligence and they are sending me back to Bredtveit today. I have only been here since yesterday and already they are sending me back. I am not sure they even bothered to track down Eddie."

"Or they don't want to disclose anything about him. Wartime secrets and all that."

"Do you think that's it?"

"It certainly wouldn't surprise me."

"I also worked at Sipo since last November. I thought I could find out more about the Nazis and make a difference while at the same time protect myself from being sent to a labor camp, but it appears to have been a bad idea. Eddie told me to keep in close contact with the Germans and continue to spy on them when he was gone."

"And then he left you and Norway behind."

"Yes, he left on a new mission."

"I am sorry, Dagmar."

"Don't feel sorry for me. I created this mess." She wiped her eyes. "I didn't mean to make this all about me. What is your situation? You obviously have been facing hardship in prison too. When did they arrest you and bring you here, or are you here from another prison for questioning like me?"

"No, I was arrested on June 3 in Kristiansand and brought here."

"They arrested me in mid-May. I have been in custody for over a month now."

"I am sorry. I can see you have lost weight." She nodded ruefully. "I'm in the same boat as you: our crime was fraternizing with the enemy."

"That is what this is all about, isn't it? It makes me sick."

"The only difference is that in your case, the enemy was actually not German at all but our British ally."

"Unfortunately, neither the Norwegian police nor British intelligence know that, or at least they can't prove it."

"Which is what makes our situations virtually identical. I'm terribly sorry, Dagmar, but that's where we both stand."

"Don't you have people to vouch for you, people who can prove that you have worked for the Home Front?"

"Yes, I have many people connected to the Resistance that will vouch for me. But I'm not sure it's going to make any difference. I have been questioned three times now by the British and twice by our police, but they don't seem to be very sympathetic to my unique situation. That's why I am here now—the British want to question me again."

"What about?"

"Siegfried Fehmer. They want to know everything about him in preparation for his war crimes' trial. They are calling me his mistress."

"But you weren't his mistress, right?"

"No, I wasn't. But we did become intimate last fall after my husband left me."

"I'm sorry that you are going through this just like me. My problem is I have no one who can vouch for my Milorg courier work or the work I performed on behalf of Eddie and the British. My Milorg control officer was killed in January and I only knew him by his code name anyway. And now the British don't want to have anything to do with me. I just wish I knew why."

"I would wager it's about maintaining secrecy. Or perhaps one branch of the British intelligence kept Eddie off the books and the other branch, the one interrogating you here now, doesn't know anything about it and can't find out even if it wanted to."

"Either way it's bad for me. By the way, what happened to Fehmer? Were they able to catch him?"

"Yes, they caught him."

"How?"

"When he made his escape, he left his German shepherd Wolfie with me. One day he called me to ask about the dog. I informed the police that he had contacted me. They tracked down the phone he had placed the call from and arrested him. It turns out he was hiding out as a regular army private in a German POW camp in Solørkanten."

"You're saying that when he called to inquire about his dog, you made sure he was discovered and arrested?"

"Yes. I believe he needs to pay for his sins."

"Did you love him?"

"Part of him. But for the things he did to my people, I also hated him. But he did free more than eighty prisoners and remove several noted torturers during the war at my request. In the end, that is worth a lot."

"Will you testify against him or on his behalf?"

"I don't know. All I know is I am going to tell the truth. He was blinded by the bright light of Hitler and was unable to see the world as it truly was. For that, he will probably be shot."

"And what about us, Annemarie? Are we to be tried and convicted just like Quisling and Fehmer when we did nothing but help our country?"

Dagmar looked at her plainly and Annemarie felt tears come to her eyes. She wanted to say something reassuring, but no words came out.

"Who will stand up for us, Annemarie? Who will tell our story and spare us from a shame that neither of us deserves?"

"Like I said before, it doesn't matter who vouches for us. Our fate has been decided. That's why I'm here being interrogated, yet again, and the British are sending you back to Bredtveit. I'm truly sorry, Dagmar. I'm afraid that in the eyes of our countrymen, we have become the one thing they will not tolerate after a collaborator."

"A *tyskertøs.*"

"It doesn't matter what we did for the Allied cause, that's all we are to them."

"So, we are scapegoats then?"

"Yes, we are scapegoats for Norway's guilt. Our national guilt for standing by and doing virtually nothing—while the Nazis took over our country and persecuted our people and the Americans, British, and Russians died by the millions to set us free."

"So that's it then. We must pay the price for our country's sins."

She nodded sadly. "I am so sorry, Dagmar."

Though the younger woman's lips quivered, her face took on a fierce resolve. "Our country may never forgive us, but we must quietly serve our sentences with pride and honor," said Dagmar stoically. "For we know what we have done for Norway."

"Yes," agreed Annemarie. "You and I—and God above—know the sacrifices we have made for our country. And that is what matters most."

CHAPTER 87

AKERSHUS FORTRESS PRISON

JUNE 20, 1945

JUST BEFORE DAGMAR stepped into the waiting police car to return to Bredtveit Prison, she stared out at Oslo Fjord. A diesel-powered British Royal Navy S-class submarine was chugging its way northward towards the main harbor with victorious seamen lounging about the deck in their jumpers and grey-brown denim battle-dress uniforms. The sleek, two-hundred-foot-long vessel sat low in the water, parting gently through the waves against a backdrop of silver-tipped storm clouds, whitecaps, and a flock of soaring seagulls. The grayish-white birds hung virtually motionless in the stiff wind above the forward deck gun and conning tower, sporting a Royal Navy ensign and a Jolly Roger of skull and crossbones, as speckles of sunlight broke through the cumulous cloud cover, highlighting the tree line at the edges of the fjord.

It was a spectacular sight, and she remembered back to the sunny days she and Eddie had spent sailing together and making love in the fjord. It saddened her to think that she would be locked away in prison because of the good times they had spent together on the fjord. But what she dreaded most was the strong possibility that when she was eventually released, she might never again experience such tenderness and passion in her life. Charming, fun-loving rogues like Eddie Chapman were one in a million, and she had certainly never met any other man like him. Thinking of the joyous times they had shared, tears came to her eyes and she paused to stare out at the British submarine and the majestic fjord all around it.

"It's so beautiful and peaceful. Can you please give me a moment?" she asked her two Milorg guards.

One of them frowned at her as if such a request was out of the question, but fortunately he wasn't the one in charge. The one who was nodded with bland efficiency and said, "You have five minutes."

"Thank you," she said with feeling, and she stepped towards the iron railing and stared out at the torpedo-shaped craft sailing past and the white-tipped sea beyond. She raised her head into the mercury-colored sky and felt the cool sea breeze on her face. For a fleeting instant, her heart lifted.

I am going to make it, she told herself stubbornly. *Even if no one is there to speak for me, I am going to tough it out and make it through this hateful time.*

She thought again of Eddie. In her mind's eye, he had the same devilish grin, pencil mustache, captivating charm, and funny sense of humor as always. Hearing their peals of laughter at the Ritz and aboard his wonderful little Swedish yawl, a little smile came to her lips. He was dressed in a Norwegian sweater with the sailor's cravat about his neck that he used to wear, and they were drinking champagne and kissing like overeager schoolchildren. And then suddenly their clothes were off and they were making love and swimming in the clear, glacial-cool waters of Oslo Fjord. He had been a wonderful, unselfish lover and she couldn't help but remember how he had made her writhe with pleasure. Then she felt a little pang of guilt at her prurient thoughts and he was gone.

Vanished.

She tried to picture him again but was unable to, as if he had transformed into an old sun-bleached photograph in which the image couldn't quite be made out.

Oh, Eddie, she thought with the tears flowing down her cheeks. *Why didn't you come back for me like you promised? Why, Eddie, why?*

It was then she knew that *he* wasn't ever coming back and that she would never see him again. It made her think of her cold prison cell and her heart again filled with hopeless despair.

But it wasn't Eddie that had let her down most: it was Norway. She had come through for her country—but her country had failed her miserably and all her wartime efforts had been for nothing. That was the stark reality of it. Her country had failed to hold up its end, and she knew her life in the post-war world—a life that had once been filled with so much hope and promise—would never live up to her youthful expectations.

For Norway had killed her inside.

AFTERWORD

Spies of the Midnight Sun: A True Story of WWII Heroes was conceived and written by the author as a work of historical fiction. Although the novel takes place during the Second World War and is a true story based upon actual historical figures, events, and locales, the novel is still ultimately a work of the imagination and entertainment and should be read as nothing more. Though I have strived for historical accuracy and there is not a single primary or secondary character in the book that is not an actual historical figure (with one exception noted below), the names, characters, places, government entities, armed forces, religious and political groups, and incidents, as portrayed in the novel, are products of the author's imagination and are not to be construed as one-hundred-percent accurate depictions. The single fictional minor character is Dagmar Lahlum's control officer, whose name has either been lost to history, or more unlikely, did not exist or was a lower-level contact and not an actual control agent. With that said, the story is based primarily upon known historical events and real people.

With respect to the events portrayed in the novel, I have tried to place the actual historical figures where they physically were during a given event and have used their actual words based on case files, contemporary transcripts, trial documents, memoirs, and other quoted materials. Like Michael Shaara in his Pulitzer-prize-winning historical novel about the Battle of Gettysburg, *The Killer Angels*, I have not "consciously changed any fact" nor have I "knowingly violated the action." Most of the scenes in the book are based on known events with specific historical figures present, but a minority are based on incidents that are generally accepted to have taken place but have unfortunately not been documented by history, or that I believe happened under similar circumstances to those described in the book but for which there is no historical record. In these cases, the interpretations of character and motivation are mine and mine alone. Thus, the book's characters are ultimately a part of my overall imaginative landscape and are, therefore, the fictitious creations of the author, reflecting my personal research interests and biases.

In the novel, I have taken one important liberty to tighten up the interpersonal connections: I have had Dagmar Lahlum and Eddie Chapman interact with Annemarie Breien and Siegfried Fehmer, when in real life these historical figures may or may not have encountered one another in wartime Oslo. However, in the handful of scenes where these historical figures share the page, their thoughts and actions are, I believe, consistent with their characters and they are typically interacting during a documented historical event that is accurately portrayed.

Below I present the fate of Norway following the war along with the legacy of the six primary historical figures and point-of-view characters of the book: Dagmar Lahlum, Eddie Chapman, Annemarie Breien, Tar Robertson, Siegfried Fehmer, and Stephan von Gröning.

THE WWII LEGACY OF NORWAY

For a country that was complicit with the Nazis during WWII and failed to thwart Nazi aggression, there was a fervent need in 1945 for Norway to find culprits—and both Dagmar Lahlum and Annemarie Breien were undeservedly snared in the post-war reckoning known as the *landssvikoppgjør* (The Settlement with the Traitors). As Richard Overy, author of *Scandinavia in the Second World War* states: "For all the discussion in present-day Scandinavia about the failure to uphold universal human values, there was a strong sense of retribution at the time against those deemed to have failed those values...in Norway, 20,000 were imprisoned [for collaboration] and 30,000 lost their civil rights." At war's end, Norway had an inferiority complex and a public-relations nightmare on its hands: it had to convince itself and the Allies—which had expended billions of dollars and spilled copious amounts of blood while Norway had cozied up to the Nazis and offered only token resistance—that it had been a steadfast resister and stalwart ally all along.

According to Norwegian WWII historian Ole Kristian Grimes, "An overwhelming majority had by the end of the war rallied around the King and to a lesser extent around the government-in-exile and around the resistance movement at home. Only a minority had participated in the more or less permanent organizations and networks of the resistance movement, but as a whole, the population identified itself with resistance and saw it as the expression of their feelings of hostility to the occupation regime and of their hopes and aspirations for liberation and the post-war period...The counterpart to this solidarity and sense of oneness and the strength of 'us' was the castigation of 'them': the quislings, traitors and collaborators of different sorts."

As part of its revisionist history in the name of post-war nation-building, the country whitewashed facts by exaggerating the feats of its most unimpeachable Resistance heroes and hunting down scapegoats with Inspector-Javert-like vengeance. The result was inevitable: many patriotic innocents like Dagmar Lahlum and Annemarie Breien were caught in the crossfire and their lives unfairly ruined. At the same time, many powerful Norwegian economic interests and factory workers whose labors directly benefitted the Nazis were never prosecuted, drawing attention to the gross unfairness during what has also become known infamously as the "legal purge of Norway." This *landssvikoppgjør*, purge, overzealous retribution, or whatever one wants to call it took place between May 1945 and August 1948 against anyone who was deemed to have collaborated with the German occupation.

As eminent Norwegian WWII scholar Tore Pryser has pointed out, the importance of several Resistance members hailed as heroes following the war was exaggerated for nation-building purposes, and a number of companies that cooperated with and profited from the Germans went largely unpunished for their "economic high treason." While the official Norwegian view of the war has focused on the opposition to German authority and the abhorrence to the Nazi philosophy, the truth is that there were 43,000 registered NS members in Norway in 1943, Norwegian farms and fishermen kept the occupying power supplied with fresh produce, and hundreds of thousands of Norwegians took part in German war-related infrastructure, "building barracks, fortifications, strategic railways and roads, airports and aluminum plants for the Germans." Yet few of these "collaborators" were tried and found guilty during the post-war "Settlement with the Traitors." Twelve thousand Norwegians also volunteered for the Waffen-SS to fight for the Nazis in the Viking Regiment. Many of them saw action on the Eastern Front, with a total of eight hundred killed. Half of Norway's police officers joined the NS or

German SS. The roundup and deportation of Norway's 767 Jews to Auschwitz was engineered by Norwegian civil servants, who drew up registers of Jews, and commanded by the very same Norwegian police who rendered rash and unfair judgment upon Dagmar Lahlum and Annemarie Breien during the post-war treason trials. Only twenty-six of the deported Jews survived.

If Germany had won the war, Norway could, thus, have presented a strong case for favorable consideration by the Third Reich. As Richard Petrow, author of *The Bitter Years: The Invasion and Occupation of Denmark and Norway, April 1940- May 1945*, states: "In Norway, Germany had the service and support of the Quisling regime," which accommodated the Germans and "looked with respect and admiration on Germanic culture. At no time, even when the tide of battle turned sharply against Germany, did the majority of Norwegians come out in active opposition to the Germans."

It is for this reason—a kind of national overcompensation induced by the shame of complicity—that Norway engaged in historical revisionism and pursued the draconian post-war treason trials. The impulse to purge Nazism, render moral judgment, and move forward in a unified democratic front resulted in the punishment of many innocents with ties to the Resistance. This same overreaching impulse is what made anyone who had ever been an NS member accountable, even those who had been placed on lists without their knowing or joined the party to spy on its members. According to social anthropologist Sindre Bangstad of Oslo, "There is nothing new in denials or whitewashing of the actual historical record as part of processes of nation-building or national reconstruction in any country of course. Yet this way of looking at Norway's World War II past has in fact persisted well into our time." Even to this day, claims Bangstad, the WWII stories that most Norwegians like to hear about are those about "blond, heroic Norwegians courageously fighting the overwhelming might of the evil Nazi German occupiers. These Norwegians actually existed, and their personal sacrifices and heroism still need recording. But the overall reality of Norway's and Norwegians' role in World War II was of course far more complex."

Unfortunately, Dagmar Lahlum and Annemarie Breien were the collateral damage of a nation that was desperate to purge its ugly past and have clear-cut heroes who actually killed Nazis and blew up ships and plants, like Max Manus and Gunnar Sønsteby.

DAGMAR LAHLUM

History shows that Dagmar Lahlum should have long ago been recognized for her wartime achievements just like Manus, Sønsteby, Haugland, and other Norwegian heroes. British and Norwegian records indicate that she not only risked her life working as an unofficial MI5 spy on behalf of Chapman and the British Secret Service, but as an operative in the Norwegian Resistance, most likely *Militær Organisasjon*, or Milorg. There are multiple lines of evidence that demonstrate her espionage credentials and dismiss the false and pernicious charge that she was a "German's tart" or Norwegian Mata Hari working on behalf of the Nazis. Though her precise role in the Resistance remains shrouded in mystery and she took many espionage secrets to her grave, her spy record on behalf of Great Britain is well-established. For this stalwart service alone, she is a WWII hero of Norway who should never have been locked up in Bredtveit Prison in 1945 by her countrymen, been convicted of treason in 1947, or suffered a lifetime of abuse and shame.

During Chapman's time in Norway, Dagmar became his skillful subagent, helping him to obtain intelligence that he wouldn't have been able to collect—or, at least, not as discreetly—if she had not been present. In other words, she added significant value to the British double agent's intelligence-gathering activities by providing him with a plausible cover, thereby enabling him to blend in and act as a sponge within the Oslo community. As Ben Macintyre, author of *Agent Zigzag: A True Story of Nazi Espionage, Love, and Betrayal*, has stated, Dagmar was "privy to all sort of interesting information; moreover, she was a vital prop. A man taking a photograph of a military installation would arouse suspicion, but what could be more natural than a young man taking snapshots of his Norwegian girlfriend?"

With Dagmar's help, Chapman was able to construct an accurate picture of the Abwehr in Occupied Norway and identify the Germans' key military installations in and around Oslo. The *British MI5 Camp 020 Report* dated July 11, 1944 (KV2 459), which describes the results of Agent Zigzag's interrogation upon his return to England in June 1944 from Norway and France, provides a detailed description of German military facilities that the double agent visited during his training work in Occupied Norway. But the list in *Appendix B–Pin-Pointing of Places of Operational Interest* also includes several installations that Chapman had increased access to specifically because of Dagmar, or that he visited with her. These include *Sicherheitsdienst* offices and lodgings; Luftwaffe headquarters; supply, tank, and armored car depots; U-boat pens along Oslo Fjord; naval yards; flak defenses; and Vidkun Quisling's fortified Gimlé Mansion on Bygdøy Peninsula that he and Dagmar stealthily reconnoitered during one of their sailing ventures.

But the beautiful Norwegian spy provided much more than cover. She discreetly took photographs of the key members of the German Oslo Abwehr: Stephan von Gröning, *SS-Oberleutnant* Walter Praetorius, *Kapitäns* Johnny Holst and Mueller, secretary Molli Stirl, and others. As Macintyre states, "Here was a complete photographic record of the Oslo Abwehr team, 'obtained discreetly' by a vague, pretty Norwegian girl no one could ever suspect of spying." In addition, Dagmar provided Agent Zigzag with the name of the Chief of the German Security Service in Norway, Heinrich Fehlis, reviled by the Norwegians as much as Terboven and Fehmer. When Chapman wanted her to get close to von Gröning, who seemed to enjoy her company, and the other members of the Oslo Abwehr to gather intelligence on them, she willingly obliged. When the two lover-spies walked the streets of Oslo or sailed the fjord, the British double agent had a built-in Norwegian interpreter to explain everything he saw and help him gather valuable intelligence on the German occupiers to use against them. And when he left Norway, she continued to perform espionage activities on behalf of MI5 at Chapman's request by keeping "her eyes and ears open for information that might later be of interest." She gathered intelligence on a German *sturmbannführer* (likely Axel Etling), notifying Chapman about the officer in a letter when he was in Occupied France awaiting his return to Britain in spring 1944. For Agent Zigzag, Dagmar Lahlum was a key Allied operative that enabled him to put together a voluminous report in his head on the German presence in Norway, a report that he was later able to deliver in detail to Tar Robertson and the Double Cross team at MI5.

With regard to her role in the Resistance, the evidence suggests that Dagmar was likely a simple courier, transmitting information and perhaps forged documents to cutouts in Oslo. The brilliant Norwegian Historian Kristina Hatledal, author of *Women Fighting: The History of Norwegian Female Resistance Fighters* based on her detailed Master's Thesis on Dagmar Lahlum and Annemarie Breien, concluded that if Dagmar in fact was an official freedom-fighter, she most likely served as a courier or in some other lower-level anonymous role (typically the only option open to female Norwegian Resistance operatives), since a more prominent position in Milorg or another group would likely have come to light during her post-war treason case. Based on British documents, Macintyre concludes plainly: "Dagmar Lahlum, model and dressmaker, was…secretly working as an agent for Milorg, the spreading Norwegian resistance network. Though neither knew it, Eddie Chapman and his 'beautiful and adorable' new lover were fighting on the same side." MI5 was more cautious. They acknowledged in their July 11, 1944 report that Dagmar worked for the "Norwegian underground movement" while having the "confidence of a British Secret Service agent," yet chauvinistically referred to her as "the girlfriend" and requested additional information from the Special Operations Executive on the nature of her Home Front service to check out her bona fides. For his part, Chapman made it abundantly clear how invaluable Dagmar had been to him as a subagent, to which MI5 reported with apparent mystification, "Chapman appears anxious at every opportunity to talk about Dagmar Lahlum."

There is a very good reason he did this: though untrained, his new Norwegian "girlfriend" proved to be a damned good spy. Furthermore, there is little question that she was working for the Resistance when she first met Chapman, and she was most likely working under a control officer she knew only by code name. During their initial encounter at the Ritz, the German occupiers' favorite watering hole in Oslo, it is obvious that she was there to gather intelligence on the enemy. From numerous first-hand accounts, she hated Germans with a passion and was terrified of them—and yet here the twenty-year-old farm girl from Eidsvoll was in the lion's den with her "Craven A cigarettes, long ebony holder, high heels, and fashionably risqué dresses" pretending to be a Marlene Dietrich-like good-time girl. As Macintyre properly concludes, the only possible explanation is that she was put up to it by the Norwegian Resistance, who likely coaxed her into giving a try at the honey-trap ruse to gain German intelligence. But the problem was she was terrified of Nazis and was at the Ritz only reluctantly. When Chapman approached her table and spoke in German, she showed visible fear and spurned his advances, and it was only later, after significant effort on his part, that he was able to win her over and convince her to have dinner with him. As Macintyre states: "Only much later did Chapman pause to wonder why a beautiful girl who hated Germans should choose to drink in the city's most notorious Nazi hangout." There's only one reason she would have done it: to spy on Germans. And she probably had to be convinced to do it by a male Milorg control officer, as she was clearly uncomfortable at the bar and around German military and intelligence figures until later when she and Chapman were a couple and he was there to protect her.

During their burgeoning courtship, Dagmar couldn't resist hinting to her lover—whom she knew early on was not German and suspected was a British spy—at her links with the Resistance movement in Oslo. For Chapman, subsequent events confirmed she was working for the underground and fighting the good fight on behalf of Norway. In the summer of 1943, following a fire set by saboteurs at the Forbunds Hotel occupied by the Germans, Dagmar disappeared from Chapman's side on the street and returned moments later to inform him that it was the work of the British Allies. How would she come by such information so quickly if she wasn't working for the Resistance? On July 10, 1943, as they were walking arm in arm through Oslo, she told Chapman to wait in the street, and then dashed into a tobacconist. She returned a few minutes later, empty-handed, looking flushed and excited, and whispered the news: "The Allies have invaded Sicily." The news of the invasion had not been broadcast on Norwegian radio, and Dagmar could only have obtained the information through contacts in the Resistance with access to banned radios. As Chapman stated under interrogation at Camp 020, "she intimated, without revealing the names of any of her contacts, that this information came through the patriotic Norwegian Jøssings," the general term used to describe members of the Norwegian underground Resistance loyal to Britain. A short time later, after he had confessed that he was a British double agent, he set her a test: to locate the Oslo headquarters of the Abwehr, which he already knew. She promptly returned with the difficult-to-obtain information that only a spy would know: the Abwehr headquarters was at 8 Jilingenberggate, and the head of station was a naval officer with four rings on his sleeve. In the late fall of 1943 at the University of Oslo, a student demonstration was taking place protesting against Quisling's continued attempts to Nazify the education system. When the police attacked and began hauling off the student leaders, Dagmar pointed to a young man being hustled away and whispered that he was a member of Resistance. Brandishing his Wehrmacht pass, Chapman intervened and "obtained the immediate release of Dagmar's young friend," but not before a loud "argument with a German soldier and a German officer in the street." Finally, Dagmar is the one who gave Chapman the name of *SS-Oberführer* Fehlis not the other way around. Given the secrecy of the Nazi police and intelligence apparatus, the much-hated head of the Gestapo, Kripo, and SD and a key instrument of Nazi terror in Norway was a man whose name would likely be known only by those well-connected to the Home Front. Collectively, these incidents demonstrate Dagmar's close ties to the Norwegian Resistance and strongly suggest she was not merely in the loop but an active member of the spy community, likely as a simple courier and transmitter of information as Hatledal proposes.

Dagmar was never a member of *Nasjonal Samling* and was without question a spy working on behalf of the Norwegian Resistance and the British government. So why was she, in a great miscarriage of justice, arrested by the Norwegian police on May 19, 1945 and locked up in Bredtveit Women's Prison? In her master's thesis entitled *War Heroine or German Mistress? The Story of Dagmar Lahlum in the Light of Other Female Resistance Fighters*, Hatledal concludes it was a combination of her intimate relationship with Chapman, her supposed fraternization with other members of the German Intelligence Service (whom she was not collaborating with but spying on), and her work for the German censoring authorities in the final months of the war that led to her arrest and incarceration. Hatledal makes a strong case that her reputation for being a "German's tart" cozying up to the enemy was intolerable for the uniformly male Norwegian authorities, particularly the police with an axe to grind who ultimately decided her case. Consequently, she was given an extremely harsh penalty for "sleeping with the enemy" even though she, unlike Annemarie Breien, never did, as Chapman was a confessed British spy who was actively working against the Germans throughout the war.

In a written statement from prison dated June 15, 1945, Dagmar referenced her contact with Chapman, whose last name she still did not know (for security reasons he told her only his first name). She rightfully maintained that she had never been a member of the NS and her sympathies had always been with the Resistance and British. She admitted to having worked for the Germans at Sipo in letter censorship but pleaded not culpable to treason. She further made clear that her job as a letter censor had been approved by Eddie, who had promised to return to Norway to clear her name as soon as the war was over if he was still alive. If he was unable to return, he had assured her that if she contacted his superiors in British Intelligence, they would help ensure that she was recognized for her wartime service on behalf of the Allies and keep her from being tried as a collaborator.

Following her unsuccessful meeting with her own countrymen to clear her name, Dagmar requested a meeting with the British in accordance with Chapman's instructions. The documents in her treason archive indicate the Norwegian police allowed Dagmar to be transferred to the English police at Akershus Prison, where Annemarie Breien was coincidentally being held. As stated by Hans Olav Lahlum, a prominent Norwegian author and historian and Dagmar's grand-nephew, "Dagmar was escorted to a meeting with official British representatives in Oslo on June 19, 1945, but they denied any knowledge of the case and she was returned to Bredtveit Women's Prison." The police report from June 20, 1945 indicates that the British firmly refused to accept her. After the inestimable service she had performed on behalf of Agent Zigzag and Churchill's England, why didn't the British help her out? The most likely possibilities are that British representatives in newly liberated Norway didn't bother (or didn't want to bother) to obtain corroboration of her story with MI5, or that they did check but MI5 refused assistance because their hands were tied due to the Official Secrets Act, or because of Chapman's perceived untrustworthiness after being cut lose for being a blabbermouth. Hatledal maintains that MI5 didn't consider helping Lahlum a priority, either because she was not an official agent with them or because they looked upon her as just another of the womanizing Chapman's many lovers, or a combination of both. Regardless of the reason, what we know for certain is that the British left her hanging out to dry and she now had no one to defend her wartime activities on behalf of the Allies.

According to Norwegian political scientist and *Aftenposten* correspondent Hilde Harbo, when Dagmar worked at Sipo censoring letters from Sweden and Norway, she had the opportunity to slip through messages to the Norwegian Resistance. Furthermore, Harbo states that she acquired the job through Fehlis's driver, *SS-Oberscharführer* Otto Paul Iredi. As Harbo makes clear, Iredi was a valuable contact if Dagmar was willing to help Norwegian Resistance fighters in an attempt to liquidate Fehlis, but it is not known whether she pursued information about Fehlis's movements from the driver or not.

Dagmar remained imprisoned at Bredtveit until she was released on November 24, 1945 after having served 189 days. During the later scandalous court proceedings in 1947, she was wrongly accused of high treason and accepted a fine, prison time, and the malicious whispers that she was a "kept woman" by the Germans rather than fight the charges in a public trial. She was sentenced to 189 days of prison time, the same number of days she had spent in remand in 1945 as her time spent in custody was considered time served. She was also deprived of voting rights for ten years. After enduring so much hardship, she wanted to get on with her life rather than face the grim prospect of an even worse verdict, for she viewed her situation as hopeless. Like a rape victim who would rather internalize the trauma rather than relive it in the charged atmosphere of a courtroom, she knew the odds were against her. Having been an anonymous Milorg operative who no longer had a control officer or other operative that she knew by name to vouch for her, she had no one in the Resistance that she could call upon. The only people she knew were cutouts. Unlike Annemarie Breien who was well-connected, Dagmar had little money, no influential persons or family members, and no legal advocate to defend her. Though stubborn and brave, she was an unsophisticated girl from the country without the resources to mount a strong defense. She had trusted too much in Chapman and the British to bail her out of her situation, and when her white-knight-in-shining-armor Eddie failed to return to Norway to rescue her and the British threw her to the wolves, she gave up all hope of exonerating herself.

Some have suggested she may have had questionable motives for her contact with the Germans during the war, and that was why she accepted the penalty, but that is highly unlikely. As demonstrated above, there is no evidence to indicate that she was a traitor and considerable evidence of her contributions to the Allied war effort as both an underground operative and unofficial MI5 spy; and it should be noted there were likely many other contributions that have gone unrecorded by history. For example, during her Agent-Zigzag-sanctioned work at Sipo she may have gathered intelligence on the Germans, as Garbo suggests. Most importantly, none of her actions and expressed emotions in the presence of Chapman are consistent with her being a German collaborator. In her words, body language, and deeds, she consistently showed a strong aversion towards, and fear of, Germans, as well as a fierce loyalty to the Allied cause, and she risked her life while working as a subagent under Chapman. Most importantly and telling, Chapman would have been arrested by the Germans in Norway and never been sent back to England, and von Gröning and the rest of the Abwehr team would have shown some visible change if she had been working for them, as Chapman pointed out during his Camp 020 interrogations. But none of that happened.

The judgment in her treason trial and her undeserved reputation as a *tyskertøs* dogged Dagmar for the rest of her life after the war. Her neighbors back in Eidsvoll whispered within earshot that she was a "German's tart," but she ignored the affronts and never told her presumptuous neighbors that she had spied on behalf of the British Secret Service and Norwegian Resistance during the war. According to Hans Olav Lahlum, a nosy neighbor once yelled after Dagmar's little niece Bibbi Røset in Eidsvoll, "Remember your aunt was a Jerry bag!" He further states that she soon returned to the more anonymous streets of Oslo and abandoned Eidsvoll once and for all when she received a small inheritance from her parents in the mid-1950s. She continued to work and pay taxes to the country that had unjustly condemned her to prison, serving as an assistant nurse aboard the cruise ship Stvanger Fjord, which sailed between Oslo, New York, and Nova Scotia, for through Chapman she had learned to love the sea. She also worked in a bookshop, then as a hairdresser, and finally as an accountant. She retired towards the end of the 1980s, but never applied for any public positions or sought to attract public attention.

According to Hans Olav Lahlum and Bibbi Røset, who was close to her and faithfully took care of her in her later years, she never had any children and lived on her own for the rest of her life, with the brief exception of a short marriage in the early 1950s. She had several lovers after the war—all older, wealthy men—but none of these relationships was ever formalized and none of them lasted. She continued to wear fashionable clothes, leopard-skin hats, and a dash of makeup until her later years, and she did not lose her looks until late in her life in the mid-1990s when the ravages of cigarette smoking and heavy alcohol consumption overtook her. One time, Bibbi caught her dancing alone in front of the mirror, when the former spy who had loved a dashing British double agent must have been thinking back to happier times.

Unbeknownst to Dagmar, Chapman repeatedly told his MI5 case officers throughout his time in England upon his return that she should be taken care of and her name cleared. But as always, his intelligence handlers, led by the hostile Major Michael Ryde, failed him and, according to Chapman, even did everything in their power to make sure that he couldn't travel to Oslo to clear her name. When he eventually made contact with her from the Canary Islands in 1992, she wouldn't speak to him on the telephone at first, so distraught was she that he had left her behind to face her vengeful countrymen alone. But she finally relented and the two ex-lovers re-established contact. Whether she actually travelled to England and the two reunited remains uncertain, but records suggest that around 1996-1997 she expected that Chapman would soon return to Norway and make public the story of her war effort. However, he was unable to follow through with his promise owing to ill health and he died on December 12, 1997.

According to Hans Olav Lahlum, "the news that Eddie had died without coming to Norway, and telling the truth about-her wartime experiences, was probably the last blow for Dagmar's already fragile mind. Her final hope for some kind of vindication turned into just another disappointment. The last years of Dagmar's life were very difficult. She was not only a heavy smoker and an alcoholic, but also suffered from Parkinson's disease and became increasingly socially isolated and undernourished. A tragic shadow of her youthful beauty, she continued to walk alone on her circuit from *Vinmonopolet* (state alcohol shop) to the bank to her flat with increasingly unsteady steps through the late 1990s." She was last seen alive by her niece Bibbi at Christmas dinner on December 25, 1999 and was found dead four days later from Parkinson's disease behind the locked doors of her flat. As Hans Olav states, "As was fairly typical for her life, the exact date of her death and the circumstances remain unclear. She was reportedly found lying on the floor among all her old clothes and empty bottles, in a somewhat unusual and defensive position. However, there was no evidence of violence and a routine police investigation concluded that no one else had been in the flat at the time of her death." Hans Olav believes that, in the end, his aunt died "alone in her home during a fight against some mental ghost from the wartime years."

She was virtually forgotten by everyone and her war effort was still entirely unknown at the time of her death, so very few people came to her funeral. Following her funeral, Bibbi found a box of letters amongst her belongings, carefully written out in English, on sheet after sheet of airmail paper. They were addressed to Eddie Chapman. None had ever been sent and Bibbi burned them all. But Dagmar had never forgotten her beloved Eddie.

She was and will forever be a true WWII hero of Norway. Though her personal honor was never restored as it should have been in her lifetime, it can and should be done today.

EDDIE CHAPMAN

Waxing philosophically on the challenges of peacetime after the war, Eddie Chapman said, "When war ends, it leaves a gap in one's life that is not easily filled. One has lived on a peak of anticipation, either of terror or excitement. Then comes the quiet after the storm when one realizes that the chances of a sudden death have become more remote. Yet one still feels oddly insecure and afraid; afraid of the vagueness and economic instability of the future." As it turns out, Chapman didn't feel that way for long following the German surrender as his recidivistic impulses got the better of him and the intrepid British double agent returned to his former life as a prince of the London underworld.

Unable to go straight, in the 1950s Agent Zigzag smuggled gold, guns, and cigarettes across the Mediterranean and knocked off a post-office van with a new criminal gang, escaping with £250,000. In the 1960s, he moved to Africa's Gold Coast, where he raked in a bundle from a complicated building contract. During the course of his resurrected felonious career, he mingled with an eclectic mix of high-rolling glitterati, common robbers, and blackmailers, naturally drawing the attention of the police. They were often hot on his tail and making inquiries into his occasionally harebrained schemes, like when he became involved in a ludicrous plot to smuggle 850,000 packets of cigarettes and kidnap the deposed sultan of Morocco.

Lieutenant Colonel Robin "Tin Eye" Stephens, Commandant of London's Camp 020 who had a surprising affection for Zigzag, had wondered on more than one occasion "what will happen when Chapman, embroiled again in crime, as he inevitably will be, stands up in court and pleads leniency on the grounds of highly secret wartime service?" He and his cohorts in British Intelligence swiftly found out. Chapman would be summoned to court repeatedly for two decades following the war, but he was never sent back to prison. On more than one occasion, he had a character reference from former colleagues confirming his contributions to the war effort. When he was charged with passing forged currency in 1948, he produced a character reference from an unnamed "senior officer of the War office"—believed to be his first and favorite case officer Ronnie Reed—maintaining that he was "one of the bravest men who served in the last war." As Macintyre says, "MI5 had not entirely welched on its debt." In 1974, he was found not guilty of striking a man on the head with a glass during a dance party during a fight over a young woman. In defense of his actions, Agent Zigzag proceeded to inform the court, "I was trained in unarmed combat for my wartime activities and I didn't need a glass to defend myself in a pub brawl. I could have killed him with my bare hands." When the jury acquitted him, he offered to buy them all drinks.

Soon after the German surrender, he found his new Dagmar. During the war, he had two fiancées—Freda Stevenson with whom he had had his first daughter Diane, and Dagmar—each in opposite war zones. He was still betrothed to Freda, who was being taken care of financially along with Diane by MI5 in Britain, when he met Dagmar in Norway. But he ended up abandoning both women after the war. Instead, he married his former love interest Betty Farmer, whom he had been wooing at the Hotel de la Plage in Jersey in 1939 when undercover police arrived to arrest him and he was forced to jump through a French window and make a run for it. He and the platinum-blonde Betty were married on October 9, 1947 in London and their daughter Suzanne was born in 1954.

It was for the most part a happy marriage that lasted fifty years, though Chapman's eye wandered often during their time together. Like Dagmar, Betty proved to be a strong and faithful soul mate despite his mood swings, heavy drinking, and desperate need for constant action and adventure. Together, they became at least modestly wealthy, owning a castle in Ireland and a health spa called Shenley Lodge in Hertfordshire, not far from the de Havilland Mosquito plant. He drove a Rolls-Royce (though he never passed a driving test), donned fashionable fur-collared coats, became known affectionately by the London newspapers as "the gentleman crook," and served as the "honorary crime correspondent" of the Sunday Telegraph. According to Betty, "He had six mistresses in his life and I used to say, when he was getting towards his end, 'You know, you had all those mistresses. How I wish there was one here now who could help me with you!'" Despite his dalliances with other women, he always came back to Betty, who was his rock. One of their post-war friends articulated best why she stayed with a hopeless Lothario like Eddie: "Better to have lived in the light than never to have had it on at all. And that's why Betty stayed." The couple remained devoted to one another until his death on December 11, 1997 at the age of 83. In 2013, Betty published her memoirs of their loving yet tumultuous time together in *Mrs. Zigzag: The Extraordinary Life of a Secret Agent's Wife.*

Shortly after the war, Chapman defied MI5's warning and tried to publish an accurate first-hand account of his espionage experiences but was blocked by the British government. A bowdlerized version of his exploits as a secret agent were serialized in a French newspaper in 1946, and in 1954 he was able to publish his memoirs as *The Eddie Chapman Story*, but they were heavily censored by the government and semifictionalized in order not to violate the Official Secrets Act. Finally, in 1966, Agent Zigzag was allowed to publish a semi-accurate but still incomplete version of his WWII espionage activities on behalf of MI5 entitled *The Real Eddie Chapman Story*, which provided scant details and was heavily excised by government lawyers. The book provided the basis for a spy film directed by his friend Terence Young, the director of the James Bond classics *Dr. No* and

Thunderball. *Triple Cross* starred Christopher Plummer as Chapman and Yul Brynner as Colonel Baron von Grunen, a fictionalized Stephan von Gröning. Filmed mostly in France during the second half of 1966 because of continuing worries over whether the British government might attempt legal action, the film bore only a superficial relation to the truth. Chapman was severely disappointed from it, as were reviewers who savaged the film as an "unsatisfactory yarn," "thoroughly dull and implausible," and "a rather shoddy, anachronistic, badly directed attempt to re-create one of the most thrilling of all war adventures."

In the early 1990s, Chapman's health began to decline from all the years of heavy drinking, smoking, and carousing. He and Betty were living in the Canary Islands, and it was at this time that he tracked down and resumed contact with Dagmar. A Norwegian woman who lived in a flat next door got into conversation with him one day and, as they talked it became clear that they both knew her. From a Norwegian reporter, he had learned that she had been arrested on suspicion of being a collaborator and had "gone through quite a bit of hell." According to Nicholas Booth, British author of *Zigzag: The Incredible Wartime Exploits of Double Agent Eddie Chapman*, when Chapman learned from the Norwegian reporter what had happened to Dagmar, he was outraged. "For God's sake, this girl had nothing to do with collaborating," Chapman told him. "She was helping me. One thing I'd like to do is clear her name." In 1992, he called her from the Canary Islands. At first, she refused to speak to him but she eventually relented. She was both horrified and excited when he called, and they talked for an hour. Over the next few years, they began what Booth describes as "a slightly stilted correspondence," sharing the kind of inconsequential reminiscences that old friends often do. "I remember you as a kindly and charming fellow, always smiling," she wrote in March 1992. According to Booth and Norwegian journalist Hilde Harbo, Dagmar visited Eddie in England just before his death in 1997. However, Norwegian Historian Kristina Hatledal casts doubt upon this, noting that at this stage Dagmar would have been in the latter stages of the Parkinson's that claimed her death in 1999 and would hardly have been able to travel to Britain.

Whether they met in person or not, Chapman promised to come to Oslo and book a suite at the Grand Hotel for them. He also promised to contact his old spymasters at MI5 to get her official recognition for her wartime service. But shortly thereafter, he became so ill that his wife Betty brought him home to England and he never made it to Norway to clear her name. On Chapman's surviving videotape recorded three years before his death in 1994, he reveals with obvious emotion how badly in the 1940s and 1950s he had wanted to maintain his promise and seek Dagmar in Norway to clear her name, but that British intelligence "found some excuse to prevent me getting back into Norway after the war." Throughout his time in England, Eddie repeatedly told his MI5 case officers that Dagmar should be taken care of but they failed him. "The bastards had not done anything about it," Chapman revealed on his tapes in 1994. "It was just a load of, 'Oh yes, we'll see that she is looked after.'" MI5 and the British War Office never lifted a finger to help his Norwegian Resistance contact and subagent that had enabled him to gain invaluable intelligence on the German war machine in Occupied Norway. In his final years, Chapman would often ask people who were visiting Norway to look Dagmar up. When a pianist friend of his who was due to appear on Norwegian television called her after he arrived in Oslo, "I asked him to dedicate one of his songs to her," Zigzag recalled. "She was delighted."

In the end, Chapman is remembered as a selfish but dashing, courageous, and lovable rogue. As Macintyre states, "His vices were as extreme as his virtues, and to the end of his life, it was never clear whether he was on the side of the angels or the devils." A family friend from Yorkshire that knew him and Betty said of him: "Eddie was a much-misunderstood soul with a brilliant mind. He was a character and that character was forged through hardship and adversity. Eddie and his peers are long gone, but not forgotten. There won't be anyone like him again." The naval spymaster Ewen Montagu of the Double Cross Committee called him, "a rogue but a very brave man," while Ronnie Reed said, "Zigzag is himself a most absorbing person. Reckless and impetuous, moody and sentimental, he becomes on acquaintance an extraordinarily likeable character." And even the unsentimental Tin Eye Stephens was forced to concede his admiration. Shortly after D-Day, he said, "The outstanding feature of the case is the courage of Chapman. Yet there is something more to the story than that, for Chapman has faced the searching inquiries of the German secret service with infinite resource. He has rendered and may still render his country great service. For that, in return, Chapman deserves well of his country, and a pardon for his crimes."

ANNEMARIE BREIEN

At the end of the war, Annemarie Breien returned to Kristiansand to be with friends and family in the Allied victory days of May, but the euphoria did not last. Her parents and relatives began experiencing police raids, and a heavily armed British and Milorg contingent busted into her residence in Oslo to arrest "Fehmer's mistress, Mrs. Langballe." Learning that she was being sought for arrest, Annemarie turned herself in to the authorities in Kristiansand, where she was detained and questioned. Being well-connected with the Resistance leadership through Jens Christian Hauge, chief of Milorg, her father Roald Breien, head of Milorg's Upper Buskerud cell, and others, she had a large support system to vouch for her work as a Resistance operative and was released from custody. However, once freed she returned to Oslo but was again arrested on June 3, 1944 and sent to Akershus Prison.

"It was a strange feeling to be carried away captive into Akershus after three years I had trudged the same way in all sorts of illicit errands for my compatriots," recounted Breien wistfully in later years. Strange it must have been indeed for a Norwegian war hero who had rescued between 80 and 90 of her countrymen from prison. Here she was, after helping smuggle Jews to Switzerland before the war and three years of risking her life in Oslo, being held in custody pending trial as if she was a common criminal like Quisling, Fehmer, or Henry Rinnan, the Norwegian head of the independent Gestapo unit *Sonderabteilung Lola* responsible for the arrest of more than a thousand Norwegians, hundreds of whom were violently tortured and more than a hundred of whom were murdered.

History has established that she performed inestimable service on behalf of the Norwegian Resistance as an intelligence gatherer, courier, go-between, and unofficial humanitarian relief worker on behalf of the Allied cause. According to

Hatledal and other Norwegian researchers, she carried letters, packages, and suitcases bearing food, clothing, and hidden money to incarcerated Resistance figures and delivered communications to her Milorg compatriots about forthcoming raids based on intelligence given to her by Fehmer—or that she was able to overhear, coax, or steal from him. She also succeeded in convincing him to soften his interrogation procedures on prisoners and to remove one or more of his most brutal Gestapo torturers from his interrogation teams. Her primary Milorg contact that she reported to was a dentist and captain named Knut Reidar Bergwitz-Larsen, and she also maintained contact with key executives in Milorg through Else Endresen, who in turn reported to Jens Christian Hauge. On the night of May 7 and 8, 1944 at Victoria Terrasse, she was an instrumental and trusted liaison between Milorg and Fehmer in helping bring about a peaceful end to hostilities and transition to Allied control.

So, the question is, despite all she did on behalf of the Home Front, why was she imprisoned and treated like a traitor by her countrymen? While most of her 40,000 Milorg comrades in arms did nothing but tromp around in the woods performing useless training exercises until April 1944 when Allied victory was imminent, she had 80 to 90 of her countrymen released from prison and garnered critical intelligence on behalf of the Allies—and yet she was the one that had to suffer incarceration and ostracism? What was her crime? Unfortunately, the answer is simple and obvious: she became unacceptably close—at least in the eyes of the Norwegian police and her countrymen—to the Gestapo's top bloodhound, the loathed and greatly feared Siegfried Fehmer.

There was no formal charge of treason, but the police were vindictive and suspicious and the investigations dragged on for more than a year and a half before her case was filed. In her defense, Annemarie was able to obtain 34 testimonials on her behalf from Milorg officers and those she had managed to have released from prison, including Jens Christian Hauge and the author-filmmaker Sigurd Evensmo. The testimonials made it clear that she had helped the war effort by securing prisoner releases, providing food and payments, and providing invaluable intelligence information to the Home Front. However, the police refused to waive the indictment for complicity with the enemy and the case was suspended only after another year. On October 26, 1946, Attorney General Lars L'Abée-Lund finally acknowledged her efforts: "The matter is settled because, in the light of the evidence available, I consider that there is no criminal offense. Mrs. Breien must, on the contrary, be said to have greatly benefitted her countrymen." But even though the criminal chief had made it clear that there was no criminal offense and that she had done important work for her countrymen, she continued to be dogged by her past association with Fehmer and the indictment against her was maintained on record for fifteen years before the Norwegian Police Board dropped it. Ironically, this was the same police department that only two years earlier had been staffed by more than fifty percent *Nasjonal Samling* Party members and had terrorized Norwegians, especially the Jews sent to Auschwitz, as much as the Germans.

As was the case with Dagmar Lahlum, the cloud of being a "German's tart" unfairly dogged her for the rest of her life and led her to be harassed in her hometown. She was punched in the face and subjected to other forms of violence.

Even though she had far more supporters, friends, and family members that had served in the Resistance during the war than Dagmar, her life after the war wasn't much better and her countrymen continued to harass her. Breien obtained a job at the United States Embassy in Oslo but was let go without any reason. More tough breaks would follow.

In June 1947, she served as the defense's main witness in Fehmer's war crimes trial, which, of course, did not make life any easier for her. But she considered telling the truth the right thing to do. In her heart, she believed she at least owed him and her country an honest assessment of the positive things he had done during his reign of terror over Occupied Norway. When she revealed on the witness stand that she had been working on behalf of the Home Front, Fehmer was very surprised. Randi Evensmo, wife of Sigurd, remembered her standing courageously on the witness stand and speaking calmly about the many cases where the Gestapo chief had proven himself helpful in releasing prisoners, and even though she drew the baleful stares of the journalists in the audience bent on promoting a black-and-white story of Good vs. Evil, Randi could tell that they couldn't help but admire her for her honesty and fortitude even if her story didn't fall neatly in line with the desired post-war narrative. At the trial, Annemarie's feelings were deeply conflicted, as they had been from 1942-1945 when she had been close to Fehmer. Her testimony, of course, didn't save the hated Nazi bloodhound from being convicted of war crimes: he was sentenced to death in June 1947 and executed in March 1948.

During her lifetime, Breien would never be able to escape her past, and even today most references mistakenly and slanderously refer to her as "Fehmer's mistress," which Randi Evensmo, whose husband was saved by her, took grave exception to, and rightfully so as we have seen. Annemarie traveled the United States in 1947 to visit her sister and to find refuge from the rumormongers. She eventually returned to Norway to work at the U.S. Embassy in Oslo, and later the NATO Northern Command headquarters at Kolsås. But rumors of her past continued to dog her, and in 1954 she was forced to resign from her job when an irresponsible journalist threatened to expose her relationship to Fehmer in a front-page story. Only in 1981 would she be awarded a war pension from the Norwegian government, after her family had fought for her case for years. It was a long and arduous 36-year wait. Thus, like Eddie Chapman but unlike Dagmar Lahlum, she received some recognition for her service to her country. But she would never receive the war medal she deserved for the 80 to 90 prisoners she saved.

After her resignation, she returned to the U.S. and remained there for the rest of her life. She died in a California nursing home on April 4, 2003, after struggling with the psychological repercussions of the war and her abuse by her countrymen. She self-medicated with alcohol for some years but was also involved in Alcoholics Anonymous and eventually also helped others through AA. In 1998, five years before her death, she proclaimed defiantly during an interview for a Norwegian magazine, "I have nothing to be ashamed of." In 2013, she was placed in 81th place of Norway's 100 most important women by World Walk (VG), the nationwide Norwegian newspaper published in Oslo. The women were voted upon in celebration of the centenary anniversary of women's right to vote in parliamentary elections, and the women selected were between the years 1913 and 2013. Interestingly, the list did not include Dagmar Lahlum though it should have.

Both Annemarie Breien and Dagmar Lahlum should be officially honored by Norway for their wartime service on behalf of the Allied cause.

SIEGFRIED FEHMER

At the close of the war, on May 8, 1945, Siegfried Fehmer left his German shepherd with Annemarie Breien and slipped out of Oslo dressed in a Luftwaffe private's outfit, attempting to escape to Sweden. He never made it and ended up instead at the German POW camp at Solørkanten, cleverly mingling with the regular army masses. But he would shortly make the mistake of calling his former lover by telephone to check up on his dog. After learning his whereabouts, Annemarie Breien dutifully notified Milorg and Fehmer was promptly identified and arrested by Sergeant John Maclean from British Military Intelligence, assisted by Norwegian police officers.

As stated previously, Fehmer's trial took place in June 1947, with Annemarie Breien, who had sealed his fate by giving away his location at Solørkanten, serving as his principal defense witness. With a strong legal background and a commanding physical presence, the Nazi officer was able to mount a strong defense. He was able to demonstrate that he had coordinated the release of a large number of Norwegian prisoners at the recommendation of Breien and that he had helped some others, but the charges were serious and included torture, sometimes resulting in death. The prosecution was able to prove that he had led the interrogations of a number of known Resistance fighters and had on occasion performed brutalities, but that he usually he left the dirty work to subordinates. Several of the most heinous tortures he performed along with the vicious Lieutenants Hoeler and Bernhard and others, documented in *The Gestapo at Work in Norway: The Road to Grini Concentration Camp*, are presented in the novel. It was said that Fehmer could turn from a friendly and charming sympathizer to a savage torturer, jumping on his victims and dunking them in freezing cold water, in a matter of seconds, like some sort of Dr. Jekyll and Mr. Hyde. On Fehlis's orders, he had been the one to prepare rules for the use of torture during interrogation in Norway. While under incarceration, he became one of the best sources of information about the *Sicherheitspolizei's* organization and work, and British intelligence officers were impressed by him: "First-rate education, intelligence above normal, excellent memory, makes excellent account of himself, imposing presence, maybe a little too smooth..." Tall and strong, with blond hair and blue eyes, he looked just like the Norwegian police sitting across from him as he attempted to justify his actions from the jury box in fluent Norwegian.

On June 27, 1947, he was charged and convicted of widespread torture, and to have sent 18 Norwegians as "*Nacht und Nebel*" prisoners to concentration camps, of which only eight returned home. "Night and Fog" was a directive issued by Adolf Hitler on December 7, 1941 targeting political activists and resistance "helpers" to be imprisoned or killed, while the family and the population remained uncertain as to the fate or whereabouts of the Nazi state's alleged offender. Most of those who became victims disappeared in these terrorist actions. The code name stemmed from Germany's most acclaimed poet and playwright, Johann Wolfgang von Goethe, who used the phrase to describe clandestine actions often concealed by fog and the darkness of night. Fehmer was sentenced to death, and the Supreme Court upheld the judgment on February 24, 1948, with two dissenting votes proposing life without parole. In the end, the judges felt that Fehmer should have known that the probability of death as a *Nacht und Nebel* prisoner was high and, therefore, he was held responsible for the deaths of those that had not survived the camps.

In his defense, Fehmer claimed that sending them away to what he believed were labor camps was far more compassionate than execution before a firing squad. He further maintained that he couldn't have stopped the NN-transfers even if he had wanted to, and again pointed out that in releasing 80 to 90 prisoners he had helped many more than he had punished. The Supreme Court majority did not agree and sentenced him to death for war crimes. On March 16, 1948, the sentence was carried out and Fehmer was shot at Akershus Fortress in Oslo.

One of the voting judges, Judge Anton Holmboe, argued in the February 24, 1948 judgment that Fehmer's strong Nazi convictions should be taken into account and his sentence reduced from death to life imprisonment. "The German view that Fehmer unreservedly endorses," the judge maintained, "is built on the belief that the state's interests take precedence over everything." He went on to explain that the Gestapo terrorist's mindset was "reprehensible" but noted that Nazi Germany was responsible for brainwashing him into being a disciple of Nazism and for compelling him to subvert himself to the state and enforce its draconian policies.

While in captivity before his execution, Fehmer wrote a long report on his experiences as a German intelligence officer from 1940 to 1945 in Occupied Norway. The document, *Meine Tätigkeit bei der Geheimen Staatspolizei: Erlebnisse, Erfahrungen, Erkenntnisse* (My Job at the Secret State Police: Adventures, Experiences, Insights), is regarded by Norwegian historian Berit Nøkleby as one of the best sources on German police activities in Norway during WWII.

An intelligent and resourceful criminal investigator, Fehmer must have known he was being manipulated to some extent by Annemarie Breien in order to secure the release of anti-Nazi Norwegian prisoners like her father Roald Breien and Sigurd Evensmo. One of the puzzling questions for historical researchers is why such a fearsome police investigator would allow himself to be bamboozled like that? Behavioral evidence suggests it was a combination of three reasons. First, he was so smitten with the seemingly innocent, alluring, and charitable Breien that she was able to deceive him into thinking that she was simply a concerned citizen and humanitarian and not a member of the Resistance. In other words, his physical attraction and desire to please her essentially blinded him to her true motives and possible connection to the Home Front. He definitely had very strong feelings for her long before they began their intimate sexual relationship in the fall of 1944, and she was able to fool him throughout their interactions between 1942 and 1945. He was clearly surprised at his trial when she confessed to having been an active member of the Resistance who had undermined him by giving his secrets away to her Milorg superiors for three years. Second, Fehmer could have released the prisoners as a gesture of good faith so that he would be in a position to negotiate with Milorg if and when he needed to. Third, he was using Annemarie as much as she was using him so that he could get closer to the Resistance. Based on historical records, it is unclear if he kept any of the released prisoners under surveillance following their release to assist in the tracking of other Resistance operatives. But it must be considered likely.

Fehmer will always be remembered as a clever criminal investigator and brave Gestapo raid team leader but a cruel and ruthless human being who stood stubbornly behind National Socialism until the final days of the war, when he seemed to realize just how monstrously evil Nazi Germany had been and what a failure it was as a governing ideology. He may have freed 80 to 90 prisoners at the behest of Annemarie Breien, but his evil deeds still far surpassed his humanitarian efforts during the war. Despite her brief love affair with the man, Breien's assessment of his legacy was blunt. Fehmer, she said, had "a well-equipped brain" but his lack of "cultural enlightenment and intellectual development" had made him "an easy target for Nazism" with his "more primitive form of self-morality than one is used to." The judges that sentenced him to death by firing squad and the Norwegian people who experienced his wartime abuse would have agreed with her.

TOMMY "TAR" ROBERTSON AND THE DOUBLE CROSS TEAM

With Allied victory and the end of the war, peace brought a new world order to Great Britain and its intelligence services as the Labor party took power in a landslide and the new threat shifted from Nazis to Stalin and his globe-gobbling Communists. The post-war change in government was keenly felt by the British Security Service whose budget was severely trimmed. The Double Cross Committee was quietly disbanded and most of the spymasters from Robertson's B1A team drifted back into civilian life, sworn to secrecy by the Official Secrets Act. It would be decades before anyone outside the inner circle knew that Double Cross, Most Secret Sources, Ultra, and Enigma, and spies like Eddie Chapman had existed. A few, like John Masterman and Ewen Montagu, eventually emerged from the shadows of the paternal British government to recount their spy stories and reap some glory, but most did not.

Not fond of the new peacetime regime, in 1948 Lieutenant Thomas Argyle Robertson gave up the spy game and retired to a Worcestershire sheep farm. He was only 39 years old. As Macintyre says, Robertson was able to tend to "his flock as gently and cleverly as he had tended the Double Cross agents." He would spend the rest of his life farming sheep in Worcestershire, giving up his Glengarry cap and McKenzie tartan trews of the Seaforth Highlanders. He was universally well-liked and his neighbors referred to him as "a good egg." His wartime legacy is secure. Among his two biggest successes of his spymastering days were fooling the Germans over the actual location of the Normandy D-Day landings in Double Cross's greatest wartime deception operation, and cleverly using Agent Zigzag/Fritz to trick the Germans into changing the target areas of the V1 and V2 rockets. Both operations saved thousands of military and civilian lives. For these successful espionage operations and a host of smaller but no less cunning ruses, he was awarded the U.S. Legion of Merit by Harry Truman, the Royal Order of the Yugoslav Crown by King Peter in a bizarre ceremony at Claridge's, and an Order of the British Empire from Britain for work too secret to be described. Upon

Robertson's retirement, John Masterman best summarized the Whitehall perspective when he commented in his memoirs: "I think his decision at the end of the war to leave the service in order to farm, was one of the greatest losses which MI5 ever suffered."

It was Masterman who published the first book describing the Double Cross spy system during the war. In 1970, Eddie Chapman's least favorite MI5 man, whom he considered an elitist snob, revealed to the world how German agents were secretly run against the Abwehr by the British for five years running to tip the scales of war. His account had been written immediately after the war, strictly for internal MI5 reading, but he had secretly kept a copy for himself and arranged with Yale University Press in the U.S for publication, thereby ensuring that the British government and Official Secrets Act could not stifle him. Entitled *The Double Cross System of the War of 1939-1945*, the book remains in print today and was an invaluable reference for *Spies of the Midnight Sun*.

The members of Robertson's team went in different directions following the war. Masterman was feted with awards and returned to academic life at Oxford; his exclusive clubs, cricket, mystery novels; and his unshakable belief that only the well-born and affluent should be allowed to rule the world. In 1945, Robin "Tin Eye" Stephens ran Bad Nenndorf, the Allied interrogation center near Hanover, a secret prison set up following the British occupation of northwestern Germany. At this German version of Camp 020, Tin Eye was tasked with extracting the truth from SS officers and spies picked up as the Allies thrust eastward across the Rhine into Germany, including Walter Praetorius, the rabid Nazi who loved English folk dancing, and two of the vilest German war criminals: SS Chief Walter Schellenberg and the murderous Ernst Kaltenbrunner. Tin Eye was soon accused of using Gestapo-like methods to extract confessions, but he was acquitted of all charges having damned his accusers as "degenerates, most of them diseased by VD" and "pathological liars." Ronnie Reed stayed on at MI5 as senior technical adviser to the security service. Between 1951 and 1957, he headed the counterespionage section, responsible for investigating Soviet moles in Britain, including the Burgess, Maclean, and Philby cases that made the British Secret Service the laughingstock of the international intelligence community. The Iron Cross presented to Chapman by von Gröning for services to the Third Reich, and then passed on to Reed as a souvenir of their friendship, remains in the possession of the Reed family. Michael Ryde, Chapman's despicable final case officer, left MI5 soon after the war and rejoined the family firm of chartered surveyors. According to Macintyre, he soon drank himself out of a job, however, and began a sad descent into alcoholism. One marriage disintegrated, and he walked out of the next, leaving two young children fatherless. While on the pub circuit, Ryde would boast of his role in the case of Eddie Chapman, a man that he had despised and considered beneath him who was by then garnering headlines as a colorful and likable master crook.

Historians are in unanimous agreement that the success of Double Cross is attributable largely to Tar Robertson, and that is his lasting legacy. As Geoffrey Elliot, author of *Gentleman Spymaster: How Lt. Col. Tommy "Tar" Robertson Double-Crossed the Nazis*, states: "It is the constant balancing and rebalancing of velvet glove and iron fist, in circumstances of extraordinary strain, without losing his sense of proportion and humor or his eye for detail, his 'networking' and organizational talents, and his imagination, that made Tar a master spymaster."

Robertson the avid cricketer died on May 10, 1994 at the age of 84 and was laid to rest in the churchyard of St. John at Birlingham, in a leafy picturesque corner of Worcestershire far removed from London.

STEPHAN VON GRÖNING

At the end of the war, Stephan von Gröning was arrested by American forces and held in a prison camp outside Bremen. With the historic family mansion at Am Wall 113 destroyed in the summer of 1944, he was homeless, destitute, and living with his sister Dorothea and her adopted Jewish daughter Alice when the U.S. Army arrived to arrest him. The Americans got lost escorting him to the prison, so the half-American von Gröning showed them the way, in perfect English with an upper-class accent. Allied intelligence revealed that he was a typical anti-Nazi Abwehr officer of the old school that had supported the July 20, 1944 plot against Hitler and he was released after only six months—while Dagmar Lahlum and Annemarie Breien were still being incarcerated and abused in Norway by their own countrymen for merely fraternizing with German officers. In the POW camp, the high-born baron whose linen had always been ironed by servants found himself pleading for handkerchiefs and toothpaste.

Upon his release, he discovered to his intense annoyance that in order to obtain a ration book in post-war Germany, and thus to eat, he had to actually find a paying job. Through family friends, he found nominal employment at the Bremen Museum, but he rarely turned up for work. It was just too painful for the former aristocrat to sink to such a mundane level. The family fortune may have vanished, but the German spymaster Eddie Chapman had known only as Doktor Graumann continued to live on his name, loyal to his class to the end just like John Masterman. He married a much younger woman named Ingeborg, and though she worked, he did not. He would lie for long hours on the sofa drinking aperitifs and postprandial cocktails and reading borrowed books.

Von Gröning seldom spoke of the war. He believed Eddie Chapman had been captured, exposed as a spy, and executed. He kept a photograph of La Bretonnière in his wallet and often thought of his daring protégé, whom he never knew had been a double agent actively working against him. The two drinking partners had always gotten along famously and Chapman had always held him in high regard. As Tin Eye said, "It must always be borne in mind that he had a very close connection and high regard for Graumann. He regards him as being anti-Nazi and liberal in his outlook." Chapman was always quick to defend his German spymaster, insisting that he was "a very able man, cautious and resourceful, but was handicapped by the poor material in the way of personnel that he had at his disposal." The two also shared an aversion for Hitler and Nazism, which von Gröning openly expressed with greater frequency with his drinking buddy once Walter Praetorius left Norway and the German war situation deteriorated. "Eddie really hated the Nazi regime," said Betty Chapman about her husband in her later years after her Agent Zigzag had passed. "The only reason he ever became so close to von Gröning was because they both despised the Nazis." For Chapman, von Gröning was a father figure.

The German spymaster and British double agent were eventually able to reconnect in the mid-1970s. According to Macintyre, Chapman bumped into Leo Kreusch in a London bar in 1974, when the German agent who had taught him to shoot at La Bretonnière informed Chapman that the man he had known as Doktor Graumann was still alive and living in Bremen. Agent Fritz penned his former spymaster a letter, in which he recounted, with affection, the times they had spent together in Nantes, Paris, and Oslo. He inquired whether his old friend knew what had happened to his sailing yawl and whether he remembered Dagmar Lahlum. "I suppose she is married now," he reflected nostalgically. Chapman described his properties, enclosing a photograph of the ancient Irish castle he had acquired, and invited the veteran of two world wars and former head of the Abwehr Nantes spy school, who was now penniless, to come to England and stay with him and his wife. "What delightful memories we could exchange...I remember how much you used to like castles," he said via letter. Though he knew his controller had lost his family's home to Allied bombing during the war, he didn't know that he was no longer a wealthy aristocrat and had fallen into a state of penury.

Somehow, von Gröning managed to cobble together enough money to travel to England in the summer of 1979 and attend Chapman's daughter Suzanne's wedding. The wedding took place at Shenley Lodge, the thirty-two-room health spa owned by Eddie and Betty. Von Gröning—at this stage an elderly, short-sighted German gentleman with a large potbelly—amused the children by reciting old-fashioned English nursery rhymes. As the party wound down, Chapman and his former German handler joined arm in arm to wander off together and reminisce about their days in Occupied France and Norway when war raged across Europe. Von Gröning offered the protégé that had double-crossed him repeated thanks for standing firm with the Abwehr and insisting that he would work for no one but the German spymaster during his return to France in 1943. "He was the luckiest man on Earth," said Chapman in 1994, acknowledging that von Gröning would have been wiped out if he had been forced to remain in the bloodbath of Russia instead of sent to Norway to look after his coveted agent.

As the last wedding guests departed, laughter and singing could be heard drifting from the garden: the faint strains of *Lili Marlene*. For Betty it was a touching moment, but she was also surprised by the strength of their bond since during the war they had fought for different countries and because Eddie had deceived his German handler throughout their time together.

"They were like brothers," she said.

Von Gröning died in 1982 and was buried in the family grave on the Waller cemetery in Bremen. In the embarrassingly unrealistic 1966 film *Triple Cross* based on their WWII experiences together, Yul Brynner plays a highly fictionalized version of von Gröning named Col. Baron von Grunen. While the real von Stephan von Gröning was an intelligent, socially refined, and ingenious but also sluggish and unmilitary man, as well as a stubborn elitist, Yul Brynner's Baron von Grunen is a stodgy Prussian who obeys all the rules. But what the screenwriters got right was the negative attitude towards National Socialism, as Brynner's character ends up being connected to the July 20, 1944 plot to assassinate Hitler.

SOURCES AND ACKNOWLEDGEMENTS

To develop the story line, characters, and scenes for *Spies of the Midnight Sun: A True Story of WWII Heroes*, I consulted over a hundred archival materials, non-fiction books, magazine and newspaper articles, blogs, Web sites, and numerous individuals, and I visited many of the historical locations in the novel. There are too many resources and locations to name here. However, I would be remiss if I didn't give credit to the key historical references upon which this novel is based, as well as the critical individuals who dramatically improved the quality of the manuscript from its initial to its final stage. Any technical mistakes in the historical facts underpinning the novel, typographical errors, or examples of overreach due to artistic license, however, are the fault of me and me alone.

In addition to the primary reference materials from British and Norwegian archives listed below, I relied heavily upon eleven secondary sources dealing specifically with the German Occupation of Norway, British Double Cross Spy System, Norwegian Resistance, and the major historical figures in the novel. These references were invaluable and included the following for those interested in further reading about the historical events and personalities presented in the book: *Agent Zigzag: A True Story of Nazi Espionage, Love, and Betrayal* (2007), *Tragic Love Story of MI5 Agent Eddie Chapman* (2011), and *Double Cross: The True Story of the D-Day Spies* (2012) by Ben Macintyre; *Zigzag: The Incredible Wartime Exploits of Double Agent Eddie Chapman* (2007) by Nicholas Booth; *War Heroine or German Mistress? The Story of Dagmar Lahlum in the Light of Other Female Resistance Fighters* (2009 Master's Thesis) and *Women Fighting: The History of Norwegian Female Resistance Fighters* (2011) by Kristina Hatledal; *Women in Secret Services: Intelligence Work in the Nordic Countries during World War II* (2007) by Tore Pryser; *The Human Flies*, "Afterword" entitled *About My Late Aunt Dagmar Lahlum–and My Novel, The Human Flies"* (2014) by Hans Olav Lahlum; *German Double Agent for the British: Dagmar Lahlum took her Secret with her to the Grave. She was a Resistance Woman and worked for British Intelligence MI5* (2007) and *Double Agent Eddie Chapman Never Managed to Clear Dagmar* (2008) by Hilde Harbo (*Aftenposten* Articles); and *Gestapo Officer Fehmer: Milorg's Most Dangerous Enemy* (1986) by Steinar Brauteset.

In writing the novel, there were many excellent historical books and articles in addition to those listed above from which I drew facts and inspiration to flesh out the German Occupation of Norway, the British and German Intelligence Services, the Double Cross Spy System, and the historical events and major figures presented in the book. The interested reader is referred to the following additional sources used to write the true story presented herein.

Norwegian Resistance, Dagmar Lahlum, and Annemarie Breien: *The Bitter Years: The Invasion and Occupation of Denmark and Norway, April 1940-May 1945* (1974) by Richard Petrow; *Scandinavia in the Second World War* by Richard Overy, *Closing a Long Chapter: German-Norwegian Relations 1939-45: Norway and the Third Reich* by Tom Kristiansen, *Hitler's Norwegian Legacy* by Ole

Kristian Grimnes, and *Conclusion* by Allan Little in *Hitler's Scandinavian Legacy* (2013), edited by John Gilmour and Jill Stephenson; *The Dark Sides of Norwegian History* (2015) by Sindre Bangstad; *How a Few Thousand Nazis Seized Norway* (1940) by Leland Stowe; *A Stand Against Tyranny: Norway's Physicians and the Nazis* (1997) by Maynard Cohen; Public Records of The Norwegian National Archives, Oslo: Treason Archives L-case Oslo pfm F. No. 418/47-Landssviksak Dagmar Lahlum and L-case Oslo pfm HNL no. 3662-Landssviksak Annemarie Breien; *Norway and the Second World War* (1966) by Olav Riste, Magne Skodvin, and Johannes Andenae; *Norway, 1940-1945: The Resistance Movement* (1970) by Olav Riste and Berit Nökleby; *Folklore Fights the Nazis: Humor in Occupied Norway, 1940–1945* (1997) by Kathleen Stokke; *Saboteurs at Work* (2017) by Thomas B. Allen; *The German Occupation of Norway* (1970) by Paul C. Vigness; *Norwegian Resistance 1940-1945* (1979) by Tore Gjelsvik; *War Heroine or German Girl?* (2015) and *Anne Marie Breien: Norwegian Resistance Woman during the Second World War* (2017) by Kristin Hatledal; *Church Resistance to Nazism in Norway, 1940-1945* (2014) by Arne Hassing; *Dagmar Lahlum: A Norwegian Mata Hari of Real Life* (2018) by Per Gjendem; *The Winter Fortress: The Epic Mission to Sabotage Hitler's Atomic Bomb* (2016) by Neal Bascomb; *The Second World War in Norwegian Film—The Topography of Remembrance* (2015) by Tonje Haugland Sørensen; *Quisling: A Study in Treachery* (1999) by Hans Fredrik Dahl; "Afterword" to Ben Macintyre's *Agent Zigzag: The Incredible Story of Eddie Chapman* (2008 Norwegian Edition) by Hilde Harbo; *Resistance Fights were Most Important: Annemarie Breien* (1998) by Randi Evensmo; *Nine Lives Before Thirty* (1947) and *Underwater Saboteur* (1953) by Max Manus; *Max Manus: An Extraordinary Man* (2018) by Bob Pearson; *During the Nazi Occupation of Norway, Humor Was the Secret Weapon* (2016) by Loni Klara.

General WWII Military History, Double Cross Spy System, Tar Robertson, and Eddie Chapman: Public Records of The British National Archives, Kew, London: KV 2/455–463, MI5 files about Eddie Chapman, Agent Zigzag, 12/17/1942-11/07/1944; *Double Agent: The Eddie Chapman Story* (2014) by Frank Owen; *Double Agent: The Eddie Chapman Story* (2011), BBC Documentary and TV Movie; *An Army at Dawn: The War in North Africa, 1942–1943* (2002), *The Day of Battle: The War in Sicily and Italy, 1943–1944* (2007), and *The Guns at Last Light: The War in Western Europe, 1944–1945* (2013) by Rick Atkinson; *The Second World War* (2005) by John Keegan; *Deceiving Hitler: Double Cross and Deception in World War II* (2008) by Terry Crowdy; *The Spies Who Never Were: The True Story of the Nazi Spies Who Were Actually Allied Double Agents* (2006) by Hervie Haufler; *Camp 020: MI5 and the Nazi Spies* (2000) by Colonel Robin "Tin Eye" Stephens; *Gentleman Spymaster: How Lt. Col. Tommy "Tar" Robertson Double-Crossed the Nazis* (2011) by Geoffrey Elliott; *The Game of Foxes: The Untold Story of German Espionage in the United States and Great Britain during World War II* (1971) by Ladislas Farago; *Operation Mincemeat: How a Dead Man and a Bizarre Plan Fooled the Nazis and Assured an Allied Victory* (2010) by Ben Macintyre; *The Deceivers: Allied Military Deception in the Second World War* (2007) by Thaddeus Holt; *The Double-Cross System in the War, 1939-1945* (1972) by J.C. Masterman; *We Have Ways of Making You Talk...World War II British Interrogation Tactics: A*

Historical Moral Study (2010) by Patrick Doerr; *Hoodwinking Hitler: The Normandy Deception* (1993) by William B. Breuer; *Wild Bill Donovan: The Spymaster Who Created the OSS and Modern American Espionage* (2011) by Douglas Waller; *The Spy Who Loved Me: 'Mrs. Zigzag' on Being Married to One of Britain's Most Celebrated Double Agents* (2013) by Jane Warren; *The English Double-Agent Who Won the Iron Cross* (2015) by George Winston; *Wait, What? How a Double-Agent Codenamed Zigzag Two-Timed Everyone* (2017) by Jeff Elder; *Into the Lion's Mouth: The True Story of Dusko Popov: World War II Spy, Patriot, and the Real-Life Inspiration for James Bond* (2016) by Larry Loftis; *Defend the Realm: The Authorized History of MI5* (2009) by Christopher Andrew.

German Intelligence Services and Siegfried Fehmer: *The Gestapo: The Myth and Reality of Hitler's Secret Police Hardcover (2017) by Frank McDonough*; *Gestapo: German Police in Norway from 1940 to 1945* (2003) and *Siegfried Fehmer: Nazi Police Officer* (2009) by Berit Nökleby; *Hitler's Secret Agents: German Intelligence in Norway from 1939 to 1945* (2001) by Tore Pryser; *The Gestapo at Work in Norway* (1942) by the Royal Norwegian Government; *Hitler's Scandinavian Legacy* (2013) by John Gilmour and Jill Stephenson (Editors); *Meine Tätigkeit bei der secreten Staatspolizei: Erlebnisse, Erfahrungen, Erkenntnisse* (My Job at the Secret State Police: Adventures, Experiences, Insights), Fehmer's detailed report written in the summer of 1945, in the Norwegian Home Front Museum, Oslo; *Introduction of Exception to the Prohibition against Use of Force at Examinations of Apprehended Persons* (1945) by Siegfried Fehmer; Public Records of The Norwegian National Archives, Oslo: War Crimes Archives L-dom 3500-Landssviksak Siegfried Fehmer; *The Norwegian Gestapo Boss Believed in Hitler Until Late* (2014) by Ola Karlsen; *The Gestapo: A History of Horror* (2008) by Jacques Delarue and Mervyn Savill; *German Military Intelligence in World War II: The Abwehr* (1984) by Lauran Paine; *German Reprisals in Norway During the Second World War* (2017 Master's Thesis) by Knut Kristian Langva Døscher; *Hitler's Spies: German Military Intelligence in World War II* (2000) by David Kahn; *In Time of War: Hitler's Terrorist Attack on America* (2005) by Pierce O'Donnell.

I would also personally like to thank the following for their support and assistance. First and foremost, I would like to thank my wife Christine, an exceptional and highly professional book editor, who painstakingly reviewed and copy-edited the novel. Any mistakes that remain are my fault, of course.

Second, I would like to thank my former literary agent, Cherry Weiner of the Cherry Weiner Literary Agency, for thoroughly reviewing, vetting, and copy-editing the manuscript, and for making countless improvements to the finished novel.

Third, I would like to thank Stephen King's former editor, Patrick LoBrutto, for thoroughly copy-editing the various drafts of the novel and providing detailed reviews.

I would also like to thank the late Austin and Anne Marquis, Governor Roy Romer, Ambassador Marc Grossman, Betsy and Steve Hall, Rik Hall, Christian Fuenfhausen, Bill Eberhart, Fred Taylor, David Boyles, Mo Shafroth, Peter Brooke, Tim and Carey Romer, Peter and Lorrie Frautschi, Deirdre Grant Mercurio, Dawn

Ezzo Roseman, Joe Tallman, John Welch, Link Nicoll, Toni Conte Augusta Francis, Brigid Donnelly Hughes, Caroline Fenton Dewey, John and Ellen Aisenbrey, Margot Patterson, Cathy and Jon Jenkins, Danny Bilello and Elena Diaz-Bilello, Charlie and Kay Fial, Vincent Bilello, Elizabeth Gardner, Robin McGehee, and the other book reviewers and professional contributors large and small who have given generously of their time over the years, as well as to those who have given me loyal support as I have ventured on this incredible odyssey of historical fiction writing.

Lastly, I want to thank anyone and everyone who bought this book and my loyal fans and supporters who helped promote this work. You know who you are and I salute you.

ABOUT THE AUTHOR

The ninth great-grandson of legendary privateer Captain William Kidd, Samuel Marquis is the bestselling, award-winning author of a World War Two Series, the Nick Lassiter-Skyler International Espionage Series, and historical American fiction. His novels have been #1 *Denver Post* bestsellers and received multiple national book awards (Kirkus Reviews and Foreword Reviews Book of the Year, American Book Fest and USA Best Book, Readers' Favorite, Beverly Hills, Independent Publisher, National Indie Excellence, Next Generation Indie, and Colorado Book Awards). His books have also garnered glowing reviews from #1 bestseller James Patterson, Kirkus, and Foreword Reviews (5 Stars). Critics and book reviewers have compared the books of his WWII Series to the epic historical novels of Tom Clancy, John le Carré, Ken Follett, Herman Wouk, Daniel Silva, Len Deighton, and Alan Furst.

Below is a list of Samuel Marquis novels along with their release dates and book awards.

THE WORLD WAR TWO SERIES

Bodyguard of Deception – March 2016 – Winner Foreword Reviews' Book of the Year Awards; Award-Winning Finalist USA Best Book Awards

Altar of Resistance – January 2017 – Award-Winning Finalist Foreword Reviews' Book of the Year Awards, American Book Fest Best Book Awards, and Beverly Hills Book Awards

Spies of the Midnight Sun: A True Story of WWII Heroes – May 2018 – Winner Independent Publisher Book Awards

Lions of the Desert: A True Story of WWII Heroes in North Africa – February 2019 – Winner Readers' Favorite, National Indie Excellence, and Beverly Hills Book Awards; Award-Winning Finalist Foreword Reviews' Book of the Year and American Fiction Best Book Awards

Soldiers of Freedom: The WWII Story of Patton's Panthers and the Edelweiss Pirates – March 2020

THE NICK LASSITER – SKYLER INTERNATIONAL ESPIONAGE SERIES

The Devil's Brigade – September 2015 – #1 Denver Post Bestseller; Award-Winning Finalist Beverly Hills Book Awards

The Coalition – January 2016 – Winner Beverly Hills Book Awards; Award-Winning Finalist USA Best Book Awards and Colorado Book Awards

The Fourth Pularchek – June 2017 – Winner Independent Publisher Book Awards; Award-Winning Finalist American Book Fest Best Book Awards and Beverly Hills Book Awards

HISTORICAL PIRATE FICTION

Blackbeard: The Birth of America – February 2018 – Winner Kirkus Reviews Book of the Year and Beverly Hills Book Awards; Award-Winning Finalist American Book Fest Best Book Awards

THE JOE HIGHEAGLE ENVIRONMENTAL SLEUTH SERIES

Blind Thrust – October 2015 – #1 Denver Post Bestseller; Winner Foreword Reviews' Book of the Year and Next Generation Indie Book Awards; Award-Winning Finalist USA Best Book Awards, Beverly Hills Book Awards, and Next Generation Indie Book Awards

Cluster of Lies – September 2016 – Winner Beverly Hills Book Awards; Award-Winning Finalist USA Best Book Awards and Foreword Reviews Book of the Year Awards

Thank You for Your Support!

If you can lend a helping hand, please post a review on Amazon (https://amzn.to/2yr3M0q), Bookbub (https://bit.ly/2RVxukV), and/or Goodreads (https://bit.ly/2KlfpbQ). Thanks in advance!

To Order Samuel Marquis Books and Contact Samuel:

Visit Samuel Marquis's website, join his mailing list, learn about his forthcoming historical fiction novels and book events, and order his books at www.samuelmarquisbooks.com. Please send all fan mail (including criticism) to samuelmarquisbooks@gmail.com.

Made in the USA
Middletown, DE
22 June 2022